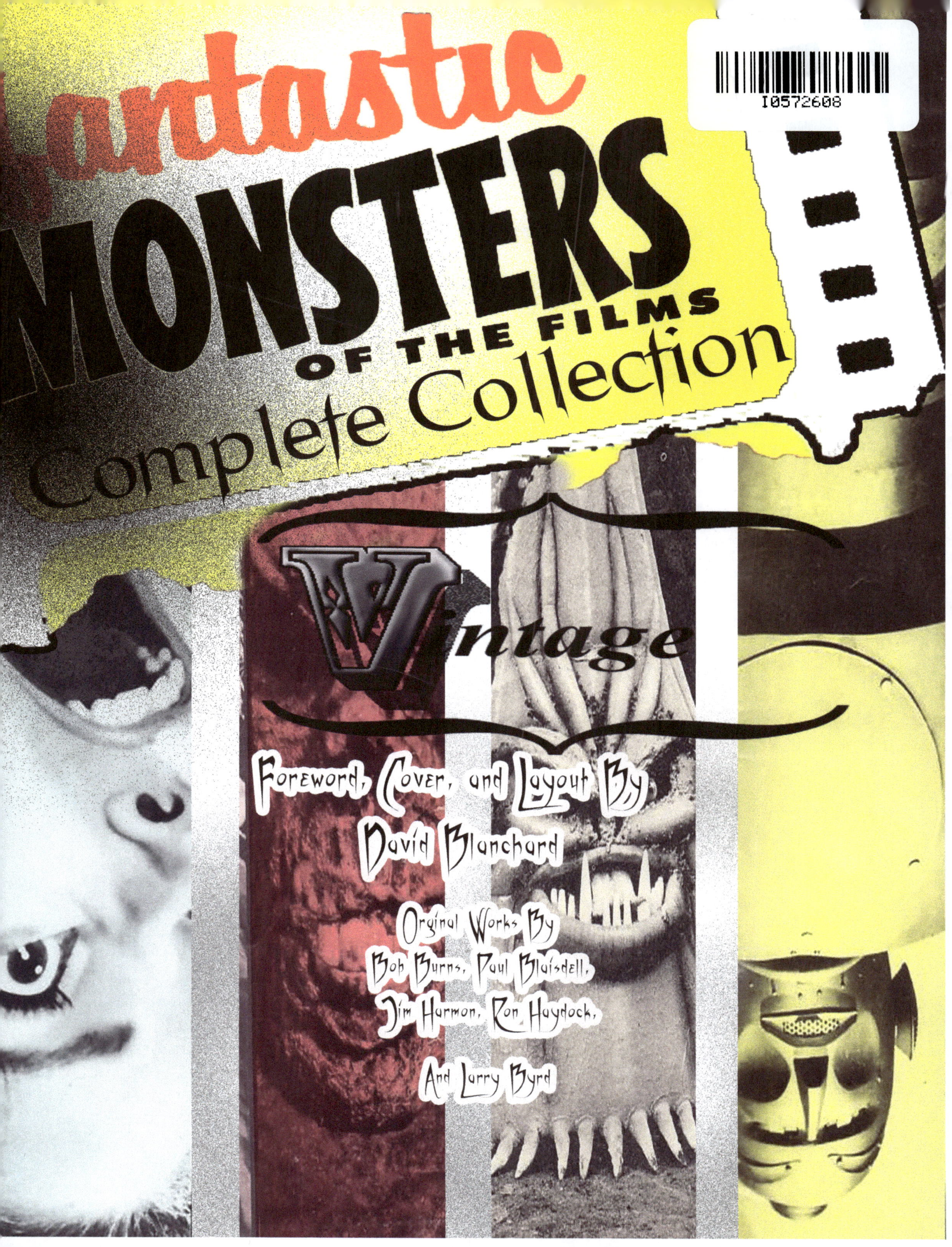

Fantastic
MONSTERS
OF THE FILMS
Complete Collection
I0572608
Vintage
Foreword, Cover, and Layout By
David Blanchard
Orginal Works By
Bob Burns, Paul Blaisdell,
Jim Harmon, Ron Haydock,
And Larry Byrd

Vintage

Fantastic Monsters of the Films Complete Collection

By David Blanchard, Bob Burns, Paul Blaisdell, Jim Harmon, Ron Haydock, and Larry Byrd

Author: David Blanchard, Bob Burns, Paul Blaisdell, Jim Harmon, Ron Haydock, and Larry Byrd

ISBN:
Digital: 978-1-939977-92-2
      1-939977-92-4
Print: 978-1-939977-99-1

Table of Contents

Foreword

'Horror guaranteed to shock you to dead or your life refunded!'-

That was the tag line of this cult monster magazine. While I love just about all things old school horror I have a sneaking suspicion that there were quite a few lives refunded.

Fantastic Monsters of the Films was not the first monster movie/ horror magazine to come out and it was by far from one of the best known or longest lasting, but it did capitalize on that golden age of the of the Hollywood horror albeit near the end of the era. (1930s-1960s) the seventies were a relatively dry period, just not for horror but many other genres, however in the 1980s it experienced a rebirth and in the late 80s to early 90s several famous monster magazines were restarted being pulled from hiatus some by their original founders other by people who loved these books growing up as young kids and now found themselves in apposition to restated these books most of the time because the rights had lapsed and there were no longer any legal ownership to the magazine names. Not to say that there weren't some prolonged legal battles. Fantastic Monsters of the Films sad to say was not one of these books.

Fantastic Monsters of the Films, FanMo as it is sometimes shorten too was created by Bob Burns a movie archivist and Paul Blaisdell a make-up effects creator, special effects creator, and actor, whose monsters graced the covers of issues 2through 6. Jim Harmon was hired to be the editor of the magazine, who would go on to edit the magazine

Monsters of the Movies in the mid-seventies and Ron Haydock to provide the writing for the magazine. A special double page spread cover was drawn for issue No.7 by Larry Byrd Depicting characters from the movie, *The Son of Frankenstein.*

The magazine stated publication in 1962 through Burns and Blaisdell's company Black Shield Productions. Each issue contained special segments such as "The Devil's Work Shop" where Blaisdell wrote articles on special effects and how these fiendish ghouls were created for the movies of the time. There was also a monster of the month, which was a full color fold out poster.

An issue No.8 was planned but never materialized do to what some consider a suspicious fire at the printers hired to print the magazine. Where the issue may have been completed or may have only been prepped to go, it along with many irreplaceable and valuable stills, lobby card and other materials were completely destroyed.

Owned by Burns and Blaisdell the financial loss was too much for the company to bear and Black Shield Productions folded in 1963 thus ending any possibility for more issues.

Now on to my role in the history of this magazine; while old copies can still be found and some reprints of individual issues have been done, this will actually be the first time that all the issues have been collected together in a single binding.

I was one of those kids who loved all those old horror movies of the black and white era and beyond. In my elementary school library I remember finding old books and magazines just like this one for the Blob, Frankenstein, Dracula, and others, for me these books were already twenty-five to thirty years old, or older as this was the late 80s to early 90s. I remember looking in the back of the books at the catalogue cards in the card pockets to see that I was the first person in several, several years to check these books out, and that my name soon became the one repeatedly listed on the cards as I would be constantly rechecking these books out. I still every now and then think about going back up to my old school to see if they still have these books in the old library to see if I they are still bury on the bottom self in the back corner being forgotten and neglected and if I can rescue them.

I can still remember the old musty smell of when I opened them, the faded pages, the yellowing of the paper. This is why I have chosen to present this book the way I have. Normally when I work with vintage material for republication I go back and clean it up, remaster it to make it look as new as possible, but I didn't feel that way with this book. I think it adds character to the item to keep the yellowed pages, the cracked images, to let its age shine through. It has always been my opinion that when it comes to horror the older more distressed something appears the better it is, and the fact that as I kid this is always the condition I found these things in maybe why I feel this way.

That is way I have done nothing to the pages of this book and have left them as is. Not to say that this has made the process of laying this book out any easier as one might think.

When I obtain an archive I get it in whatever the condition the scanner scanned it in, so in other words I get the good the bad and the ugly, and man was there some ugly with this project. Most of the time I am remastering old comic books, so everything is an illustrated image, but this was a magazine with pictures, pictures I have no idea what the originals looked like. In the first issue in the archive was a double page spread with what looked like pieces from another page placed on top of it covering up parts of the pictures and a section of text, at the moment I left it, for there was no way for me to fix it because I didn't know what it was supposed to look like underneath. So I concentrated on just completing the rough initial layout to see where everything was going to go and adjust thing accordingly. Which lead to more issues the archivist(s), I don't know if it was one person who scanned all issues or various ones contributed what they had to complete the archive. They would on the monster of the month poster scan one page facing one direction then scan the other half facing the other direction and upside down so I would have to try and figure out the best way to fix and present the poster in the book, as in this book the poster will not fold out. They also included for most of the issues how the poster would look as on solid picture in its proper upright position. Which I did like and included those in the book. But this and the fact that these magazines were never meant to be laid out back to back as one publication, with front and back cover included threw off the layouts for the double page spreads, so I've had to alter and manipulate the layout to get things to display properly which was slightly easier for the e-book edition versus the print edition.

Then finding that the cover for issue No.4 had been written on and the archivist(s) didn't scan the back cover for issue No.7 that was the special wrap around cover, this then led me to have to scour the depths of the internet to find replacements for these images. This in the end actually worked out for the best, because I found the replacements and a better copy of the cover for issue No.5 and a few other pages.

I also had to figure out the thing not to fix because they were original mistakes, like the cover of issue No.5 says the monster is the voodoo woman, but most monster movie aficionados say it is the she creature, an erroneous mistake that was originally published so I left it as such. And then there were the magazines claims to have more color images than ever before, but these were just old black and white film still with various color filters placed over them, not in color as we would think of it.

And this is where I leave you to experience a complete collection of cult classic monsterdom. While I don't make the same shocking claim to guarantee to shock you dead I do hope that you enjoy this nostalgia look back into yester years when monsters were stop motion, guys in rubber suits, when they set the ground work and standers for the future, and more than animated CGI images on the big screen back to when they were fantastic monster of the films.

-David Blanchard

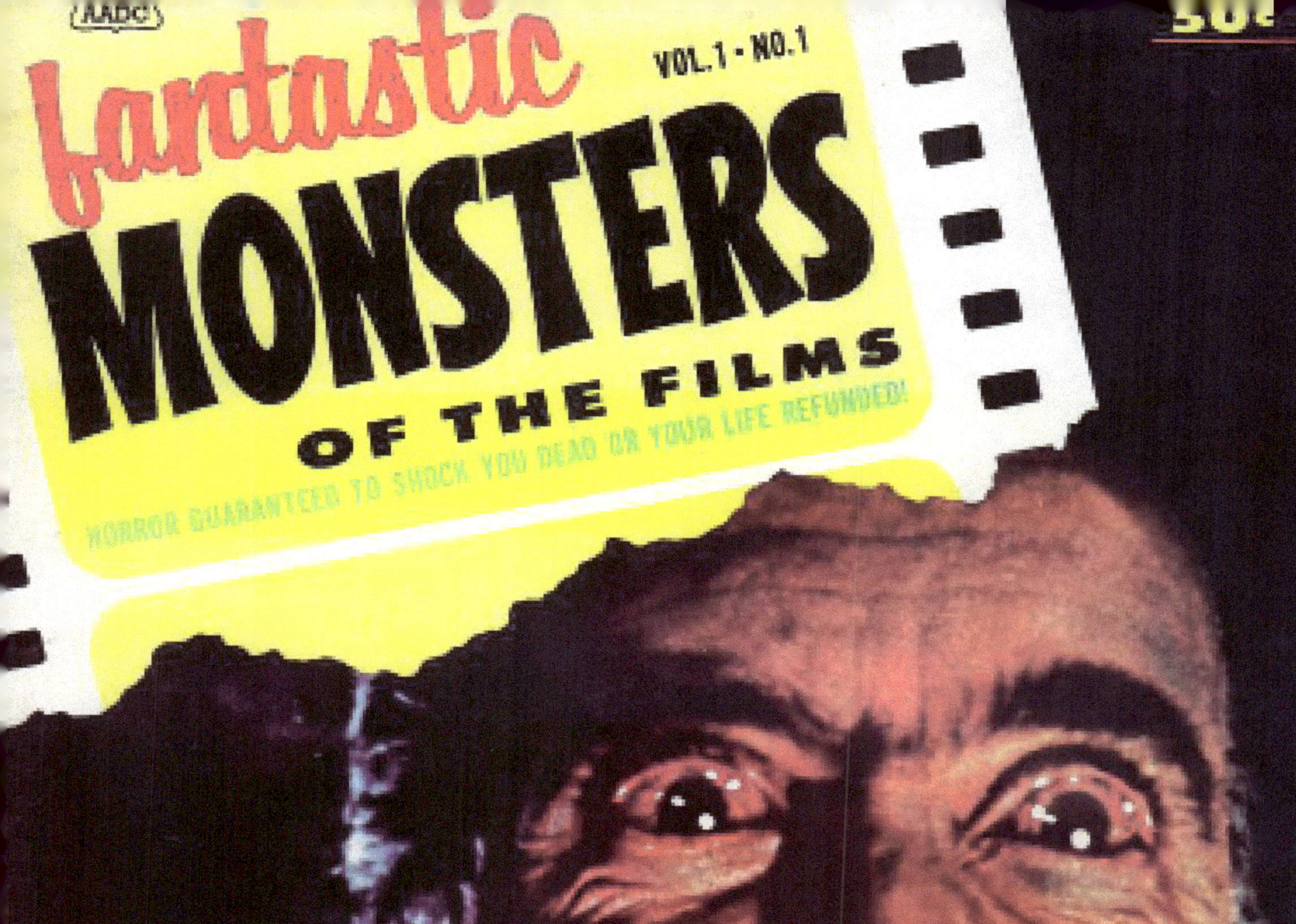
AADC
VOL. 1 - NO. 1
50¢
fantastic
MONSTERS
OF THE FILMS
HORROR GUARANTEED TO SHOCK YOU DEAD OR YOUR LIFE REFUNDED!
INSIDE!
Full Color
MONSTER
PINUP
HORROR FICTION
by Robert Bloch
AUTHOR OF
PSYCHO
Hammer Films' HORROR OF DRACULA — released by Universal International

Gathered from the most extensive morgue of monster mags this side of Transylvania, and with special added shots by our own Hollywood staff, *FANTASTIC MONSTERS'* Premiere Collector's Edition presents the widest (and wildest) spectrum of spooks and space scenes ever captured between covers. Whether you're young.

Whether you're young, or just young in heart (whose?), we know you'll agree that *FANTASTIC MONSTERS* is the monster movie and fantasy film buff's dream come true. In short, a perfect nightmare.

Besides the pictures and articles that speak for themselves—in fact, scream out loud in color—you'll find short-short stories by Robert Bloch, the *Psycho* who likes to shower us with pointed entries, and staffer Jim Harmon who, this issue, takes Poetic license with a classic tale or two in the hopes of winning for himself an *Edgar*.

So sit right down and enjoy this sizzling stake of shock we've served up. And believe us, when it comes to dishing out Collector's Items, this stake will be rare.

THE EDITORS

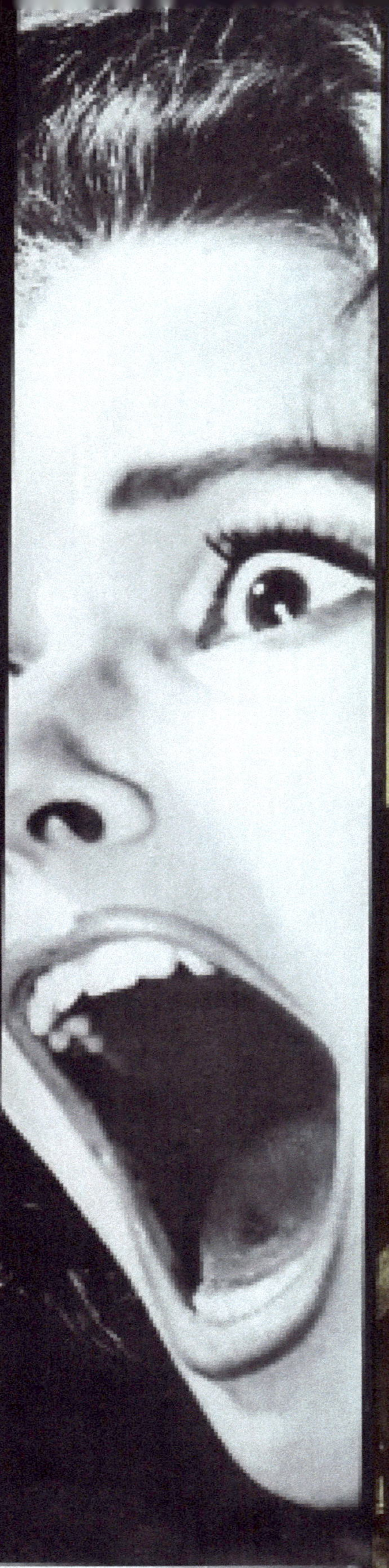

The Can Terrors are only one of the feature attractions in FANTASTIC MONSTERS' three-ring Circus of Horrors

Screams of fear and fun are waiting for you in each and every issue of this, the greatest magazine show on Earth

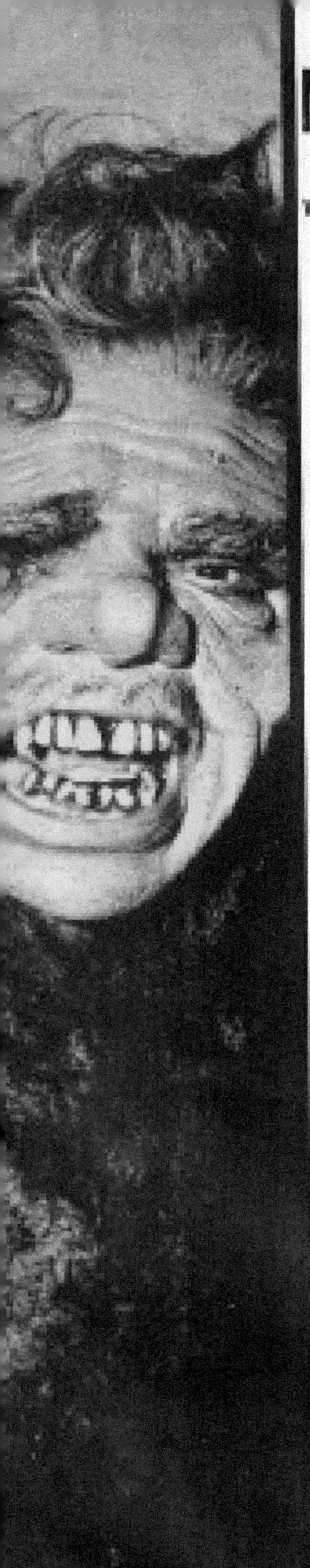

fantastic MONSTERS OF THE FILMS

VOL. 1 • NUMBER 1

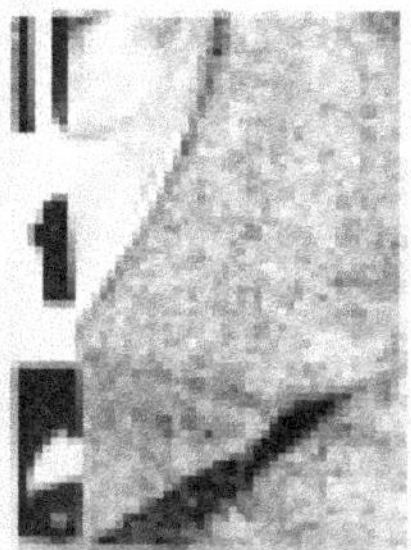

COVER: Christopher Lee in HORROR OF DRACULA; courtesy of Hammer Films and Universal-International Pictures

BACK COVER: (1) BEAST WITH A MILLION EYES (2) Bert I. Gordon's THE MAGIC SWORD (3) COUNT DOWNE

RON HAYDOCK
editor

PAUL BLAISDELL
editorial director

BOB BURNS
research editor

JIM HARMON
associate editor

CREDITS & ACKNOWL-EDGEMENTS: Larry Byrd, Cayuga Prod., Columbia Pic., Alex Gordon, Bert I. Gordon, Hammer Films, Milt Moritz, Estelle Nathan, Bob Smith, Glenn Strange, Larry Talburn, Universal Pic., Johnny Weissmuller

VOLUME 1, NUMBER 1, FANTASTIC MONSTERS OF THE FILMS. PRICE 50c PER COPY. Published bi-monthly by Black Shield Productions Inc. Mailing address: Post Office Box 141, Topanga, California. National Advertising Representatives: Harbor Company, 860 North Fairfax, Los Angeles 46, California. Entire Copyright 1962, by Black Shield Productions Inc. Nothing may be reprinted in whole or in part without written permission. Printed in U.S.A. Return postage should accompany unsolicited manuscripts and pictures; the publisher accepts no responsibility for return. Any similarity between people and places mentioned in the fiction and semifiction in this magazine and any real people and places is purely coincidental.

CONTENTS

You're mad, my friend, if you think those softly beating wings behind us belong to a Vampire Bat! Everyone knows there is no such thing as a Vam——

VAMPIRE BATS IN MY BELFRY

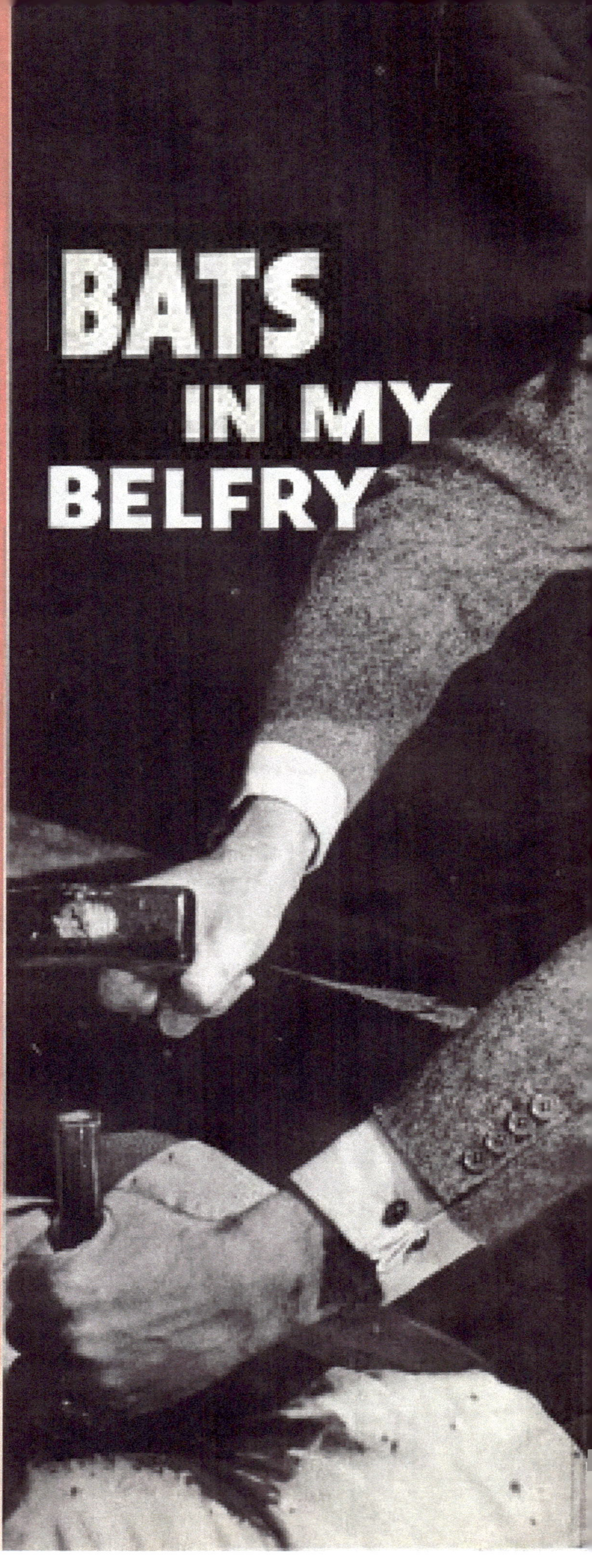

The hours between sunset and sunrise are not the wisest time to go roaming about the shadowed graveyard—as any loyal Transylvanian can tell you. These bewitching hours, Legend has it, are when Things of the Night take flight, and flap fun-lovingly off in search of human prey—humans who don't say their prayers.

Though the bat people have been with us in story and song for hundreds of years now, today's Transylvanians contend there is a new vampire menace facing the world: the modern bat-man.

This present-day danger is able to walk about in the daytime, cast a reflection in a mirror, even do *without* sleeping in his or her own Monogram coffin (or a Universal one too).

And the only way we can destroy these Things is by a double-cross.

Vampires nowadays are *twice* as deadly as ever.

Fortunately, heroes with a stake in the vampire's business are springing so fast, you wonder where the yellow went.

Universal pictures, naturally, had been years ahead of their time when they produced the thun-

turn the page

Terror team of Bela Lugosi as the vampire and Matt Willis as the werewolf frighten the night-lights out of Nina Foch in RETURN OF THE VAMPIRE (Columbia, 1948)

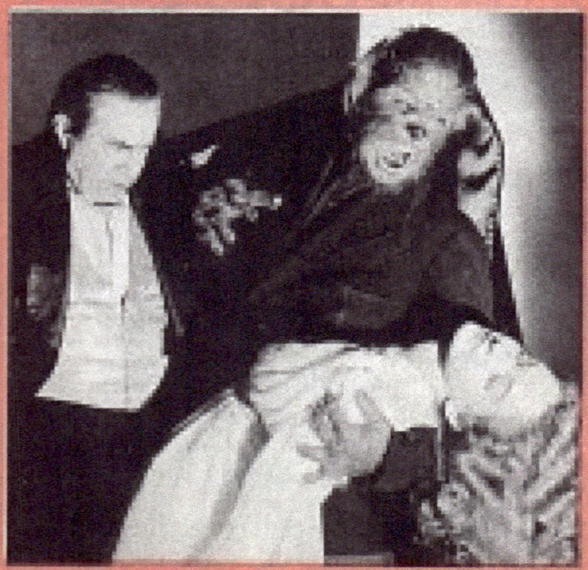

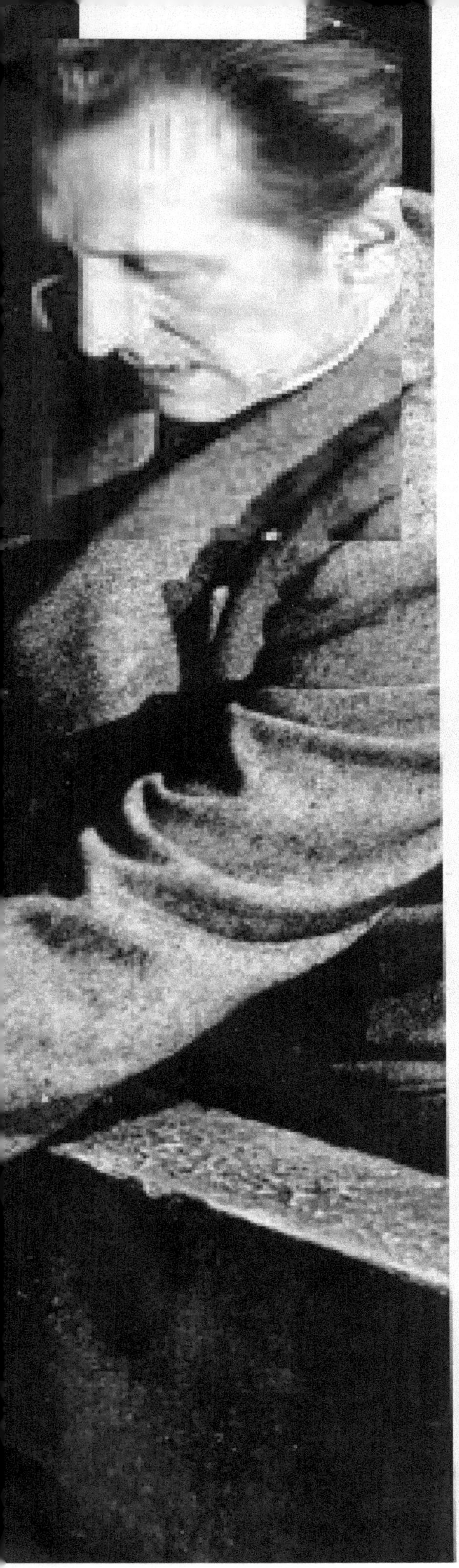

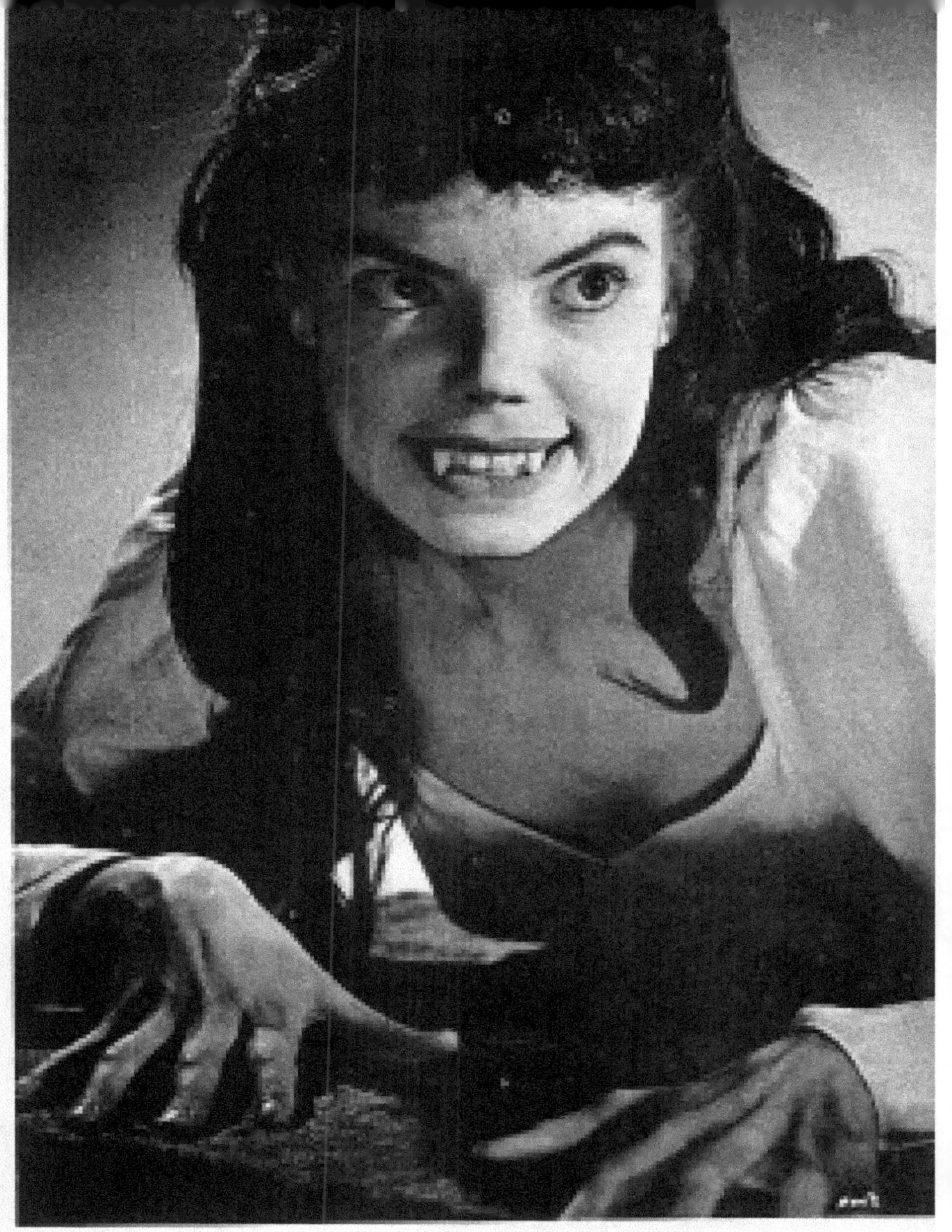

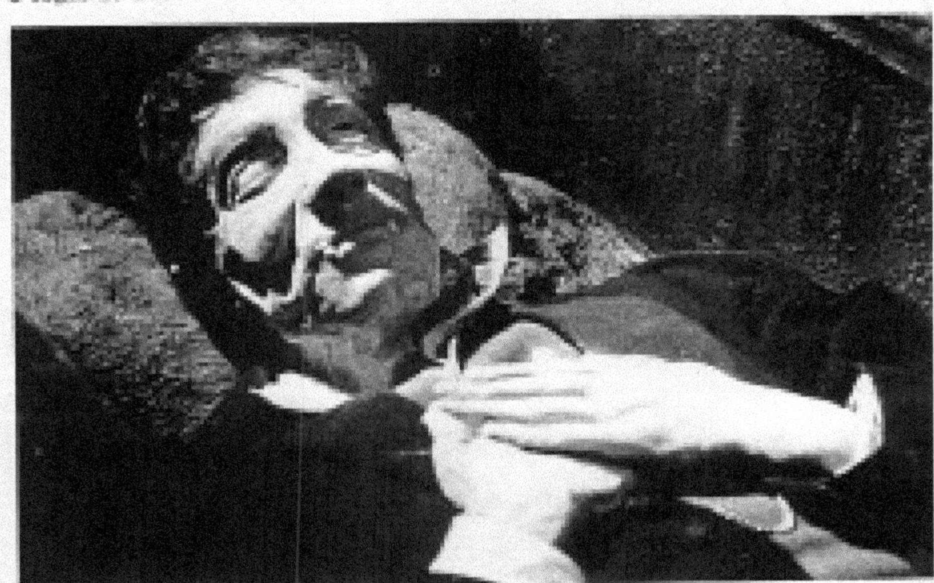

(Left) Professor van Helsing (Peter Cushing) instructs his students in the fine art of destroying vampires in HORROR OF DRACULA. (Above) One of the many BRIDES OF DRACULA is Andree Melly (Universal, 1960). (Below) Vampire victim John van Eyssen takes to a coffin in Dracula's mausoleum (HORROR OF DRACULA)

5

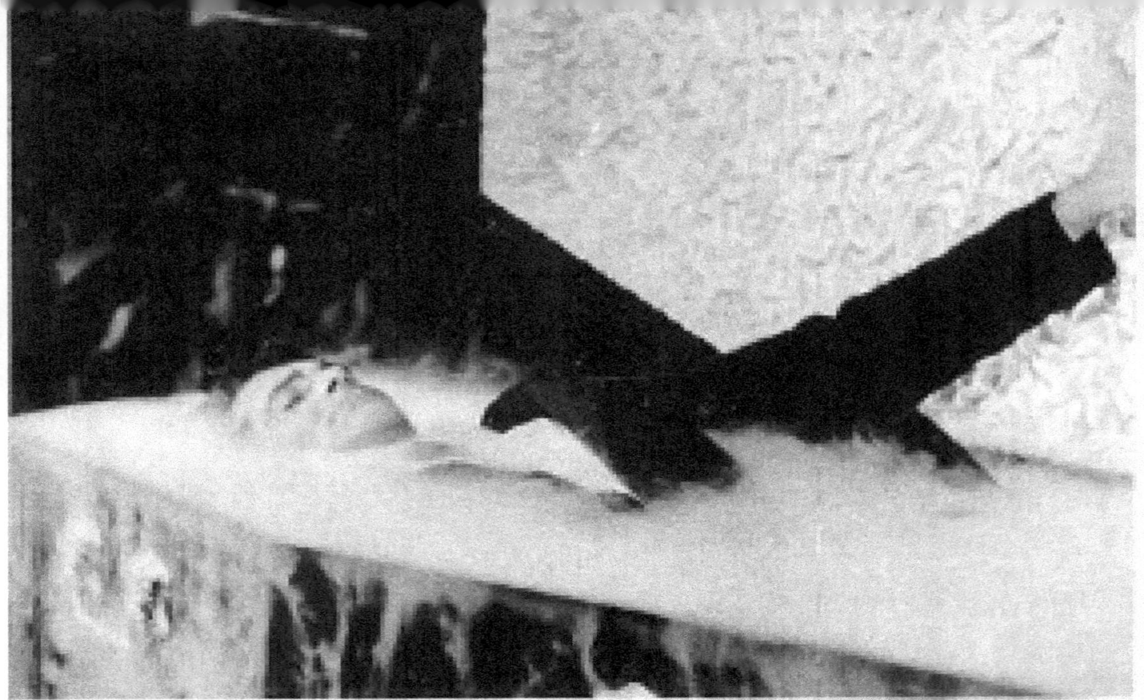

(Above) It's time for the RETURN OF DRACULA as Francis Lederer rises from his silver-tipped coffin (United Artists, 1958). (Below) King of the Vampires—Bela Lugosi

Count Christopher Lee spreads HORROR OF DRACULA for Hammer Films (Universal release, 1958)

derous Flash Gordon serials of the late '30's. But now we realize this commendable studio had also been time-tapping tomorrow when filming Son of Dracula in 1943.

In one scene of this descendant drama, Universal depicted the modern vampire.

Lon Chaney Jr., starring as the sinister son, paraded past a full-length mirror which reflected his fearsome figure!

However, as Alex Gordon, Hollywood hit-maker of fantasy films, told us recently:

"There is only one true vampire version—that which Bela Lugosi made world famous in the original Dracula. No other can ever hope to compare to it."

The King of the Vampires, Most Dreaded of Draculas, will be remembered as the sharpest fiend ever to bite the dirt in Hollywood.

Complete with coffin and cape, Bela still continues to scare up nightmares for everyone who sees his toothy smile on the screen.

But Bela the Bat did not stop his career with just one vampire flight. For years he returned again and again to haunt theatres with his incisive presence.

Bela was Dracula-like for Columbia's Return of the Vampire.

Devil Bat saw him raising the roof with flying creatures that drained the local villages.

Once again as the original Count, Bela frightened the daylights out of one-time night club comics Abbott & Costello when they visited him at an eerie island castle in Universal's Abbott & Costello Meet Frankenstein.

Bela went bats again in Mark of the Vampire.

There have been other winged wonders who have soared the Silver Screen:

turn to page

TERRORS from

Rod Serling, talented author-host of the CBS teleseries, **The Twilight Zone**, has presented many fascinating and intriguing flights into fantasy during the several seasons he has amazed millions of America's viewing public.

One of his most widely-heralded and often discussed single plays is the terrifying little tale called **Eye of the Beholder**.

In a wink, we see a future where a young woman, her head wrapped in bandages, is pleading with her doctors to perform plastic surgery to remold her face to normal.

White-masked faces and skilled hands begin the incisions; and when the fateful day arrives, the bandages are unwrapped to reveal the face of a hauntingly beautiful girl.

But, in this world of the Future, everyone wears the same, hideous, grotesque face. The girl who departed from the norm was a freak too hopeless for surgery to help.

FANTASTIC MONSTERS, for the first time anywhere, presents a photo of the Average Man of the Future! ●

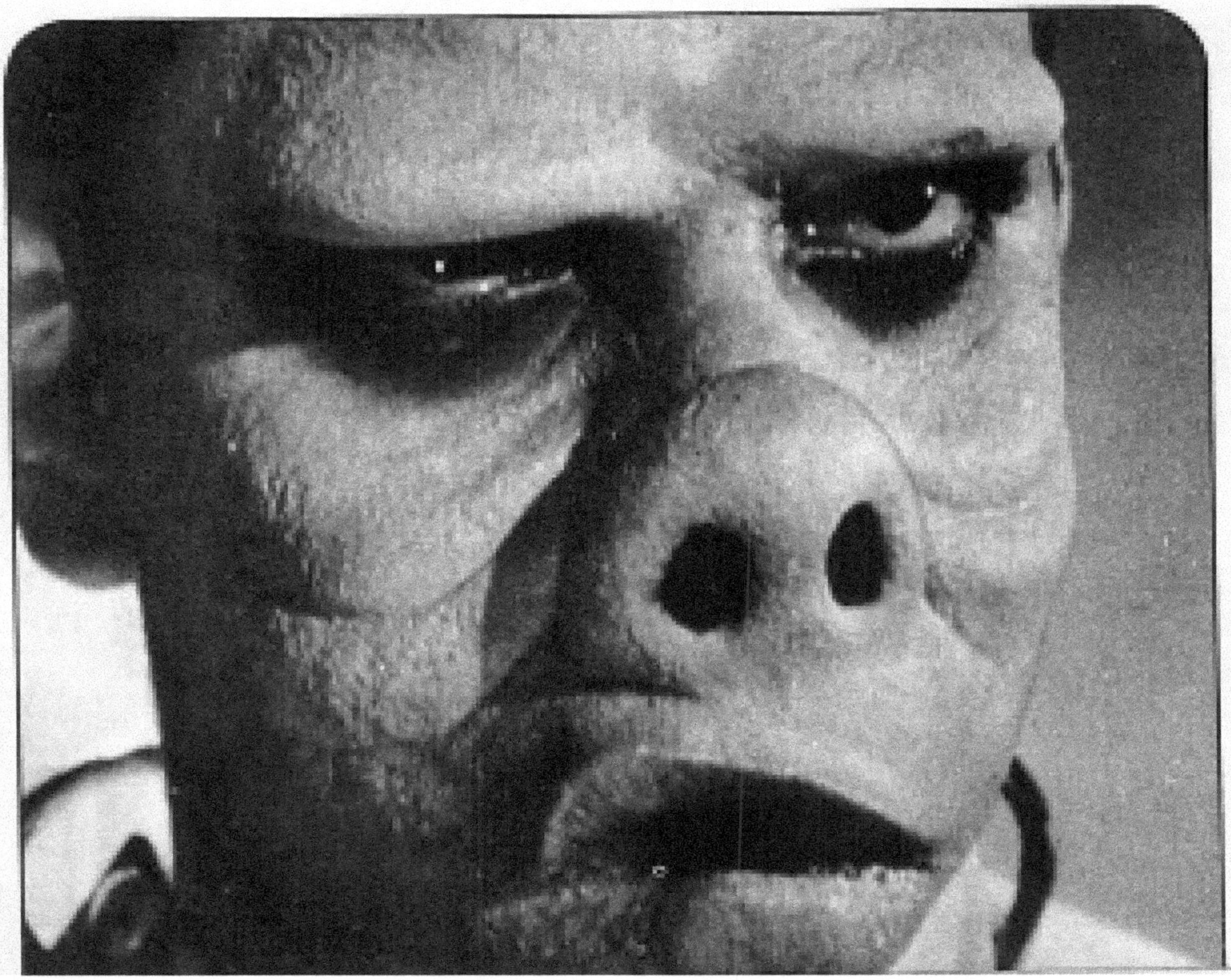

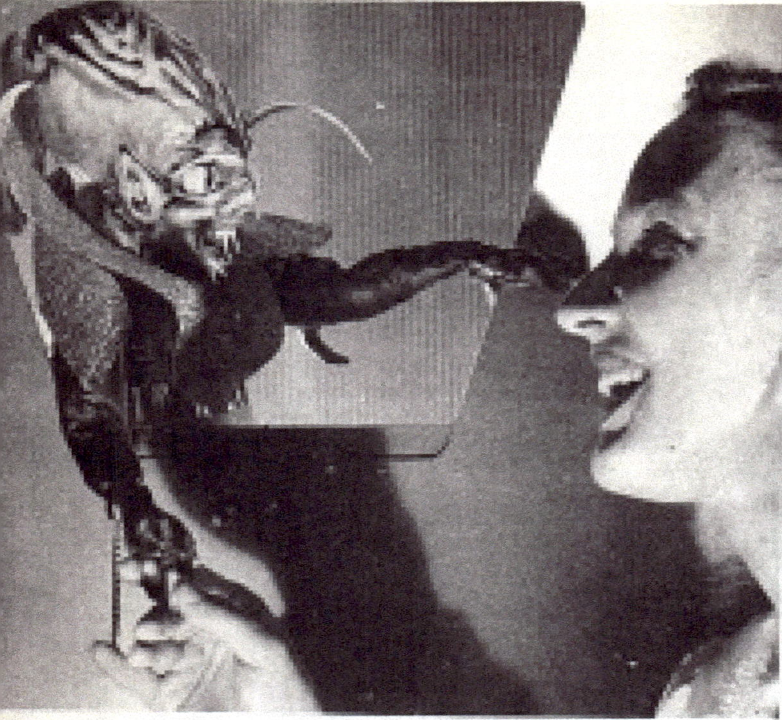

I am still having a problem trying to explain why my creature in **Beast With a Million Eyes** is missing 99,998 orbs! As a matter of fact, I even had to explain it to *Fah!*'s editor!

There is, however, one simple answer:

You've got the wrong beast.

In the film, the monster that appears with the hypnotic spiral superimposed over him is actually the slave of the **Beast With a Million Eyes**. The true "Beast" is never shown.

One of the reasons we used the twin-eyed stooge was because the special effects for this film were on an extremely tight budget. There is a popular misconception about Hollywood Monster Makers. The plain truth is we do not always work on Million Dollar Movies, and we do not take home Million Dollar Paychecks. Often we have to work with limited funds in a budgeted amount of time. When the Big Money is not behind the film, we have to exercise even more imagination to create those "wonders" for the motion picture screen.

So all you monster fans who are looking for economical ways to work with your favorite hobby—making monsters—might follow these photos we set up for you.

First of all, you will want to get the materials you need.

That "special gooey rubber" you may have seen mysteriously mentioned in other magazines is really *liquid latex*. Today, you can purchase liquid latex at hobby, hardware, and arts & crafts stores all over the country. Instructions for its proper use are included. If you happen to have no luck obtaining the latex at any of these places, try contacting one of the local distributors for any of the big rubber companies through your telephone directory.

But remember: liquid latex is the sap of the rubber plant, period! Any-

turn to page 52

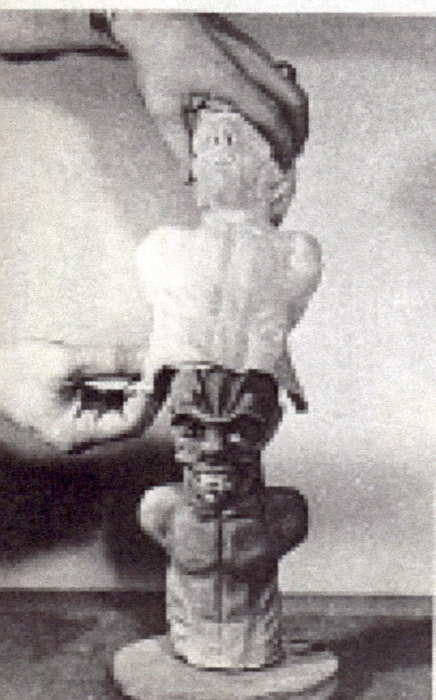

(Above, left) Shape monster from modeling clay — one with either a drying or oil base. (Above, right) Apply latex. Build up layers of rubber. Follow instructions on bottle and refer to this article. (Left) When "cured," slit the rubber up the back and work it off the clay form. Repeat for arms, legs, etc.

DEVIL'S

Hollywood Monsterdom's youngest master of special effects, Paul
Blaisdell, takes you behind-the-scenes to introduce do-it-yourself
Monster-Making

WORKSHOP

HORROR'S
HAIRIEST
HORROR

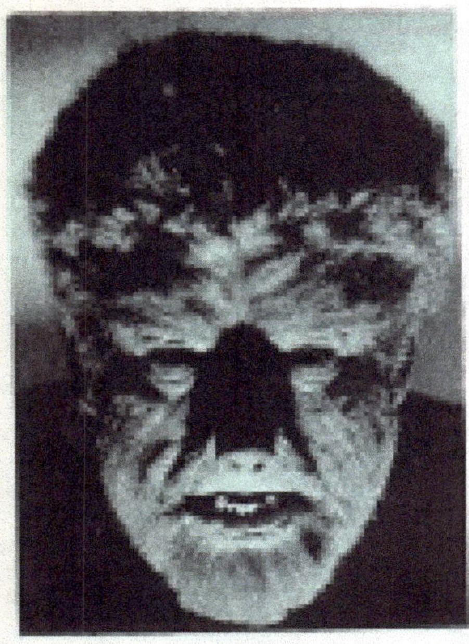

*"Even a man who is pure
     in heart,
And says his prayers by
     night,
May become a wolf when
     the wolfbane blooms,
And the moon is full and
     bright."*

By day, he was a respectable young man; but by night, he prowled the land.

So goes the wooly legend of the werewolf who was in Universal Pictures' classic shudder flicker, *The Wolf Man.*

With a cast starry enough to decorate a Halloween sky (Evelyn Ankers, Bela Lugosi, Claude Rains, Warren Williams, Ralph Bellamy, Maria Ouspenskaya, and Lon Chaney Jr. as the canine primate) *The Wolf Man* went slinking about the Universal soundstages, barking at cameramen, and whistling wolf-calls at the script girls.

The *Curse of the Wolf Man* was upon Chaney, and the *Curse of the Werewolf* fell over the theatre audiences who yet recall the menace that prowled the cloudy mists of the moon.

The hair-raiser starts tamely enough.

Lawrence Talbot (Lon Chaney Jr.) lopes home to his father's castle after a long absence and is soon rubbing noses with his childhood sweetheart, the fair Gwen Concliffe (Evelyn Ankers), now the manager of her father's tourist snare, the local gift shop.

turn the page

Inspector Montford beats it for the Talbot mansion to question Larry.

Montford, Dr. Lloyd (Warren Williams), and Sir John Talbot (Claude Rains) listen attentively to Larry's story of how he killed the canine giant that had attacked Jenny.

But all insist that the wolf fangs on Larry's chest must all be in his head; there have been no wolves in the region since Larry left. The inspector believes Talbot killed Bela the Gypsy, mistaking him for a wolf during his beastial attack in the night.

Larry retraces his trail to the gypsy camp the following night and talks to Bela's mother, Maleva (played by Maria Ouspenskaya). She obligingly informs him that her son was a werewolf, and now that Larry has been bitten by a wolf man, he will also feel the teeth of the curse.

Talbot is disinclined to accept the fact he is a monster, but the fear grows until he is running in circles with the thought that he may be transformed into a wolf in the full of the moon.

His dread of the Curse reaches its summit when, by dawn, he learns of another brutal murder and finds the spoor of a wolf in his room!

Larry decides that for the safety of the village people, he must leave the area.

But while saying goodbye to Gwen, he reads the Mark of Death in the palm of her hand.

Realizing there is not enough time to escape before the full moon rises

Noticing a rack picketed with walking sticks, young Talbot is attracted to a cane upon which is mounted a silver wolf's head. He sniffs around after information about the unusual design of the stick, and Gwen tells him the five-pointed star represents the Sign of the Beast, and that the wolf's head is that of a werewolf.

"Old Wives' tales," growls Larry, purchasing the cursed cane.

That night, a gypsy carnival arrives in town, and Larry, Gwen, and her girlfriend Jenny decide to take part in the frolic.

While Gwen and Larry trot off by themselves, Jenny's fortune is read by Bela (Lugosi) the Gypsy. In the girl's trembling hand, Bela spies the Sign of Death!

Suddenly, Gwen and Larry hear Jenny shriek!

Young Talbot roars towards the fortune teller's tent and comes upon a beastly sight—a huge wolf attacking Jenny!

Larry slams his silver-knobbed walking stick into the skull of the beast, finally beating the night creature to death.

But panting in victory, Larry discovers he has his own wounds to lick: the bite of the wolf phantom.

The next day Larry awakens to hastily explore a wolf's head and the mark of the pentagram etched faintly on his bared chest. He recalls with a nagging, irresistible fear Gwen's tale of the Curse of the Werewolf.

That same morning, Police Inspector Montford (Ralph Bellamy) whips together a search party to hunt the forest for clues to Jenny's murderer. The villagers uncover Bela the Gypsy's battered corpse—and Larry Talbot's bloody cane alongside it.

gain, young Talbot confesses his terrifying tale to his father. Sir John stubbornly refuses to believe his son changes into furry beast.

Sir John himself is about to join the villagers in a search for the crazed killer when Larry insists he be strapped to a chair in his room. The elder Talbot is docilely obliging, then leaves the castle for the hunt, taking his son's wolf-headed walking stick with him.

Soon the pale circle of moonlight lies full in the sky, and Larry Talbot slowly begins to change into the form of a ferocious Wolf Man in one of the most shocking scenes ever viewed on the screen!

He bursts his bonds and crashes out of his room, growling his contempt at Gillette and the moon.

Meanwhile, back at the branch, Gwen is searching the woods. She comes upon Maleva the Gypsy Woman sitting blandly in her wagon. Maleva tells Gwen that she should not attempt to locate Larry Talbot while the moon is full and a werewolf prowls the grounds.

Paying no attention to Maleva's irritating timidity, Gwen dashes further into the foggy forest.

Lurking behind a tree, eyeing her every movement, is the shadowy form of the Wolf Man!

Without warning, the beast lunges at Gwen!

Gwen's scream echoes through the woods, and Sir John, still with the search party, hears her cry and races wildly to her aid.

He spots the Wolf Man and Gwen, and charges the creeping creature. Using his son's cane, Sir John mercilessly beats it upon the furry head of the werewolf, finally slaying his son.

The villagers, close on Sir John's heels, reach the scene of horror.

They find the older Talbot standing terror-stricken over the lifeless body of the Wolf Man. As they stare down at the form, the features slowly melt into the face of fun-loving Larry.

The Wolf Man's bones will be buried 'neath the constant moon forevermore.

But . . .

When the wolfbane blooms . . . ?●

Matinee Menace

Rocketship fueled? Ray-Gun charged?
Then strap yourself into your acceleration
couch and get set to blast-off into
the serial sky, shot through with comets
of doom and stars of peril

Commando Cody, Sky Marshal of the Universe, defends Earth from invading RADAR MEN FROM THE MOON (Republic, 1951)

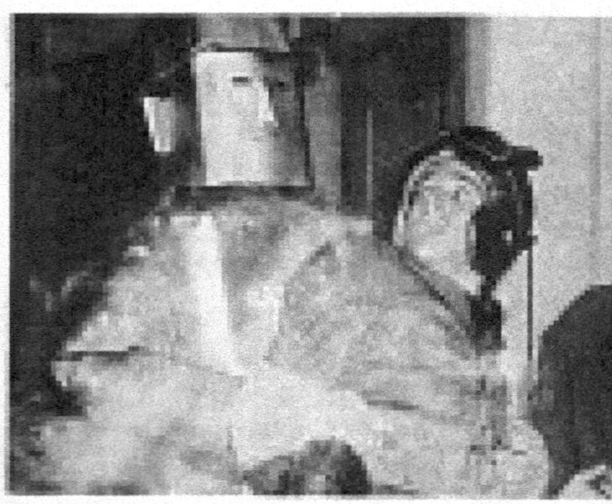

The Video Ranger (Larry Stewart) needs the aid of a COL. ICEBOX in this scene from Columbia's CAPTAIN VIDEO, serial cliffhanger of 1951.

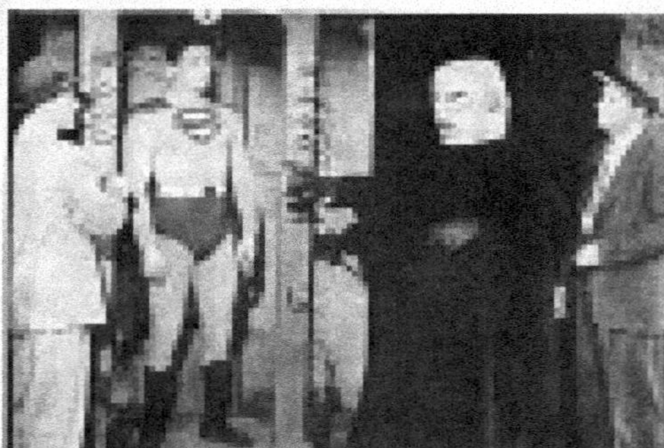

Superman is noticed to the villain's gad job by Mister Transmitter, Kirk Alyn as the Man of Steel in ATOM MAN VS. SUPERMAN. (Columbia, 1950)

Surrounded by a sizzling display of film flames, Lois Lane, girl reporter for a great metropolitan newspaper, leisurely sinks to the floor of the burning building

Hungry flames begin to lick at her toes as an ominous fog of silver smoke fills the room, curtaining off the slender sob-sister.

THEN—an Earth-shaking gong thrills through you, and you see a circle of black sweep across the theatre screen!

Is this the end of Lois Lane?

Will she be burned to death in this inferno? Or will she manage to escape from a horrible death?

These questions wind-milling in your head, and popcorn buttering in your hand, you return to the theatre next week just in time to catch sight of a scarlet and blue caped figure sweeping down from the skies to smash through the walls of Lois' fiery tomb.

It's Superman!

The indestructible Man of Steel scoops up the stunned and stunning reporter and flies her to safety.

Nyoka the Jungle Girl surprised by an unidentified fiend in Republic's JUNGLE GIRL, based on the famous novel by Edgar Rice Burroughs.

Once again the Man of Tomorrow has saved the day—and his girl-friend's life!

So begins episode 11 of Columbia's serial sensation, Superman, starring Kirk Alyn as the invulnerable immigrant from the planet Krypton, and lovely Noel Neill as Lois Lane.

Heroes and heroines have been thrilling serial audiences for over 50 years, starting with What Happened to Mary in 1912. There has been an endless parade of perils packing the picture house:

Tristram Coffin jetting through the stratosphere as King of the Rocket men;

Don Winslow of the Coast Guard washing over the Scorpion;

Captain Video rocketing into time and space to match ray-guns with Vultura, prominent Pretender to the title "Dictator of the Universe";

Bela Lugosi gesturing hypnotically as Mandrake the Magician;

Batman and Robin teaming against Dr. Daka, who assembly-lines zombies.

Whether the cliffhangers lasted 12, 13, or 15 (even 115!) chapters, we were always guaranteed to be at the ringside of the greatest thrills and spills Earth-side or elsewhere.

Relive the daring (if you dare the reliving) of Superman, Captain Marvel, Sky Altitude, Buck Rogers, Brick Bradford, Congo Bill, Bruce Gentry, Batman, Commando Cody, Crimson Ghost, and hundreds of others in future issues of FANTASTIC MONSTERS, where there's always another episode coming up in Hollywood's serial story! ●

The King of All Monsters, KONG, wrestles with a Tyrannosaurus in the jungles of Skull Island. See champion screamer Fay Wray perched up in the twisted tree, watching the tussle?

This Tyrannosaurus Rex claws out of Nassour Studios' BEAST OF HOLLOW MOUNTAIN (United Artists release, 1956)

The triple horrors, the Triceratops, wage war against each other as Cesar Romero and friends look on in this scene from Robert L. Lippert's THE LOST CONTINENT (1951)

DAWN AGE BEASTS

Leapin' Lizards and Flying Ones too — Part One of the history of monster menaces from Earth's dim red past

The last dinosaur emitted a final bellow of loneliness and frustration that echoed and re-echoed throughout the steaming jungles of the world in which he lived. He toppled to earth like a gigantic prehistoric steam shovel—and the crash of his massive body brought to a thundering climax the Great Era of Pre-History in which he existed.

We will probably never really know exactly why he died: changes of climate, shortages of food—we can only guess. But we do know that the Tyrant King was dead, and the world was now safe for the Age of Mammals—and the Age of Man.

Today in the world's many museums we can see models of nature's experiments with living monsters, and detailed reconstructions of their bones. And, thanks to the laboring technicians in Hollywood, we've also seen these very same creatures "live" again, in the fantastic films of the cinema screen.

At the theatres, we've witnessed dinosaurs crashing through their Dawn Age jungles, sometimes hunted by Man, oftimes plagued by other ferocious beasts. In some films, the prehistoric pets have charged into our teeming cities, creating panic wherever they lumber.

The Brontosaurus was a tame, vegetarian friend; the Tyrannosaurus Rex, a flesh-eating fiend. However, all of the dinosaur clan have at one time or another been carefully recreated and operated by Filmdom's Masterminds—makeup men, special effects departments, and animators. Through Hollywood, we have been taken back a million years in time to the days and nights when the skyscraper-high beasts reigned.

Although Hollywood frequently makes the mistake of placing dinosaurs in fictional environments, credit is due Universal-International Pictures for allowing the Elasmosaurus from *Land Unknown* to romp around in his correct element.

In real life, the Elasmosaurus (meaning metal-plated lizard) swam through the inland seas of North America, near an area which is today known as Kansas. Huge and fearsome, very little escaped his swiftly-snapping jaws, propelled by his serpentine neck.

The Lost Continent showed us the terrible Triceratops—curious creatures who might very well be the great-great-great grandfather of what is today referred to as the Western Horned Toad.

Although the Triceratops (translation: "3 horns on the head") would prefer eating radishes to readers, more than once did they battle each other for such delicacies as prehistoric potatoes.

In *The Lost Continent*, these triple-horned terrors lunged and snapped at one another constantly with their beak-like snouts. Bullets bouncing off his saurian hide, one even ended up making like an

turn to page 24

*

A prehistoric peril, the Elasmosaurus, surges from the murky depths of an unfathomable warm water oasis near the South Pole in LAND UNKNOWN (Universal Pictures, 1957)

BLACK LOTUS

by ROBERT BLOCH

Pedalling this Rosy Horror is Robert Bloch, Grave Fancier whose Biers Made Milwaukee Famous before Hollywooding such Tele- and Cine-magics and Tomb Tomes as THE COUCH, PSYCHO, CABINET OF DR CALIGARI, YOURS TRULY — JACK THE RIPPER, and . . .

This is the story of Genghir the dreamer, and of the curious fate that overtook him in his dreams; a story old men whisper in the souks of Ispahan as other old men once whispered it in fabled Teraa, five thousand years ago. What portion of it is truth and what portion only fantasy, I leave unto your judgement. There are strange sayings in the banned books, and Alhazred had reasons for his madness; but as I have said, the judgement rests with you. I but relate the tale.

Know then that Genghir was lord over a distant kingdom in the days of the griffin and the fleet-winged unicorn. Rich and powerful was his domain, and peaceful and well-ruled withal, so that its sovereign need occupy himself only with his pleasures.

Handsome was Genghir, but formed as a woman is formed, so that he cared

turn the page

LOTUS, from page 19

not for the chase or manly combat. His days were spent in rest and study, and his nights in revelry amongst the women. The functions of government rested upon the shoulders of Hassim el Wadir, the Vizier, whilst the true sultan dallied at his pleasures.

Grievous was the life he led, and soon the land was torn by dissension and corruption. But this Genghir heeded not at all, and Hassim he ordered flayed for misuse of office. And there was revolution and killing throughout the land; and then a fearful plague arose; but all this Genghir minded not, even though two-thirds of his people died. For his thoughts were alien and far away, and the weight of his rule he felt as a feather. His eyes knew only the musty pages of enscrolled books and the soft white flesh of women. The witchery of words and wine and wenches cast a spell upon his senses. There was dark magic in the black-bound books his father had brought from ancient conquered realms, and there was enchantment in the old wines and the young bodies that his desires knew, so that he lived in a land of unreality and dreams. Surely he would have died were it not that those left in the land, after the plague, had fled to other kingdoms, leaving him in an empty city. The report of their going never reached his ears, for well his courtiers knew that those who brought displeasing news were beheaded. But one by one they slipped away, taking with them gold and precious jewels, until the palace lay deserted under a sun that shone upon a barren land.

No longer did the women rest within the zenana, or disport as nymphs beside the amber pools. The sultan turned to other pleasures from the realms of Cathay, and in robes of velvet black he lay and toyed with the juices of the poppy. Then did life become indeed but a dream, and the opium-visioned nightmares took on the semblance of events and places mentioned in the eldritch volumes that he read by day. Time became but as the lengthening of a monstrous dream. Genghir ventured forth into his gardens no more, and less and less did he partake of food and wine. Even his books he forgot, and lay for all the time in a drugged sleep, nor heeded the coming and going of the few followers that remained within his retinue. And a silence of desolation fell upon the land.

Now it came to pass that opium and other drugs were not enough, so that Genghir was forced to seek recourse in other and more potent distillations. And in one of the curious evil books he read of a subtle potion brewed from the juices of the Black Lotus that grows beneath the waning moon. Dire and dreadful were the warnings of the scribe regarding the concoction of this forbidden preparation, for its genesis was deemed unholy, and the dangers surrounding its use by a novice were couched in trenchant terms. But Genghir thirsted for the lurid magic of its dreams and for the promise of its delight, nor would he be content until he should taste of its forbidden ecstasy.

His palace stood dim and deserted, for in the latter days the remnant of his sycophants and hearts had departed from the dusky halls whose cheap splendours had long since been

"Do we carry Tanna Leaves?"

bartered for the true delights found only in the land of opiate dreams. There now remained but three faithful servitors to guard Genghir on his couch of visions, and these he called unto his side and commanded them to journey forth and seek the venom-distilled beauty of the Black Lotus, in the hidden swamps afar of which the cryptic book had told. And they were much afraid, both for him and for themselves, because they had heard curious legends; with one accord they besought him to recall his words. But he grew angered, and his eyes were seen to flame like opals, whereat they departed.

A fortnight passed ere one of them returned—a fortnight during which the dreamer tried in vain to beguile his satiated senses with the common reek of the white flower. Overjoyed was he when the slave returned with his precious burden and brewed from it the blissful juices of nepenthe, following the injunctions set forth in the curious book. But he did not speak of his journey, or venture aught concerning the fate of his two companions; and even the dazed dreamer wondered why he kept his features veiled. In his eagerness he did not inquire, but was content to see the philtre carefully compounded and the pearly-hued liquor inserted in the nargileh. Immediately upon the completion of this task, the servitor departed, and no man knows the manner of his going, save that he lashed his camel far across the desert, riding as though possessed by demons. Genghir did not note his genii-beset progress, for already he was enraptured at the thought of what was to come. Indeed he had not stirred from his divan in the palace chambers, and in his brain was naught but the thirsty demand of desire for the strange new thrill fore-told in the elder lore. Queer dreams were promised to him who who durst inhale the fumes, dreams of which the old book dare not even hint—"Dreams which surpass Reality, or blend with it in new and unhallowed ways." So spoke the scribes, but Genghir was not afraid, and heeded only the promise of delights it was said to hold.

And so it was that he lay on the couch that evening and smoked his hookah alone in the deepening dark-ness, a dream-king in a land where all but dreams was dead. His divan over-looked the balcony high above the empty city, and as the moon rose, its crescent-given rays glistened upon the iridescent bubblings of the white fluid in the great bowl through which the smoke was drawn. Sweet indeed was the essence's taste, sweeter than the honeycombs of Kashmir or the kisses of the chosen brides of Paradise. Slowly there came stealing over his senses a new and delightful languor —it was as if he were a creature free-born, a being of the boundless air. He gazed half-seeing at the bubbles, and suddenly they bubbled up, up, up, un-til they bathed the room in a veil of shimmering beauty, and he felt all identity vanish in their crystalline depths.

Now ensued a period of profound and mystic sadness. He seemed to lie within the graven walls of a tomb, upon a slab of pale-white marble. Shrill funereal pipings seemed to echo from afar, and his nostrils were titillated by the distilled aromatic in-cense of the sepulchral lily. He knew himself to be dead, and yet he re-tained the consciousness that was his own in life. The timelessness of com-mon dreams was not his lot; centuries passed on leadenly, and he knew every second of their length as he lay within the tomb of his fathers; en-mausoleumed upon a slab covered with stone that was carven with demon-like basilisks.

Long after the odors and the music had faded from the darkness in which he lay came the advent of corruption. He felt his body grow bloatedly puru-lescent; felt his features coagulate and his limbs slough off into charnel, oozing slime. And even that was as an instant in the weary, dragging hours of his eternity there. So much longer did he lie bodiless that he lost all conscious recollection of ever having possessed one, and even the dust that had been his bones lost all significance to him. The past, present and future were as naught; and thus uncon-sciously Genghir had revealed unto him the basic mystery of life.

Years later the crumbling walls clove thunderously asunder, and shards of debris covered over the de-caying slab that housed naught but an undying consciousness. And even they were overcast by dust and earth, until there was but nothingness to mark the sight of the proud tomb where once lay the lords of the house of Genghir. And the soul of Genghir was as nothingness alone amongst nothing-ness.

Such was the substance of the first dream. As the flicker of his soul ex-pired into everlasting darkness within the earth, Genghir awoke, and he was sweat-bathed, trembling with fear, and as pale as the death he feared. And anon he turned the pages of his book to where it spoke of the Lotus and its prophecies thereof and this he read:
The first dream shall foretell that which is to come.

Whereat Genghir grew much afraid, and closed the book in the ensilvered moonlight, then lay back upon his couch, and tried to sleep, and to for-get. But then there came stealing upon his senses the subtly sweet odor of the essence, and its magic englam-oured and engulfed, till he grew fran-tic with the insidious craving for all its sinister soothing. Forgotten was fear and prophetic warning; all dis-solved into desire. His fumbling fin-gers found the hookah, his feverish lips closed upon the stem, and his being knew peace.

But not for long. Once again the opaque mists of roseate, sweet volup-tuousness parted and dissolved, and the enchantment of rapturous, inef-fable bliss faded as a new vision su-pervened.

He was himself awaken and rise from the couch in the light of dawn, to gaze haggardly upon a new day. He saw the wretched agony of his being as the drug wore off its potency and left his body racked with spasms of exquisite pain. His head seemed to swell as if about to burst; his rotting, benightmared brain seemed to grow inside his skull and split his head asunder. He beheld his frantic gropings about the deserted chamber, the mad capers of grotesque agony that made him tear his hair and foam epilep-tically at the mouth and gibber ter-ribly as he clawed with twitching fin-gers at his temples. The white-hot mist of searing anguish sent him reel-ing to the floor, and then it seemed as though in his dreamconsciousness there came to him a horrible longing to be rid of his torment at any cost, and to escape from a living hell to a dead one. In his madness he cursed the book and the warning; cursed the ghastly lotus flower and its essence; cursed himself and his pain. And as the stark biting teeth of his torture bared still closer to the roots of his sanity, he saw himself drag his rigid, paralytic body to the outer balcony of his deserted palace, and with a grim-ace of agony greater than can be sensed by sanity, he raised himself slowly to the rail. Meanwhile, as he stood there, his head swelled and bloated to monstrous, unbelievable proportions, then burst rottenly asun-der in a ghastly blob of gray and
turn to page 63

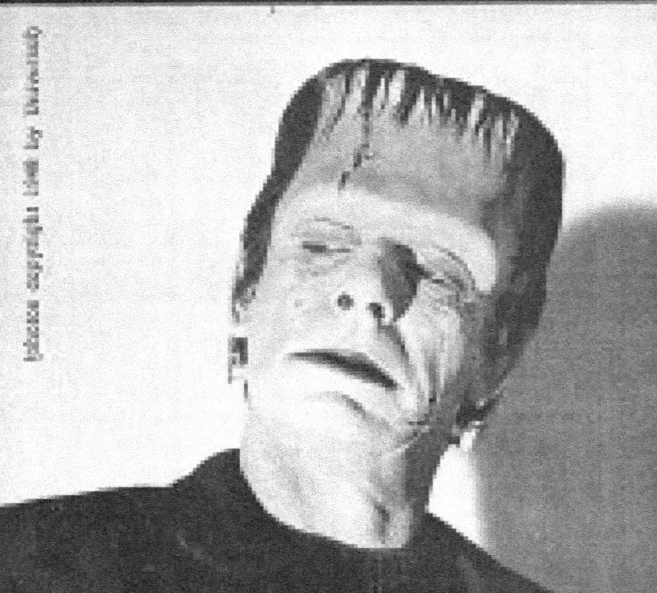

Horrors In Hollywood

Glenn Strange as the Frankenstein monster takes you with him on a typical shooting day, proving it's better to be a filmed fiend than a taped hero

"Wake up, dear—it's time for work, and you haven't shaved yet." Shooting days mean rising early, like at 5 in the morning. 1 ▷

"Since you clowns won't come peacefully . . ." It's up to Frankie-Glenn to get the film rolling. ◁ 4

"Smile, Lou—you're on camera." Frankie puts the famous comedian through his paces. 5 ▷

"Hoo Boy! The director said it's time for lunch!" A break in shooting is always a welcome relief. ◁ 6

"I bake the best cakes this side of Betty Crocker," a Universal starlet tells Frankie-Glenn. 7 ▷

"Nuts, I can hardly squeeze into my shoes anymore." Then it's a march to the Universal studios to begin monsterly duties for a new fright flicker. ◁ 2

"Arms, fellows — please!" Stars Abbott & Costello are holding out for bigger pay, and also holding up production. 3 ▷

don't miss

"So you finally found the mousetrap I placed in your lunchbox, eh?" Wolf Man Chaney says, "Fangs for nothing, you woke with a joke." 8 ▷

the next FANTASTIC MONSTERS when we rejoin Glenn Strange, Lon Chaney Jr, and Bela Lugosi on the set of Universal Pictures' ABBOTT & COSTELLO MEET FRANKENSTEIN.

FAMILY RECREATION

HUNTING: The hunting of your life. Big game species Mule Deer, are abundant. Duck, Quail and Geese are plentiful.

FISHING: A fisherman's paradise. Huge Rainbows, Brook Trout and German Browns abound in Alpine-like lakes and mountain-fed bottom streams.

FOR THE FAMILY: Riding, swimming and all sports. Camping and picnicking sites of unbelievable scenic grandeur.

INSURE YOUR PROFITABLE TOMORROW

Yes, wise investors are buying in TWIN RIVER RANCHOS. America's largest corporations who buy in advance of population explosion are also investing in Nevada. Anaconda Copper has just completed a $32,000,000 plant. North American Aviation, Curtiss-Wright and Kaiser Steel have secured building sites. U.S. Census Bureau Fact: Nevada is the Nation's fastest growing state—8 year population increase, 70%, highest in U.S.A.

TAX RELIEF: No State Income, Gift or Inheritance Tax. The low Real Property Tax is actually limited by the State Constitution.

THE TOTAL COSTS

The full price of the title to your 2½ acre Rancho is only $495.00. Total payment schedule is $10.00 down, and $10.00 per month, including 6% interest. You are not required to do anything to your land. You can live or vacation on it, or simply watch its value grow, then sell all or part of it for a profit. Your profitable tomorrow is here TODAY in TWIN RIVER RANCHOS.

THE BOOM THAT HAD TO COME IS NOW ON IN NEVADA. Ground floor buyers are reaping fortunes from small initial investments. A factual example of skyrocketing values is Las Vegas, Nevada. Land in Las Vegas that originally sold for $300.00 an acre now sells for $20,000.00 an acre, a profit of 1000%! Buyers who took advantage of low opening prices have become wealthy. The ground floor opportunity of Las Vegas is gone. BUT ANOTHER AREA OF PROSPEROUS NEVADA IS NOW BEING RELEASED FOR PUBLIC SALE!

This area has such a tremendous growth potential, such a fantastic unlimited future, that wise investors have purchased large acreage. Bing Crosby's ranch was one of the largest ranches in the county. James Stewart is Honorary Sheriff. Yes, the smart experienced investors have sensed the future and are buying TWIN RIVER RANCHOS in Elko County, Nevada.

TWIN RIVER RANCHOS has all of the factors needed to boom . . . to prosper . . . to skyrocket its land values. Located on the level, fertile lands of Rich Elko Valley, The Ranchos have the backdrop of the statuesque Ruby Mountains. The sparkling Humboldt River actually forms one of the Ranchos' boundaries, and is a valuable asset of the property. Every Rancho fronts on a graded road. The City of Elko, with its long established schools, churches and medical facilities is a friendly neighbor only 10 miles away!

NOW! DON'T MISS THIS OUTSTANDING OPPORTUNITY

TWIN RIVER RANCHOS Dept. 1358
27 Water Street • Henderson, Nevada

MAIL COUPON TODAY

Yes!—Reserve acreage at TWIN RIVER RANCHOS for me — $495 for each 2½ acre parcel— payable $10 down and $10 a month including 6% interest. No other charges. Send purchase contract and map showing exact location of my holding. You will return me $10 deposit if I request same within 30 days. I enclose $10 deposit for each 2½ acre Rancho desired.

SIZE ACRES	DOWN	PER MO.
2½	$10	$10
5	20	20
7½	30	30
10	40	40

Name _______________________

Address _______________________

City _______________ Zone ____ State _______

Indicate No. of Ranchos _______ Total enclosed $ _______

DAWN AGE, from page 17

African Rhino charging a man.

King Kong, the most menacing monster of them all, had his own share of Dawn Age Beasts to compete with.

In one of the most spectacular animation sequences ever put on film, Kong pitted himself against the Tyrannosaurus Rex, "the king of the tyrant lizards."

Set in the steaming tropical jungles of Skull Island, ape and reptile snapped, punched, kicked and clawed. They toppled trees, shook the earth, roared, bellowed and hissed—while stunned audiences sat breathless in their theatre seats, watching the beastial bout.

Remember the Tyrannosaurus stopping to scratch his ear before he plunged headlong into combat with the mighty Kong?

This was just one of the many thoughtful details the animators included in the thundering sequence to make the gigantic lizard seem more life-like.

The Tyrannosaurus' wicked facial expressions, his lunging serpentine neck, and the nervous twitching of his tremendous tail were all the result of deliberate planning too.

The Brontosaurus also braved in *King Kong*.

Hurtling his giant bulk through a mist-swirling swamp, Brontosaurus ran down a frightened group of explorers and commenced to snap them up, one by one, like Dawn Age dog biscuits.

One unfortunate explorer thought he might escape the wrath of the beast by shinning up a tree. It was a mistake—it was also the explorer's last scene in the film.

While all this violence and excitement livened up the screen, the monster's actions were almost entirely fictional. In reality, the bellicose Brontosaurus sought plant-food much more than he did people-food.

Tyrannosaurus Rex returned again in all his fury in Nassour Studios' production, *Beast of Hollow Mountain*.

Like most all movie monsters, the ravenous reptile worked long and hard to cause a great deal of damage and nightmares to star Guy Madison and others in the Cinemascope feature.

The Tyrannosaurus' animated antics in *Beast of Hollow Mountain* were aided by a new picture process labeled Regiscope, whatever that means.

In color and wide screen, Hollow Mountain's big bad beast ran rampant through the Mexican forests, stomping on all—human or otherwise—in his path.

Of course, Hollywood's biggest error has always been placing men and dinosaurs together. Whether yesterday or today, the towering reptiles and King of the Mammals have never co-existed.

But the table has been so full of thrills, no one could ever object to such loose history and great movies.

Mystery Museum

Rare photos from the crypts of
FANTASTIC MONSTERS

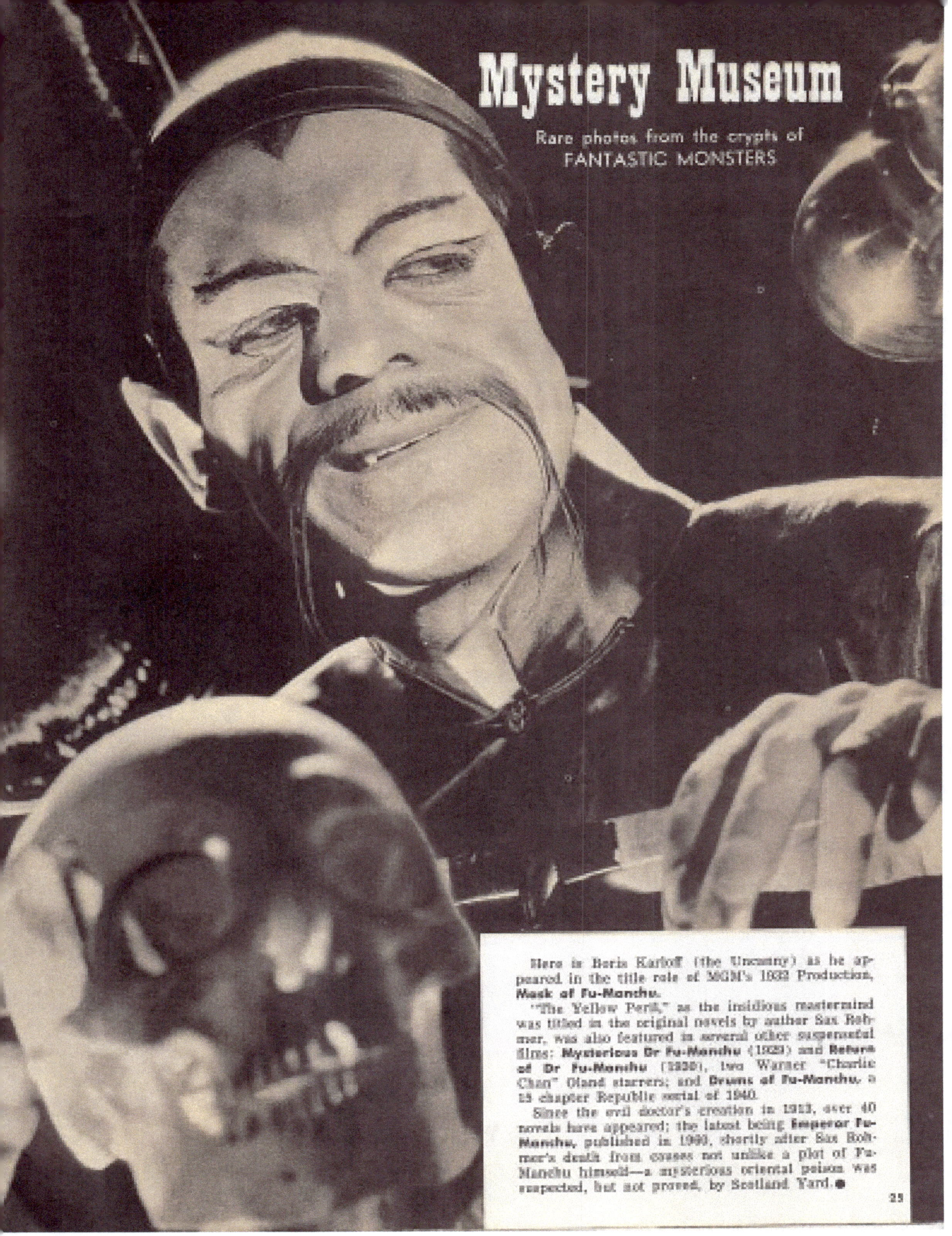

Here is Boris Karloff (the Uncanny) as he appeared in the title role of MGM's 1932 Production, **Mask of Fu-Manchu.**

"The Yellow Peril," as the insidious mastermind was titled in the original novels by author Sax Rohmer, was also featured in several other suspenseful films: **Mysterious Dr Fu-Manchu** (1929) and **Return of Dr Fu-Manchu** (1930), two Warner "Charlie Chan" Oland starrers; and **Drums of Fu-Manchu,** a 15 chapter Republic serial of 1940.

Since the evil doctor's creation in 1913, over 40 novels have appeared; the latest being **Emperor Fu-Manchu,** published in 1960, shortly after Sax Rohmer's death from causes not unlike a plot of Fu-Manchu himself—a mysterious oriental poison was suspected, but not proved, by Scotland Yard. ●

DESTINATION MOON

Man's Eternal Dream — the final conquest of outer space, and the exploration of our nearest planetary neighbor, the Moon. Here, for the first time anywhere, is the prophetic story of a science fiction film which is still as timely as today's headlines

Jim Barnes (John Archer), president of an aircraft corp., supervises the production of a rocket capable of journeying to the Moon.

Years before film producer George Pal placed actor Rod Taylor in an H.G. Wells Time Machine, even b e f o r e he caused worlds to collide or launched an Academy Award winning Martian invasion on Earth, he was determined to take a celluloid journey by rocketship to the Moon. And after 48 months of a staggering amount of work and research, Pal's *Destination Moon* loomed up on the world's theatre screens, and rocketed into a permanent niche in Hollywood's Motion Picture Hall of Fame.

F i l m e d in technicolor, against the beautiful and authentic outer space scenery designed by technical artist Chesley Bonestell, *Destination Moon* held audiences everywhere spellbound. The film even had some Europeans wondering if America actually had reached Luna!

The science fiction epic posed tremendous problems for the small army of technicians who worked on it, and solutions were arrived at in ingenious ways. To produce the unwinking stars in the inky blackness of space, over 1,500 automobile headlights were connected by miles of wire to a back-drop consisting of 400-feet of black velvet. A life-size spaceship cabin and airlock were scientifically constructed in an enormous rotating drum, so the actors could walk with the "free fall" effect of no gravity.

Upwards of 130 men labored for two months to construct the vast and rugged surface of the moon. The actors themselves had to learn to float in the air, and walk up walls. (They were aided in their efforts by Steinway wires and special harnesses.)

To achieve the effect of a crushing acceleration, as the turn the page

The ship is finally completed. Then, with the powerful thrust of its atomic engines, it hurtles spaceward, its sole destination—the Moon.

Dr. Cargraves (Warner Anderson) hands a special pill to space-sick Joe Sweeney (Dick Wesson)

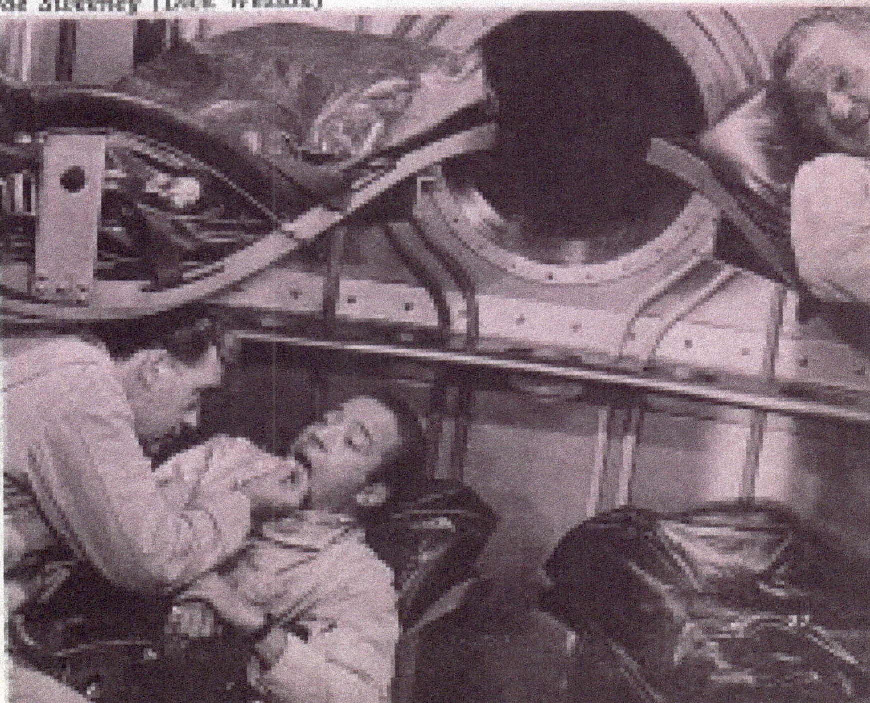

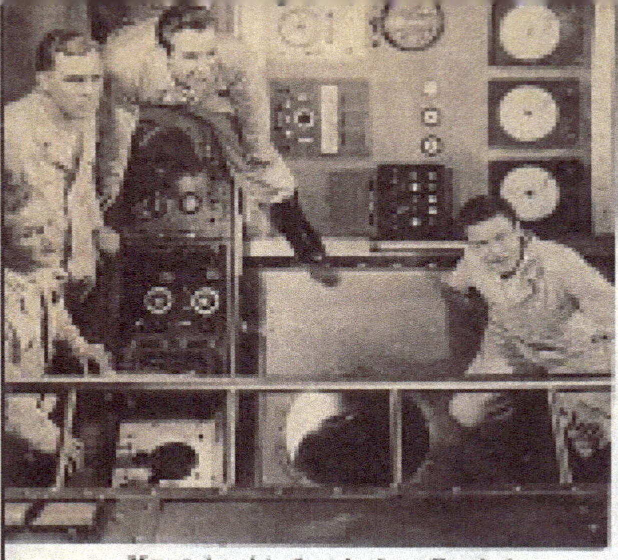

Man takes his first look at Earth from outer space, awestruck at the magnificent sight of our planet orbiting in the black void. Barnes gives each of the astronauts magnetized boots to keep them from floating about the ship now that they are in free fall

Discovering Sweeney has greased the ship's radar antenna (causing it to freeze), three of the men go out onto the hull to repair the damage. Cargraves floats away from the Luna, and Barnes straddles an oxygen bottle, rescuing him.

spaceship *Luna* blasted from Earth, near-invisible rubber membranes were stretched across the actors' faces when they lay pinned to their couches.

The marvellous $35,000 space rocket contained a startling array of meticulously authenticated dials and gadgets. They represented the careful calculations of researchers, physicists, astronomers, and a host of other specialists, who worked over the dummy instruments as conscientiously as if they were literally intending the mock spaceship to orbit the Moon.

To obtain a feeling of greater depth in some of the moon scenes, midgets were substituted for the regular actors. Bounding across the lunar surface in their colorful spacesuits, near a reduced model of the rocket, they provided scenes which gave perspective.

The actual story itself was a refreshing departure from the all-too familiar Hollywood cliches. Adapted from the novel *Rocketship Galileo* by Robert A. Heinlein, the film seriously concerned itself with the problems of four daring Columbuses who take the theatre audiences with them on the first well-planned, but extremely perilous, expedition to the Moon.

The men, Dr. Charles Cargraves, Jim Barnes, General Thayer, and Joe Sweeney were portrayed by Warner Anderson, John Archer, Tom Powers, and Dick Wesson. In the picture, these pioneer astronauts were united by the common ideal, that if we are to exist in our present status, beyond our generation, we must get to the Moon, and get there first.

By pooling the not inconsiderable resources of atomic physicists, industrialists, and others, an adventuresome but practical new spaceship design became a reality.

At 3:50 A.M., in the pre-dawn blackness of the Majave Desert, the 150-foot long rocket, the *Luna*, lifted its silver body from the sandy floor and roared into the unknown.

In less than four minutes, it was 800 miles from Earth, rocketing into interplanetary space at the unheard of velocity of 32,000-feet-per-second!

Passing from the Earth's shadow into the brilliant perpetual glare of the sun, the great atomic engines shut off, and the man-made projectile streaked for the Moon, in free fall and utter silence.

Aboard the silver ship, Cargraves, Barnes, Thayer, and Sweeney found that they would

turn the page

(Above) Landing on the Moon, the spacemen begin exploration of Earth's natural satellite.

(Below) They must lighten the ship if they are to return home, and the adventurers begin by ripping out the heavy instruments.

DESTINATION, from page 39

have to adjust themselves to many new experiences—ranging from walking on walls in magnetic boots to eating sandwiches upside-down while travelling at seven miles a second.

Halfway to the Moon, the discovery of a frozen radar antenna led three of the astronauts to don their spacesuits and crawl out onto the ship's hull for repair work. While checking the rocket tubes for possible blastoff damage, Dr. Cargraves became detached from the hull, and Barnes barely rescued him in time by using one of the Luna's oxygen bottles as a miniature spaceship. Utilizing the nozzle of the oxygen tank, he jetted after the floating scientist, then returned them both to the ship.

The four adventurers finally landed their rocket in the lunar crater Harpalus, high in the northern latitudes of the moon. A busy exploration period followed. The crew examined the timeless, pitted surface of the Moon, engaged in astro-photography, and checked for valuable mineral deposits. Impressions of sights never before seen by human eyes were radioed back to a waiting Earth. And, at last, the time came to return to the mother planet.

Now a horrifying predicament was discovered.

With the little amount of fuel left in its tanks, the Luna was carrying too much weight to pull free of the Moon's gravity. It looked as though one of the space travellers would have to remain behind—forever. Even when the ship was stripped of every movable object, including the radios, it was still many pounds too heavy.

As the men discussed the terrifying thought of one of their number remaining on the Moon, Joe Sweeney, the radio man, quietly slipped into the last on-board spacesuit and left the ship, voluntarily offering to give up his life so that the others could return to Earth.

Barnes, the youthful industrialist, hit upon a scheme for lightening the ship still further, and frantically called Sweeney back.

Still in his spacesuit, the radio man was instructed to file a small notch under the outer airlock door. He then attached his suit to an empty oxygen cylinder with a length of rope. Placing the rope in the filed groove, he hung the cylinder outside the Luna and closed the door.

The airlock was pumped full of air and Sweeney removed his 50 pound suit. He retreated to the control room through an inner door.

The inner door was sealed, and the outer one opened by remote control. The vacuum of the airless Moon rushed into the chamber, and the suit was pulled across the floor and out of the ship by the weight of the heavy oxygen bottle.

With a collective sigh of relief, the men closed the outer airlock door for the last time, and strapped themselves in their couches. The Luna rose on a towering column of orange flame—plunging into space, heading for Mother Earth, and home; and to the cheers of enthusiastic movie-goers for the man who made it all possible, the talented George Pal. ●

Revealed at last
shocking scenes from Your Past

"Spotlighting my favorite scene from a fantastic film is easy," writes Larry Byrd, fright flicker fan and editor-publisher of the amateur monster gazette, *Terror*.

"I choose the death scene of Ygor the Shepherd in Universal's *Son of Frankenstein*, with Boris Karloff intoning goodbye to the bearded Bela Lugosi."

Do you have a favorite scene you'd like us to capture in this department.

Write us about it. Published letters will earn the actual photo from *FANTASTIC MONSTERS'* "Wanted" catalog!●

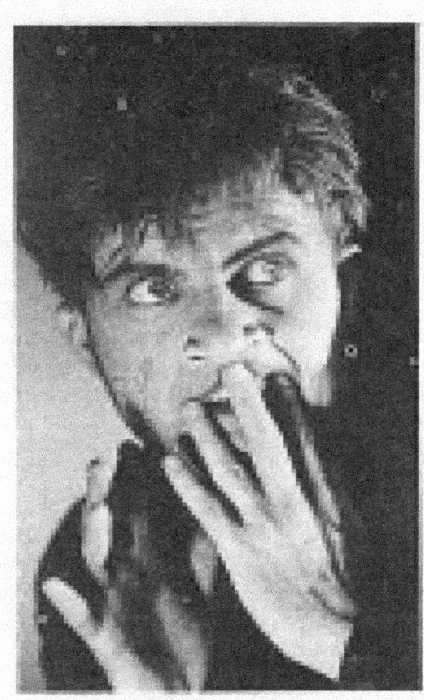

I DIED SCREAMING

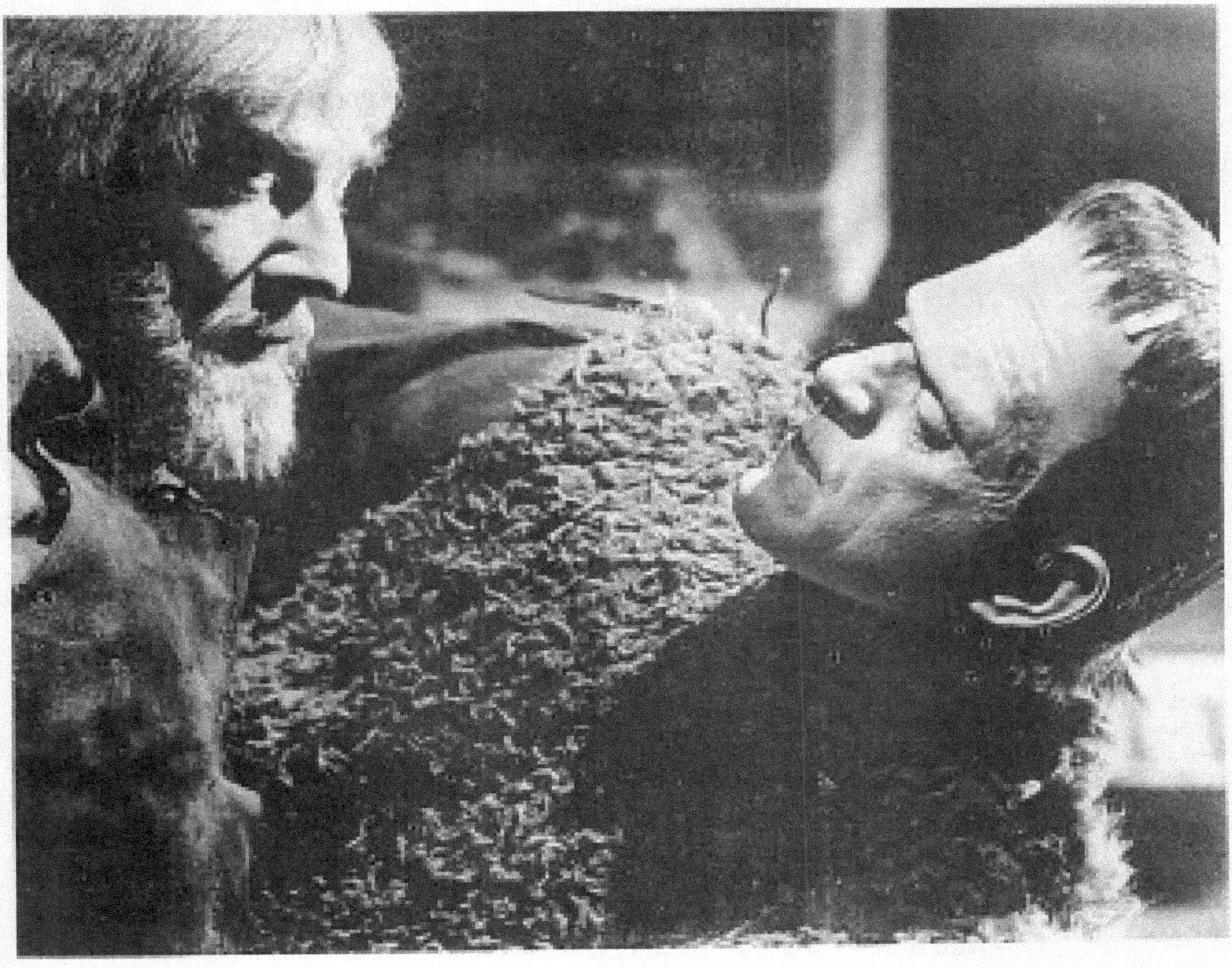

Killer Diller Ape

Jungle Johnny Weissmuller, Crowned Prince of the Dark Continent, pits himself against Africa's hairiest menace, a rampaging half-human creature, in the Columbia thriller, KILLER APE

In his every film, Jungle Johnny Weissmuller has been forced to break from monumental dangers. Big John has rescued misplaced safaris, plunged into angry torrents, splashed into crocodile herds' private lagoons. He has been trapped by a brain-snapping collection of troubles from an unabridged Catalog of Doom:

Fighting jealous gorillas as **Tarzan the Ape Man**;

Protecting his prize skull from voodoo witch doctors in **Valley of the Head Hunters**;

Turning back the clock for million-year old monsters in Jungle Jim's trip to **The Forbidden Land**;

Swinging into the teeth of vampire bats when **Tarzan Escapes**;

Singeing the Fire-Demons on the trail to **The Devil Goddess** . . .

The list could go on with struggles with rib-fracturing pythons, bull-dozing elephants, confidently grinning tigers, and royally angry lions, chest-drumming baboons, non-vegetarian sharks plaguing his vacations. But now a terribly upset 8 foot, 6 inch ape man gives Johnny his toughest test as Hollywood's King of the Jungle.

Columbia Pictures' monkey-murderer, **Killer Ape**, made in 1953, was filmed by the Kings of the Serials, producer Sam Katzman and director Spencer G. Bennet; with the scripting of Carroll Young and Arthur Hoerl, familiar travellers on the pathways of the Hollywood jungles.

The fast-paced action adventure gets off to a running start when Jungle Jim (Johnny Weissmuller) comes upon a tribe of natives who are trapping wild animals for white hunters.

Questioning them, Jungle Jim learns the animals are being used as guinea pigs by the hunters' boss, a biologist named Andrews.

Unknown to both Jim and the natives is the fact that Andrews has been experimenting to perfect a drug which can paralyze the minds and bodies of men. He is using the jungle creatures for his research tests. After formularizing the convenient drug, Andrews intends to sell it to a totalitarian nation with all its blood-icing possibilities for tyranny over the human race.

Jim warns the natives not to hunt for animals in the area where a fierce killer ape lurks.

"This half-man, half-hairy one has killed before," Jungle Jim tells the Africans. "And now he has the taste for man-blood."

But the tribesmen refuse to listen to his warning.

One of the natives enters the off-bounds country of the giant ape man, and is easually slaughtered by the lumbering creature.

Because he was in the vicinity of the murder when it

turn to page 54

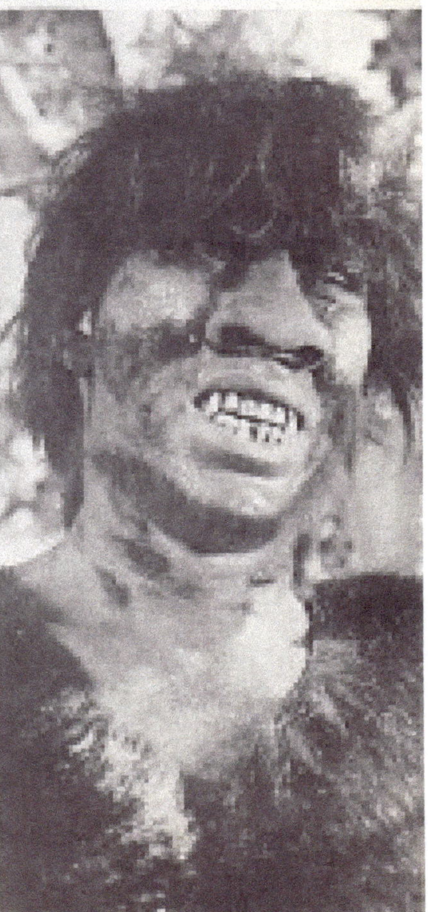

"Shotgun or no shotgun, buddy, I'm just not going to marry your daughter."

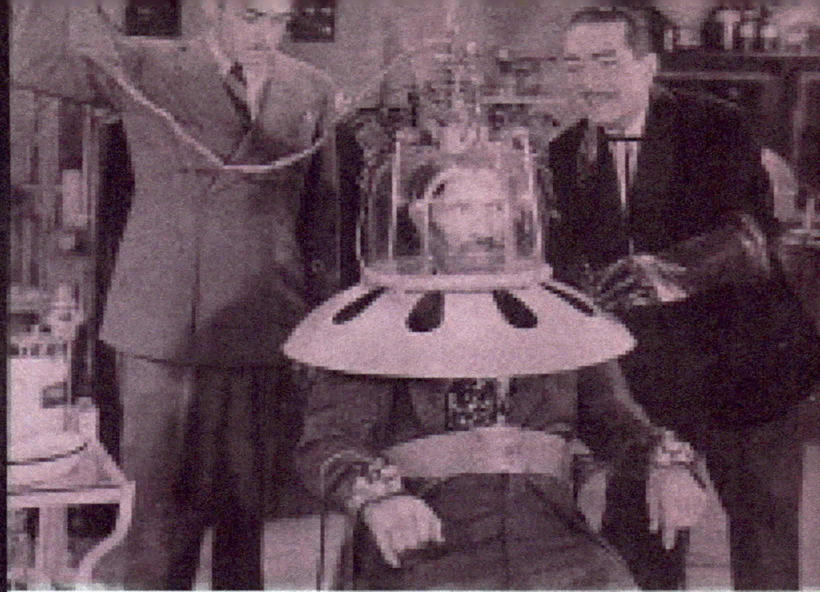

"So you guys have invented a new cure for headaches—all I want is an aspirin tablet!"

Dead Time Tales

A Little Added Dialogue Makes Monsters Better Than Ever

"I say, I wonder if my Blue Cross policy covers this sort of thing?"

"Mother, the new neighbors want to borrow a cup of blood—my blood!"

"You chase the cat around the house just one more time and I'll disconnect your rheostat for good."

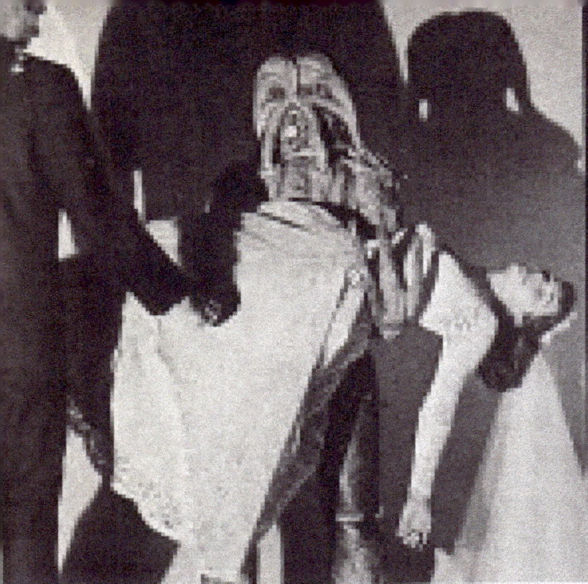

"I'm terribly sorry sir, but our Bridal Suite is occupied."

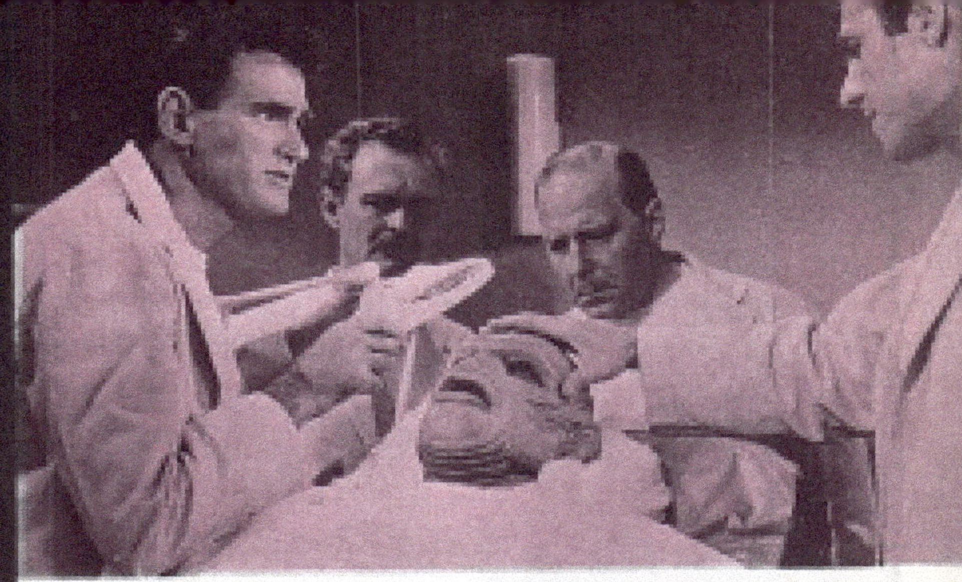

"Next time we have a plastic surgery operation to perform, keep your eyes on the patient—not on the nurse."

"But mother, it's my first High School Prom —can't I go out without you just this once?"

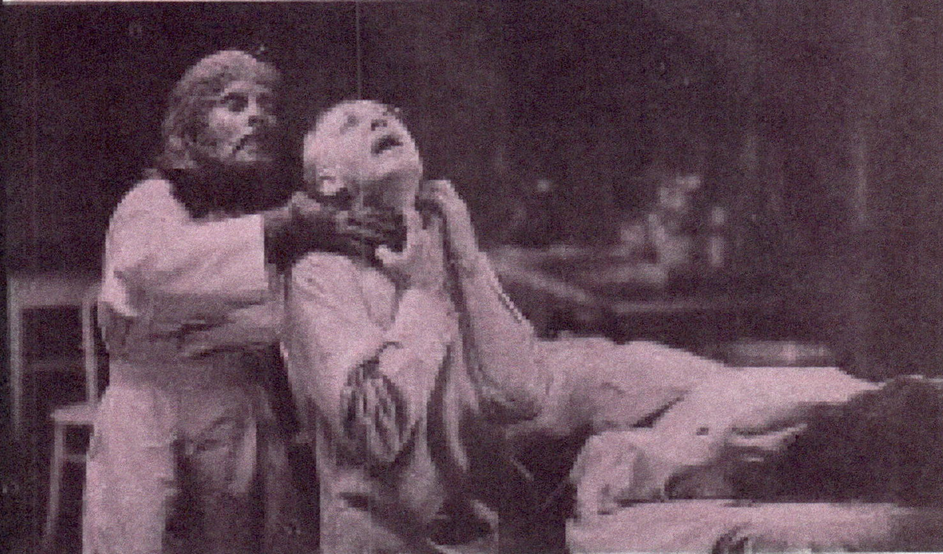

"But, son, even if she did follow you home, I still say you can't keep her."

"So she wasn't no Marilyn Monroe—what do you expect on a blind date?"

"I'm sure your son has a beautiful voice, Mr. Novack, but I still don't feel I want him in the school's glee club."

FLASH
FIGHT

Earth's mightiest warrior blazes an interstellar trail to combat a Warlord intent on conquering the Universe

GORDON'S FOR LIFE

The possessed Warlord of the planet Mongo—Ming the Merciless. (Charles Middleton in Universal's *FLASH GORDON*, 1936)

Our world was reeling under the tremendous impact of hurricanes, earthquakes, and skyscraper-high tidal waves caused by mysterious rays from outer space. These cosmic forces were hurled from **Mongo**—an unknown planet whose threatening face was growing even larger in the star-studded sky as it plunged millions of miles across the Solar System.

Suddenly, the first rocketship from Earth came screaming down through the scarlet clouds of Mongo. Inside rode three people—the square-jawed blond pilot, **Flash Gordon**; the beautiful **Dale Arden**; and the rocketship's bearded inventor, **Dr. Hans Zarkov**.

This interplanetary trio was Earth's one hope against molten destruction!

With a flaming crash, the spaceship tore into a jutting mountain peak on alien Mongo. As Flash and his crew crawled from the craft's smouldering wreckage, they found themselves menaced by two flame-spitting **dragons** hungry to eat them alive!

So began Flash Gordon's legendary fight for life.

This is how things were in the first chapter of Universal's celebrated **Flash Gordon**, a 1936 serial. The 13 episodes starred film Tarzan, Buster Crabbe, as the dragon-fighting Flash Gordon; Jean Rogers as Dale; and Frank Shannon in the role of Zarkov.

With sword, rocketship, and ray-gun, Flash & Co. battled the forces of destruction the length and width of Mongo. And, near the climax of the final, fabulous chapter, the embattled trio successfully managed to rescue our world from universal catastrophe.

Flash's greatest enemy, Ming the Merciless (played by Charles Middleton), was Emperor of Mongo. The destruction of Earth was his first step in conquering the universe. King Ming, time and again, nearly stamped out Flash's life as Earth's champion strug-

turn the page

Buster Crabbe as Flash Gordon brings forceful aid to his fighting friends, Prince Barin, Zarkov, and Happy Hapgood, who are under attack from the Forest People. Scene from *FLASH GORDON'S TRIP TO MARS*.

Flash smashes way through battalions of walking robot bombs to blast Ming

gled to save the Solar System from Ming's fanatical mission.

The second and most popular Flash Gordon serial was **Flash Gordon's Trip to Mars** (1938), another Universal Pictures entry.

Once again Earth was rocked by disastrous forces from outer space, the new project of a vengeful Ming, who had transferred his base of operations to Mars. With the help of Queen Azura (Beatrice Roberts), ruler of the Red Planet, Ming was aiming the atomic beam of his mammoth **Nitron Lamp** at Earth. The death-dealing Nitron ray was extracting vital elements from the atmosphere, and creating holocaust on our world.

Flash, Dale and Zarkov took up Ming's new challenge and sped across the gulf of space to Mars, where they fought to smash the towering Nitron Lamp, and collapse Ming's plans for making himself Dictator of the Universe.

The bitter Ming struck back with a third plot in 1940 when **Flash Gordon Conquers the Universe**, the last of the Universal chapterplays.

The **Purple Death Dust** (which left a vivid mark on the foreheads of its victims) was scattered over our planet by the sly Warlord, who was once again enthroned on Mongo. In taking up the Pursuit of Justice this time, Flash and his allies had to smash their way through battalions of walking robot bombs before discovering an antidote which would counteract the effects of the deadly particles.

In the closing moments of the 12 episode cliffhanger, Emperor Ming disappeared in a splitting explosion of his laboratory; and Flash, Dale and Zarkov returned victorious to a wildly cheering Earth.

The indestructible Flash Gordon retired after fighting for his life for Universal, but then in 1955 back he came in a European-made TV series starring Steve Holland.

Where he will make his next lightning-like appearance we can't say. But if you get impatient waiting for the blond hero to rocket across your home or theatre screen, you can always find him in **Fantastic Monsters**, captured in action by our Flash cameras.●

Prince Baris (Richard Alexander) and Flash ready themselves for out-of-this-world action.

Danger in outer space challenges Flash and friends in this scene from the Flash Gordon TV series, starring Steve Holland, Irene Champlin, and Joe Nash.

They're NEW!
HOLLYWOOD MONSTERS!
IN STANDARD 2 x 2 COLOR SLIDES
EACH SLIDE DIFFERENT—EACH SET DIFFERENT!
EACH SLIDE WITH ITS OWN MOVIE TITLE ! ! !
SET 1 —   THE SHE CREATURE—ALL
SET 2 —   THE SPIDER
              INVASION OF THE SAUCER MEN
              THE BEAST WITH A MILLION EYES
              IT—THE TERROR FROM BEYOND SPACE
SET 3 —   IT CONQUERED THE WORLD—ALL
SET 4 —   VOODOO WOMAN
              HOW TO MAKE A MONSTER
              THE BEAST WITH A MILLION EYES
              IT CONQUERED THE WORLD
SET 5 —   INVASION OF THE SAUCER MEN—ALL
ABSOLUTELY TOPS IN COLOR AND NOVELTY. PROJECT THEM LIFE SIZE
GREAT FOR PARTIES, HALLOWEEN, THOSE INTERESTED IN THEATER ART
MAKE-UP, ETC.
ANY SET OF FOUR SLIDES, ONLY $1.00 !   OUR PRESENT SUPPLY
LIMITED, SO ORDER TODAY. ALL SLIDES AND FILMS ARE GUARANTEED
YOU MUST BE SATISFIED !
INVASION OF THE SAUCER MEN
IT CONQUERED THE WORLD
INVASION OF THE SAUCER MEN
THE SHE CREATURE
IT CONQUERED THE WORLD
GOLDEN EAGLE FILMS
Topanga   California
1   2   3   4
O.K.! RUSH ME SETS NO. □   □   □   □
I'M ENCLOSING $
NAME
ADDRESS
CITY   ZONE   STATE
IF I'M NOT HAPPY WITH THE SLIDES, I'LL RETURN THEM
UNDAMAGED, WITHIN TEN DAYS, FOR A FULL REFUND—
—LET'S GO !

Favorite Fiends of Filmland

That's the terrifying role Vincent Price creates for Columbia Pictures' 1954 3-Dimension entry, **The Mad Magician.**

As with most of the fright features in which he starred, Price (who has lately become synonymous with the dream-books of Edgar Allan Poe) met with a disastrous finish on screen, but remained unharmed at the box-office.

Three tons worth of balcony crushed him in **House of Wax,** a headhunter's poison arrowed him in **Green Hell,** he crumbled to dust in a falling house (Usher, that is), and returned to the **Tower of London** to get drowned in a vat of wine.

But as **The Mad Magician,** Price went out in a blaze of glory: he fell victim to one of his own deadly illusions, a flaming crematorium with a temperature of 3500° fahrenheit!

And there are new deaths in store for Price.

With him, it's a way of life. ●

The Great Gallico, world's foremost master of illusion and disguise who, when he goes corpse-crazy, uses more knowledge of mortality than any other mortal.

MATINEE IDOL

Fighting Rex Barrow, conqueror of space, devout newspaper reporter—he takes on the devil of an opening as a one-man battle against cosmic crime when Flying Saucers decide they want Rex's job—Space Conqueror.

Judd Holdren, Captain Video in the Hollywood movie serial version of the television epic, returned to the serial screen two years later in 1953 to star as Rex Barrow for producer Sam Katzman's *The Lost Planet*, directed for Columbia by Spencer G. Bennet from the George H. Plympton - Arthur Hoerl script.

Rocketing to Ergro, the lost planet, Holdren—Fighting Rex himself—encounters and countermands dazzling menaces and deadly machines wheeling around him, robots of the planet's severely disturbed ruler, Dr. Grood, who chants "Today, the Earth—Tomorrow, the Universe."

In his fight for the stars, Rex Barrow wins his stripes after a Prysmic Catapult through space, into the range of a Cosmic Cannon, to be sent sky-high by a Degravitizer, into the whirlpool spin of the Axial Propeller, only to fall back to Ergro for the Thermic Disintegrator, and finally to get thoroughly shook-up by the Sonic Vibrator.

But even these or all of Ergro's sixty dread death devices in the cosmic chapterplay couldn't stop Fighting Rex from proving to Grood that he's the serial screen's battle king. ●

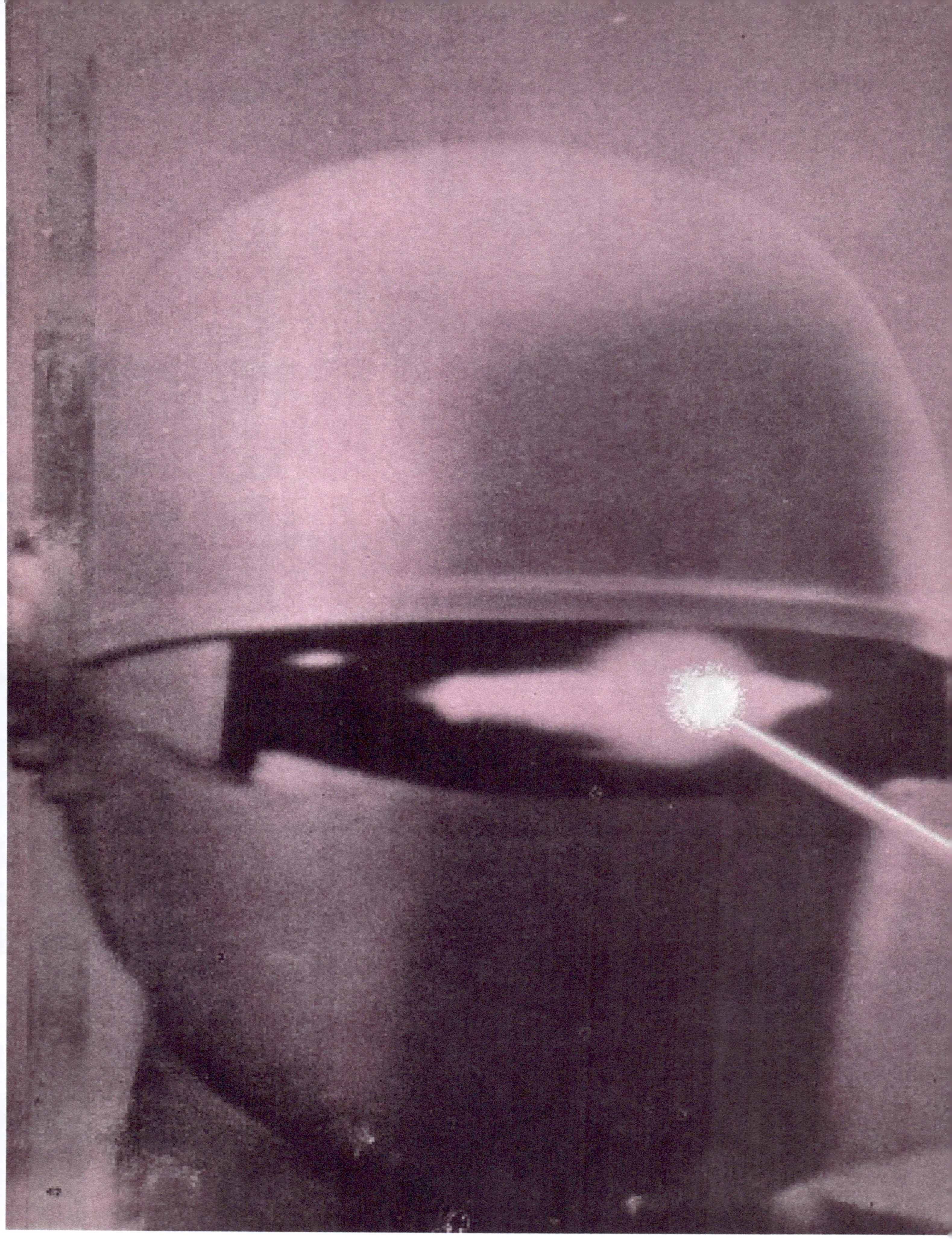

day the earth stood still

The classic science fiction story of a Super-Being who came from another galaxy to threaten our world with nuclear destruction

Radar screens lighted with the strange blip, and newscasters flashed the word around the world. People everywhere began searching the skies.

And then it came . . .

An unearthly humming roared into a doom-like thunder as a great spaceship touched down near the Washington Monument. It was a saucer of burnished silver that caught the fire of the dipping sun.

Troops from nearby Fort Meyer were immediately rushed to the scene. They cordoned off the alien craft, taking familiar military precautions against a completely new situation.

The District of Columbia police arrived to hold back the crowds of curious people. Tanks, machine guns, and other defensive weapons were focused on the saucer. Radio and television reporters were portably installed to inform the waiting world.

The Earth waited impatiently, tensed, not knowing what to expect from this first non-human visitor. For two hours all was silent in the area of the spaceship.

And then, a narrow, silver ramp slid from the ship.

Soldiers gripped their guns, and the police thoughtfully drew their revolvers. A hush was on the crowd.

Now, down the protruding ramp walked the first man from a world other than ours.

He wore a shimmering one-piece spacesuit. Atop his head was a transparent helmet, and in his hand he held an odd instrument.

The spaceman studied the throngs around him, and found all eyes on him.

He raised his arm in salute, and said, "I am Klaatu. I come in peace."

turn the page

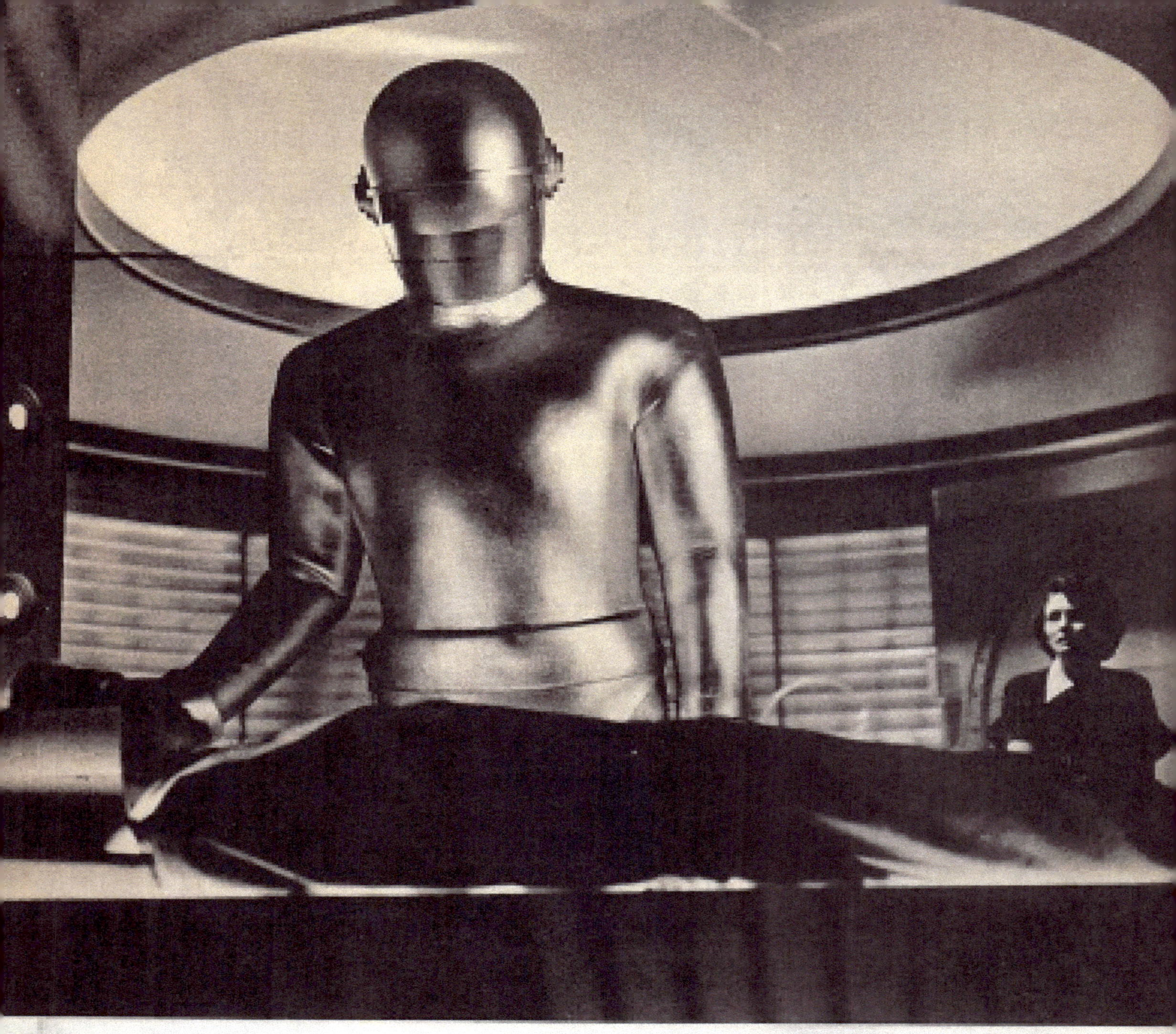

As he spoke, he lifted the strange object in his hand. Before he could say anything further, a well-trained soldier fired his rifle at the foreigner.

The man from the saucer pitched to the ground.

As the army and police approached the body, there came new movement inside the unlatched air lock.

An 8-foot robot plodded mechanically down the ramp, to the blood-stained grass.

Gort!

With a sweep of his fiery eye, the monster machine disintegrated all of the guns and rifles in sight. Deeply disturbed, the soldiers, police and crowds ran.

With a weak gesture, Klaatu halted the robot in his trail of destruction, dead in his tracks. Fears subsiding, medical officers crept out and hurried Klaatu into an ambulance and spirited him to the Walter Reed Hospital.

Sometime after in the hospital, Klaatu conversationally informed a Presidential Secretary that he must speak to all of the world's leaders to warn them of the dreadful consequences Earth would face if she did not turn to the ways of peace. Impossible nonsense, he is quietly assured.

Late that night, using alien means, the Man from the Stars left the hospital unnoticed. But not for long.

His sudden disappearance sent the city into a rage of fears and suspicion.

Klaatu sought out the one man whom he thought could help him: Professor Jacob Barnhardt, an Einstein among scientists. On hearing Klaatu's story, the professor agreed a meeting of the world's foremost scientists should be held in Washington. To impress the importance of this meeting, Barnhardt suggested Klaatu give a world-wide demonstration of his unique powers. The visitor agreed with a slow nod.

At noon the following day, Earth was in a state of confusion and shock.

Electricity ceased to function.

Cars would not operate.

Phones would not work.

Clocks ticked to a standstill at 12 noon.

For 30 minutes, the Earth stood still.

A national emergency was declared. Orders were given to capture Klaatu —dead or alive!

The spaceman's good intentions were doubted by all sane men.

Under an assumed name, and wearing everyday street clothes, Klaatu moved into a boarding house. He met Helen Benson, her young son Bobby, and a suspicious Tom Stevens. Ste-

turn the page

DAY, from page 45

vens spied out Klaatu's true identity and spilled the information to the authorities.

Emergency units closed in for the kill.

A frantic chase through the city, a telling shot, and the Messenger from the Stars lay mortally wounded. Before he died, he gave a weeping, ashamed Helen Benson three words to speak to the giant robot, Gort.

The fate of the world was to rest on those three words.

Helen ran to the spaceship, as Gort was preparing to destroy the city. The mammoth being menacingly approached her. At last, she found courage enough to speak the three words.

"Klaatu . . . barada . . . nikto!"

The robot stopped.

From his 8-foot height, there came a glint of metallic understanding.

Helen silently moved out of the robot's way, seeing it rumble into the city. Minutes slid by before Gort returned, Klaatu's dead body lying across his arms. The girl followed them into the flashing interior of the spaceship.

Gort led Klaatu to the coils of a weird machine, and Helen watched with numb amazement as Klaatu slowly regained his spilled life.

Helen looked around her. The room glowed with masked lights; unreadable dials, and shimmering control switches. And then—before her stood Klaatu!

The meeting between the scientists and Klaatu was held at the saucer. Warning them that our planet should not dare threaten the patterned peace of the universe by atomic war. The moment Earth endangered the peace, other planets would know Earth could not be trusted when she would reach the stars. Our planet would be destroyed by a race of beings such as Gort.

His grim mission completed, Klaatu made his goodbyes to Helen and the scientists, and slowly re-entered the spaceship.

As the vortexing silver disk rose into the night, the minds of men everywhere turned over the warning. Business would be resumed as usual, but for this moment they thought of *The Day The Earth Stood Still*.

This "A" treatment of a science fiction theme from 20th Century Fox in 1951 was based on the story, *Farewell to the Master* by Harry Bates. The cast featured Michael Rennie as Klaatu, and Patricia Neal as Helen Benson, in addition to the amazing atomic man, Gort.

The thriller's production problems were Earth-stopping themselves.

A full-scale spaceship isn't the easiest thing to construct. Ask John Glenn. 20th's final result proved to be a flying disk spanning 350-feet, budgeted at $100,000. The ship stood 25-feet high. Since the script called for no visible opening of any kind in its contour, set designers incorporated an invisible split in its side which was sealed with soft plastic and coated with a silver paint. Every time the disk was opened and closed, workmen had to reseal the split. Through this invisible seam, an intricate gangplank was made to protrude.

And leave it to Hollywood to build a flying saucer that flies!

The 350-foot interplanetary spaceship threatened to take off from its moorings during production when high winds invaded the studio's backlots.

Actress Patricia Neal had a grudge against Gort, the 8-foot robot, even more than the disc that saucered.

Most of her grief occurred during the night scenes when the scenario called for her to approach the spaceship and Gort. Robert Wise, the director, instructed her she was to look at the mecho-man, then start running.

The light that was Gort's beady eye unfortunately blinded her, and when she spun around to run, she couldn't see where she was going. Rather than spoil the take, Miss Neal ran anyhow, stumbling over an unseen guide wire and banging up her knees. By this time, she realized that her misfortune would add to the scene's realism, so she lurched up and started to limp away.

This time she tripped on a light cable.

Taking a strategic rest on her face, Miss Neal looked up to see Gort bending down. He picked her up in just the way an 8-foot iron man would do it.

Patricia later stated that she didn't know how she would reap revenge on the robot, but she just might throw a wrench into his transmission next time, instead of a wrench in his path.

The construction of Gort gave the head prop man some troubles too. He was tossed a ahead of blueprints from the art department and was told to deliver, within one week, the following: "One 8-foot, 8-inch mobile man-like robot. Should look like 'fluid metal', whatever that is, and have a single, electric body-blue lucite eye."

The robot proved to be the prop man's toughest nut to crack. But bolting back to work, he achieved the appearance of fluid metal, by sewing spun-glass cloth onto an 8-foot, 8-inch mold of a human figure, and spraying it with solidifying lacquer. After it hardened, he cut this armor from the dummy in sections — arms, legs, breastplates, and backplates. Over this he poured sponge rubber, and painted the sections a bright silver color. The assembled robot had hinged joints, permitting movement, and a suggestion of softness, or skin, over his hard lacquered skeleton.

Gort was given an all-seeing eye made from a finely ground 8-inch crystal of lucite. Lighted by blue bulbs in its head, the glow increased as his ire was lit at Earth's tragic race towards destruction. ●

FRANKENSTEIN MONSTER MASK

Most realistic we've seen! Fits over entire head! Has shiny metallic bolts along forehead, and the famous electrodes at neck. Green skin, grim lips and scars! Hair, black! Carefully cut ear slits, nostrils, and eyes give adequate hearing, ventilation, and sight! Great for photography, parties etc! It's your own personal Frankenstein monster mask. Fits out of this world! Only $4.00, postpaid. Also ¾ mask which covers only front of head. With elastic holder. $2.50 postpaid.

ALLIGATOR HAND PUPPET

"See you later, alligator!" Best hand puppet we've seen in a long time! Made of realistic latex rubber, extremely well detailed! "Two-tone" hide coloring, light and dark brown! Pink mouth and white teeth, with black eyes! Made to order for you 8mm movie fans! Here's "miniature" for your own home movie productions! Great fun for the kids too! Flexible and articulated! Whole puppet show in itself! Only $1.00, postpaid.

MAD LAB CAMERA

Looks like expensive sub-miniature camera, but wait until you press the secret button! Lens swings open, and with a terrific squeal, a "Killer Shrew" leaps out! Camera has viewfinder, dummy winding knob, carrying case, realistic lens mount. Authentic black crinkle finish with silver-gray trim! Furry "Killer Shrew" and "monster" concealed inside. Lens locks in place until you push the shutter release! You'll have your friends jumping for the ceiling with the MAD LAB CAMERA! Only $1.00, postpaid

MAD LAB HYPO

Life-size 6 inches, fully extended! Needle appears to pierce "victim's" skin! Concealed button gives illusion of hypo filling up with "victim's" blood! Can also be used in reverse, to "inject" blood—then show hypo apparently empty! The illusion is absolutely perfect, even close up! This glittering, wicked-looking instrument is quality made of crystal clear styrene plastic, with metal head and "needle"! Scientific calibrations marked along body! Don't use around friends with weak stomachs! Only $1.50, postpaid

MONSTER FEET

Horribly distorted monster feet, with twisted toes and snarled claws! Slip over your shoes, and go shuffling after friends! Feet cover entire foot and ankle! Heavy duty latex. In realistic flesh color, with black toenails and claws! Great fun for parties, or to complete your monster outfit! Wear them down the street at night if you like screaming neighbors! Only $5.00, postpaid

MAD MONSTER BUTTONS

Screamsational! Newest rage! 6 big, different 3½ inch badges, with 3-D monster heads in color! Molded vinyl plastic, with heavy film backing! Complete, with pin! Can be worn on sweater, jacket; or can be pasted on books, doors, automobiles, etc. Terrific for groups and clubs, parties and picnics! Have a different monster each day! Badges include: Wild Monster man, Zombie Bazzak, Female Vampire, Mummy, Vampire Man, and Frankenstein monster! Only 50c each, postpaid; or $2.50 the set!

MR. BONES, THE POCKET SKELETON

Your own spooky mascot! Take Mr. Bones wherever you go. He's 7 inches tall, well detailed, made of vinyl-like rubber! Even feels creepy! Flexible and springy, the slightest movement sets him shimmying and shaking! Hang Mr. Bones from car mirror, or pin him to your jacket! Sit him down on desk, or table! For you shutterbugs, MR. Bones makes a sensational prop for table-top photography. Only 75c, postpaid

UNLUCKY 13 RATTLESNAKE

13 unlucky inches of wriggling rattler! Coloring fools everybody, even inches away! "Flexite" vinyl formula makes snake feel cool and slimy to the touch! Sure cure for nosey friends! Just put this rattler where they're bound to snoop! If you want shrieks and howls at your next get-together, this UNLUCKY 13 RATTLESNAKE is for you! Camera fiends who like to shoot miniatures can turn rattler into huge "python" in table-top scenes! Only 75c, postpaid

DEVIL SPIDER

Ugh! What a little horror this guy is! Made of vinyl rubber, for that "creepy" feel! 2 inches in diameter, he really gets the screams when you lower him on a thread or send him skittering across the floor! Well detailed in black, with rough texturing! 8 wiggling legs start vibrating at the slightest touch! Slip him in your pocket, hang him from a car mirror, dangle him in a doorway! If you have any friends left afterwards, they'll never forget the time they combed the DEVIL SPIDER out of their hair! Only 50c postpaid

MAN MOON MASCOT!

Poor little Moon Man! Looks like he's "way out there", and he can't get back. This lovable little guy is all head, hands, and feet. Put him on a lamp shade, p i c t u r e frame, note book, or car mirror, and these things become his "body".

He's fun-tastic, a n d made of soft, durable, flesh colored plastic, with pink ears, and bright red eyes. Your own personal moon Mascot!

Only **$1** postpaid.

CASTLE DRACULA
TOPANGA, CALIFORNIA

SPACE-TRIX!

Three magnetic models of the Sun, Earth and Moon, attractively lithographed in seven colors. They come complete with descriptions of many mystifying scientific illusions, that YOU can amaze your friends with!

Floating planets on a pencil! Whirling worlds! These are a few of the tricks with the "interplanetary magnets". But you'll soon be making up your own illusions, as you become familiar with their powerful magnetic fields.

Over an inch in diameter. Well made, strong and durable. Can be slipped into the pocket, for impromptu demonstrations.

Only **$1** postpaid.

CASTLE DRACULA TOPANGA, CALIFORNIA

VAMPIRE DEVIL RING!

Shades of Count Dracula! It looks like it came straight from his castle, in the Carpathian Mountains! A gleaming, scowling, silvery Devil's head. Great for club or costume make-up.

Deeply curved horns, brow, nose, beard and "vampire fangs". These are set off by flaming simulated ruby eyes. Good quality and massive. A real conversation piece!

Let us know your ring size with order. **$1**

· **Castle Dracula**
Topanga, California

"""

HOW TO BE A VAMPIRE VICTIM IN ONE EASY LESSON

Here's the opportunity you've been screaming for!

Be a Vampire Victim— right in your own home!

It's as easy as pulling wings off a bat!

Simply punch two straight pins through the vampire's fangs, making sure the sharp points are facing you.

Now slowly bring this page towards your neck, all the while moaning and groaning softly (for effect).

Then quick like a bunny, jab the page into your neck!

Wasn't that fun?

Try it on the members of your family — they'll die laughing!

THE TWO TALE HEART

The Unwritten Tales of Edgar Allan Poe, Transcribed by Jim Harmon — the story's end may have been final as death, yet there came something after

I
CASK AWAY

. . . I had completed the eighth, the ninth, and the tenth tier . . . there remained but a single stone to be fitted and plastered in . . . But now there came from out the niche a low laugh that erected the hairs upon my head . . . There came forth in return only a jingling of bells . . . I forced the last stone into its position; I plastered it up. Against the new masonry I re-erected the old rampart of bones. For half of a century no mortal has disturbed them. In pace requiescat!

—EDGAR ALLAN POE,
The Cask of Amontillado

For the worst part of half a century I have not been able to rest in peace.

The jingling of the jester's bells are always here with me in my tiny apartment, the taste of the Amontillado wine turned vinegar on my withered tongue. I am trapped as no man has been trapped, suffering suffocation that no mortal has ever before known, and always the laugh and the bells ringing in my ears, becoming one, a whisper of a knell, a jest of doom, and nowhere to escape in this, the confines of my world.

I rot alone, not the Fortunato fortunate in his easy tomb, but I, the mason who sealed my gullible comrade behind a wall of his folly. I, Montressor, who has lived on to strong, respected old age, with yet many years to enjoy my wealth of fortune and friends. If it were not for the bells!

turn the page

by Jim Harmon

HEART, from page 51

The cask of Amontillado emptied with the years, celebrating births, mourning deaths, and as the level of the wine fell so grew my aversion to the bells. Aversion, I say, but yet it was not so negative a thing, as a positive one. It became my mission to destroy bells. A bribe to the town crier earned me this, and I contributed food and drink to the strengthening of his voice. I tithed heavily to the church to slow and rest their bells, but at last I was called upon to leave the city.

In my country house, I removed all clocks except the honest face of the sun dial. My servants were fetched by a pitch-pipe like the sailors of foreign seas. So strong became my mania against the bells, that when a stupid child was in my garden ringing a music box out of tune with a latch key, I was seized with a fit that left my left arm and the limb on that side of mine, immovable.

Many of the leading physicians of the country attended me and most assured me that my trouble was chiefly a melancholy nature, and that I should find gayety and sport. Not a few, however, assured me that my singular, and unexplainable, hatred of bells was so great that if I were exposed to their ringing again it might mean a fatality. In this I concurred more heartily than in the opinions of fools who said I should seek their ways.

Yet, I had paid for this advice, and I would lose more (indeed, I realized, perhaps all) if I did not heed it.

My invitations to my many friends were sent out, and all were invited to my country house for food, wine, and dancing. Many were the lovely ladies of the countryside, even from the distant city that knew my house. A fine orchestra was assembled, all string and wind instruments, none of the tinkling monstrosities of the Swiss, I ascertained.

And as the gay ball began beyond the walls of my private chambers, I sat alone, bitterly nursing the final drags of a wine far inferior to the Amontillado that was gone with my youth, and my dancing legs.

There came to pass a chance happening. As I fingered the glass, the ball of my thumb rubbed the rim and brought forth a ring, such as happens to all people one time or another. In horror but fascination, I repeated the experiment, r u n n i n g a fingertip around the fine crystal glass and producing the vibrations of a second definite ringing. It was not the ringing of a bell, but the ringing of a wine.

With a cry I fell to the floor, and I lay here still, knowing that the physicians and my own fears were correct in the thing that could cause my death.

If the wine's knell was not enough, the ladies of the ball have circled in sweet solicitation, and doubly, for a moment more, I am surrounded by the ringing of the belles.

II
MASTER KEY

It is with heavy heart that I take pen in hand to write the last words I shall ever be able to record about my friend, M. Dupin, the greatest detective in France during the 1800's. My American compatriot, the esteemed Edgar Allan Poe, has previously shaped my poor words into better form, telling you how Dupin exposed the horrid monster ape responsible for the Murders in the Rue Morgue, how the great detective solved the Mystery of Marie Roget, and how he finally uncovered the Purloined Letter. Now I alone remain to recount these final and moments.

"My friend," Dupin said, breezing into my quarters, "I must quit the country of France at once and for ever."

"What?" I cried. "This is impossible. You cannot simply disappear."

"I have before, and I may again," Dupin confided.

"But why?"

"Politics," the detective shrugged in his nervous, abrupt manner. "The distinguished D—— is once again in power, and he remembers me unkindly for finding his cleverly concealed correspondence. If I do not flee, I will pay with my freedom, perhaps my life."

"I'll do anything to help that I can," I assured Dupin. "But where will you go?"

"There is only one place. 'Cross the channel to England. I will set up a new life for myself there."

"What do you know of that fog-bound land?"

"More than you know about me, old fellow. I have my small secrets. Yes, England has been another home for me. I have two homelands, and thanks to that criminal Napoleon, D——, each will be locked to me, one fastening me in, the other without. But enough, I must be off by midnight."

"We'll take my carriage to the boat," I said readily. "But you are the greatest detective in France, in literature, in the world. Dupin, things cannot be as bad as you make them out?"

The detective pointed an angular finger at me. "Two, I tell you, sure-locked homes."

Then he laughed, and smiled cryptically. ●

WORKSHOP, from page 8
one who tells you he has a "super-secret special latex" is trying to make a sap out of you!

Incidentally, that odor which curls your nose when you open the bottle is ammonia. This keeps your latex from coagulating into solid rubber golf balls.

After creating your own monster, you will want to give it a home to haunt.

From your local hardware store, you can obtain "chicken wire" mesh, or hardware cloth. Shape the metal hardware cloth into mountains and caves. Cover with wet plaster. The plaster should also be available at the hardware store. It comes as a dry powder. Next, add water to the powder, following the instructions on the container.

Model railroad landscaping gives you trees and bushes to add to the atmosphere of your weird world.

Or, you might get some twigs and "plant" them in the plaster while it is still wet.

One thing to keep in mind is that creating "monsters" and "monster worlds" is a challenge to your imagination and creativity. It all takes time and patience—ingredients which only you can contribute.

In future issues, we'll be conducting a Monster Clinic for those of you who are having problems creating your creatures and special effects.

Address all cards and letters to *Devil's Workshop*, in care of this magazine. ●

BATS. *from page 6*

John Carradine, distinguished Shakesperian actor, followed the immortal Lugosi when he played Dracula on a country weekend visit to the **House of Frankenstein** (1945), and repaid by hosting **House of Dracula** (1945), both for Universal. In this second homecoming, Carradine tried to rid himself of the vampire curse, but he retained the bat blood.

When it came time for the **Return of Dracula** in 1958, Francis Lederer was paged to portray the grim grandson.

Christopher Lee, fresh from the king-size grave in **Curse of Frankenstein**, terrorized in technicolor as Dracula M. This was Hammer Films' excellent remake of the original Bram Stoker tale, forged under the banner, **Horror of Dracula**. Count DracuLee swooped to world wide fame with his modernized menace.

If you're looking forward to Things to Come, keep your eyes up (for forms flying the face of the full moon), and your collar anchored down. ●

Secret Skull Ring!

Mystic skull symbol of the ancient Aztecs, later copied by the fierce pirates who sailed the seven seas. The romance and adventure is all embodied into the unique and latest style of this massive, quality ring.

Sculptured cheek bones, teeth, and sparkling simulated ruby eyes are blended into a finger encircling curve on this exciting new ring. Gleaming silvery finish, too.

Please state ring size when ordering.

$1
Only $1 postpaid.

Castle Dracula
Topanga, California

KILLER, from page 22

happened, Jim falls under suspicion. his reason for wanting the territory to remain unexplored is questioned.

Journeying to the camp of the white hunters, Jungle Jim learns some of their plans. Andrews quickly decides Big Jim knows too much to stay alive.

Jungle Jim soon finds he is facing death wherever he turns—the natives are out to sacrifice him, believing he has murdered one of them; Andrews and his henchmen are after him because he knows of their cold-blooded plans; and the hulking ape man is now hunting in the area where Jim is trapped!

While searching for Jim, the hunters stumble on the killer ape and manage to cage him after a violent struggle. They deliver him to Andrews, who is jolly at the thought of using the beast man in his experiments.

Jim the Jungle King learns of the ape man's capture and beats the trail for Andrews' camp, where he meets up with the giant man ape in a cave filled with explosives!

Suddenly, the horror bursts his bonds and jumps Jim! The sparks

from a torch which Jim is using to ward off the blows of the killer ape catch on the dynamite cases and set them blazing!

Barely does Jungle Jim dash out of the cave before the entire area goes up in a crisping explosion—burying the mindless beast in a prefab tomb.

The natives attack Andrews' outpost after Jim convinces them it was actually the killer ape who had so viciously murdered one of them.

The warriors, led by Jungle Jim, pounce on the insane scientist and his cutthroats, and once again there is a lull in the danger-packed jungles of Africa.

Filing away the Killer Ape in his collection of menaces, Johnny Weissmuller now awaits his next test of jungle manhood. ●

Makes a terrific club ring, or just wear it for "good luck"; Gleaming silvery finish, with blazing simulated ruby eyes. Looks like the mystical snake, often associated with secret Caribbean Voodoo rites!

Deeply sculptured snake head has metal "fangs", and protruding red f o r k e d tongue. A massive, quality ring of superior design. The photo doesn't do it justice.

Don't forget to give us your ring size, when ordering.

$1
Only $1 postpaid.

CASTLE DRACULA
Topanga, California

Confessions of a Mad Mummy

Out of the best-forgotten tombs comes the Pharoah's landlord; an embalmed Egyp-enigma who threatens a bandage rebellion

I am a mummy.

Most people don't appreciate all that goes into being a mummy. It isn't exactly a snap getting to be 5000 years old. That's a lifetime job.

As I enscroll these hieroglyphics and snacks (do you smell rags burning?) I'm haunted by the monstrosities that try to pass themselves off as fully-wrapped mummies today. When I was a mummy's boy, King Tut would never have allowed any of these poor preserves to be caught dead in his

turn to page 65

things to come

Crystal Balling
the coming Year of Fear,
as forecast by Hollywood's
Mediums of the Macabre

"More grue in '62," affirms James H. Nicholson, American-International Pictures president, commenting on his forthcoming fantasy film schedule.

Among the titles already registered by AIP are the Alexander Dumas classic, *Iron Mask*; "X", the brand of eyes of a far-seeing fiend; something bravely listed as sci-fi humor, *The Maid and the Martien*; *The Haunted Village* (Mayor Vincent Price, of course); *Survival after the Big War* (a fantasy); and H. G. Wells' *When the Sleeper Wakes*.

Conjure Wife, a novel by Fritz Leiber, will be released by AIP under the title *Burn Witch Burn* (A novel by A. Merritt, made famous years ago). Witch scripters, Charles Beaumont and Richard Matheson, both have choice acting roles in producer Roger Corman's latest, *The Intruder*, based on Beaumont's own fine novel (Dell, 50c).

While Robert "Rocketship X-M" Lippert is busy opening *The Cabinet of Dr. Caligari* (Robert Bloch is inside, going Psycho all over again), Alex "Underwater City" Gordon is planning to pop out from behind Poe's *Masque of the Red Death*. Gordon also intends to blanket the world with his *Killer Smog*.

Vincent Price, Peter Lorre, and Basil Rathbone in scenes from AIP's new TALES OF TERROR

Currently before the British cameras, Ian Fleming's best-seller of Secret Agent James Bond against the oriental super-criminal, *Dr. No* (Signet, 50c). And at the neighboring studios of Hammer Films, Herbert Lom (Captain Nemo in *Mysterious Island*) portrays the third *Phantom of the Opera*.

Tarzan Goes to India with stuntman Jock Mahoney as the new ape man. On the trail of Tarzan, ex-tree swinger Johnny Weissmuller is negotiating with Desilu Studios for an around-the-world adventure teleseries.

CBS Radio on Sundays serves stories in the dark on *Suspense* (authors like Robert "Mysterious Traveller" Arthur; stars like Jim Bowles, once in the middle of Jack, Doc & Reggie) while television will be hoping you understand *Tales of the Unexplained* and *Famous Ghost Stories*, the last one hosted by Vincent Price.

S-F writer Ray Bradbury journeys to *The Twilight Zone* with his "I Sing the Body Electric".

Having escaped from Caligari's Cabinet, Robert "Psycho" Bloch, one-time collaborator with Poe, even when he was several years Edgar's junior, has had so much favorable response from his western *Thriller* that he has been asked to do the weekly 90-minute *Virginians* next year. FANTASTIC MONSTERS understands Bloch will do one about a marshal, who wears a ruffled shirt, and keeps his mother in the fruit cellar. ●

THE CLIFF MONSTER!
It's Your Turn Now!
8 MM – 2.00   16 MM – 6.95
FILMLAND MONSTER
They're NEW!
The "Big Four" – blended together on one film!
Your Hollywood horrors can come home to roost!
ALL ON ONE FILM !
8 MM – 2.00   16 MM – 6.95
GOLDEN EAGLE FILMS   TOPANGA, CALIFORNIA
GOLDEN EAGLE FILMS   TOPANGA, CALIFORNIA
ORDER BY MAIL

THE MAGIC SWORD

Producer Bert I. Gordon unsheaths an enchanted blade which hacks a trail through the terrors of darkness

Amazing Colossal Man, Beginning of the End, Attack of the Puppet People, and the exquisitely *Tormented;* these films were spawned in the rapid imagination of Bert I. Gordon, young Hollywood motion picture producer-director, often cited as the High Priest of Cinematic Wizardry.

His latest big screener, *The Magic Sword,* is no exception to the Gordon Rule of always leave 'em living—sometimes.

It is his most ambitious project to date; Gordon put all of his power into the creation of this realistic movie magic.

Over 18 months of exhaustive planning went into the filming of the Eastman Color extravaganza.

A master of special effects himself, Gordon has combined all of the known technical illusions (animation, split-screen, travelling mattes, super-imposition) with his own special techniques; to line up the weirdest menagerie of creatures you ever nightmared of.

turn the page

The brave knight St. George boldly faces the wrath of the double-dreaded, double-headed dragon

He left no cinema stone unturned in bringing to life a film unlike anything that has ever been audienced by a stunned public.

Starring in the United Artists release are Basil Rathbone as the sly sorcerer, **Lodac**; Estelle Winwood as **Sibyl**, the bungling witch; Anne Helm as the beautiful **Princess Helene**; and Gary Lockwood in the role of **St. George** of dragon fame.

George's magic stallion is renown in its own right. **Bayard** is a subtle characterization by **Silver**, on an acting vacation from The Lone Ranger.

The action-laden fantasy gets off to a skin-tingling start when George learns that Lodac the Loathsome has kidnapped Princess Helene. To counteract the seven deadly curses which the mad sorcerer Lodac has set upon anyone who attempts to rescue the fair princess, George's foster-mother, the whacky witch Sybil, presents the knight with invincible armor, Bayard (the fastest horse in the world), and a magic sword called **Ascalon**.

Utilizing the sword's convenient powers, George brings to life the seven bravest knights in history; and they all take to the high roads of medieval England to save Helene from being fed to Lodac's two-headed, fire-breathing dragon!

On the road to the sorcerer's castle, George and his men encounter four of Lodac's curses:

A **25 foot Ogre** attacks them, and kills two of the knights

The life of a third knight is claimed when he pitches forward into the **Boiling Crater of Death**

A vicious **vampire woman** destroys another of the warriors

And the fourth curse is a **scorching fireball** which sears two more knights to death

Meanwhile, Sybil is brewing new magic for George to use in his battle against Lodac's curses. But her bumbling brew instead deprives the legendary hero of all the magic he already has!

George and St. Patrick, the remaining knight, become trapped in the Cave of the **Fifth Curse**, inhabited by hideous **Green Fire Demons** who consume Patrick. George, h o w e v e r, breaks to safety, and goes it alone to Lodac's gloomy, treacherous castle.

Once there, he is snared by the sorcerer's menagerie of evil, blood-curdling creatures—**horrifying hags, beastial bird-men, wicked warlocks, and perilous pin-headed people!**

Other prisoners in the medieval suburb, whom Lodac's black magic has made only inches tall, break out of their cage and saw George's bonds with his magicless sword. The knight's wits are keen even if **Ascalon** has lost its magic edge, and trusting them he mounts Bayard and attacks the twin-

headed dragon, who is having Princess Helene for dinner.

While the valiant George engages in a mis-matched battle with the menacing monster, Sybil finally stumbles upon the correct magic formula, and George's sword regains all of its vacationing powers. With it, the knight slays the flame-belching dragon and swoops up Princess Helene.

Sybil, changing herself into the blackest of panthers, goes after the fleeing Lodac and fangs him, breaking his evil spells and freeing all who are under them.

George uses the not inconsiderable powers of the Magic Sword to restore the seven famous knights of history to life again, then he and the beautiful Helene are married.

And everyone lives happily ever after; as you may have already guessed.

In order to create an appropriate mood throughout the filming of **The Magic Sword**, producer-director Bert I. Gordon purposely began filming his spectacle on the 13th day of the month.

He even held a party on the set when the 13th day of production happened to fall on a Friday!

"Nothing superstitious about me," Gordon grinned, knuckle-tickling a piece of wood.

It was fortunate he knocked on wood though.

In his quest to rescue Princess Helene from the scaly dragon, St. George, in the story, faced many tense, near-death moments. But Gordon and his crew of technicians were not without **their own** moments of anxiety.

When no one could locate a tame black panther to use in the picture, Sir Tom, a 190 pound mountain lion, was paged for the role. He was treated to an ebony spray, then put through his paces by his trainer.

One of Sir Tom's chores was to jump from a castle wall to the floor below; but producer Gordon discovered that the lion would have to be **set free** to accomplish this feat. No ropes or chains could be placed around the half-wild animal's neck as they would have showed up in the film.

Realizing this, Gordon instructed everyone but a skeleton crew to leave the sound stage where this scene was being shot. The cameras began to grind away, and Sir Tom made a perfect leap from the mock castle wall.

Then everyone's hearts started leaping to their mouths as Sir Tom made a tour of the sound stage, moving in and out of feet of Gordon and his nervous crew, who had to remain standing absolutely still until the trainer could leash the lion.

Commenting on the number of scenes in which Sir Tom had to be

turn the page

SWORD, from page 41

set loose on the set, Gordon, biting his lip, said, "Too many!"

The fire-breathing dragon which St. George slays in The Magic Sword is actually only 20 feet in length, although in the film it looks a menacing 150 feet. The monster, which took four tedious months to construct, is operated manually by six men on the inside. Gordon could direct the roaring fire from either of the dragon's two fire-proof heads because gas jets had been installed behind each scaly face.

As he was directing the twin-headed creature during the filming of an important scene, he called out, "Fire head #1", and suddenly everything went wrong.

Instead of bellowing forth a searing breath, the dragon inhaled and got a classic case of heartburn.

The men operating the monster ducked serious injury, and the monster was checked out A-OK.

Having roared its last for The Magic Sword, the dragon has now been lovingly boxed away, as movie maker Gordon plans to make future use of his hot new creation.

The Magic Sword being Bert I. Gordon's biggest and costliest fantasy flicker to date, the amiable producer-director was asked how he intends to encore.

"Do you know," he mused, "I've been wondering about that myself . . ."

There's one thing—no matter what type of tingling tidbit of terror Bert I. Gordon produces in the future, he will have to top his own dazzling screen illusions sliced up by The Magic Sword!●

LOTUS, from page 21

scarlet putrefaction, from which arose the stupefying scent of black lotuses. Then, with a single inarticulate cry of horror and despair, he crumpled and toppled from the balcony, to spatter himself in red madness upon the court below.

At this instant he awoke, and his teeth shook inside his mouth as he gagged and retched in terrible repulsion. He felt old and decrepit, and the tide of life ebbed in his veins. He would have fainted were it not for the revivifying fumes of the nargileh that still smouldered beside him. Then unto himself he swore a mighty oath to abandon the ways of the dreamer forever, and rose to his feet and took unto himself the book and turned the pages to the passage of warning, wherein he read this rune:

The second dream shall show what might have been.

Then there descended upon him a resignation and a black despair. All of his life unrolled before him once again and he knew himself for what he was—a deluded fool. And he knew also that if he did not go back to his drugged slumber there would come to pass the horror of his second dream, as it foretold. So, wearily, and with queer wonder in his heart, he clasped the book to his bosom and betook himself once again to his couch in the moonlight. And his pale fingers lifted the hookah to his ashen lips once again and he once more knew the bliss of Nirvana. He was under the compulsion of a sorcerous thrall.

. . . Oh night-black lotus flower, that groweth beneath the River Nile! Oh poisoned perfumer of all darkness, waving and weaving in the spells of moonlight! Oh cryptic magic that worketh only evil . . .

Genghir the Dreamer slept. But there was brooding ecstasy and mystic wonder in his dreams, and he knew the beauty that lies in twilight grottoes on the dark side of the moon, and his brow was fanned and his slumbers lulled by the pale wind that is the little gods who dance in paradise. And he stood alone in a sea of endless infinity, before a monstrous flower that beckoned great, hypnotic petals before his dream-dazed eyes, and whispered unto him a command. In his vision he glanced down to where a dagger hung by his side, in his jeweled stomacher of sultanship.

And there came to him a sudden gleam of understanding. This before him was the Black Lotus, symbol of the evil that waits for men to sleep. It was casting a spell upon him that would lure him to death. He knew now the way of atonement for the past and the release of his enchantment— he must strike!

But even as he moved, the great flower shot out one velvet petal steeped in the cloying scent that was a wind from the gate of heaven. And the black petal entwined itself about his neck like a loathesome and beautiful serpent, and with its succubi-like embrace sought to drown his senses in a sea of scented bliss.

But Genghir would not be frustrated. The allurement of delight left him cold, but his numbing brain commanded him. He raised the silver dagger from his side and with a single blow, slashed off the twining collar from his neck . . .

Then Genghir saw the flowers and the petals vanish, and he was left alone in a universe of mocking laughter; a dim world that rocked with leering mirth of idiotic gods. For an instant he awoke to see a ruby necklace encircling his bare throat; to realize monstrously that in his dream he had cut his own throat. Then, on the bed of moonlight, he died, and there was silence in the deserted room, while from the dead throat of Genghir the Dreamer little drops of blood fell upon an open page of a curious book; upon a curious sentence in oddly underlined letters:

The third dream brings reality.

Nothing more remained, save the all-pervading scent of lotus-flowers that filled the nighted room.●

CONFESSIONS, from page 55

tomb more than once.

This proves into what a state of decay the mummy profession has withered.

I believe that we dead people have a right to some respect. Dying isn't the easiest way to make a living. But these young upstarts just blunder along and fall into the crypt business.

It's really a grave affair.

Some of these modern mummies simply will not do. How can they pass for dead when they have never really lived the part?

I've seen a monster movie or two. Tom Edison showed me one. And I know why they call these films "horrors."

The acting alone would earn the tag. Some of the corpses, in particular, are really rotten.

If there's one thing I know about, it's being dead. And it's obvious to me that many of the bodies in the movies have never been dead a day in their lives.

The cemeteries, tombs, and graveyards of Hollywood are loaded with fine, competent, experienced corpses. But do they ever get to work in the movies? No. Living actors, like Christopher Lee, are phoneyed up with a lot of makeup to look like us.

I ask you: is this fair?

Having reached a respectable age, my views deserve some attention. Believe me, when a 5000 year old Mummy talks, people listen.

The practices of Hollywood horror film makers are unfair and discriminatory. Actors such as Vincent Price, Basil Rathbone, and Lon Chaney Jr. get all the best roles in the monster movies because they belong to an exclusive little group who all have something in common:

They breathe.

Yes, the sad truth of it is that to get anyplace in Hollywood today you have to be alive.

I call this prejudice.

Here I am—a deceased Mummy; very cultured (you should see my germ vat), kind to rats, bats, and spiders; and never once have I worked in a Roger Corman film.

Just as I think the next Tom Mix western should feature real Indians, so I feel the forthcoming Lon Chaney thriller should star real dead people.

There is no substitute for real dead people.

Somehow the audience always knows the difference.

Remember, all you dead ones out there in Cemeteryland—if we all rise together, it is well within our power to raise a big stink. We mustn't let Hollywood slam the lids on our faces any longer.

And, with that, your friend, the Mad Mummy, concludes the final minutes of Local 6x6.

(You'll have to admit that I went all-out this time, and really took the wraps off!) ●

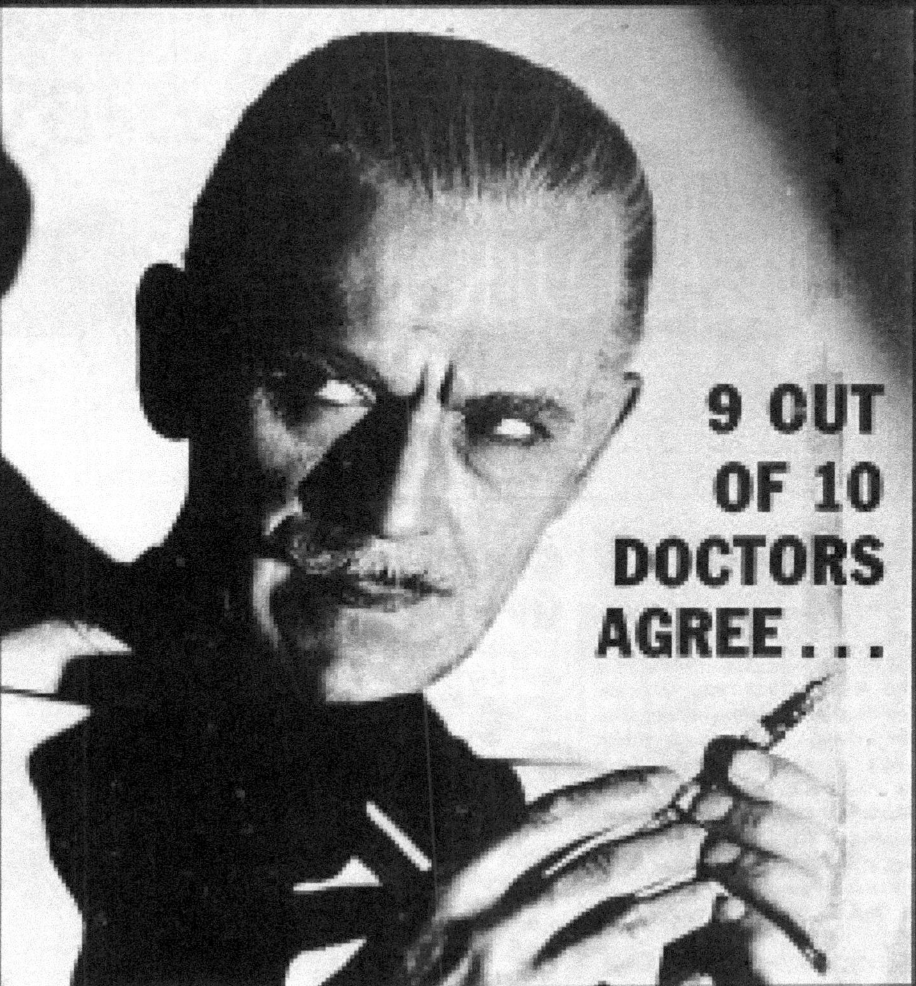

SLAYER
brings faster pain

Contented Normalcy is often caused by complete freedom from strain, minor aches, tenseness and other comforts.

When you take *Slayer* aspirin at bedtime, you increase your sensitivity to these sensations. Thus, *Slayer* doesn't make you ache, it *lets* pain come *naturally.*

And when you wake up you feel wonderfully miserable, with a heavy trace of the "sedative hangover" always following a good drugged sleep.

So when no discomforts are bothering you, feel pain *better* with *Slayer.*

COFFIN CORNER

I always believed the first Frankenstein film was made in 1931, by Universal, starring Boris Karloff. Recently I read where this was not so. Was there an earlier film?—**Bob Scharf, Cleveland, Ohio**

It's a little known fact the 1931 Karloff classic was actually the second Frankenstein film. The original was produced by none other than Thomas A. Edison at his Black Maria Studios in NY in 1898.

Being tremendous followers of motion pictures which have featured comic strip characters, we are wondering if you can give us any information on the Buck Rogers serial; and, if possible, the titles of the episodes.—**John & Tom McGeehan, Santa Ana, Calif**

Buck, as portrayed by Buster Crabbe in 1939, rocketed his way through 12 chapters in all, the names of which are Tomorrow's World, Tragedy on Saturn, The Enemy's Stronghold, Sky Patrol, Phantom Plane, The Unknown Command, Primitive Urge, Revolt of the Zuggs, Bodies Without Minds, Broken Barriers, A Prince in Bondage, and War of the Planets. The cliffhanger was released by Universal.

A friend of mine told me there have been almost 12 different movie versions of Dr. Jekyll & Mr Hyde! I told him he was as batty as Dracula. Am I right?—**Barry Mohr, Johnstown, Pa**

Your friend is off by 2. The very first screen adaptation of the Robert Louis Stevenson story was in 1908, filmed by Selig. 6

GHOULDEN OPPORTUNITY

Gather 'round all you ghouls and guys because here's the chance you've been waiting for—become a noose reporter for Transylvania's greatest export, **Tombstone Times.**

All you have to do is send in the horrifying news of what is happening at your local cemetery, or school; or information about your monster club.

Dig up photos of your gorgeous girlfriends and sisters, or your hungsome boyfriends and brothers.

Let the World of Monsters know what you are brewing these days!

Don't delay—be a **Tombstone** reporter today!

Address all cards, letters, neatly wrapped bombs, and photos to:

Tombstone Times
c/o Fantastic Monsters

other silents followed: 1910, 1912, 1913, 1919, and 2 in 1920 (one a German flicker). Talkie versions were made in 1932, 1939, and 1941. And there have been countless sequels, such as Son of Dr Jekyll and Abbott & Costello Meet Dr Jekyll & Mr Hyde.

Once and for all—is there a plant called "wolfsbane"? I say there is, but none of my monster friends believe me!—**Larry Talburns, Roberts, Texas**

Yes, wolfsbane does exist; but it is not the type Lon Chaney Jr. is familiar with. Wolfsbane is a yellow flower, a poisonous plant, from which drugs to relieve pain are obtained.

TOMB IT MAY CONCERN

Introducing COUNT DOWNE, spinster editor of the monster world's greatest newspaper, Tombstone Times

ATOMS & EVE

London—Scientific hysteria was made here by **Alan A. Harris, M.D.** (Mad Doctor) of Bradford, England, when he astounded the British medical authorities by presenting them with the first fan-made monster.

Doctor Harris, who comes from a family of inventors (his great grandfather perfected the Harris Wheel), claims he has discovered how to produce ultra-violent rays which give life to dead tissue. For years he had been experimenting in secret; and finally, after hundreds of failures, he has succeeded in bringing to life a creature which he calls Gorgonus.

The unfortunate mishap with the Harris monster is that it feeds on human blood. And to make matters worse, the doctor told **Tombstone Times,** "The creature's atoms have started acting up, and every hour on the hour a new Gorgonus is created!"

London is in a state of shock due to these unforeseen developments with the Harris horror; and the last report to reach our ears (all three of them) stated that the original Gorgonus has just been signed by Hammer Films to star in their forthcoming remake of the classic **Birth of a Nation.**

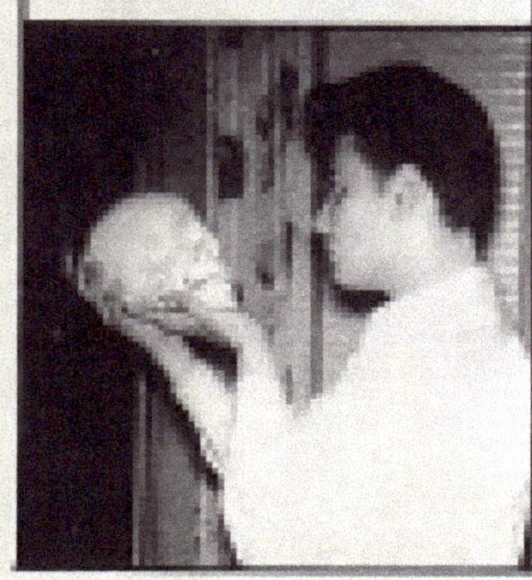

SKULLDUGGERY

Kathy Roberts (above) of Burnsville, Calif., and Donald Glut of Chicago, Ill., are pictured here with two of their friends — only they insist are real boneheads.

HAUNT ADS

Bernie Bubnis Jr., 65 Walnut Ave., East Farmingdale, Long Island, NY, is in the market for glossy stills and posters from science fiction, horror, and serial films. Bernie also would like to purchase bundles of fanzines and old comic books featuring super-heroes . . . . All fans and followers of the jungle man, Tarzan, are invited to become members of **The Burroughs Bibliophiles**, the only authorized ape man club. Interested devotees should write to the group's secretary, **Robert Horvath**, for complete membership information. Robert's address is 1 Luce Ave., 5, Morrison, Pa . . . . Collectors of stamps, books, and recordings can probably find what they want if they contact **Billy Hoover**, Walnut St., R2, Manchester, Tenn . . . **John & Tom McGeehan**, 405 East 5th, Santa Ana, Calif., are looking for someone who will sell them the first dozen issues of **Sky Altitude** comics. "We'll pay $5 for each issue," John & Tom write . . . , Another Califan, **Don Sheppard**, wants to hear from all who have movie pressbooks, posters, stills, and scripts for sale. Don himself has a list of monster film material to sell or trade, so write him at 2771 San Marino, Los Angeles 8, Calif . . . . Writing fantasy short stories is the hobby of fan **Charles McNulty** of Beaumont, Idaho . . . . Calling all monsters! **Paul Mitchell**, 1404 Ostrander, La Grange Park, Ill., would appreciate hearing from those of you who are interested in the Creature from the Black Lagoon pictures . . . . Comic book fans and readers would do well to get their super-claws on issues of *Alter-Ego* fanzine, edited and published by **Jerry Bails**, 1710 Kenwood Dr., Inkster, Mich . . . . **Jim Broecker** is selling his vast collection of sci-fi paperbacks and has a catalog ready for those who contact him. Jim will trade for hardbound copies of the Tarzan and Commander Birdman novels. His address is 4336 No. Lawndale, Chicago, Ill ●

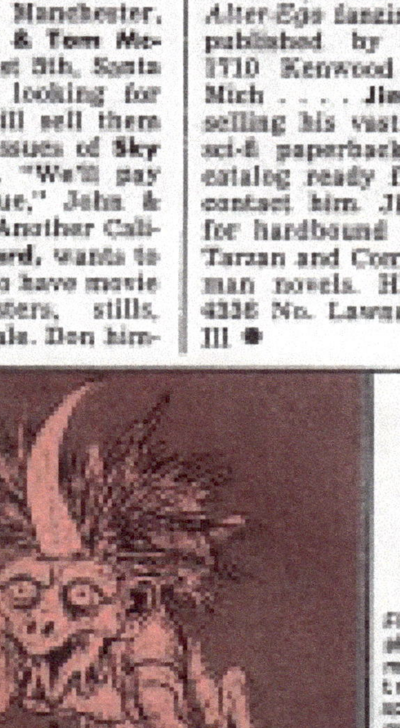

First, exclusive shots of the farmade creature Gargantis, scanned in the mad lab of Alan A. Harris of Bradford, England.

Slaymate of the Month

Is it Beauty? Or Jekyll? Count Dawno making after a hard day's slice? No. It's Monster Makeup Fan Lionel Comport of Burbank, Calif.

MONSTER
OF THE
MONTH

American-International's
She Creature

Up from the silent green depths of the Pacific Ocean comes a monster born of shadow and slime. The She Creature, an almost human water-breather who swam across the theatre screen in four spine-cooling films.

According to AIP producer, Alex Gordon, the creation of the She Creature required more sweat and ingenuity than it took to scare up the Frankenstein monster. Alex himself poured through dozens of books on underwater prehistoric creatures, then had 76 sketches of scaly bodies made, and 32 of the gilled skull.

After the form was finalized, months of tests with the rubber and plastic She Creature suit went on, until the day the monster walked.

The She Creature performed in 1956, in a film of its own name, *The She Creature*. The AIP feature scored so high with monster aware audiences that a year later the female horror was starred in *Voodoo Woman*. The head alone appeared in the studio's *How To Make a Monster* (1958), and was seen full length again in *Ghost of Dragstrip Hollow* (1959).

The awesome amphibian retired after the *Dragstrip Hollow* comedy, setting a near record as one of the longest and hardest working monsters in show business. ●

There's Something
BIG Coming Up . . .

. . . in each and every
terror and thrill-packed issue
of FANTASTIC MONSTERS,
the scare-sational film magazine
created specially for YOU!

In future issues, You Are
There when:
— the deadly TARANTULA
spins its spidery web of
gripping fear!
— Frankenstein, Dracula,
Mummy, and a coffin load
of other nightmarish creatures
cause a fright in the night!
— daring spacemen
discover the terrifying secrets
of THE LOST PLANET!
— exclusive coverage is
given fantasy film classics
like NOSFERATU, 7 FOOT-
PRINTS TO SATAN, and
METROPOLIS!
— mysteries from the
eerie TWILIGHT ZONE
are revealed!
— IT CONQUERS THE
WORLD
— Flash Gordon, Buck
Rogers, and Sky Altitude
rocket through time and space
in search of amazing
adventures beyond the
wildest dreams!
Plus a castle-ful of fiendish
features and frightening
photos guaranteed to make
your pulse pound and
your blood boil!

Don't walk, don't run — take a GIANT STEP to your news-stand
to reserve YOUR COPY of the next FANTASTIC MONSTERS!

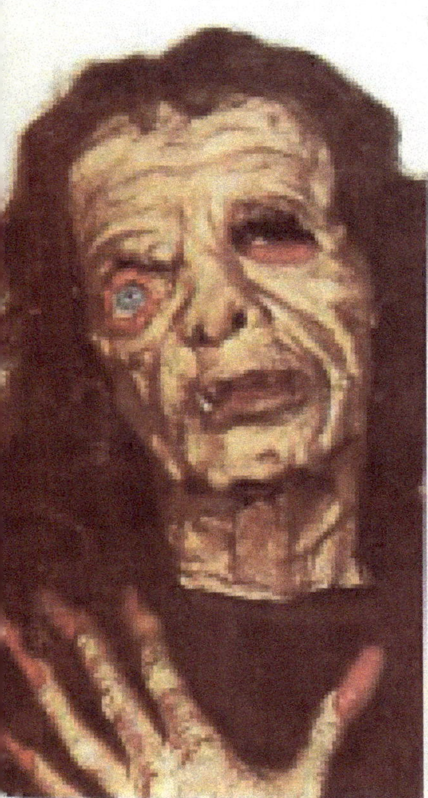
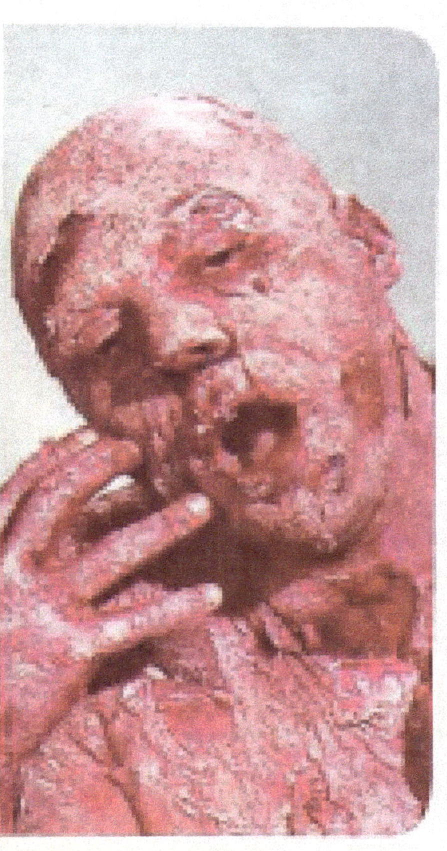

VAMPIRES
WEREWOLVES
MONSTERS
GHOULS
ROBOTS
FIENDS
MUMMIES
mutations
Wierd Creatures
MADMEN
the supernatural

OFFICIAL
PUBLICATION OF THE FANTASTIC
MONSTERS CLUBS
Rules and Membership Information Inside

AADC
fantastic
MONSTERS
OF THE FILMS
VOL. 1 • NO. 2
50¢
HORROR GUARANTEED TO SHOCK YOU DEAD OR YOUR LIFE REFUNDED!
3-D HORRORS
COME ALIVE
INSIDE!

WORLD'S GREATEST MONSTER MAGAZINE

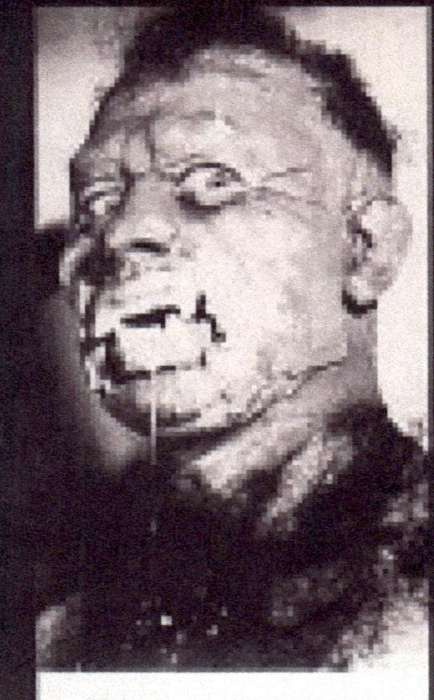

Witches with switches, riding brooms through the night; orange-yellow pumpkins, grinning eyes glowing bright; on Poe's black cats and goblins and fiends: here come the monsters—it's Halloween.

And if young Frankensteins, Draculas, and Wolf Men parading throughout darkened streets, armed with packed bags of candy and mischief, aren't enough for you this time of year, we here at *FANTASTIC MONSTERS* have scared up an additional cauldronful of creatures and lurking horrors to come tapping at your waxed windows in this special Halloween issue.

But it's a treat, not a trick, you're in for when you unlock the squeaking door to Karloff's Castle and step into the strange and whacky realm of The Twilight Zone. The Devil's Messenger is there to conduct a tour which includes a lunch break where 3-D terrors come lurching off the pages at you.

If you find you have trouble returning to This Island Earth, we've got Captain Marvel on stand-by, to flash to your rescue.

Unless, that is, he's too busy battling Varan.

However, we think you'll survive even this chill-chocked issue. Remember the old saying: There's nothing to fear but fear itself — and that's enough.

THE EDITORS

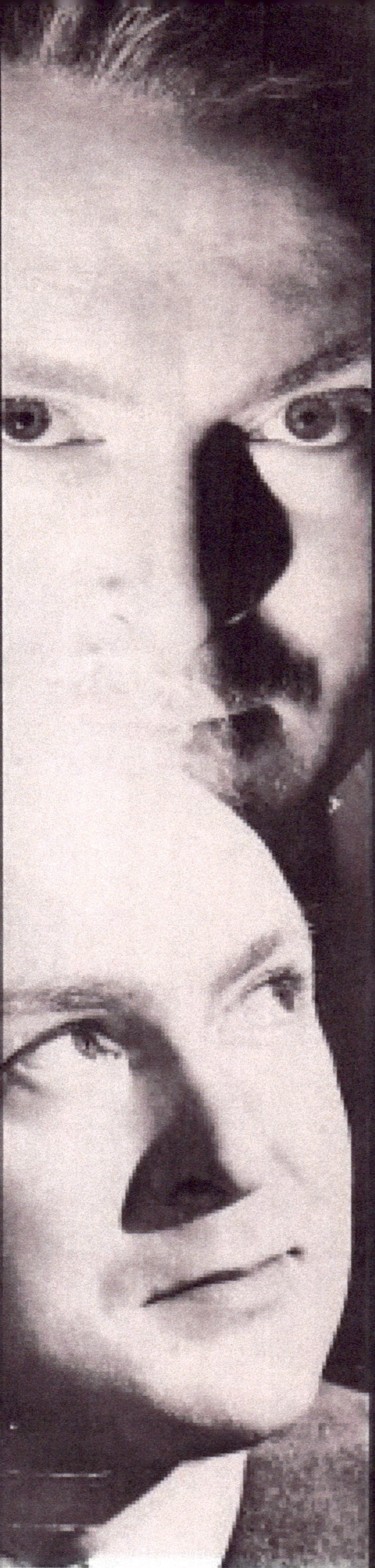

Keep your spirit up
by reading
FANTASTIC MONSTERS

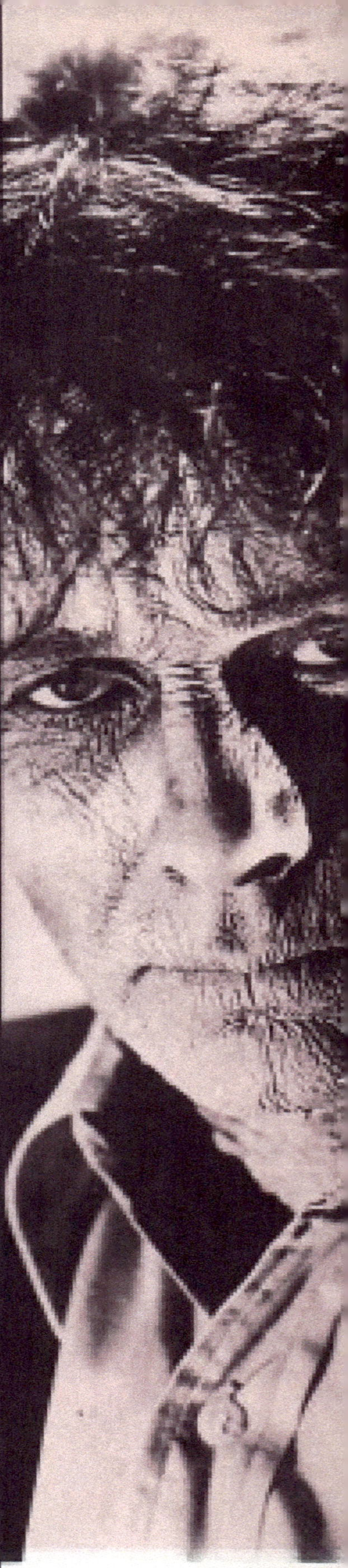

Face it — this is
the magazine with the
new wrinkle

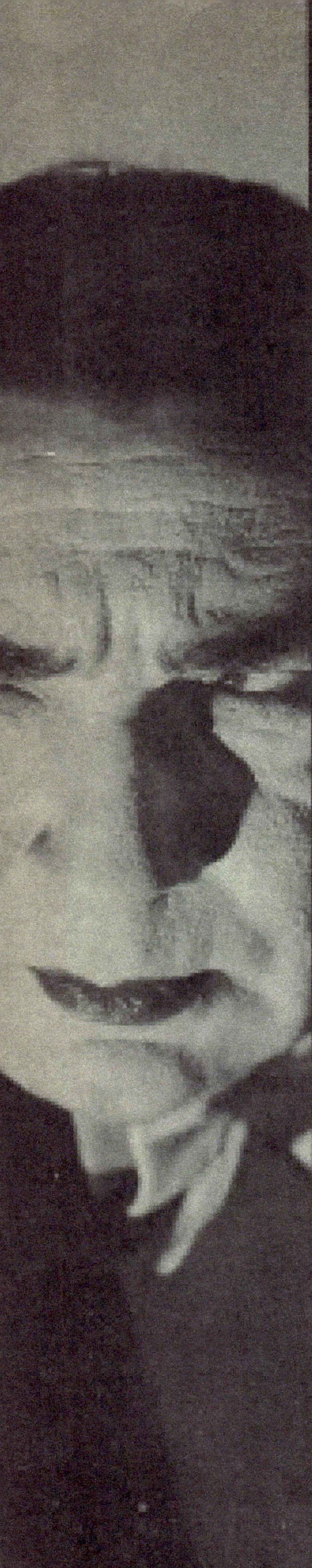

fantastic
MONSTERS
OF THE FILMS
VOL. 1 • NUMBER 2

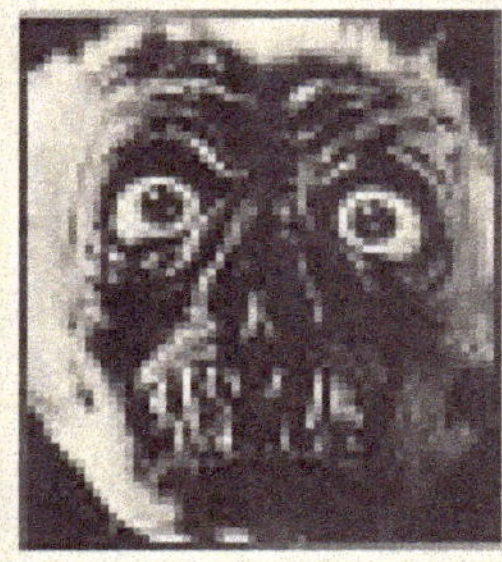

COVER: From American-International's Pictures' HOW TO MAKE A MONSTER

RON HAYDOCK
editor

PAUL BLAISDELL
editorial director

BOB BURNS
research editor

JIM HARMON
associate editor

CREDITS & ACKNOWL-
EDGEMENTS: Kirk Alyn;
Larry Byrd; Cayuga Prod;
Lon Chaney Jr; CBS-TV;
Columbia Pic; George Fa-
ber; Kenneth Hertz; MGM;
Mike Minor; Milton Moritz;
NBC-Radio; Bill Pearson;
Vincent Price; Republic
Pic; Bob Smith; Glenn
Strange; Universal Pic;
Warner-Bros; Mark Tener.

VOLUME 1, NUMBER 2, FAN-
TASTIC MONSTERS OF THE
FILMS. PRICE 50c PER COPY.
Published bi-monthly by
Black Shield Publications
Inc. Mailing address: Post
Office Box 541, Topanga,
California. National Advertising Representative: Harbor Company, 862 North
Fairfax, Los Angeles 46,
California. Copyright Copyright 1962, by Black Shield
Publications Inc. Nothing
may be reprinted in whole
or in part without written
permission. Printed in U.S.A.
Unsolicited manuscripts must
be accompanied by stamped,
self addressed envelope;
the publisher accepts no responsibility for return. Any
similarity between people
and places mentioned in the
fiction and situations in
this magazine and any real
people and places is purely
coincidental.

We guarantee
you'll go bats about
this issue

CONTENTS

TWIN SHOCK SHOW
A night at your local theatre with Crown-International Pictures' latest and greatest offerings is a guarantee of thrilling monster mayhem and chilling outer space jitters

Varan
The Unbelievable
Monster

With film stars Myron Healey as Commander James Bradley and beautiful Japanese actress Tsuruko Kobayashi as Anna, his wife, the incredible beginnings of Varan the Unbelievable take place on one of the smaller islands of the Japanese Archipelago where Bradley is conducting experiments to change salt water into fresh.

In his experiments, Bradley uses untested chemicals much to the chagrin of the natives of the island. They tell him that legend says a giant prehistoric creature lies beneath the water of the lagoon and warn him that his experiments may disturb the feared monster.

Bradley ignores the warning.

And the dreaded sea beast, Varan, rises from the salty floor of his kingdom, its chaotic behavior resulting in total destruction of everything and everybody before and around it.

Army units pour all their fire power into the reptile, to no avail. Then, suddenly as it arose, Varan disappears beneath the waves again. Bradley and his men wonder where it will strike next—and they don't have long to wait to find out.

The city of Onida becomes the playground of the legendary monster. All the inhabitants are evacuated, and hundreds of army units begin their all-out war on Varan. Every modern weapon is used—heavy artillery, rockets, planes—but again to no avail.

Bradley arrives at the conclusion that if his chemicals were responsible for Varan leaving the lagoon, possibly a heavier concentration exploded directly on him will destroy the monster.

Bradley's plan appears to succeed, but not until we see most of the Japanese city destroyed. At least for the time being the monster is repulsed, having retreated back to its underwater home.

But is it dead? Will it appear again? No one really knows . . .

(Above, left) Stars Myron Healey and Tsuruko Kobayashi flee from the rampaging prehistoric monster. (Above & Below) VARAN THE UNBELIEVABLE wreaks havoc and destruction as it claws out against mankind

FIRST SPACESHIP ON VENUS

Man takes up his most darir challenge

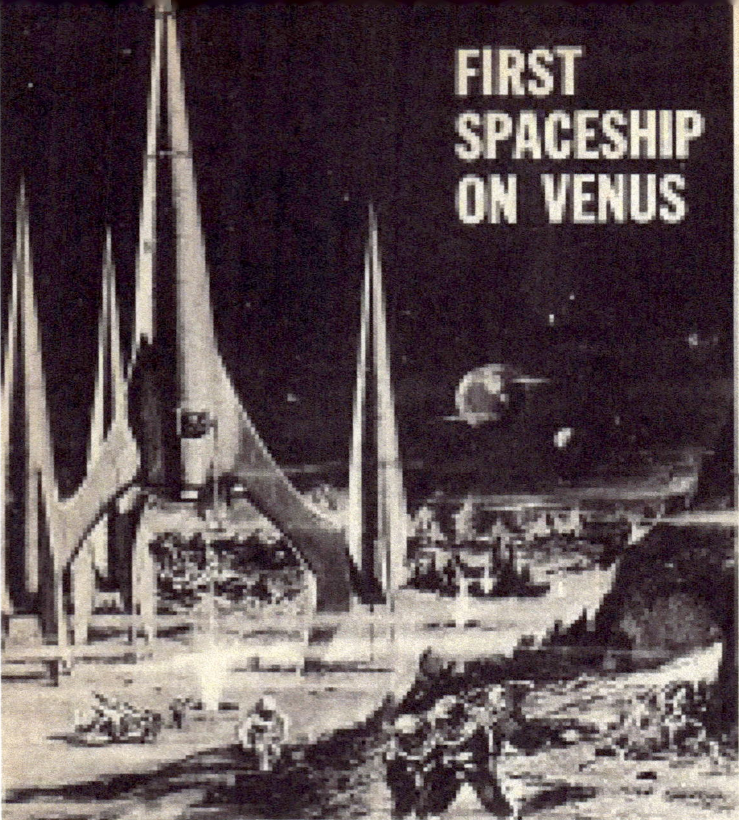

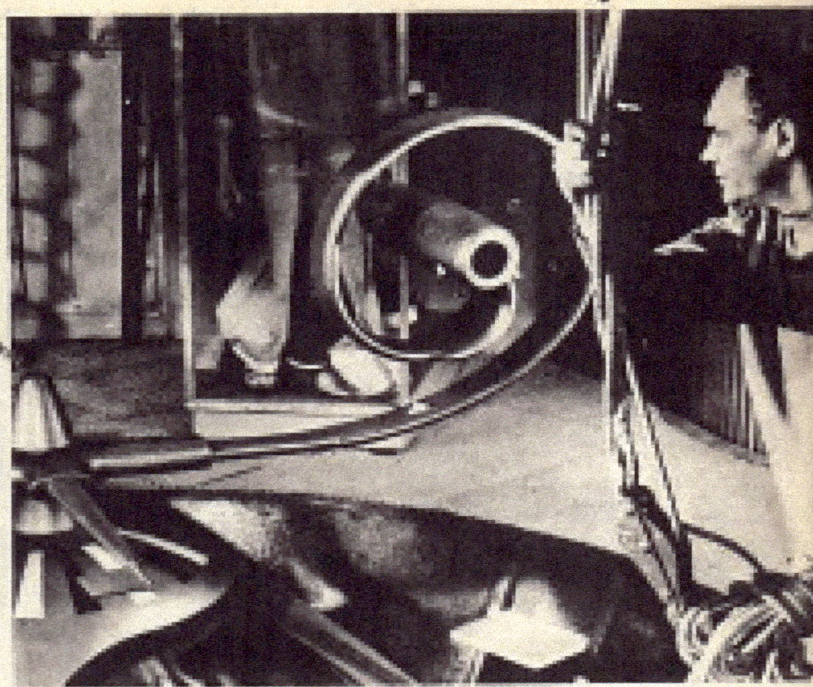

(Above, right) Inside the ship, enroute to Venus, the spacemen prepare to meet the impact of a storm of meteorites.

(Below) The interstellar Columbuses, using their Astraicle scout ship, begin their search of the gaseous Venus.

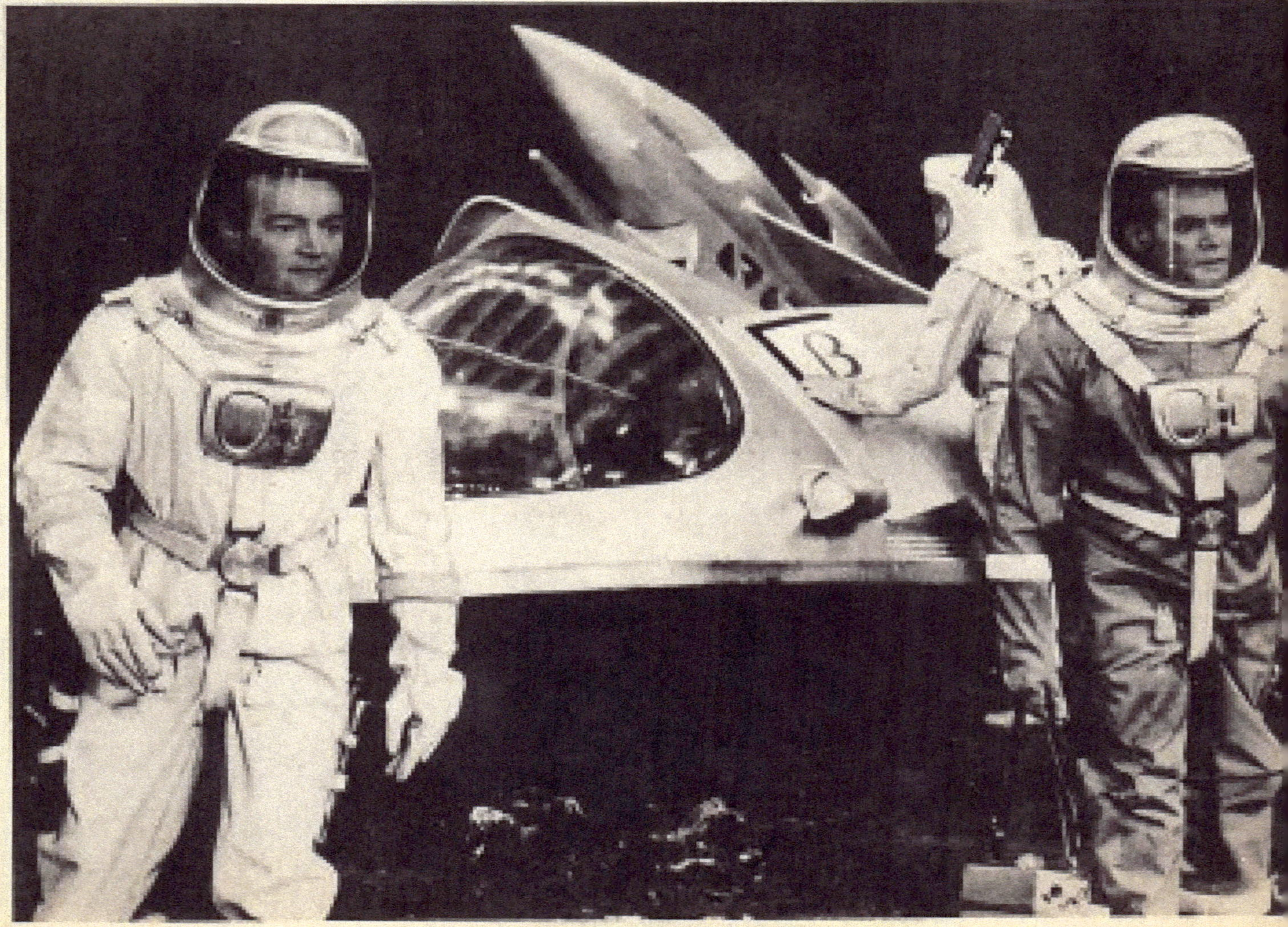

e rockets through the unknown to Venus

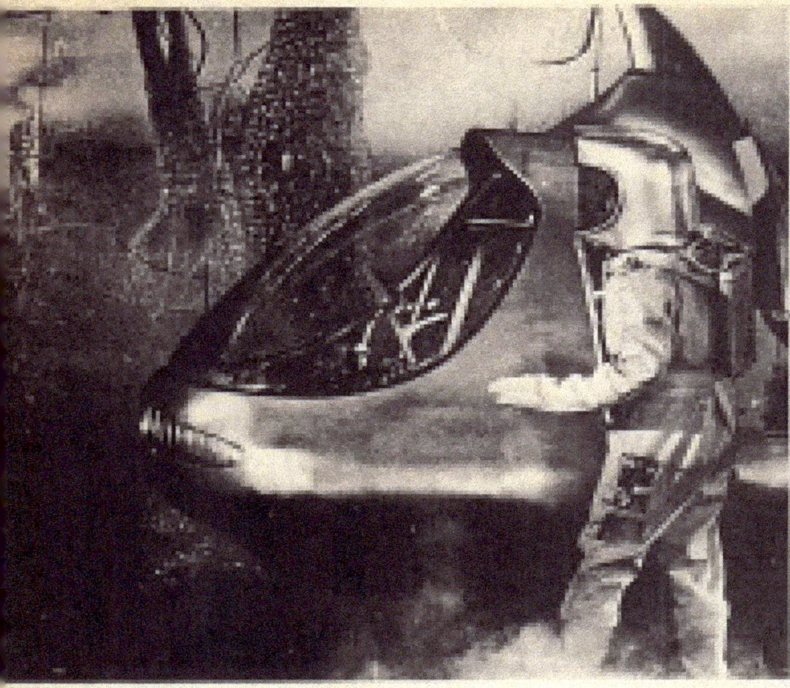

This second Crown-International film of the evening is noteworthy because for the first time in motion picture annals the screen graphically portrays every breathless, thrilling moment of a space flight from Earth to Venus and its return; from the blast-off to touchdown.

Eight international astronauts, seven men and a woman (with femme star Yoko Tani and male lead Oldrick Lukes heading the interstellar safari), comprise the crew of the spaceship. You are literally aboard the sleek space projectile as it streaks through the solar system, at eight miles per second, passing the moon and an already-established Earth outpost, Lunar Station III. You are there as the crew braves a staggering shower of meteorites, and finally pierces the mysterious, gaseous layer surrounding Venus.

And you're with them as they land on Venus, and discover the Vitrified Forest, the weird Venusians' invasion-control center; as they brave the deadly, crawling quicksand and struggle against the staggering Venusquake, a radiation tempest raging uncontrolled.

If you want chills and thrills, Crown-International has come up with the shock double-bill for you—*Venus the Unbelievable* and *First Spaceship on Venus*.

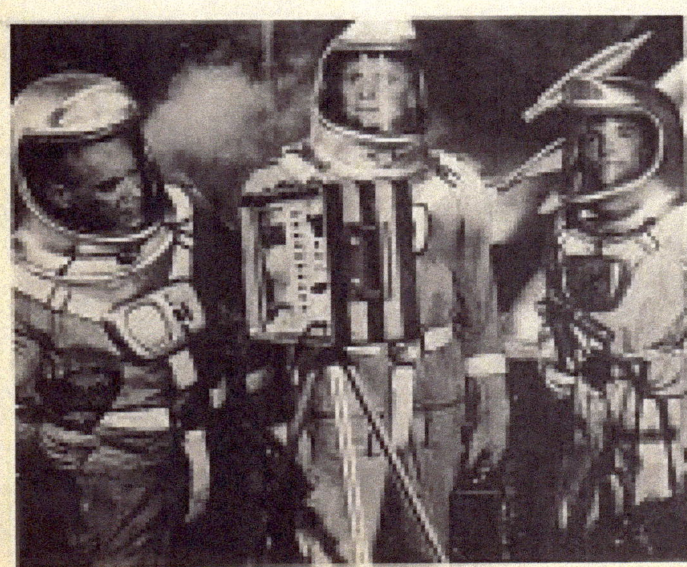

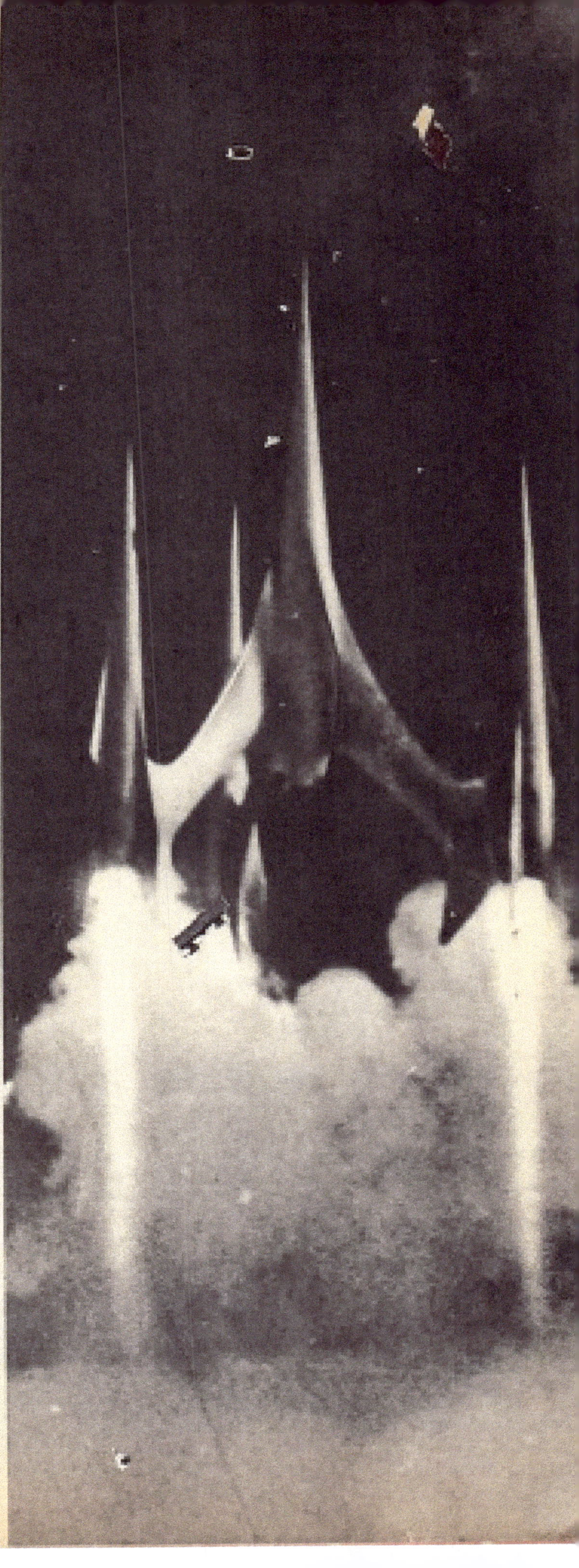

With his fine Egyptian hand, the Bandaged Bard of the Pyramids is quick to draw a parallel between two of Moviedom's Mummy Epics

MAD MUMMY WRITHES AGAIN

As faithful readers of *FANTASTIC MONSTERS* will recall, I was brought back to life in the editorial offices of *Black Shield Publications* last issue. We Egyptians used to go in for disemboweling in the old days, but I think it is an even crueler and unnatural punishment to wake up to find yourself being carted around by four members of the editorial staff: Haydock, a young Basil Rathbone type who is plugged into an electric guitar; Blaisdell, a mustached artist in a yachting cap; Bob Burns, a dark-haired serial hero type, wearing cowboy boots and a can of flea powder in his pocket; and finally a well-fed chap who looks like a bust of Napoleon (a real bust) and who wears a sportshirt with a T-M Bar brand on it. They call this one Gem Harmon (the gem, I think, because he is a diamond in the rough).

I tell you there I was, a poor helpless corpse being carted by those four—honest to Isis, you would have thought it was a funeral.

But the FanMo staff isn't a bad lot if you like the type—human beings. They offered me a job reviewing movies for them. Since I knew nothing

Right: Boris Karloff as the unwrapped Im-ho-tep, having a cup of Tana leaves. Left: Christopher Lee, while still in favor with the Pharaoh, judging a line of Vestal Virgins.

about contemporary life, or about movies, and even had trouble reading and writing, they told me I had all the usual qualifications for a motion picture reviewer.

After getting an advance, I bought a new suit of clothes; and I must say I don't care a great deal for the new styles. Those new Band-Aids with their little red centers make me look like I have measles all over. A mummy my age—five or six thousand—doesn't have kid ailments like that.

In my first column last time, I blew off a little steam. Well, actually, it was a cloud of vapor from some brewing Tana leaves. But now, I intend to do a calm, objective review of two productions about my kin.

First of all, let me calmly and objectively say that all moviemakers should be sealed in their own film cans, with a length of footage around their throats!

Movies are unfair to mummies!

To start off, look at *The Mummy* starring Boris Karloff. And to start off, it goes well. The 1932 Universal Pictures production begins similarly to Hammer Films' 1959 Universal-International release of Christopher Lee as *The Mummy*.

Both features open in Ancient Egypt with a love-smitten priest (Karloff, Im-ho-tep; Lee, Kharis) mooning over a comely star as a high priestess. When the Pharaohs start making furrows in the heart of the priestess for stepping out of the chorus line of Vestal Virgins, the priest attempts to revive the corpse of his beloved by using the forbidden Book of Thoth.

The priest is captured in both films and is severely chided for his misdeed. After his tongue is ripped out, he is wrapped alive in bandages and crammed into a coffin to wait out the centuries as a guard of the dead priestess-princess.

Then in the two pictures, as the parallel continues, two vile teams of grave robbers, archaeologists, if you will, descend on the pyramids. (I sat in the audience yelling "Yankees, Go Home" until somebody told me they were British.)

The terror twins continue a similar path with the Mummy (at last, the star of the picture) coming to life in his attractive set of threads, and scaring the archaeologists into insanity, which is where they belong. (I

turn to page 46

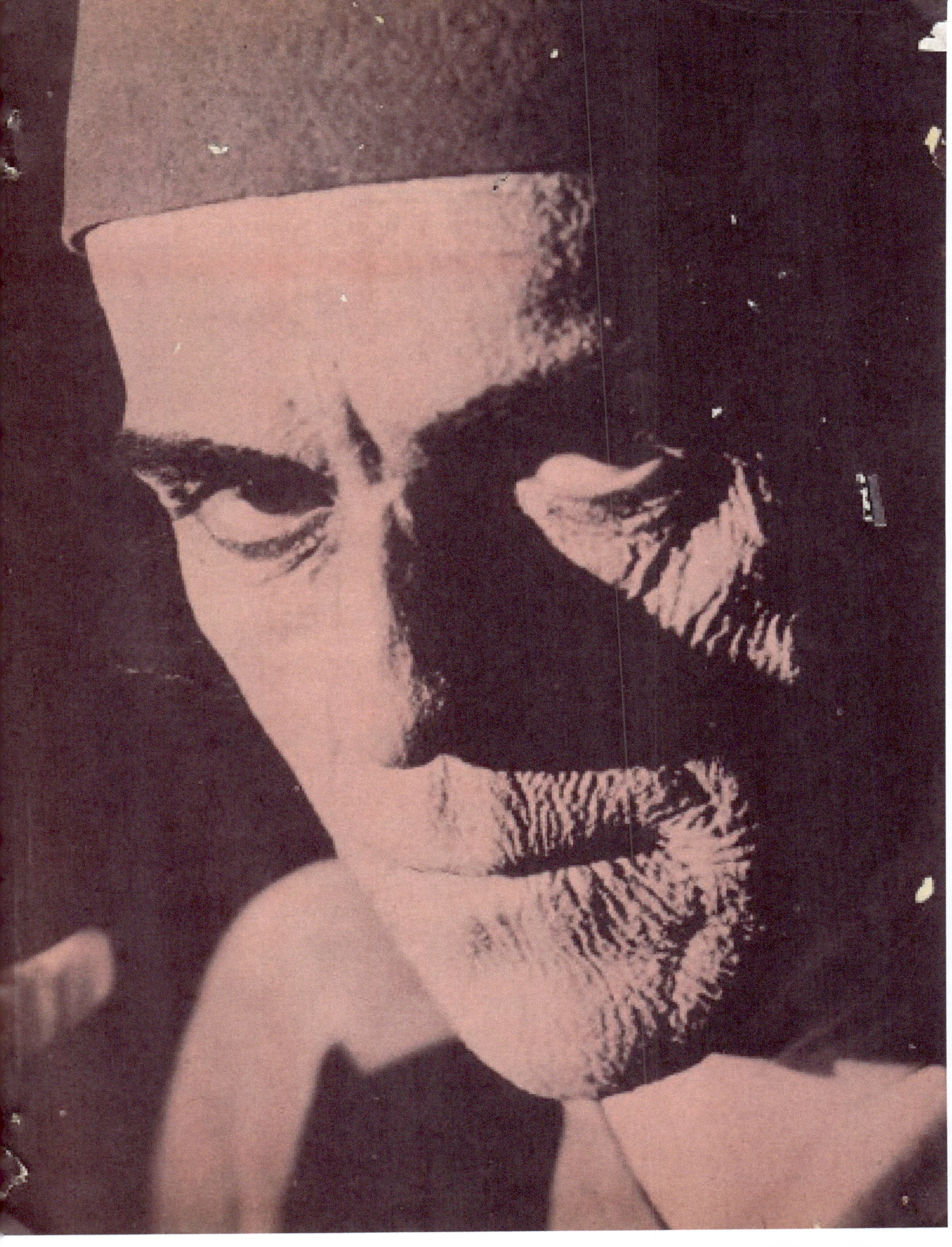

The Man With The Rubber Face

by JOHN MARIM

The trouble with being a struggling young actor, thought Don Dell (it was once Donald Delbert), is that the struggle wears you out, especially if you don't eat regularly. He wanted to do a horror movie, but not as the human skeleton.

Dell strolled the hot sidewalks past MacArthur Park, near Seventh and Alvarado Streets in Los Angeles. This was where many of the actors, writers, and beatniks in L. A. hung out, ones that couldn't afford the rent in the Hollywood district.

He was a tall, blond young man, very handsome, and well aware of it. Regarding himself in the plate glass windows he passed, windows of pawn shops, radio-TV repair stores, eateries, he frowned ruefully. A sportshirt and jeans didn't do enough for him at all. He needed some new clothes, some "front" clothes; then maybe a producer would notice him. He needed money to make a splash, and by this time, he was about ready to do any-

turn the page

RUBBER, from page 11

thing to get it.

He looked into the window of one of the pawn shops, and halted on the baking sidewalk, only beginning to shadow with afternoon. There were some suits inside. A friend of his had once found a brand new $150 suit with only a small tear in the lining for $6.00. Not that he had five dollars, at least not to spare. But still —

Then he saw it.

Right in the window, it was. The small hand-lettered sign read:

KARU CREIGHTON'S PERSONAL
MAKE-UP KIT
Make me an Offer

Dell looked at it. It didn't look like a fake. All of it was there, the base, the grease paint, bits of face hair, trimmers, appliers, more, all of it in an old worn wooden case with a lid mirror that was beginning to flake off from the back, leaving a faint dust of black snow across the still lake of the glass.

This might be a good gimmick, Dell thought. Go to an audition with this thing, maybe make a spiel about Karu passing it on to him as a kid, or something. Besides, he simply wanted the thing. He needed it. It could make a splash. So he was going to have it. That was only logical.

He walked to the entrance of the pawn shop, down a short flight of stairs, the display windows being ground level but the store having a basement entrance. Probably the building was the design of a New York builder who had moved to California.

Karu Creighton, Dell thought. He had been one of the truly great stars of silent movies, and had even made some fine early talkies. Many people seemed to think that Lon Chaney Sr. had been the only one making movies in the silent era, but there had been others. The great actor, John Barrymore, had departed from his romantic roles for *Dr. Jekyll and Mr. Hyde*, and even Karloff had started back then. There had been a number of others, perhaps not so famous, including Karu Creighton. He had not worked for a major studio like Universal, unlike Chaney, and had never received the publicity others had. But Creighton was a great horror man — even today his movies played in small art theatres and before film societies. Where Chaney had been known as the Man with a Thousand Faces, Creighton was called the Man with the Rubber Face.

The cool of the basement was a relief from the heat of the street, but with the cool came a chill at the memory of the first Karu Creighton movie Dell had seen as a boy, a revival of an early talkie, *The Rolling*. In it, Creighton had portrayed a man who only had bones on one side of his body, the other side hanging limp and hideous, the flesh almost liquid.

The tinkle of the store bell brought Dell back to the present.

"Hi, there," called the hefty pawnbroker. "What'll it be today, Bud?"

"That make-up case in the window," the actor said. "I'd like to see it."

"You want to buy it?" the store owner said, eyeing him sharply.

Dell shrugged. "I might. If it's what I want."

The pawnbroker hesitated, then said briskly, "Okay, I'll get 'er right out for you, Buddy."

Dell waited while the big man went to the front of the store, climbed up a few wooden steps and hauled the case from the window. Returning to the counter, carrying the kit open, he put it down.

"A bug on the old silent movie stuff, huh?" the pawnbroker said. "I get one of you guys in here every so often. Want stuff on Clara Bow, Doug Fairbanks, William S. Hart. I had a pile of old movie posters in here a couple of months ago. Might get some more."

"I'm an actor," Dell said. "I just wanted a make-up kit. I don't care who it belonged to."

"Didn't you ever hear of Karu Creighton? He was big, very big. But eccentric. That's what ruined him in pictures."

"Really?" Dell said politely.

"Sure, I got all the inside dope on things like that," the big man said. "You know, like Ken Maynard had to quit the movies because his horse, Tarzan, died, and Tom Mix couldn't make talkies because he was really a deaf mute—"

Somehow, Dell doubted both of these stories.

"What about Creighton?"

"He wouldn't make movies nowhere but New York City during the months of December, January, and February. That was okay in the early days — there were studios back there then— but when everything moved to Hollywood, all his stuff had to shot on location, and it got expensive. When he wouldn't listen to reason—"

"How much for the case?" Dell asked.

The big man grinned. "You saw the sign. Make me an offer."

"Ten dollars," Dell said.

"What?" yelled the pawnbroker. "I asked for an offer, not an insult!"

The big man slammed down the lid on the case, on all the magic and mystery inside, and threw the catches.

"You bum!" he screamed at Dell. "You came in here off the street and make me an offer like that for a valuable piece of property like this! I wouldn't sell it to you now, no matter what, not if you offered me a hundred!"

The hulking form pushed Dell aside with a thrust of a hairy hand and stormed back towards the display window.

Feeling his face flaming with anger, Dell tried to think clearly. Obviously, a slob like this didn't deserve a rare item like that make-up case. The store was deserted, shadowy, the interior invisible from the street. The actor's eyes darted over the litter of pawned items, and found the inevitable musical instrument, a trumpet.

Mr. Pawnbroker, Dell thought, your day of judgment has arrived. It is time for the Last Trumpet.

As the big man finished replacing the case in the window and started back down the short flight of wooden steps, Dell came around behind him, and brought the musical instrument crushing down on his skull.

The pawnbroker lay on the floor, too broken even for pawning.

As Dell removed the case from the window, he thought it would serve a slob like that right if he were dead.

THE CASE WAS A PHONY!

Dell stormed up and down his tiny room, literally beating his head with his fists. All that trouble for nothing.

Finally, he lit up a cigarette and sat down to examine the case critically.

He should have known that the hair pieces and the like would be so old and dry they would fall apart, and some of the make-up containers were absolute fakes. The nose putty container, or rather what was labelled nose putty, when opened revealed a shiny tin interior, completely clean and odorless, as if it had never contained anything.

The case still looked authentic, the wooden box. It had the right initials —K. C. The actor ran his fingers along the wood, and it parted under his hands. Coming apart? he thought. He was sorry he had done it now. The pawnbroker was a bull, of course, up the next day, screaming his head off, but now Dell had t— You can get in big trouble over something like that.

But now he saw the case opened on a pre-conceived seam. There was something inside.

In the secret compartment was a small bottle, wrapped with paper.

Dell unrolled the paper, and read:

My Formula for a Rubber Face, by Karu Creighton

To whoever is clever enough to find this: The bottle contains the distillation of a chemical formula which was given to me by a very old East Indian in my early days in show business, working a small circus. With an injection of this formula, a great plasticity of the flesh is possible, so that the skin itself can be molded into new shapes. But with this gift goes certain responsibilities and hazards . . .

Dell stopped reading.

"What a gimmick," he said to himself. "What a great gimmick!" He chuckled to himself. "This really ought to make a splash."

turn to page 62

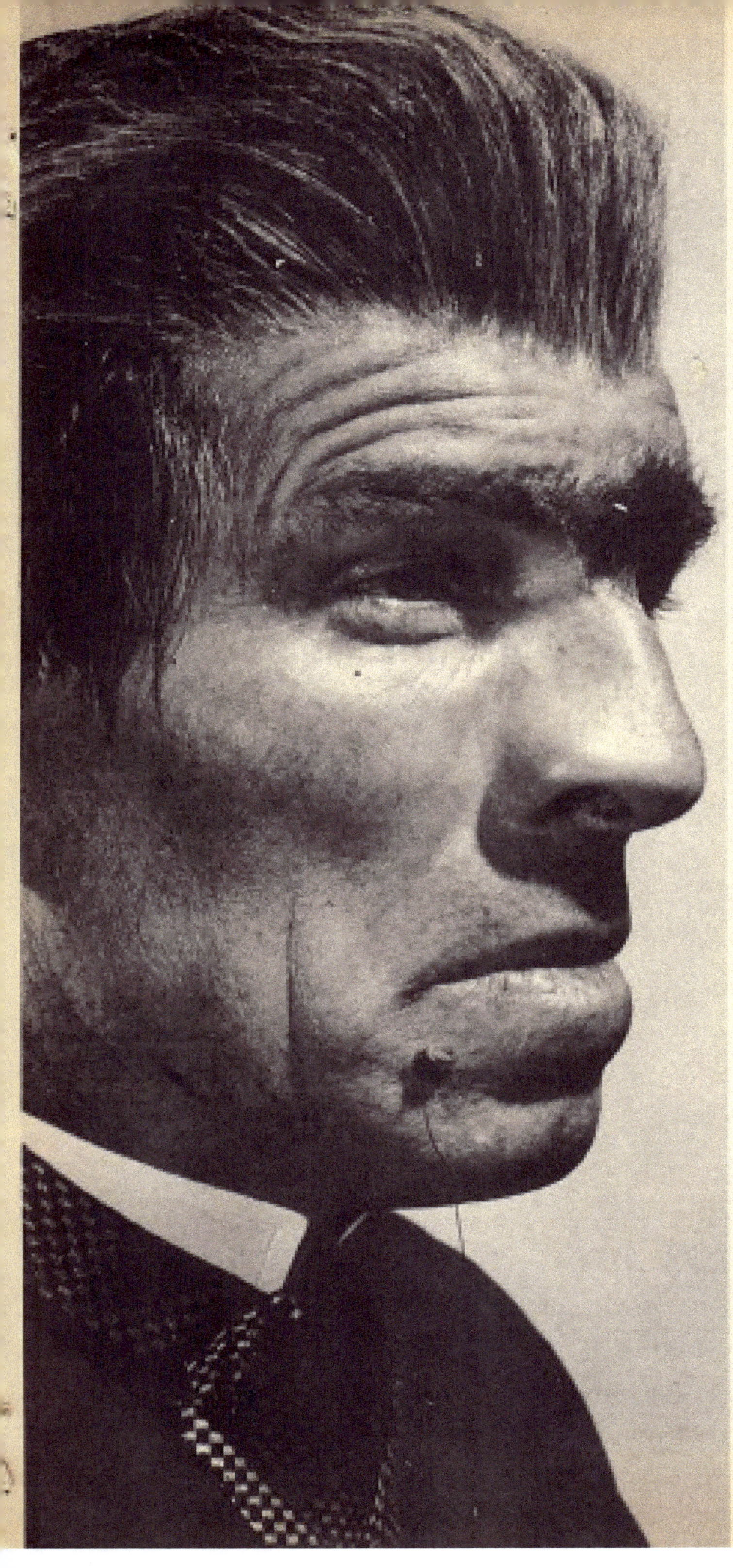

Monster Mugshots from the Private Morgue of FANTASTIC MONSTERS

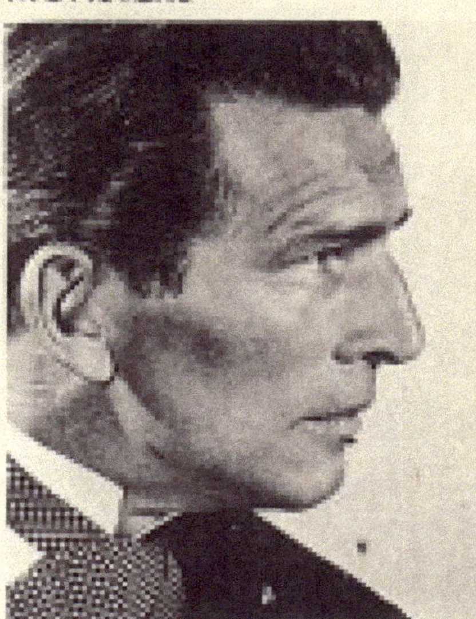

Mystery Museum

The theatre's most challenging dual-role, *Dr. Jekyll and Mr. Hyde*, has rolled up a long list of performances: John Barrymore (stage and screen), Frederic March, Spencer Tracy (movies). Television got into the act with its own adaption of the Robert Louis Stevenson classic thriller on CBS-TV's "live" drama series, *Climax*, in July, 1955—scripted by *Visit To A Small Planet*'s Gore Vidal.

As the fun-loving doctor whose transformation to a human monster took place on T.V. before th[illegible] millions, Michael Rennie d[illegible] the luxury of a camera pause to crea[illegible] the elaborate makeup malformations in four of his six facial changes.

Although two of the six metamorphoses were recorded prior to the "live" presentation on tape and integrated with the action, Rennie performed a quartet of queer transformations before millions on open cameras by deftly clutching his tortured face, then pressing on heavy eyebrows and other monstrous makeup undercover of his flying fingers.

Only by his accomplished acting could Michael Rennie meet the challenge of *Dr. Jekyll and Mr. Hyde* for this one-time "live" performance—not to be seen again, except in the pages of *FANTASTIC MONSTERS* ●

How a werewolf disguised himself as a monster from watery space to stand in for a friend on television—proving a fiend on channel two is a fiend true-blue

DAY THE SHE CREATURE INVADED TV

Special Article by Bob Burns

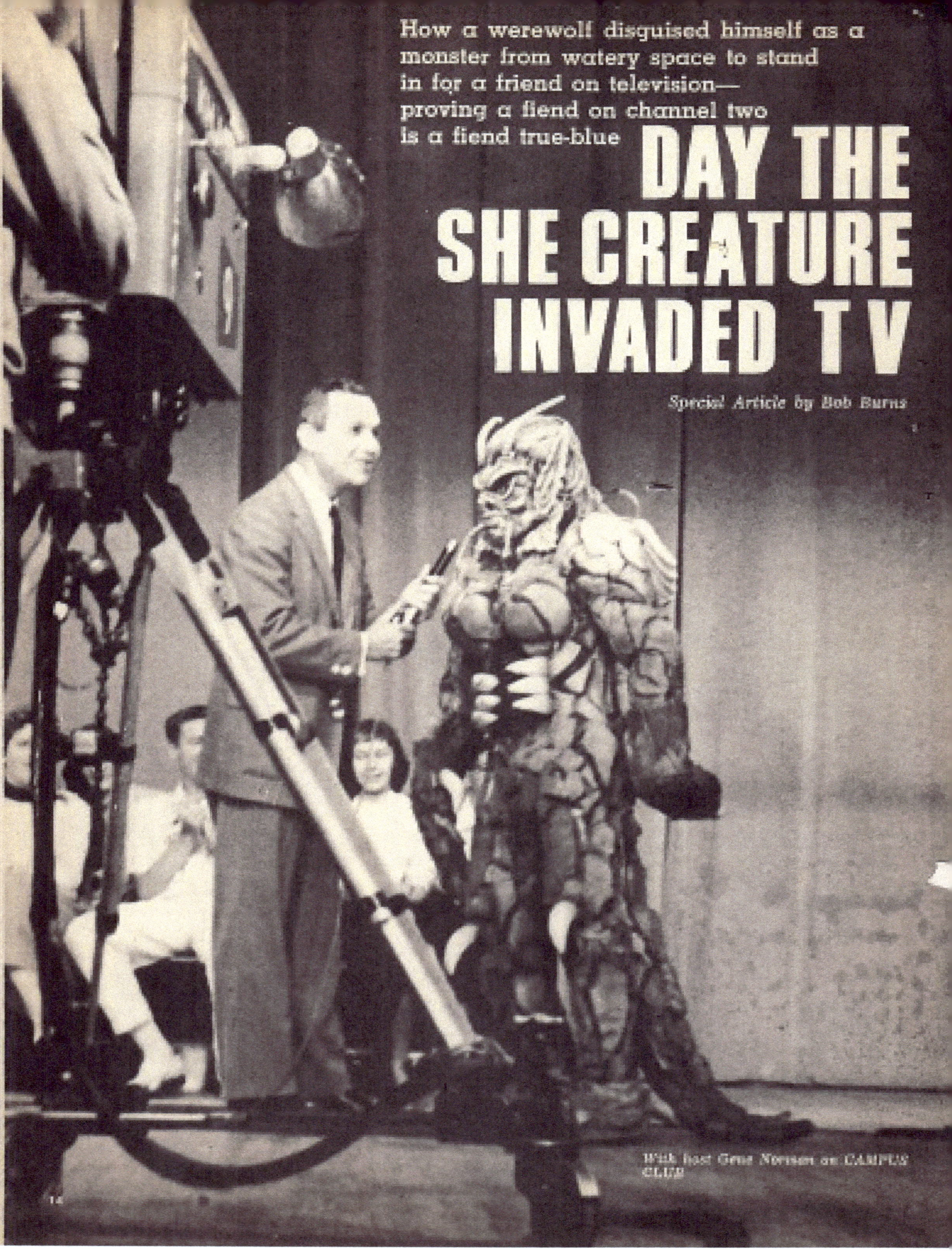

With host Gene Norman on CAMPUS CLUB

One afternoon some time back, when I was expecting to spend a quiet evening at home, I asked my wife to hand me my head.

"Which one, dear?" Kathy inquired.

I explained that I wanted the one in the middle of the rack, the one with fur and blood all over it—the goodlooking one—when the telephone rang.

"Bob Burns, Monster," I said, lifting the receiver.

"Bob," an excited voice babbled at me, "I'm in desperate trouble. They want me to go on television as the *She Creature*. If I do, they'll find out what I really am!"

Agreeing with my friend, an actor too well known in Hollywood to be named, I listened while he asked me to be the *She Creature* for him on television. (That way no one would ever discover the *She Creature* was really human.)

Balancing my head on my knee, I scratched it thoughtfully and finally consented.

The movie, *The She Creature*, was opening all over the Los Angeles area. American-International Pictures, the studio that released the film, wanted to promote it on television, and the actor who wore the weird costume actually was not available for the appearances on TV, as he explained to me on the phone. I was a collector of horror masks and materials, and had done some previous monster work on TV, in Texas. Since I was about the same size as my friend, and had seen him do the part when AIP was filming the picture, he asked me to stand in for him.

With the aid of a friend, Lionel Comport, another horror man, I managed to get over the first hurdle, set up by racetrack tout Louis Quinn— this in the days before he did "Roscoe" on *77 Sunset Strip*.

While sitting out the 60 minute wait before the Quinn interview, Lionel took off my *She Creature* head for me, then put it back, suggesting he needed a drink, even if I didn't.

There was a Coke machine in the basement of the TV station, so we got into the elevator and started down. Somehow, we had managed to get the elevator all to ourselves.

When the doors rolled back to reveal the basement, it also showed us two attractive young secretaries — and they saw us.

Their screams and footsteps faded into the distance like an old "Hi-Yo Silver Away . . ."

I wonder if they ever got to their floor?

Finally, at the machine, I found it difficult to hold a pop bottle between my two claws, so I slipped off my huge monster gauntlets and drank the Coke through a straw stuck in the mouthpiece of the *She Creature* mask.

Just then, another cute secretary strolled by, a triplet for the other two, and saw the *She Creature* drinking a Coke. Even the sight of my human hands could not soothe her, and she ran screaming off to convince her two friends she had just seen a monster walking around, one with a tongue that hung out, big as a Coke bottle.

As Lionel and I walked back towards the elevator, two other girls sitting at snack tables didn't even look up from the book they were discussing, "The Man Who Made Maniacs."

It was now time for the first TV appearance of the *She Creature*.

On *Quinn's Corner*, Louis and I gagged it up for a good (I hope) ten minutes, playing it strictly for laughs. Since it was three in the afternoon, the station didn't want any irate mothers saying we scared their kids so bad they weren't able to enjoy the murders on *Martin Kane, Private Eye*.

We had opened with Quinn sitting at his desk, giving everybody a big smile of welcome, when I came in through the window behind him, and

turn to page 37

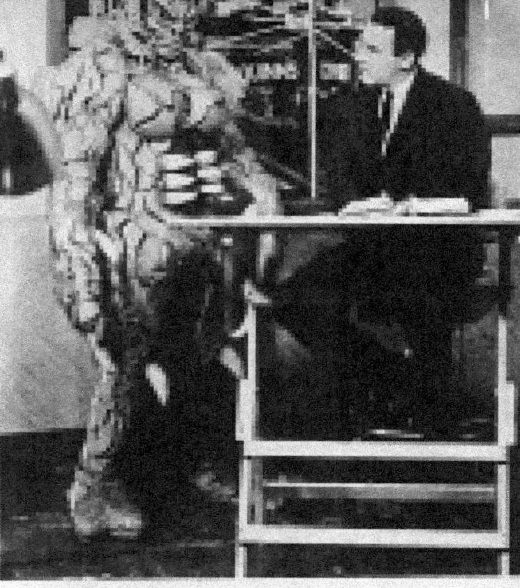

"Cuddles" the Creature being interviewed by Louis Quinn on QUINN'S CORNER

Above: The fearsome SHE CREATURE competes with high school girls for the marshmallow-on-the-string. Below: Taking time out for a Coke between appearances

In this tour of the Devil's Workshop, you're going to learn how you can make your own miniature werewolf.

The first step is to carefully sculpture the head, using your favorite brand of modelling clay, white or colored. For convenience in working, mount the clay on a stick or pencil. A bobby pin makes a good modelling tool.

Take plenty of time to shape the head, if you want this little wolf man to be a realistic model.

When finished modelling, you're ready to make a plaster mold of the head. Build a simple box of thin wood, or strong cardboard, to hold the liquid plaster and the head. The plaster may be obtained at your local hardware store. Mix with water, following the directions on the package. Use a "throw-away" container, such as a large paper cup, or coffee can, for your mixing. When the plaster is a thick, creamy consistency, pour it into the box until the box is half full.

Set the clay head, face up, half-way into the wet mixture. Now set two small balls of modelling clay into the corners of the mixture, half-way, just like the head. Let the mixture harden, then remove the two clay balls, leaving the head right where it is.

Brush vaseline over the entire hardened surface of your mold, and into those two "sockets" left by the clay balls. Brush it right up to that clay head — all around. It's not necessary to put it directly on the head, however. The vaseline will keep the top half of your mold from sticking to the bottom half.

Mix a second batch of plaster with water, and fill the remaining half of the box right up over the head. Before the plaster hardens, tap the box gently on the table to coax any trapped air bubbles to rise to the surface. You may notice how the plaster becomes warm as it "sets up"; when it is cool and hard, you're ready to peel the sides of the box away.

Locate the "seam line" of your mold, and carefully following it around with a screwdrive, pry the

THE DEVIL'S

Lon Chaney Jr. as the Wolf Man in Universal's House of Dracula

16

two halves of your mold apart. When the two halves are separated, you will notice that you have "registration pegs", thanks to those clay balls you put in earlier. The mold will now fit back together in exactly the same way, every time you use it.

Remove the clay head. If any scraps of clay are left in the mold, scrape them out carefully with a wooden toothpick.

You're now ready to cast the head in plaster.

From your local hobby, or arts and crafts store, obtain liquid latex molding compound. Brush it into the two halves of the mold carefully, following the directions on the bottle. Build up to the desired thickness, a layer at a time, allowing sufficient time for each layer to "set". We recommend five or six coats. If you want to save that brush, wash it thoroughly with soap and cold water, before the latex dries in the bristles.

When you've allowed time for the liquid latex to dry, or "cure", according to the directions that came with it, remove the two halves of your werewolf head from the mold and "seam" them together with more liquid latex, or a little glue. For the finishing touch, use a fine brush and carefully color the head with colored India inks.

Hands and feet may be made for the wolf man in the same manner as the head. A "body" may be constructed very simply with pipe cleaners, and two big corks. Glue the corks together like an hour-glass. This becomes the torso. Twist three or four pipe cleaners together and cut two equal lengths for the legs, and two more equal lengths for the arms. Make a smaller length for the neck. Attach the pipe cleaner arms, legs, and neck to the corks, and the head, hands, and feet to the pipe cleaners. Wolf man pants and shirt may be altered doll clothes, or you may prefer to make them out of colored paper.

Your miniature werewolf can now become a desk mascot, or even a subject for an 8mm home movie. If you wish to use him for miniature photography, you might, as a final touch, construct a little world for your werewolf to prowl in. ●

A hair-raising experience, when you build your own werewolf

WORKSHOP

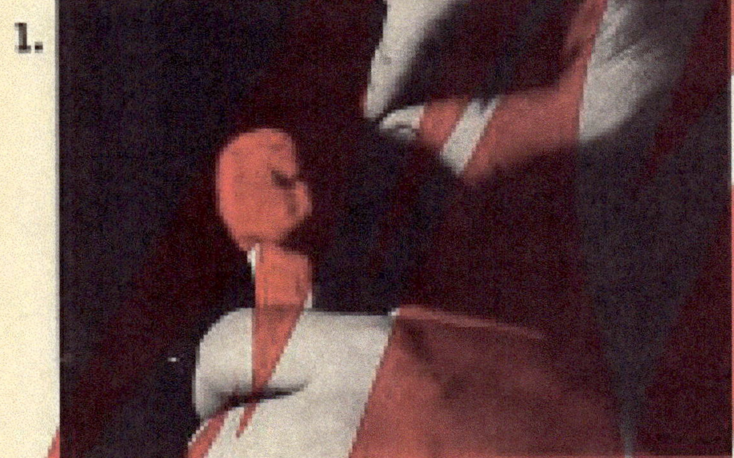

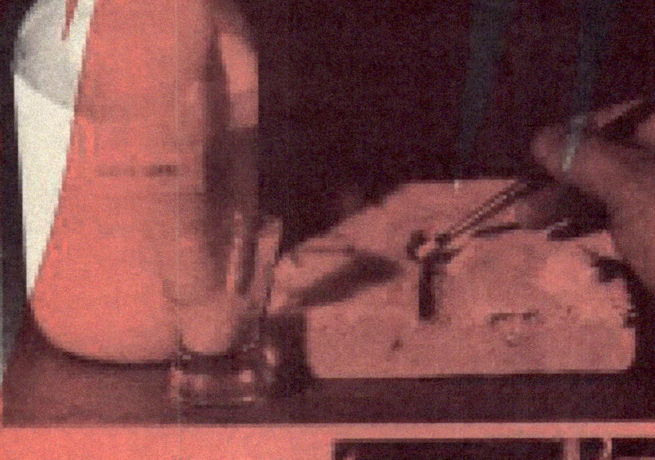

1. A werewolf head is made from modelling clay. A bobby pin is a useful tool for sculpturing this miniature. 2. The bottom half of the plaster mold, with the clay head placed halfway into the wet plaster. The clay balls will make "registration pegs". 3. Painting liquid latex rubber into the molds. A glass of cool, soapy water is handy for cleaning the brush. 4. The completed Wolf Man, in his own miniature w o r l d. He's painted with colored India inks.

THIS ISLAND EARTH

When *This Island Earth* is discussed, the scene most likely to be recalled in technicolor detail is the one in which the bug-headed Mutant takes off in hot pursuit of Faith Domergue, a girl well worth pursuing.

Certainly, the king-size cockroach in this Universal - International release is one of the screen's most memorable monsters. His heavily veined, double-compartmented head towering above the soft-fleshed humans on the eerie planet, Metaluna, makes a striking picture. The effect is no stroke of luck, either, but the result of tedious work by U-I's master makeup men, who also gave the screen the cultural heritage of Frankenstein, Dracula, and more recently, the Creature from the Black Lagoon.

Yet there is much more to this movie than just a buggy masterpiece. Recently, FANTASTIC MONSTERS opened its film vaults and removed its copy of this epic to view it for our report. All the color and excitement is still there; all the fearsome thrills of the stalking insect, immune to bullets, bombs and Raid. But there is more.

Faith Domergue's delicate, haunting face is a reminder of the fact that she is one of moviedom's most beautiful women.

She is as lovely and lively off the screen as on. She is helpless enough as a heroine to raise Bela Lugosi himself from his coffin, not to mention inspiring a bug-man to new heights of horror.

Opposite Faith in *This Island Earth* are rugged Rex Reason and brooding Jeff Morrow, both of whom have become Western stars on Television. In *This Island Earth* they portray a young scientist and a somewhat sinister alien.

Faith, Rex and Jeff head one of the most skilled and accomplished casts in space film annals.

The motion picture, released in 1955, was over two and a half years in preparation. It was adapted from the novel by star science-fictioneer, Raymond F. Jones. Universal Pictures paid one of the most unbelievable figures in cinema history for the film rights.

Catching the lucky assignment of producing the film was the ever popular William Alland, who fathered *The Space Children* and Broadwayed *The Colossus of New York*. Bill avers that this was one

Silver Spaceships, Whirring Saucers, Bug-Headed Monsters, Beautiful Heroine, A Brave Man Without a Gun, all Combine in one of Hollywood's Most Lavish and Well-Conceived Science-Fiction Spectaculars

Exeter and Metaluman assistant at the controls of the INTEROCITOR.

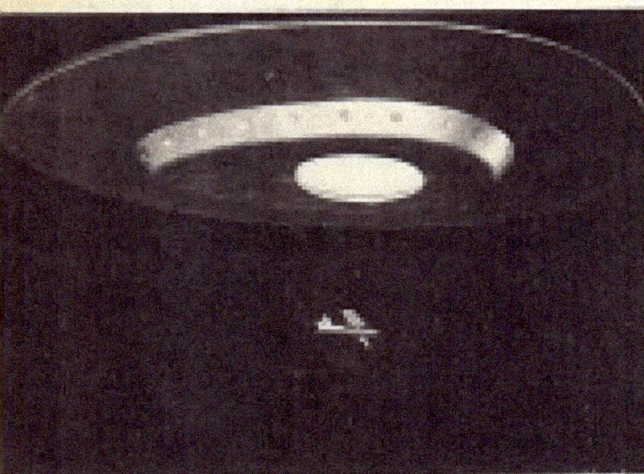

of his toughest jobs, and often recounts amusing stories of what happened during the filming of *Island*: Like the time when Faith and Reason were trapped in a colossal plastic tube, and when Jeff Morrow stepped between the poles of an electric arc to see how the special effects men managed the illusion, and other incidents that revealed the cast and crew had as much fun and excitement making the production as the audience did in seeing it.

The tides of *This Island Earth* sweep in with turbulent winds — strange currents hurl a plane piloted by Cal Meacham (Reason) out of control. A strange green ray—almost like Hal Jordan's power ring beam familiar to magazine readers, stabs down from the sky and scoops up the falling jet, allowing it to land safely.

Later, Cal begins to give serious thought to the origin of green rays that scoop up airplanes, but his perceptive thoughts are interrupted by the arrival of a catalogue apparatus at his laboratory. Even though he is a well-known scientist he is completely unfamiliar with the items shown.

Finally, the parts for one of the unorthodox instruments listed in the catalogue arrive. Cal turns his fine hand to fashioning a working model of the device, an *Interociter*.

Cal fits together his super-science jig-saw, and turns it on—not knowing what will happen. The triangular screen lights up and Cal sees the face of a man with white hair.

It isn't Hoppy on the TV screen, but the high-domed, silver thatched Exeter (Jeff Morrow) who asks Cal to come to his secluded workshop in Georgia.

The curious young scientist undertakes the trip, hoping that there will not be any more grave

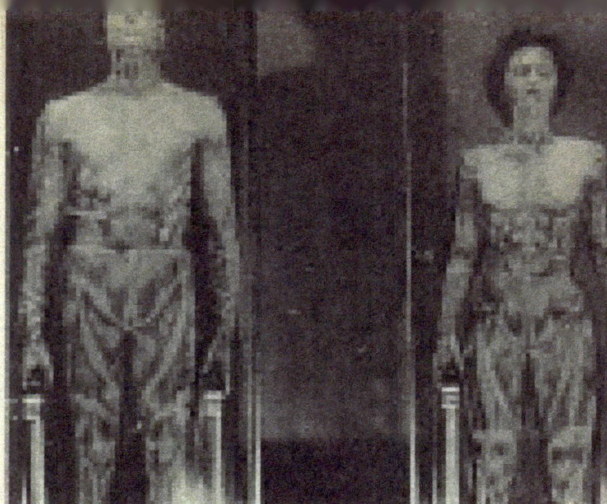

Passing through the Space Thermo Barrier, all must undergo changing of rate of metabolism

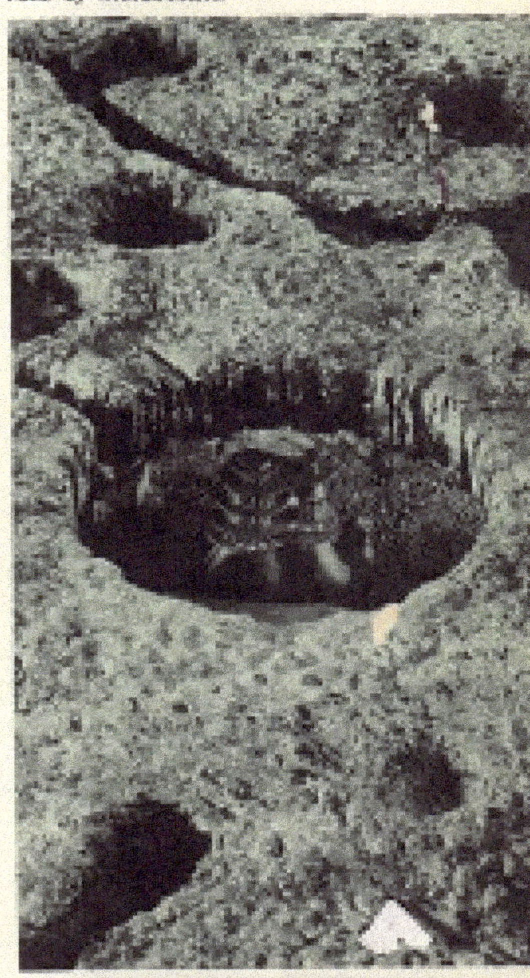

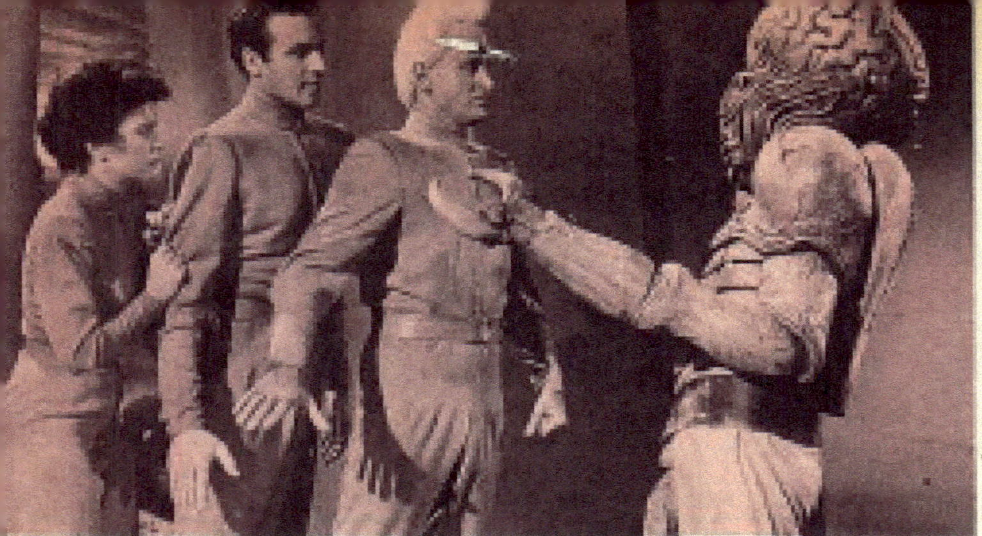

Meeting the Monitor, supreme head of the Metaluna government

The bug-headed Mutant attacks.

In her conversion chamber, Faith Domergue is menaced by dying Mutant

undertaking involved.

The plush establishment in Georgia apparently is inhabited solely by Exeter's relatives — they all have the same towering dome; thatched with silver hair. Cal encounters a comely co-ed from his Ivy League days, striking Ruth Adams (Miss Domergue).

The impressive Exeter reveals little to the two college alumni, and as they proceed through a course of experiments to discover a source of nuclear fusion other than Uranium, the two begin to suspect that Exeter isn't exactly excellent as a security risk.

Cal and Ruth decide the white-haired Exeter family is a little too far out to really be in, and set about eloping.

But as Cal and Ruth make a try for the wide open spaces, Exeter steps in to tell them they are going to be headed for some very wide space en route to the planet Metaluna. Both the young scientists take this information without the wink of an eye in as stoic a demonstration of sheer courage as the screen has ever boasted.

The kindly Exeter assures them they have nothing to fear, then turns a crimson death ray on several other lab assistants making a break for freedom, destroying his massive secret laboratory in a classic temper tantrum.

Meanwhile, Ruth and Cal have made it as far as a light plane, but as the physicist pilots the ship through the white clouds, a green ray once again fans down over the aircraft and the plane is sucked up into a mammoth flying saucer as deftly as a teen-ager strawing up a nickle Coke.

The two young scientists are given a crook's tour of the saucer by kidnapper Exeter, and they react with the same admirable stoic calm to the communication that they are traveling lightyears through interstellar space to the grayhead's home world, Metaluna, a planet fighting for its existence against cosmic forces of destruction held at bay only through the use of atomic power.

"That's a tough racquette to serve," murmers sympathetic, athletic Cal.

But things are getting worse, Exeter avers, because their stockpile of Uranium is running out. Now they need a new source of energy, a source Meacham and Ruth must discover for them.

A simple enough task for Cal Meacham, but he rankles at being forced to work at it, particularly off salary.

But there is no more rankling time left — the flying disk saucers down to explosion shaken Metaluna, to find it nearly a dead planet, with only a few

turn to page 40

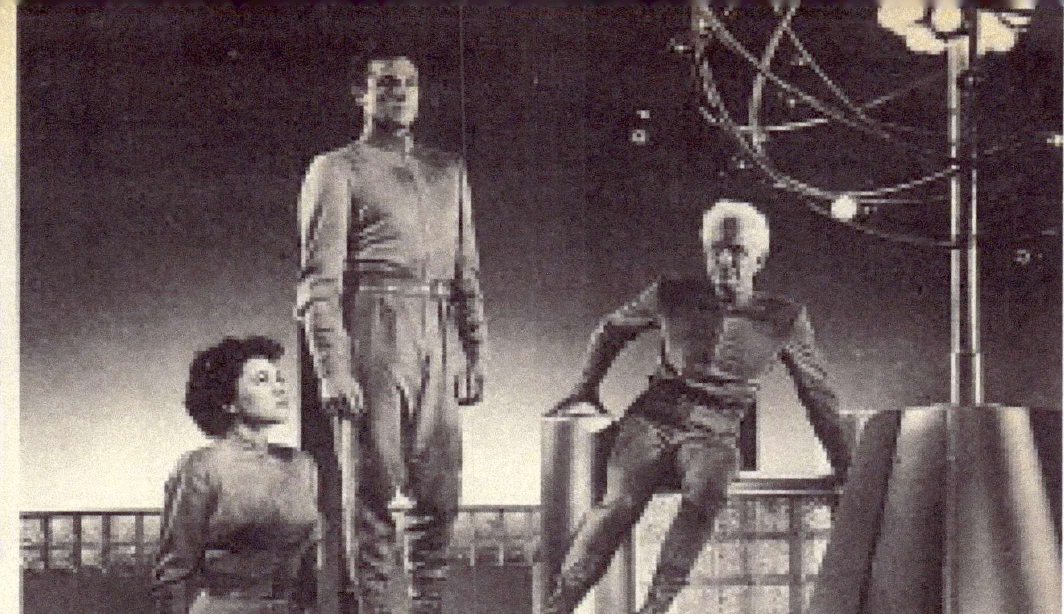

Enemy Planet, Zahgon, challenges Metal-una ship

Lon Chaney Jr. the Maestro of the Macabre, whose catalogue of menacing and memorable scream creations number those of the radioactive and Indestructible Man, the howling Wolf Man, and the super-charged, electrifying Man Made Monster, has now conceived a chilling new screen concept for the King of All Monsters — the Devil himself.

"What with the New Frontier, single-button suits, and taped television," Chaney told staffer Bob Burns at the Hollywood preview of The Devil's Messenger, "I wanted to modernize old Mephistopheles, and bring him right up to date."

In the film, Chaney portrays the Devil without elaborate makeup or costume, with a sense of (unearthly) humor, and a tongue-in-cheek approach.

A new twist, preview attendees agreed — but Lon Chaney in The Devil's Messenger is nevertheless his old diabolical self.

Produced by Kenneth Herts from an original script by Leo Guild, the story concerns Satan Chaney providing his attractive but deadly assistant Satanya (played by vivacious Karen Kadler) with unearthly devices which readily make earthlings candidates for perdition.

Satan's beautiful messenger spreads havoc on earth for him, bearing his gifts from hell:

An ordinary camera which leads to the self-destruction of a magazine photographer who has brutally murdered a woman he had never seen before.

A miner's pick, which an anthropologist uses to unearth a girl trapped for millions of years in a block of ice, his obsession to free her from her frozen grave driving him to murder.

And a crystal ball, through which Chaney, as Satan, turns the tables on a killer.

Watching with devilish glee as these three victims make their entrance to the pits of hell, the Devil then cooks up his most fiendish, maniacal plot.

He wants the entire human race to commit mass suicide.

And to hasten earthlings to their oblivion, Satan directs his messenger to deliver a formula of his own devising to the world.

The formula, he reveals, contains the secret of the five hundred-megaton bomb, enough nuclear energy to destroy all living beings on the face of our world.

Will the Devil's hellish plan work?

You'll have to see the film and its terrifying surprise finish to find out.

You can't miss this one.

It would be best not to.

Unless, that is, you'd enjoy receiving a gift specially prepared for you by Satan Chaney, and delivered to your doorstep by The Devil's Messenger. ●

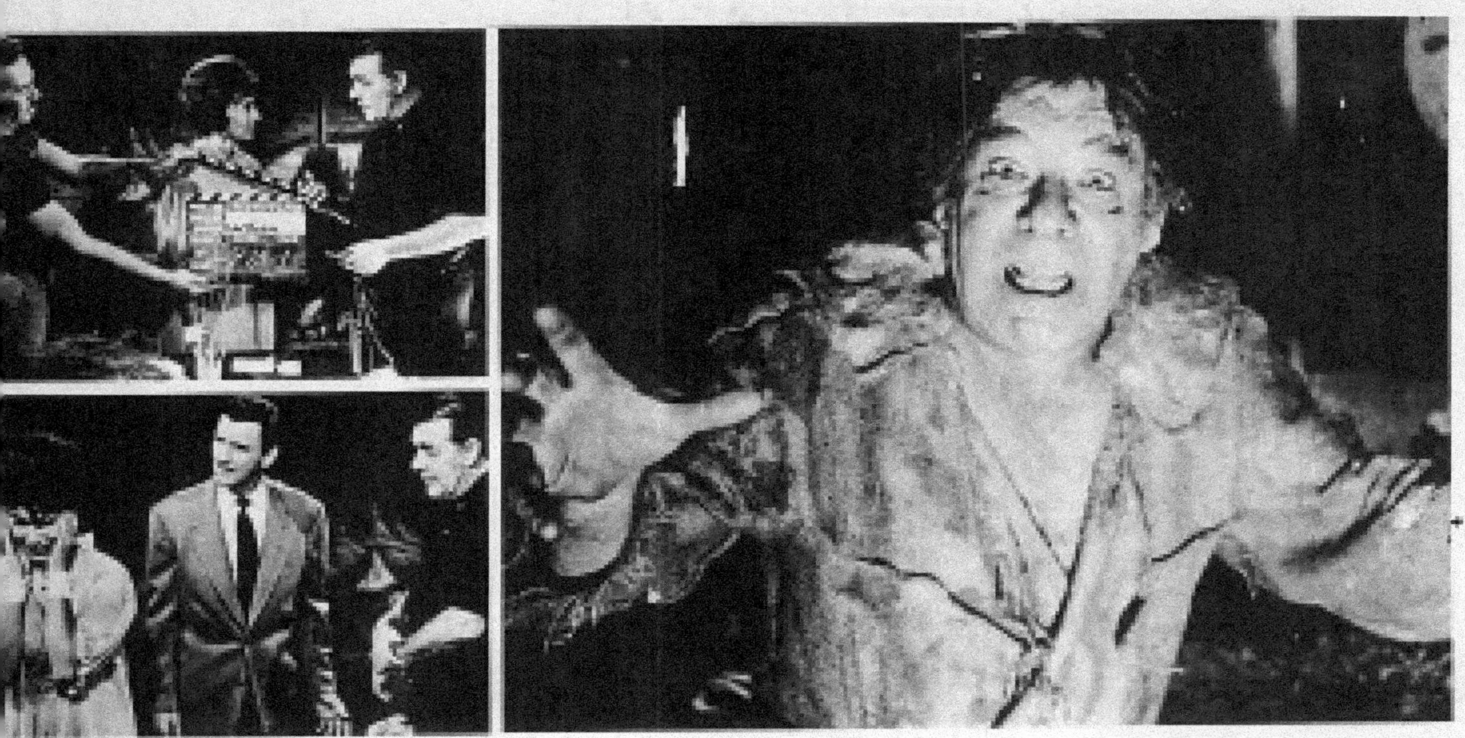

Lon Chaney is back, as evil as ever A Fantastic Monsters Movie Preview

INTO THE THIRD

DIMENSION

Swimming in the waters of the Amazon River is the ill-bred Gill Man.

You see the armor-skinned Gill Man swimming towards you out of the depths of the motion picture ocean, reaching out to you.

At arms length, you see a fist batter away the face mask of Vincent Price to reveal a horror you could reach out and touch . . .

You could see great spaceships blasting away from you, sailing higher and higher, seemingly going out of reach—and out of the theatre.

One of the past marvels of movies is just as far out of reach these days.

Not since Warner Bros first introduced sound to motion pictures had there been such a stir of excitement in Hollywood.

In 1953, the word spread like the Red Death—something new and different was being added to films—third dimension, an unfathomable process which projected images in real prospective, with depth, as well as width and height.

Warner's, the studio that developed this amazing process as it had talking pictures some 25 years earlier, termed it "Natural Vision". Based on the principle of human eyesight, this breath-taking illusion of screen depth not only fully rounded performers and the backgrounds, it also hit you between the eyes with hurtling chairs, leaping fires, collapsing buildings, cannon-fired shells, even sending the actors and actresses themselves plunging out of the silver screen, right into your lap.

And soon, the producers were lapping their folding money with glee. You never knew quite what to expect when you donned the weird cardboard-rimmed pair of stereoscopic glasses handed out when you entered the theatre, except that you were going to be sitting in the audience with what appeared to be a bunch of Martians.

With the dawn of this remarkable film development came the beginning of a two year span of the weirdest, maddest, and most uniquely thrilling movies yet.

A horror thriller really kicked off the 3-D daze: House of Wax, produced by Warner Bros., starring

by RON HAYDOCK

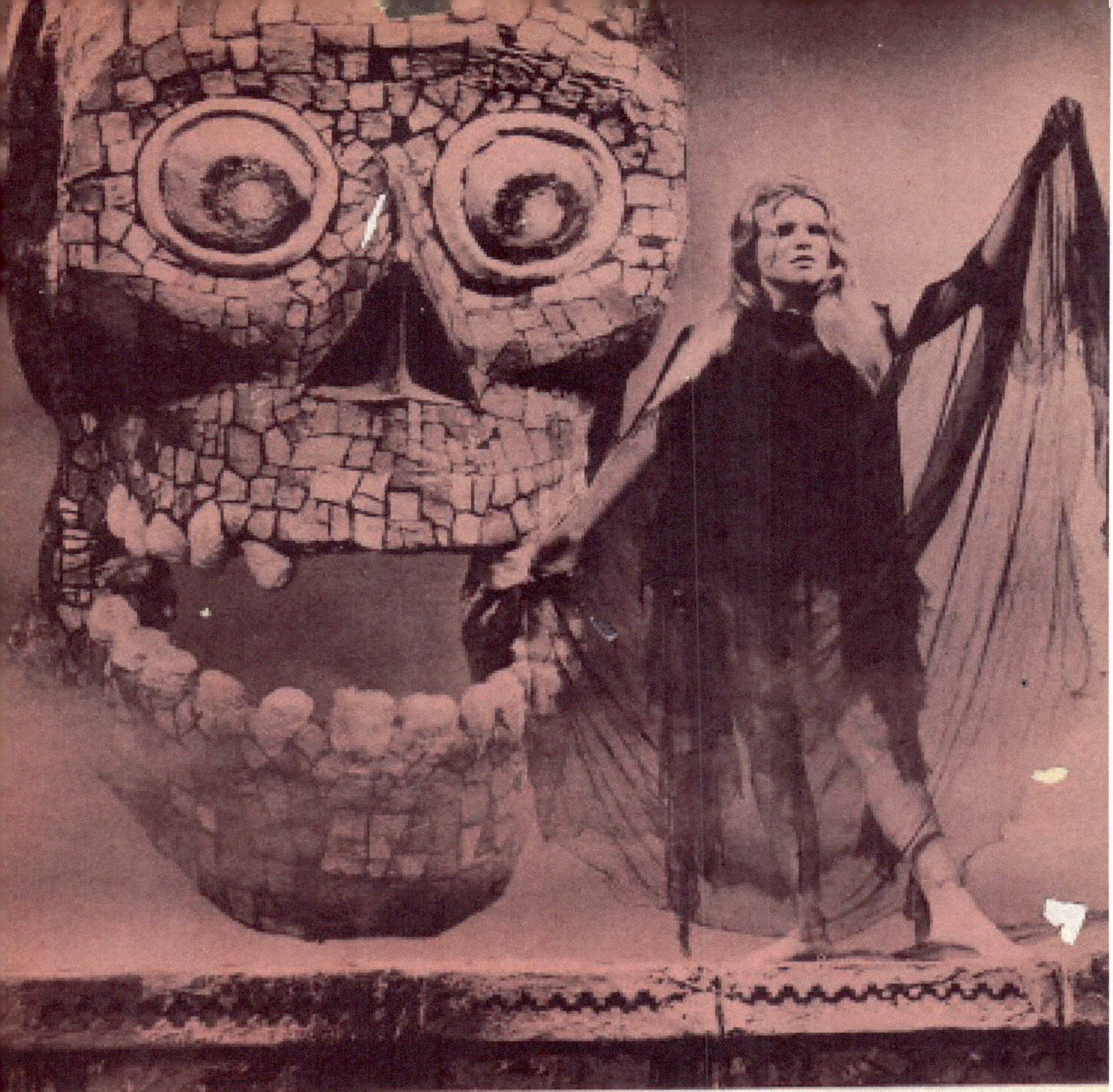

Vincent Price, Phyllis Kirk, Frank Lovejoy, and Paul Picerni (recently an "Untouchable").

In this colorful shocker Price showed the depths he could rise to as a monstrous sculptor who terrorizes early 1900 New York by murdering his strangely reluctant victims, then artfully molding them into wax statues.

The film was a remake of another mouldy production made by Warners, in 1933, *Mystery of the Wax Museum*, with champion screamer Fay Wray, surely one of the most put-upon girls in movie history.

In what is considered a classic sequence in the 3-D remake, frightened Phyllis Kirk pounds away at Price's mask until it cracks, splinters, and falls away. Behind it lies a scarred, burned and mutilated mon-

Above: A peek into the world of terror when you don The Mask. Below: Up from the sewers of Paris comes nostril-flaired Karl Malden, in the scene of The Phantom of the Rue Morgue.

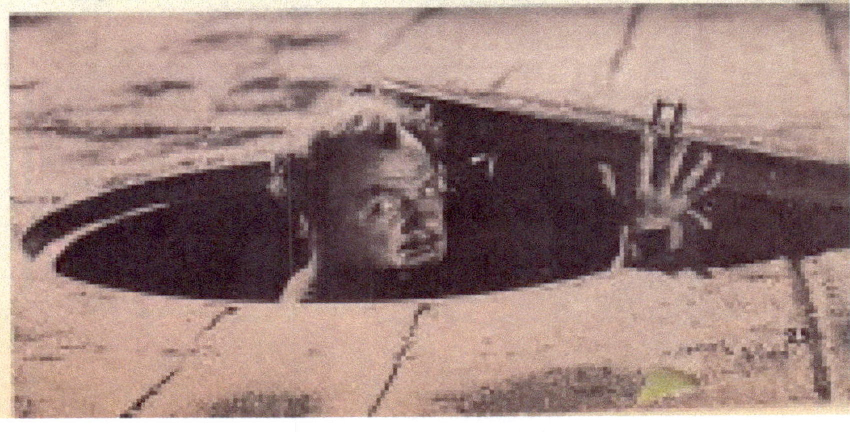

Above: The unearthly Xenomorph, as seen in Universal's It Came from Outer Space. Below: Earthling discovers the glowing spaceship, realizing It Came from Outer Space

strosity.

Two dimensions alone were enough to create screams from theatre audiences. In 3-D, with all of the thrill-producing realism of life, it is a bit of film history which can never be forgotten by those who shuddered through it.

A flaming rocketship from another planet came screaming out into the theatre in the opening frames of *It Came from Outer Space*, to create another memorable moment.

Universal-International's initial science-fiction entry in the 3-D sweepstakes, based on an original by author Ray Bradbury, featured Richard Carlson as the astronomer who first discovers the uninvited arrival of interplanetary visitors, the weird and one-eyed Xenomorphs. Fortunately, Carlson and the state troopers halted the creatures' nefarious conduct on our planet before too many of them had slithered out into the theatre aisles.

A horrible little film in the quickie swing to 3-D was *Robot Monster*, produced by Al Zimbalist who a few years ago gave us Denny Miller as Tarzan the

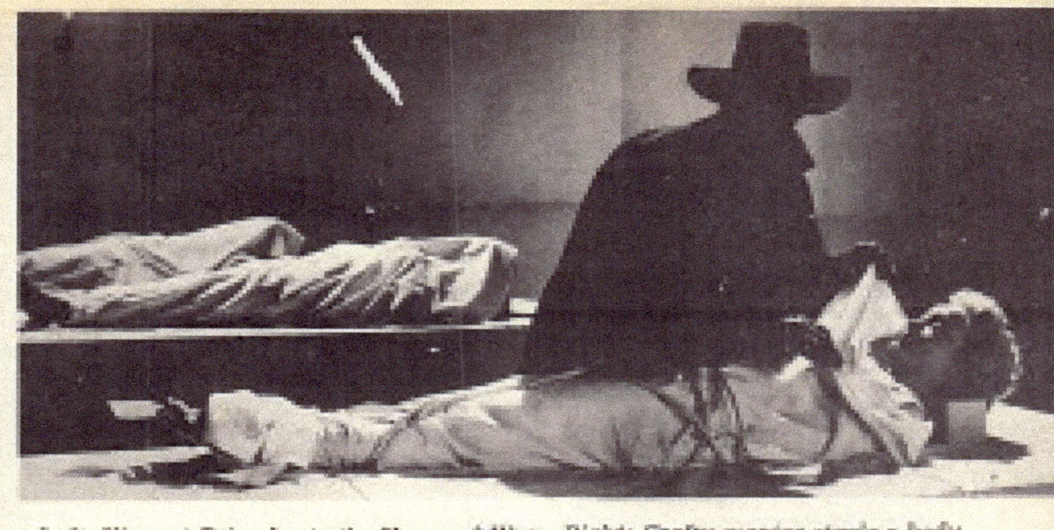

Left: Vincent Price hosts the House of Wax. Right: Crafty maniac steals a body from morgue (House of Wax). Below: Vincent Price trapped as the House of Wax melts.

Above: Gog, a Frankenstein of Steel, attacks Richard Egan. Below: Scene from the hairy 3-D chiller, Gorilla at Large. Center: Vincent Price as The Mad Magician for Columbia.

Ape Man.

Funny-looking, and I do mean funny, moon monsters attacking and hoping to conquer Earth was the crushing bore of cymbalist Zimbalist. A lawsuit claimed that the film wasn't even real 3-D, that the theatre was just running two ordinary prints at once.

TV star George Nader plodded through the 3-D script, looking for its depth, but realizing all the while that this was one challenge no man could meet. Even a trick cue couldn't have helped.

Robot Monster may currently be seen under a new title, *Monsters from the Moon*.

Universal came back strong in 1954 with the very first 3-D "character" monster. The studio, famous for its Wolf Man, Frankenstein, and others, introduced the gilled water-breather, *The Creature from the Black Lagoon*, to a breathless audience.

Richard Carlson returned to the stereo screen as the leader of a scientific expedition which comes upon the eerie lagoon monster in the upper reaches of the Amazon River.

More than one moviegoer was splashed when the superbly-filmed 3-D underwater sequences drifted on the screen.

Following closely on the scales of the Universal Gill Man was *The Phantom of the Rue Morgue*, a Warner Bros release, based on the story by Edgar Allan Poe.

Sultan, a wild gorilla, all wooly and a yard wide, was the featured attraction of this color extravaganza.

After Sultan had been caged by Paris police, Goliath, another beast from Tarzanic jungles, was loosed by 20th Century-Fox for *Gorilla at Large*.

Goliath's escape creates like pandemonium when it cuts the circus pad, and finally climbs a carnival roller coaster, only to get sent on its last ride with some lead, and winds up dead, man, dead.

The film sports a good cast with Lee Marvin, Lee J. Cobb, Cameron Mitchell, Raymond Burr, Warren Stevens, and Anne Bancroft. So far, the New York Drama Critics have not awarded any Gold Medals here. (Rumor has it Goliath was up for a nomination though.)

Many customers also went ape when Allied Artists baffled us with *The Maze*, casting Richard Carlson (again?) in the role of a young Scotsman who falls heir to a mysterious castle which hides a gruesome secret.

A secret, like a gigantic frog!

The overwhelming success of Universal's first Gill Man epic of the previous year was the reason for a sequel, *Revenge of the Creature*.

Captured in its Amazon home, the watery Gill Man is transported to Ocean Harbor, Florida, where it promptly escapes and blankets the city with horror. In the last reel, the Creature, badly wounded by hunters' guns, drops into the ocean, disappearing beneath the onrushing waves — and leaving the story line wide open for yet another sequel—should the public demand it.

They did, and Universal filmed the third and last Gill Man movie the next year, but not in depth.

Gog was fashioned by United Artists, in color.

Built to serve man, this four-armed robot machine could think a thousand times faster than any human, also move a thousand times faster. turn to page 40

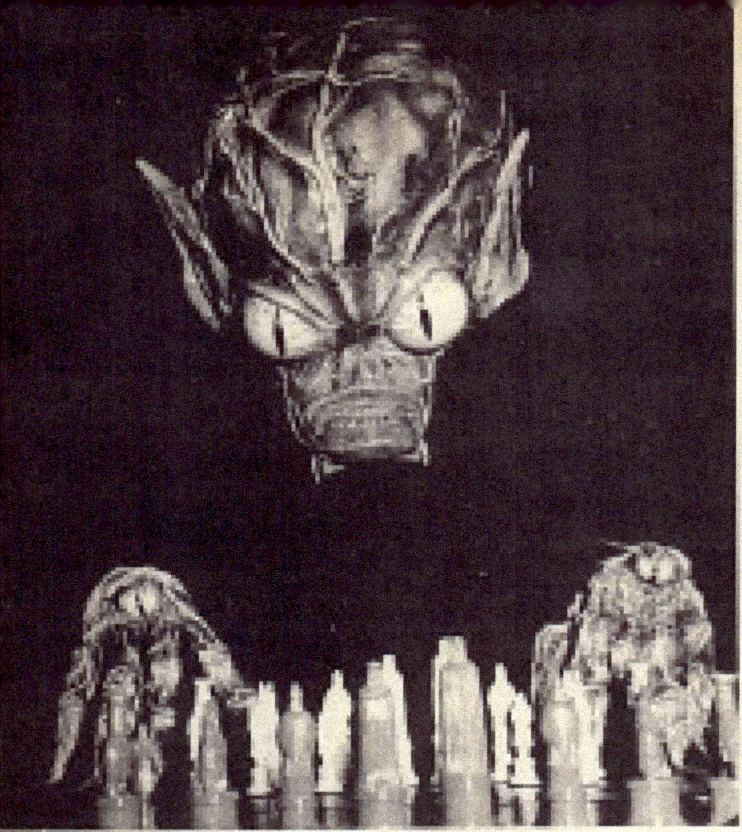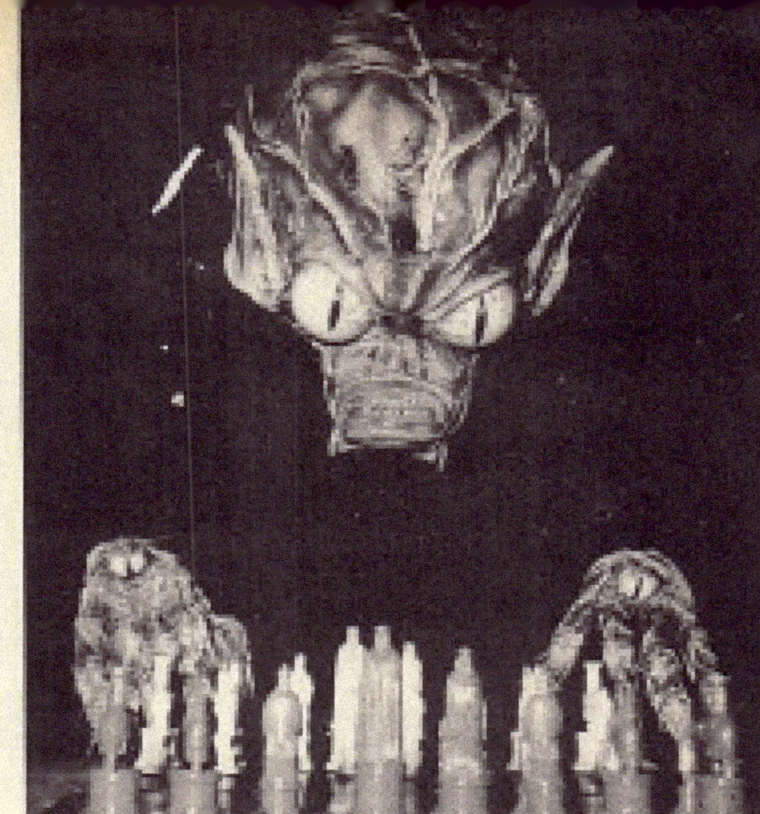

Instructions for Viewing 3-D Photos...

To view these photos, in shocking 3-D, use a rectangular mirror, although an oval one will do. The important thing is that the shortest side of the mirror should be as long as the height of these stereo pictures. Put the edge of the mirror between the photos, perpendicular to the page.

If the mirror has only one reflecting side, try placing that side so as to reflect the right-hand photo. Make sure the mirror and the picture are lined up together.

Center your eyes by lining your nose up with the edge of the mirror. Now close your left eye, and stare at the mirror with your right eye. Tilt the mirror a trifle, if you have to. Open your left eye, and concentrate on the left hand photo with both your eyes. The left hand photo will give you a true 3-D image.

For some, it will take a little practice. Others might find it more convenient to use the left eye to stare at the mirror.

Give it a good try, and you can have your Fantastic Monsters in 3-D!

●

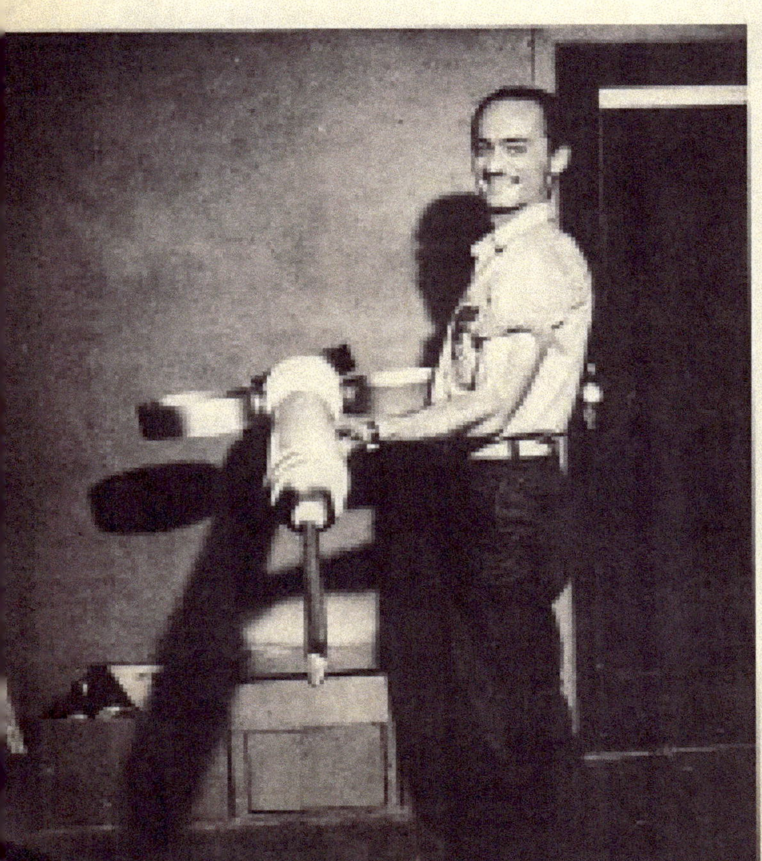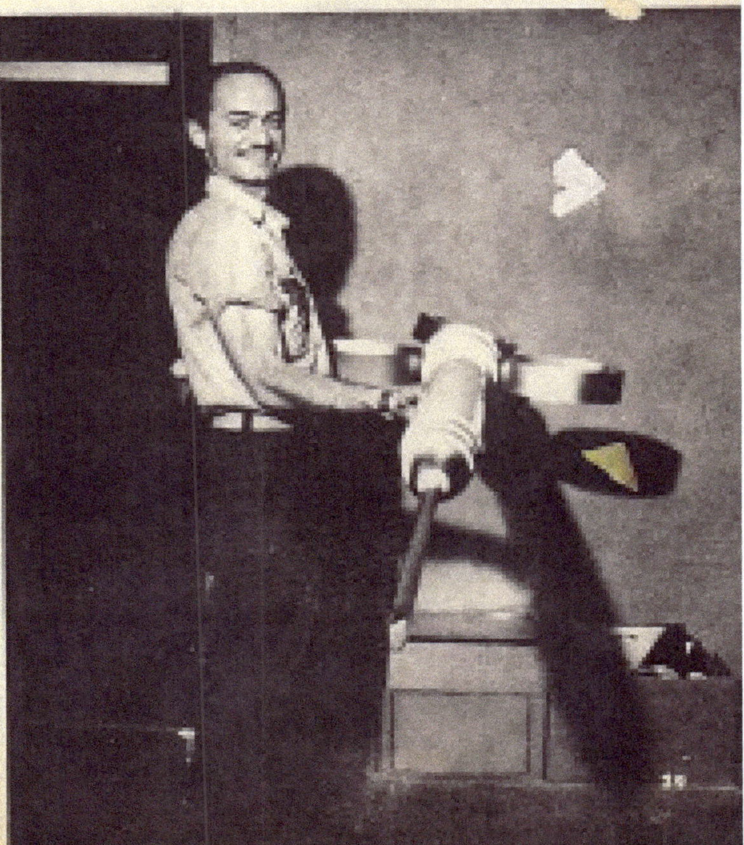

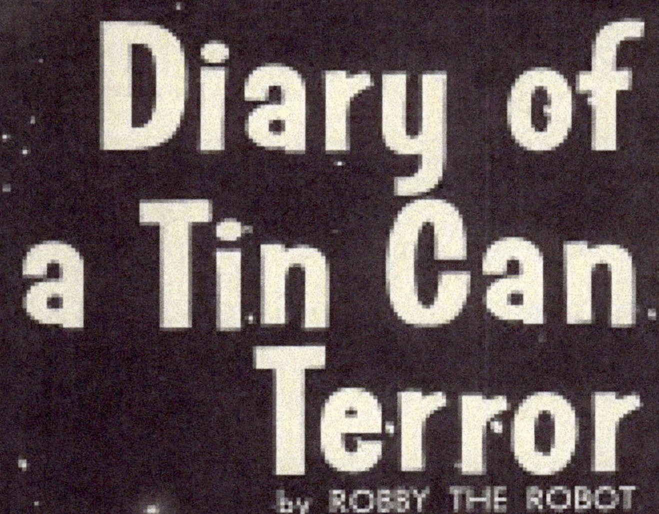

Diary of a Tin Can Terror

by ROBBY THE ROBOT

When I was hatched from a sardine can in 1955, I was christened with a bottle of castor oil as "Robby". That's short for "Robot"; not that we electronic men care much for shorts.

They care a lot about a robot's feelings. *They* call the first man "Adam"; not "Manny". Couldn't *They* have got the lead out and named an iron man something with class, like "XR-One"?

The "They" I refer to are commonly called People. Personally, I sometimes think they have a few cogs missing.

The flawless product that I am can be traced back a hundred thousand years to the first wheel. I am a direct descendant of a distinguished line of metals and an extinguished group of chemicals. Even this typewriter I'm working with is a second cousin, relatively speaking.

Seven months from the time I was conceived, I saw the light bulb of day. I was a burnished body, seven feet, two inches tall, and a sturdy 1600 pounds. I was mauled with more bolts than popcorn on the theatre floor of a double-feature matinee showing the latest chapter of *Captain Marvel*.

Although I had no childhood, I did have to learn to walk, and that's when I had my first accident. My arms felt like pig-iron, and once when I leaned over I lost my balance and fell flat on my axis.

You should have seen the commotion.

They yelled and ran around like somebody had thrown a monkey-wrench into the works.

Above: Walter Pidgeon bets visitors on Altair 4 that I can do everything asked of me except cannot bodily harm. (I take no chances—not with my glass jaw.)

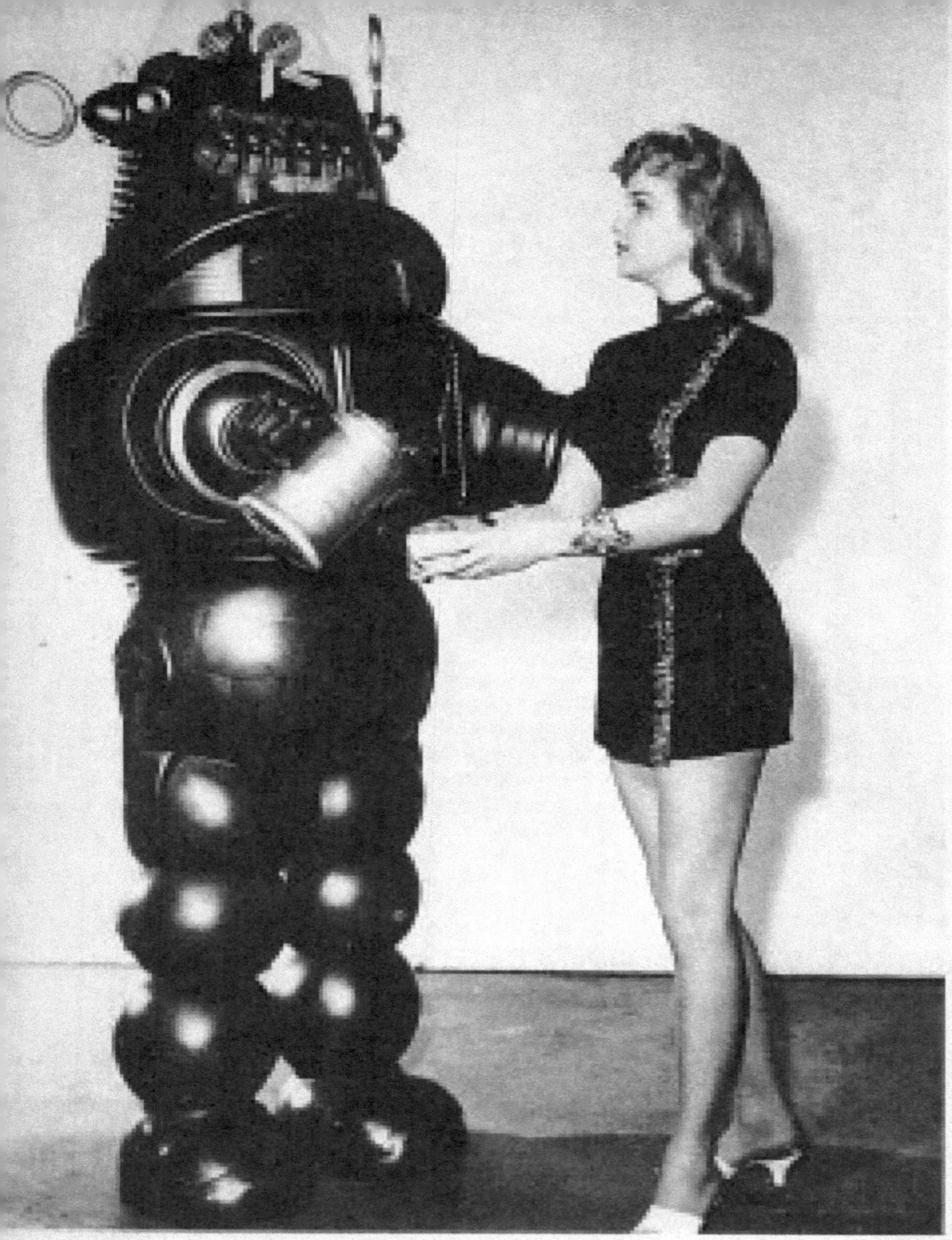

But the only damage was to the wood floor.

It caved in.

They finally secured a crane, hoisted me onto a ten-ton truck and took me to the hospital. There They amputated my heavy steel arms and grafted on a pair made of aluminum. After that I moved around with such facility that I even thought of getting a set of irons and taking up golf.

But times weren't golden for me, not while They were around, bold as brass.

They immediately dispatched me to school, and I had to learn all human knowledge. Two days later, I graduated.

My first job was starring in a science-fiction movie called *Forbidden Planet*, produced by a boss of the Theys, Nicholas Nayfack, who, as it turned out, became my biggest booster (next to my 900 volt batteries).

I made good.

The Theys all over the world liked me, and as a result there was enough of what They call money to gear up for another movie about me and my relatives.

Then I made my second picture and, although I still liked producer Nayfack, he pulled a fast one on me. Just when I was beginning to get the circuit-pattern of normal, everyday human beings, he gave me to somebody I couldn't even scan—an invisible boy. And he compounded the dirty trick by casting the part with an eleven year old They.

Furthermore, the film was labelled after this kid you can't see—*The Invisible Boy*, whereas it should have been engraved *Robby and the Invisible Boy*.

I'd like to have given Nayfack a piece of my electronic brain, but if I had, he wouldn't have been able to lift it.

However, inexplicable and improgramable as They can be, I do feel right at home in science-fiction movies, what with casts including Univac computers, Nikes, rockets, satellites, and all kinds of gadget-members of my family.

The only trouble is—Mr Nayfack, are you listening?—I haven't been able to bolt out of the clink for a metallic movie since 1957.

At this rate, I just may get rusty. ●

Above: Anne Francis always liked the way I made coffee at MGM during the breaks on the set of FORBIDDEN PLANET back in 1955. With Anne around, the stuff percolates right in my grip. Below: Here I am with Phillip Abbott, Diane Brewster, and Richard Eyer, THE INVISIBLE BOY himself. Below right: In FORBIDDEN PLANET, my mechanical brain was so superior to humans', I had to take over the wheel of the spaceship en route from Altair 4 to Earth

reached over to tap the cheerful Louis on the shoulder with a scaly claw.

Undaunted, Quinn had gone on to talk casually with me on the little fine points of monster film-making, and even sympathized with me about how the poor monster never wins in horror movies.

The bit with Gene Norman was going to be different.

For one thing, on his *Campus Club*, Norman had a live audience of school kids, and he was going to surprise them with the *She Creature*.

They were surprised, all right. The next moment turned into a time of terror.

I was scared stiff that I might get trampled in the mad rush they made up onto the stage, practically driving me through the backdrop, scales and all.

Finally, Norman restored order, and it was time for fun and games.

After we talked about the picture for awhile, Norman asked "Cuddles" —that's the *She Creature's* pet name, not mine—to join in the marshmallow-eating contest. Admittedly, marshmallow eating is fairly simple—but it does get a little harder when the marshmallow is on a one foot string, and you have to drag it up to your mouth by eating the string. Pure string, I found, tastes nothing like string beans.

Finally, I made it and got my prize — two tickets to see *The She Creature* at my local theatre.

Growling, I gave them to the runner-up.

Then, at the end of a perfect day, Lionel and I headed for the vault—for films—that I had used as a dressing room. As the elevator opened on the 2nd floor, one of the same secretaries we had met in the basement was standing there, her mouth open.

I decided to say something to quiet her. "Don't worry, honey," I said, "I'm not a She Creature. I'm a man."

But, alas, she just ran off screaming again.

Lionel Comport helped me out of the horror suit, after I had been in there for some four hours. And by that time I was drenched in sweat, just as if I had been in a steam cabinet. I lost three pounds doing the TV spots, but the movie studio figured that it was better I lose pounds than they lose dollars.

Anyway, I may have suffered, but nothing could kill the *She Creature*. You'll probably be seeing her on TV again soon, but this time in the original film.

Old monsters never die, they just look that way. ●

Collector's Curse

by Jim Harmon

"I know the identity of the monster who stalks our village by night and preys on our townsfolk," Allard, the collector, announced to his new neighbor, Borgous, late one September evening in his foothills home.

Borgous' eyes, blacker than the burning night outside, narrowed. "How could you know the murderer's identity? You stay here with your stuffy books, and stamps, and trinkets and know nothing of the business of the great world around you."

"True," Allard admitted, knocking pipe embers onto the fireplace logs, "I am a collector of many things. It is because I collect the books of blackness, the tomes of the unspoken, I know the one who rips open the throats of the helpless to be a lycanthrope, a werewolf."

Borgous laughed too loudly for the comfortable fireplace talk. "Nonsense. You read too much, and count your old coins too often by firelight. The night conjures up its demons too readily for you."

Tapping new tobacco into his pipe, Allard regarded the newcomer carefully, the lean face, the dark eyes, the coarse black hair. "Don't make the mistake of taking me for a fool, Neighbor. I collect facts, not fancies."

Climbing from his comfortable chair by the fire, Borgous stalked the large, oak-beamed room, glaring here at the crossed sabres in the collection of ancient weapons, eyeing the bookcases of cobwebbed volumes there.

"You should come over by daylight sometime," Allard suggested, "and get a worthwhile look at my collection."

The tall man spun around, his eyes catching the red flames in mirrored reflection.

"There is nothing here worthwhile, including yourself, old man," he said. "Tell me, what would you do if you found yourself alone with this killer of the night?"

"Why," Allard said, moving surprisingly swiftly to a mounted wall collection of arms, "I would seize this—a Blunderbus pistol. It is capped and primed, its funnel mouth capable of firing pieces of scrap metal, anything shoved into it."

"And what could you fire from it to stop this supposed supernatural beast?" Borgous inquired, his lips drawn back in mirth.

Allard moved again. "I would fire a silver coin from this case."

"Any item from your collection would be useless," Borgous informed the old man, moving closer into the circle of firelight. "You erred. The killer is not a werewolf. He is a vampir."

"Vampire?" Allard cried in surprise.

"Yes," Borgous moistened his wine-colored lips. "And regardless of legend, a silver bullet can not slay the Winged One, only wood driven through his heart may claim him for Hell. As you are about to find out, Neighbor."

With haste born of terror, unheeding the words of his strange guest, Allard seized a coin from the collection case, rammed it into the barrel of the ancient pistol, then fired it at the distorted shape falling upon him with the wings of darkness.

As the sound of the shot died, so did one of the figures in the light from the leaping flames of the logs.

"But how could the coin-bullet slay Borgous if silver can not kill a vampire?" the Burgermeister demanded of old Allard at the constabulary. "Had he lied?"

Allard struck a new fire to his pipe. "The jagged shards from my coin did kill the vampire, Borgous. Fortunately, I am old and my collection very extensive. In that coin case, I had a novelty piece from a gypsy carnival—a wooden nickel." ●

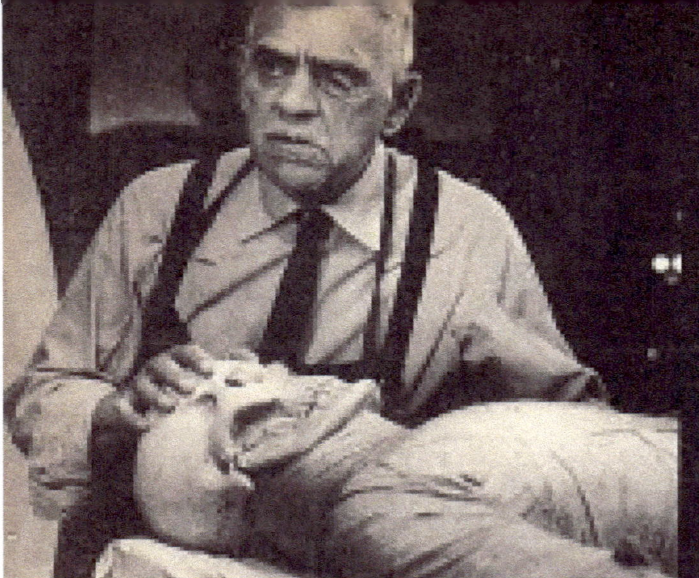

Thank goodness I only used that antiseptic for an eyewash, and not for dandruff

She won't hurt you, Peter

Dead Time Tales

From the captured files of Mother Goose Pimple

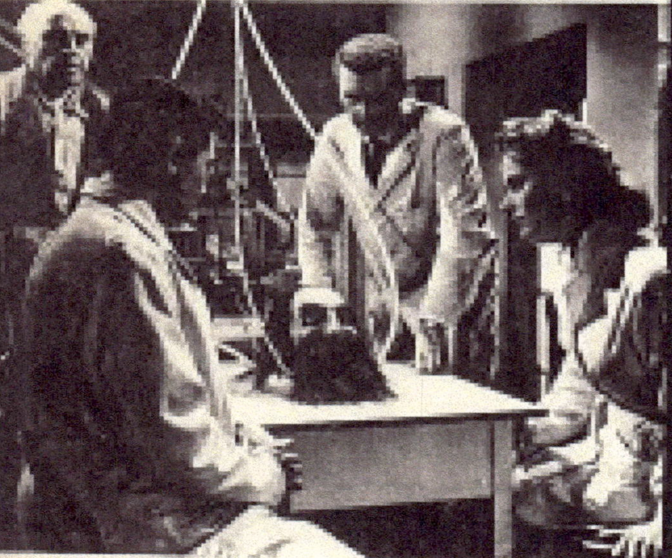

All right this once, Ben, but next time wait for me when you take out torus'

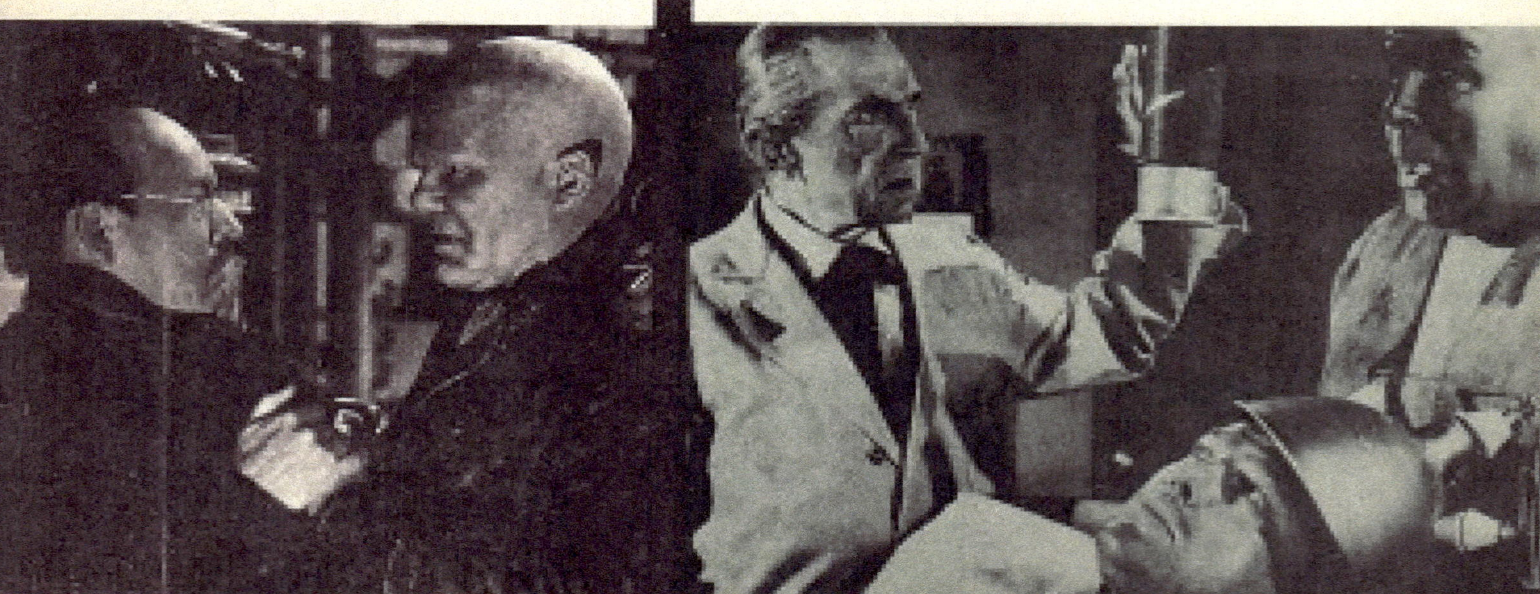

I should have suspected any hair-restorer you sold

How did he ever get a silly thing like that stuck on his head in the first place?

Get it? You jump out at Gladys, then I rush up, make like a big man, and . . .

Helen, are you positive you want to marry this man?

Got another nickel, Joe? I think I saw Mars for a sec.

I tell you I'm a good dentist, Flash. I've done wonders for Charlie there

Big deal. You have a bug in your eye

You're right, he's dead. You may work out as a new Watson after all

Photos at right reading from top to bottom: The mysterious Scorpion and his thugs prepare a death trap for an unsuspecting Captain Marvel. Professor Bentley, Billy Batson, and Dwight Fisher in the hidden tombs of Scorpio. The mighty man of marvel routs villainous Siam natives.

effects of the ray into a disintegrator that utterly destroys anything in its path!

Meanwhile, Billy has wandered inquisitively into another section of the tomb, where a gaunt, white-robed figure of incredible age steps from shadows. Tall, bearded, the stranger tells Billy that he is the wizard Shazam (Nigel de Brulier), that he has waited untold centuries in the tomb, "Neither alive nor dead, as you know life and death," for this day. This day, the wizard says, is the day when the menace of the Scorpion is loosed upon the world! This day is the day when the world needs a hero to defend it from the Scorpion!

"Speak my name!" the wizard commands, and as Billy pronounces the word *Shazam* he is enveloped in a cloud of smoke as thunder booms ominously in the tomb. When the air clears, in the place of young Billy is the magnificent figure of Captain Marvel, clad in a scarlet costume of standard supercharacter tights with yellow satin trim at the wrists and waist, and with a golden thunderbolt, symbolic of the source of his power, emblazoned on his chest.

Shazam reveals to Captain Marvel the meaning of his—Shazam's—own name and Captain Marvel's magic word. Formed from the initial letters of six great figures, a weird conglomeration of gods, legendary heroes and historical persons, The Word gives Captain Marvel an attribute from each.

From Solomon, wisdom; from Hercules, strength; Atlas, stamina; Zeus, power; Achilles, courage; and from Mercury, speed.

I remember the first time I saw that miraculous change back during the Captain Marvel serial's original release in 1941. There are others who remember it, too.

Doddering graybeards in their twenties and thirties remember this hero of their childhood. Teenagers and those younger, rarely privileged to see a revival showing of the serial,
turn to page 57

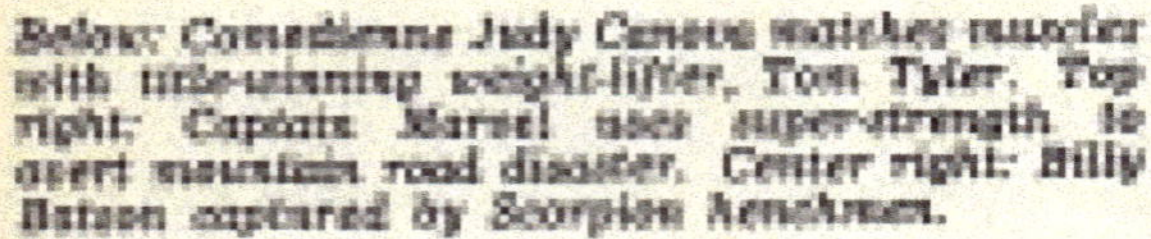
Below: Comedienne Judy Canova matches muscles with title-winning weight-lifter, Tom Tyler. Top right: Captain Marvel uses super-strength to avert mountain road disaster. Center right: Billy Batson captured by Scorpion henchmen.

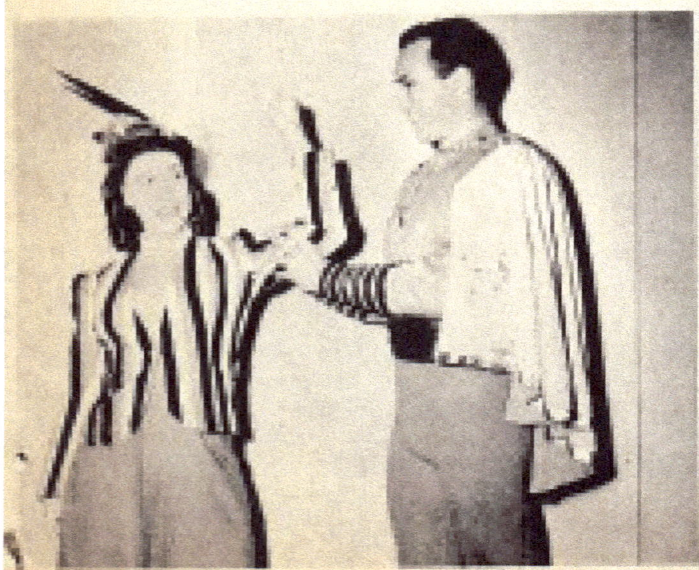

DIMENSION, from page 38

It could kill a thousand times faster too, turning it into a Frankenstein of Steel.

One of the last of the stereo thrillers of any type was Columbia's late entry, *The Mad Magician*, with Vincent Price doing the berserk honors.

Price was the Great Gallico, world's foremost master of illusion and disguise, who becomes homicidally mad and seeks revenge on his taunters.

His victims were burned alive in a specially-built, blazing crematorium. Some of them, though, lost their heads when they faced his whirling buzzsaw.

With the last head rolling merrily off into the theatre aisles, Hollywood closed its 3-D lenses, believing the public was tired of wearing the stereo glasses, and renewed their efforts in other screen developments, like Cinemascope and Cinerama.

As recently as a year ago, though, a brand-new fright flicker shot partly in 3-D was released.

The Mask, from Warner Bros, took us into the uncanny world of third-dimension via a type of red and blue filter-glasses which were popular during the 3-D comic book craze of 1953-54.

The surrealistic depth scenes presented in *The Mask* were truly an astounding and awesome sight — undoubtedly the most creative and significant efforts since the days of *King Kong* and *The Invisible Man*.

When the next horror or monster will be popping out at us, no one knows. Television has, for the past ten years, been quietly experimenting with the illusion, hoping one day to bring it into every home. One of their early attempts at 3-D televising was the one-time popular science-fiction adventure program, *Tom Corbett, Space Cadet*.

The 3-D cycle of the past is by now permanently carved in the History Niche of Motion Pictures. It was a period of thrills and chills like nothing ever witnessed or experienced before. Those who were a part of it, will never quite forget it. Those who missed it, will have to offer a prayer to the Cinema Gods for another revival.

In reality, and in illusion, with 3-D, the movies took a step forward. ●

EARTH, from page 20
Metalunans alive.

One of Exeter's extant countrymen is the Monitor (Douglas Spencer), chief of the planet, an ancient, imposing figure enthroned before the space-traveling trio.

The Monitor communicates that he plans to take over Earth for his people, in spite of Cal and Ruth explaining all the troubles he would be letting himself in for on Earth. (Coming from there, they know.)

Irritated by the young couple's stubborn refusal to help exterminate their own race, the Monitor orders them into a machine that will rob them of their will power and destroy their minds for anything but routine work.

"It looks like the tubes in a giant TV set," Ruth gasps in horror.

Even as they are fed to the monstrous device, the outlaw planet, Zahgon, strikes against Metaluna, and the world lunges into its death-throes while the Metaluna slaves, the half-human insect Mutants, revolt in flesh-tearing terror.

Mauled by one of the bug-eyed, bug-headed monsters, Exeter nevertheless manages to free Ruth and Cal, and in a change of his soft heart, helps them escape the doomed world.

Once again with the Earth's atmosphere, Cal and Ruth pilot their stored airplane to safety from the flying saucer, which a dying Exeter fatalisticly dives into the night sea.

So ends one of Hollywood's more attractive space adventures.

A large part of the film's attraction (Miss Domergue aside) lies in the work of Bud Westmore's U-I makeup department in creating Jeff Morrow's and the other Metalunans' alien heads, and of course in fashioning the memorable Mutant.

With a head five times the size of normal — the Mutant, not the justifiably proud make-up chief — the Metaluna monster has a brain that is completely visible. This reflection of scripters Franklyn Coen and Edward G. O'Callaghan reveals bulging eyeballs to rival Eddie Cantor, interlaced with night-after veins, supported by facial muscles even more visible than Kirk Douglas'.

At the command of Director Joseph Newman, the creature's cranium pulsates around five layers of lips, while lobster claw hands dangle to its ankles. Despite a cost of $24,000, the Mutant has found it difficult to find further work because it is considered to be type-cast as a Metaluna monster.

THIS ISLAND EARTH remains a landfall of spectacular action in a universe of super-science that grows ever closer to us Earthlings as we travel further into the future each day of our lives. ●

I particularly enjoyed the article on Flash Gordon in your great first issue. It might be of interest to you to know that I have one of the largest collections of early Alex Raymond newspaper comics of *Flash* in the world.

I have a few suggestions. I notice you mentioned Tom Mix in a list of serial stars. I remember one Tom Mix serial with rockets and ray guns on the range. What was the name of that one? And could you run an article and some stills on it?

FANTASTIC MONSTERS covers movies and even television, but aside from a passing mention of the still-going *Suspense*, there was nothing on radio. How about articles on some of the old horror-fantasy radio shows like *Lights Out, I Love a Mystery, Stay Tuned for Terror*? Or better still — could you run some of the old stories themselves?

Bill Thailing
Cleveland, Ohio

For Bill and Gordonites everywhere, here's spaceman Flash again. The Tom Mix serial, released by Mascot Pictures in 1935, was the Miracle Rider — Ed.

MORE VAMPIRES

I'd like to add a few additional titles of vampire films to the list given in last issue's "Vampire Bats in My Belfry" — Universal's *Curse of the Undead*, made in 1959; American-International's *Blood of Dracula* (a teenage she-vampire); *The Vampire*, with John Beal; Mexico's *Castle of Monsters*; and, of course, (I'm surprised you missed it) the original silent film classic *Nosferatu*, produced in 1922 in Germany.

Al Eck
LaGrange, Ill.

GHOUL CALL from Fellow Monsters

MUMMY SPHINX?

As far as I'm concerned, the *Mad Mummy* is the most ridiculous and idiotic character I've ever heard of! Any reader who likes that bandaged boob ought to have all of his heads examined!

I suppose that next you're going to give us the *Deranged Daddy*, or something equally nonsensical!

Don Sheppard
Los Angeles, Calif

How about the Batty Baby, *Don?* —Ed.

MONSTER MAKER

I've been building my own movie monsters for over a year now, so I was glad to see the article on "*Do-It-Yourself Monster Making*" in your magazine. I'm sure that this type of feature will help a lot of us to create bigger and better monsters for our home movies.

Ray Gerstle
Chicago, Ill.

RED, WHITE & GRUE

FANTASTIC MONSTERS is the most colorful magazine I've ever seen! How did you guys ever do it?!

Grant Gardner
New York, NY

We used a large box of crayons —Ed.

POE AWARD

In your first issue's editorial you jokingly referred to one of the fiction pieces — "*The Two-Tale Heart*" — having a chance to win a writing award called an "*Edgar*". I know this was only a pun, but there really is such an award, isn't there?

Jerry Smithers
Key West, Fla

The "Edgar" is presented to the writer of the best crime novel of the year by the Mystery Writers of America organization. Author Robert Bloch won one for his Psycho. *— Ed.*

CALLING KRYPTON

I'm very glad to see that in future issues you'll be giving us articles on the comic book character *Superman.* I recall seeing when I was younger a serial in which he matched superwits with an arch-scientist called *Atom Man.* The entire film was so much better than anything *Superman* did on TV.

But when will you have the mighty Man of Steel in your pages?

Dick Crenshaw
Laramie, Wyoming

The Krypton Comet is scheduled to hurtle through a near-future issue, Dick, in an exclusive article written by the actor who portrayed Superman on the screen, Kirk Alyn — Ed.

ROOMS FOR IMPROVEMENT

Hoohah! Admit it — you made a mistake when you listed the release dates of *House of Frankenstein* and *House of Dracula* as '45 and '46!

The years should be '44 and '45!

Judy Langenscheidt
Waco, Texas

We stand corrected — Ed.

PRO & KAHN

I very much enjoyed the fiction pieces in FANTASTIC MONSTERS #1. The Robert Bloch story was great, but I preferred the two shorties by Jim Harmon.

Bradford Knight
Washington, D. C.

No one's intelligence was insulted by Bloch's "*Black Lotus*" story, but I can't say the same for Jim Harmon's "*Two-Tale Heart*".

Henry Kahn
Woodridge, N. J.

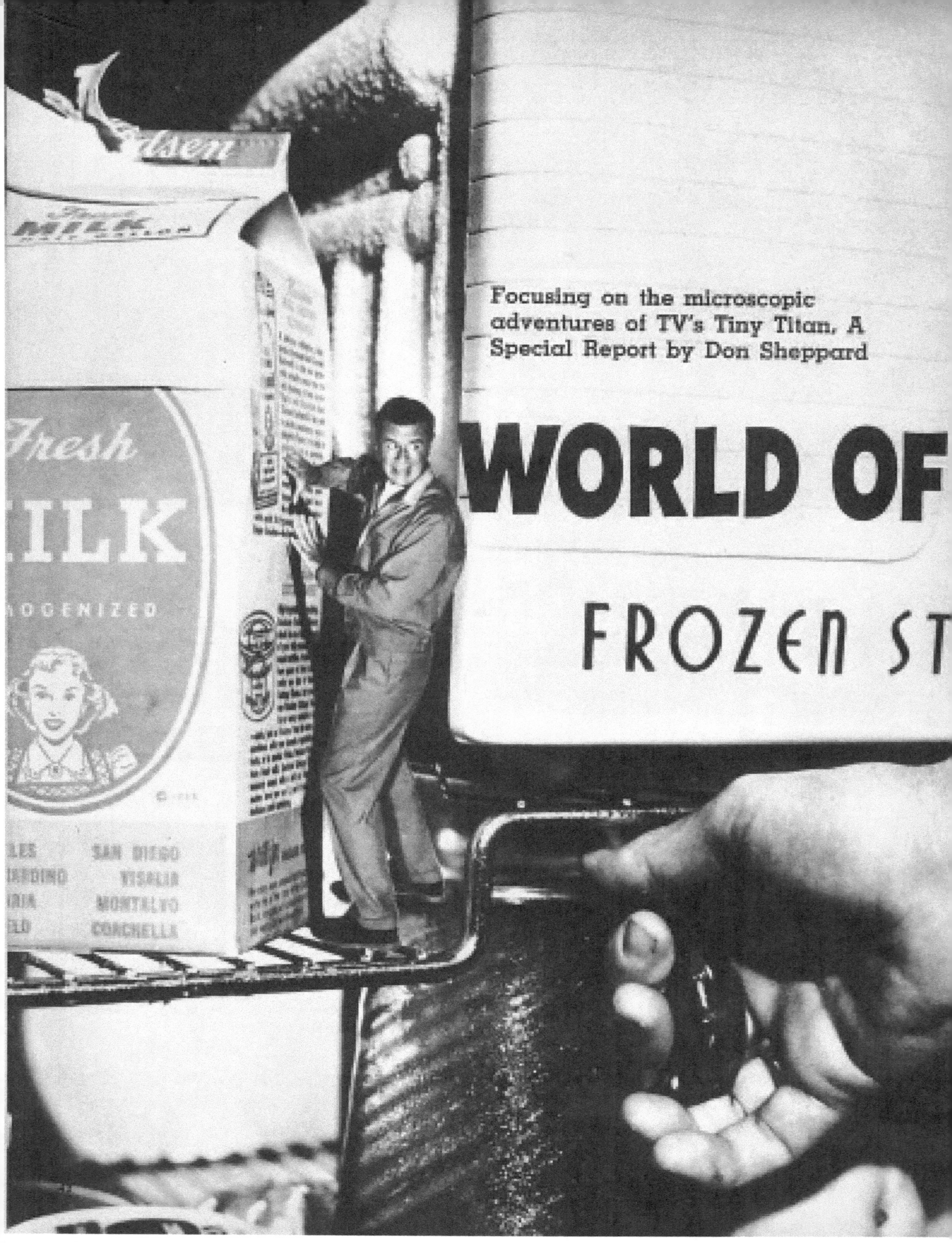
Focusing on the microscopic
adventures of TV's Tiny Titan, A
Special Report by Don Sheppard

WORLD OF

FROZEN ST

Fresh
MILK
HOMOGENIZED

SAN DIEGO
VISALIA
MONTALVO
COACHELLA

Picture in your mind a giant insect, towering over you, its wriggling antennae poised menacingly from a massive height of more than eight feet, its huge bug eyes glaring down at you contemptuously.

Fear-stricken at the awesome sight of this mammoth monster, your first instinct is to run, get away before it strikes.

Then you look around again, fastening on other Kong-size items:

A ruler measuring 12 feet instead of 12 inches;

Pencils, four to seven feet in length;

A telephone so large it would fill an entire office;

Books with covers nine by twelve feet;

Ash trays, five feet in diameter . . .

You'd think you were in a world of giants.

And you'd be right.

Especially if your name is Mel Hunter—a government agent who has diminished in size from a six-footer to a six-incher because of exposure to a strange new radiation.

This is the science-fictional theme of *World of Giants*, the most startling and exciting television series of its kind ever seen by this viewer.

The microscopic adventures of agent Hunter, which

GIANTS

by Don Sheppard

Top: Hunter travels to his various counter-espionage assignments in this special attache case, devised by producer Alland's program. Left: Trapped in creampuffs, agent Hunter is about to be served for breakfast. Far Left: Miniken Mel gets put inside a refrigerator and nearly freezes to death.

are distributed both here in America as well as Europe by CBS Films Sales, were produced for the Columbia TV network by William Alland, who himself spawned *The Space Children*, investigated *The Land Unknown*, and had audiences goggle-eyed when *It Came from Outer Space* was released.

Marshall Thompson is starred as Mel Hunter, who, while on a special mission for the government, becomes the victim of radiation, and involuntarily shrinks to a six-inch height.

The mission, behind the Iron Curtain, leads to his presence at a rocket research site where a new propulsion fuel is being tested. The fuel explodes, and Hunter is near enough to the blast to be affected by the radiation emitted from some unknown ingredient in the mixture.

In less than a month's time, he shrinks to a mere six inches. But despite his new size, he is retained in the government service to work as a counter-espionage agent with a full-sized man, his partner, Bill Winters (played by Arthur Franz). Together they carry out assignments in which miniken Mel's stature can be utilized most effectively.

For instance, in one episode Hunter slips into a lady's pocketbook to get hold of a spy system's code that was written in the form of a recipe.

In another, "Off Beat," he climbs inside a piano at the risk of being crushed by the felt hammers, searching for some valuable art that has been smuggled into the country.

"Rainbow of Fire" sees him hiding under a hat worn

turn to page 68

Left: Straining to dial a phone call to his headquarters, Mel Hunter realizes he'll have to use a ruler as a crowbar to remove the receiver from the hook. Above: The six-inch agent invents a pen-sized tear gas gun which he uses effectively from behind some flower pots against a flock of "giant" carrier pigeons. Right: Hiding in the coin return of a slot machine, Hunter is bombarded by a deluge of 50-cent pieces.

MUMMY, from page 5

had a nice comfortable tomb until some of those grave robbers came and dug me up, and now look at me —working for a monster magazine. I never thought I'd be caught dead doing that. But I have been.)

But, here is where Karloff (Im-ho-tep) and Lee (Kharis) take divergent paths.

This is mainly due to the fact that in 1959, when the Hammer Films production was released, Nina Wilcox Putnam, author (with Richard Schayer) of the original screenplay for Universal, was in London, and she brought pressure against Hammer to surpass its *Mummy* because she claimed they did such violence to her original story. Or perhaps that the *Mummy* did such violence to people. But in spite of Miss Putnam, you just can't keep a good Mummy down.

As you may have gathered, I don't care much for movies about monsters —Mummies, in particular. We always get killed; and we appear so unsympathetic when we kill people (it is seldom explained that we have a good reason for our mass murders). But reluctantly I must admit that both the Hammer and old Universal versions of *The Mummy* have something on their side—even if it isn't me.

Karloff, as Im-ho-tep, drops his bandages and walks the land as a man, in contemporary dress. Behaving not unlike a vampire, he seems to have hypnotic powers of the occult to force people to his will, and to have command of the ancient magic of the Nileland. Karloff is certainly no Frankenstein, at least not in this picture. That is, he is no lumbering super-human ox, invulnerable to bullets and blade. It seems that he is trying to imitate Bela Lugosi, who had just made the successful *Dracula* shortly before Karloff's *Mummy* was released.

On the other hand—on both hands, as a matter of fact—Chris Lee retains the bandages of the Mummy, and prowls the night, dripping green mold from the tomb; acting much like the Mummy which appeared in *The Mummy's Hand*, as enacted by one-time Captain Marvel and all-time Western star, Tom Tyler; and also like the version of the Egyptian menace carried on by Lon Chaney Jr. in a series of films which included *The Mummy's Ghost*.

Im-ho-tep with his subtle occultism, and sly, sinister looks actually creates a more eerie, scarey mood—if you don't go to sleep during the dull stretches featuring mushy love scenes between young scientist Frank Whemple (David Manners) — with two names like that, you know what kind of a guy he is — and the somewhat simple-minded darling, Helen Grosvenor, as portrayed by Zita Johann.

The story of Kharis, the unstopable gift-wrapped monster, is no work of art, but it is lively entertainment and there is no danger of drowsing off. As Kharis rips aside iron-gratings, survives shotgun blasts, and smashes through plateglass, the racket will keep you alert if nothing else.

In the original Universal *Mummy*, the Mummy itself only served as a buildup for what was really just a variation on the old vampire theme. Edward van Sloan (as Professor Muller) finally destroys the creature exactly as he, in the role of Professor Van Helsing, staked out a claim on Bela Lugosi in *Dracula*. There was very little new in the film, even 'way back in 1932.

Of course, Christopher Lee as Kharis follows the tradition of Tyler and Chaney Jr. — even to using the name "Kharis" — but this lurching, muscle-bound body wrapped in rags remains a visually interesting creature, perfect for the screen, whereas the Karloff story would be better in book form.

In both pictures, the youthful heroine is represented as a reincarnation of the Mummy's last love, one which he must reclaim to satisfy the Gods of old Egypt. As Edward van Sloan destroyed Im-ho-tep, so Kharis is ended by Peter Cushing, who notably enough also played Professor van Helsing in *Horror of Dracula*. With Cushing in their movies, Hammer has created something new in horror films — the continuing sympathetic hero to combat a string of menaces: van Helsing, Sherlock Holmes, or here in *The Mummy* as the heroine's husband, John Banning. Since horror films are one of the few kinds of movies being made, they have to provide audiences with what they have always wanted in mysteries, westerns, and all types of pictures—a hero, as well as a threatening villain.

I can proudly say that the Mummy is perfect for playing on one of Mankind's oldest fears, the *Walking Dead*. There is nobody quite as dead as a corpse wrapped in the dusty cloth of five thousand years, and nothing more upsetting than to see it walking.

Of course, deep down, the fear is not of the dead walking but the doubt that nags with wondering if the dead ever really do walk again, anytime, anyplace, or is the sleep dreamless?

If you think my tune has changed in the middle of this review, just remember mummies are deeper than you think—six feet deeper, at least. ●

MAD LAB RADIO

It appears to be one of those little imported transistor radios, but just turn it "on". WOW! The dummy speaker flips to one side and a "killer shrew" jumps out, with a wild squeal! Mad Lab radio is all metal, lithographed in four colors. Has fold-down carrying handle, three dimensional dummy dial and working "off-on" switch, which pretends "sleep". YOU invite your buddie, or girl friend, to turn on your Mad Lab radio, then watch them climb the wall, when the squealing "shrew" leaps out at them! Only $3.00, postpaid.

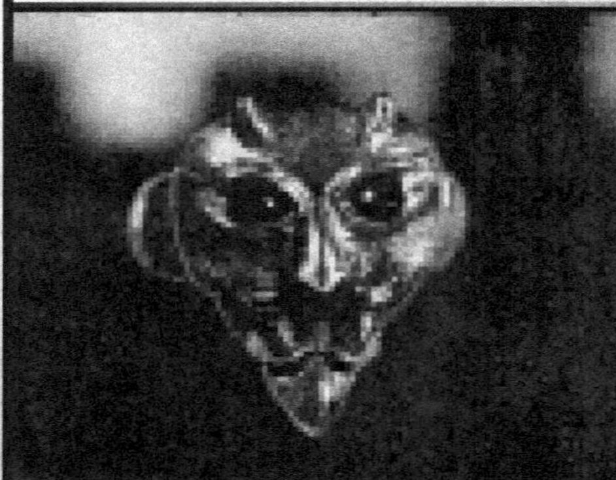

VAMPIRE DEVIL RING

Shades of Count Dracula! It looks like it came straight from his castle, in the Carpathian Mountains! A gleaming, scowling, silvery Devil's head. Great for club or costume make-up. Deeply carved horns, brow, nose, beard and "vampire fangs". These are set off by flaming simulated ruby eyes! Good quality and massive. A real conversation piece! Let us know your ring size with order. $1.

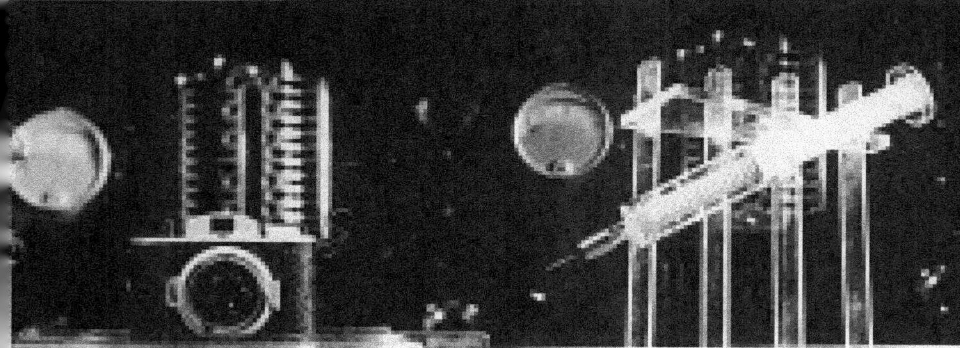

MAD LAB CAMERA

Looks like expensive sub-miniature camera, but wait until you press the secret button! Lens swings open, and with a terrific squeal, a "Killer Shrew" leaps out! Camera has viewfinder, dummy winding knob, carrying case, realistic lens mount. Authentic black crinkle finish with silver-gray trim! Furry "Killer Shrew" and "squeals" concealed inside. Lens locks in place until you push the shutter release! You'll have your friends jumping for the ceiling with the MAD LAB CAMERA! Only $1.00, postpaid!

MAD LAB HYPO

Life size! 6 inches, fully extended! Needle appears to pierce "victim's" skin! Concealed button gives illusion of Hypo filling up with "victim's" blood! Can also be used in reverse, to "inject" blood— then show them apparently empty! The illusion is absolutely perfect, even close up! This glittering, wicked-looking instrument is quality made of crystal clear styrene plastic, with metal head and "needle"! Realistic calibrations marked along body! Don't use around friends with weak stomachs! Only $1.50, postpaid!

MAN MOON MASCOT

Poor little Moon Man! Looks like he's "way out there", and he can't get back. This lovable little guy is all head, hands, and feet. Put him on a lamp shade, picture frame, note book, or car mirror, and these things become his "body". He's fan-tastic, and made of soft, durable, flesh colored plastic, with pink eyes, and bright red ears. Your own personal moon Mascot! Only $1 postpaid!

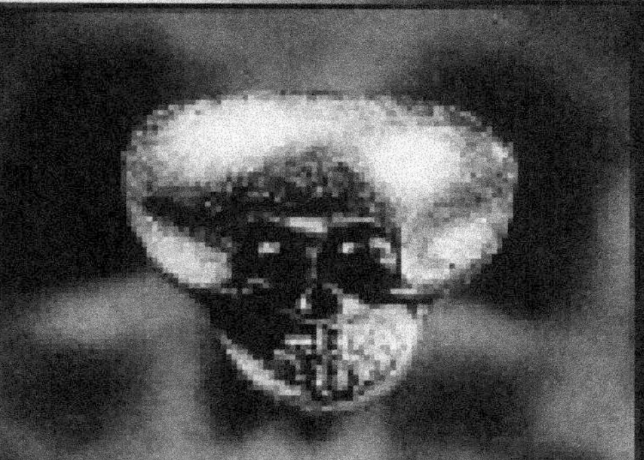

SECRET SKULL RING

Mystic skull symbol of the ancient Aztecs, later copied by the fierce pirates who sailed the seven seas. The romance and adventure is all embodied into the unique and latest style of this massive, quality ring. Sculptured cheek bones, teeth, and sparkling simulated ruby eyes are blended into a finger encircling curve on this exciting new ring. Gleaming silvery finish, too. Please state ring size when ordering. Only $1 postpaid.

MR. BONES, THE POCKET SKELETON

Your own spooky mascot! Take Mr. Bones wherever you go. He's 7 inches tall, well detailed, made of vinyloid rubber! Even feels creepy! Flexible and springy; the slightest movement sets him shimmering and shaking! Hang Mr. Bones from car mirror, or pin him to your jacket! Sit him down on desk, or table! For you shutterbugs, Mr. Bones makes a sensational prop for table-top photography. Only 75¢, postpaid!

UNLUCKY 13 RATTLESNAKE

13 unlucky inches of wriggling rattler! Coloring fools everybody, even inches away! "Flexite" vinyl formula makes snake feel cool and slimy to the touch! Sure cure for weak friends! Just put this rattler where they're bound to snoop! If you want shrieks and howls at your next get-together, this UNLUCKY 13 RATTLESNAKE is for you! Camera fiends who like to shoot miniatures can turn rattler into huge "python" in table-top scene! Only 75¢ postpaid!

DEVIL SPIDER

Ugh! What a little horror this guy is! Made of vinyl rubber, for that "creepy" feel 2 inches in diameter, he really sets the screams when you lower him on a thread or send him skittering across the floor! Well detailed in black, with rough texturing! 8 wiggling legs start vibrating at the slightest touch! Sit him in your pocket, hang him from a car mirror, dangle him in a doorway! If you have any friends left afterwards, they'll never forget the time they combed the DEVIL SPIDER out of their hair! Only 50¢ postpaid!

CASTLE DRACULA, TOPANGA, CALIFORNIA

NOVELTIES, JOKES, GAMES

*Rush me the following:*______________________________

____

____

____

*for which I enclose $*______________________________

NAME (PLEASE PRINT)________________________________

ADDRESS____

CITY ________________________ ZONE ______ STATE __________

If I'm dissatisfied with my purchase, I'll return it within one week for a full refund

GIANTS, from page 44

by a donkey, completely confusing his adversaries by making it appear as if they own a talking burro.

Many times, too, Hunter can be found wedging himself between volumes in a book case to observe enemy agents at work.

Needless to say, the scene designers and property men involved in the production of the fascinating series had to think big. In fact, I learned that to create the illusion that Hunter is just six inches tall, they had to build scenery and props 12 times larger than normal for every scene in which Marshall Thompson, a six-footer, appears.

One *World of Giants* episode required the use of 50-cent pieces 15 inches in diameter. Another required test tubes 15 feet high, flower pots seven feet high, a standing lamp 35 feet high, and a woman's comb five feet long. A special tear gas gun that is to miniken Mel Hunter the size of a fountain pen was actually five feet in length.

A trellis that Hunter climbs in "Death Trap" was covered with roses and petals as big as elephant ears, and thorns as big as daggers. The prop men even had to produce a postage stamp for an oversized box that was to be shipped to Washington, D.C. The stamp was a foot high, and was carefully marked to appear as if it had just gone through a giant postage metering machine. String used to wrap the package was actually a length of heavy sailor's rope.

Even a mud puddle couldn't be just a mud puddle. It had to become a small pond, 34 feet across.

There was also a typewriter with keys measuring four by six inches in size. Imagine typing a letter on that!

Producer Alland evidently spared no expense in the creation of the seventy-plus props used in various episodes of *World of Giants*. All told, they cost nearly twenty thousand dollars.

And the series itself nearly costs atom-sized agent Hunter his life many times over, as each week he is confronted by hungry squirrels, playful possums, gopher traps, sand-crabs, pouncing felines, and, of course, the nefarious do-badders, the spies themselves.

World of Giants is a refreshing albeit imaginative and thrilling journey into the wacky realm of fantasy. They say that everything good comes in small packages. This is a king-sized package of miniature wonders that you can't afford to pass up.

But, HANDLE WITH CARE.
Mel Hunter might be inside. ●

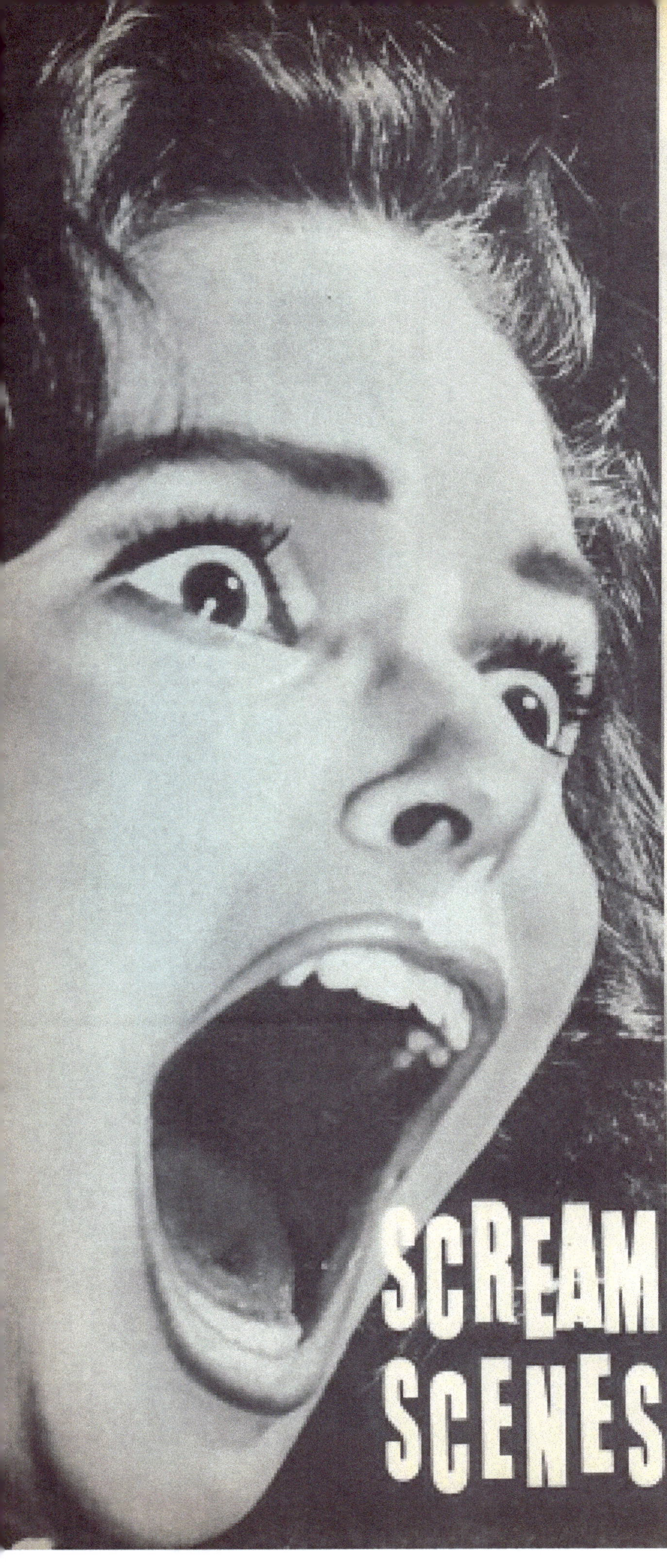

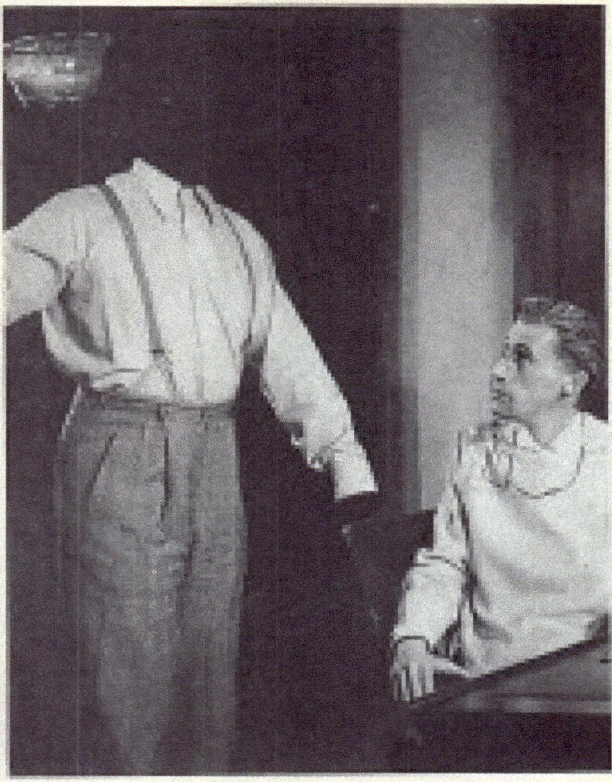

"I've seen a lot of so-called 'photos' of the Invisible Man," peeves reader Susan Storm of New York City, "but he always either has his head and hands bundled in bandages or else an artist has drawn in his features. What I would really like to see, for a change, is a picture of the Invisible Man where I can't see him!"

That's a reasonable request, Susan. Here is a scene from Universal's 1944 terror chiller *The Invisible Man's Revenge*, with John Carradine as Dr. Drury and (note how well you can't see him) Jon Hall as Griffin, the man without any visible means of support.

ScREAM SCENES

CASTLE OF

Today, after the countless millions upon millions of words written about Karloff the Uncanny and his progression from a truck driver to the immortal Frankenstein Monster and onwards, there are very few corners of the earth where the name William Henry Pratt is known.

William Henry Pratt was born in Dulwich, England, on November 22, 1887. You mean you've never heard of him? Well, there are few people who have. But there are very few corners on the earth where *Boris Karloff*, the name Mr Pratt adopted upon entering his theatrical career, is not known. To the majority of people, the name Boris Karloff is synonymous with horror.

Karloff's story has been told and retold, and then again and again, so many times over we doubt there are areas of his much-acclaimed career which are not known by now.

However, there is a visual category to the Karloffian History that has seldom if ever been depicted.

Here, then, is Mr Pratt, as you've probably never seen him before, in photos from some of his most famous and often chronicled motion pictures.

There has never been any one quite like Boris Karloff—or for that matter, never any thing

KARLOFF

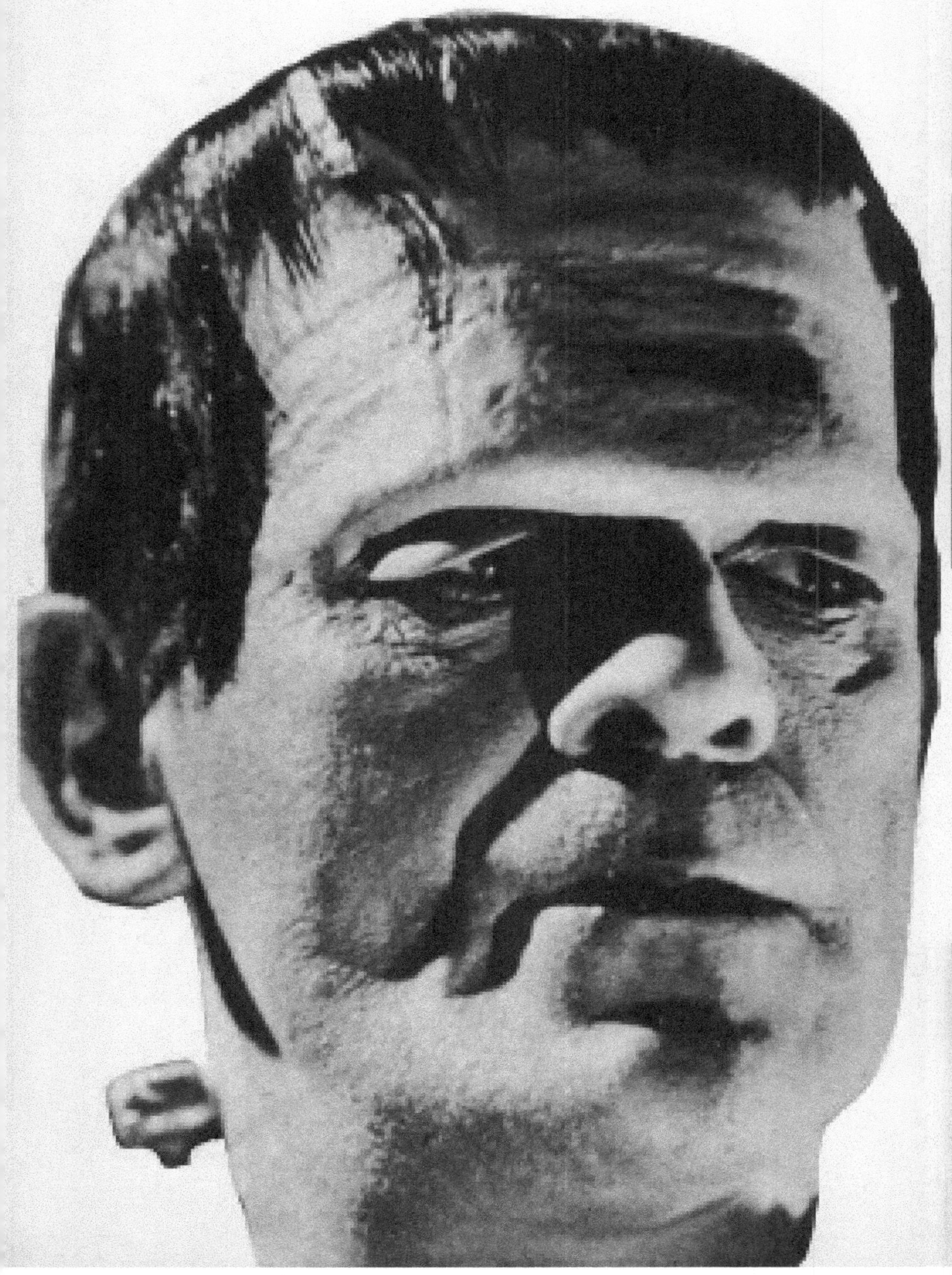

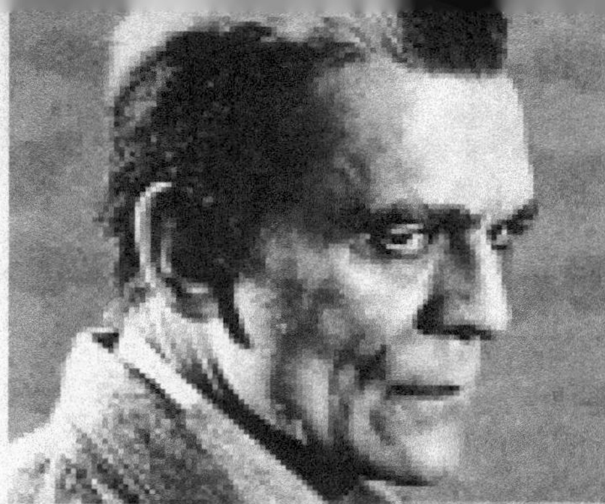

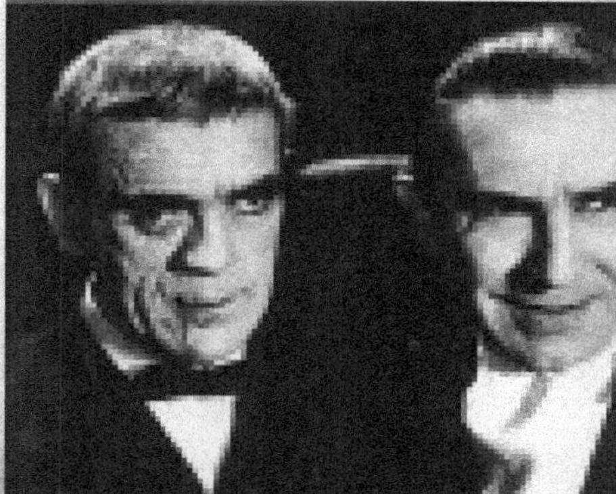

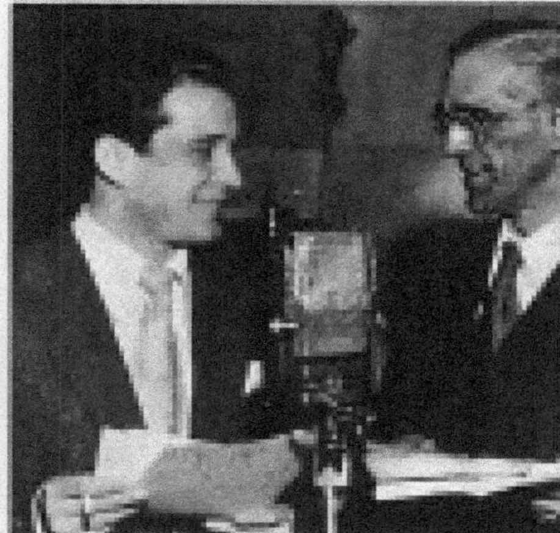

Reading from top to bottom the photos shown are Karloff as the Master of The Walking Dead *for* Warner Bros, 1936. *Premier terrifiers of the screen, Boris with* Bela Lugosi *as they appeared in* Edgar Allan Poe's classic, The Raven (Universal, 1935). *With singer Perry Como at the rehearsal of a* 1948 NBC *song & scare radio special. Karloff as "The Mad Swami" in Universal's* Abbott & Costello Meet The Killer *(1949)*

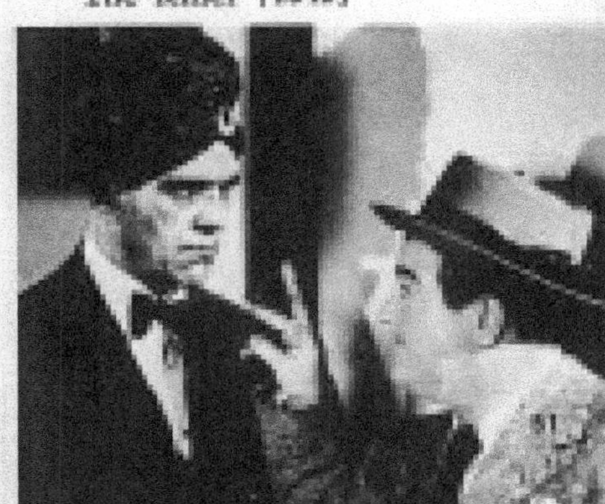

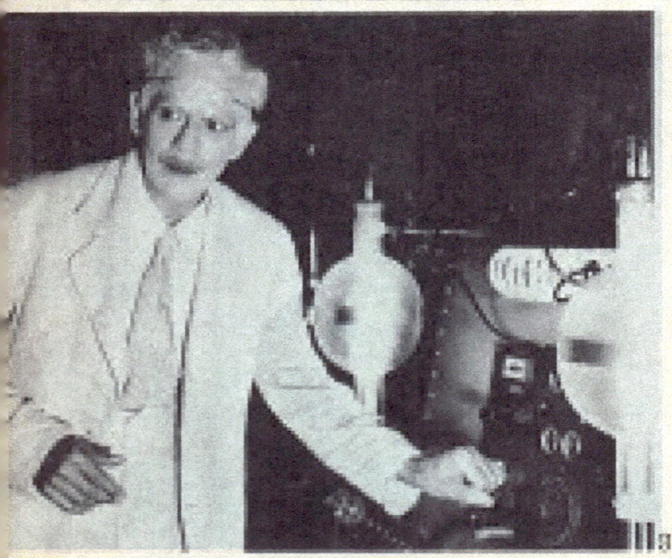

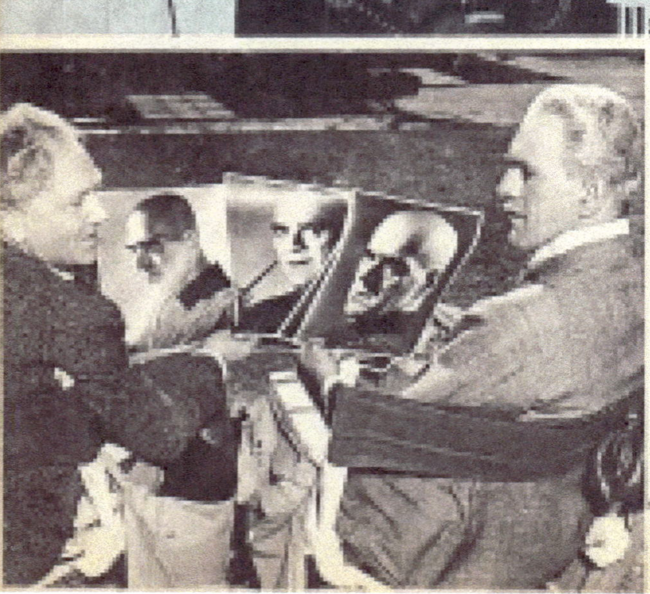

1. *Starring as Voltan, who aids in unlocking the sinister secret behind Universal's Strange Door in 1951*

2. *The duty-bound General Pherides, trapped on the Isle of the Dead for RKO in 1945*

3. *Comic mad scientist in Columbia's The Boogey Man Will Get You (1942)*

4. *Off-camera, Boris shows fellow actor Stanley Ridges shots of himself taken while filming Tower of London (Photo by Ed Jones, on the Black Friday set for Universal in 1940)*

5. *Boris attempts to rule the world behind The Mask of Fu-Manchu (MGM, 1932)*

6. *The Ghoul breaks from his padded cell to terrorize superstitious villagers (1933)*

7. *Gaudet, a prisoner of Devil's Island (Warner Bros, 1935)*

8. *The Black Castle's well-meaning physician (Universal, 1952)*

Morgan, Universal's weird drama, The Old Dark House, constructed in 1932

The two sides of Boris Karloff are shown here in this rare scene from Abbott & Costello Meet Dr Jekyll & Mr Hyde (Universal, 1953)

HORRORS IN HOLLYWOOD

photos copyright 1948 by Universal Pix

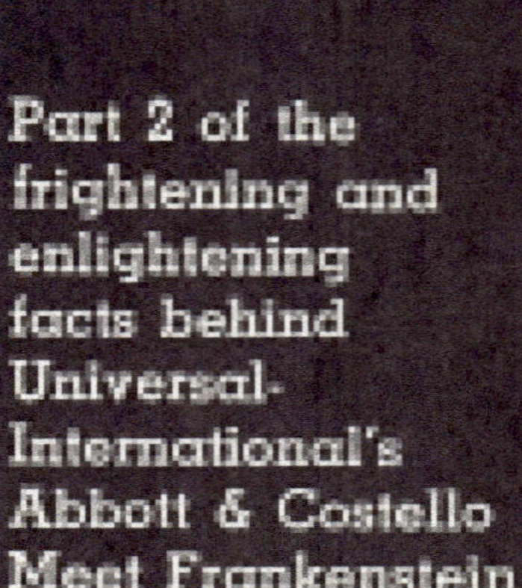

Part 2 of the frightening and enlightening facts behind Universal-International's Abbott & Costello Meet Frankenstein

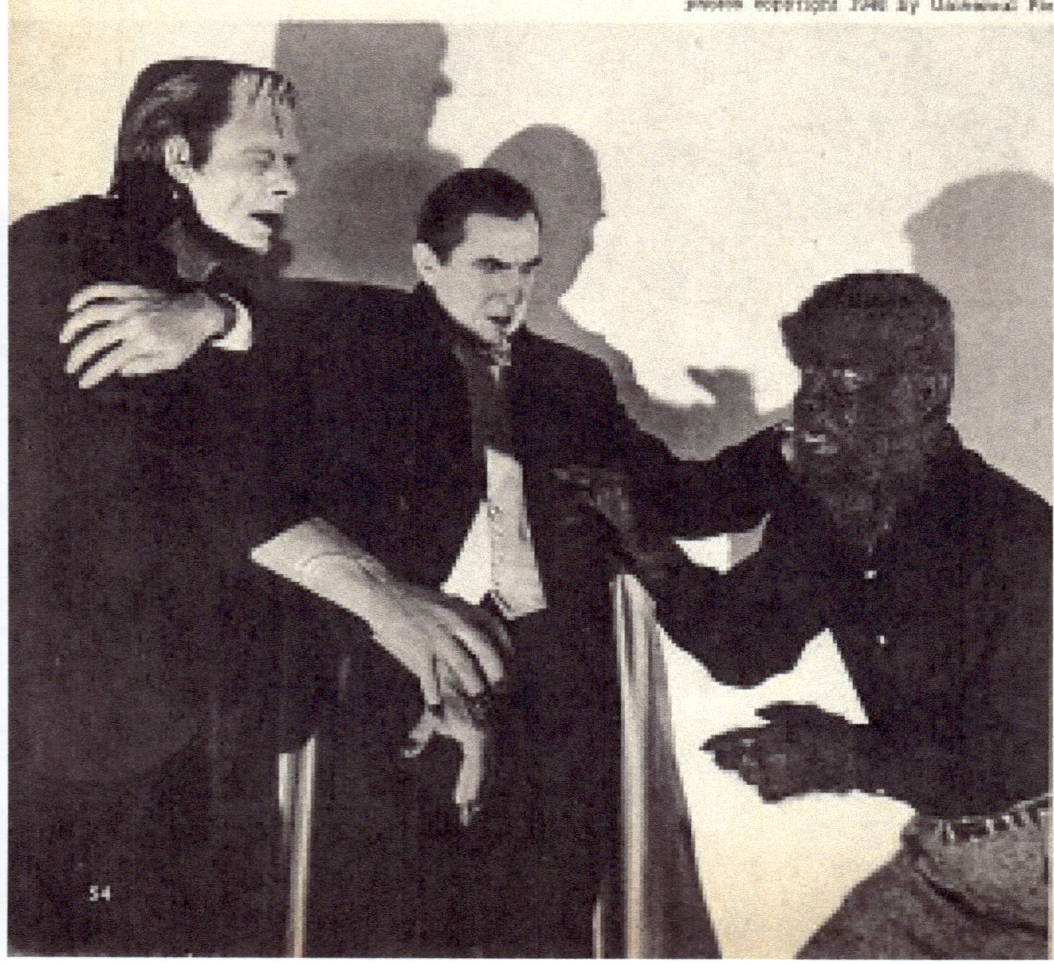

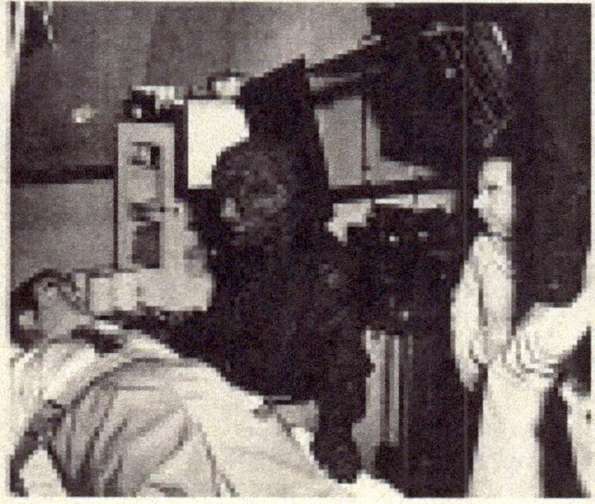

Director Charles Barton warns Lon Chaney Jr to stop biting nails—particularly coffin nails

"Peaches and scream it's not, playing the role of a monster like Frankenstein," Glenn Strange reported one Black Friday. "Sometimes the old bean aches with it all."

Strange rapidly lent conviction to his words with a few of his memorable experiences starring as the legendary Frankenstein Monster for Universal's *House of Frankenstein* in 1944 and *House of Dracula*, one year later.

The splitting headaches that constantly cleaved him after wearing the massive horror disguise for a few hours were only the first flashes of his troubles.

"That, and the fact I had my face scarred by the heavy use of makeup. That spirit gum will leave you looking like a ghost, it takes off so much skin. One more movie and I could have played the Living Skeleton instead!"

Lon Chaney Jr. also at the party where *Abbott & Costello Meet Frankenstein*, had his own skin to worry about for the many monsters he had brought to life in film.

Like Glenn, Chaney owned face scars from wearing deep-rooted makeup for the Wolf Man, the Mummy', Frankenstein's Monster, and others too monstrous to mention.

"But," Glenn pointed out, "when Lon and I did the Abbott & Costello comic horror in 1948, we didn't have to worry about losing our skins any-

more—thanks to those two great Universal makeup men, Jack Kevan and Buddy Westmore."

Kevan, especially for the film, devised not only a new type of sponge-rubber Frankenstein mask for Glenn, but also a pliable wolf head for Lon Jr.

And for the first time on the screen, Chaney as the wild and wooly Wolf Man was able to register facial emotions. The mask, built up by Westmore, replaced the previous makeup clap which made the horror's hairy face rigid.

With these ingenious masks, not only were hours saved in each morning's makeup schedule, but also the actors could appear in their ghoulish roles with no pain and no more sweat than any other player when the day's shooting was over.

The idea for the Bud Abbott and Lou Costello funfilm-chiller was born during a conversation the hilarious duo had with their writer, John Grant, Strange explained.

Grant and the two clowns had established a successful pattern where the rotund and hapless Costello struggled against perils, confusions, contradictions, and complexities put in his path by the lean, sardonic Abbott. Both Bud and Lou were now anxious to veer sharply away from the story backgrounds they had covered so successfully

turn the page

cessfully in previous features.

Menacing foils for Costello were discussed, and in rapid order the nefarious names of Frankenstein, the Wolf Man, and Dracula were suggested.

The idea of Abbott & Costello getting themselves tangled up with the three terror titans received a hysterical nod from the Universal scenario department.

And before any of the three movie monsters could even say "Boo!", they were already face-to-face with the notorious laugh-getters.

With Glenn as the Frankenstein Monster, Chaney Jr as the Wolf Man, and Bela Lugosi at his toothsome best as Count Dracula of Transylvania, the film primarily concerned itself with the vampire's attempt to transfer Costello's brain to the Monster.

Although Drac was unsuccessful in his educational project, the brainstorm for making such a feature resulted in one of the most famous (or infamous) motion pictures in Hollywood history.

"As long as I live," Glenn Strange told us, "I'll never forget working with Bud and Lou. Out of all the many films I've made, this one is my favorite. It was a laugh a minute, both on-screen and off."

One of the off-screen gags, thought up by Glenn and Lou, was actually seen in the film.

The script called for Costello to sneak around the wax museum of Dracula's castle and suddenly bump into Glenn as the Monster. The comedian was to act frightened at this point. End of scene.

But when the two of them got together on the weirdly-lit set, they decided to do a turnabout just for the howl of it.

While the cameras were grinding, Lou stumbled on the Monster and stood petrified. The man-made creature took one look at the round-faced comic, raised his arms with fright, and ran screaming from the cobwebbed museum.

Director Charles Barton and producer Robert Arthur both joined the laughter, and the gag stayed in the print.

This initial combination of the two famous comedians meeting up with monsters, human or otherwise, was so well received by audiences that by popular demand Abbott & Costello later went on to plague and bewilder Boris Karloff as "The Killer," the Invisible Man, the Mummy, and the gruesome-twosome of Dr Jekyll & Mr Hyde.

"Being a movieland monster isn't always the easiest role to do," reminisced Glenn Strange, long a Western actor, currently bartender Sam in CBS-TV's Gunsmoke. "But if I had to be Frankenstein and renew acquaintance with Bud and Lou all over again, I'd be the first one back at the castle." ●

Above Bela Lugosi and Glenn swap shop talk outside the Universal picture morgue. Below and right, A Strange Pair—(left) Glenn and his daughter Janine (age 8) on the set of MEET FRANKENSTEIN in 1948, and (right) Glenn and Janine circa 1962

discover a hero of superb conception, played by a magnificent star and backed by special effects never topped in all the years of movie serials.

Readers of comic books, bored by a steady diet of incredible monsters from outer space, beneath the sea, and other unlikely locations, haunt collectors' shops and find, colorfully chronicled in the dust-laden pages of bygone decades, the adventures of a magical figure who was to become the world's best-selling comics hero with a monthly circulation of over two million copies.

They discover Captain Marvel, the World's Mightiest Mortal, brought to life by Republic Pictures in The Adventures of Captain Marvel, a twelve chapter thriller.

Come back with me to that time I first saw Captain Marvel on the screen. Let's transfer ourselves back to those days before World War II, and for just a little while be kids standing outside a small-town movie theatre, reaching into our blue jean pockets for the reassuring feel of the coins that will take us past the box office and into the enchanted darkness of a Saturday afternoon kid show. Posters tell of the cartoons, the two (or three!) features we'll see, and, thrill of thrills, a multi-colored sign as big as a ten-year-old advertises the first chapter of a new serial starring Tom Tyler, the long-time western star who had only recently broken character to snatch us with The Mummy's Hand.

Tom Tyler is starred as Captain Marvel, the red-suited flying hero we've all been goggling at in Whiz Comics and Captain Marvel Adventures, and it looks like a real corker.

We buy our tickets, make our way past the candy stand, and when the serial comes on with Chapter 1, we can see that it's going to be a corker indeed!

We sit, thrilled and stunned at the transformation of the young boy into a grown man of unlimited power. We whisper the word ourselves, but we find it can only happen up there on the magic movie screen.

At the wizard's command, Captain Marvel speaks his name and is magically transformed back to Billy Batson. The wizard tells Billy that he need only pronounce the magical word, "Shazam," to be turned to Captain Marvel in times of danger. And so off we go onto one of the great film adventures of all time.

Rejoining the party of archaeologists, Billy learns that they have decided that the Scorpion is too powerful a weapon to place in the hands of any one man. They leave the golden figure in the tomb, but each takes one lens so that no member of the party can use the ray without the consent of the others.

Bothered only by attacking native tribesmen (rescued by Captain Marvel) and by a bridge over a mountain gorge that collapses as they drive across it (Captain Marvel saves them), they all make their way safely back to America.

Once again on native soil, the serial takes a turn for the routine. A mysterious hooded villain, known also as the Scorpion, seeks to gain control of all five lenses, by trickery—and by violence.

One by one the lenses fall to the Scorpion as the archaeologists, joined by Tal Chotali, Billy, Betty, and Whitey, hold periodic councils to fight the threat.

A series of magnificent cliffhangers cap the passing chapters. In one, Captain Marvel himself is rendered unconscious by a rigged electrical device, and carried down a conveyor belt to a falling guillotine as the chapter ends.

In another, one of the greatest of all special effects is used to create the sight of an entire mountain melting to lava with Captain Marvel trapped inside!

In other chapters, Billy Batson (played by Frank Coghlan Jr.) is the intended victim as, true to Shazam's instructions, he uses his magic power to be transformed to Captain Marvel only in moments of dire danger. But if, as Billy, he is knocked out, bound and gagged and left to die in an exploding airplane, a bombed shack, a sinking ship, he cannot call upon Shazam.

Of course, Billy-Marvel is not the victim in every cliffhanger, not by a long shot. One of the best of them has Betty Wallace knocked out and trapped behind the wheel of a madly-careening automobile; in another Betty and Billy together are exposed to a death-trap as they open a safe which will automatically set off twin machine guns aimed at the very spot where they stand!

All the time, the Scorpion is getting the lenses one by one. Finally, in a frantic race to head off worldwide destruction by a now invincible madman, the entire surviving cast make their way back to the tomb in Siam, passing through a tornado en route, only to be captured, bound, and—you could guess it—gagged by those selfsame tribesmen.

Gloating in triumph, the Scorpion mounts the five lenses in the golden idol and destroys a few innocent bystanders, just to show how well it works. He has Billy brought before him, having guessed that Billy is somehow capable of the magic transformation to Captain Marvel, and demands that Billy give him the secret or die.

As the Scorpion removes Billy's gag, the brave youth says, "I'll not only tell you how I become Captain Marvel, I'll show you! Shazam!"

Boom! Captain Marvel appears, rips the hood from the flabbergasted Scorpion, and reveals him as none other than . . . Professor Bentley!

Bentley is killed in the eruption of a convenient live volcano, and as Captain Marvel stands once more in the Tomb of Shazam, he is magically transformed to Billy without having spoken the name of the wizard.

Instead, the voice of Shazam himself is heard, explaining that now that the menace of the Scorpion is no more—Marvel had thrown the golden idol and the lenses into the volcano, just for good measure—he is no longer needed and so his powers are being withdrawn.

Thus ended the great film adventures of the even-greater Captain Marvel, the super hero who out-supered Superman.

The serial was reissued in 1953 under the misleading title, The Return of Captain Marvel, a nifty little piece of deception also used in the re-release of Captain America, another comic book adaption into the world of serials.

The lucky few can still see The Adventures of Captain Marvel today. An occasional private showing is arranged at which the whole twelve chapters—they run almost five hours altogether—are shown in a single evening. Even more rarely the serial is shown as it was made to be seen—one chapter at a time, over a period of twelve weeks. Probably that is the better way to see it. There's an awful lot of plot packed into twelve episodes. It took five screenwriters to produce the script: Ronald Davidson, Norman Hall, Archie Heath, Joseph Poland, and Sol Shor. The musical score (it was a gem!) was by Cy Feuer, who recently composed the music for the hit show Bye Bye Birdie. There were even two directors: William Whitney and John English.

But if you are hoping that there will ever be a real revival of this wonderful character, you are doomed to disappointment.

Captain Marvel may have out-supered Superman, but National Comics, the owners of Superman, out-lawyered Fawcett Publications, who owned Captain Marvel and his whole Shazam-begotten family.

National's lawyers got Fawcett to sign a consent decree in 1952, agreeing to bury Captain Marvel deeper than the waste from an atomic reactor, in exchange for National's dropping a long-outstanding lawsuit against the rival firm.

So except for those rare and semi-clandestine showings, chances of seeing Captain Marvel are slim.

It's sad indeed, it seems unjust; but these graybeards in their aged twenties and ancient thirties can cling to that golden memory. And youngsters of today can keep on the alert for those rare revivals, and maybe, some Saturday afternoon in a decrepit old movie theatre in an old neighborhood, discover what it was like to view the mighty Captain Marvel. ●

The imaginative Rod Serling, Emmy award winning host and curator of THE TWILIGHT ZONE

Terrors From The Twilight Zone

You're travelling through another dimension—a dimension not only of sight and sound but of mind—a journey into a wondrous land whose only boundaries are those of the unlimited nightmarish imaginings of the far out Rod Serling

Below, Andy Devine, veteran comedy actor, stars as a confirmed teller of tall tales who more than meets his match when he encounters creatures from another planet, in "HOCUS POCUS AND FRISBY." Right, Science-fiction author Charles Beaumont casts a careful eye over the pawn of Satan (played by Robin Hughes) that he had created for "THE HOWLING MAN" episode of THE TWILIGHT ZONE. Far right, "THE FUGITIVE," ruler of a fantastic planet beyond our solar system.

Midnight may be the witching hour . . . moonrise the time when creatures rise and werewolves howl. But the true time of terror . . . the time of fear and foreboding . . . the time of fantasy and phantoms, is twilight time.

It is in the dying hours of the day, in the last dim moments before darkness overcomes and envelops day in a black shroud, that imagination runs wild. Then, the unreal becomes real. Fancy becomes fact. Shadow becomes substance. In twilight time, nothing is impossible.

That is the premise on which the imaginative mind of Rod Serling created his Emmy-winning series, The Twilight Zone, for the CBS Television Network.

The unlimited possibilities of the "impossibles" which can occur in the mystic twilight zone would be grist for any writer's mill or mind. But in the hands of Rod Serling, what might have been "just another fantasy series," won television's highest award: The "Emmy" of the Academy of Television Arts and Sciences.

It brought Rod's total number of Emmy's to five, and must have made his adulthood as "wonderfully happy" as his growing-up years.

Serling, creator, primary writer, and host of The Twilight Zone, was born on December 25, 1924, in Syracuse, N. Y. The childhood he remembers so pleasantly was spent in Binghamton, N. Y.

But any teen-age dreams he had of a writing career were blasted from his mind by war. Hitler blitzkrieged Poland. Pearl Harbor was bombed and World War II burst into furious flame.

Rod Serling's happy childhood suddenly was over. He quickly grew up as an army paratrooper. The blood, sweat and tears of three war years in the Pacific did not stifle his desire to write, however.

He used the experience to soak up the deep insight into human beings which a writer must have. Serling listened to and observed his fellow troopers. He learned their speech, their character traits, their philosophies and ideas.

The unreality of war itself may have planted in his mind a subconscious idea for a later Twilight Zone story. In any event, as Serling used the tools of war, he also acquired the tools of writing.

by Dan Gilbert

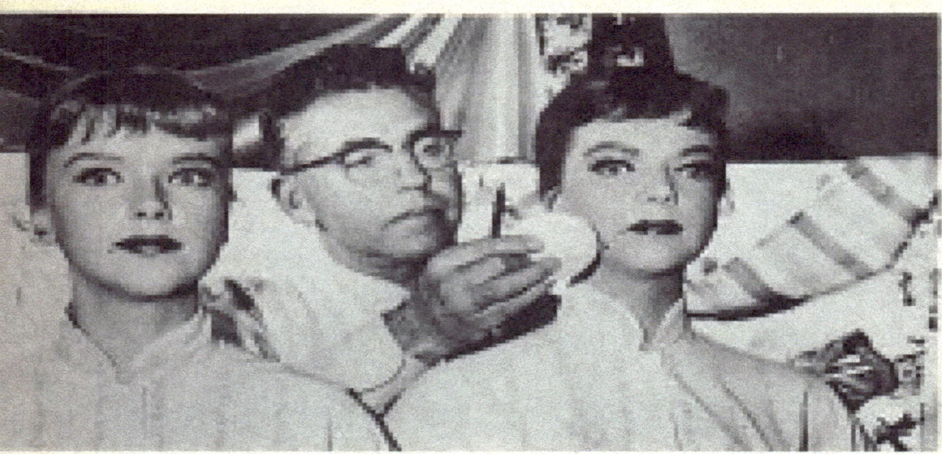

After the war, his first step towards a career as a writer was to enter college on the GI Bill. He enrolled in little Antioch College in Yellow Springs, Ohio, deliberately choosing a small school because he believed its environment to be the best kind in which to let literary ambitions grow.

Two years before graduation, he took a partner in his efforts to obtain recognition as a writer. He married Carol Kramer. As Mrs. Rod Serling, Carol has been a major source of strength to her husband in his struggle to reach the top pinnacle of television.

Soon after their marriage, Rod and his bride went to New York. There Rod worked as an apprentice radio writer under Antioch's work-study plan, which provided for actual radio writing experience in addition to academic study.

As a raw recruit to radio, Rod quickly moved up in rank. A first success was winning $500 second prize in the *Dr. Christian* script competition. Then, he wrote for such famous radio shows as *Grand Central Station*, on CBS. At the same time, he returned to Ohio, and was hired as a staff writer by WLW, Cincinnati, one of America's outstanding radio stations.

By the time television was ready for the masses, Rod was ready for television. His TV credits included such top-rated shows as *Luz Video Theatre*, *Armstrong Circle Theatre*, *Fireside Theatre*, *Ford Theatre* and *Kraft Theatre*.

It was *Kraft Theatre* which catapulted Rod Serling to eminence as a television writer by televising his famous "Patterns." This television masterpiece and classic won Rod his first "Emmy," the Sylvania Award, and the Christopher Prize.

Successes tumbled on successes for Serling with the advent of *Playhouse 90*. Rod's unforgettable scripts for "Dark Side of the Earth," "The Velvet Alley," "Rank and File," "Requiem for a Heavyweight," and "The Comedian," clearly established Serling as a writer of first rank. He won two more "Emmys" for "Requiem" and "The Comedian." He also received the Peabody award for "The Comedian,"

turn to page 62

Upper left, Serling at the gateway to Heaven in the story "CAVENDER IS COMING"
Center, Makeup man Charles Schramm puts the finishing touches on the department store mannequin created in the likeness of actress Anna Francis for "THE AFTER HOURS"
Below, Burgess Meredith, as "MR. DINGLE, THE STRONG", paces with space creatures who make him the smartest man in the world
At Right, The dog-faced nurse from "PRIVATE WORLD OF DARKNESS"

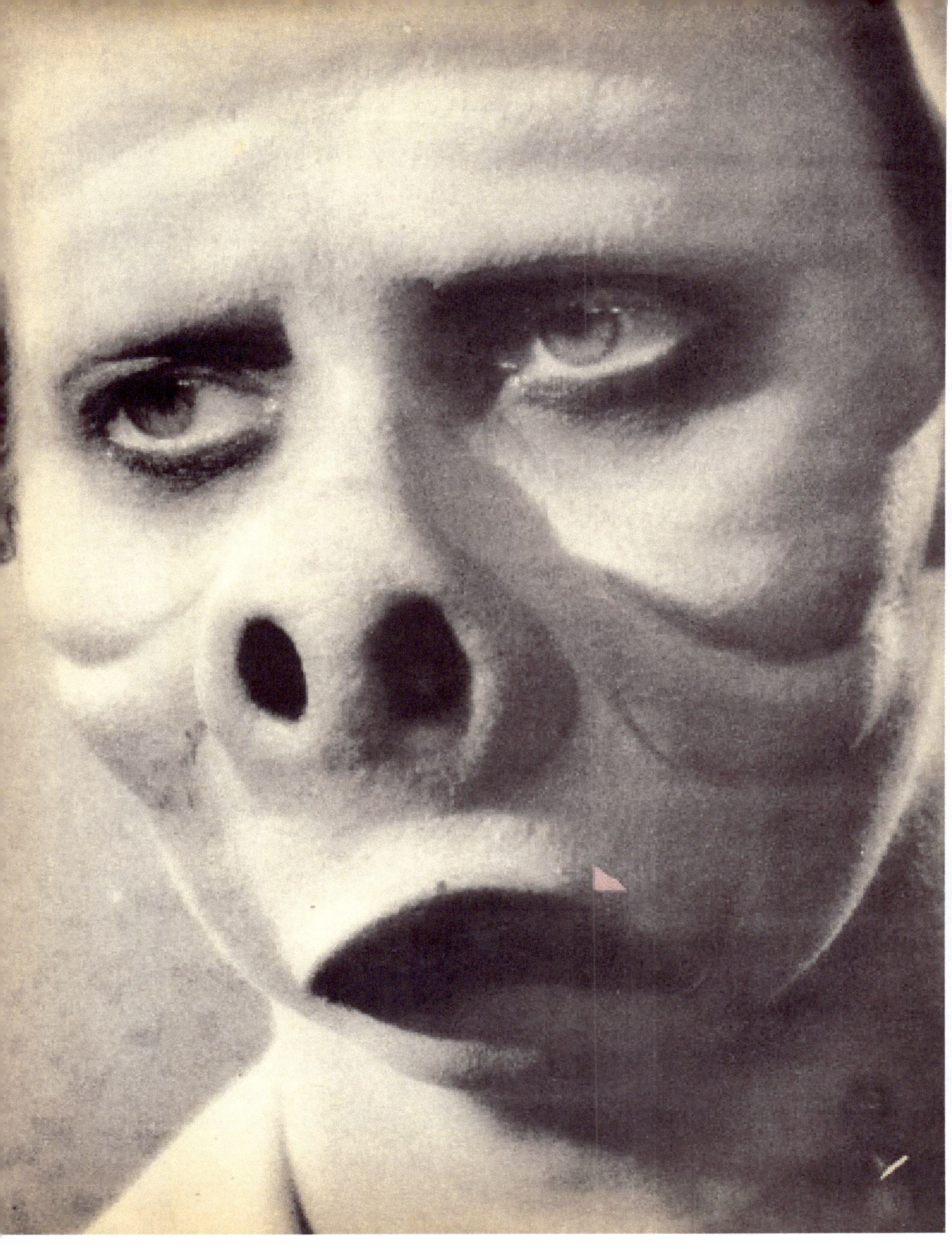

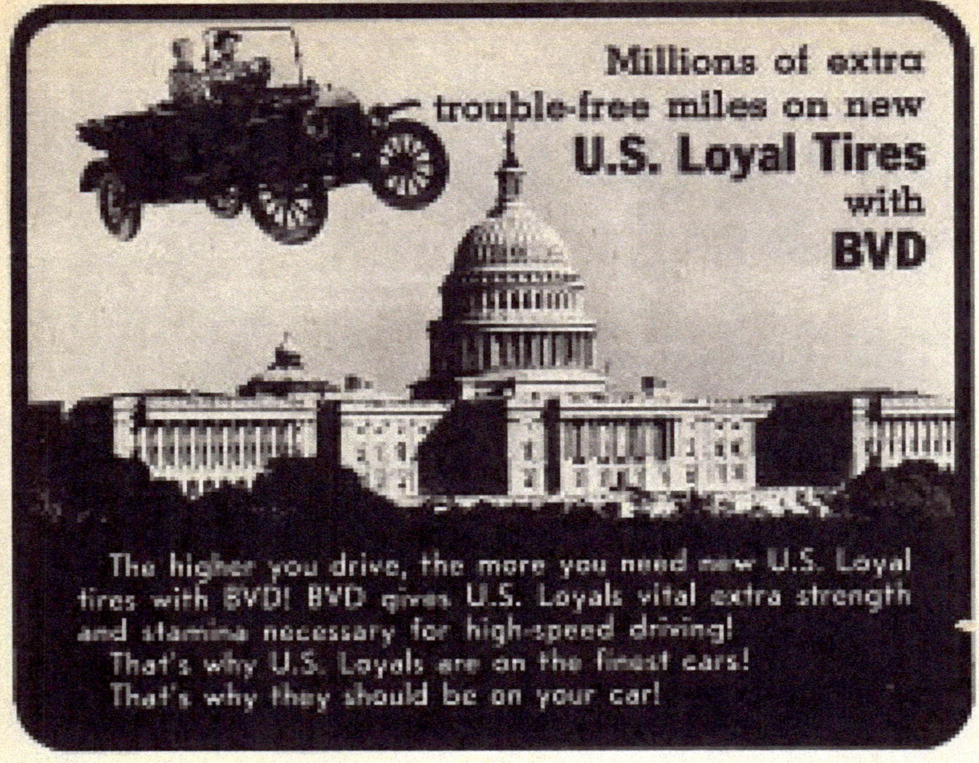

RUBBER, from page 12

He quickly read the label and looked deeper into the compartment for the instrument he needed to take the formula. He found it.

Dell took a dose of Karu Creighton's formula in the specified amount. Tensely, he went over to the dresser in the small room. He threw up the window shade so the sunlight would give him a well-lighted view of his face. Standing in the brilliant sun a moment, he nervously threw open the window to relieve the stifling heat of the California summer.

His eyes looked back at him strangely from the glass. Glassily from the glass, he thought, almost giggling. He pulled back one eyelid, for closer inspection. It stayed pulled back, with a curious oriental look.

That was it! Creighton realized. The Orient. Or at least, the Far East.

An India Rubber man, a real one, that's who had given Creighton the formula. That's how he had been the "Man with the Rubber Face." And now, Don Dell could recreate his roles, even The Halfling. He could make a fortune!

He tried all the roles he could recreate. Dell sculpted his face into weird gargoyles, and pious saints, into the visage of the Hunchback and of the Frankenstein monster . . . Strange face that, but there were stranger ones . . .

His mind went back to The Halfling, that thing with almost liquid flesh he had seen Creighton do when he had been a boy. He tried it. He tried letting his arm hang limp, like plastic. It was easy.

But then in ridiculous alarm, he tried straightening his arm out. It . . . wouldn't . . . straighten . . .

Dell looked at his face in the mirror, the face that wasn't changing of his own accord, but that was flowing into new weird contours.

Suddenly Dell remembered what the pawnbroker had told him of Creighton, and just as abruptly he knew why the old actor had made all of his monster films in New York in the winter.

Dell looked up at the bright, hot California sun. And screamed. Once.

. . .

Mrs. Hudson pounded on Don Dell's door angrily.

"Less noise, Mr. Dell!" the landlady said. "You and them wild friends of yours got to keep your voices down!"

When there was no response, she tried the door, found it open. She entered, sniffing noisily.

"Empty," she observed. "What's that rubber smell?"

Finally, she saw the pool of shiny liquid, on the carpet, near the dresser.

"He's going to have to clean that stuff up himself," she said. "Looks like that rubber stuff that was used to patch up tires with in the old days. Messy. Melts and runs all over Nell's Half Acre in hot weather like this. Okay in the winter, but stop this time of year. Wonder if he's stealing tires and fixing them up. . .?"

Mrs. Hudson left the room, talking to herself, leaving the puddle of liquid rubber on the floor that had once been alive, never realizing that Don Dell had at last made his big splash in the world. ●

TERRORS, from page 61

the first time the award was ever given a writer.

His Twilight Zone series, in addition to adding to his collection of "Emmys," also has been given many other outstanding awards. And the object of all this honor and fame is a compactly-built, sun-tanned, intense, but down-to-earth fellow who speaks the language of the average guy as easily as he talks in literary language.

So busy at the typewriter that an occasional swim in the family pool is his principal recreation, Serling keeps regular office hours. The pool is strategically located just outside the door of his writing studio at his Pacific Palisades home, enabling him to jump up from his desk and into the pool between pages of a script.

The rest of the family, besides Rod and Carol, includes daughters Jody, 10, Nan, 7, Beau, an Irish setter, and George, a beagle. Rod is always fighting the clock to have time with his family.

His business-like approach to writing, his solid connection with the real world, may seem paradoxical, compared to the wildly-imaginative scripts for The Twilight Zone.

But as in twilight time, so in the mind, anything is possible, and the story limits of The Twilight Zone episodes are limited only by the imagination of Rod and his primary writing colleagues, Charles Beaumont and Richard Matheson. Creatures from outer space, tales of terror, psychological dramas and pure fantasy have come out of the twilight zone.

"Private World of Darkness" was pure horror: the tale of a hideous race of the future in which the abnormal became the normal. "The Fugitive" was the tale of a king on holiday from another planet, who befriended and entertained a little girl.

"Hocus Pocus and Mr. Frisbie" had Andy Devine destroying creatures from outer space with a secret weapon, his harmonica. In "The After Hours," a department store mannequin came to life and was sent into the human world to observe humans.

One of the funniest episodes was the story of "Mr. Dingle, the Strong." Two experimental teams from different planets made Mr. Dingle, alternately, the strongest and smartest man in the world. These powers enabled him to overcome the bullies and wise guys who made his life miserable.

Every episode has had such a fresh and interesting approach, it might well be asked of Rod Serling, "What are you going to do for an encore?" CBS has the answer to that. The good news for fantasy fans is that, starting in January, 1963, The Twilight Zone" goes to one hour in length.

So, away with the witching hour, the hour of moonrise, and bring on the hour of The Twilight Zone and the remarkable Rod Serling. ●

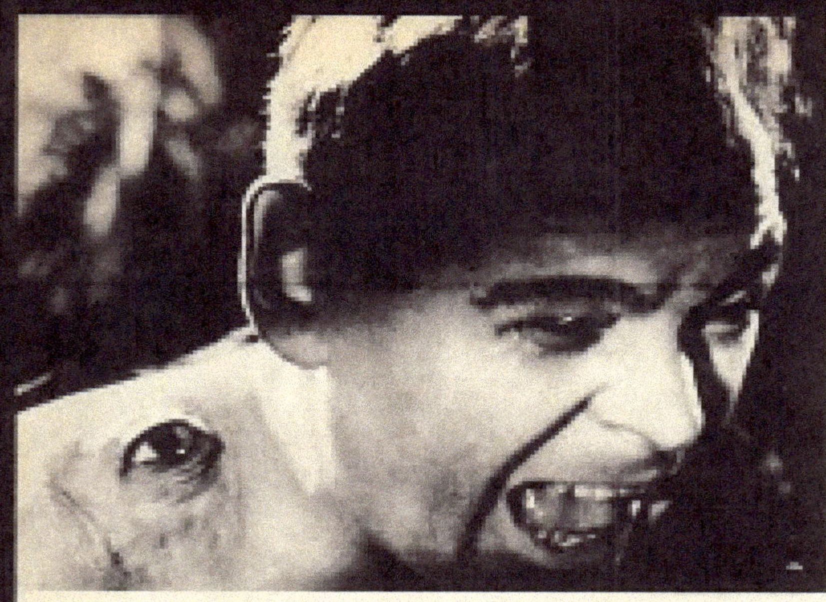

Scanning the future flights of fantasy looming up in Hollywood's Try-Fright Zone

HORRORSCOPE

Above, THE MAN-STER, currently making eyes pop out at local theatres

Below, Moonmen capture Earthlings in new Mexican space feature, CONQUISTADOR DE LA LUNA

"The beast is yet to come," courageously puns Roger Corman, who has soared up over 50 feature productions. Corman plans to uncage Edgar Allan Poe's *The Raven*, rebuild *The Tower of London*, become a tourist on *Sinbad's Magic Voyage*, and finally, get in *The Race for Mars*.

While *The Hands of Orlac* fingerpaint the screen with blood again (the first time was in a 1924 silent classic), *The Fire Serpent* will be scorching celluloid for Rainbow Films. An *Alien Seed* is being cultivated by writer John Kelley, and Jerry Lewis plans an about-face as the troublesome doublesome *Dr Jekyll and Mr Hyde*.

MGM spooks all with *A Haunting*, while it helps Oscar-owner George "Time Machine" Pal cage scripters Ben Hecht and Charles Lederer for *The Circus of Dr Lao* (also a Bantam Book, 50c).

Searching for *The Village That Wandered* is producer Charles "Mysterious Island" Schneer, who also plans placing *The First Men on the Moon* early next year.

Herman Cohen, man behind *Teenage Frankenstein* and *Blood of Dracula*, called with the news that he will be conducting a celluloid tour through his *Black Zoo*, after which he'll be aiming at *Target Moon*.

Curse of Kemu-Shek, an avenging Egyptian mummy, chilled faithful radio listeners to CBS recently; while later, flying saucers landed to convince radio fans *You Died Last Night*, scripted by Robert Arthur. *The Second Door* lead to matter transmission, written by the audio play's star, onetime Gangbuster, Robert Reddock. You'll find *Suspense* in the Sunday radio lineup.

And you'll find humor in the lives and film deaths of Boris Karloff, John Carradine, Lon Chaney, and others as author Leo Guild tells it in his funny, funny new book *Hollywood Screwballs* (Holloway House, 60c).

Ex-Tarzan Gordon Scott dons an Italian loincloth for his starring roles in *Maciste Against the Vampires*, *Maciste in Hades*, and *Maciste Against the Monsters*. Former "Jane" in the Burroughs ape-man films, Maureen O'Sullivan, is currently swinging on Broadway, *Cradle and All*.

The Black Robed Ghost is wrapped up in Jack "Dragnet" Webb's *True* tee-vee. Robert Bloch, synonymous with *Psycho*, is off on a *Treasure Hunt* for the Webb series.

William "Zotz" Castle sends his greetings from *The Old Dark House*, which he is exploring in England. He wants us to know he'll be filming a whacky one after *House*—*My Brother Was an Eagle*, with a hero, even he admits, is a real bird-brain.

VOLUME 1 ☆ ☆ ☆ ☆ ☆ FIVE SCAR FINAL — ALL THE NEWS UNFIT TO PRINT ☆ ☆ ☆ ☆ ☆ NUMBER 2

COFFIN CORNER

I recently saw *The Man of a Thousand Faces*, in which James Cagney portrays Lon Chaney Sr. I thought Cagney's makeup was so terrific that I'd like to know who created it for him.—PAUL MITCHELL, LOUISVILLE, KY

Bud Westmore and Jack Kevan, mask and makeup specialists long associated with Universal horrorama, are the ones who take the credit. For more information on them, see "Horrors in Hollywood" in this issue.

I live and breathe werewolf films and movie serials! And never in my life have I seen a serial hero like Sky Altitude! Would you please list for me all the cliffhangers in which he's been featured?—LARRY TALBURNS, ROBERTA, TEXAS

The deformed flying leader of the famed Super Squadron made his debut in 1936, in Sky Altitude. Two years later, Sky Altitude Meets Zoltar; and in 1940, Sky Altitude Vs Maniac Master. A little-known film, released in 1946, was Son of Sky Altitude, a full-length feature.

Is there any way I can contact horror movie producers, Roger Corman and William Castle? — DOUG BOBADLO, BROOKFIELD, ILL.

Roger Corman may be reached through American International Pictures, and William Castle at 1628 No. Gower. Both are in Hollywood.

For years and years now I've been trying (without much luck) to learn the identity of the actor who was *The Shadow* on radio. I've heard it was Orson Welles, but I find that hard to believe. Can you help me out? —JACK PACKARD, REDWOOD CITY, CALIF.

Yes, Orson Welles did at one time play the invisible Shadow; but the most popular actor in that role was Brett Morrison who, back in 1938, produced, directed, and starred in a special radio adaptation of Bram Stoker's Dracula.

BUZZ GORY SPACE DERANGER

If you think this is silent film star Rex Max Navarro or British actor Helmut Dantine, you're wrong. It's Count Downe, blasting out with another edition of Tombstone Times.

Monster Fan Mag Launched

"*Horrors of the Screen* is devoted to the realm of motion picture suspense and fantasy," writes editor *Alex Sowa* about his great new fan publication. "It is designed for those who enjoy and appreciate the art of cinematic terror."

Within the 44 thrill-crammed pages of Alex's first issue of *Horrors of the Screen*, you'll find stills of Bela Lugosi, Peter Cushing, Vincent Price, Christopher Lee in addition to features and articles on silent and current horror films, plus a photo-packed review of *Curse of Frankenstein*.

"Copies are going fast," Alex tells us. So if you don't want to miss gasping to *Horrors of the Screen* #1, send Alex your 50c today. His address is 469 Union Ave., Brooklyn 11, NY.

HAUNT ADS

. . . Comic book fan Ross Fass is anxious to obtain original artwork by noted comic magazine artist, Joe Kubert. If you have any for sale, you can reach Ross at Rt 1 - Box 161, Suisun (Rockville), Calif . . . Bob Harper has a list of monster movie items for sale. Contact him at 11 Eastwoods Lane, Scarsdale, NY . . . Wanted by Don Sheppard, 2771 San Marino, Los Angeles 6, Calif: stills, presses, posters, anything at all from the serials *Sky Altitude* and *Sky Altitude Meets Zoltar*. "I'll pay top prices for whatever you have on my favorite serial hero," Don adds. . . . Nicholas Cerrone is in the market for back issues of

64

PETER CUSHING FAN CLUB

Victoria Priester extends an invitation to all the many fans of British actor Peter Cushing (star of Horror of Dracula, The Mummy, Hound of the Baskervilles, etc) to join her Peter Cushing Fan Club.

In addition to free membership photos, club card, and monster contests, there is a special club journal detailing the latest film adventures of Cushing.

For full information on membership, contact Victoria at 6 Courtland Drive, Montgomery 6, Alabama.

California's Larry Byrd presents the latest issue of his monster gazette Terror to horror film star Vincent Price on the set of Price's recent chiller, aptly titled, Tales of Terror.

the fanzine Ape. If you have any for him, write him at 821 Girard Rd, Toms River, NJ . . . Larry Talbarus, 931 No. Valley, Burbank, Calif, has his claws out for photos from movies like The Wolf Man and Destination Moon. He also wants pix of Glenn Strange and Lon Chaney Jr . . . An ape call goes out to Tarzan fans everywhere from Jules & Tom McGeehan. All interested jungle man devotees are asked to write John & Toni. Their address is 406 E. 5th, Santa Ana, Calif . . . Rudy Franke wants all fans who have photos from Flash Gordon and Tarzan films for sale or trade to write him. Drop him a line at 5448 Foothill Blvd, Oakland 1, Calif . . . If you have pressbooks from Curse of Frankenstein, Revenge of Frankenstein, Creature from the Black Lagoon, or I Was a Teenage Werewolf up for sale, contact William Armstrong, 241 Pleasant St, Providence 6, Rhode Island. Bill is in the market for the above . . . Back issues of comic books are wanted by James Brown, 5th Control Co., Material Bn, Barstow, Calif. He is particularly interested in titles like All Winners and Spectre . . . Jim Biz, 2743 San Marino, Los Angeles, Calif, is interested in hearing from those of you who have actual discs or tapes of old radio programs like Inner Sanctum and I Love a Mystery. He also wants westerns, sci-fi, comedy radio shows (any type at all). Will trade or buy.

Drac Is Back

Bob Christy of Chicago, Ill, poses as the infamous Count Dracula, in this scene from one of his home horror movies, Planet of Satan, co-produced with fan Bob Greenberg.

Monster Clan

Head of his own monster clan is Frank Stobrina, alias Glenn Normale of Burnsville, Alabama. Other famous members of Frank-Glenn's cult are Peter Lawsford, Sctven Martin, and Gary Bishop.

SECRET MESSAGE FOR FANTASTIC MONSTER CLUB MEMBERS ONLY

GYSRLGSDUWCSBXW
CGDLRGOWRMYWXU
GIPZWOWFSYELATL
SDNRLWCDZLKRUAL
WTTRSCELCGOLVC

(Use decoding key on back of your membership card.)

JOIN fantastic MONSTERS CLUB NOW!

A new world of supernatural pleasures for those brave enough to join!

Join the most exciting monster club of them all.

Send coupon today!

FREE MONSTER PHOTO

BLOOD RED MEMBERSHIP CARD

FULL YEAR'S SUBSCRIPTION TO OFFICIAL FANTASTIC MONSTERS OF THE FILMS MAGAZINE

EXCLUSIVE MEMBER'S BULLETIN WITH SECRET MESSAGE . . . STRANGE FACTS

He got caught without his copy of **FANTASTIC MONSTERS**--- next time this happens to you, be prepared!

SEE COMPLETE PHOTO REVIEW OF THIS ISLAND EARTH IN THIS ISSUE ON PAGE 18

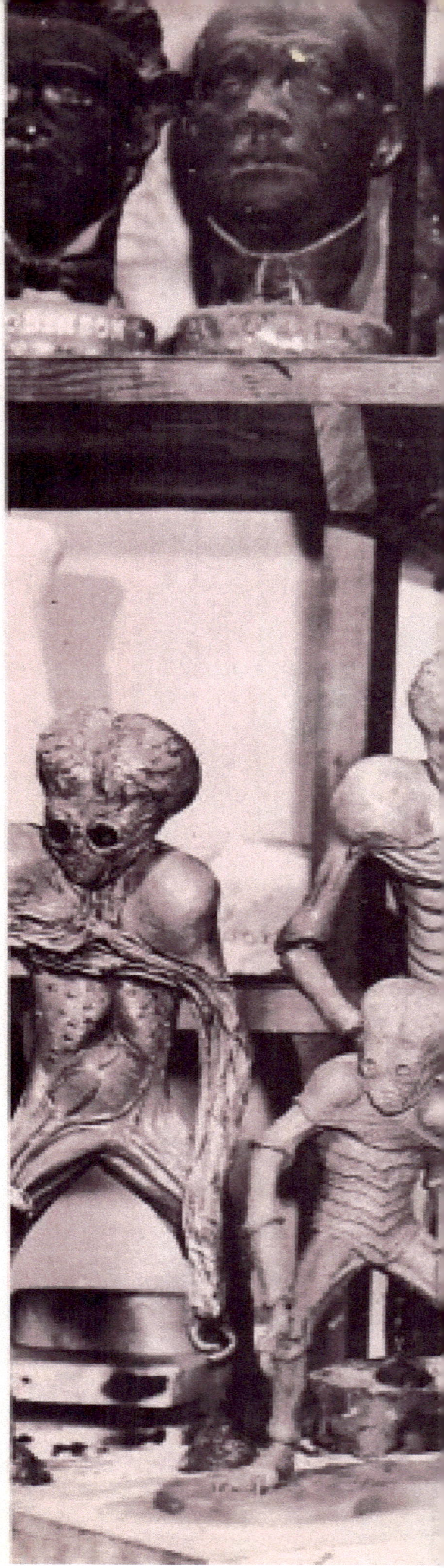

Universal-International's
Metaluna Monster

MONSTER OF THE MONTH

The bulbous head, five times the size of a human's: the brain, completely exposed. Apoplectic eyes projecting like glowing half domes, a network of underlying veins plainly visible. Strained facial muscles, on the surface.

The cranium, pulsating with each heartbeat. Five tiers of interlocking mouths—one serving double purpose as a nose. Hands dangling to the ankles, lobster-like claws replacing fingers. A shell, like an armadillo's, covering the spine.

It all adds up to the Metaluna Mutant—an eight foot creature from another world, half human, half monster—easily one of the most nightmarish of all grotesque figures ever to reach the technicolor screen.

The Mutant slithered forward in This Island Earth, a Universal-International science-fiction production of 1955.

This special specimen, created especially for the film by Bud Westmore (pictured here), U-I makeup veteran, had a total construction cost of over $24,000. The horrendous suit was the product of ten months of special design and development by Westmore and his monster-happy associates.

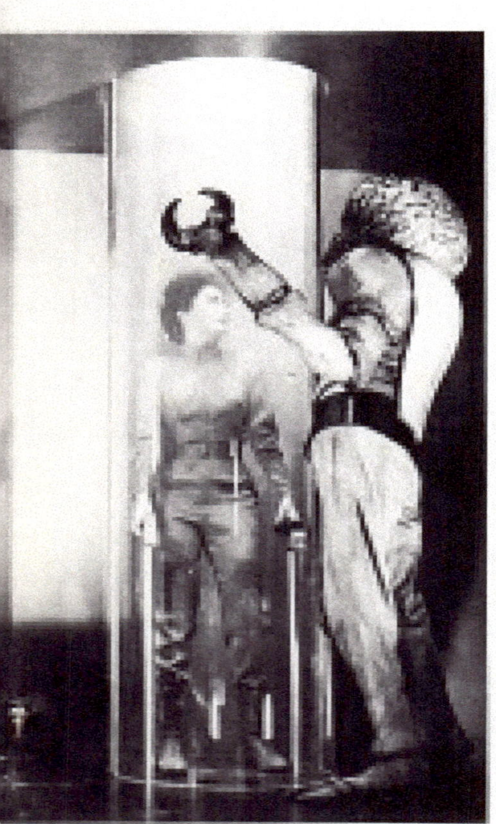

FANTASTIC
MONSTER
OF THE
MONTH

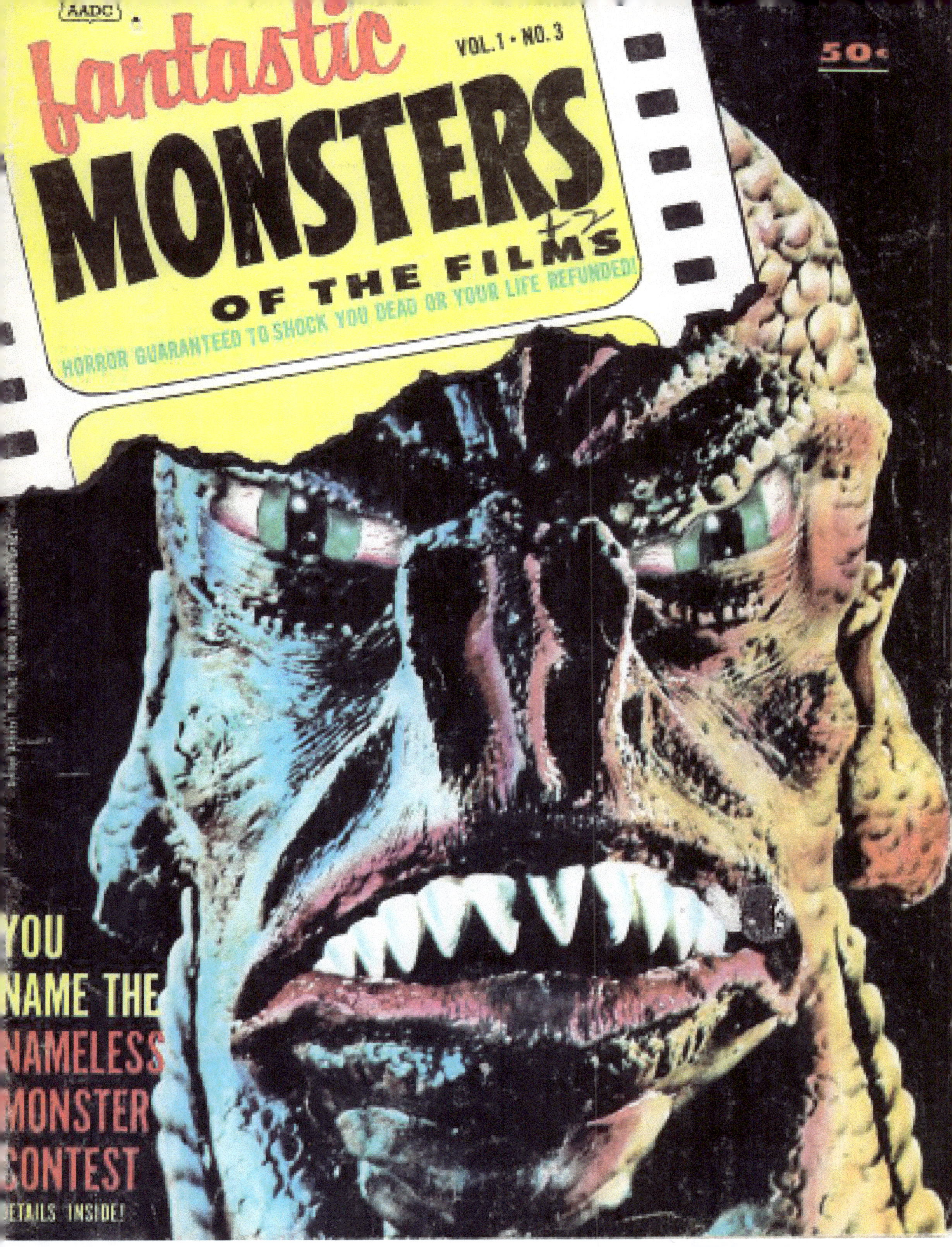

AADC
VOL. 1 - NO. 3
50¢
fantastic
MONSTERS
OF THE FILMS
HORROR GUARANTEED TO SHOCK YOU DEAD OR YOUR LIFE REFUNDED!
YOU
NAME THE
NAMELESS
MONSTER
CONTEST
DETAILS INSIDE!

Scratch a monster, find a man.

That's the story of a remarkable filmland personality who is a legend in his own time —Mr Boris Karloff. We met up with Mr Karloff on the set of his latest picture, The Raven, and beneath all that monstrous makeup usually masking his features we discovered one of the kindest and most sincere people you could ever have the pleasure of getting to know. The many hours we spent with Dear Boris, rekindling old monsters and memories, will be warmly remembered in the times to come.

We bumped into Psycho's Robert Bloch, also on The Raven set, and stopped to chat with him about Stay Tuned for Terror, a radio series which he created in the middle '40s. FanMo's own radio historian, Jim Harmon, who this time around has covered the wireless adventures of Jack, Doc & Reggie, has promised us a complete report on the Bloch series in a future issue. Harmon, it will be of interest to many, has one of the largest collections of radio programs, both on tape and disc, in existence today.

Also on hand herein is novelist Jameson Harvey serving up a quick dish about a cave monster combatting magic, a behind-the-scenes feature on the talented individuals responsible for producing our favorite type of entertainment, and, of course, that embalmed Egyptian enigma, The Mad Mummy, this time hurtling through space to Mars.

See you in eight weeks.

THE EDITORS

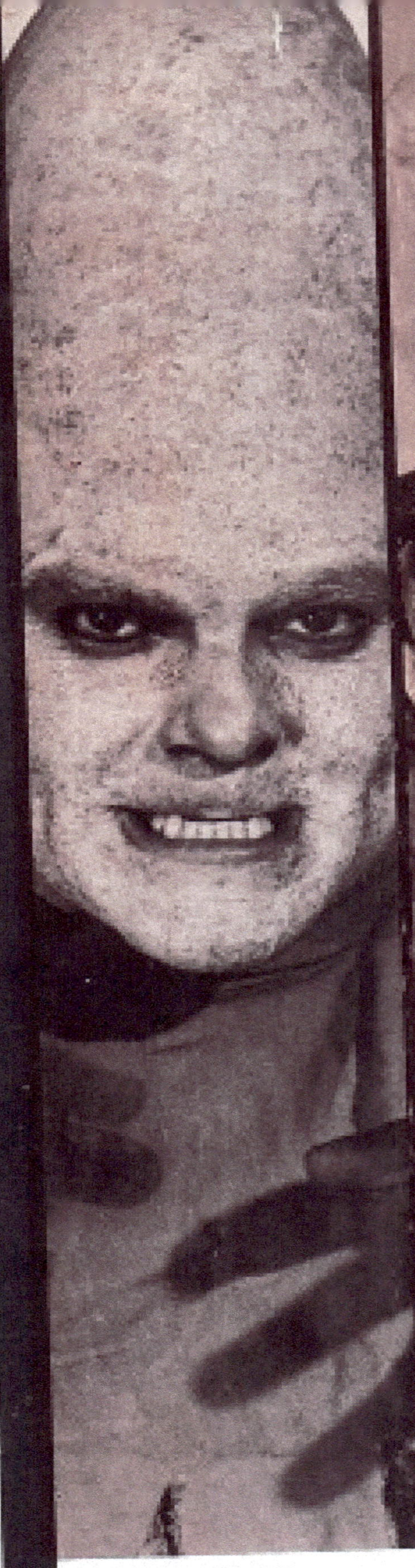

FANTASTIC MONSTERS, the thrill and chill magazine that's ahead of all the rest!

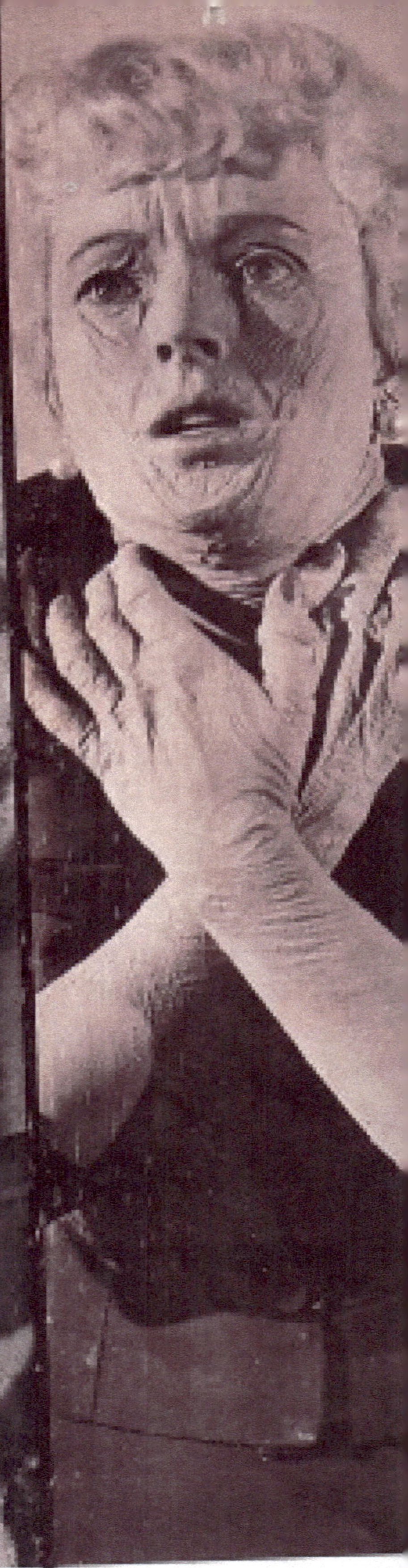

It's no choke that you're in for a colorful treat with this Rare Collector's Issue!

fantastic MONSTERS OF THE FILMS

VOL. 1 • NUMBER 3

COVER: IT — THE TERROR FROM BEYOND SPACE. A United Artists release

RON HAYDOCK
editor

PAUL BLAISDELL
editorial director

BOB BURNS
research editor

JIM HARMON
associate editor

CREDITS & ACKNOWLEDGEMENTS: Kirk Alyn; AIP; Richard Bernstein; Robert Bloch; Larry Byrd; Jack Cash; CBS-Radio & TV; Columbia Pic; Gene and Roger Corman; Golden Eagle Films; Alex Gordon; Bert I. Gordon; Dick Jebel; Boris Karloff; Will Kuenne; Larry, Moe, & Curly Joe; Mad Mummy; Fay McMullin; Mike Minor; Carleton G. Morse; Jack Nicholas; Paramount Pic; George Romero; Vincent Price; Sam Sherman; Ray Smith; L. S. Snyder; Glenn Strange; David Szurek; Mark Tenney; Universal Pic

VOLUME 1, NUMBER 3. FANTASTIC MONSTERS OF THE FILMS. PRICE 35¢ PER COPY. Published bimonthly by Black Shield Publications Inc. Mailing address: Post Office Box 141, Topanga, California. National Advertising Representatives: Member Company, 862 North Fairfax, Los Angeles 46, California. Contents Copyright 1963, by Black Shield Publications Inc. Nothing may be reprinted in whole or in part without written permission. Printed in U.S.A. Unsolicited manuscripts must be accompanied by stamped self addressed envelopes; the publisher accepts no responsibility for return. Any similarity between people and places mentioned in the fiction and similarities in this magazine and any real people and places is purely coincidental.

CONTENTS

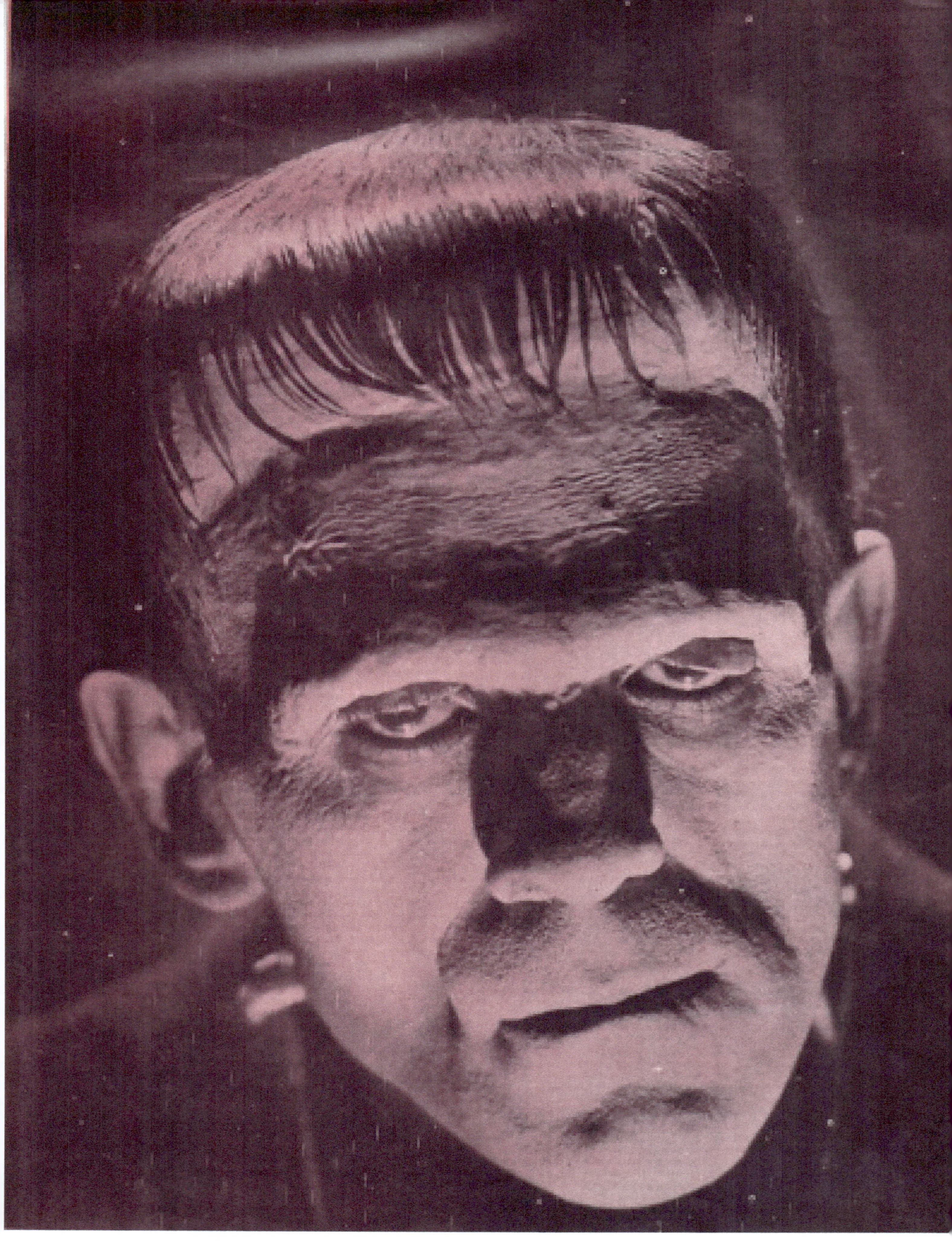

How To Make A Frankenstein Monster

Take one part actor, two parts nose putty and greasepaint, add one part makeup man, then blend mixture well with the most important ingredient of all, if you have it—ten parts patience

by Don Sheppard

Everyone, it seems, would someday like the chance to play the role of a movie monster, growling and clawing out at the world, having a field day wrecking a mad scientist's lab frightened the daylights out of the local villagers, and, of course, be chased over fog-shrouded moors by citizens with blazing torches.

It sounds like fun.

But it isn't.

Any actor who ever was a ghoul, zombie, monster, vampire, or what-have-you, could tell you being a man-made horror isn't the easiest way to make a living.

This interviewer caught up with the greatest monster man of them all, Boris Karloff, on the set of his new picture The Raven, and asked him what it's really like to be a filmland creep.

What the Master of Horror had to say on the subject is something to be carefully considered by all budding Karloffs, Chaneys, or Lugosis.

Above: Makeup master Jack Pierce applies the infamous Frankenstein head and face to Karloff's own. Left: Monster Authority, Boris Karloff. Below: Karloff and Ernest Thesiger in BRIDE OF FRANKENSTEIN

A touching moment in BRIDE OF FRANKENSTEIN, the best in the series (Elsa Lanchester is the Monster's Mate).

Top: SON OF FRANKENSTEIN, Basil Rathbone, meets with his father's creation. Below: Bela Lugosi and Dear Boris in SON OF FRANKENSTEIN.

During the filming of his three Frankenstein movies (*Frankenstein*, 1932, *Bride of Frankenstein*, 1935, and *Son of Frankenstein*, 1939), Boris Karloff had to check in each morning at Universal Pictures at six o'clock sharp, where he was met by a sleepy-eyed Jack Pierce, the ace makeup specialist. For Karloff, or for any actor in his position, the next six hours were the most gruelling.

From six o'clock till noon, Pierce was plastering on Karloff's facial and arm makeup. Karloff, practically strapped to the makeup chair, sat motionless while Pierce applied the thick, greenish-gray greasepaint. Bloody scars were trenched on Karloff's forehead, scalp, neck, and wrists; and collodion and cotton made the fire-wrinkled skin of cheek and hand. There were aluminum neck spikes (popularly known as the Monster's electrodes), and steel braces for the arms.

At twelve o'clock, Pierce would begin fitting on the shoes, which weighed 11 pounds, five ounces apiece. They were size 24.

Then came the final touch in creating Frankenstein's monster — helping Karloff on with the padded suit two inches thick, which he wore under his clothes from neck to ankles.

As a rule, one o'clock signalled the completion of makeup, and "Dr. Frankenstein" Pierce and his monster breathed a sigh of weary relief as they sat down to a hasty lunch before it came time for Karloff to thump off to the set for eight hours of acting.

All told, Karloff's makeup as the Frankenstein Monster weighed 62 pounds. On screen, he towered seven feet, seven inches. Of this height, seven inches had been added to his head, and nine inches to his feet.

Each day, from 30 to 45 minutes were spent in making up his hands alone! So heavy was this makeup that if Karloff attempted to open his left hand unaided he would have broken the fingers.

When Karloff made *Bride of Frankenstein*, he had to receive Infra-Red Ray treatment and massage to stimulate circulation in his legs and arms and to relieve pain in his injured left side. He had hurt his side in the first scene of the film, where he drowned the burgermaster in the flooded cellar of the mill.

A typical shooting day saw Karloff home about nine in the evening, with just enough time to study the next day's script, then catch some well-earned sleep before the four o'clock alarm rang off.

With the production of a monster film running anywhere from three weeks to three months, and with the monster actor having to be subjected each day to the agonizing and tiresome ritual of an eight-hour makeup job, an actor's endurance is sorely tested. To quote the authority, Mr. Boris Karloff, "You've got to have patience!"

Tearing up the local village may sound like fun, but I'm one would-be monster who would rather be in the audience than on the screen. ●

Karloff injured himself during the shooting of this scene.

THE DEVIL'S

How do you like your trick photography — with monsters?

All of us, at times, wish we could photograph a "monster" that we didn't have to build; one that would "act" all by himself, too. Surprisingly enough, there are many such "monsters" available — in the family of reptiles we call lizards. Most of them are no further away than a walk through the country — or to the nearest pet store.

A trip to the library can tell you, in a pleasant hour of reading, which "monsters" are available in your neck of the woods. Nearly all lizards, with few exceptions (notably the poison-spitting Gila Monster of the Southwest!), make fairly good pets. Their average intelligence is on the level of a parakeet, and in many respects they're more interesting to watch (and photograph).

Now before you molding-and-casting fiends throw down your plaster and walk out of this session of the DEVIL'S WORKSHOP, think about a couple of cinema super-extravaganzas, like The Lost World and Journey to the Center of the Earth; remember the Iguanas and the baby Alligator?

Okay then, let us tell you about Lizzie. She's one part Alligator Lizard and one part ham — as you can see by the pictures! Strictly a Western gal, she stays on the Hollywood side of the Rockies, from Canada to Mexico. Around here, she lives in a glass fish tank (minus the water, of course), furnished just like her world outside, where she was caught. Male Alligator Lizards can't be tamed, but after a month of gentle handling and feeding

#1

#2

#1—"A guy gets thirsty under those hot photo-flood lights."

#2—"It looks like I'm tossing this Jeep over the goal line!" — see text.

#3—Give your saurian friend something to climb: he'll climb it! — HO gauge light tower.

#4—Two good models, ready to go to work.

#5—"He forgot to put a nickel in the meter. Let's give him a ticket!" Lizzie and friend check out the "campsite".

#3

#4

WORKSHOP

by Paul Blaisdell

(live insects and water from an eye dropper), she decided to pose for us, so we named her Lizzie (naturally). We even got a few of her relatives to help out, too.

It seemed as though the Alligator Lizards would work out fine, pretending to tear up an explorer's campsite, in a short movie scene. These days, it's no trouble at all to get an endless variety of interesting props from the local model store. A miniature jeep and trailer kit was available, so they became the "key props" in our miniature scenery, which we purchased from the same model store.

In a movie, no one would expect the explorers to stick around, so except for a quick "cut" shot of our heroes running for the tall timber, we might think that our Alligator Lizards would have the scene to themselves.

From this point on, it was up to us and the lizards. When Lizzie climbed up on the jeep to get a drink from an eye dropper, held just out of the scene, we slowly pulled the jeep over with a thread. In the completed scene, it looked as though she'd deliberately pushed it! When Lizzie's girl friend rushed "off stage" after the fleeing explorers, she was actually rushing to get a meal worm (available as reptile food, at the local pet store), which we held in a pair of tweezers. You get the idea — the lizards always looked like they were doing one thing, when they were actually doing some-thing else.

With a little patience and kindness on your part, you'll find that the lizard of your choice makes a fine 1,000,-000 B.C. type of "monster", although we won't say that a Horned Lizard really looks like a Triceratops, nor an Alligator Lizard like a Teleosaurus. But you have to admit there's a nice family resemblance there.

There are some Dos and Don'ts to keep in mind, when working with lizards! Limit the time you keep your saurian friends exposed to concentrated sunlight, or under photoflood lamps. Surprisingly enough, too much heat can be harmful to most lizards, and they don't like it. Check the sur-

turn to page 62

9

THE CAVE CREATURE

by Jameson Harvey

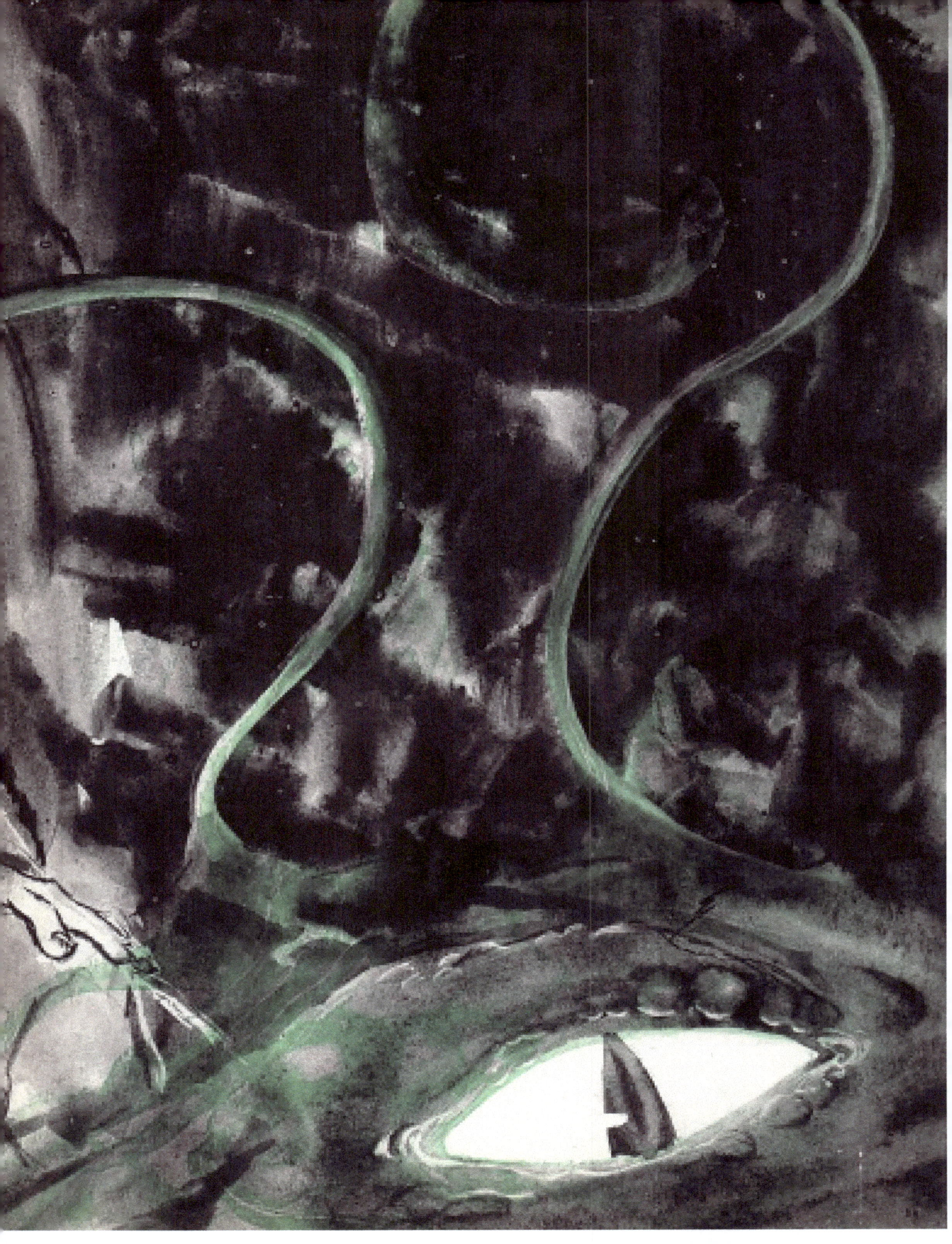

As the door opened, he appeared half drowsing over a chemistry school book.

The elderly man came into the room, closed the door softly behind him, and approached the bed.

"Studying hard?" the old man asked pointedly.

Bob looked up at the weathered face above him, creased with stern lines on either side of the mouth, but revealing clusters of laugh lines around the eyes.

"I guess so," Bob replied.

"You aren't going to learn much about chemistry from something like this," the old man said, snatching a fallen magazine from the floor like a prize. "Monsters . . . ghouls . . . the occult . . ."

The old man sighed and sat on the edge of the bed carefully as if afraid to wrinkle the covers.

"You're a sweet, wonderful guy and loads of fun. But as a steady boyfriend . . . . I just can't see you."

"Bob," he said seriously, "your father is a chemist. I am an archaeologist. How can you be so—so unscientific?"

Bob said nothing.

"An old woman has all the superstitious people in this desolate country believing that there is a ghost or a werewolf or some such lurking in the cave in the gorge, but I'm surprised at you believing it, trying to find out from those dusty old books whether the monster should be killed with a wooden stake or a silver bullet . . ."

"It . . . it's a little more complicated than that, Grandad," Bob said at last.

"While you are staying with me, I'll teach you what I know your father and mother would wish me to teach you—that the only thing to fear is ignorance," the old man said. "There is something in that cave—probably the last lobo wolf in this part of the country. But it's nothing science can't take care of. The science of ballistics in this case. I'll go out with my rifle tomorrow. And take you with me."

Bob knew it could be a matter of life or death if he was right. And perhaps more life or death as we understood them was at stake.

"Well, Mr. Magician, why don't you conjure up your monster?" demanded Bob's grandfather when they had penetrated several hundred yards of the cave's tunnel.

Bob played his flashlight ahead of them, but there was nothing ahead but darkness and cold walls.

Mephisto, the big farm dog, sat down beside the old man and waited for the two of them to move on.

"I'll show you some magic," the old man said, picking up his rifle and pointing it into the darkness ahead of them.

"Mephisto, stay here with the boy," the old man said, advancing.

A moaning wind swept through the tunnel, and at Bob's side Mephisto growled a warning as the hair stood up on his neck.

Suddenly Mephisto leaped past Bob and after the old man.

The roar of the rifle. Again and again. Mephisto snarling and snapping. And then the knifing scream of stark terror.

Bob wanted to run. He wanted to run to the help of his grandfather, and he wanted to run to safety, out of the cave, far away. But he stayed where he was.

It was in the book, all in the book. It said it would be this way. But he had read the book and believed he had the secret, the secret of controlling the monster by ancient magic.

"Primum Movens Wamphi! Evil of the Earth Obey in the name of the Mad!"

Bob ran now, ran forward into the darkness that the flashlight could not penetrate.

"Primum Movens, Shibchet! Not in Desert heat nor Hell's fire but—" he called in bellowing greeting "Hail Winter Wamphi!"

There was a slithering in the darkness, a slithering of retreat, withdrawal, submission?

No.

A tentacle wrapped around his ankle, its slim hair-like protuberances wrapping around his leg delicately.

His heart was beating in fury now.

What could be wrong?

He had said the incantation just the way the book had said. He had greeted winter with a hail—

Winter, hail?

Or Winter Hail? As in sleet and hail, not the hail of greeting.

The translation could have been wrong, a grammatical error in the old book. . . .

He was being dragged forward, closer, and now he could see. The thing cast up a strange light of its own, and he saw.

Writhing in the tentacles of the monster were his grandfather and Mephisto. One evil black-eye glistened like wet marble, and there was a . . . mouth . . .

This was it. The last of the great snake monsters that had once infested the earth—Gorgon, Medusa, and this, the last of their kind, huddled the centuries through in a frosty Dakota cave, feared and worshipped by the Indians before the coming of the white man to this icy cave.

Ice.
Hail.

Snakes hated water, and according to mythology could not cross running water. And as for frozen water, that was the key.

As he was drawn nearer the gaping mouth, Bob clawed at the water that had dripped down the walls of the cave and frozen into icicles.

He flung the spear of frozen water.

"Hail Winter Wamphi!"

The icy missile sang straight and true into the eye of the oldest of beasts. With a whining sigh of resignation and perhaps of relief, the creature melted back into the shadows. And was gone.

Grandfather Adams sat on the bed beside Bob and Mephisto.

"How did you find out the right thing to do, the secret lost for so many centuries?" the old man asked quietly.

"I did what you and Dad always taught me," the boy said. "By researching, examining, I discovered the truth."

The old man smiled, n o d d i n g wearily.

"The scientific method," the old man said. "It is the scientific method that is important, and that is exactly what you used. Yes, science searches in all directions for the truth, not just in one. Or at least it should."

The old man picked up a copy of a supernatural horror magazine from the bed, and stood up.

"Maybe I should do a little scientific research before I turn in." Grandfather Adams said.●

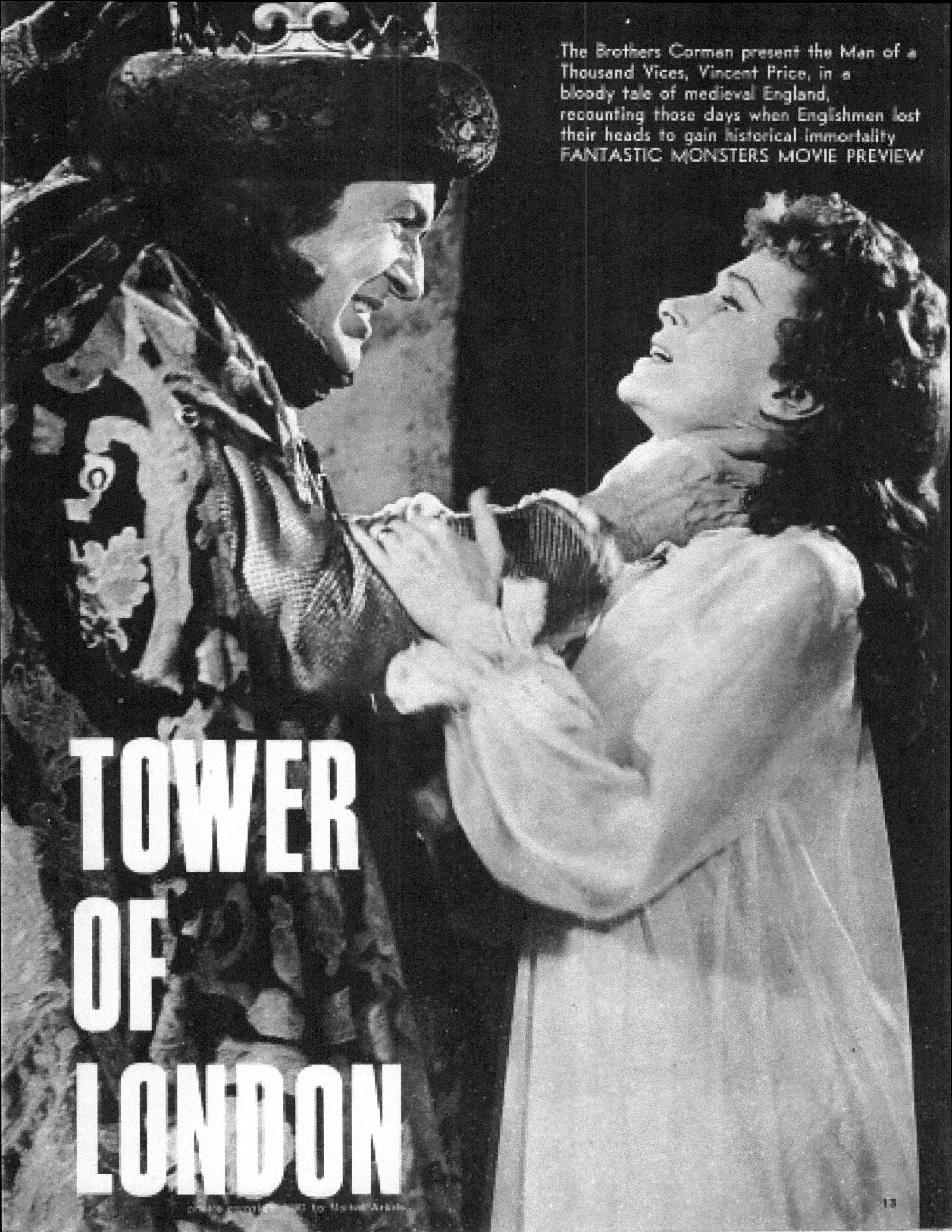

TOWER OF LONDON

(Above) Vincent Price, the new King of Terror, plots his newest fiendish deed. (Below) The price of being a traitoress to his cause can be excruciating, as Vincent proves in this scene.

That master specialist of movie macabre, Vincent Price, is once more up to his theatre chilling tricks, again flickering the silver screen with his deadly presence. This time Price recreates one of history's all-time arch-villains, Richard III, the ambitious man to whom the bodies of murdered wife, brothers, nephews, and friends were merely stepping stones to his claiming the throne of England in 1483.

The film, Tower of London, released by United Artists, ironically marks Price's return to this bloody era in Britain's history. In 1939, Price was featured in Universal Pictures' accounting of the grim happenings at the Tower of London, in the role of Clarence (brother of Richard), and sharing the honors with co-stars Boris Karloff and Basil Rathbone. The new Tower, however, boasts the fact it is not a mere remake of the Universal construction.

Responsible for razing the old Tower and rebuilding the new are two of Hollywood's most successful young motion picture executives, the brothers Corman, Roger and Gene. Roger, Edgar Allan Poe's favorite director (House of Usher, Pit and the Pendulum, The Raven, etc), lists Tower as his 60th feature in less than eight years—a remarkable feat in this Age of the One-Eyed Monster, television.

Roger's brother Gene, who has recently produced the much-awaited film version of Charles Beaumont's fine novel The Intruder, is chiefly responsible for the new concept of character seen in Tower of London. Delving deep into the motivations of history and personality, Gene developed the current concept of Richard III to fit a Grand Guignol theme, then delivered the scripting assignment to writ-

A plotter in knight's armor puts Price in a daze.

Bruce Gordon proves to Price that he is untouchable.

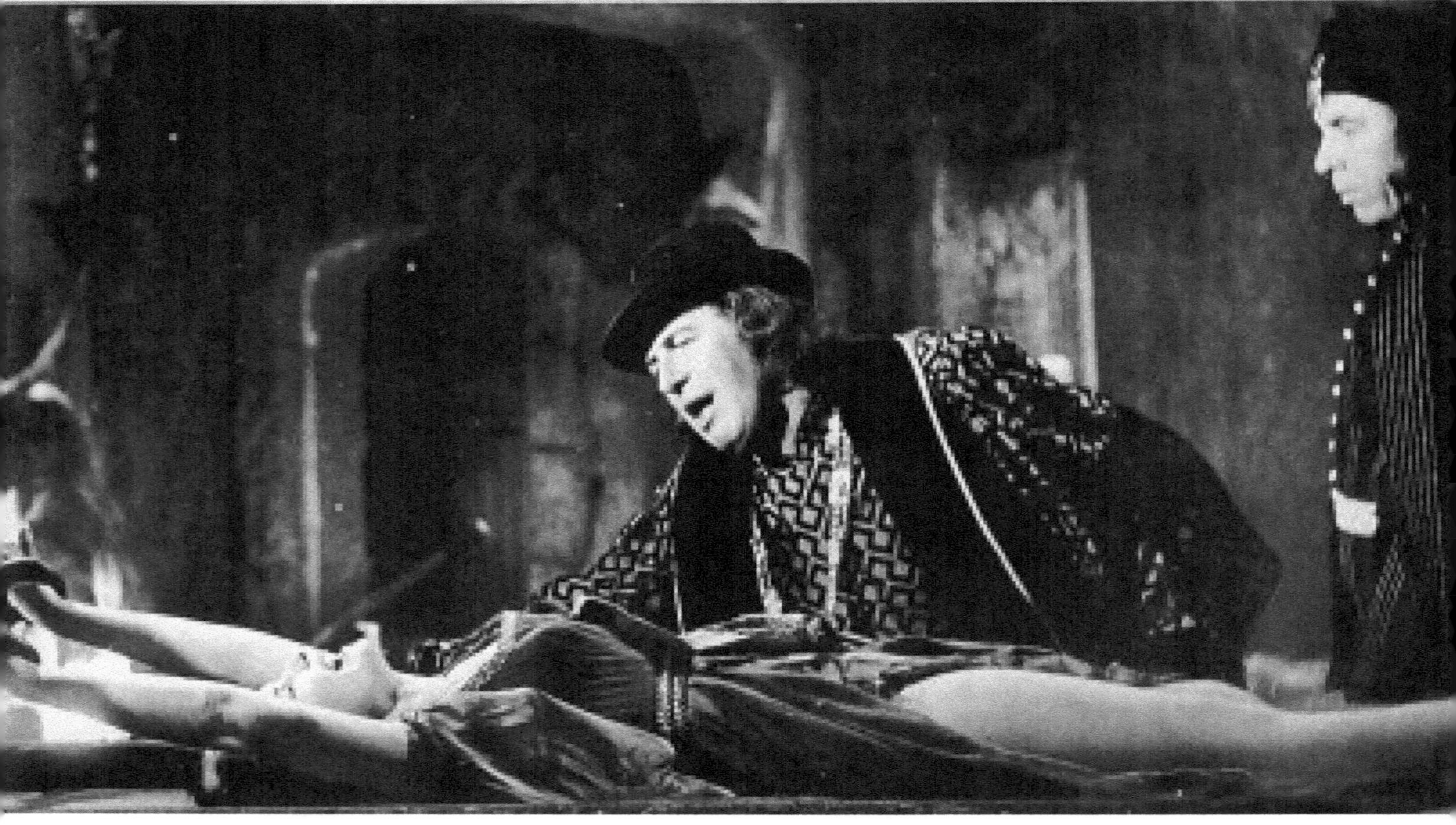

era Leo Gordon and Amos Powell.

The Cormans' picture includes a full catalog of the torture instrumentation of medieval punishment and horror: the rack, iron maiden, lash, and other deathly devices are all seen in the course of Richard's diabolical campaigning for the crown. A rare head cage, into which a hungry rat is placed, is one of the more unusual torture devices Vincent Price as Richard III finds use for. (The rat, however, is a white pet dyed to look repulsive.)

The Tower itself, frequently referred to as "The Bloody Tower" in the course of its grim history, was re-created by Daniel Haller, noted art director who has served Roger Corman's scenic needs in the filming of the Poe stories. Temporarily placing Edgar Allan aside, Haller has constructed the Tower of London complete with wine cellar, great dining hall, foul-smelling dungeons, battlements, and living—and dying—chambers.

Authentic 15th century costumes, furniture, decorations, armor, and rare, valuable weapons are among the many inanimate attractions the brothers Corman have sprinkled on their latest effort. The weapons used in the climactic battle scenes, for example, matched in every way the weight and description of the tools of war in the days of Richard III. One mace was literally a museum piece, having been picked up on the battlefield after Richard's last battle.

The actors who donned the complete fighting armor had to also don long underwear, football shoulder and hip pads, to prevent bruises and chafing from the heavy metal. Price, though, received special treatment because of his six foot, four inch height. Vincent's suit armor was custom forged due to the fact that he exceeded by several inches the average height of the average warrior of the Middle Ages.

The cast around which Price plots to proclaim himself King of England features a n o t h e r notorious arch-villain, the bootlegging and Ness-fighting prohibition gangster Frank Nitti—in the person of movieland heavy Bruce Gordon. Another notable in the Cormans' cast is the truck driver's favorite Bus Stop waitress, Joan Freeman, now shoving aside the cups and saucers to serve the Queen of England as her lady-in-waiting.

The combination of Roger and Gene Corman and Vincent Price, in a tale of the terror-filled days of the Tower of London when heads rolled by the minute and tyranny was the topic of the day, is a cinema combination hard to beat.

Don't miss it. ●

In the role of King Richard III, star Vincent Price leads his crusade against usurpers of the crown.

Above: Janice Logan, Charles Halton, Victor Kilian, Albert Dekker, and Thomas Coffey in the opening sequence. Right: Albert Dekker as Dr Thorkel, the Cyclops, captures Janice Logan. Below: Dr Cyclops and his Radium Chamber

Dr Alex Thorkel clawed helplessly at his pair of spectacles. Smashed, he thought fearfully. Without them he would be blind and at the mercy of the *little ones!*

No. Only one lens was broken—he still had one eye left to see them, to pursue them.

Cackling, Thorkel clamped the half-ruined glasses over his weak eyes, and glared around the room, the naked bulb overhead shining like a spark of evil on the single thick lens, magnifying the glittering eye behind it grotesquely.

Now, he thought, I can seek them out. The little people who were trying to destroy him, his deadly enemies who were twelve inches tall.

The twelve inch high, would-be assassins hid from the looming monster towering above them, the huge slick-headed creature with a single burning eye, the mad giant, *Dr Cyclops.*

The year was 1940. In the United States, the threat of war hung on the horizon like a summer storm. Most Americans didn't see the threat, because they refused to look; Hollywood was offering them some good entertainment to look at instead.

For people who didn't want to think about Hitler, Paramount presented another monster—the classic celluloid creature, DOCTOR CYCLOPS.

One of the first full-color fantasy movies, this Dale Van Every production was directed by Ernest B. Schoedsack from the original screenplay by Tom Kilpatrick.

The screen version (from Charles Strong's novel) was headed by capable character actor Albert Dekker, who, as Cyclops, towered above such tiny humans as Janice Logan and Tom

THE

Quick as a wink, he shrunk people to pinhead-size and filled the movies with wide-scream terror in the days of narrow screen and narrower escapes

BIG
EYE

Charles Halton, in the hands of the madman

Coley. These actors were of course of normal measurements, but they were reduced on the screen to baby pygmies in never surpassed movie miniaturization.

You can still find people who have never seen this picture; but harder to find than a soap opera on radio today is a true fan of fantasy and horror who hasn't heard of its fame.

The picture began with the arrival of a select group of workers at Alex Thorkel's lab to assist him with his radiation experiments.

The laboratory, secreted far into the dark, feverish jungles of Peru, became a place of danger to Bill Stockton (Coley) and Mary Phillips (Janice Logan) when they came under the suspicion of neurotic, angry Dr Thorkel.

Seeing them as potential rivals, thieves who would snatch away his brilliant discoveries, Thorkel lured Mary, Bill Stockton and three other men into his radiation chamber and bathed them in the sparkling fires of radium.

The five people tried desperately to escape from the terrible chamber, then fell one by one, exhausted.

When Stockton at last opened his eyes he discovered that Mary was the size of a doll. So was he and the others! The unknown properties of the radiation had shrunk all of them down to twelve inches in height, leaving them at the mercy of a madman.

Somebody up there hated them, and it was Thorkel. Realizing that the tiny people would soon grow up on him and regain their original size, the scientist had to take further action. The first step was to grab up a butterfly net and pursue the waspishtongued, insect-sized Dr Rupert Bullfinch (Charles Halton). Finally netting the protesting mite, the scientist popped the diminutive doctor into a bottle of lethal chloroform-vapor.

Witnessing this murder of one of their fellows, Stockton, the girl, and the two remaining men darted into the deep shadows of the surrounding jungle—scampered for their lives.

The little people fled through rivers of rain only to come face-to-snout with the king of all crocodiles which suddenly loomed before them, large as a prehistoric monster. A nightmarish battle for survival thrashed the jungle growth; a fury of lashing armored hide and soft human flesh.

When the stillness came, the river creature was dead. But now the exhausted humans had to face the crazed Cyclops who stood over them with a shotgun that looked like twin cannons.

The roar of the shotgun tore away the life of one of the party, and as Thorkel set fire to the grass where they hid, the two men and the girl who remained were forced to gallop away. By luck, they found a place of concealment—Thorkel's portable insect specimen box.

Returning to his home base, the scientist set the specimen box down, and went to sleep.

Inside the box, the men and the girl stirred.

The trio hid Thorkel's spare glasses, and sought out the gigantic shotgun that had taken one of their own number. Working together, they aimed the weapon and fired.

The blast tore away Thorkel's spectacles, but unfortunately not his head. Recovering his now single-lensed glasses, Cyclops prowled madly about his lab, tipping over boxes, knocking over bottles and containers, blasting away with his shotgun.

Outside, the pursuit continued right to the edge of the hundred feet deep pit, the radioactive source of Thorkel's Radium.

One of the harassed humans was out on the plank that spanned the fiery pit. Thorkel discarded his gun to belly out on the wood support to crush his tiny victim with his bare hands, but the board splintered under his weight, and he dropped.

Grabbing the windlass rope (used for lowering his peculiar radiation accumulator machine), Thorkel clung in bubbling terror.

At last, Bill Stockton thought, as he used a broken scissors blade like a broadsword, slashing the rope through to drop the murdering Cyclops into the fires of an atomic hell.

Alex Thorkel was dead! but the fame of a great movie, Dr Cyclops, lives on. ●

Thomas Colby carries   half a pair of shears for a weapon

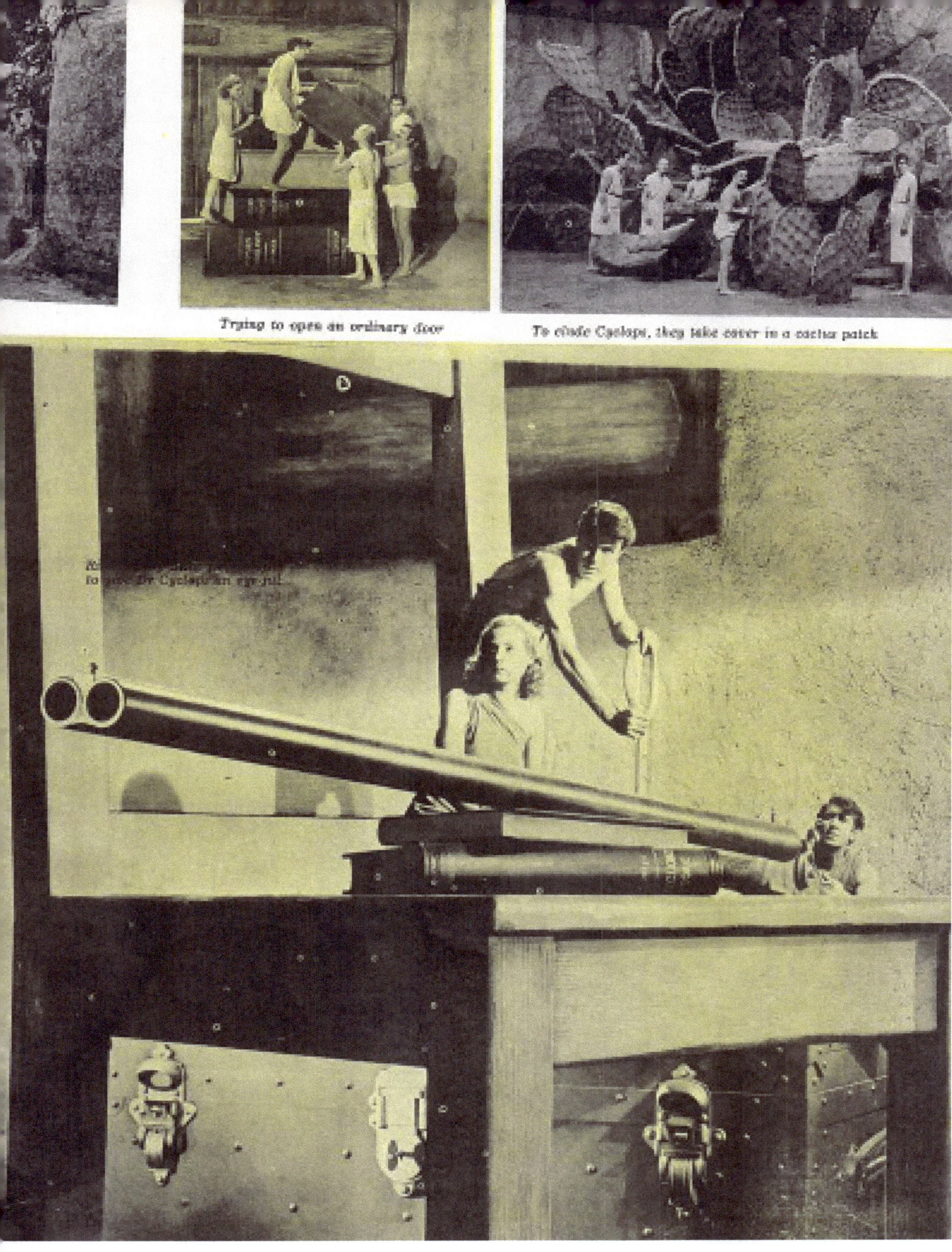

Trying to open an ordinary door

To elude Cyclops, they take cover in a cactus patch

Special effects ace and creature-creator *Paul Blaisdell*, pictured here with his *Venusian horror* from IT CONQUERED THE WORLD. *Blaisdell's other movie monsters include* THE SHE CREATURE, INVASION OF THE SAUCER MEN, IT — THE TERROR FROM BEYOND SPACE, *and* VOODOO WOMAN.

The teenage Wolf Man and Frankenstein Monster were united for HOW TO MAKE A MONSTER, *thanks to the talents of producer Herman Cohen (far left) and AIP makeup chief Philip Scheer.*

Behind every grotesque face, there's a hand — behind each helpless heroine's shriek, a writer — and for every Frankensteinian horror, an ace creator

MASTER MAGICIANS of Movieland

In the bygone days of the dragon and the unicorn, it was observed that "The juggler and the sleight-of-hand artist appear oft on our stages, but the spells of the true magician oft appear in his absence!"

So it is with the modern magicians of monsterland.

We rarely see these men of movie magic, but we know them by their spells that "oft appear" on the silver screen.

FANTASTIC MONSTERS presents a picture symposium of these special filmland personalities — the magicians of Hollywood whose writing, producing, and directing have built the fantasy factory that produces our favorite type of entertainment. ●

▲ Illustrated by sketches he himself made, Ray Harryhausen (left), the Dynamation Expert, points out to producer Charles H. Schneer how he intends to show live actors with giant land crabs for a sequence in THE MYSTERIOUS ISLAND.

Makeup Magician Dan Striepeke was chosen to create the weird and wonderful creatures seen in Bert I. Gordon's spectacular THE MAGIC SWORD. ▼

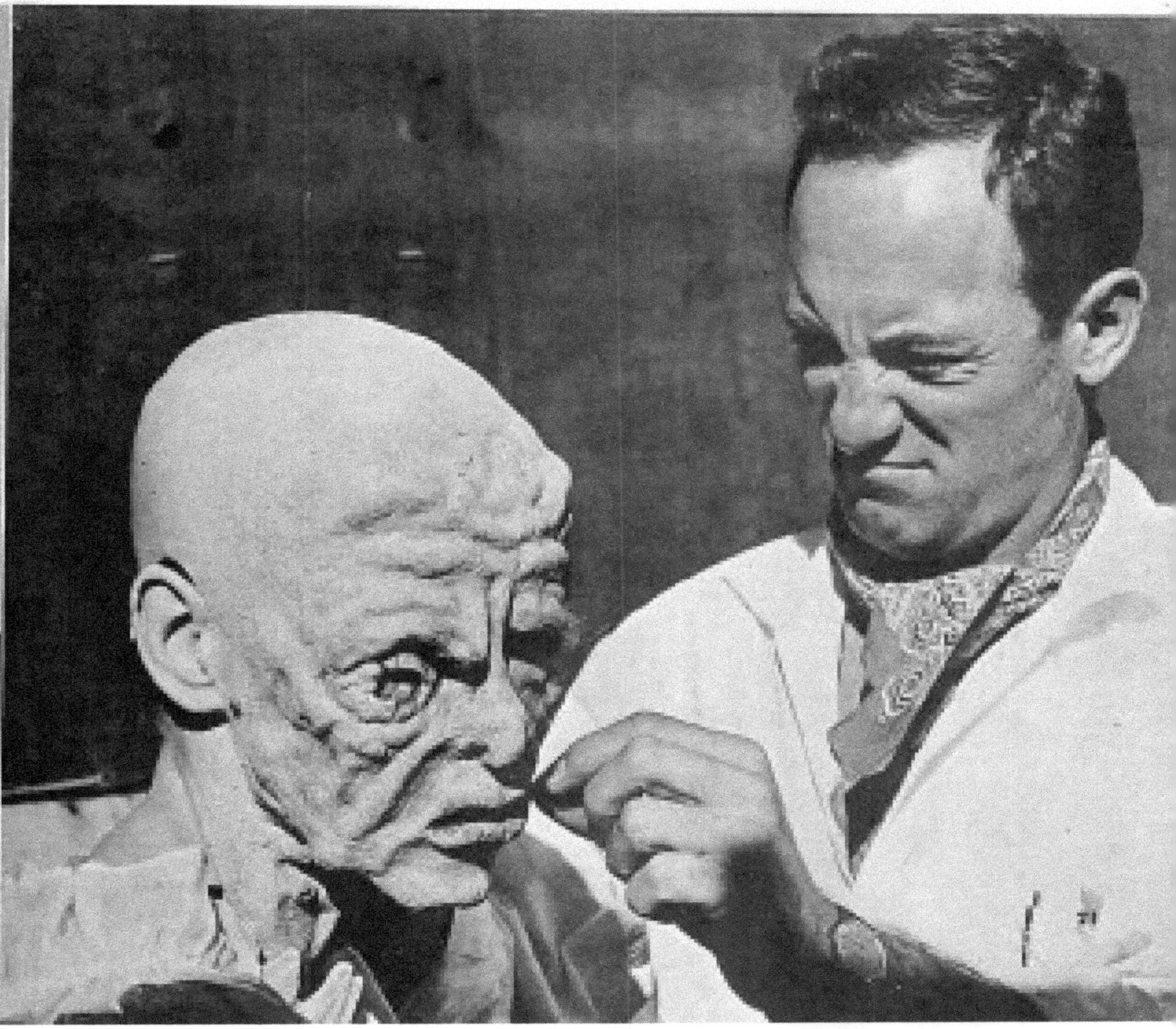

Director Spencer G. Bennet (left) and producer ▲ Alex Gordon, backstage. Famed for his serial directing, Bennet put Superman, Blackhawk, Purple Monster, Batman & Robin through their cliffhanger paces — while producer Gordon launched an ATOMIC SUBMARINE, stirred up THE SHE CREATURE, and recently discovered THE UNDERWATER CITY.

Director Virgil Vogel (middle) poses with one of THE MOLE PEOPLE while star John Agar looks on. ▼

On a lunch break during the filming of HOUSE OF USHER are James H. Nicholson (left), president of American-International Pictures, Vincent Price and Barbara Steele, co-stars of the AIP production. ▲

Jack Pierce, creator of Dracula, Wolf Man, and the Mummy, had a five and a half hour make-up job on his hands in transforming Glenn Strange into the roaring Frankenstein Monster for Universal's HOUSE OF DRACULA. ▼

Theatre audiences have been gasping and ducking every time producer William Castle conjures up another of his imaginative film gimmicks, his latest being THE OLD DARK HOUSE. ▼

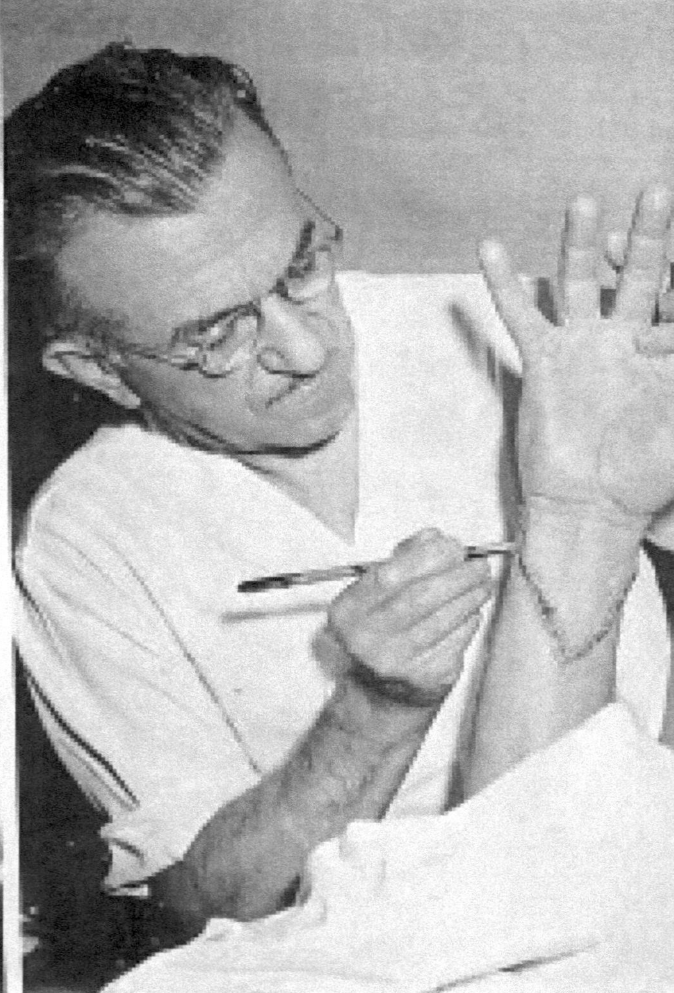

The acknowledged new High Priest of Cinematic Wizardry, producer-director-writer and special effects ace, Bert I. Gordon, on location for his excellent TORMENTED. ▼

When it comes to filming the strange tales of Edgar Allan Poe, producer Roger Corman (left) is the man for the job. Corman, whose new thriller is THE RAVEN, is seen here with star Vincent Price on the set of PIT AND THE PENDULUM.

The Man of a Thousand Faces, and the men who created each one—Bud Westmore (left), head of Universal's makeup department, James Cagney as the Lon Chaney Hunchback, and Jack Kevan, who made the monster. ▼

The unequalled Master of Suspense, Alfred Hitchcock, in one of his more serious moods. The Master has just released THE BIRDS, is shaping THE MIND THING, and is hosting his great CBS-TV hour suspense series.

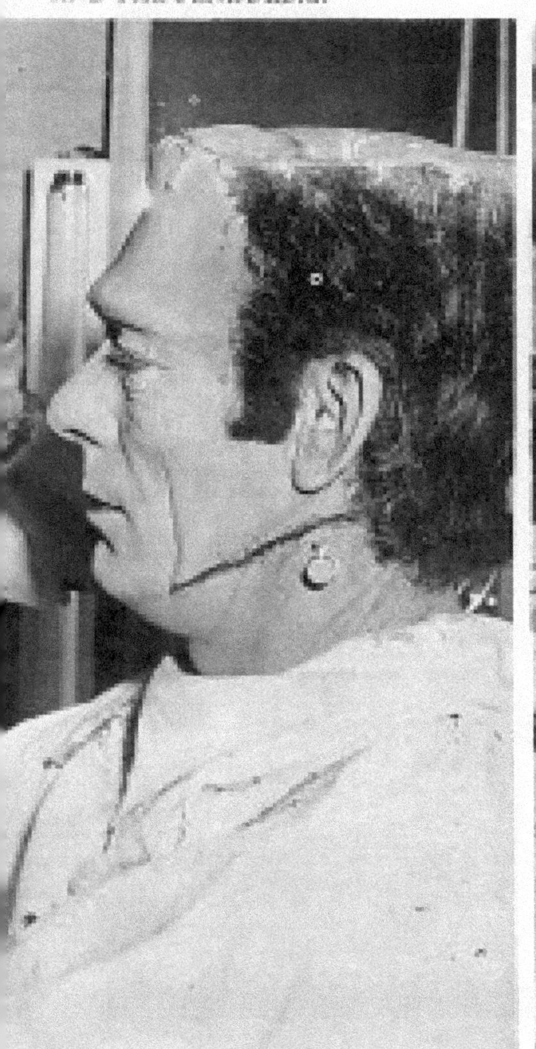

Top: James Allardice is the veteran writer who is responsible for creating all those wonderfully witty comments with which Alfred Hitchcock opens and closes each segment of his teleseries. Below Left: Ray Bradbury, Dean of Science-Fiction Writers. The author of such classic works as THE MARTIAN CHRONICLES and THE ILLUSTRATED MAN, Ray has contributed to films with features like IT CAME FROM OUTER SPACE and BEAST FROM 20,000 FATHOMS. Below Right: The Man Who Went PSYCHO, Mrs. Bates' favorite son—Robert Bloch. Bob, whose cinema credits include CABINET OF DR CALIGARI and THE COUCH, has just completed the screen adaption of Bradbury's short "The Black Ferris", and is currently scripting for TV.

SCREAM SCENES

"Out here in El Paso, we hear a lot about the wolves of the range," writes reader Mix, who tells us his friends call him Tom, "but I'm a modern, red-blooded, monster-loving Westerner, and my favorite kind of beast is a werewolf."

FANTASTIC MONSTERS' biggest booster in the Lone Star State tells us he has a picture of every movie werewolf in his photo collection — except one.

Pardner, your description of the missing monster is a mite vague, but staffer Jim Harmon came up with the answer (our Associate Editor, incidentally, has written several books on the subject of wolves, and is, as Authentic Science Fiction puts it, a "noted American scientist"). Harmon turned the film's title over to Bob Burns, the Research Editor (whose specialty is werewolves), and Bob turned his scene-by-scene still collection from the film over to Editorial Director Paul Blaisdell for him to apply his award-winning artistic ability to selecting the best shot. After a four-way telephone conversation with our leader, Ron Haydock, who once wrote a song that mentioned the full moon (something that affects werewolves) we are able to present reader Mix with this selected scene from The Undying Monster, the 20th Century-Fox Production starring furry-faced John Howard, filmed in 1942.

Frankly, Tom, it was more trouble than it was worth. No more letters from you, please. ●

THE DEVIL COMMANDS

And Karloff obeys, bridging the gap between the living and the dead, in a Columbia Pictures thriller-chiller

by Larry Byrd

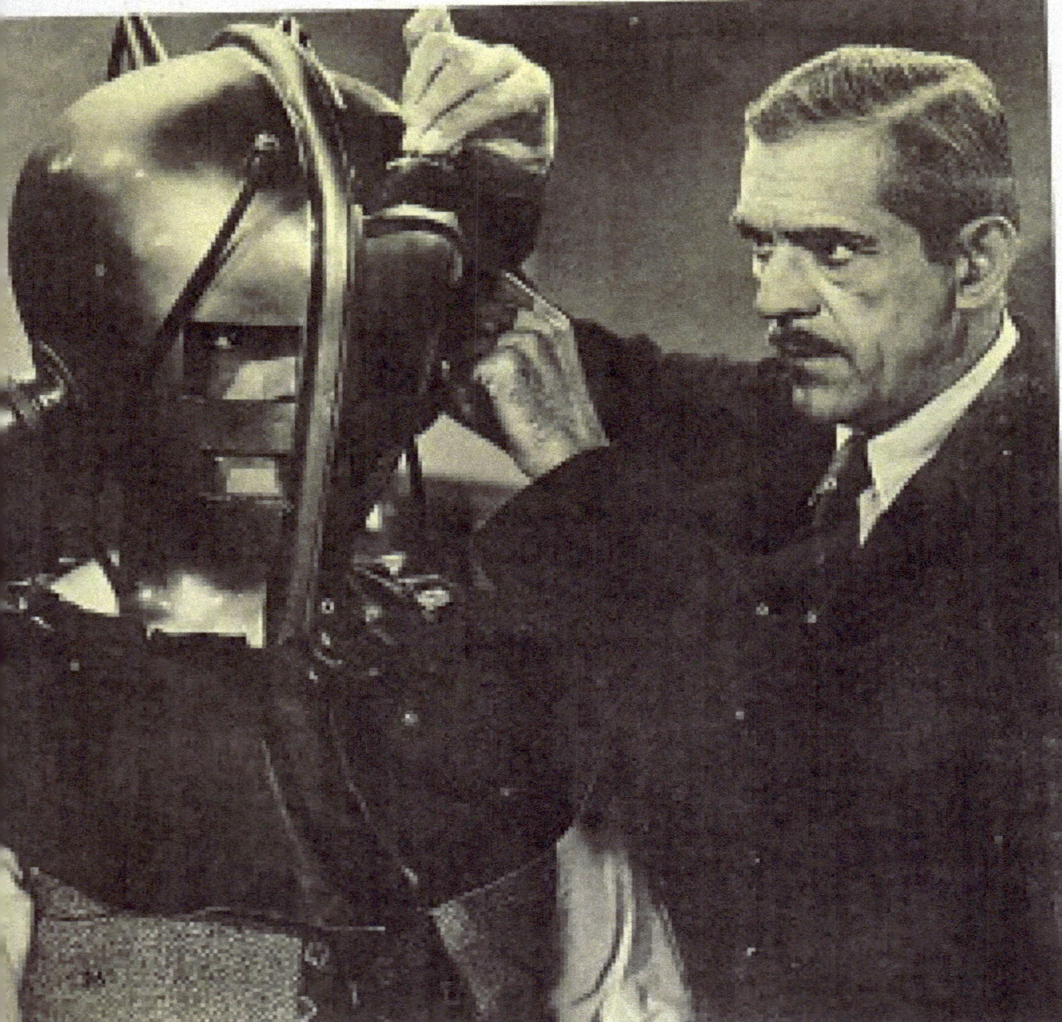

The cold, blue laboratory lights glinted and shimmered on the metallic armor of the weird, insulated figure seated in the corner of the room. The atmosphere tingled with the pungent smell of ozone, as the high pitched whine of the generators increased in volume. Instrument needles crawled across their dials and lighted panels went mad as the warning colors of their blinking lights increased alarmingly.

The armored figure twitched suddenly, as ever increasing voltage was pumped into its brain. The ear-like glass antennae on either side of the domed helmet glowed and sparkled. The face was inscrutable behind the tinted glass of the visor.

A light of expectation illuminated the face of Doctor Julian Blair. Perhaps this time he would triumph. Perhaps this time he would at last succeed in sensitizing a human mind with high frequency radiation to the point where it could communicate with the world beyond the grave, and make the age-old mystic's dream come true. To talk with the dead!

For years, Julian Blair had sought the secret of life beyond the grave, and every new experiment seemed to bring him closer to his goal. His electrical apparatus and the armored casing that enclosed his subjects had been improved and expanded until they dominated the entire laboratory, just as the incredible idea of communication beyond the grave had expanded until it dominated every waking moment of his thoughts. His

Mrs. Walters, the spirit medium, conducts a séance

daughter, Anne, and his former assistant, Richard Sayles, had become increasingly alarmed as his single-mindedness of purpose threatened his overworked brain with insanity.

Having pushed his illegal experiments to their limit, he finally killed his housekeeper with high voltage discharges from his unique electrical machines.

Desperate for another subject, he found, at last, what well might be the ideal person to help him pierce the barrier of death—Mrs. Walters, the famed spirit medium. Having devoted her own life in attempts to communicate with the world of departed beings, she agreed to help Blair in his illicit experimentation.

Yet, for all of Doctor Julian Blair's scientific knowledge and Mrs. Walters' experience in the world of the occult, this experiment also came to a disastrous end. The spirit medium died in Doctor Blair's mad robot-like casing, and in so doing perhaps became part of the very world of death that she ironically devoted her life to seeking out!

Questioned by Dr Sayles, played by Richard Fiske

His mind slipping away under the strain of what was fast becoming a series of scientific murders, Blair, in a fit of fanatic desperation, attempted to induce his own daughter Anne to undergo the test of his electrical bridge between the living and the dead. As he attempted to force her into the apparatus, he was interrupted by the arrival of his former assistant, who frantically tried to rescue Anne from her insane father. As Richard pulled Anne to safety, the activated electrical bridge between life and death built up to an insane crescendo of power. The pulsations of high-voltage energy and high-frequency radiations were at last beyond the ability of even their inventor to control. With a final thunderous blast, the fantastic machine exploded, killing Doctor Julian Blair and reducing itself forever into a harmless fused mass of coils, tubes, generators and insulators.

Perhaps somewhere in the smoking, sparking debris lay the answers to the secret of life and death that Doctor Julian Blair had attempted to discover for himself, alone and unaided by any scientific discovery. When the Devil commanded, Julian Blair had obeyed, and ultimately paid the price that the Prince of Darkness extracts from his victims.

Adapted in 1941 from an original story by William Sloane, The Devil Commands was typical of an era of low budget pictures that starred the redoubtable Boris Karloff. Mr. Karloff, to his everlasting credit, managed to carry most of these pictures "on his back" with his typical portrayal of solid, believable menace, backed by a convincing and hard working cast of supporting characters.

Particularly commendable was the portrayal of the medium, Mrs. Walters, by Anne Revere. Her "other worldliness" was calculated to send shivers down the spines of those who expected shivers to be the sole weapons of Boris Karloff. This haunting couple worked long and hard to lend a living atmosphere of conviction to the scientific gadgetry so artfully constructed by the special effects man to create the impression of a laboratory.

Amanda Duff as Karloff's daughter and Richard Fiske as her boyfriend managed to establish a solid base around which the screen's greatest portrayer of mad scientists revolved. As the heroine and hero of *Devil Commands*, they finally managed to thwart the efforts of the mad scientist who had the usual problem of all mad scientists: trying to move out of this world, and into the next.

Perhaps it's just as well Karloff never achieved his goal. We'd have all been disappointed if we had to leave the land of make-believe without witnessing Mr Karloff's cold-blooded sacrificing of human lives to further his own inventions! ●

Mrs Walters and Dr Blair, hypnotised by the spark of life

Don't shoot, Dadda! We're engaged!

Stoned again, huh?

That kid of mine is pretty clever with his hands, huh, Clarence?

Dead Time Tales

Swiped from Mother Goose Pimple's new book I Slit You Not

Ella, you know perfectly well you are standing on my foot, don't you?

No, no, you can't have it! It's my Magic Friendship Ring!

But the spirit of Santa lives in every one of us . . .

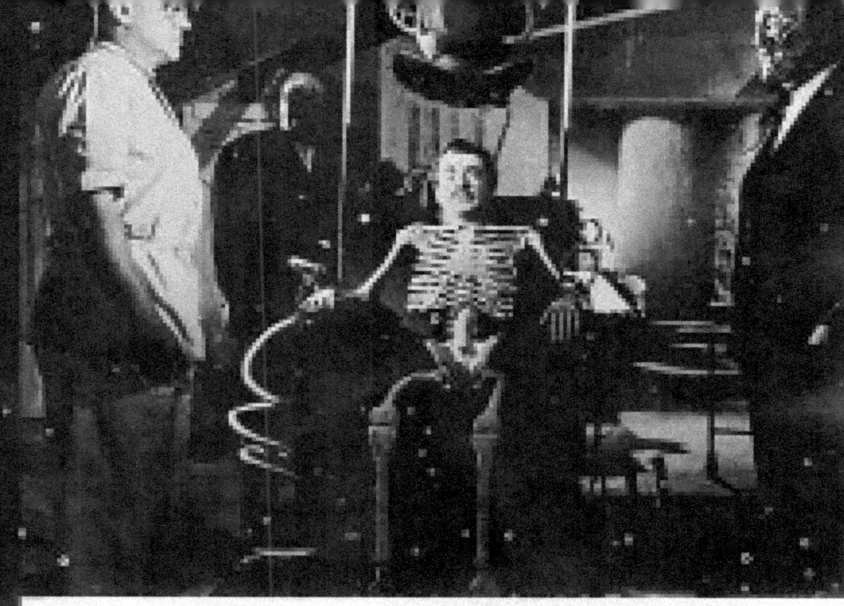

And here, Smedley, is a classic case of iron deficiency anemia . . .

Golly, Judy, you Americans sure have fun on the Fourth of July!

He's coming! The white horse and the Indian are with him and he looks mad!

Smells a bit, doesn't it?

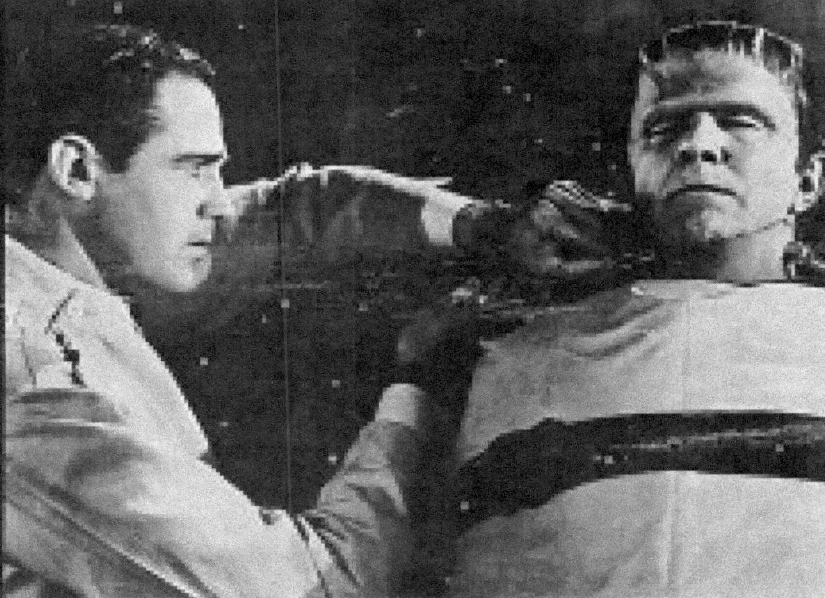

Mr. Dewhurst, I hope next time you will be a little more careful about sticking your head into television sets!

Name The Nameless MONSTER CONTEST

Win a Giant Kong-Size Monster Pin-Up of Your Favorite Fantastic Monster or Horror Star!

There's nothing to buy — nothing to sell!

Anyone can enter!

The Colossal creature (seen on the right) from Golden Eagle Films' THE CLIFF MONSTER is waiting for a name only YOU can give him!

All you have to do is think up an original name for this Nameless Monster, fill out the entry blank coupon below, and mail it in!

Name the Nameless Monster contest is as easy to enter as pulling wings off a bat!

Grand prize winner will receive a giant, premounted — size 30"x60" — monster pin-up of his or her choice! Would it be Karloff, Wolf Man, She Creature, Lugosi, others? You tell us!

25 2nd PRIZES — big color monster movie posters, like the ones you see at theatres, for your clubroom or den!

25 3rd PRIZES — glossy filmland monster photos, terrific for framing!

THIS IS THE MONSTER CONTEST YOU'VE BEEN SCREAMING FOR!

READ THE OFFICIAL CONTEST RULES! GIVE THE NAMELESS MONSTER A NAME! SEND IN YOUR COUPON! DO IT NOW!

OFFICIAL ENTRY BLANK COUPON

NAME THE NAMELESS MONSTER CONTEST
TOPANGA, CALIFORNIA

Here is my ORIGINAL NAME for the Nameless Monster:

_______________________ . If I am judged WINNER by

FANTASTIC MONSTERS-GOLDEN EAGLE FILMS, I want a

GIANT MONSTER PIN-UP of _______________________

Name _______________________

Address _______________________

City _______________ Zone _____ State _______________

OFFICIAL CONTEST RULES

1. Mail the ENTRY BLANK COUPON below, along with your ORIGINAL NAME for the Nameless Monster.

2. You may enter as many times as you wish, but each name must be accompanied by A SEPARATE ENTRY BLANK COUPON — no facsimiles or copies of the ENTRY BLANK COUPON will be accepted.

3. The FANTASTIC MONSTERS-GOLDEN EAGLE FILMS NAME THE NAMELESS MONSTER CONTEST closes at midnight, March 31, 1963. All entries must be postmarked before then to be eligible.

4. Winners will be judged on the basis of originality and thought.

5. Anyone may enter — except employees of Black Shield Publications, Inc., and Golden Eagle Films, its affiliates or families.

Zarkov and Gordon, pursued by Azura's airships. Below Left: Flash and friends, Dale Arden, Dr Zarkov, Happy Hapgood, and Prince Barin of Mongo. Below Right: Ming the Merciless plans evil with his High Priest

Flashing across interplanetary space is the "Ancient Race" riot, that Cotton-Cuddled Corpse, the Mad Mummy, coming to call on the yellow-haired youth of Mongo

"One of these days, kid—right to the moon!"

That's what I'm told somebody used to threaten. It's a pretty awesome threat certainly, but being told you are headed for Mars is even more unsettling.

After all, I just got here (after being d e a d for several thousand years), and I would just as soon not leave again.

Still, to Mars I was going. That was the written memo I got when I reached my desk at the offices of FANTASTIC MONSTERS.

Immediately I headed for the editor's office to protest. I figured on making a good impression with my new set of threads—tweed bandages.

There the surly, rewrite-demanding editor informed me that the Martian trip was part of my duties as the FanMo movie reviewer.

Why, I demanded, did I need to go all the way to the Red Planet just to view a film?

The hawk-faced, beady-eyed, blue pencil-wielding editor told me to re-read his memo.

Looking at the paper again through the slits in my face wrappings, I read:

Mummy:
This issue you take TRIP TO MARS
        Your Master, the Editor

Of course, the editor informed me, the full title of the movie I was to take on for the current issue was *Flash Gordon's Trip to Mars.*

I grinned, suggested he give me a raise (how does he expect a man to live on six Tana leaves a week?), and he kicked me out of his office.

With no choice in the matter, I headed for FANTASTIC MONSTERS' file room and film library. The huge

MAD MUMMY'S
TRIP TO MARS

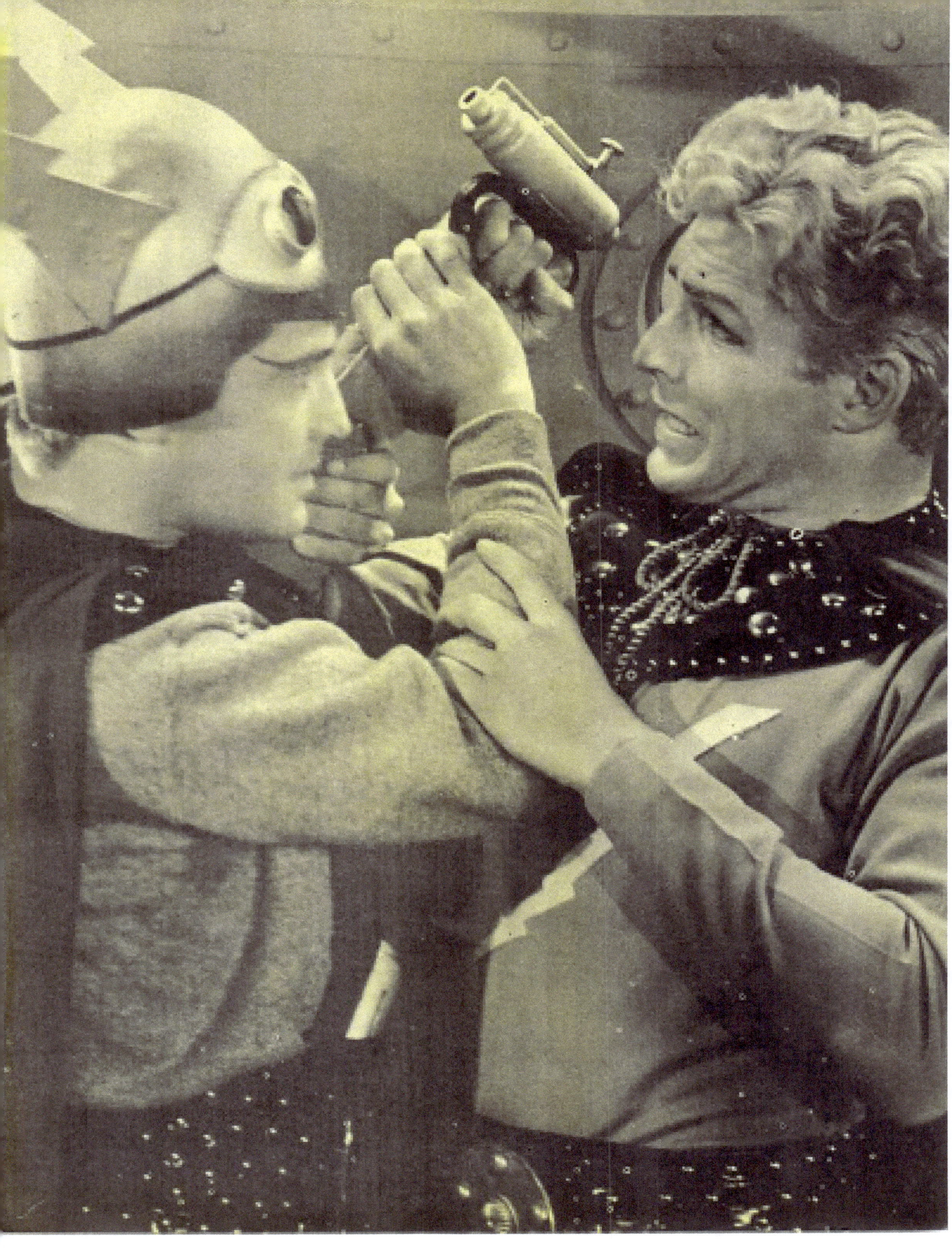

Flash takes prisoner Zarkov to Queen Azura's palace

Trapped in the Martian tomb

place is like a tomb, but even that didn't cheer me up much.

I did note with some small satisfaction that the simple-minded editor was wrong about the movie's title. Sort of. The 1938 Universal serial was released as *Flash Gordon's Trip to Mars* all right, but there was an edited-down feature film brought out as *Mars Attacks the World*; and the serial version plays on TV under the title *Space Soldiers' Trip to Mars*.

I set up the projector and reeled the film off.

It starts off great!

Mammoth storms rage across the face of Earth. Empire State Building-size tidal waves smash against the shore-lines of all continents. Great cities topple, nations tremble.

It looked like all human life was going to be wiped out, but there is always something to louse up things when they are going good.

In this case, it's the bearded Dr Zarkov (Frank Shannon), who is building a rocketship to go to Mars. The egg-shaped crate looks a little risky to me: I doubt if NASA would ever approve it.

But Flash Gordon, the big blond cheese (swim champ Buster Crabbe), is so hot to get into the spaceship he parachutes out of an airplane to get to the launching site. Maybe the fact that the plane is being pulled apart by one of the storms raging across the world has something to do with it.

Meeting up with his girlfriend, Dale Arden (Jean Rogers), Flash goes to the bearded inventor.

"Flash," Zarkov says, "I think the cause of Earth's destruction comes from Mars. We must go there and stamp out the source of the danger."

As the mammoth storm outside rips away one wing of the house, Flash agrees that it would indeed be best to make a fast getaway.

Blasting t h r o u g h interplanetary space, the Earth Trio discover a stowaway, the nosy young reporter, Happy Hapgood. He says he wants to help out. Personally, I think he just wanted to get in out of the rain.

turn to page 62

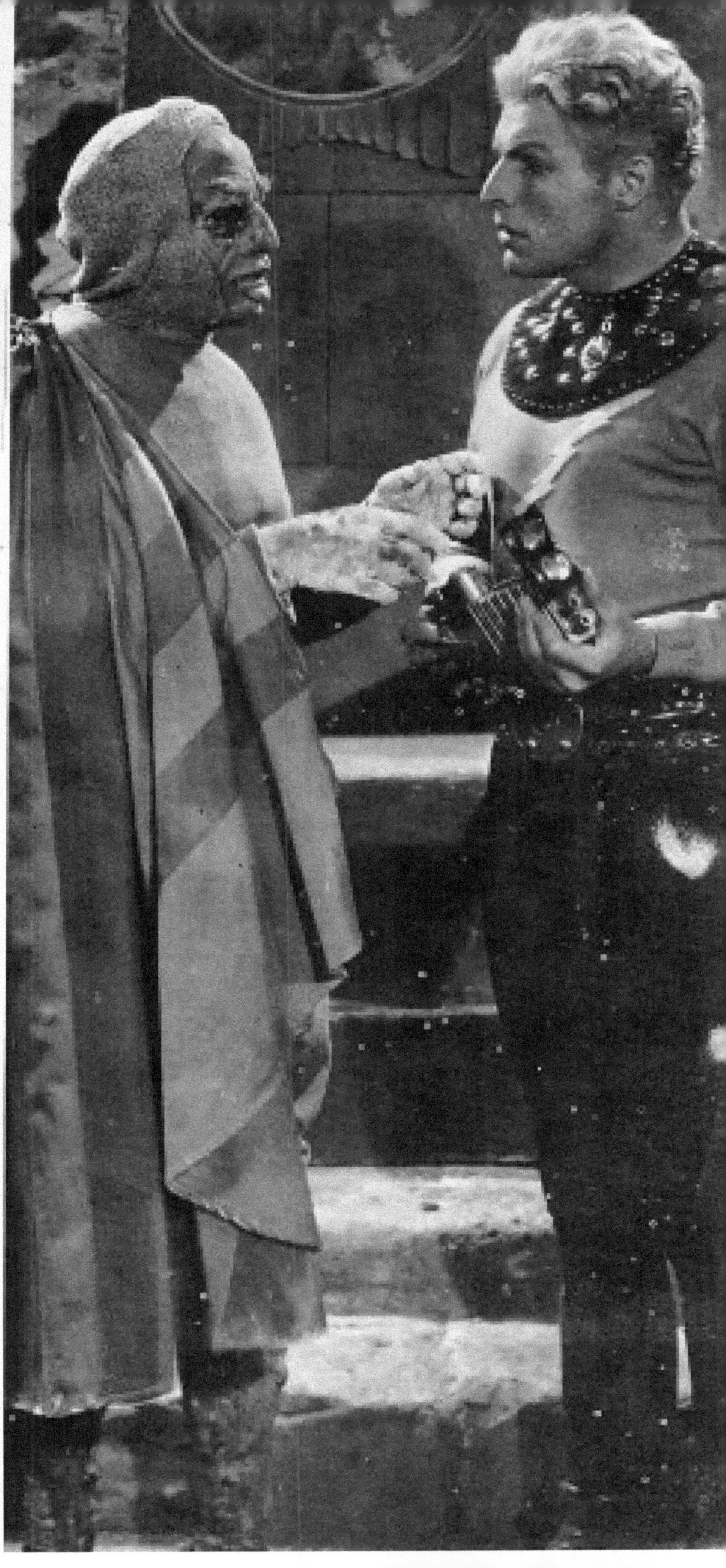

"You must capture Azura and wrest from her the secret of her clay curse," the Clay King tells Flash.

As a train waits eerily in the darkness, and the clock chimes midnight, a man flees through the night from a hideously disfigured hunchback, dispatched by a scarlet-robed High Priest of an ancient cult, sent to slice off the hounded man's head and carry it away to distant Tibet.

This is the wild, wonderful thriller you may have heard on the radio in the 'forties or fifties, or have seen adapted to the screen in a 1945 Columbia release. Both the motion picture and the original radio series that inspired the film were called *I Love a Mystery*.

There were two other pictures in the movie series about detectives Jack Packard (Western veteran Jim Bannon on the screen) and Doc Long (Barton Yarborough). The *Unknown* was a tale of a haunted Southern mansion, sinister grave robbers, secret passages, and a prowling cloaked phantom of the night, who carried a crying baby doll. In 1946, *Columbia* let us see behind *The Devil's Mask* to reveal a story of a sly hypnotist, a man who spoke from the grave, and a fiend who shrunk human heads to the size of a gnarled fist.

These were the three stories inspired by *I Love a Mystery* in the movies, but there were many others on the air during the Golden Age of radio. The rest of this report on ILAM will concern itself with the broadcast exploits of Jack Packard, Doc Long, and their third pardner (who did not appear in the film version), Reggie York.

Sometimes working as operators for the A-1 Detective Agency, the Three Comrades investigated the supernatural, hidden jungle temples, and weird super-criminals — much like such adult evening programs as *The Shadow*; but the ILAM radio series was serialized in the style of the afternoon adventure kings, *Captain Midnight, Tom Mix, Superman*. The chapters were made distinctive in that each one was presented as one act of a play, a dramatic unity without breaks, a format used in the soap operas about noble wives, pioneered in the early thirties on *One Man's Family* by the writer-producer-director of both the *Family* program and ILAM, Carlton E. Morse.

Today, one of the greatest of all fantasy-adventure writers in any medium, Carlton Morse is one of the two scripters of radio character series to have won the Peabody Award, radio's "Oscar".

Recently, a letter from Morse came to a *FANTASTIC MONSTERS* staff

turn to page 46

I Love a Mystery — and so do millions of fans of the Modern Musketeers, Jack, Doc and Reggie, Timeless Radio Heroes, Inspiration for Three Chilling Movie Thrillers

TERROR IN THE AIR

Special Report by Jim Harmon

Extreme upper left: *Doc Long of HBS (Jim Boles)* guest stars with *Fat Man* sleuth, *Jay Scott Smart*. Box at left (L to R): *Michael Raffetto*, 1939 *Packard; Russell Thorson*, 1949 *Packard; Jim Boles, Tony Randall* as *Mutual* friends *Doc & Reggie*. Right: *Carlton E. Morse* and editorial associate *Jim Harmon* at radio master *Morse's estate, Seven Stones*.

Left: Jack and Doc (Jim Bannon, Barton Yarborough) are shown The Devil's Mask itself. Below left: The Unknown prowls menacing Packard and Long's dolls. Below: Jefferson Monk (George Macready) learns from the High Priest there's a tall price on his head in the first filmed I Love a Mystery.

Kirk Alyn, one-time Superman, again takes off like a Big Bird as Ace of Eagles, Blackhawk

MATINEE IDOL

One of the all-time serial kings is handsome, iron-jawed Kirk Alyn. The role of chief of the multi-lingual aviation adventurers group, Blackhawk (a 1952 Columbia Pictures release), offers Alyn an excellent chance to show his fine acting ability. He has also portrayed several comic strip heroes including Clark Kent (the Man of Steel) as well as a number of hardhitting detectives. Editor Ron Haydock learned from the still active and versatile actor that Alyn had also been offered the opportunity to characterize Captain America, Batman, and Flash Gordon at various times, but declined because of previous commitments—and, perhaps, an allergy to peroxide.

In the role of the chief Blackhawk, Kirk Alyn braves dangers ranging from fisticuffs near whirling airplane propellors to leaps from swooping aircraft into the rumble-seat of cruising convertibles to continue the rumble. He goes through all of this in order to clear one of the six Blackhawks (serial veteran Rick Vallin) from a false charge of treason, and bring to justice a gang of international criminals threatening the peace of the world.

The serial was produced by Sam Katzman and directed by Spencer G. Bennet. The staff of script writers was headed by George Plympton.

Script author Plympton told staffer Jim Harmon the studio had its problems with the Blackhawks as portrayed in the original Military Comics and the old ABC radio program. The speech accents of this international group were so varied and complex, the writer feared theatre audiences would need a course at Berlitz Schools of Language to understand Andre or Olaf saying "Dey vent dotaway" or "Ve vill head zem off at zee landing strip".

Fortunately for serial fans, these fifteen chapters are understandable and enjoyable, one of the last great milestones in the tradition of sky high continued cinema, and a credited starring role for sometimes anonymous Superman, always super serial star, Kirk Alyn. ●

A captive Marilyn Manning is given a tour of the Cave of Mummies by host Kogah, latest Fairway-International release.

HORRORSCOPE

The three Opera Phantoms—Lon Chaney, Claude Rains, and the newest, Herbert Lom. Relax: it's Madness by Terror for Mexico's Dr. Cyclops.

American-International's Big Ones boast the Big Three: Boris Karloff, Vincent Price, and Peter Lorre. American-International contracted them to star in a thriller series smacking of the Universal heydays of Karloff, Lugosi, and Chaney Jr. First up is a remake of the 1935 chiller The Raven, starring the three terror titans; their own separate AIP films follow.

Behind-the-scenes on the new Raven are House of Usher-Tales of Terror talents. Roger Corman, producing and directing the Richard Matheson screenplay. Another from AIP is Samson and the 7 Miracles of the World, starring tree-swinger Gordon "Tarzan" Scott free-swinging against Mongol warriors to destroy an entire city single-handed.

* * *

Jerome Curse of the Faceless Man Bixby is scripting two indies, Sea Demons and Fantastic Voyage, while island plant monsters is the budding plot of The Night Crawlers, from Murray Leinster's Monsters from the Earth's End (Gold Medal, 35c).

TV's favorite slapstick pie-hurler has disked Soupy Sales Up in the Air with hit tune "My Baby Has a Crush on Frankenstein".

* * *

"You've just heard another tale well-calculated to keep you in . . . Suspense!" And, the announcer Sunday, September 30, 1962, might have added: And you'll never hear another.

Suspense e n d e d. Johnny Dollar closed his last crime case. Radio died.

The rock 'n' roll went on, the conversation continued, but all that made radio great was gone. Now everyone who can remember the Golden Age of Radio will speak of radio as a close relative, now dead.

That Sunday the final dramatic shows went off radio. There are a few religious dramas on AM, an occasional ancient classic on FM, but all the great, popular characters went with Dollar's final signature, the last well-calculated Suspense.

Raymond opened no more the squeaking door to the dark dread of the Inner Sanctum. The Shadow at last knew what evil lurked in the hearts of broadcasting executives and advertising men. Not even the silver bullets of the Lone Ranger could stop the vampire of television from sucking the lifeblood from its older, more imaginative, better-loved b r o t h e r, radio.

Radio will never die in the memory of all those who rode with Tom Mix, flew with Captain Midnight, hopped a freight with Jack, Doc and Reggie.

Listen, broadcasters—the buzz of the Green Hornet, the air whoosh of Superman, the growing rumble of protest from the public. We're coming! We remember radio, and we'll never let you forget it.

You can never destroy magic. It never dies. It only sleeps. ●

The Slapstick Trio get Space Sick when they are stuck with some Menacing (But Merry) Martians in the new Columbia triumph — THE 3 STOOGES IN ORBIT

3 STOOGES MEET THE MARTIANS

by Ron Haydock

As we go to press, six men — two Americans and four Russians — have been rocketed into orbit around the Earth.

No, we have to make that nine men.

Columbia Pictures has added three to the ledger on the American side with Larry, Moe, and Curly Joe. With a few lenses and solar power in the guise of sunlight, Columbia has launched the Three Stooges way out there by laugh-propulsion.

In this, their fourth feature-length movie (*Three Stooges Meet Hercules, Snow White & the Three Stooges,* and *Have Rocket, Will Travel* were 1, 2, 3), Larry, Moe, and Curly Joe are bottom, middle and top banana on a television epic which must slide into a new format, or fall on hard times.

Booted out of their apartment for unpaid rent, about to lose their video berth, the Stooges answer a "Rooms for Rent" classified ad and stumble into a cheerless castle dubbed Hawk Hill Manor. Their new landlord is a wild-eyed inventor, Professor Danforth (Emil Sitka). His pet project is a vehicle to revolutionize warfare — a submarine-helicopter-tank. Sort of a helisubtank.

The mad scientist would, of course, have a beautiful daughter, Carol (Carol Christensen), but his servant, William, is a bit off-beat even for a hip mad mechanic — the servant is a Man from Mars.

William (Norman Leavitt) yearns for Danforth's invention, because the Martians are under the impression that only this remarkable craft can halt their planned annihilation of this planet.

The United States Air Force, in the uniformed presence of Captain Andrews (Edson Stroll), is dispatched to arrange a test of the invention for the top brass. Andrews also manages to get down to brass tacks with pretty Carol.

Ransom Bill (as William is sometimes known) botches his first attempt at snitching the nutty bundle of bolts that is the machine. Consequently, two more aliens, Ogg and Zogg (George Neise and Rayford Barnes) are fired to Earth to grab the scientific wonder and turn Earth into pure energy. Dan-

Professor Danforth (Emil Sitka) displays a model of his Helisubtank. Below: The amazing, super-scientific Helisubtank goes on

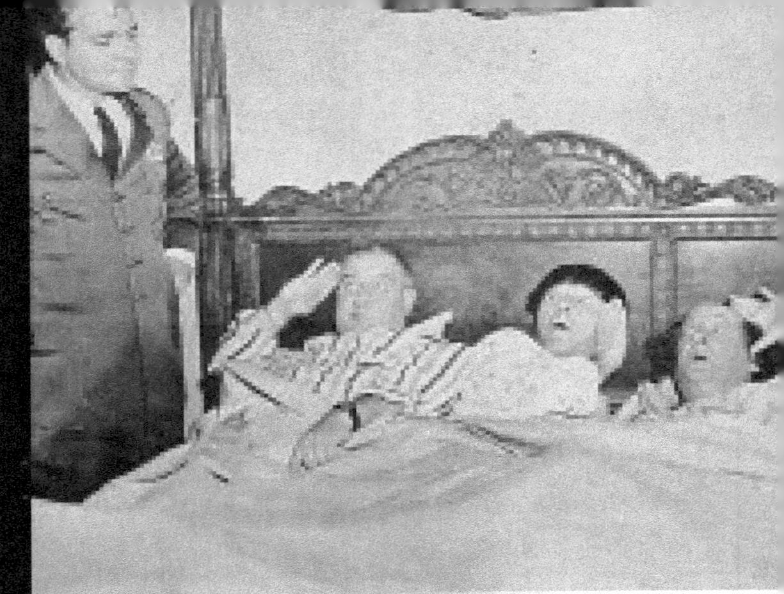

Don Lamond, host of Los Angeles' KTTV-TV Three Stooges show, has the role of Colonel Smithers in the new film. Don is also Stooge Larry's son-in-law

Below: Ogg and Zogg prepare to blast Earth

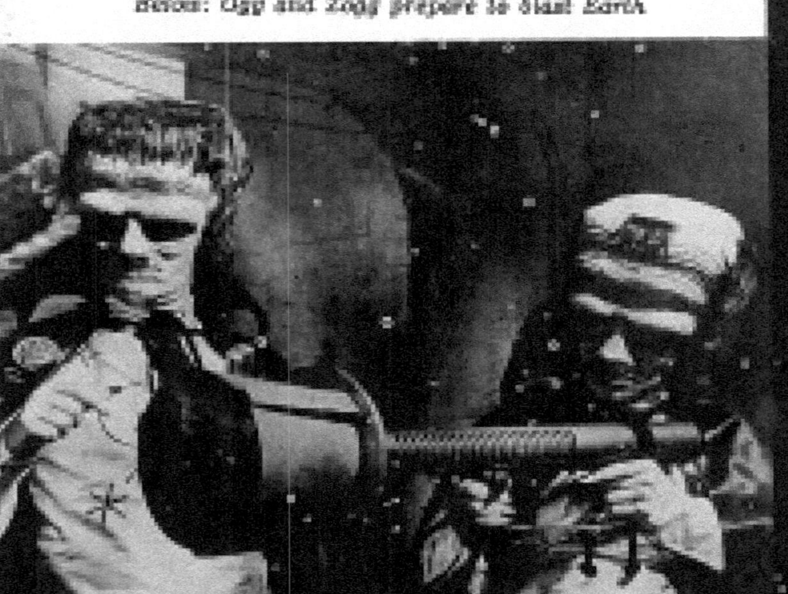

Below: Martians Hubie Kerns, Nestor Paiva, and Gay Way in Red Planet conference

Above: Larry, Moe, and Curly Joe find themselves on their way to Mars in the ridiculous invention piloted by Ogg and Zogg. Below: Cutting up on the Martian Space-A-Phones between scenes

forth vows to the Stooges he will whip up a fabulous new cartoon development for their drooping TV show if they will lend a hand in preparing his machine for the Fly Boys' USAF test and guard it against Martian spies.

The test fouls up, permitting the Martians to capture the device. The Three Stooges are trapped into going along for the rocket ride, clinging to the outer hull in magnetized spacesuits as the ship blasts off for the Red Planet.

A wild series of misadventures follow with Ogg and Zogg attempting to wipe out Earth; the Army, the Air Force, and Navy blast away at the Martian duo, and the Earthling Trio trys to zig-zag the crossfire.

The weird warfare and the weirder helisubtank, can't be described in words, only in a picture — *The 3 Stooges in Orbit*.

No strangers to TV with their ever-galloping comedy re-runs, the Stooges outdo themselves in this role as TV comics.

Also, this movie gives producer Norman Maurer a chance to film some effective scenes employing his newly-patented process, *Artiscope*. Artiscope permits filming "live" action — Larry, Moe and Curly Joe in a zany free-for-all — with automatic translation of the photographed people into the line drawing of cartoons. The result is an animated cartoon of figures drawn by machine, no human artist needed.

Maurer himself, along with comic strip artist Joe Kubert, illustrated and wrote *The Three Stooges* comic books which were originally published by the St. John company. Another Maurer contribution to funny books was his method of making 3-D drawings in red and blue for tinted spectacle viewing. This resulted in the world's first 3-D comic magazine, *The Adventures of Mighty Mouse*—one of the few comics ever written up in the Encyclopedia Brittanica.

Even more impressive in the 3 Stooges movie than Artiscope, perhaps, is the $15,000 thirty-foot-long submarine - helicopter - tank combo, still another brain-child of multifaceted Maurer.

This triumph of mad science is powered by a jeep, fitted into the bottom of the sub hull, and can actually make a top speed of 85 mph when breaking away from aroused film critics. Moving on tank treads, connected to the jeep's rear wheels by chain drive, the Stoogecraft has a 7½ hp golf cart motor spinning the monstrosity's blades at 300 revolutions per minute.

Middleman Larry, spending a morning's filming riding around in the abomination, came down complaining of feeling helisubtank sick. Worried producer Maurer rushed him to the studio hospital, and in a few minutes Larry snapped back with three variously-labeled pill bottles.

"Have to take one of each," Larry gulped. "The doctor isn't sure whether I'm sea-sick, car-sick, or air-sick!"

But Larry's problems are small compared to those he and his space-happy chums spin into while *in Orbit*.

The movie may not advance space science, but it will pep up ticket sales. For everybody who loves the great and almost vanished art of slapstick this picture is a must. ●

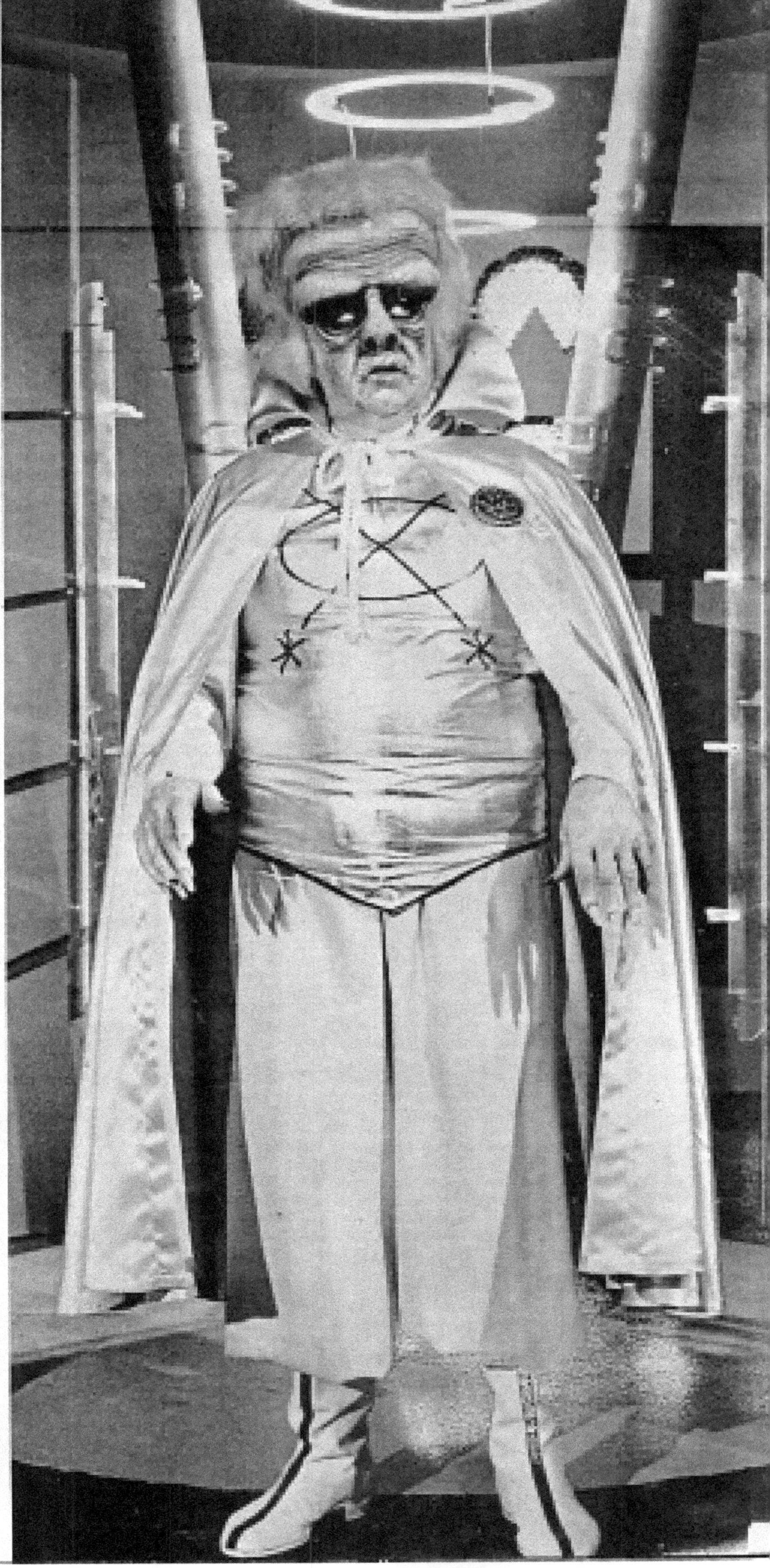

The *Warlord of Mars*, played by *Nestor Paiva*, who in 1942 attempted to bring doom to *Don Winslow of the Coast Guard* as the *nefarious Scorpion*.

member, a long-time admirer and correspondent of the master of radio drama. The latter revealed that Morse had returned from his vast Southwestern ranch to his mountain-top castle overlooking a great West Coast city, and that there was an opportunity for another visit.

Two of the FM staff drove several hundred miles through the night to finally begin climbing the curving, perilous mountain road, at last passing through the open gate of the electric fence to the forecourt of the towering stone structure that serves Carlton Morse as a summer home.

Morse, a sturdily built man of middle age or better, proved to be quiet but friendly.

In his Cadillac-showroom-size living room, Morse was eager to talk of the serious novel he is now writing. He also provided the information for this article.

The ILAM author revealed that there were some thirty-eight serial stories of Jack, Doc, and Reggie, averaging fifteen chapters each (down to five for *The Corpse in the Compartment,* murder on a transcontinental train; up to twenty-odd for *The Twenty Traders of Timbuktu,* African adventure).

Others among the serial thrillers were *My Beloved Is a Werewolf*—the tale of a wife who suspected her mate of strange prowlings, and the *Stairway to the Sun.* The "Stairway" led to a lost plateau on which resided a race of super-beings who controlled world destiny from their ancient temple. The temple was surrounded by a jungle infested with prehistoric monsters and inhuman submen. One of the high points of the story was a wild cross-country freight train ride with a fat, evil Maestro and his hypnotic slave, the beautiful Natsha. The trip took the happy band to the town of Bury Your Dead, Arizona.

The three central characters of the series were portrayed by vivid radio personalities in the original broadcasts from Hollywood, starting on NBC with half-hour weekly chapters in 1939, and ending the first day of 1945 with 15 minute daily chapters on CBS. In Hollywood, plain-spoken, rugged, Jack Packard was played by Michael Rafetto, who lives in well-earned retirement today. The two fine actors who were Doc and Reggie met early deaths, but are today remembered as radio legends. As the young Englishman, Reggie York, Walter Patterson's portrayal was perfect. And, as perhaps the best loved of the trio, easy-going, Texas-drawling Doc Long, the unforgettable Barton Yarborough.

Although Morse revealed that the characters of Jack, Doc, and Reggie were actually based on the original actors who played them, the threesome's legend outlasted some of their originators. In 1949, the Mutual radio network arranged for Carlton Morse to repeat his famous stories in New York City. This time the cast was Russell Thorson, Jim Bowles, and Tony Randall (now a movie comic) as Jack,

Doc, and Reggie. Mercedes McCambridge repeated some of her original Hollywood roles in New York, even after winning her movie Oscar.

Up until 1952, ILAM repeated many of its famous stories:—

In *The Fear That Creeps Like a Cat* an insane scientist again studied fear by letting a mountain lion loose on a deserted island with an unarmed man (such as Doc Long). The mansion-prowling phantom, who cried like a baby, renewed his pursuit of the three poor little rich Martin girls, *Faith, Hope,* and *Charity,* and, of course, Morse's most famous story demanded repetition. This was an epic about a hidden temple in the middle of the Central American jungles, which was inhabited by black-robed priests and priestesses who had the power to come and go through the air between the staggeringly high stone ledges that climbed the fabulous Temple of Vampires.

For a moment rest your eyes and view the giant screen of imagination that was radio . . .

The train whistle screams, a voice calls "I Love a Mystery", and the eerie organ plays *Valse Triste* hauntingly. The ancient clock strikes five—Five o'clock in the Temple of Vampires in the midst of the Central American jungle. Jack Packard and Doc Long climb a stairway up the side of the sting tower . . .

DOC: Honest to my Grandma, son, what's the use of climbing this overgrown staircase? We was up one just like it.

JACK: There's one difference. We weren't up *this* one.

DOC: Yeah, I suppose. Jack, how come you left Reggie guarding Sunny and the boy, not me?

JACK: Because I thought Reggie would make a more reliable guard.

DOC: That's a fine doggone thing to say . . . Hey—here we are at the top, and just like I told you. Same as the other.

JACK: Uh-huh. The ledge is the same, but not that wall. Look.

DOC: Hey, son—a door. There's a door in the wall.

JACK: Even a red-headed Texan ought to be able to figure that out . . . Doc, what are you doing now?

DOC: I'm opening up the door. What did you expect?

JACK: Maybe we had better see where it leads.

DOC: Funny pictures cut in the rock. People in long black robes, just like that hombre, Manuel . . .

JACK: Shut up, and give me a hand here.

DOC: I think it's coming . . . .

JACK: Look out, Doc!

DOC: Hey! Bats! The place is full of bats! Thousands of red-eyed, furry bats! Flying right in our faces! I can't stand 'em!

JACK: Doc, look out for the edge of the ledge! It's a couple of hundred feet straight down . . .

Valse Triste sings out again.

These are some of the thrills that are suggested in the Columbia theatre features now televiewing on the air, but they are part of the magic that can only be captured by the now unused wonder of radio. ●

MAD LAB RADIO

It appears to be one of those little imported transistor radios, but just turn it "on". WOW! The dummy speaker flies to one side and a "killer shrew" jumps out, with a wild squeal! Mad Lab radio is all metal, lithographed in four colors. Has fold-down carrying handle, three dimensional dummy dial and working "off-on" switch, which releases "shrew". YOU invite your buddy, or girl friend, to turn on your Mad Lab radio, then watch them climb the wall, when the squealing "shrew" leaps out at them! Only $1.00, postpaid.

VAMPIRE DEVIL RING

Shades of Count Dracula! It looks like it came straight from his castle, in the Carpathian Mountains! A gleaming, scowling, silvery Devil's head. Great for club or costume make-up. Deeply carved horns, brow, nose, beard and "vampire fangs". These are set off by flaming simulated ruby eyes. Good quality and massive, a real conversation piece! Let us know your ring size with order. $1.

MAD LAB CAMERA

Looks like expensive sub-miniature camera, but wait until you press the secret button! Lens swings open, and with a terrific squeal, a "Killer Shrew" leaps out! Camera has viewfinder, dummy winding knob, carrying case, realistic lens mount. Authentic black crinkle finish with silver-gray trim! Furry "Killer Shrew" and "squealer" concealed inside. Lens locks in place until you push the shutter release! You'll have your friends jumping for the ceiling with the MAD LAB CAMERA! Only $1.00, postpaid.

MAD LAB HYPO

Life size! 8 inches, fully extended! Needle appears to pierce "victim's" skin! Concealed button gives illusion of Hypo filling up with "victim's" blood! Can also be used in reverse, to "inject" blood— then show Hypo apparently empty! The illusion is absolutely perfect, even close up! This glittering, wicked-looking instrument is quality made of crystal clear styrene plastic, with metal head and "needle"! Scientific calibrations marked along body! Don't use around friends with weak stomachs! Only $1.50, postpaid

MAN MOON MASCOT

Poor little Moon Man! Looks like he's "way out there", and he can't get back. This lovable little guy is all head, hands, and feet. Put him on a lamp shade, picture frame, note book, or car mirror, and these things become his "body". He's fun-tastic, and made of soft, durable, flesh-colored plastic, with pink ears, and bright red eyes. Your own personal moon Mascot! Only $1 postpaid.

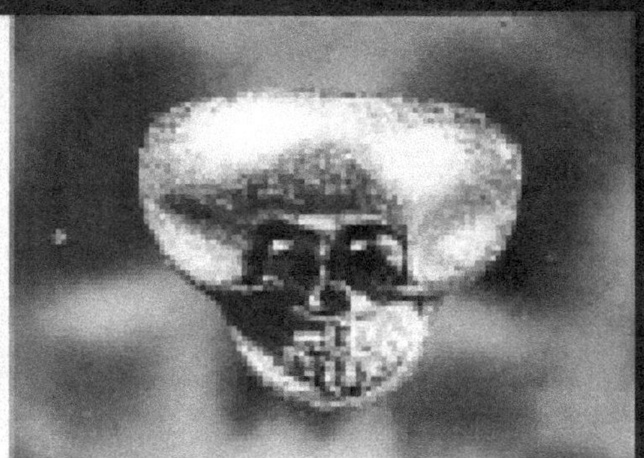

SECRET SKULL RING

Mystic skull symbol of the ancient Aztecs, later copied by the fierce pirates who sailed the seven seas. The romance and adventure is all embodied into the unique and latest style of this massive, quality ring. Sculptured cheek bones, teeth, and sparkling simulated ruby eyes are blended into a finger-encircling curve on this exciting new ring. Gleaming silvery finish, too. Please state ring size when ordering. Only $1 postpaid.

MR. BONES, THE POCKET SKELETON

Your own spooky mascot! Take Mr. Bones wherever you go. He's 7 inches tall, well detailed, made of vinylized rubber! Even feels creepy! Flexible and springy, the slightest movement sets him shimmying and shaking! Hang Mr. Bones from car mirror, or pin him to your jacket! Sit him down on desk, or table! For you shutterbugs, Mr. Bones makes a sensational prop for table-top photography. Only 75c, postpaid

UNLUCKY 13 RATTLESNAKE

13 unlucky inches of wriggling rubber! Coloring fools everybody, even inches away! "Fleshy" vinyl formula makes snake feel cool and slimy to the touch! Sure cure for nosey friends! Just put this rattler where they're bound to creep! If you want shrieks and howls at your next get-together, this UNLUCKY 13 RATTLESNAKE is for you! Camera bugs who like to shoot miniatures can turn rattler into huge "python" in table-top scenes! Only 75c postpaid

DEVIL SPIDER

Ugh! What a little horror this guy is! Made of vinyl rubber, for that "creepy" feel! 3 inches in diameter, he really gets the screams when you lower him on a thread or send him skittering across the floor! Well detailed in black, with rough texturing! Its wiggly legs start vibrating at the slightest touch! Slip him in your pocket, hang him from a car mirror, dangle him in a doorway! If you have any friends left afterwards, they'll never forget the time they chased the DEVIL SPIDER out of their hair! Only 50c postpaid

<table>
<tr><td colspan="2" style="text-align:left">

CASTLE DRACULA, TOPANGA, CALIFORNIA
NOVELTIES, JOKES, GAMES

Rush me the following: _______________________

____

____

____

for which I enclose $ ______________________

NAME (PLEASE PRINT) _______________________

ADDRESS __________________________________

CITY _______________ ZONE ____ STATE ________

If I'm dissatisfied with my purchase, I'll return it within one week for a full refund

</td></tr>
</table>

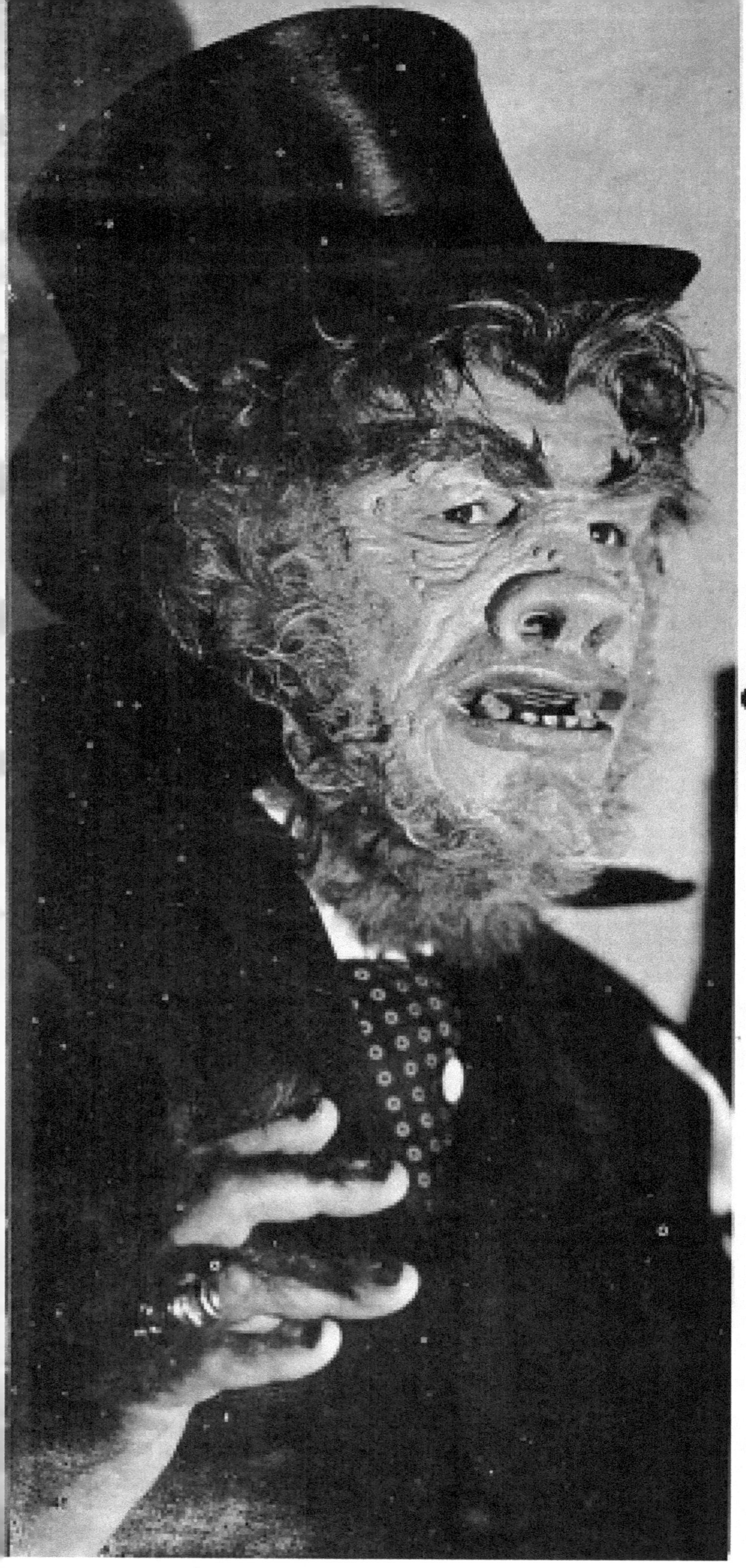

Favorite Fiends of Filmland

"An actor's most versatile tool is his own face," Boris Karloff recalled, when cornered by *FaM*'s Bob Burns, on the set of his new theatre thriller *The Raven*. "I felt I could handle any type of role without elaborate makeup. For a lot of years, stage, screen, TV audiences were content to see me as I am.

"But there was no living down this reputation for horror that I seem to have built up since the outset of my screen career. The demand for monstrous characterizations kept recurring, so there remained nothing to do but satisfy it."

The King of Horror recalled that in 1953, just 21 years after he created his Frankenstein Monster for Universal Pictures, he was back on the lot starring in the dual role of Jekyll and Hyde for Universal - International's horror comedy *Abbott & Costello Meet Dr. Jekyll & Mr. Hyde*.

The British star who had marched through the early Frankenstein films in an iron-clad costume to intimidate audiences now donned a wolf-like mask which covered his entire head for his role with the two notorious laugh-grabbers.

On the same sound stage where he once brought life to the immortal Monster of Frankenstein, Karloff the Uncanny metamorphised from a suave English doctor to a fur-faced fiend, hot on the scent of Abbot & Costello, proving that nothing can mask the genius of Karloff. ●

Alien creatures vs. a nightmare on Earth

by Paul Blaisdell

Somewhere across the city, a church bell sleepily tolled the hour of midnight as the two strangely attired figures moved silently through the puddles of moonlight in the littered alley.

"This planet's atmosphere is choking me, Zilnik!" hissed the heavier of the two. "Let us return to the spaceship for atmosphere suits."

"There is no time, Gilno," breathed the other. "We must capture our specimen and go as quickly as possible before an alarm is given."

"Then here is our chance," whispered Gilno. "I sense an Earthman less than fifty arts away. Quickly now; and if we can't take him by force, use your weapon."

Mike crouched against the warm bricks of the factory near the mouth of the alley, and reflected bitterly on the passing thundershower that had soaked his coat, and left him shivering in the chill night air.

The soft rustle of clothing barely warned him in time as he ducked and spun to face his shadowy assailant.

A blunt object thudded into the wall he'd been leaning against as he lashed out savagely with his hairy fist, burying it in his opponent's stomach. A chopping right cut off a groan of pain in mid-air, and the figure crashed into a pile of boxes six feet away.

Mike let out a grunt of surprise as he straightened, and a second assailant landed heavily on his back. Lunging forward, he sent the figure flying over his shoulder in the direction of the first, then turned and ran for the mouth of the alley and safety.

He never saw Zilnik rise painfully to his feet and level a flowing rod at his retreating back, but he felt the shock as the purple ray splashed over him in a shower of iridescent sparks and his brain sank slowly into oblivion . . . .

It was sometime later, when the silver spaceship flashed past the orbit of the moon, that Zilnik limped painfully into the control room, gingerly feeling his discolored third eye with one of his intermediate tentacles. With a sigh, he eased himself onto the pneumatic cushions.

"Gilno, I had no idea that the Earthman fought so savagely," he wheezed. "Even now, when we have him safely in a cage, it frightens me to look at him. Nevertheless, I shall attempt to communicate with him."

It was with visible effort that Zilnik forced himself to stand squarely in front of Mike's cage. Drawing himself up to his full sixteen inch height, he pointed to himself and spoke slowly in his native tongue.

But the only answer he received was th[illegible] [illegible]ting stare of a pair of luminous eyes . . . eyes that belonged to [illegible] [illegible] biggest alley cat in Flagstaff, Arizona! ●

MOVIE PREVIEW by Douglas Higley

Toho Productions rings up the clash of the mile-high monster champions of two great nations, in a film bout destined to be the most talked-about tussle of the century

KING KONG vs GODZILLA

The Toho Films locker room was a scene of confusion that one history-making morning. From every corner of the world came the reporters with their pencils; photographers clutching speed cameras, the greatest heroes of the sports world — a thousand tense and anxious people, huddled together, silently awaiting the Great Moment.

The Japanese police force were on hand, forming a cordon around the mammoth Toho lot, on their toes keeping the restless crowds back, but even their own disciplined thoughts stealing back to the lockers.

Then They came . . . first one, then the other, crashing through the crowds, passing inside studio gates, to where the press waited inside.

Kong, the ape King of Skull Island, was the first to arrive, scarcely paying attention to the many questions hurled up at him by the news-hungry reporters as he cleared the way for himself with a growl and checked in at the scales.

The crowds fell back again, and the newsmen murmured, as Kong cocked a confident eye to the newcomer, Godzilla,

turn to page 52

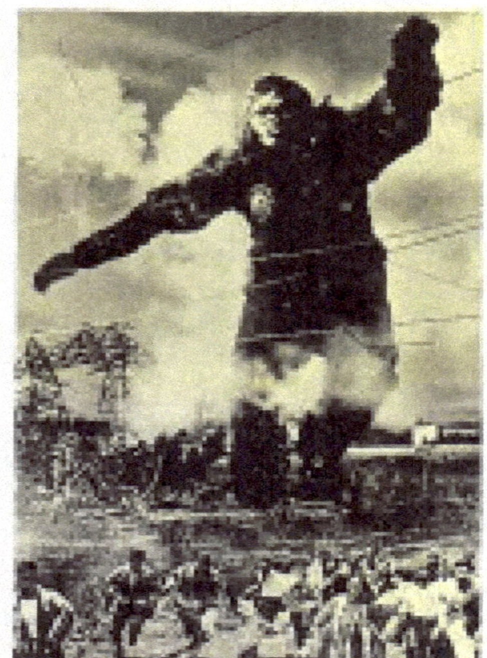

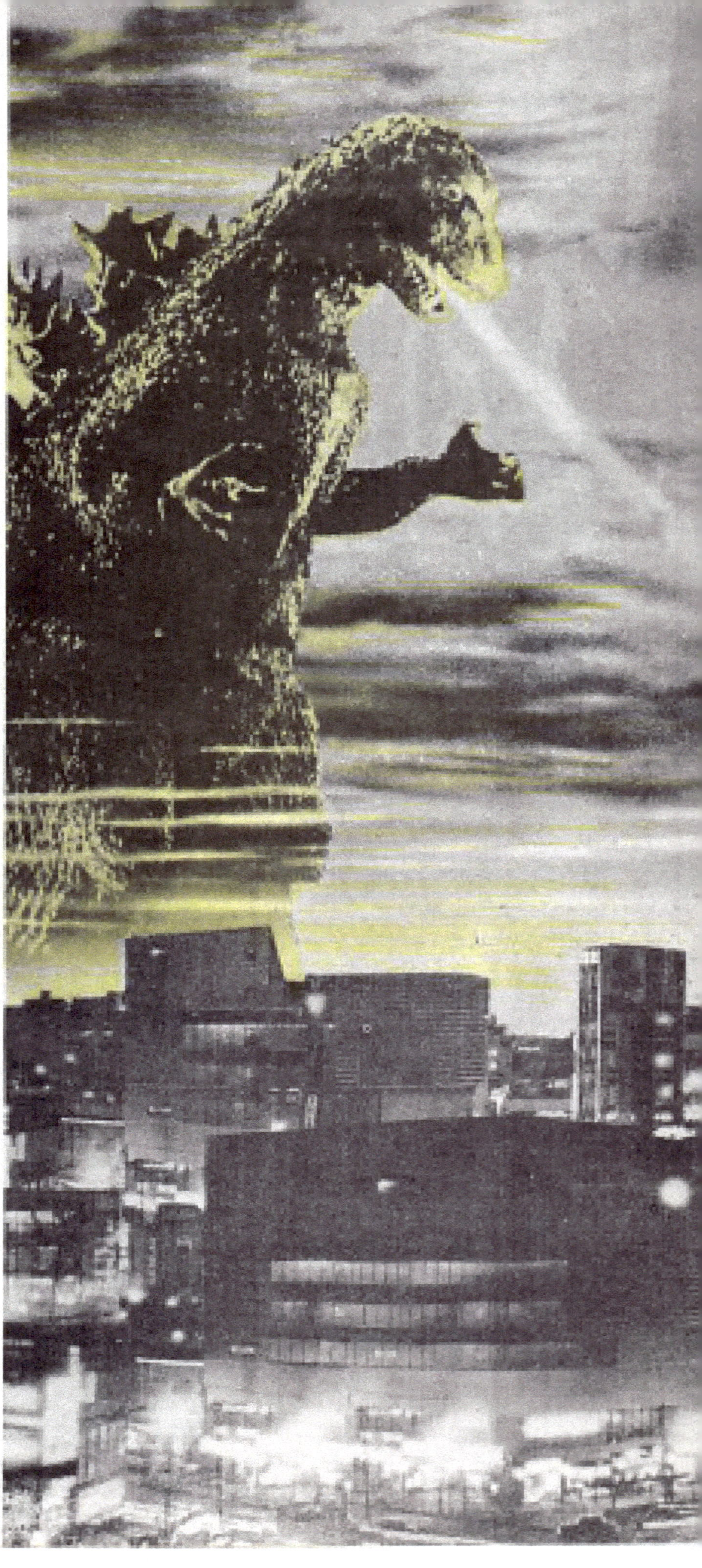

KONG, from page 50

the prehistoric monster he was to war against in a few minutes.

Godzilla stomped up to Kong at the scales, his 100 yard long scaled tail twitching anxiously.

The matchmaker stepped out of a crowded doorway, making his way to the two mighty opponents. The newsmen grabbed for their notebooks, the sports heroes stood in awe, and camera bulbs flashed.

The scales tipped, and pencils hastily scrawled out the facts . . .

Height—KONG, 148 ft; GODZILLA, 164 ft

Weight—KONG, 55 million lbs; GODZILLA, 44 million

Age—KONG, 29 (born in 1933); GODZILLA, 8 (born in 1954)

Category—KONG, mammal; GODZILLA, reptile

Nationality—KONG, American; GODZILLA, Japanese

Punch—KONG, the confidence to KO any and all opponents; strength is his greatest asset; swings a devastating hook; GODZILLA, one flip of its powerful tail and a whole city is in ruins; weakest point is a frontal attack

Technique—KONG, excellent, almost human-like; GODZILLA, belches out searing radioactive flames, its deadliest weapon

Stamina—KONG, age is his greatest handicap, but cleverly covers it with experienced know-how; GODZILLA, young and completely without fear; takes the initiative in any fight

Speed—KONG, like a jetliner, his attacks are well-planned and smooth. GODZILLA, slow, but nearly invincible in fights at close quarters.

Title—KONG, Monster Champion of USA; GODZILLA, Monster Champion of Japan . . .

All the facts were in.

The twin champions stomped out of the locker room, the grim determination

to win blazing in their large, alert eyes. They knew this was the battle of the century, and that there could only be one victor . . .

Kong, who had been re-discovered by Toho on the distant Faro Island, was confident he could easily overcome that young upstart they called Godzilla.

Godzilla, awakened from its eight year slumber in the frozen Arctic Ocean by the Toho matchmaker, special effects wizard Eiji Tsuburaya, glanced at his opponent, the mighty ape Kong, grinning to him that the Old was about to be replaced by the Young.

The two colossal champions lurched

Turn to page 65

there's something sneaking up on you

Most sleepers aren't too shocking, unless they have been sleeping the sleep of the dead for a long time, but Hollywood manages to come up with a shocker sleeper every once in a black and blue moon.

"Sleeper" is the term movie-folk use to describe a picture produced on a fairly low budget that hits high at the box office. When it comes to horror pictures, a new film called *Terrified* looks like one sleeper that will wake up to a big success.

Terrified is certified with a lot more class than most of its low-fi (financial, that is) screen mates. The film is directed by Lew Landers, who was in charge of the original Universal *Raven*, one of the few films with both monster masters, Bela Lugosi and Boris Karloff; and the new release's writer-producer is Richard Bernstein, who previously helmed epics that are now inescapable on TV, such as *The Phantom from 10,000 Leagues*.

Rod Lauren is starred, and some think he is even a classier singer than Fabian. Along with one-time Victor discer Lauren is Miss Tracy Olsen, who has climbed off *The Couch* at Warner's for the Bern-Field Production. Rounding out its shivering cast, *Terrified* has seared up an attractive ghost from the past: Barbara Luddy, star of radio's theatre where every play was a *First Nighter*.

First nighters at the opening of *Terrified* will find two college boys (Lauren and Steve Drexel) squared off against each other in a triangle. The point of the triangle is Miss Olsen, who plays a night club hostess whose brother was driven out of his mind by an unknown enemy, her daddy rubbed out in an unsolved murder, and her mother killed in a fatal way.

With her luck running like this, the girl thinks the best thing to do is to go to the haunted ghost town (constructed by Bern-Field on the Hal Roach Studio lot) along with her two boy friends to find out what hideous horror left her brother so mouth-frothingly *Terrified*.

They find out. ●

The Phantom Fiend, man of mystery. Below: Robert Towers is up to his neck in trouble and limestone

FANTASTIC FOUR

I'm confused. Perplexed. Bewildered. About the staff of FANTASTIC MONSTERS. I mean, if what I think is true, then for the first time in the history of horror magazines we have a mag (FanMo) that is actually assembled by people who have been connected with terror movies, in one form or another.

Is Paul Blaisdell, the editorial director, the same Paul Blaisdell who created and built the creatures in *Invasion of the Saucer Men*, the monster suit for *It — Terror from Beyond Space*, the *She Creature*, etc.? Is associate editor Jim Harmon the same Jim Harmon who writes such great and far-out science-fiction stories for magazines like *Galaxy* and *If*? Is research editor Bob Burns the same Bob Burns who has been called "Horror's Hottest Newcomer", and who I've been reading about in other monster magazines? And, finally, is editor Ron Haydock the same Ron Haydock who has written so many interesting horror movie articles for those "other" monster magazines, as well as articles for fan mags like *Terror*, *Ape*, *Please*, *Beyond*, *Alter Ego*, *Cinder*, *Comic Collector*, *Escape*, etc, etc?

If all this is true, well, I find it hard to believe that I'm finally reading a monster magazine which is edited by people who actually know what they're talking about!

Harold Aeschliman
St. Petersburg, Florida

To answer all your questions in one word — Yes! But you left out our contributing editor, the Mad Maestro. He's got more horror knowledge crammed into his withered brain than all of us stacked together — even if he is a bit too wrapped up in himself — Ed.

ADULTUS IGNORAMUS

I consider myself an adulte even if I am 12 and I think you're magazeene is stuped and is reading by only stiped people, as adultes got BETTER ways to spend money. Then by reading stuped monster magazeenes like your's.

Phil Philfrick
Toronto, Canada

Agreed, Mr. Adulte — you should spend you're money on dikshonairies — kindergarten style — Edatur.

BLOOD MONEY

I thought you might be interested to know that I lost an entire pint of blood over the recent movie *Poe's Tales of Terror*.

Here's what happened.

Wanting to see the film very badly, but being of weak mind and empty pocket, I therefore went to the local blood bank where I was paid four whole dollars for a pint of my red stuff. This not only paid my way into the show, but also bus fare and a couple boxes popcorn.

Larry Byrd
Leavenworth, Kansas

We're wondering if you enjoyed the film though. If you didn't, Terror's producer, Roger Corman, should be glad to refund your money — drop by drop — Ed.

BUTTON-DOWN FROWN

I was recently in a book store looking at the new issue of FANTASTIC MONSTERS when this well-dressed man carrying a copy of U.S. News and World Report walked up to me, and said, "You read that monster stuff, and I read this intellectual material. I make $80000 a year, and you make $10,000. I just don't get it."

He slowly walked away, throwing the magazine over his shoulder. Poor guy.

Robert Watson
Phoenix, Arizona

Which goes to prove you can't judge a reader by his monster magazine — Ed.

TO BE CONTINUED

If you are going to do the film stories of Superman, Batman & Robin, Crimson Ghost, Rocket Man, and others, would you please do it with chapter-by-chapter descriptions? Comic strip style? Each issue you could run the following chapter. Instead of reading "Continued Next Week", you could have "Continued Next Issue."

Manuel Maese
El Paso, Texas

What do you other readers think of Manuel's serial idea? — Ed.

GIANT REQUEST

Being a fan of all monsters, I'm especially interested in stop-motion photography. That is, animated miniature models such as in the great *King Kong*, the superb *Mighty Joe Young*, etc. I hope you will feature lengthy articles on these "giant" horrors, and also their creators, people like Ray Harryhausen and Willis O'Brien.

And if humanly possible, could you have a color fold-out scene of *Mighty Joe Young* or *Beast from 20,000 Fathoms*?

Larry Richardson
Burlington, N. C.

Since you're a fan of prehistoric monsters, you should find this issue's "Devil's Workshop" of special interest. Also, you'll find stop-framist Harryhausen featured in our special behind-the-scenes article. — Ed.

SATISFIED READER

With your first issue of FANTASTIC MONSTERS, you have accomplished for us monster fans what no one else in the monster magazine field has yet done, and probably never will do. You've given us a magazine with not only color covers and color pages inside, but also intelligent writing.

In the other monster magazines you'll find gore, sex, sick jokes, and just an average selection of fantastic photos. FANTASTIC MONSTERS No. 1 was in direct contrast. It consisted of little gore, no sex, few sick jokes (which, by the way, were funny in some cases), and an array of the finest photos I've ever laid my eyes on.

And your color pages, whether green, red, blue, or yellow, really give your magazine the look of good, clean monster loving.

Keep up the good work.

Harvey Ovshinsky
Detroit, Michigan

What can we say but that we'll be doing our best with all future issues to give you readers the type of fantastic filmic magazine your enthusiastic cards and letters have told us you want — Ed.

CALL from Fellow Monsters

POP GOES THE MONSTER

In FANTASTIC MONSTERS No. 2 you had a story on the old 3-D movies that I enjoyed very much. I'm only 12 years old now, so I never got to see any 3-D pictures like *House of Wax* or *The Maze*. I have seen some of them though, but only on television, so not in 3-D.

Do you think that 3-D movies will ever come out again? Not on television in 2-D, but in the theatres like ten years ago.

I sure hope so, because it must have been great to see the Black Lagoon creature swimming out into the audience, and spaceships zooming out at you, too.

Les Cuccio
Twin Rivers, Wisconsin

It's very doubtful that theatres will be running new 3-D films, even re-running the old ones, in the near future, Les. For the present, movie studios are satisfied with Cinemascope, Cinerama, Todd A-O, and the rest. However, where there's hope, there's life, as the old saying goes — Ed.

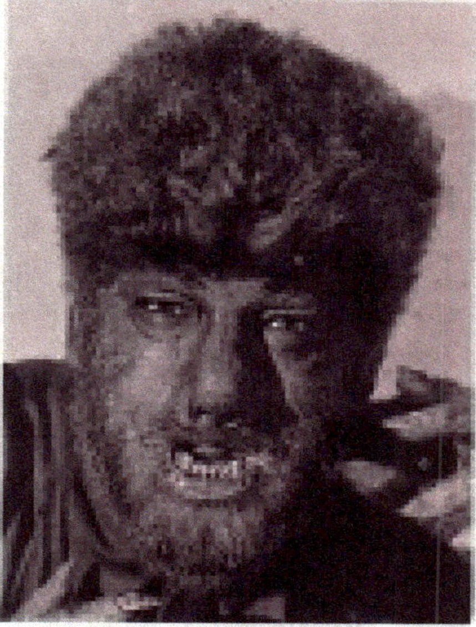

NO PLACE FOR SPACE

Why not leave space movie stories like *Flash Gordon* and *Day the Earth Stood Still* to magazines like *Spacemen*? After all, FANTASTIC MONSTERS is supposed to deal exclusively with Frankenstein, the mummies, werewolves, and vampires.

Bill Drumeller
Richmond, Virginia

See next letter, Bill — Ed.

NOT ENOUGH SPACE

Your story on *Destination Moon* in No. 1 was excellent! I never saw this movie, and I enjoyed reading about it, and seeing all those photos! *Day the Earth Stood Still* was just as good, and I liked it because I did see this movie and found it fabulous!

The *Flash Gordon* article, though complete, was too short. I think you should have a few good, long articles instead of many short ones.

David Coleman
Rochester, New York

How does the length of the Flash feature in this issue measure up against your space-minded yardstick? Ed.

FICTION FRICTION

Cut out the fiction stories. We can go to the newsstand anytime and buy paperback novels.

John Dulaney
Oklahoma City, Okla.

See how much money we're saving you? — Ed.

FRADKIN COMMENTS

I truly think that your magazine is the one I have been waiting for. The other monster mags are not worth the paper they're printed on.

Although some of them at times have run some pretty good photos, they have never bothered to take the time to report on the films in an intelligent way, like you do. Maybe they just don't know anything about the films to begin with. And I especially like the way you get into the sidelights with special effects, a field that I am very much interested in.

I've just finished reading Robert Bloch's *Black Lotus* in No. 1, and I hope that he will never start writing movie reviews for you like he did for other competing magazines. Whenever he does, he just sounds silly. I liked *Black Lotus* very much, even better than his *Psycho*.

Things I'd like to see in future issues are articles on *The Time Machine*, *War of the Worlds*, *Beast from 20,000 Fathoms*, *Forbidden Planet* and *20,000 Leagues Under the Sea*; color pin-ups of Robby the Robot, any Phantom of the Opera, and Gort from *Day the Earth Stood Still*; stories on the Jekyll and Hyde pictures, and Frankensteins; life histories of Karloff, Lugosi, both Chaneys, Christopher Lee, Vincent Price, Peter Cushing.

In all though, I think you've got the greatest magazine in the world. But, please, don't ever lower your standards to the level of your competitors. This is why I feel your *Dead Time Tales* and *Mad Mummy* are a complete disgrace to your otherwise fine and intelligent publication. I think that if you do continue with these two things, sooner or later the rest of your quality will drop. And then down goes FANTASTIC MONSTERS to become nothing more than the rest of the monster magazines — silly and stupid.

Lloyd Fradkin
No. Hollywood, Calif.

This is the Mad Mummy speaking— Watch your mouth, Fradkin! Do you realize you have INSULTED ME TWICE? First you say that I'm a disgrace to this magazine, then you start knocking Dead Time Tales! Did you know that I am the one who captions all the photos for this feature? May the unwholly wrath of Imhotep, Ananka, and Fabian be upon you forever! (EDITOR'S NOTE: Don't forget, Lloyd, there's three sides to every pyramid.)

BELFRY OF BELA

Bela in his one-time appearance as the infamous Frankenstein monster, seen here in a scene from FRANKENSTEIN MEETS THE WOLFMAN with co-star Lon Chaney Jr (Universal, 1943)

Lugosi, Crowned King of Vampires, in a rare collection of photos from those nights of terror when he countered the challenge of the stake to take up as his other self, Master of Movie Menace

Right: Bela as the deaf mute servant in THE BLACK SLEEP

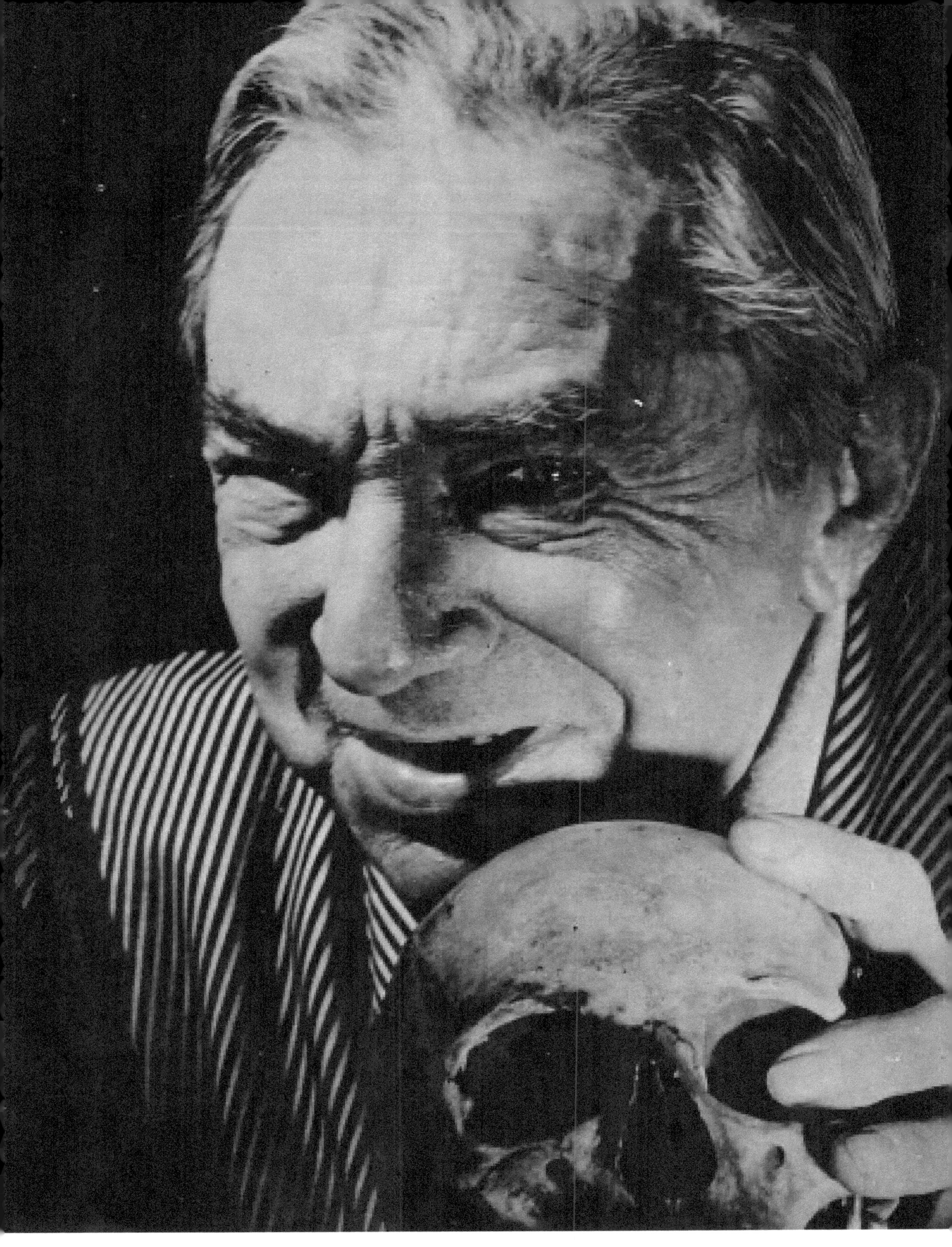

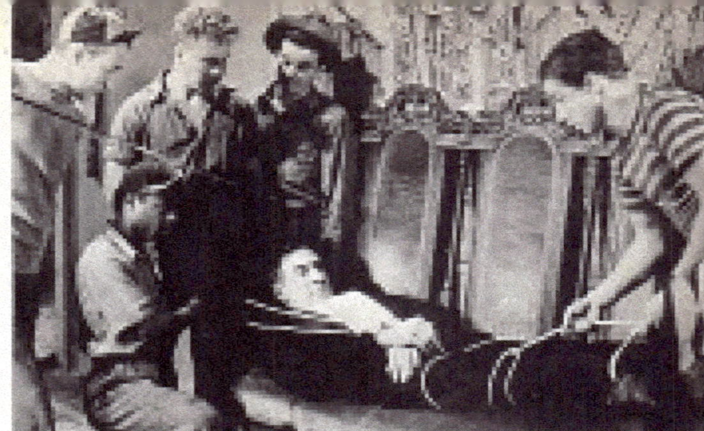

Lugosi meets the ageless Bowery Boys in SPOOKS RUN WILD, 1941 release from Astor Pictures, produced by serialdom's Sam Katzman

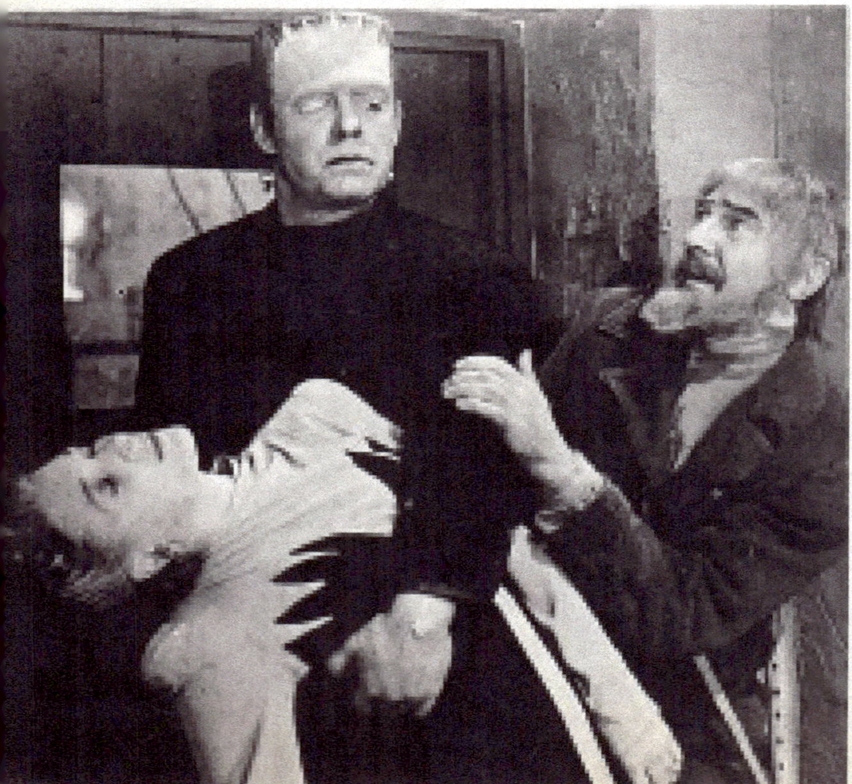

Molly Lamont was SCARED TO DEATH when she played opposite Bela in 1947. Below: Lon Chaney Jr and Evelyn Ankers, confronted by Bela as Ygor the Shepherd in GHOST OF FRANKENSTEIN, Universal, 1942

With Kay Kyser, Dean of the College of Musical Knowledge, for RKO's 1940 hit YOU'LL FIND OUT. Below: Boris Karloff in the role of killer Bateman meets his match in Universal's Edgar Allan Poe chiller THE RAVEN, released in 1935

THE VOODOO MAN, High Priest of Black Magic (Monogram, 1944)

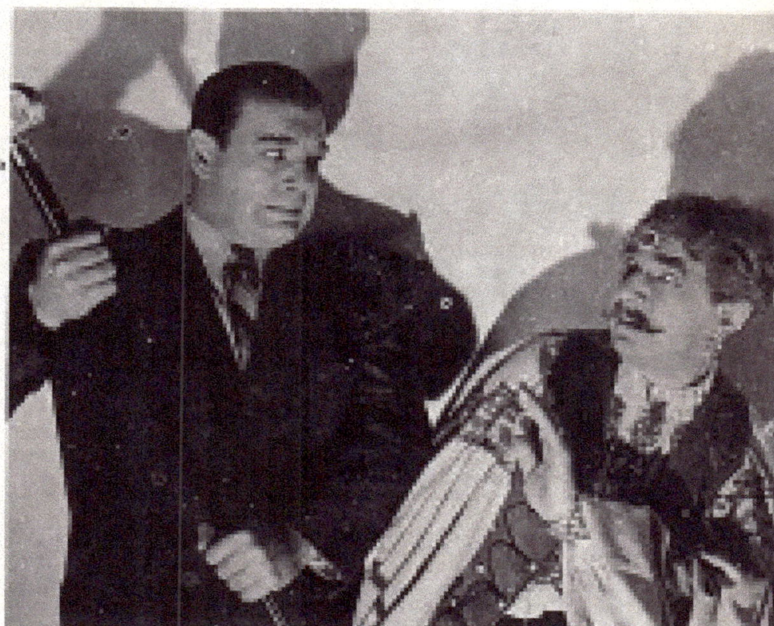

Universal signed Lon Chaney Jr and Bela to match caresses again in 1941 for THE WOLF MAN classic. Below: Lugosi as the snooping servant Joseph for RKO's THE BODY SNATCHER

Lugosi in a non-menace role for Fox Films' WOMEN OF ALL NATIONS

WORKSHOP, from page 9

face of your miniature landscape every five or ten minutes. You can give your lizard a "hot foot" very quickly under photoflood lamps. *Never* pick a lizard up by its tail. Most lizards have tails that break off automatically, when grabbed. It's a form of protection. Although the lizards will grow newer, shorter tails, neither you nor they will appreciate the wait!

Some lizards that you might find worth "looking up" are: the Whiptail Lizard, many species found all over the Central and Southern United States, coast to coast. Horned Lizards, or Toads as they are sometimes called; eight species covering the entire Western half of the country. The Desert Iguana and Chuckwalla, two vegetarians from the Southwest. The American Chameleon of the Southeast, so familiar at fairs, carnivals and pet stores; and the Swift, a large family of some fifteen species found in nearly every part of the country.

Study and learn all you can about your four legged "monster" friend; fix him up like "he never left home" and you'll both have a long and happy life together — both in and out of your horror films. ●

MARS, from page 37

Before you know it, Flash, with his unerring skill, has managed to smash the rocketship into one of the mountains of Mars.

But before the intrepid foursome can clear the crash site, the shock troops of the Queen of Mars, alluring Azura (Beatrice Roberts), have landed their airships and are soon tangled up with the blond champion of Earth. Since it's only a few dozen to one, Flash routs them in, shall we say, a hurry.

But reinforcements drive the Earth people into Caves of Mars.

Then the type of thing you might expect to happen in a dark cave on the Red Planet, happens. Trapped in the rocks, Dale begins to crack up. She babbles that she saw people coming out of the walls. Flash and Zarkov exchange knowing looks, and the good doctor reaches for his pocket straight-jacket.

Just then, the real stars of the picture appear—the Clay Men.

These handsome devils, the Clay Men, look almost exactly like mummies. Now I understood why the editor had assigned me this picture.

Dragging the Earthlings before their wise, virile, mummy-like King (C. Montague Shaw), the Clay Men hold Dale and Happy prisoner while Flash and Zarkov are sent in captured Martian uniforms to capture Queen Azura and force her to free her clay curse from the Clay Men.

At the royal abode, Flash pretends Zarkov is a prisoner who has to be delivered to the Queen. The Martian sentry turns on a light beam bridging the chasm, telling Flash and his "prisoner" Zarkov to cross on the Light Bridge.

"Th's stupid Earthman never saw a Light Bridge before and seems fearful of walking out on a beam of light."

"Dr. Jekyll isn't in right now . . . may I take a message?"

Flash says to the sentry. "You go first!"

Flash makes his capture of Queen Azura as soon as he gets to the throne room; but now he meets his old enemy, Ming the Merciless of Mongo (Charles Middleton)—the real source of the danger to Earth, what with his giant Nitron Lamp that is extracting all the vital elements from our atmosphere.

Captured, Flash is thrown into a dungeon with other recent catches: Dale, Happy, and Zarkov.

But before they can begin to enjoy their cozy tomb-like prison, Flash's old pal from Mongo, Prince Barin (Richard Alexander), tunnels in and frees the Earthlings.

Soon re-captured, Queen Azura is carried off by Zarkov and Gordon in a Martian flying sled. Power-seeking Ming orders his men to shoot down his Earth enemies and his rival for Martian authority, Azura.

After the crash, the dying Azura gives the blond Earthman the magic jewels that will return the Clay People to human. "Despite her evil black sapphires," chokes out Flash, "she was a pearl at heart."

The Queen's death turns her Martians against Ming, and as Flash Gordon leads the attack, a turn-coat shoves the Mongo maniac into a disintegrator beam.

Flash Gordon is left with nothing to do but to return to Earth with his friends and receive the cheers of a New York celebration.

To celebrate the 25th Anniversary of the first Flash Gordon serial, made in 1936, titled simply *Flash Gordon*, a *FanMo* correspondent interviewed Flash himself, Buster Crabbe.

Playing the tape of the interview, I learned that Buster had had some narrow escapes off-screen, such as the time a giant swim tank he was in cracked into shards that threatened to slash our Flash as he splashed away from the crash.

Even Serial King Buster Crabbe admits that the Flash Gordon epics were the greatest chapter plays of all time.

They weren't too bad, I admit, if you like films about living people. Personally, my favorite serial is *Adventures of Captain Marvel*, starring Tom Tyler.

After all, Tyler once played the title role in *The Mummy's Hand*. ●

KONG, *from page 83*

into the ring, roped off by only the stars.

Kong smacked a giant fist into an open palm, readying himself for the sound of the gong.

Godzilla twitched his tail, wiping out a Japanese suburb, then turned to his opponent, throwing him the silent challenge known only to the greatest of contenders.

Matchmaker Tsuburaya reached out a hand to strike the gong, and the world was silent.

The Great Moment loomed up on the horizon . . .

If you're one of those who haven't yet seen the films of this titanic struggle, and haven't heard the final outcome, you'd better make it a point to catch it when it plays in your town. This is a bout with clouts guaranteed world-shattering. ●

His hair is so wonderfully brittle and matted, so deathly alive with grayness. With *Miss Scare-all*, it's easy to keep haircolor old . . . to keep gray showing. This is why more werewolves use it than all other haircolorings combined.

Hairdressers too prefer *Miss Scare-all* because it not only is the most effective way to keep and glorify gray, but it also keeps the hair in its desirable un-natural condition.

Try *Miss Scare-all* yourself. Tonight. Takes only the passing of a full moon before it acts. Scream Formula or Regular.

OOZE

FANG EXTRA

NOOSE

TOMBSTONE TIMES

R.I.P.

VOLUME 1 ☆ ☆ ☆ ☆ ☆ FIVE SCAR FINAL — ALL THE NEWS UNFIT TO PRINT ☆ ☆ ☆ ☆ ☆ NUMBER 3

Monster Clubs

Nosferatu, Inc., is, in the words of president Alexa Szekely, "an organization for those who are interested in the Nosferatu (vampires) and the Undead. We are a monster club, movie company, catering service for Halloween parties, and a do-it-yourself insane asylum all rolled into one." The fun-and-fang loving group invites all devotees of the macabre to contact *Nosferatu, Inc.*, 154 West Chanslor Ave., Richmond, Calif.

Jerry Younkins' Greater Detroit Monster Society is in the process of an all-out 1963 membership campaign for horror fans in their area. If you live in Detroit or thereabouts, you can write Jerry at 827 Notre Dame, Grosse Pointe 30, Michigan.

The American Bela Lugosi Fan Club is spearheaded by Bill Obbagy, 11806 Forest Ave., Cleveland 20, Ohio. The first issue of Bill's club magazine, *The Lugosi Journal*, is just out; and all your old Count Downe can say about it is that it's an issue every monster fan from here to eternity should have in his files. Write Bill for full membership info.

Another fine horror journal is the one you receive when you join *Monsters Club*. Members are also entitled to club cards, monster photos, and the special vampire glo-fang. President Craig Stock will fill you in on the details if you write 5803 Shore Parkway, Apt. 21, Brooklyn 36, New York.

COFFIN CORNER

I think I've seen every Boris Karloff movie except the one in which he tangles with comic strip detective Dick Tracy. Could you please give me its correct title, so I can watch for it when it comes on TV? — ANDREW F. ADAM, KNIGHTSVILLE, ALA.

The film you're referring to is RKO's *Dick Tracy Meets Gruesome*, made in 1947, with Ralph Byrd as Tracy. Ex-Tarzan Lex Barker is also in the movie.

Can you tell me something about Patricia Laffan who played *The Devil Girl from Mars*? — RICK MAJOR, HOLLOWAY, PA.

Sure, Rick — what do you want to know?

About a year ago I heard that Hammer Films of England was planning a TV series on *Frankenstein*, with Peter Cushing in the role of the monster's creator. What ever happened to this proposed program?—BENTLEY ASHLEY, HOLLYWOOD, CALIFORNIA.

The series never saw the light of night, Ben. However,

CRY OF THE APE MAN

Calling all Tarzan fans!

Here's a foursome of fanzines right up your treetop, all dedicated to the white ape Tarzan and the other immortal characters created by the one and only Edgar Rice Burroughs.

Vern Coriell's *Burroughs Bulletin* and companion zine *Gridley Wave* are sent free to members of The Burroughs Bibliophiles, the only authorized ERB fan club, so you'll have to join this active and still-growing organization to receive your copies of these two excellent publications. Contact the club's secretary Robert Horvath, 1 Luce Ave., 5, Montoson, Pennsylvania, for complete membership information. *Gridley Wave* No. 4 features a great article on the newest film Tarzan, Jock Mahoney.

Erbania is the work of Canada's No. 1 Burroughs fan, Peter Ogden. Issue No. 12 (just out) contains stories and articles on the life of Burroughs, in addition to an index of the Tarzan Sunday comic strips and a profile on Tarzan's greatest enemy. Copies can be had for 30c each. Pete's address is 489 Dougall Ave., Windsor, Ontario, Canada.

Editor Camille Cazedessus Jr. describes his *ERB-dom* as "an illustrated, authoritative magazine devoted to Edgar Rice Burroughs and the characters he created." One dollar will return you five issues of this great zine. Write Camille at 8203 Jefferson Hwy., Baton Rouge 8, Louisiana.

the pilot film, *Tales of Frankenstein*, is currently playing on local TV stations across the country. Keep checking the TV listings in your paper. And it's Anton Diffring, not Cushing, who finally snatched the role of Dr. Frankenstein,

KEEP YOUR EYES OPEN FOR
THE NEXT GREAT ISSUE OF fantastic
MONSTERS

MONSTER
OF THE
MONTH

Universal-International's
Creature from the Black Lagoon

Our stand-out fold-out this time stars Universal's three-time winner, The Black Lagoon Creature. Only three other monsters in Universal's long history (the longest history of any studio in Hollywood) have been screened a trio of times. Joining Frankenstein, Dracula, and the Wolf Man, the Creature makes a worthy, modern entry.

The list of the Creature's films is impressive—*The Creature from the Black Lagoon* in 1954, starring Richard Carlson, Julia Adams, and Richard Denning, followed by *Revenge of the Creature* ('55) starring John Agar, Lori Nelson, and John Bromfield, and finally *The Creature Walks Among Us* ('56) with Jeff Morrow and Rex Reason.

Notice anything unusual about those credits? Unlike Universal's earlier horror hits starring Karloff, Lugosi and Lon Chaney Jr, the actor playing the title role doesn't even get his name in the billing. The real "star" is uncredited.

Smarting at this injustice, partly because our own editorial director Paul Blaisdell played several monster stars himself without his name in lights, we have researched the fact that in all three pictures in the underwater shots the Creature was swimmer Ricou Browning, and when the Creature Walks on land it is TV's *Tales of Frankenstein* monster, Don Megowan.

Unless monsters get proper credit, we fear they will be revolting.

Bud Westmore (right), head of U-I's makeup department, adds a few final touches to one of the models of the Gill Man. Model was later duplicated as an outer skin in foam rubber and plastic, "inherited" by Ricou Browning (left), Florida's noted underwater swimmer

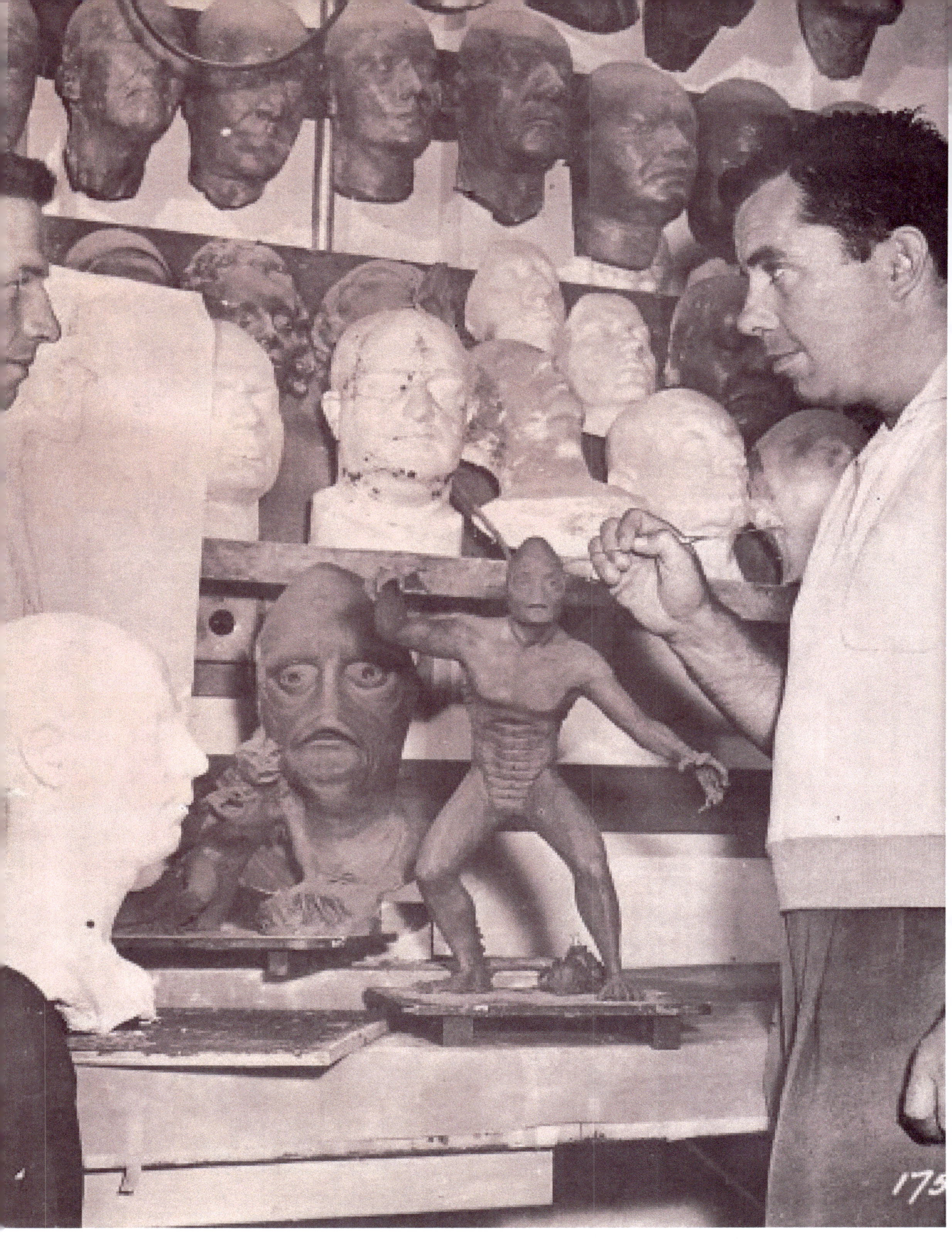
175

FANTASTIC
MONSTER
OF THE
MONTH

50¢
fantastic
MONSTERS
OF THE FILMS
HORROR GUARANTEED TO SHOCK YOU DEAD OR YOUR LIFE REFUNDED!
DEFEND
HORROR
FILMS by
VINCENT
PRICE

WORLD'S GREATEST MONSTER MAGAZINE

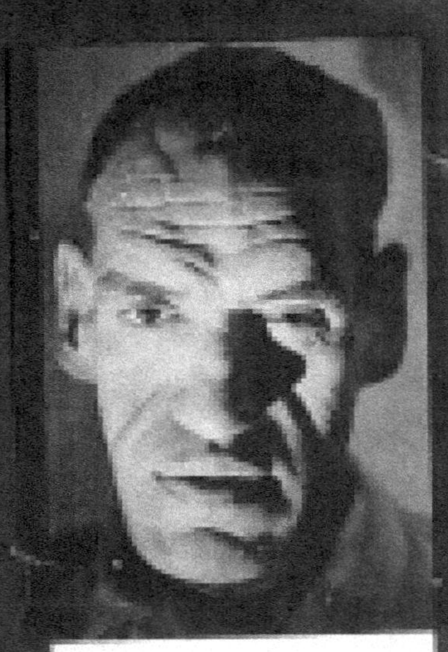

We don't know about your town, but here in Hollywood the TV stations have gone horror happy, particularly on *Saturday* evenings. If you've got the nerve, you can see a seven-hour-long shudder line-up of both old and new fright films, including one show hosted by a real "live" creep.

Strange Tales of Science Fiction kicks off the picture parade with thrillers like *King Kong* and *The Thing*, followed by the ever-popular *Shock Theatre* and its horde of Frankensteins, Draculas, and invisible men. *Attack of the Crab Monsters* is one of the films you're liable to catch when you tune in *Chiller*, but the best is saved till last — *Jeepers' Creepers*, starring a wild-eyed, maniacally giggling ex-horror producer named Jeepers, who runs creepers like *The Black Room*, *Devil Bat*, and *Mask of Fu Manchu*.

Which brings us to pointing out that we've spotlighted Jeepers and his menagerie of TV monsters in this issue. Also on tap you'll find Vincent Price on the subject of horror films, and Kirk Alyn, the movies' Superman, detailing the hazards of being the mighty Man of Steel. FanMo's beloved Mad Mummy takes on the teenage monster epics, and we think Lon Chaney Jr is well-represented in Chamber of Chaney.

And for the giant color pinup we've got Karloff as Frankenstein, Chaney as Wolf Man, and Peter Lorre—guaranteeing this issue to be an All-Time Collectors' Edition.

We hope you agree.
THE EDITORS

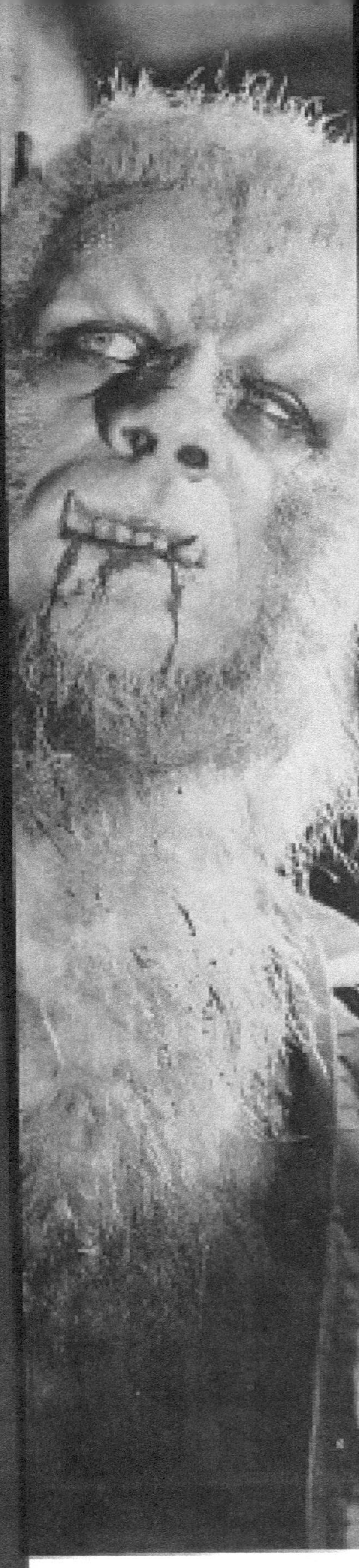

This is a howl of a Collector's Issue!

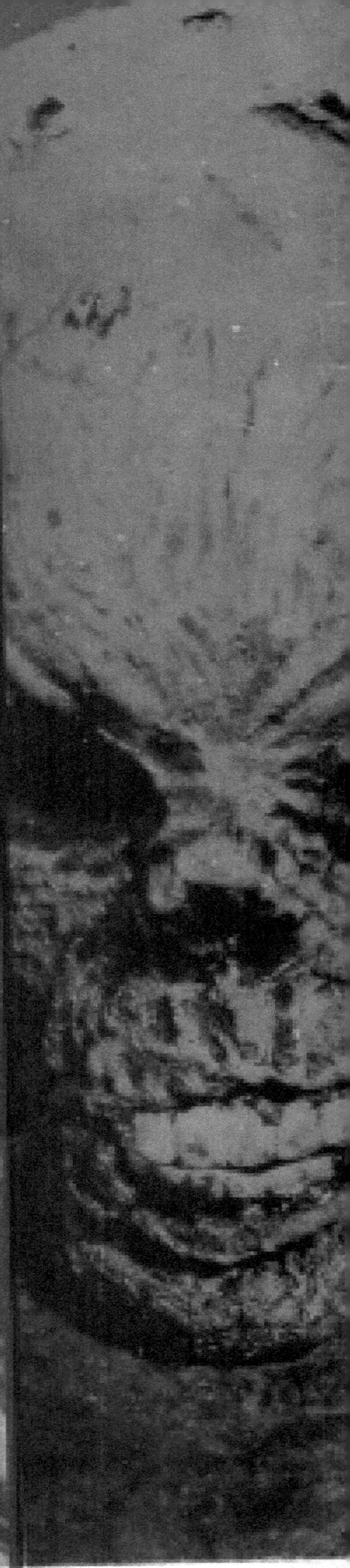

You get the inside lowdown on horror classics in FANTASTIC MONSTERS

CONQUERED THE WORLD

by Bradford Knight

A Nightmare Monster from Outer Space Threatens to Doom the Human Race

What you're about to read actually happened—on the cold, misty morning of April 10, 1956.

The setting was Bronson Quarry, California, and at the far end of the narrow canyon lay a pile of smouldering wreckage. Bits and pieces of a smashed, streamlined hull still identified the wreckage as a far-reaching U.S. satellite space probe that had come to a mysterious and untimely end.

Although it was said the satellite had originally climbed into the darkness of space with a cargo of electronic equipment, it had apparently crashed back to Earth under the guidance of a visitor from the planet Venus.

There was a stir in the smoke-shrouded debris, and something resembling a great toadstool detached itself from the shattered machinery. It laboriously eased its great bulk across the canyon floor and into the steaming Hot Springs Cave entrance, a few hundred feet from the crash. Pausing in the mouth of the cave, the Venusian turned and raised impossibly long arms. High-frequency radiations emanated from the weird antennae at the top of its pointed head, and the rays spread across the countryside in an ever widening circle. Car engines stopped, electric motors died, and gas flames and all sources of energy ceased. Wherever the creature's influence touched, It Conquered the World.

turn the page

General Pattick (Russ
Bender) tries to beat off
a flying sting-ray.

This actually happened on that morning April 10th—in front of the camera crew that was shooting a science-fiction movie for American-International Pictures. When Roger Corman, the director, yelled "Cut!", Freddie West, the cinematographer, helped his crew reload the 35mm Mitchell Camera, while Bill Clary, the still photographer, cranked up his Rollei in anticipation of another of the shots you see on these pages, and monster maker Paul Blaisdell detached himself from inside the Venusian horror for a breath of foggy fresh air.

If you liked your science-fiction films to really "blast off", It Conquered the World had more than its share of action. Scripted by Lou Rusoff, the film was an adaptation of an original idea by AIP president James Nicholson and Paul Blaisdell, who dreamed it up on a Sunday afternoon in the Spring of '56. Never one to put things off, "Nick" turned energetic producer-director Roger Corman loose on the job, with the result that the picture was all wrapped up and previewed at the Iris Theatre in Hollywood on August 29th, only a few months later.

The story concerns itself with the projection of a giant satellite into outer space, the launching site being under the direction of Dr Paul Nelson (played by Peter Graves). Nelson's scientist friend, Tom Anderson (Lee Van Cleef) is opposed to the project. Having previously tangled with government red tape and the rejection of all his pet theories, he hints that the satellite project might bring on an invasion by creatures from other worlds.

When the satellite finally vanishes from its orbit, Anderson, using a powerful interplanetary radio of his own design, contacts a being from Venus, who by this time has taken control of the missing satellite and brought it crashing back to Earth.

"Won't you come into my parlor?" But beautiful Beverly Garland doesn't seem to appreciate the gracious invitation.

the Venusian convinces Anderson that with his help it can free mankind forever from all forms of war and destructiveness.

Sending out its own 'helpers'— tiny flying sting-ray creatures — the Venusian gains control over the leading citizens of Beechwood, home of Nelson and Anderson and the city adjacent to the satellite installation. The deadly little flying creatures dominate the people by attacking them and injecting electronic receivers into the backs of their necks. Once having accomplished their objective, the creatures die; but by then, the individual is already under the powers of the master Venusian.

Nelson destroys the flying thing which is sent after him, but when his wife, Joan (Sally Fraser), succumbs to the control of the Venus horror, he is forced to kill her.

Anderson's wife, Claire (Beverly Garland), who has come to despise her husband's partnership with what is obviously an alien invader, goes to the cave where the monster lurks, and attempts to kill it with a rifle. She dies in the attempt. Even a squad of infantry, arriving a short time later, loses a skirmish with the all-powerful Venusian. Anderson, jarred back in reality by the realization that the alien has murdered his wife, finally destroys the monster in turn, wielding a flaming blowtorch in a last, suicidal battle. And his friend Anderson, coming last into the scene, observes the folly of enlisting the aid of others to correct our own mistakes, when such corrections must only come from within ourselves.

AIP's film provided 71 minutes of fast-paced screen entertainment. A'ded by the scoring of Ronald Stein, and the snappy film editing of Charles Gross, it delighted the young in heart all over the country.

Special mention should be made of the comedy relief provided by Johnathan Haze and Dick Miller, as infantry men. Their efforts alleviated what otherwise might have been an over-serious presentation of the subject matter.

turn to page 62

Above left: Soldier Jim Knight and bazooka go down before the onslaught of the Venusian invader. Above: Disillusioned scientist Tom Anderson attacks the invader with his blowtorch when bullets fail

You can make a plaster cast of your face. It need not look exactly like you, but it will be the right size. Model of The Terror of Venus in clay, over the plaster face.

Plaster cast is made over the clay "monster". Carefully separate the casting from the mold with a screwdriver. Be sure the plaster is hard. Latex is brushed in layers, until the desired thickness is built up.

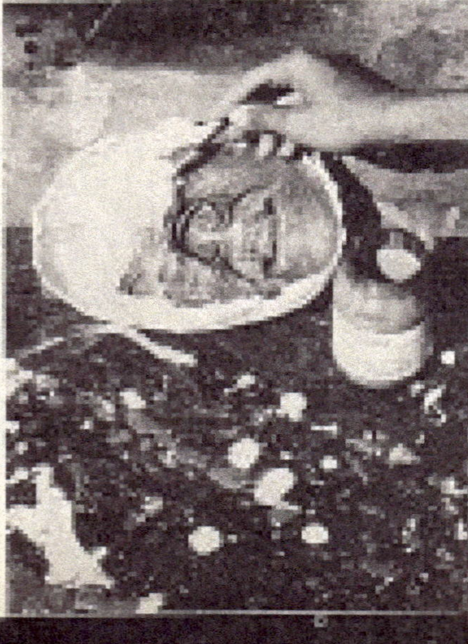

Malone's Monsters Pay Off

When we interviewed teen-age Bill Malone of Lansing, Michigan, recently, we were not only impressed by the quality of his work, but by the fact he made it pay for itself through sales to a local drug store chain. Bill finds time to do this in spite of the fact that he's the head of his school make-up department, and produces and directs his own series of short movies called *Adventures into the Unknown.*

In this issue of *The Devil's Workshop*, Bill creates his own original *Terror of Venus* mask especially for the readers of *Fantastic Monsters*. He also gives us the following instructions:

"At your local hobby, or arts and crafts store, obtain three pounds of modelling clay, a pint of liquid latex and a bag of plaster. You will also need an old bucket or bowl to mix your plaster in, and an old paint brush for the latex.

"Work the clay with your fingers until it's soft and pliable, then slowly and carefully build a heavy clay mask over the entire front of your head. Rub a little vaseline into your hair and eyebrows before you begin, to avoid the unpleasantness of the clay 'pulling' when it's removed. If you wish to avoid turning blue while this operation is underway, it's also advisable to leave small airholes for your mouth and nose.

"When you feel the clay is of sufficient thickness to hold its shape without the help of your head, remove it and place it carefully on your work table, the outside 'up'. Mix a little of the plaster with water according to the instructions on the package, and brush a couple of quick coats onto the clay to 'stiffen' it.

"After the plaster has hardened, reverse your plaster-clay 'head' and it has now become a mold. Brush or pour fresh plaster into this mold, building it up to a good strong thickness; at least a quarter of an inch. When this plaster is completely hard, it will be a rough 'form' of your face. Pull, break, or peel the softer and thinner plaster-clay mold away. From this point, you will no longer need it. You now have a rough replica of your own face, over which you will design your own tailor-made mask.

"Over this replica, you may now build a design of your choice with modeling clay. Mine was The Terror of Venus (see photos). Smooth and blend the contours of the clay into the plaster, to insure a life-like fit to your own face. For added realism, you can even put pores in the skin with the head of a pin. Be sure that the entire plaster replica is covered with at least a tissue-thin coating of clay. Rub the finished product with a light coat of vaseline before the next step.

"Make a thick, heavy plaster cast over this design. Pry the plaster cast apart from your clay-covered original design with a screwdriver. This cast will now become a mold for your latex rubber. Carefully clean all bits and scraps of clay out of it with a piece of pointed wood. Fill this mold about a third full of liquid latex. 'Slush' the latex around the inside, or spread it around with the old paint brush until even layers are built up. A base color may be imparted to the latex by slowly mixing in poster paint with an eye dropper. Let the liquid latex dry, or 'cure' in the sun; or bake in an oven at 200 degrees for an hour.

"After the latex is 'cured', dust the inside of the

turn to page 46

DEVIL'S

7. Finished product is horrible! Just like they make them for Hollywood.

WORKSHOP

"THE MONSTER OF PLANET X"

by Redd Boggs

The airlock door of the spaceship changed open, and the ladder extended with a purr of well-oiled machinery. Steve Noon clicked his visor into place and jogged down the ramp onto the ruddy sands of the strange planet.

Stunted gray vegetation spread out in all directions toward the dim horizons. The retro-rockets of the spaceship had blasted a huge charred patch in the undergrowth, but at the edges the tough little plants seemed almost undamaged. After a long wary look to all points of the compass, Steve strode across the blast area and began to examine the plants with the professional eye of a planet scout.

As he bent over the nearest plant, a tiny movement at the corner of his vision made him turn instinctively, and as he did so, something plucked lightly at the point of his left shoulder. He brushed himself off, wondering if he had been bitten by an insect of some sort. He hadn't seen any living thing on this world except for the stunted little plants.

Then something pinged off his stelaglas visor and bounced to the sand at his feet. He knelt down and retrieved it. A tiny round shot, half the size of a BB, lay dented and scarred in his gloved hand. Steve studied it puzzledly, then glanced sharply at the empty landscape. He saw nothing, so he advanced a few steps. Then a rain of shots hit him.

They clattered off his space armor and visor without hurting him. But they were irritating, like a cloud of swarming gnats. Steve waved his arms to ward away the missiles, and stalked angrily through the undergrowth, kicking wildly at clumps of plants in his path. Suddenly his boot hit something with a hollow boom. A metal sphere the size of a washtub bounded into the air from the force of his kick, its side caved in and gaping open. Three or four tiny creatures no bigger than field mice fell from the hole, twisting in midair and squealing thin-

turn to page 19

I WAS A TEENAGE MAD MUMMY

Are all Monsters Teen-Agers? Or vice-versa? FanMo's Own Wrapped-Up Rumbler reveals he Himself is Sweet Sixteen (Thousand)

The movie theatre was rather crowded, but when I shuffled in wearing my latest grave-green moldy bandages I managed to find a seat, and sit back to watch a gigantic non-stop program of teen-age monster movies.

As I sat there munching hot-buttered Tana leaves, I wondered why these teen-agers in the audience didn't perform one of their fun-loving group activities the editorial staff at FANTASTIC MONSTERS had described to me. It's known variously as the "riot" or the "rumble". It bears some resemblance to the "Twist", I understand.

If I were a teenager—and I'm not (disregard that silly heading the editor put up there about me being sixteen thousand, when I'm only five thousand)—I think I would resent the insult these pictures present not only to my manly mold, but to my intelligence.

The first on the program seemed typical of the rest. I Was a Teenage Frankenstein starred gray-haired Whit Bissell as Prof. Frankenstein, who looked like an even older teen-ager than Tab Hunter. His assistant, Phyllis Coates, (as Superman's girl friend Lois Lane in the older TV episodes she developed a false sense of security) snoops around and finds him building a monster out of parts of the highest class human bodies (teenagers), but decides not to mention it to anyone. After all, she's making $45.00 per week and she doesn't want to rock the boat. But then, when the Monster finally murders someone, she decides it is time to tell somebody

turn the page

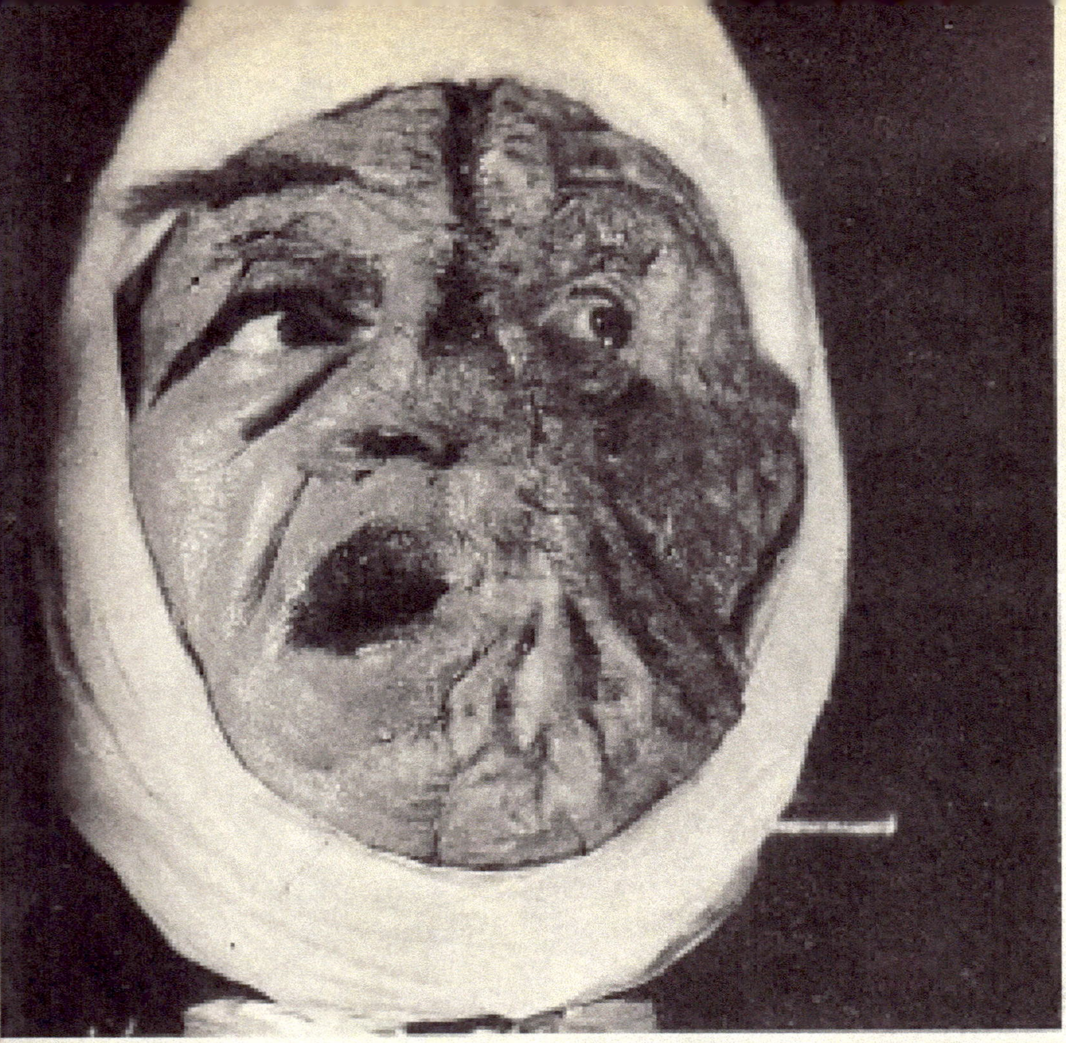

about all this. So she tells Dr. Frankenstein (who already knows), and he feeds her to the crocodiles. Later, his creation feeds him to the crocodiles, just before the Monster blunders into some live wires—one of the few live things about this production.

I next had to peek through my bandaged eye-slits at something called *Frankenstein's Daughter*, all about some more teen-agers, including a female teen-age Frankenstein in a black-leather jacket. This picture could really have used that crocodile pit!

Speaking of crocodiles, there were some of them in *Tarzan the Ape Man*, starring Denny Miller. At first I wondered why this picture was on the program but then I realized that it should have been called *I Was a Teen-Age Tarzan*. While Tarzan and I come from the same continent—Africa— I've never met him. But I never thought he looked like a vacant-faced, somewhat unhealthy-looking boy — even as a kid. Denny (Scott) Miller has joined TV's *Wagon Train*, showing a continuing love of animals, I suppose. But as for this picture, it was nice to be able to see in it most of the stock scenes from one of my favorites, *King Solomon's Mines*. After all, Sol was one of my best friends.

One of Miller's friends, another TV cowboy in *Bonanza*, Michael Landon, had to confess *I Was a Teenage Werewolf*. Screen Writer Ralph Thornton brings off a fairly interesting story here for Producer Herman Cohen and director Gene Fowler, Jr. in this American-International Picture. As a troubled high school student, Landon seeks help from a gray-haired doctor, Whit Bissell. Right away, I began to suspect something was going to go wrong.

Bissell calls himself Brandon here, but he acts like Frankenstein again and starts an experiment that causes Landon to revert to a pre-evolution animal state, to become a Werewolf.

He's just a crazy-mixed up cub Werewolf who just wants love and understanding, a pat on the snout, a rub of the pelt, but when he gets kicked around he begins to snap at people—and into them, for that matter. Finally, he is shot down like a mad dog.

The moral of the story, I suppose, is never trust one of those sneaky scientists.

In *Teenage Zombies*, another disreputable scientist, a woman named Dr. Myra (Katherine Victor) has trapped three comrades, Regg, Skip and Morrie (has a familiar ring, those names) with their three girl friends on her own private island where she is conducting experiments to turn the entire population of the world into zombies—her mindless slaves! I dozed off in this one but when I woke up the story was going along nicely.

One of Dr. Myra's Zombies was out terrorizing a Western town, threatening rugged Sheriff Bob Lehman (Stuart Wade). Unfortunately, it developed that I had missed the end of the Zombies, and we were now into *Teenage Monster*, a "huge hairy imbecile." The audience seemed to love this picture.

turn to page 59

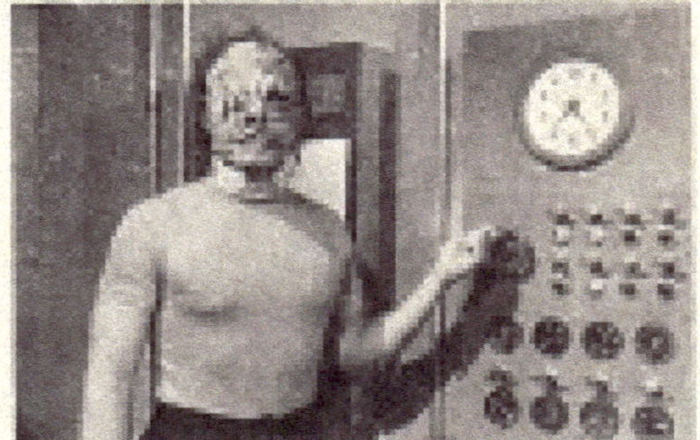

Above: Because of her toothache, Frankenstein's Daughter almost outrages a Mummy like me—but I can still rap her sore. Right: Teenage Frankenstein elevator operator doesn't find his car terribly crowded. Below: Denny the Ape Man and friends give dirty looks to banana poachers.

THE VAMPIRE AND THE BALLERINA, from the film of the same title

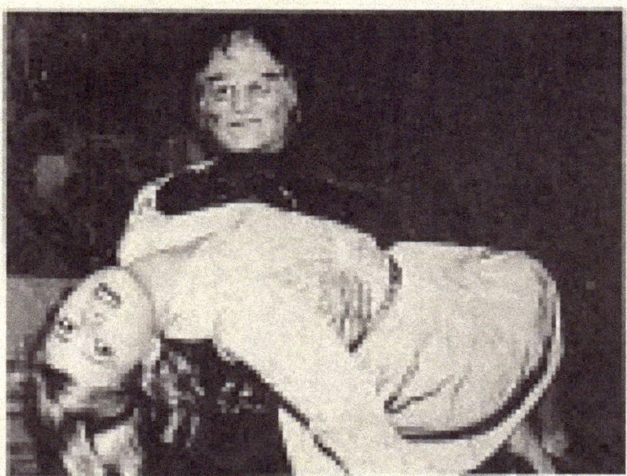

Mexico's own Tarzan, Baru, swings through the trees again in BARU'S SAVAGE WORLD

Charting the terror lanes on Hollywood's Map of Monsters to Come

HORRORSCOPE

Following American-International's release of *The Raven*, the studio's fifth Edgar Allan Poe story in two years, AIP topper James H. Nicholson told us he would be filming ten more Poe classics during the next five years.

Nicholson said this decision was made because of "the outstanding box office successes scored by *House of Usher*, *Pit and the Pendulum*, *Premature Burial*, and *Tales of Terror*. These ten new Poe productions, budgeted at from $750,000 to one million dollars each, will star Vincent Price and be produced and directed by Roger Corman.

First of the ten thrillers scheduled for filming is *The Masque of the Red Death*, to start in April. The others are *The Haunted Palace* (script by Richard Matheson), *Murders in the Rue Morgue*, *The Gold Bug*, *A Descent Into the Maelstrom*, *The Four Beasts In One*, *Ligeia*, *The Angel of the Odd*, *City In the Sea*, and *The Thousand and Second Tale of Scheherazade*. All will be in Panavision and color.

And in case you don't believe there are others beside Nicholson and Corman producing horror films these days, here they are:

Vampire and the Ballerina, from United Artists, tells the tale of a troup of beautiful maidens who are threatened by human bats wanting to rejuvenate their own circulatory systems.

MGM's *The Haunting*, produced and directed by Robert Wise, boasts a new 25mm Panavision lens developed especially for the bizarre ghost effects seen in the film. In the cast you'll find Dagwood Bumstead's one-time movie boss, Jerome Cowan.

Vincent Price (again?) stars in Eddie Small's Nathaniel Hawthorne's *Twice Told Tales*, originally titled *The Corpse Makers*, scheduled for early April release. Another chiller due in April is the *European Wolf Woman*, with Laurette LaPlanche doing the hairy honors.

Joe Stefano, scripter of Bloch's *Psycho*, is currently writing the pilot for a new science-fiction teleseries, *Stand-By*, to be aired by ABC. Also on tap for TV is a half-hour animated series, *The Adventures of Rod Rocket*, from Jim Morgan's Space Age Productions. And keep an eye out for an upcoming segment of CBS-TV's *Rawhide*, "Incident at Spider Rock", featuring Lon Chaney Jr.

Ray "Sardonicus" Russell's new novel, *The Case Against Satan* (Paperback Library, 50¢) is now a gleam in the eye of a major movie studio. William Castle, producer of *Sardonicus*, recently completed *The Candy Web* for Columbia.

While Shirley Jones is taking a *Moonswift*, Al Zugsmith is preparing *The Great Space Adventure*, and indie producer Jerry Bloom is not far behind with his *Space Animal*. ●

With its great black bird, *The Raven*, American-International hopes to dig its claws into a history making film that will fly at the same altitude as the Charlton-charioted *Ben Hur*, or the asp-bit Aphrodite, *Cleopatra* with Queen Liz. Such hopes are seldom voiced about horror and fantasy pictures, but AIP may make it. After all, they have magic on their side.

Poetic Ravens have been flying across the movie screen ever since a 1915 silent, even including a memorable pairing of Karloff and Lugosi in a Universal chiller of the '30s, but AIP's entry is a bird of a different feather. The feature, not a mere re-hatching of other Ravens, has brought together for the first time on the screen the remarkable talents of three titans of terror who have been thrilling us for a collective total of over 75 years.

Vincent Price, Crown Prince of Horror and star of a host of AIP films based on Edgar Allan Poe's immortal works, is joined by Peter Lorre, unforgettable menace of Fritz Lang's M (which started his long trail of terror), and of course, Boris Karloff, an actor who played the part of a man-made monster some years ago, as well as starring in the earlier (1935) version of Poe's *The Raven*.

With this Triumvirate of Terror appearing together, the film seems well on the way to being "history making."

The eerie script is by Richard Matheson, celebrated science-fiction author of the novel and screenplay, *The Incredible Shrinking Man*; and it touches on Poe's rhythmic poem with the ominous Raven, its deathly tapping at the door, and its final perch on the bust of Pallas Athena, the Greek Goddess of Wisdom, to quote its cryptic "Nevermore . . ." But there the resemblance between film and verse ends—the balance being to Matheson's credit. turn the page

Visiting the mammoth RAVEN set, AIP vice-president Sam Arkoff (with cigar) and president Jim Nicholson gagged it up with Price and Lorre

Swooping down on unsuspecting theatre audiences, THE RAVEN gives the bird to a trio of bewitching wizards

On-the-spot coverage by Ron Haydock

MALICE IN WONDERLAND

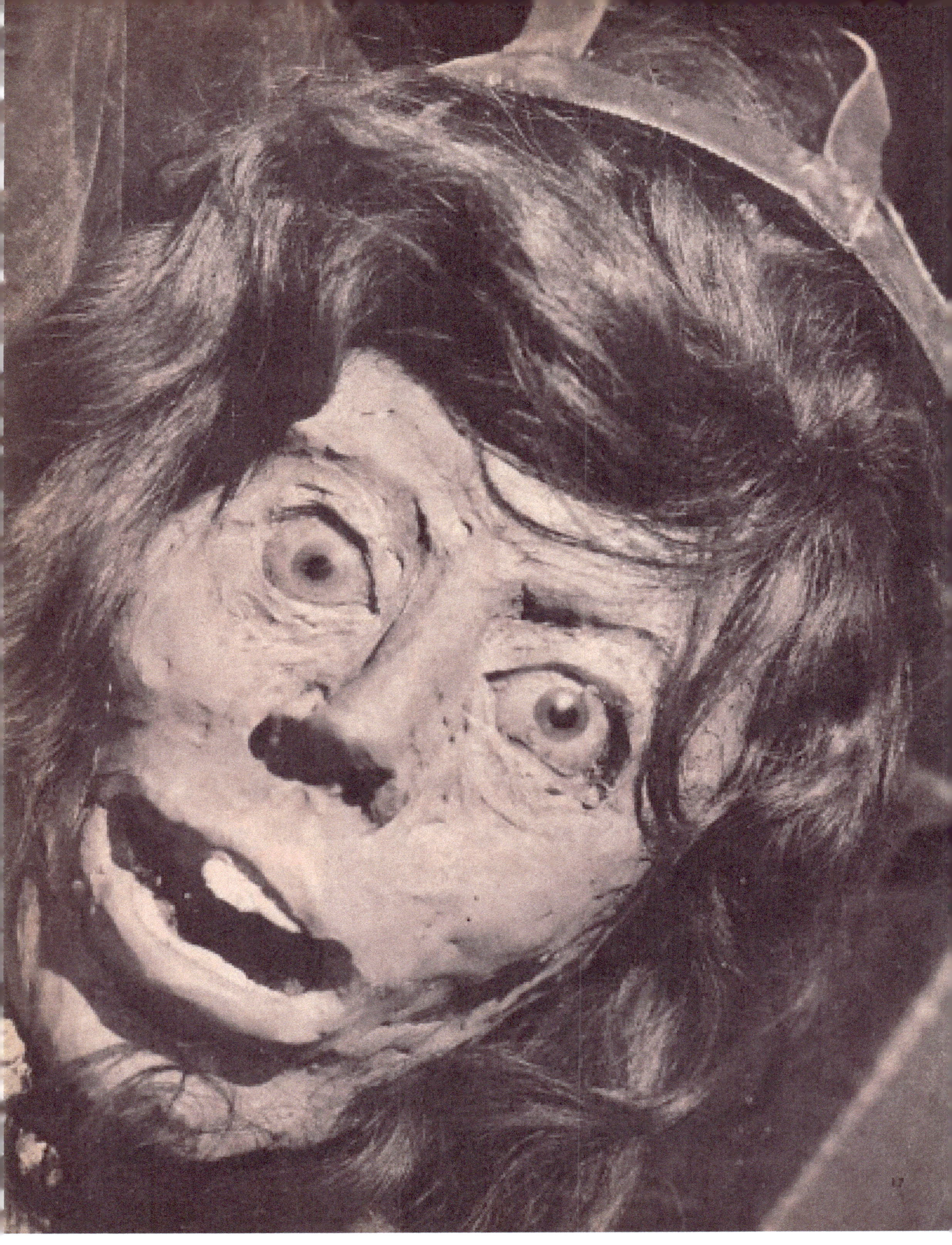

American-International's *Raven* quotes the tale of three magicians who practice their sorcery in primitive 16th century England, in an era ruled by superstition, magic, and fear. One of the wizards, Dr Erasmus Craven (Vincent Price), is living with his daughter, Estelle (Olive Sturgess), and mourning the apparent death of his wife, Lenore (the beautiful Hazel Court). Craven encounters Dr Bedlo (Peter Lorre), who has been magically transformed into a raven for daring to challenge the unlimited powers of Master Magician, Dr Scarabus (Boris Karloff).

Bedlo seeks Craven's aid in reversing the magic, and the interplay of these three powerful men and their fantastic fight for power utilizes famous screen shock devices like return from the dead, hypnotism, medieval torture, and more.

The addition of Great Britain's Hazel Court is a welcome one. All too often have AIP's films starred a top-flight star such as Price, but backed up by a supporting cast of comparative screen newcomers who could use a few more hours at their favorite acting class. Miss Court, certainly no inexperienced or unknown talent, has proved herself in well over 200 leading television roles and dozens of features, and has the distinction of adding greatly to fine Hammer Films like *Curse of Frankenstein*.

While watching the filming of *The Raven*, I couldn't help but remark again to Roy Smith, AIP publicity man, that this really is an historically important production, for more than the obvious collection of Price, Lorre, and Karloff. Although Price and Karloff have worked together in films and stage plays in the past, this was the first time they ever were Good vs Evil in a horror film. Price, the new King of Terror, and Karloff, the Grand Master of Menace, tossed magic at each other repeatedly, and in more than one scene Boris relied upon his experienced knowledge of the uncanny to teach that "young upstart" Vincent a few new tricks.

The Raven, with its subtle touches of finely played comedy, also produced some moments of uproarious laughter during filming.

There was, for example, the scene in which the raven (Jimmy, by name) was to perch upon the Athena bust, supposedly talking to Price. Actually, Lorre was off-stage, mike in hand, feeding the bird its lines. However, Jimmy, nervous because of all the people working around him, became especially irritated whenever director Roger Corman would cry "Action!", and would immediately flap its wings and fly off.

After trying to shoot this scene a number of times, the script girl suggested to Roger that he say "Go!" instead of "Action!" This always worked with horses in western movies, and Roger, never one to waste valu-

turn to page 57

Lorre is hypnotised by a magic fireball.

Above: Jack Nicholson, Hazel Court, and Karloff entertain an enthusiastic Olive Deering. Below, left: Roger Corman, ace director, and Dear Boris discuss a script change.

Below, right: Karloff and Price, after being told they were each given a subscription to *FANTASTIC MONSTERS.*

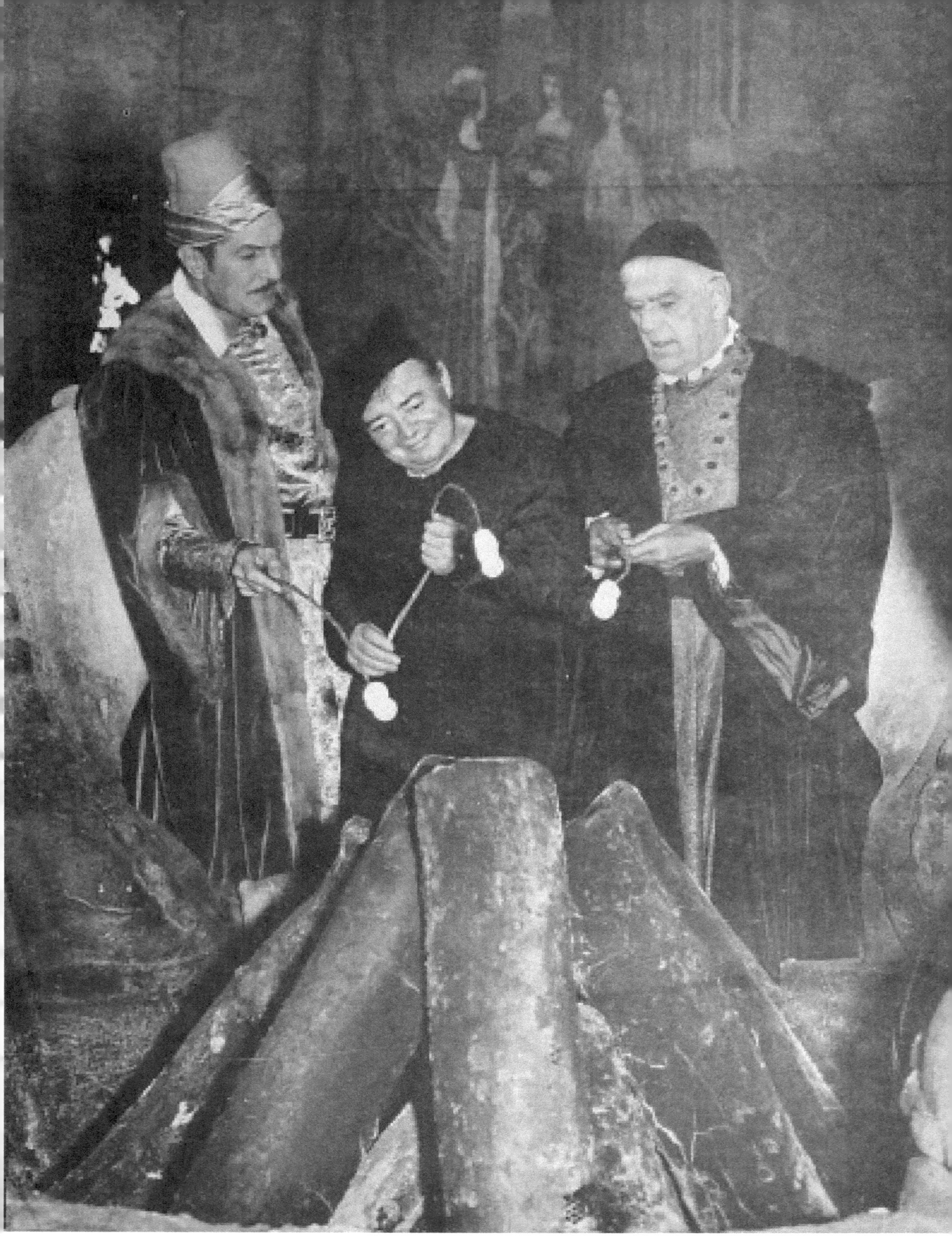

able time in production, decided anything was worth a try.

The set was lit again, and everyone scurried off into the darkest recesses of the sound stage.

Vincent ran a hand through his bird-mussed hair, quietly murmured the lines he was to speak to Jimmy, and Peter cleared his throat, clutching the mike. Roger, glancing around to satisfy himself that all was ready, said, "Go!"

The raven blasted off, upsetting the bust, leaving its shattered shards lying there like a discarded first stage rocket.

While the wreckage was removed and the bird coaxed down, Roger Corman turned his back to the set, shaking his head sadly.

I could sympathise with him.

After all, performing the picture five times since 1915, *The Raven* should have known his lines.

Of course the lines that lead up to the box office for *The Raven* can be pretty well predicted in advance. With Karloff, Price, and Lorre on hand, AIP—the studio built on horror—has no worries.

In fact, Corman is so confident of this picture's success that he tells me *The Raven* is only the first of a series of films in which the Terror Titans will star for AIP. Karloff and Price are scheduled to be working on the second as you read this in FANTASTIC MONSTERS, and Price and Lorre will be at each other's throats again for the third.

Boris Karloff, under studio policy, is scheduled for top billing by himself in forthcoming AIP horrors. To use my position as FanMo's editor to editorialize for a moment, I believe Mr Karloff has been absent too long from the screen, and I applaud AIP president Jim Nicholson for bringing him back to theatres in quality productions, so unlike the cheap "quickie" atmosphere Karloff has worked in during the past ten years, though even there managing to add class.

And, as the start of The Return of the Master, *The Raven* marks a great, top-flight production. ●

Toasting marshmallows between takes in the giant gargoyle pit.

Vincent Price discovers you can't keep a good dead man down.

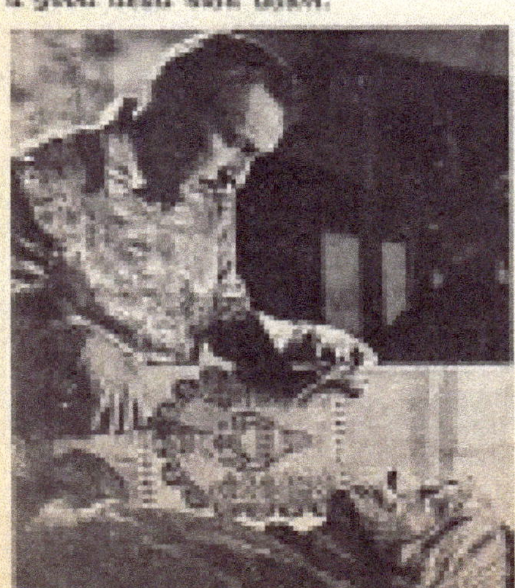

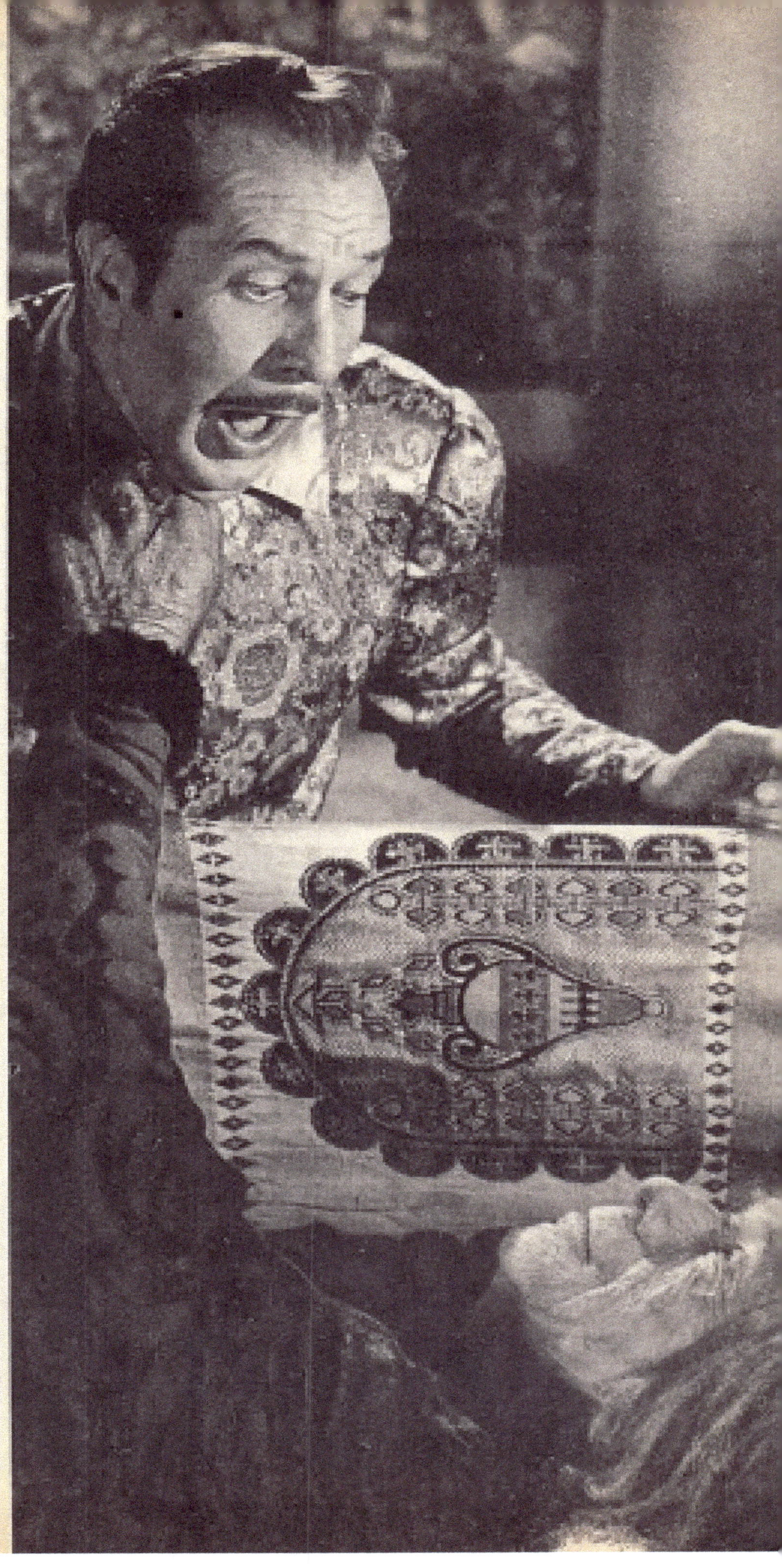

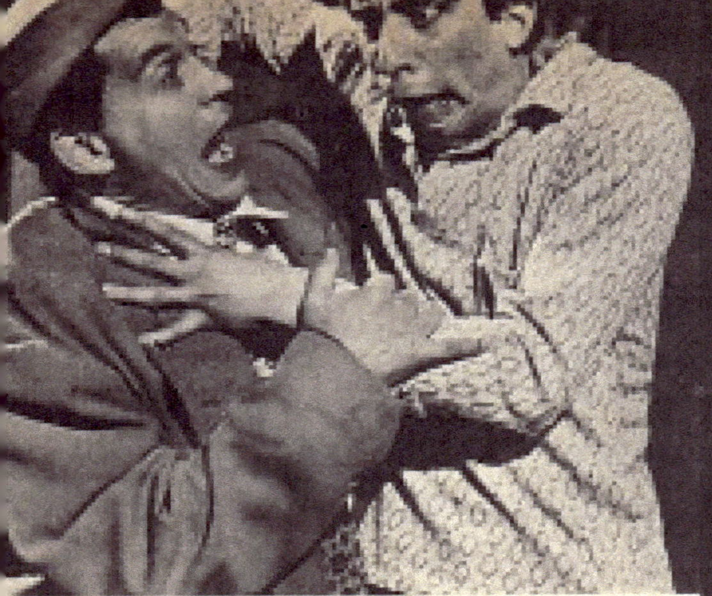

Hoppy! Hoppy's back on TV! He's back, he's back!

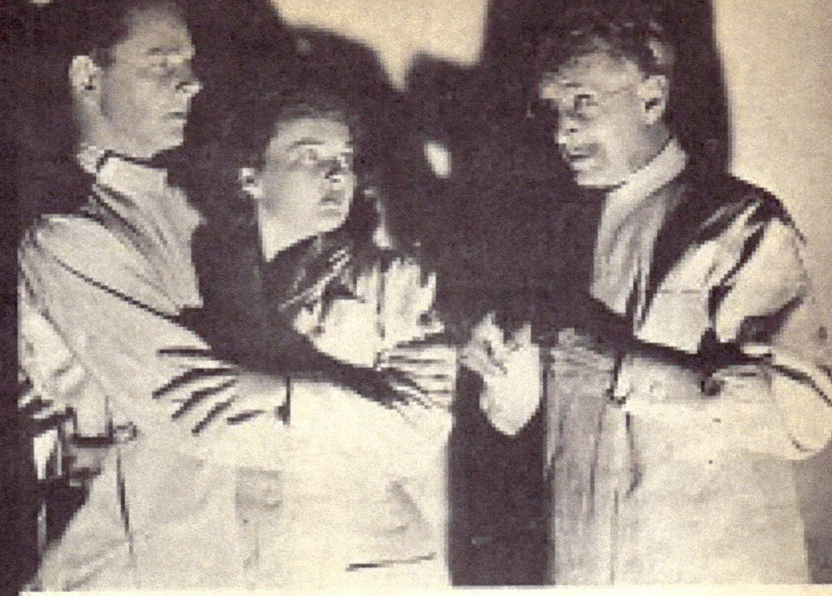

Now, now, my dear, a vaccination isn't nearly as bad as you think.

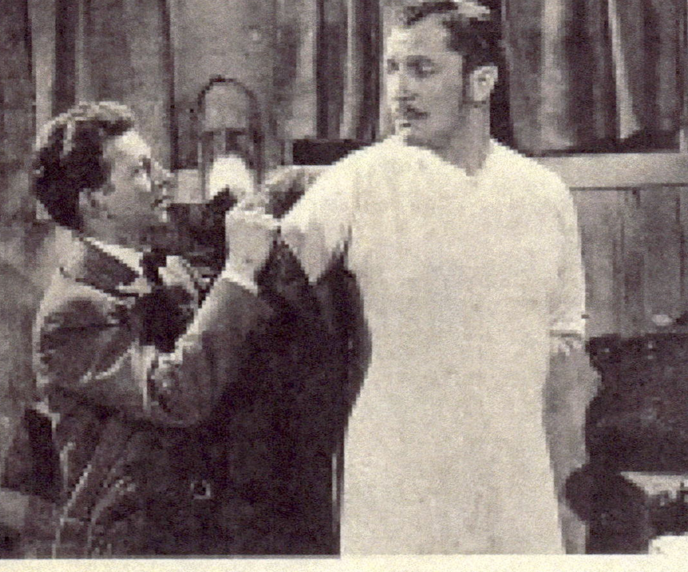

Donald, when I got up there on that speaker's platform and took off my coat, I could have died!

Dead Time Tales

From the pilfered files of Mother Goose Pimple

You know, Bud, an electrician works regular hours, gets good pay. Now being an electrician . . .

Okay, guys, I guess we got him cornered. Now, Dave, I hope you at least managed to hold onto the leash!

Left: James Bond, England's top secret agent. Right: Doctor No, evil genius of the atomic age. Below: "Going Down?" Most of James Bond's enemies usually do

Secret Agent James Bond takes on a Power-Mad Scientist intent on Controlling the World

Not since Boris Karloff's portrayal of the evil Dr Fu-Manchu in 1932 has the screen witnessed the equal of the sadistic, power-mad Dr No, whose warped scientific genius holds a remote Caribbean island in the palms of his clicking artificial hands. To counter Dr No's scheme to conquer our planet would take an almost super-human hero, and author Ian Fleming has provided us with just that type of champion: James Bond, England's foremost secret agent.

Add to the above ingredients a honey of a girl named Honey for our hero to rescue, and you have a fast-moving, contemporary science-fiction story with a fresh new cast of characters that will make even the most jaded of you thrill seekers sit up and take notice. And there's plenty to notice, too, besides the main characters; like a futuristic nuclear laboratory diverting missiles from Cape Canaveral, and a mechanical fire-spitting dragon.

In recent years, the fantastic and action-laden stories of agent Bond have captured the admiration of millions of people the world over. Not too long ago, a public announcement indicated Bond's literary creator, Fleming, was one of President Kennedy's favorite authors.

Always keeping an eye open for the latest and liveliest scientific "gimmicks", writer Fleming has had his indestructible hero tangle with such items as a super rocketship, a hydrofoil yacht called The Flying Saucer, an atomic submarine, and a streamlined train that was used in an attempt to loot Fort Knox. Tempering his imagination with colorful, sophisticated writing, Fleming has managed to ring the bell on the best seller list many times.

And now, United Artists has brought his most famous adventure tale, Dr No, to life.

In all fairness to the producers of the film, Harry Saltzman and Albert Broccoli, a great deal of effort was exercised to maintain the authenticity and flavor of the original book. Most of the location shots, for example, were actually filmed in the colorful and picturesque West Indies where the insidious Doctor was supposed to have literally ruled his island with an iron hand.

In FaMo's opinion, Sean Connery, a rugged Scottish-born actor, makes an excellent choice to play James Bond, while his honey of a heroine is lusciously portrayed by newcomer Ursula Andress. Joseph Wiseman, the well known Broadway and Hollywood actor, is a perfectly villainous Dr No.

To those of you who are familiar with such Bond novel thrillers as Moonraker, Goldfinger, and Thunderball, it's going to be a treat watching some of Fleming's famous (and infamous) characters coming to colorful life when you see Dr No. To those of you who are not acquainted with secret agent Bond, we heartily recommend this film. Your introduction to this daring hero and his evil, steel-fingered nemesis will be well worth the price of admission. ●

Evil is hatched by the kiloton, in the atomic laboratory of Doctor No. Below: The mysterious Doctor No prepares to divert another missile from Cape Canaveral.

THE INSIDIOUS DR. NO

A Fantastic Monsters Movie Preview

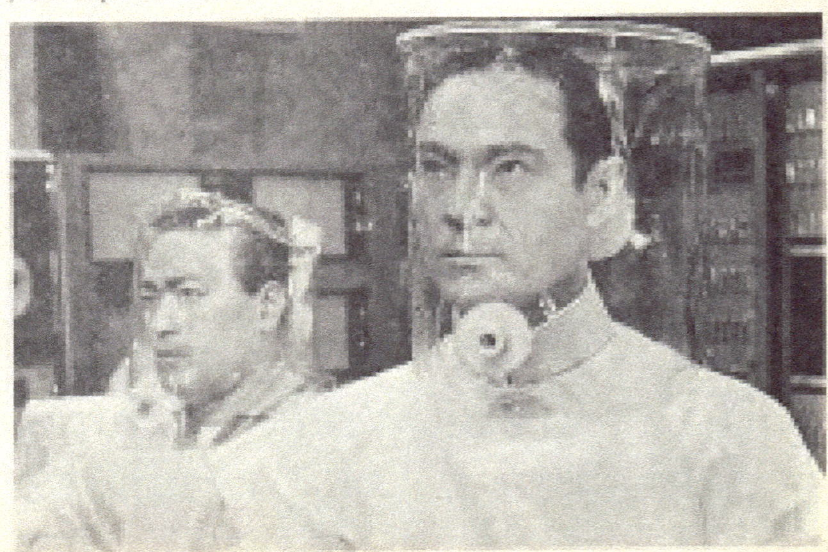

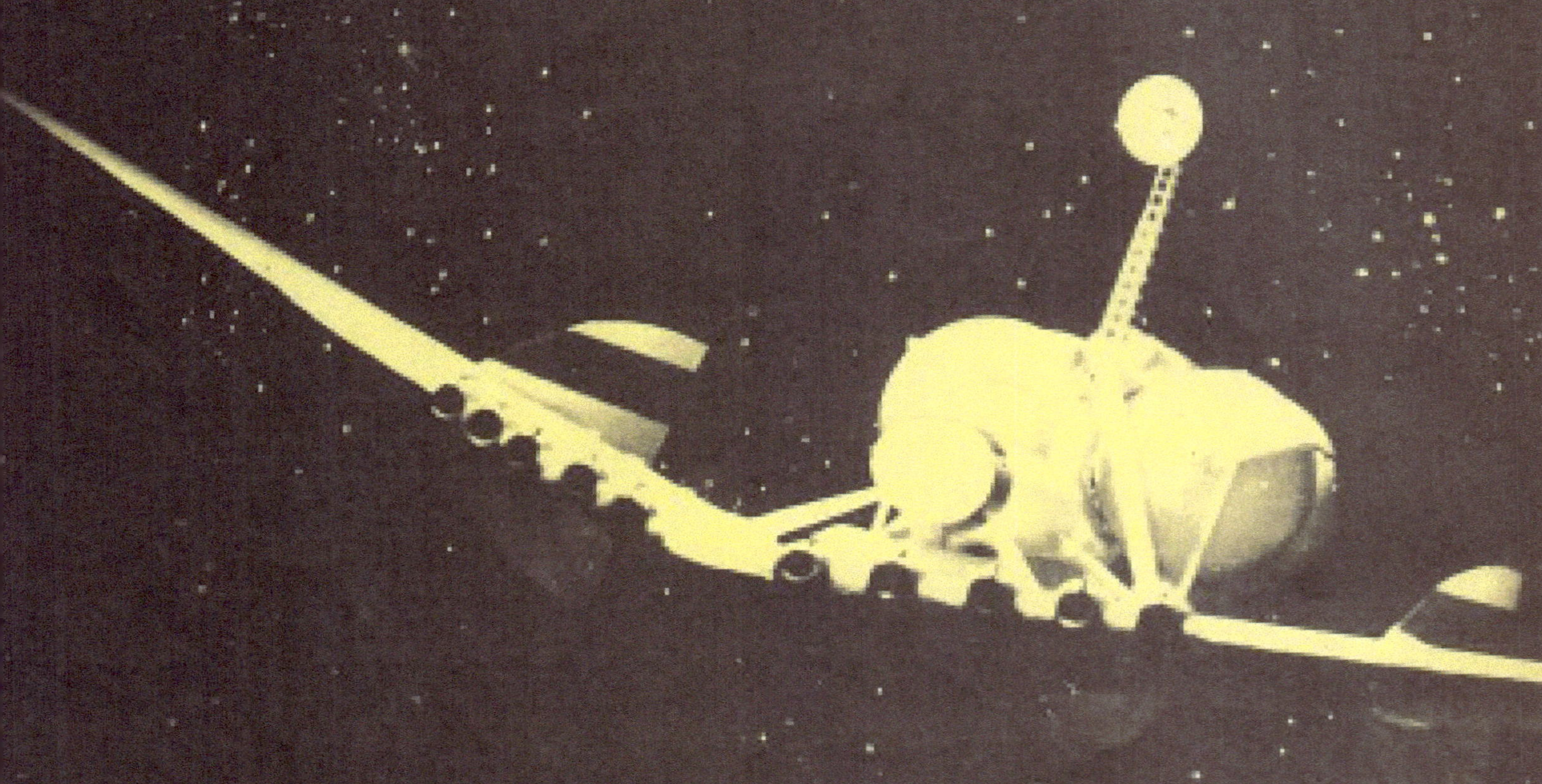

THROUGH SPACE AND TIME

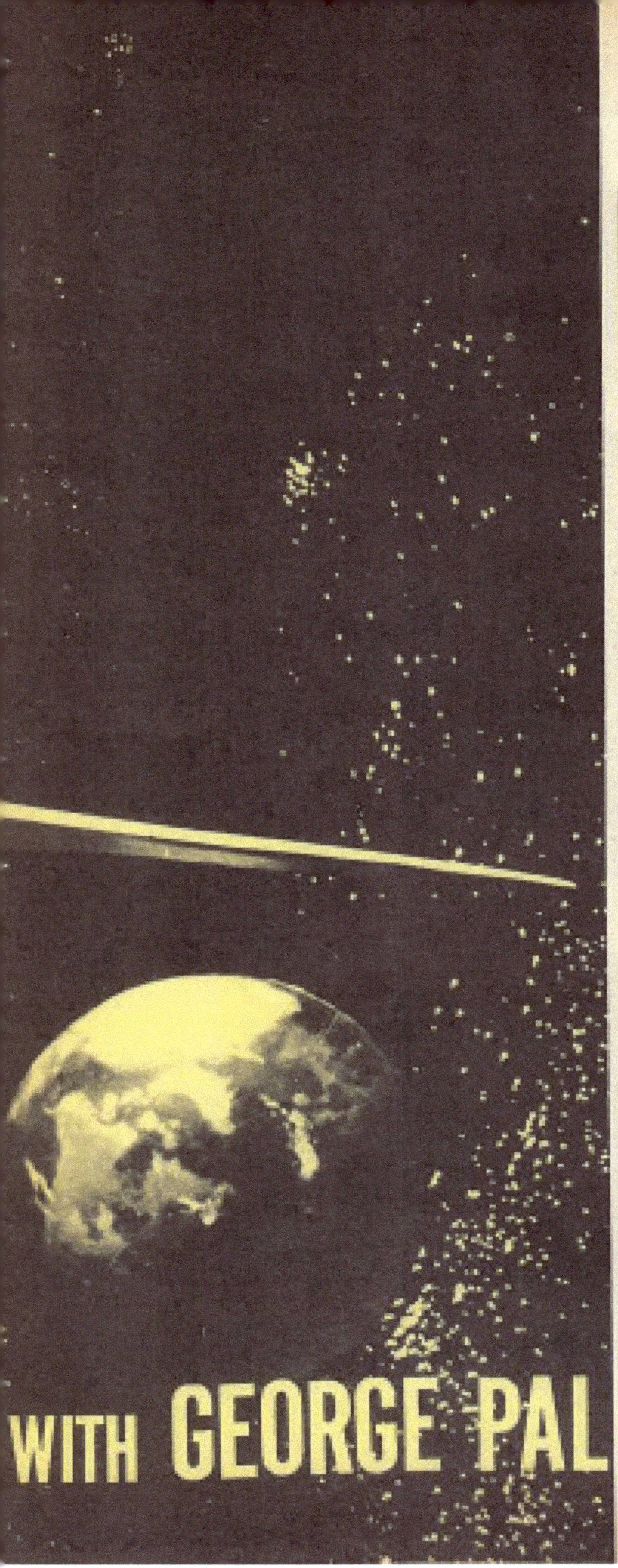

WITH GEORGE PAL

The biography of the man who conquered the Impossible Worlds of Science Fiction and brought them down to Earth

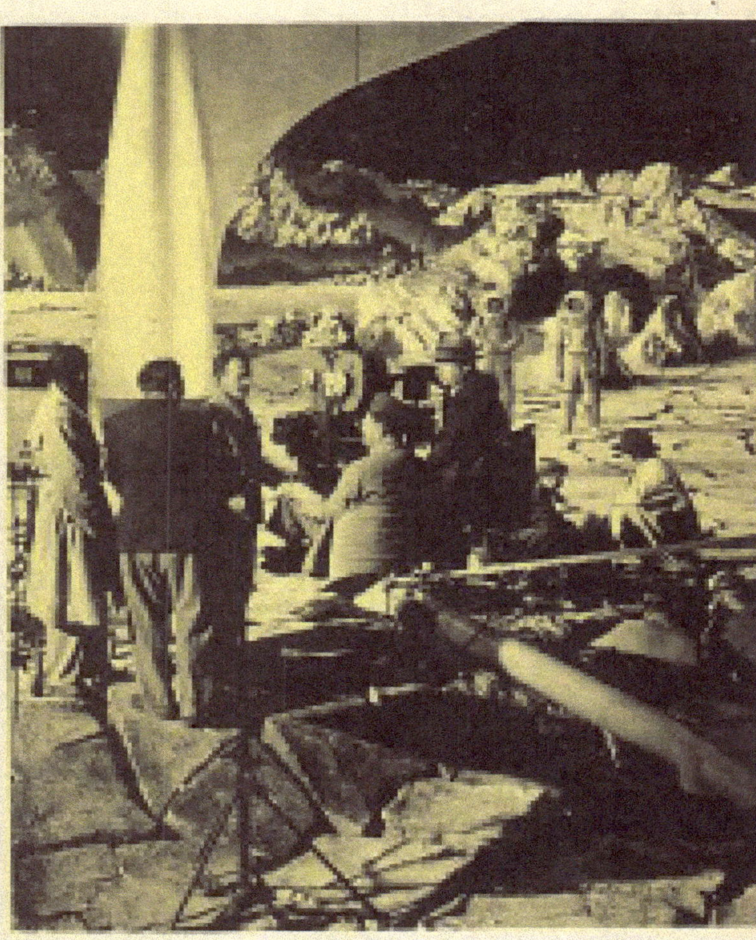

(above) On the set of *DESTINATION MOON* in 1950
(below) *The Master of Movie Marvels—Mr George Pal*

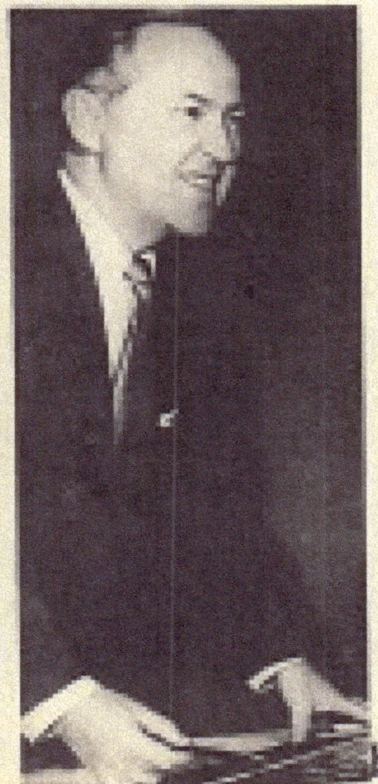

He has landed a rocket on the moon, spun planets through stellar wastes into collision orbits, peopled a dying world with spindly, malevolent beings who covet our own; he's whisked audiences to Mars, endowed a man with the ingenuity to traverse the fourth dimension, and delighted a world with gossamer tales of fairy folk.

He's a quiet man with the mildly improbable name of George Pal, and he's accomplished all this within the space of a decade.

He holds six Academy Awards for technical excellence and is the acknowledged Wizard of Hollywood

turn the page

by Mike Minor

—an honor in an industry accustomed to a sweepstakes hand like Walt Disney. The first of the Oscars came in 1943 for stop-frame animation techniques demonstrated in the remarkably Pal Puppetoons, a series of short subjects which stemmed from early experimentations in Europe prior to World War II, and featuring delightful puppet creations.

A young architect just emerged from the Budapest Academy in Hungary, George Pal found that the eating habits of his profession were rather slim. As it developed, an anatomy course landed him a job as animator at Hunnia Films—and with it, the hand of his childhood sweetheart, Zsoka Grandjean. In search of a realistic salary, Pal drifted to Berlin's UFA cartoon studio, where he prospered though his knowledge of the German language was nil.

But this was the Germany of the late 1930's, and events which chased him from Berlin to Holland, where he opened his Endhoven Studios, were also to drive him from Europe once the Wehrmacht began to roll and Europe crumble.

One continent's loss was another's gain, however, and in 1939 Pal arrived in Hollywood to produce his Puppetoons for Paramount. By 1945 and the war's end, he was a naturalized citizen and an established personality.

Closely associated with Pal, in a combination 15 years strong, is an attractive lady of invariable strength and devotion who, with her own family to manage, somehow maintains equilibrium for a producer accustomed to creating cataclysms. Gae Griffith has been burning the midnight oil for years, clearing paper work and practical obstacles in the paths of Pal's films, insuring their timely arrival on the screen. Though her hours are hectic and rest rare, Miss Griffith has a flashing smile and congeniality which has placed her on growing terms with everyone from stagehand to star.

But even her wildest moments on the Puppetoons could hardly have prepared her for Pal's next leap: feature production.

Pal released his first feature film in 1949, through United Artists. The Great Rupert, starring Jimmy Durante and an animated squirrel whose pack rat antics with money stole the show, provided Pal with knowledge he put to use in his next production, a film which was to revolutionize an industry's thinking and inaugurate a whole genre of celluloid fantasy.

For persons unacquainted with the filming of Destination Moon, the tribulations involved are meaningless. You sink all personal funds, plus those you can borrow, into a film that raises eyebrows for its unique problems and improbable solutions, and you see so-called Hollywood experts shake their heads woefully at your plans, and you approach insanity, or ulcers.

$586,000 saw the film through with its glorious celluloid dreams and technicolor wizardry intact. It had been one long lightning nightmare for cameraman Lionel Lindon, but his polished lensing set the S-F bugs'

turn the page

(left) One of the famous PAL PUPPETOONS (above) Cover from issue #1 of PUPPETOONS comic magazine, with Captain Marvel introducing the Pal creations

(above) Safety nets were hung below floating spacemen in DESTINATION MOON (below) In 1955, Pal sent six scientists to Mars in CONQUEST OF SPACE

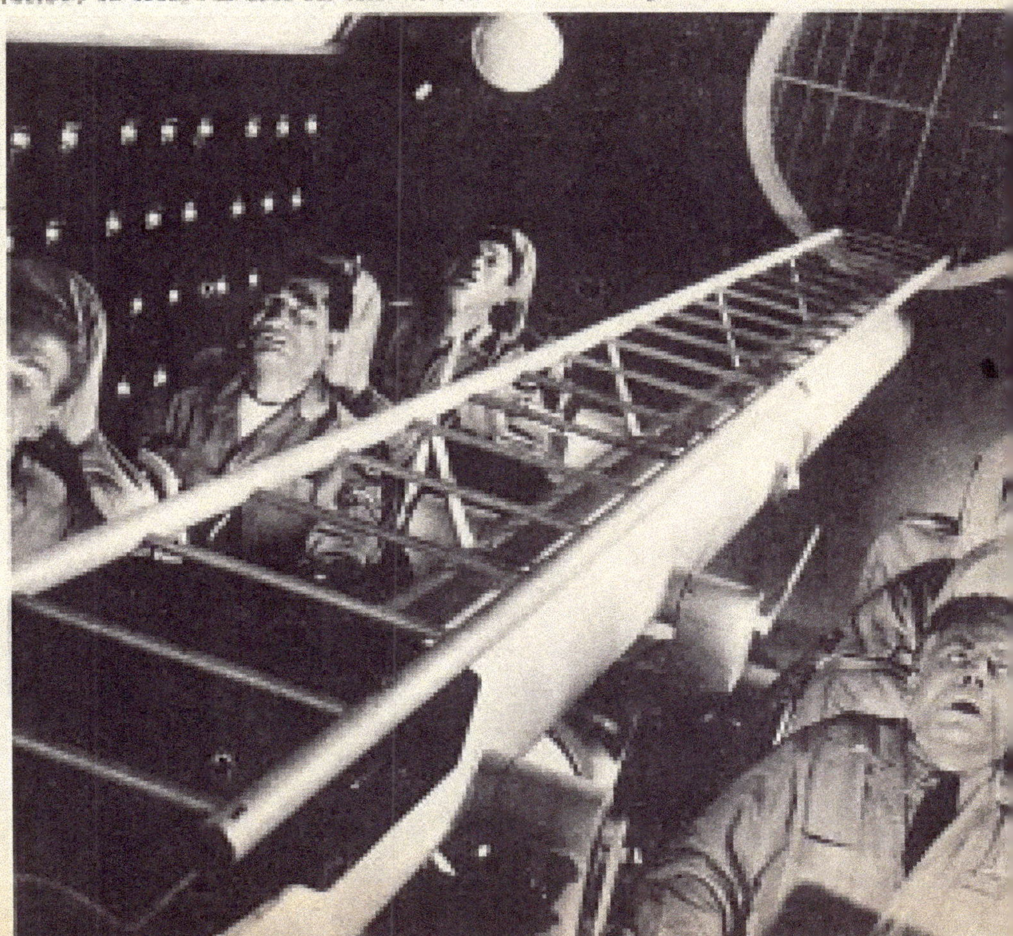

pulses racing and introduced whole generations to the possibilities of serious screen science-fiction. Pal's rocket, designed by artist Chesley Bonestell, lifted off with a roar that sent box-office receipts soaring, and the film that began as a party conversation between author Robert Heinlein and Pal became the film attraction of 1950 and direct precursor of all such future films, finally earning that year's Academy Award for Best Special Effects.

The initial success of the moon trip prompted Pal's second venture into space, this one for Paramount. When Worlds Collide had been purchased by the studio in 1934 as a Cecil B. DeMille extravaganza. Judged too radical for its time, the property had been shelved—until Pal's arrival and subsequent purchase.

How do you picture the annihilation of a world, the exodus of a handful of humanity via rocket to a new Eden? With the artistic assistance of Bonestell, you produce a rocket every bit capable of traversing the stellar wastes he has painted. With special effects ace Harry Barndollar, your visual phenomena leave audiences gasping as your tidal waves surge through New York City, and your volcanoes vomit incandescent filth upon a buckling Earth. The emotional strain is heightened by Leith Stevens' score, just as in the moon film, and a new sensation is the red dwarf star, looming ever larger on a steadily disintegrating horizon.

And so people marvel at the cataclysms you have brought in for just under a million dollars, convincing

turn to page 48

George Pal re-discovered ATLANTIS, THE LOST CONTINENT for MGM in 1961. Here, one of the stars discovers the buddha-like statue of an Atlantean god.

(below) Gigantic spaceship is poised and ready for takeoff to planet Zyra in WHEN WORLDS COLLIDE

(above) Warner Anderson, Dick Wesson, and John Archer ask the musical question—"How High the Moon?"

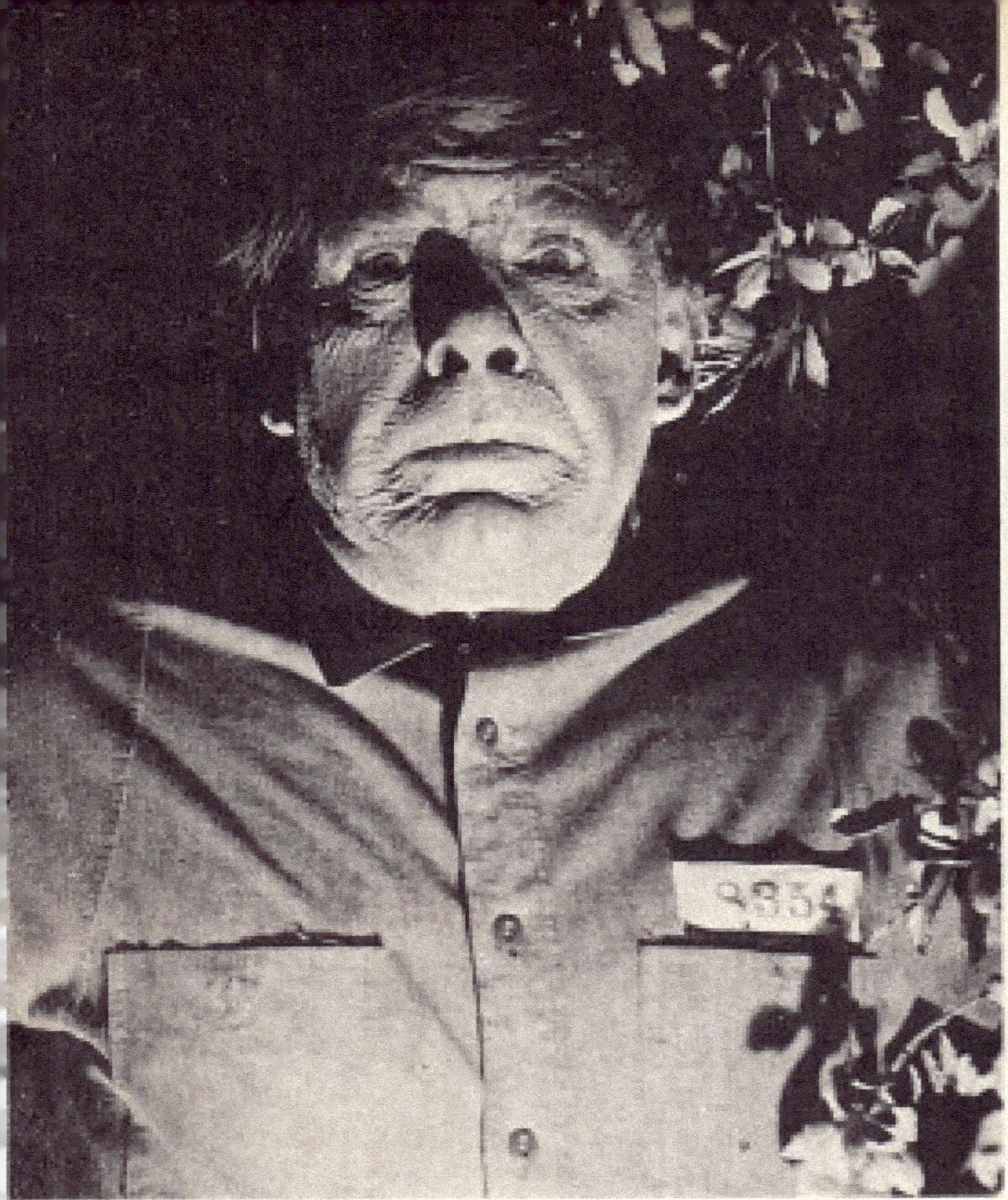

Right: Chaney shocked all as THE ATOMIC MONSTER for Universal in 1941. Below: The TV series HAWKEYE AND THE LAST OF THE MOHICANS saw Lon starring as the Indian Chingachgook. Left below: In Republic's 1936 serial spectacular THE UNDERSEA KINGDOM, Lon was featured as underwater warrior Hakur. At right: In one of his recent films, THE DEVIL'S MESSENGER, Lon played wily Satan to perfection.

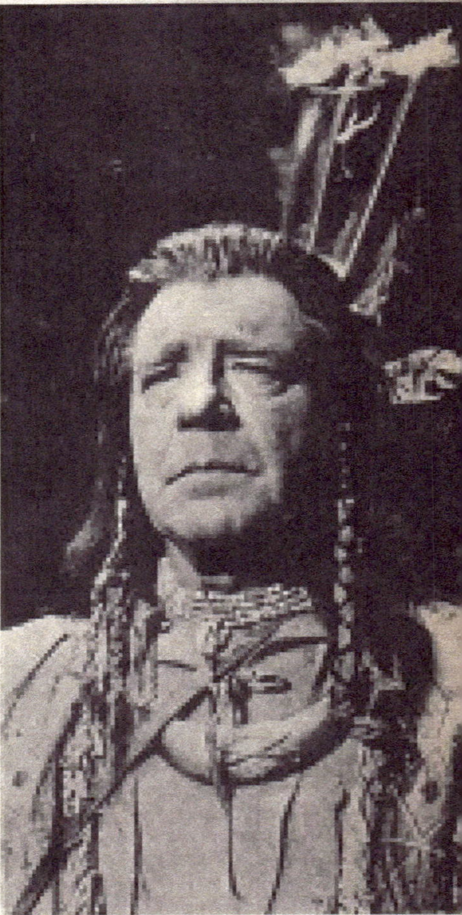

Lon Chaney Jr., Son of the Man of a Thousand Faces, in a Collectors File of Photos as he marched on in his father's Immortal Shock Steps, proving he was the screen's new master character actor.

CHAMBER

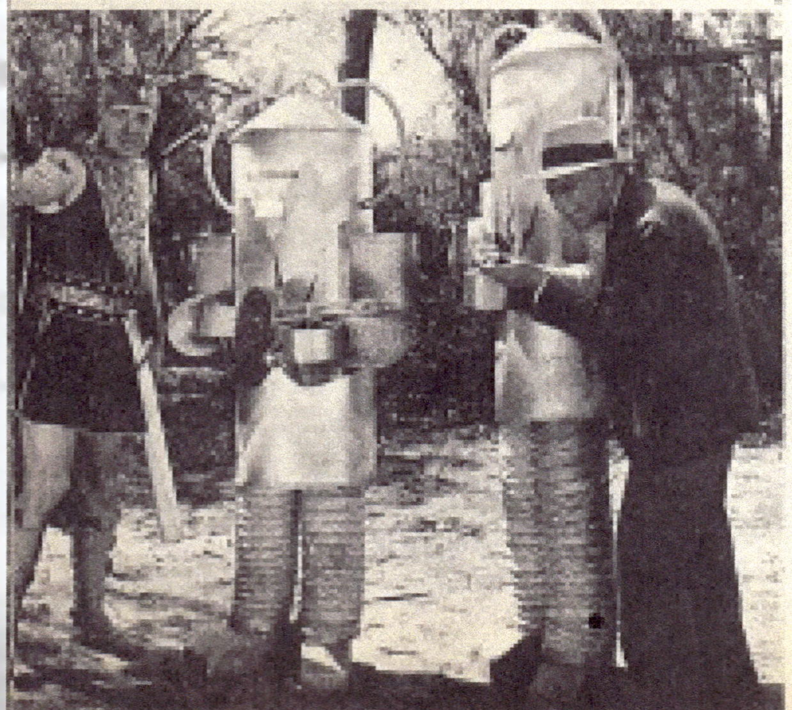

OF CHANEY

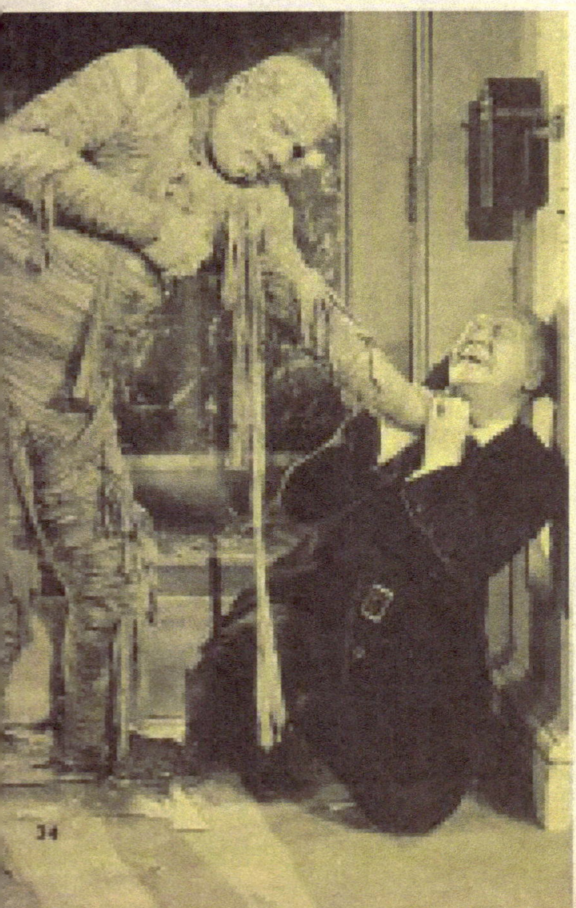

Above: Lon was the one-eyed prehistoric caveman Magno in the classic dawn-age drama ONE MILLION B.C., from United Artists in 1940. Left: The Mummy, Chaney style, reached out again in 1944 to strike terror into the hearts of those who played opposite him in Universal's THE MUMMY'S GHOST. Below: The Chaney Wolf Man snarls again—this time at an unsuspecting Lou Costello in ABBOTT & COSTELLO MEET FRANKENSTEIN (Universal, 1948). Right: Starring as the Frankenstein Monster in Universal's 1942 horroroso GHOST OF FRANKENSTEIN.

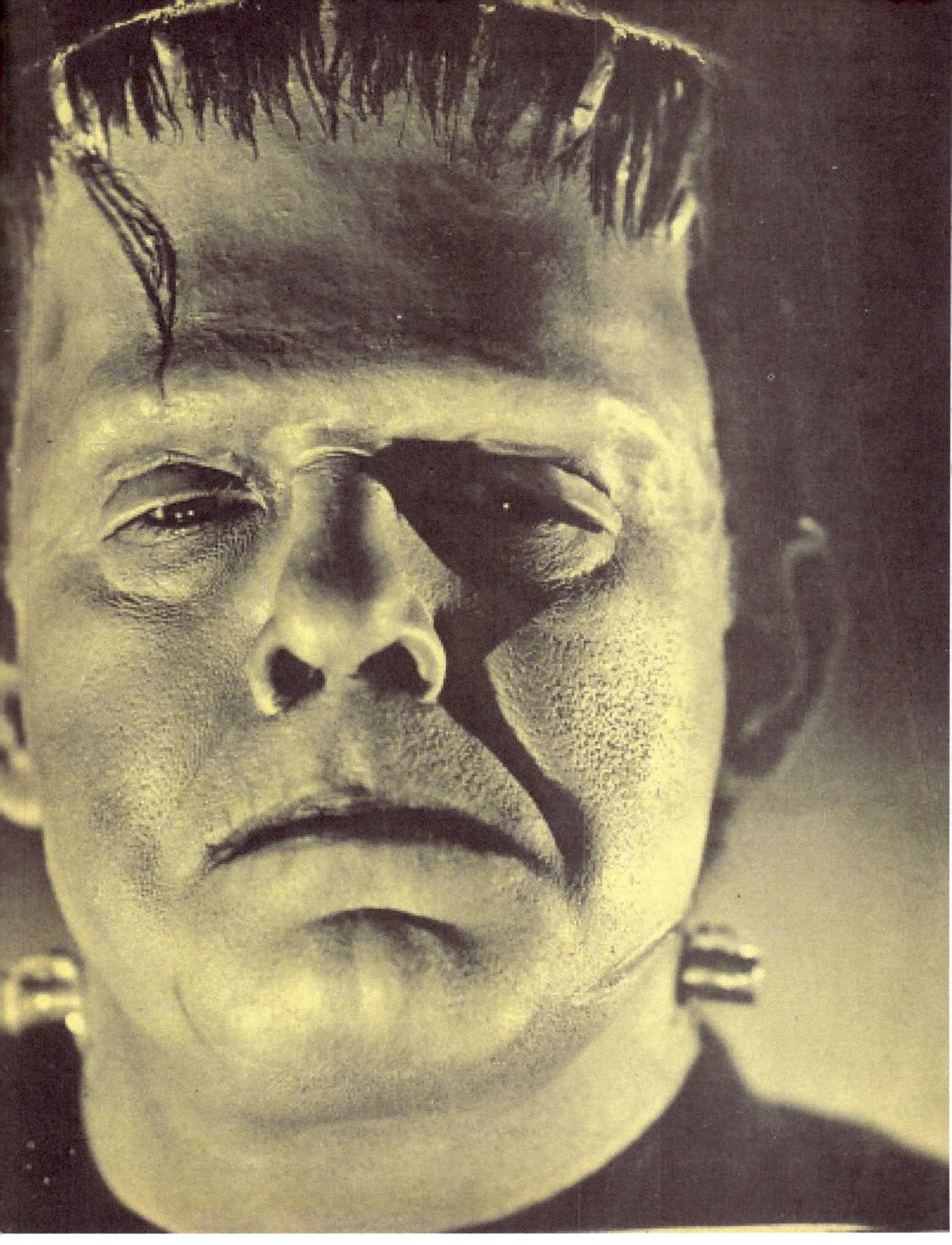

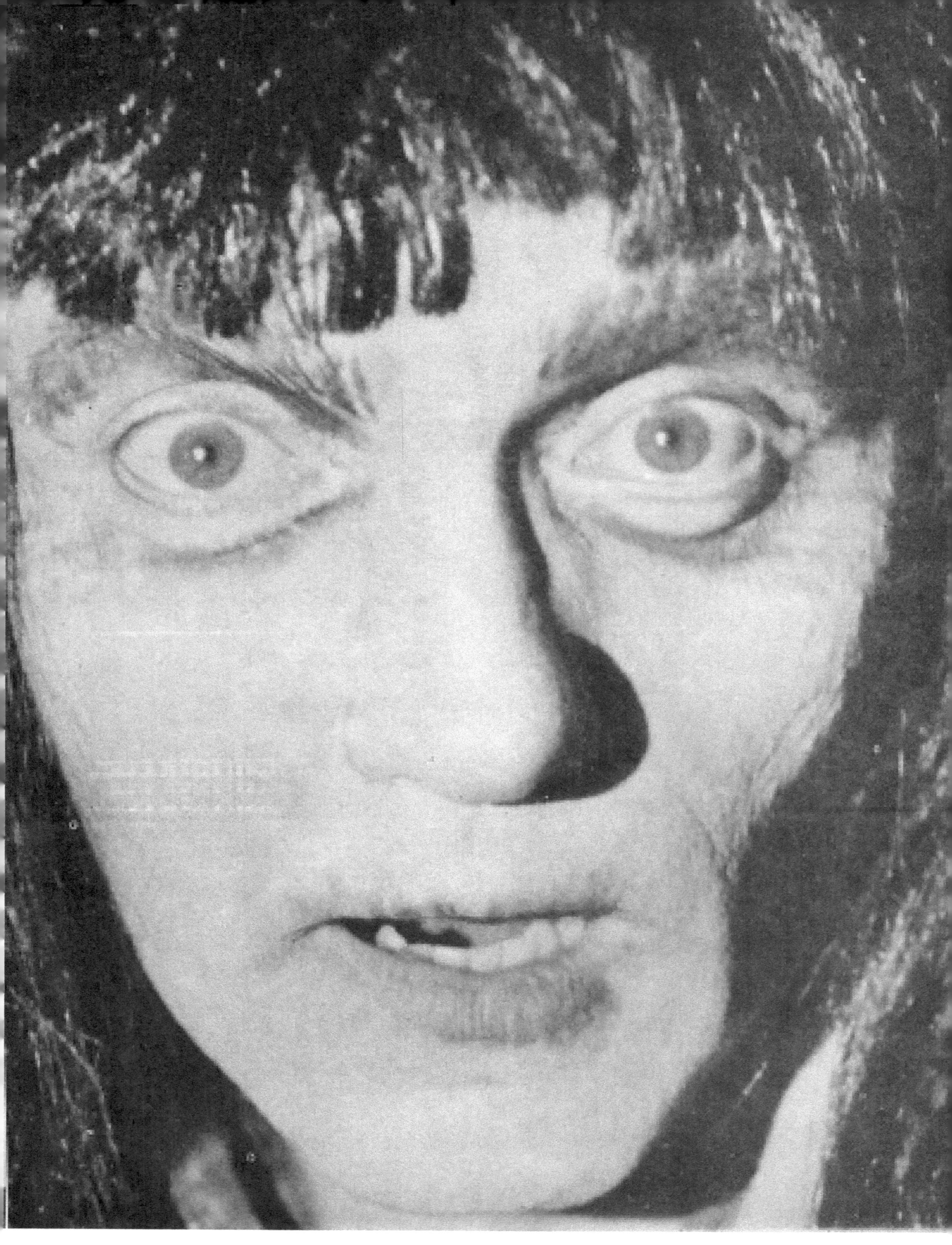

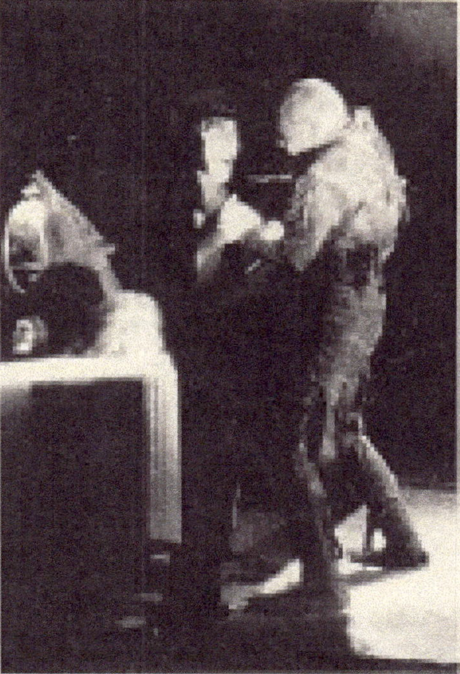

Jeepers summoned me from my coffin by burning Tana leaves.   *Above: After the show, I put Jeepers back in his box.*

Below: Jeepers and his hairy friend Boris

MAD MUMMY GETS JEEPERS

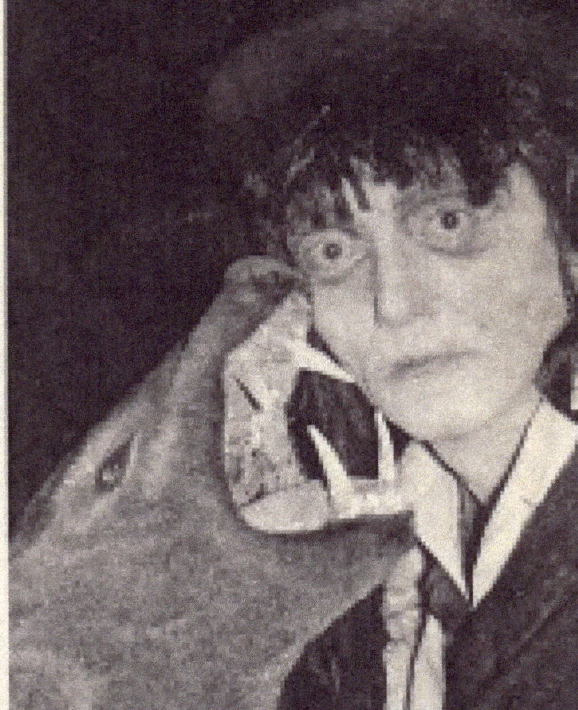

Have you ever been hauled out of a comfortable coffin to attend a tea party hosted by a creepy has-been horror producer in an abandoned, spider-webbed television studio? I hope you haven't because I wouldn't want to have anything to do with somebody like that. One Mad Mummy is enough.

I had hardly closed my eyes from watching an exhaustive parade of youthful monsters (see "I Was A Teenage Mad Mummy" in this issue—Ed) when the editor of FanMo called to tell me that I should leave immediately for a TV station where I was a guest star on a "live" (I use the term loosely) horror program. I objected on the grounds that it was still daylight outside, and that he had his nerve calling me up at such a ridiculous hour. But he insisted, and resolving to someday have his nerve —and a few of his bones—I went down to KCOP-TV, Channel 13 in Hollywood.

At 13, I met the host of the horror film show, Jeepers, a fellow with long hair down to his shoulders, a dead gray face, and hollow eyes. He was petting Pumpkin, his pet white rat, when I made my grand appearance. Jeepers was okay, but there were some real weird characters there — Jim Sullivan, who writes and produces the TV show originally called Jeepers' Creepers, now Theatre 13; a slim blonde girl, Miki Edgerton, who supplies special material and who reminds me of a High Priestess I once knew; and an impressively efficient brunette, Director Betty Turbiville.

Finally, they introduced me to the chap with the rat—Jeepers himself, an ex-horror movies producer. Jeepers told me that the movie he was showing on his show that night was The Mummy's Curse, and that I would make a perfect guest. He also told me that the biggest star ever on his program was Vincent Price, a week or two before. Naturally, I smarted at this ingratitude, and we became fast friends immediately—but he managed to tear loose from my grip right

turn the page

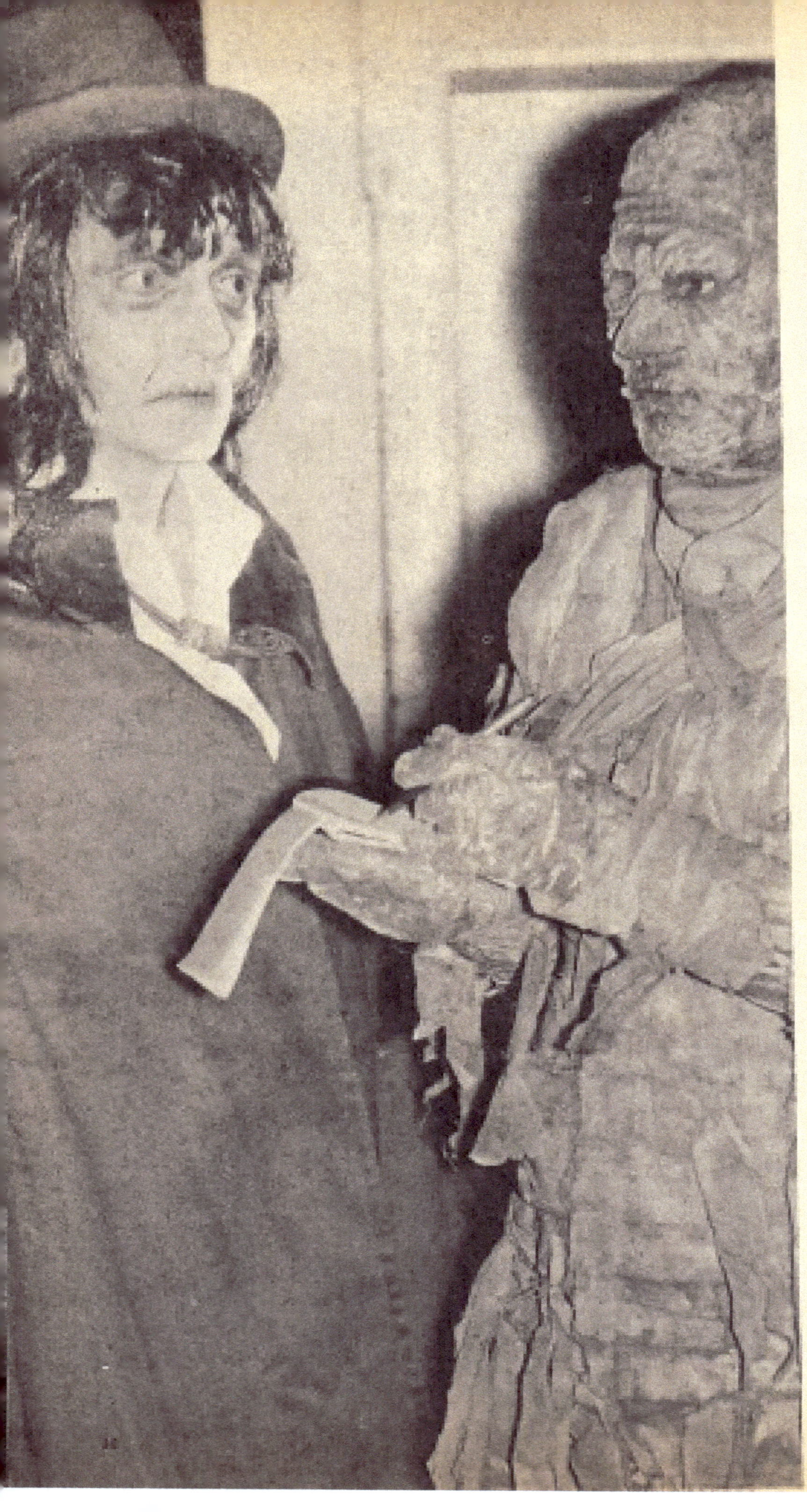

away. (These has-been producers are wiry little devils.)

The rehearsal for the TV show on Saturday, Dec. 1, 1962, proceeded. Three-quarters of the FanMo staff was on hand: Editor Ron Haydock (my arch-enemy) research chief Bob Burns, and editorial associate Jim Harmon, all asking stupid questions of Sullivan, Turbiville, and especially Miki. KCOP Program Director Bob Guy dropped in to supply some information, but he had to be off soon on other business.

Evidently, the Jeepers show was Sullivan's idea which he worked out with Guy. They discovered Jeepers himself when they and Miki started to sweep out an abandoned section of the KCOP studio. Personally, I think they should have kept sweeping.

While FanMo photographers, swell Kathy Burns and Gene Hogan, snapped their Brownies, Jeepers introduced me to his family. Of course, I had already met Pumpkin, the rodent, but he presented me to Boris, the stuffed Werewolf head that talks back to him, a small skull called Doris, a large skull (Doris' Aunt Minnie) a lizard named Billy Joe, and a shrunken head known as Julie. Personally, with all this stuff around, I think this Jeepers must be some kind of nut.

During rehearsal, Jeepers and I ran through our bit—but he ran faster than me.

Just before air time, somebody tried to introduce Jeepers to cigarettes but he threw away the evil weed angrily. While he might drink blood before his youthful fans, he would never set a bad example for them by smoking. (And let me say here that neither do I smoke—anything except Tana leaves.)

Finally, the show went on, and so did I. Jeepers made a big thing of summoning me from my coffin by burning Tana leaves, and I made a big thing out of strangling him. In fact, strangling him to death was becoming one of the big things in life to me.

We were still struggling at the end of the show, but this time over a noose (next Saturday night at 10 Jeepers was going to run Karloff's Before I Hang. I won't tell you how it all came out) but Jeepers will be back on his program next week, and I'll have my column in the next issue.

So obviously nobody won—except, we hope, the TV horror fans. ●

PLANET X, from page 11

ly. The rain of shot had stopped abruptly.

Steve paused, reached down, and picked up one of the tiny creatures. It was the only one that lay where it fell. The others regained their feet and scuttled away before he could grab them. He cupped it in his hand and looked at it with growing astonishment.

The creature was a six-legged thing with two thin tentacle-like arms. Its head was quite human in shape, but covered with green fur. Its face looked like that of a teddy bear—all the more so because the creature, like a doll, had never been alive. It was only a clever replica of a living creature.

Steve felt a sudden frustration. Had he been attacked by an army of animated toys? He crushed the small replica in his gauntled hands and watched the stuffing sift out. He threw the useless thing over his shoulder and strode forward.

The creatures had not retreated far. They had taken a stand close enough to reach him immediately with a fresh barrage. He paused a moment to judge the trajectory of the tiny missiles, and as he did so his helmet radio buzzed loudly. Automatically he nudged the receiver button with his chin, then froze in utter horror and disbelief. A woman's voice crackled through the earphones.

"Steve?"

He looked unseeingly at the far horizon. So far as he knew he, Steve Noon, was the only human being on Planet X—in fact, the only human being in a whole star cluster half a hundred light years across. He had penetrated this unknown region of space in his one-man scout cruiser, and he hadn't heard a human voice since leaving the solar system more than six months ago.

"Yes!" he croaked, clenching his fists.

"This is Helen. I've got the spaceship telescope trained on an alien city about ten kilometers due west. They're going crazy over there. A big army is being mobilized, and I think their scientists are cooking up big medicine. You've beaten them so far, but you'd better move fast now. They're bringing up high explosives and an air echelon and possibly death rays. Luck, Steve!" The transmitter clicked off.

"Right! Thanks," Steve said, squinting westward through the red sunshine. Now that he considered the matter, he remembered that the Powers-That-Be had changed things at the last minute. By heaven, he shouldn't have forgotten! The new plans called for man-wife teams to explore planets instead of lone scouts. Helen was his wife!

He squared his shoulders resolutely and marched forward to attack the city Helen had spotted. From time to time he encountered regiments of tiny six-legged creatures deployed to intercept him. He rushed forward kicking and flinging his arms, hurling metal fortresses and creatures in all directions. The tiny bodies that plummeted to earth and lay still were always artificial doll-like replicas.

He crushed them in his big hands and tossed them over his shoulder as he walked on.

At length he entered the city. He blinked in surprise that he hadn't noticed it from above as he descended from space. It was a large city full of tall, weirdly shaped buildings. Small fast-moving vehicles swirled frantically around his feet.

He crunched forward, pushing buildings aside as he walked. Towers toppled and crashed into the canyons of streets, halting traffic and flinging the tiny vehicles into the air. Through his earphones he could hear the rumble of falling masonry and the cries of the tiny six-legged creatures as he plowed on.

He advanced to the city square, a large plaza with a pond and many statues and halted uncertainly. A high thin whine was building up in the turbid air, and he swiveled his gaze anxiously to all points of the sky. Finally he saw them, scooting fast and low out of the setting sun: a dozen stubby-winged aircraft the size of pigeons. Their power dive was fast and vicious. He flailed at them frantically with both hands, but struck down only one of them. The others peeled away at the last instant, snarling past his ears at high speed. One of them made a tight turn and screamed down again, zooming directly at his face. As he covered back, trying to bring up his hands in time, a blue flash winked hotly from the nose of the craft.

Steve Noon fell heavily, crushing buildings over a two-block area under his sprawling body. As final darkness rushed over him, he saw the triumphant air squadron bank swiftly and streak off in the direction of the spacecraft. When they completed their mission there, the war would be over!

* * *

The lights came on in the projection room. The Director climbed to his six legs and beckoned with one long tentacle-like arm. "Zov, the rewrite job to put a second alien in that invading spaceship was clumsy and unconvincing. Make it more realistic and we'll reshoot that scene."

"Right, chief!" Zov started to scurry away, but the Director continued. "The scenes where the monster picks up and crushes the soldiers are too fakey. You can see the stuffings squeezing out. Let's watch that." He turned and signaled to the projectionist. "Now I want to see that last scene again."

As soon as the screen lit up again, he sat down and studied the form of Steve Noon as he battled the air armada. "Half a million we spent to build that creature," the Director said wearily, "and it still looks fakey, Zov. Fakey as all creation. Nobody will be scared by such an obvious clockwork machine. You can see the wires when he walks."

On the screen Steve Noon fell again, toppling tiny buildings. Looking closely with a professional eye the Director noticed that the fall had broken Steve's face. The metal framework glistened through the torn papier-mache and behind it loomed the dark hollow of his skull. ●

TEENAGE, from page 14

The next thing that happened made me think the bill of movies had finished, and was starting over again. But then I saw it was still another picture: *How to Make a Monster* which included the make-up of the Teen-age Werewolf and the Teen-age Frankenstein in another James H. Nicholson-Samuel Z. Arkoff winner from AIP.

Personally, I have been a Z. Arkoff fan ever since I used to see him with Flash Gordon in the funny papers and the Universal serials. Or is that the same one? After *Make a Monster*, *Teenage Werewolf*, *Teenage Frankenstein*, I'm not sure whether I'm seeing double or not.

While at first glance, I thought AIP had the teenage monsters sewed up like Frankenstein's skull, I found out other studios could get into the act, even Warner Bros.

In one of their most adventurous steps since the first talking picture, Al Jolson in *The Jazz Singer*, Warners proudly presented *Teenagers from Outer Space*.

Actually, this was not exactly a teenage monster epic because the teenagers from the stars were not monsters. They were perfectly normal-looking, pleasant young fellows who shot their ray guns at people and turned them into skeletons.

But David Love as Derek proves that there's really no such thing as a bad boy.

Derek stops turning people into skeletons, and even helps save Earth from a gigantic rampaging beast, the Gorgon, and from the invasion of his own alien people.

Still stinging from the final dying curse from his fellow space invaders in their native language—"F-bk!"—Derek turns to Dawn Anderson (Earthling Betty) for the love and understanding he never got from his alien parents, who happened to be electronic brains in charge of a garbage disposal plant on his home planet.

Teenagers from Outer Space was a fitting climax to a great program of movies, a fine fourteen hour bill.

In case you wonder where you can get so much entertainment as all this, for 35c—the only place is a theatre on Main Street in Los Angeles, or in the private theatre for magazine staff members where I saw it. Our own Ron Haydock was there, sitting next to the editor of *Spaceman*, and the editor of the new *Mass Science Fiction*.

Of course, the movie program lasted so long that some of the audience went in as teenagers and came out as young adults, abandoning their rock 'n' roll records right and left.

Considering what I'm paid for doing this FanMe column, I collected the records and am peddling them door to door. I guess teenagers really do like monsters like us mummies, because very few of them have shown much sales resistance to me. ●

MYSTERY LOVER

Much as I liked your fine third issue, the interesting article on radio's *I Love a Mystery* by Jim Harmon was not long enough.

While he mentioned that Michael Raffetto, Barton Yarborough, and Walter Patterson originally played Jack, Doc & Reggie in Hollywood, and that the NY cast was Russell Thorson, Jim Boyles, and Tony Randall, he didn't mention that Jay Novello took over as Jack Packard for a brief time.

Temporarily replacing Doc Long was John McIntire (now *Wagon Train* boss) portraying Irish adventurer Terry Burke; and Forrest Lewis (comedy cop star of Disney's *Absent Minded Professor*) played a mysterious Frenchman named Michael — who sounded so much like Peter Lorre that Lorre's studio insisted Lewis be given name credit to prove it wasn't Peter. A Swede named Sven, and two girl characters—Mary Kay Brown and Jerri Boskee—also at one time were one of the Three Comrades.

After ILAM left CBS Radio in 1945, two years later ABC had a radio series of complete half-hour stories (instead of the former serial chapters) with Raffetto and Yarborough again as Jack and Doc but with a new Reggie —Tom Collins (who was also radio's *Chandu the Magician*). This 13 week series was titled *I Love Adventure*.

Not many people know that Carlton E. Morse, author-producer of ILAM, did 52 half-hour shows that seemed to be ILAM under a different name —*Adventures by Morse*. Jack and Doc seemed to be called "Capt. Bart Friday" and "Skip Turner" here. I remember one ABM story *Land of the Living Dead* had zombies, werewolves, vampires, prehistoric monsters, black airplanes, man-eating plants, beautiful priestesses, and jungle temples. While not as imaginative as ILAM, it was pretty good.

        JAY S. KRAMDEN
        MOUNT CARMEL, ILLINOIS

Pictured above is Barton Yarborough, better known to reader Kramden and other ILAM fans as Doc Long —ED.

MONSTER CLUB

I am a member of your *Fantastic Monsters Club* and I just received my first copy of the club fanzine *Fright!* along with my membership card and monster photo. I think it is all the greatest.

        GEORGE FINE III
        LAKE VILLAGE, ARKANSAS

If you haven't joined the FanMo Club yet, better turn to page 16 and sign in please—ED.

MARVEL-OUS

Of all the stories on Captain Marvel that have appeared in movie thrill magazines, Dick Lupoff's article (*Movies' Mightiest Mortal*, FanMo No. 2) far surpasses all others. The photographs were better and the text much more informative.

        TIM TUTTLE
        DURAND, MICHIGAN

Writer Lupoff returns to our pages next issue with the adventures of another comic book favorite, Spy Smasher. Don't miss it—ED.

STRANGE REQUEST

I really enjoyed the story on Glenn Strange playing Frankenstein you had in issue 2. You told about a lot of things I always wondered about, like how the idea for *Abbott and Costello Meet Frankenstein* came about.

I think Glenn Strange was the best Frankenstein, even better than Boris Karloff or Lon Chaney. I hope you write more stories on Glenn Strange and have a lot of pictures that have never been used before.

        NORMAN BENSON
        NEW YORK, NY

Here's a photo of Glenn we don't think you've seen before, Norman. With him is his daughter Janine and grandson Mike—ED.

TIME PROBLEM

I'll bet I can stump you! I'll bet I can ask for something that you can't show me! I want to see a color photo of Boris Karloff as the Frankenstein Monster.

It would be impossible for you to have a COLOR PHOTO because he made his Frankenstein movies in the '30's and there was no such thing as color photographs then.

So let's see how good you really are! Unless you've got a time machine you'll have to admit defeat.

        WALT BAUMAN
        FORT WORTH, TEXAS

Please turn to the back cover, Walt. It'll only take a second—ED.

STERLING SERLING

Thanks for a great article on Rod Serling in FanMo 2.

My concern for Rod Serling resulted from two experiences. When our class was assigned a report based on what we intend to be as adults, I chose Mr Serling as a "victim" to my questions pertaining to a writing career. He sent me a two page reply answering my questions and more besides.

With his help I received an "A" for the report. Sometime later, when I was doing a project on television writing, Mr Serling sent me a shooting script from one of his *Twilight Zone* episodes.

All this, plus the fact that he's a gifted writer, has put him on the top of my list.

        HARVEY OVSHINSKY
        DETROIT, MICHIGAN

MAD MUMMY MUMBLINGS

I think, and I'm sure most of the other readers do too, that the Mad Mummy is a waste of paper.

        DAVE HALL
        GREENVILLE, ARK.

No matter what some of your other readers may tell you, please don't fire the Mad Mummy. I like him. He's funny.

        DICK KLINGMAN
        HOLLYWOOD, CALIF.

Who are you guys trying to kid?

        JOHN KRABEC
        DOVER, DELAWARE

CALL from Fellow Monsters

Do you realize that you've made History with the Mad Mummy? The Mad Mummy is the World's First Continuing Character in a Monster Magazine! Kongratulations!

JIMMY GUYER
URBANA, ILLINOIS

FRANK FACTS

Regarding the early Frankenstein films:

In issue 1 you said that Thomas Edison made one in 1898. I have a U.S. Copyright Index which says the Edison *Frankenstein* was made in 1910.

Also, in 1902 there was a copyrighted *Frankenstein's Trestle* produced by American Mutoscope and Biograph Co. Your guess is as good as mine what it was about.

CHRIS COLLIER
BRISBANE, AUSTRALIA

Do any of you other readers have information on these pre-Karloff Frankenstein movies? If you do, please write us—ED.

QUICKIE COMMENTS

Your 3-D article in 2 was a terrific piece of work.

ALAN SIMONS
ALEXANDRIA, VA

Have more full-length face pictures of Frankenstein, Dracula, and the Wolf Man.

JAY JOHNSON
ALGONA, IOWA

The *Devil's Workshop* is a fine idea. Most of your readers probably dream of making their own monster make-ups and can certainly profit by this department.

RORY COKER
ATHENS, GEORGIA

It's nice to see a more serious approach taken to these types of films.

H.B. BARNS JR
DAYTON, OHIO

Somehow the colors in *Fantastic Monsters* are actually more annoying than anything else.

LARRY IVIE
NEW YORK, NY

It's about time some monster magazine got the idea of using color monster photos for their covers. You were the first.

R. ROBERTSON
MONROVIA, CALIF

I like the way you've grouped photos of Karloff and Lugosi together for *Castle of Karloff* in 2 and *Belfry of Bela* in 3.

BOYD FLETCHER
BALTIMORE, MARYLAND

Fantastic Monsters has very good fiction stories—worthy of reprinting in pocketbooks.

DARREL PAYSON
MILLBURN, N.J.

Your mag has very little advertising, and I think your readers appreciate that.

JAMES CORCORAN
FALLON, NEVADA

BAT MAN

Do you think you'll have some extra space in a future issue to print a picture of me as Dracula?

VICTOR WISCOVITCH
LOS ANGELES, CALIF

No—ED.

MORE QUICKIES

Douglas Higley's article on *King Kong vs Godzilla* (FanMo 3) was really written in an off-beat style, and I enjoyed it thoroughly.

MARLENE HERTUCA
BERWYN, ILLINOIS

I'm getting sick and tired of seeing Vincent Price starring in AIP Poe films. Isn't there anyone else around to star in films these days besides Price?

BILL PAGE
OKLAHOMA CITY, OKLA

You did a real fine job on *Master Magicians of Monsterland* in your third issue. This was the first time I saw pictures of the people behind-the-scenes in horror films. Thanks.

JEAN PAZDAN
NORTH RIVERSIDE, ILL

I was rather disappointed in your first issue's vampire article. You can do a lot better.

GREGORY HEFFERNAN
MILWAUKEE, WISCONSIN

The terrible Pteranodon, giant prehistoric glider, concedes a contest to KING KONG. He didn't want Fay Wray anyway.

DAWN AGE BEASTS STRIKE BACK

by Paul Blaisdell

They come from steaming swamps and fern-laden prehistoric jungles. Roaring, squealing, and hissing, they pass glowing molten lava beds and rumbling smokey volcanoes—until at last they tumble out onto the silver screen of the motion picture theatre in all their fighting fury.

The Dawn Age Beasts have returned . . . .

One of the more recent films where the dawn age beasts got in their licks at the world of humans was the 20th Century Fox remake, in 1960, of Sir Arthur Conan Doyle's classic novel *The Lost World*, produced and directed by Irwin Allen in color and Cinemascope. Pitted against the beasts were Michael (*Day the Earth Stood Still*) Rennie, curvaceous Jill St. John, and Claude (*Phantom of the Opera*) Rains.

One of the highlights of the picture was a beautiful battle between a baby alligator and an iguana, both disguised as dinosaurs. Whether these two species just hate each other on sight, or whether it was the same alligator and iguana left over from *One Million B.C.* and still harboring a grudge, we'll leave up to the acute judgment of the audience.

This current version of *The Lost World* used real lizards rather than the animated dinosaurs of the original *Lost World*, produced in 1925 and starring Wallace Beery, Lloyd Hughes, and Bessie Love. In this earlier film, rubber models and double exposures were used to duplicate authentic replicas of actual dinosaurs. Judged by today's standards this version might appear to be a little "stiff", but in 1925 it had audiences frantically gulping popcorn sauced with real butter instead of margarine, and starring cage-eyed at every gunshot that

turn the page

Top: *Stegosaurus, Triceratops, Brontosaurus,* and *Tyrannosaurus Rex* all flee from the earthly upheaval of *THE ANIMAL WORLD.* Above: Attacked by a *Tyrannosaurus Rex* in *THE LAND UNKNOWN.* Left: The awesome *Allosaurus* struts his stuff, to prove a new method of animation for American-International Pictures, Courtesy of Golden Eagle Films. Right: The mighty *REPTILICUS* from American-International.

whined harmlessly off the armor-plated saurians that thundered across the screen.

Although the gunshots were the same, we switched to margarine and those live South American lizards in the 1960 Fox version of *The Lost World.* Now this reporter has no objection to South American lizards, but if some of our own talented Alligator lizards (see Devil's Workshop, FANTASTIC MONSTERS 2) don't start mailing themselves to the Screen Actor's Guild with placards saying "Mealworms for me in '63", they're missing a bet. After all, SAG just unanimously voted to do anything short of Hari Kari to bring film production back to American actors.

Bridging the gap between 1925 and 1960 will give us the all-time favorite of 1933, *King Kong.* Among the prehistoric pushovers laid out by the animated ape was the terrible Pteranodon Ingens ("Toothless flyer"). This realistic replica was almost authentic. During his use, Pteranodon lacked sufficient horsepower in his shoulder muscles to flap his enormous wings for any length of time, so he relied on updrafts from mountains and cliffs to prolong his soaring flights. A fantastic failure of old Mother Nature, he finally vanished into the mists of geologic time along with his dinosaur cousins.

As a movie menace to fearless Fay Wray in *King Kong,* he performed admirably; but in real life, he preferred fish to females and clobbered his suppers by skimming warm inland lakes in the manner of the present-day pelican.

"I'll have fun in '61," was the motto of the awesome Allosaurus ("Other lizard"), hatched on the insert stage of Golden Eagle Films. This granddaddy of the Tyrannosaurus Rex carved his kingdom out of the less powerful reptiles among which he lived. The carnivorous cut-up had the manners of a mastodon, but his man-sized forearms did little justice to his boarding house reach. Although the forearms helped to hold down his prey, they lacked the length to convey food to his multi-toothed mouth. Oddly enough, his descendants of a later age did even worse. The oddball arms became flipper-like appendages that were almost useless.

The brawny Brontosaurus thundered to life again in *Dinosaurus.* Capering more in keeping to his real-life self than previous prototypes, this lovable lout was laid out by a terrible tempered Tyrannosaurus, who was slain in turn during a spectacular duel of saurian versus steam shovel.

The Giant Behemoth was another animated special effect, which managed to play an effective game of "London Bridges Falling Down". Looking almost like a Brontosaurus, but not quite making it from a historical point of view, we'll have to put him in Movie History as a Brontowhatzis, pending further word from the producers, who must know more unusual types of dinosaurs than I do.

The Animal World was probably the last technicolor word in contemporary historical authenticity. Released by

turn to page 47

PAL, from page 21

them your four-foot, $7,500 rocket is actually a 400-foot colossus on the screen, while the takeoff and landing on planet Zyra required ten weeks to shoot—and again you win an Oscar for Special Effects.

Two projects occupied Pal's attention in the following years: a fictionalized biography of master magician Harry Houdini, and War of the Worlds. Houdini assumed aspects of a weak but nonetheless interesting chronicle starring Tony Curtis and Janet Leigh. Whatever shortcomings the script and subject matter contained for contemporary audience taste were balanced by ingenious casting; for Curtis died a most tortuous and photogenic death in the last reel, to the accompaniment of leaping feminine hearts. A shame that the preparation and stamina required were passed off as just so much film trickery by hardened critics. In War of the Worlds, however, Pal had a tiger . . .

And so once upon a time a vast studio called Paramount gathered all its talented craftsmen, and all its resources (known as special effects), and many of its busiest minds called writers and artists — and all these lovely people gathered about a man who told them they were all to have fun with a certain story by a Mr. Wells. Two years, $2,000,000 and one planet Earth later, they had made legitimate screen history with the film adaption of H.G. Wells' War of the Worlds. Ulcers are the stuff Hollywood dreams are made of, and Pal's new prodigy had spawned many.

Miniatures were unparalleled. $1,000,000 of the budget was spent on the designs of art director Al Nozaki alone. "The concept was painful in coming," he recalls, "but Pal agreed on the final details, and we rolled in winter, 1952." The machines the deniizens from Planet 4 operated resembled aerial mantas, sporting craning cobra eyes whose fiery rays were superimpositions of flaming welding rods. Nozaki's Martian creature resulted from a quick sketch; and this "last minute" idea became the screen's finest extra-terrestial scene. Built by Charlie Gemora, and impersonated by the short-statured actor known for his gorilla role in Ingagi.

the monster was constructed of sheet rubber, paper mache, and rubber tubing. Strictly a one-shot affair, it lasted just through shooting. The 1953 Oscar was bestowed on the special effects of this magnificent adventure.

A short story entitled Leiningen Versus the Ants by Carl Stephenson in Esquire, 1938, became The Naked Jungle in 1954. The script introduced the shivery hordes of instinctual death which descended on the lush plantation of the film's star, Charlton Heston. Accompanied by Amphitheatrof's nervy Tonalities, effects man John Fulton and cameraman Ernest Laszlo traced the Marabuntas' deadly trek and ultimate demise through spectacular flooding of the plantation—a new Pal miracle.

On the heels of such excellence came Conquest of Space, loosely based on the Bonestell-Ley bestseller. Strictly weak-line Pal, it fumbled its potential. It's been said that eventually everyone but Pal had a hand in the production, and this is apparent in the hocus-pocus result.

The pedestrian script's routine father-son relationship clouded the potentially thrilling installation of a manned satellite and subsequent Mars expedition. A boisterous Brooklyn electronics man provided comic relief, but the General went mad anyway. The climactic Mars trip was a disappointment. We're off to Mars! What do we see there? Obvious tabletop horizons, weak effect shots, and a contrived "Marsquake" at precisely the moment of takeoff. The crew safely lifted from Mars, but the film never got off the ground.

Bouncing back in 1958, Pal took the wraps off Tom Thumb. Shot for pennies in the beautiful woodlands of England, his Toyland became a spritely lad in the guise of Russ Tamblyn, who joined in with the ingenious Puppetoon characters. MGM released the film, and signed Pal to produce additional features under their banner, the first of which proved to be another Wellsian excursion.

Long on Pal's mind had been The Time Machine, a favorite screen candidate of the late author's family. And so as Gae Griffith took a deep breath, Pal plunged into the new film with

the old passion—and The Time Machine took form.

How do you film a trip through time? "Have you ever seen those time-lapse films in which the shutter has produced an extreme exaggeration by condensing a whole day into a few moments of footage? This was the basis for our thinking—this suggested an approach," says Pal. The approach necessitated the assistance of Projects Unlimited, animation-effects studio responsible for the film's Oscar-winning effects. A street underwent 25 years aging in split-seconds; an apple tree blossomed, bore fruit, and withered in seconds by means of oil paintings; and superimposition placed time traveler Rod Taylor among the Sphinx and halls of the future. A fitting touch was the inscription on the amazing Time Machine itself: "Manufactured by H. George Wells."

From marvelously grotesque Morlocks and subterranean mysteries, it was a hop to an amazingly poor Atlantis. The kindest approach to this film is to say the least. Aside from the familiar Pal touch in a handsome Atlantean submarine, all departments were extremely poor, and all the more pitiable considering the years of thought devoted to the subject and its wasted potential.

Suggestions of a Time Machine sequel had to be submerged for a Film First: the merger of MGM and Cinerama to tell Pal's story of The Wonderful World of the Brothers Grimm. Two impressions received on the set were the reduction of scale to compensate for the ultimate magnification on the curved screen, and the time spent in physical delay shifting cumbersome Cinerama equipment as "live" actors, fairies, and a particularly ingratiating Pal dragon flashed its 90 feet of bejeweled amber and emerald magnificence across the screen.

Thus, with another first behind him, adding to his successes and occasional failures—and the tragic loss of 30 years' mementos in 1961's disasterous Bel Air fire— the man born George Pal Jr on February 1, 1908, in Cegled, Hungary, prepares now for his "most ambitious project:" the filming of Charles Finney's ephemeral Circus of Dr Lao.

As yet, there is no end to the George Pal phenomenon. ●

WORKSHOP, from page 8
mold with talcum, to keep the rubber from sticking to itself. Pull the latex out of the mold gently and carefully, and you now have your own original rubber mask. Additional shading and coloring may be added to the mask with regular make-up and grease paint. If you wish, you can make a back to this mask by following the same procedure as in the construction of the front. The two halves may be "seamed" together with liquid latex, or rubber cement."

Fantastic Monsters is always interested in hearing from readers who have made step-by-step photos and instructions of their own original "how-to-do-it" projects. This issue, we extend our particular thanks, and a check, to teen-age Bill "Make 'em pay off" Malone. ●

IN DEFENSE OF HORROR FILMS

by VINCENT PRICE

It's time that motion picture critics started taking so-called "terror" or "horror" films seriously—that is, the legitimate films of this genre based either on recognized classics or on original stories by our leading writers.

Two things have been established about these exciting motion picture products—the public and the acting profession take them seriously, and enjoy them. Top film producers, like American-International Pictures, will attest to mass public support of such thrillers as *Pit and the Pendulum*, *The Premature Burial*, and *Tales of Terror*, all based on the classic writings of Edgar Allan Poe.

As for myself, and I speak for a majority of serious actors, these Poe pictures were fun to make, and were a source of great satisfaction to me as an actor. They presented a dramatic challenge to me which ordinary films, with their superficial "reality", cannot offer.

The real challenge to any actor worth his salt is the opportunity to convincingly portray "unreality". After all, isn't the original premise of acting, the actor's raison d'etre, or reason for being, the art of make-believe?

A perfect case in point is my latest film, *The Raven*, based on Poe's fine terror poem. I was additionally privileged to be able to work with, in this picture, two of Hollywood's finest actors, Peter Lorre and Boris Karloff; and I am sure that they appreciated the challenge of making Edgar Allan Poe believable as much as I did.

Unlike any other type of motion picture, the terror or horror thriller offers the serious actor unique opportunity to fully exercise his craft and critically test his ability to make the unbelievable believable.

I also believe that such films as *The Raven* are additionally important to American culture at a time when "method acting", and the sordid stories it usually accompanies, is considered in some quarters as a true reflection of American life. Actually, these "method dramas" are representative of only a very small segment of our people.

It is in this time that the "fairy tale" quality of Poe's writings furnishes a very necessary and healthy entertainment escape valve for the American public.

Let those who condemn the thriller and horror pictures recall, too, that along with Westerns, this type of entertainment was responsible for the original success of our great motion picture industry.

As for me, I'd rather take youngsters to see an Edgar Allan Poe film anytime than subject them to the amours and perversions of the sick, sick denizens of the backwoods and gutters of America. I think that most decent-thinking Americans feel the same way about entertainment for themselves, as well.

Let's have more imaginative terror stories produced with our top talent and brains, and let's have less time-wasting and corrupting epics of degeneracy. ●

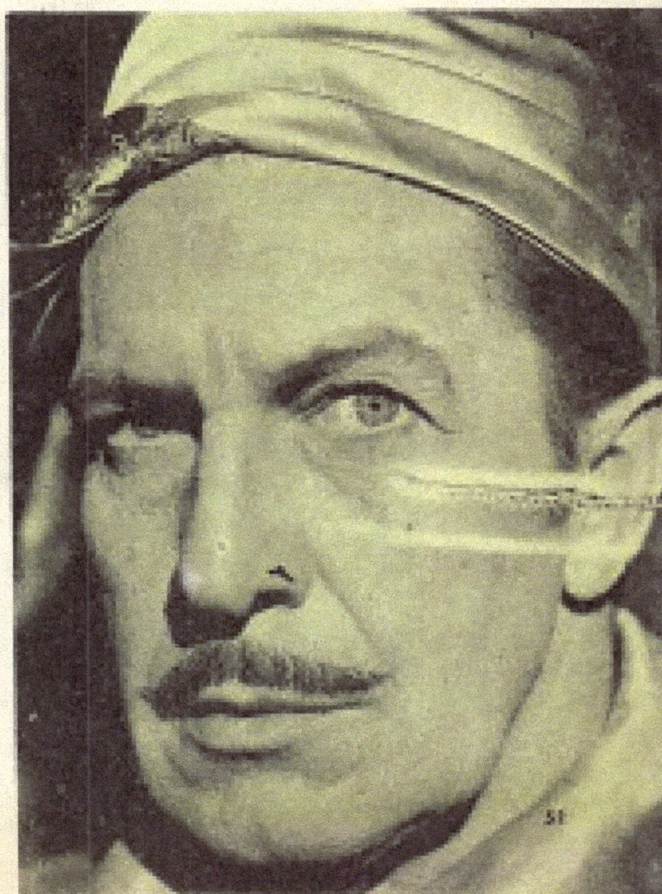

Memoirs of a SUPERMAN

by KIRK ALYN

The inside, under-the-cloak story of the first time SUPERMAN burst onto the screen in living action, told by the ORIGINAL Movie Man of Steel, Kirk Alyn — Yesterday or Today, the Greatest Man of Tomorrow of Them All

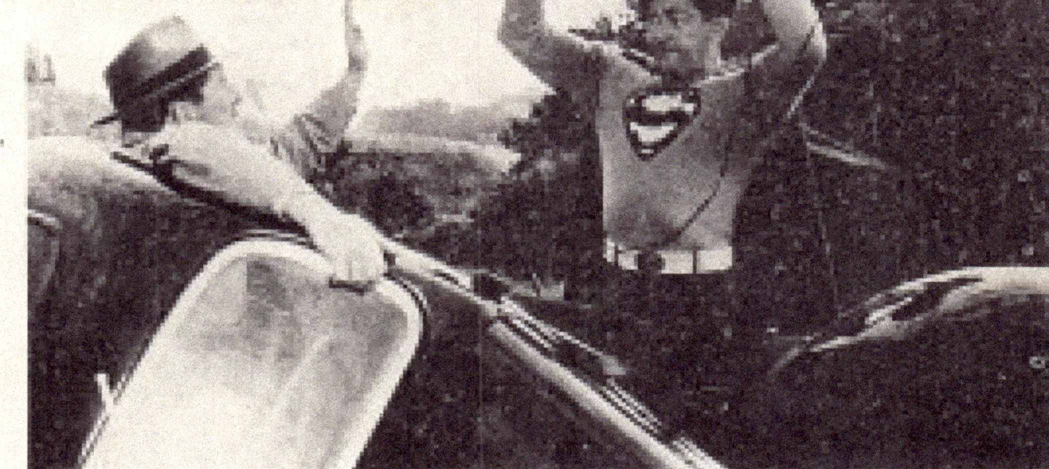

Superman holds bad guy Jack Ingram at bay. Below: Kirk and comedian Bob Hope before game time at Soldiers' Field in Chicago.

I guess every kid imagines at some time or other that he can fly or has other supernatural powers. Playing make-believe is one of the greatest pleasures of childhood. I was grown up when the experience came to me, but it wasn't all pleasure, I can tell you.

I never dreamed when I left New York in 1943 to visit my friend Red Skelton in Hollywood that I would leave the Broadway stage for a motion picture career, much less that one day I would be wearing a skintight costume and saving the world.

My first chance to be super-human came through Republic Pictures, where I was working in westerns. This was in 1943, and the studio was planning to make a Captain America serial. Even though the role appealed to me, I had to refuse it as I was already signed with another studio for a musical. My second opportunity came four years later.

I read in the Hollywood trades that producer Sam Katzman, for whom I had recently completed two features, Little Miss Broadway and Sweet Genevieve, was casting for the lead role in a serial based on the popular Superman. I'd been following Superman's adventures in the comic strips since 1940, and certainly knew what type of character he was, but I never gave the casting of the picture a second thought. So it came as a genuine

turn the page

Rescuing Lois and Jimmy can get to be a problem.

Once again the mighty *Superman* rescues an unconscious Lois Lane and *Jimmy Olsen (ATOM MAN VS SUPERMAN, 1950).*

shock soon afterward to pick up the telephone and hear Sam Katzman tell me that he wanted me to play Superman in his serial.

He asked me to rush down to his office at Columbia because representatives from Superman's Publishing company, National Comics, were waiting to take a look at the fellow he had convinced them would be "perfect" for the part. Before I could say a word, Sam hung up.

I wish that someone with a camera could have been there to capture the stunned expressions on the two National men when I walked into Sam's office. "This is Superman?" they cried in horror, pointing convicting fingers at me.

Unfortunately, Sam hadn't given me the chance on the phone to explain to them that I was growing a beard and had let my hair grow for two months in order to play a role in another film.

Sam remained confident, though, and had me put on a pair of glasses and a hat over the beard and long hair, to display me as Clark Kent, Superman's secret identity. I was more than a little stunned when Mr Katzman said, "Take off your clothes so you can flex your muscles." I told the National people that my qualifications for the newspaper man role included studying at Columbia University's School of Journalism, where I also wrote for the college paper. They didn't laugh, but said that, minus the heavy beard and with a good haircut, I would be acceptable.

We began filming the picture in early January, 1948, for summer release, but before I stepped in front of the cameras as Superman, I spent a solid four weeks working out at a gymnasium, getting in shape. I knew this was going to be a strenuous role because there would be no double for me. I was to do all of Superman's stunts myself.

The first day of shooting finally came, and I remember how conspicuous I felt when I put on the pale blue and brown Superman costume for the first time. The colors were changed from the original bright red and blue because the picture was in black and white, and reds and blues do not film well.

I understand that when you test for a Tarzan picture you wear your suit rugged. I wouldn't know about that, but I do know that being Superman is no easy job. The director, Spencer Bennet, who had directed me in a Republic serial a few years before, had me leaping, running, jumping, fighting, and carrying people around eight to ten hours a day for the entire 28 day shooting schedule. I was completely exhausted when I got home each night, and it came as no real surprise to discover that after the serial was finished I had lost nearly 20 pounds.

Superman was, in my opinion, a good serial, filled with plenty of action and excitement. George Plympton, Katzman's head writer, wrote a script that was very faithful to the comic books, telling of Superman's coming to Earth as a baby, his growth to super-manhood, and his adventure with the Spider Lady, who was plot-ting to control the world. The casting of Superman's friends—Noel Neill as Lois Lane, Tommy Bond as Jimmy Olsen, Pierre Watkin as Perry White—realistically brought Superman's comic book companions to "life".

Spence Bennet, George Plympton, and I spent many hours planning how I should play Superman and Clark Kent in the serial. We decided, for example, that as Superman I should never hit a "bad guy" with my fist because a real Superman would knock the fellow's head off with just a simple punch, being as powerful as he is depicted. So I had to "tap" the villains unconscious, or knock their heads together lightly. We also had Clark change his voice whenever he spoke so no one would guess that he and Superman were one and the same; and I even had to have a long curl hanging over my forehead just like the character in the magazines.

The serial was released in the summer of 1948, but by that time I had forgotten about it. I was then at Republic where I had to turn down my second super hero role, *King of the Rocket Men*, because I was shooting another film, *Federal Agents vs Underworld*, with Rosemary LaPlanche and Carol Forman who played the Spider Lady in the Superman picture.

However, as fate would have it, *Superman* was so highly successful—it was made for $350,000 and grossed nearly three million—that before I knew it Sam Katzman was on the phone again, telling me we were going to do a sequel, *Atom Man vs Superman*.

All of the people in the first serial were gathered together again, and back I went to leaping, running, and fighting, but this time only losing eight pounds. Plympton's sequel had Superman crusading to save the world again, and it was just as well-paced as the original serial, though more fantastic. In one scene I was sent into the Empty Doom far out in space, but using super-wits I managed to make it safely back to Earth.

Directors, I've learned through years of experience, have a habit of getting so preoccupied with their story line that they sometimes forget that the fiction they are creating is not necessarily fact. Spence Bennet, though the most considerate director I've ever had, was no exception.

For one sequence in *Atom Man*, I had to run into a burning barn, pick up an unconscious Lois and Jimmy, and carry one under each arm to safety. Noel, who was Lois, weighed 105 pounds, but Tommy Bond was a hefty 160. We rehearsed the scene five times, to synchronize camera moves, special effects of the fire and various other technicalities, and I was ready to call it a day.

Then Spence said, "O.K. This will be a take." The cameras rolled, and back I dashed into the barn, choking on the smoke, lifted Lois and Jimmy, all 265 pounds, and ran back out past the camera, trying hard not to drop them. Spence yelled "Cut, cut, cut!" and came up to me.

"Kirk," he said, dead serious, "this will never do. You're straining yourself. I can see the veins popping out

turn to page 62

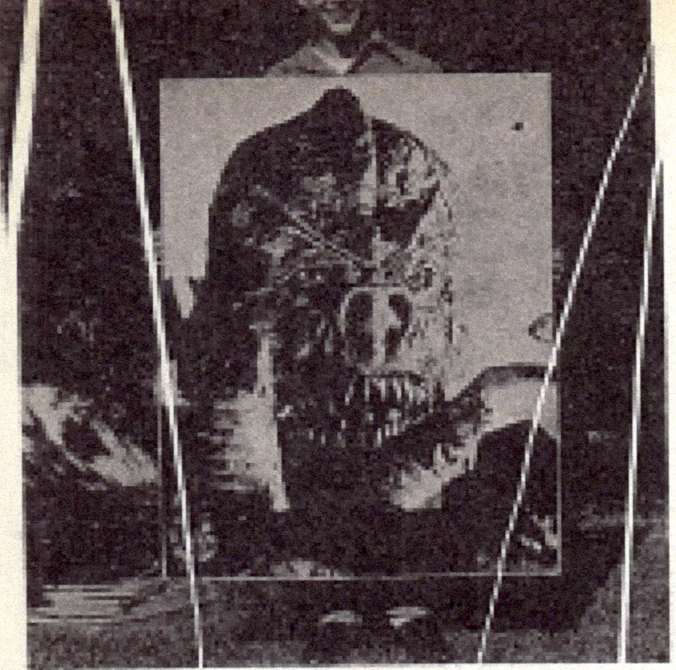

Name The Nameless MONSTER CONTEST

Win a Giant Kong-Size Monster Pin-Up of Your Favorite Fantastic Monster or Horror Star!

There's nothing to buy — nothing to sell!

Anyone can enter!

The Colossal creature (seen on the right) from Golden Eagle Films' THE CLIFF MONSTER is waiting for a name only YOU can give him!

All you have to do is think up an original name for this Nameless Monster, fill out the entry blank coupon below, and mail it in!

Name the Nameless Monster contest is as easy to enter as pulling wings off a bat!

Grand prize winner will receive a giant, premounted — size 30"x40" — monster pin-up of his or her choice! Would it be Karloff, Wolf Man, She Creature, Lugosi, others? You tell us!

25 2nd PRIZES — big color monster movie posters, like the ones you see at theatres, for your clubroom or den!

25 3rd PRIZES — glossy filmland monster photos, terrific for framing!

THIS IS THE MONSTER CONTEST YOU'VE BEEN SCREAMING FOR!

READ THE OFFICIAL CONTEST RULES! GIVE THE NAMELESS MONSTER A NAME! SEND IN YOUR COUPON! DO IT NOW!

OFFICIAL ENTRY BLANK COUPON

NAME THE NAMELESS MONSTER CONTEST
TOPANGA, CALIFORNIA

Here is my ORIGINAL NAME for the Nameless Monster:

_______________________ . If I am judged WINNER by

FANTASTIC MONSTERS-GOLDEN EAGLE FILMS, I want a

GIANT MONSTER PIN-UP of _______________________

Name _______________________

Address _______________________

City _______________ Zone _____ State _______________

OFFICIAL CONTEST RULES

1. Mail the ENTRY BLANK COUPON below, along with your ORIGINAL NAME for the Nameless Monster.

2. You may enter as many times as you wish, but each name must be accompanied by A SEPARATE ENTRY BLANK COUPON — no facsimiles or copies of the ENTRY BLANK COUPON will be accepted.

3. The FANTASTIC MONSTERS-GOLDEN EAGLE FILMS NAME THE NAMELESS MONSTER CONTEST closes at midnight, March 31, 1963. All entries must be postmarked before then to be eligible.

4. Winners will be judged on the basis of originality and thought.

5. Anyone may enter — except employees of Black Shield Publications, Inc., and Golden Eagle Films, its affiliates or families.

After being accused by Hollywood's more cynical citizens of making pictures that were horrors, Leo Gorcey and Huntz Hall took their Bowery Boys for a real excursion into Monsterland with *The Bowery Boys Meet the Monsters*, which Allied Artists loosed in 1954 on a world barely recovered from the Korean War.

All their nightmares began when they hitch-hiked out to the country, to call upon the seldom-seen owners of a vacant lot back in the city, with an eye to getting permission to use the lot as a baseball field for Bowery neighborhood kids.

But the owners, the Gravesend family, turn out to be a quartet of beings that even the Bowery Boys think weird: Dr Derek (played by John Dehner), who is planning to transplant a sub-normal human brain into the cranium of his vitamin-fed gorilla, Cosmos; Brother Anton (Lloyd Corrigan), a maniac with a walking erector set called Gorog; their spinster sister, Amelia (character actress Ellen Corby), who happens to have her own amusing hobby: lovingly caring for a cannibal plant which feeds only on human flesh; and lastly, there is Grissom (off-screen: Paul Wexler), a vampirish creature secretly planning his own batty violences—aimed, of course, at Gorcey and Hall, whose necks look soft, as well as their heads.

Nothing could be more satisfactory to Dr Derek and his resourceful relatives than the sudden thunderstorm which forces the two Bowery Boys to spend the night at the house of horrors.

Derek, ever hopeful to obtain the brain of a human with a low I.Q. to transplant to the skull of Cosmos, his ape, decides that Hall has just the lack of mentality for the job.

And Gorcey himself is chosen by Amelia as just right to be fed to her cannibal plant, grown tired of its long diet of canned dog food.

With Grissom the vampire-man, Gorog the robot, and Mad Anton on hand, Gorcey and Hall are soon involved in a merry, scary chase throughout the crocks and crevices of the haunted house, the fearsome foursome hot on their steps. And it's down to the lab in shrieks when the boys are forced into the open, just as their brains soon will be.

Just when everything seems hopeless for them, and Derek is sharpening his scalpel, help bursts in—in the persons of Louie of the Bowery sweetshop and two more of the Bowery Boys, Dave Condon and Bennie Bartlett.

Having now learned why Gorcey and Hall had not returned the previous night, Louie (played by Bernard Gorcey) and the others free their troubled chums. And with the aid of Gorog the robot, help turn the operating tables on the terror-togetherness family, finally handing them over to the ready police.

Meanwhile, back at the Bowery, baseball fiend Gorog, the metal man, displays a great screwball. A scout from the-then Brooklyn Dodgers signs the pitching robot to an iron-clad contract, while those crazy mixed-up kids, the Bowery Boys, remain as perplexed as they have been for the last 30 years. ●

Cosmos the ape points out to Leo Gorcey the tight spot he's in.

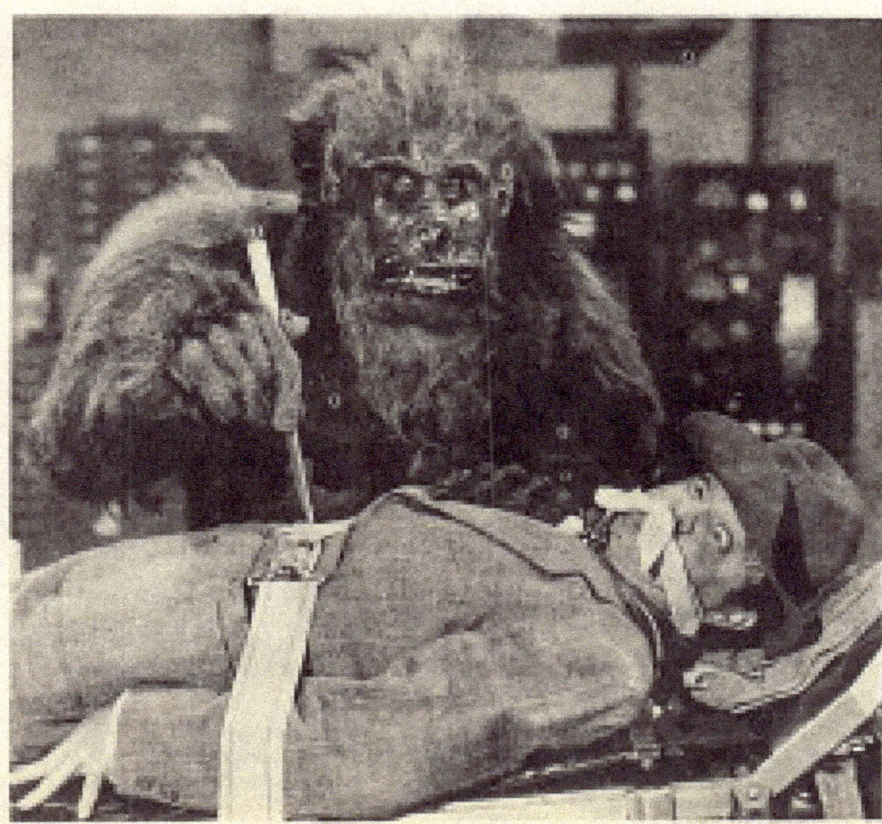

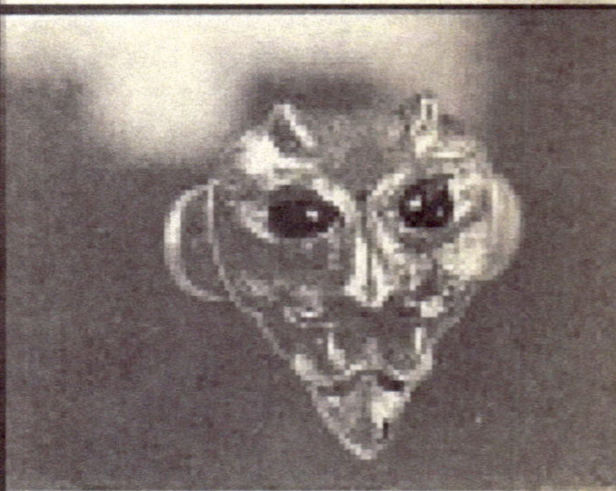

MAD LAB RADIO

It appears to be one of these little imported transistor radios, but just turn it "on". WOW! The dummy speaker flips to one side and a "Killer shrew" jumps out, with a wild squeal! Mad Lab radio is all metal, lithographed in four colors. Has fold-down carrying handle, three dimensional dummy dial and working "off-on" switch, which releases "shrew". YOU invite your buddy, or girl friend, to turn on your Mad Lab radio, then watch them climb the wall, when the squealing "shrew" leaps out at them! Only $1.00, postpaid.

VAMPIRE DEVIL RING

Shades of Count Dracula! It looks like it came straight from his castle, in the Carpathian Mountains! A gleaming, scowling, silvery Devil's head. Great for club or costume make-up. Deeply carved horns, brows, nose, beard and "vampire fangs". These are set off by flaming simulated ruby eyes. Good quality and massive. A real conversation piece! Let us know your ring size with order. $1.

Favorite moments from fright-bound movies, as selected by You the Readers

SCREAM SCENES

FANTASTIC MONSTERS reader Charles Kagay, president of The League of Horrors and Evil in Kettering, Ohio, writes us that "The scene we of LOHAE have chosen as our favorite Scream Scene is from the 1942 Universal Pictures production, Ghost of Frankenstein—which, incidentally, we all believe is the greatest horror movie we have ever seen. The photo we would like to see is lightning striking the Frankenstein Monster (Lon Chaney Jr), and chipping pieces of hardened sulphur from his monstrous body."

After receiving Charles' special request, we bolted down into FanMo's Photo Vaults to select this electrifying still—and we hope Charles and his League of Horror Fans will get a charge out of seeing it in these pages. ●

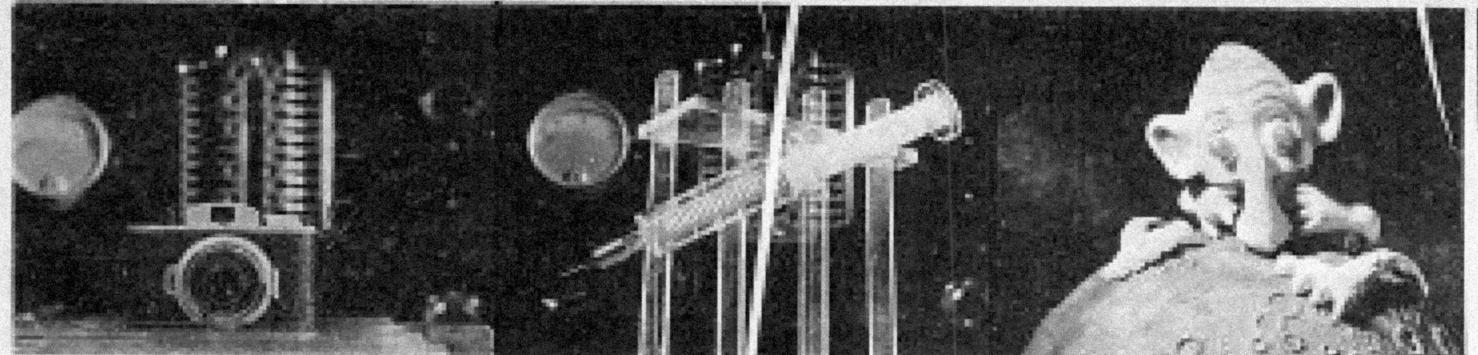

MAD LAB CAMERA

Looks like expensive sub-miniature camera, but wait until you press the secret button! Lens swings open, and with a terrific squeal, a "Killer Shrew" leaps out! Camera has viewfinder, dummy winding knob, carrying case, realistic lens mount. Authentic black crinkle finish with silver-gray trim! Furry "Killer Shrew" and "squealer" concealed inside. Lens locks in place until you push the shutter release! You'll have your friends jumping for the ceiling with the MAD LAB CAMERA! Only $3.00, postpaid

MAD LAB HYPO

Life size! 6 inches, fully extended! Needle appears to pierce "rubbery" skin! Concealed button gives illusion of Hypo filling up with "rubbery" blood! Can also be used in reverse, to "inject" blood—thus show Hypo apparently empty! The illusion is absolutely perfect, even close up! This glittering, wicked-looking instrument is quality made of crystal clear styrene plastic, with metal head and "needle"! Scientific calibrations marked along barrel! Don't use around friends with weak stomachs! Only $2.50, postpaid

MAN MOON MASCOT

Poor little Moon Man! Looks like he's "way out there", and he can't get back. This lovable little guy is all head, hands, and feet. Put him on a lamp shade, picture frame, note book, or car mirror, and these things become his "body". He's fan-tastic, and made of soft, durable, flesh colored plastic, with pink ears, and bright red eyes. Your own personal moon Mascot! Only $1 postpaid.

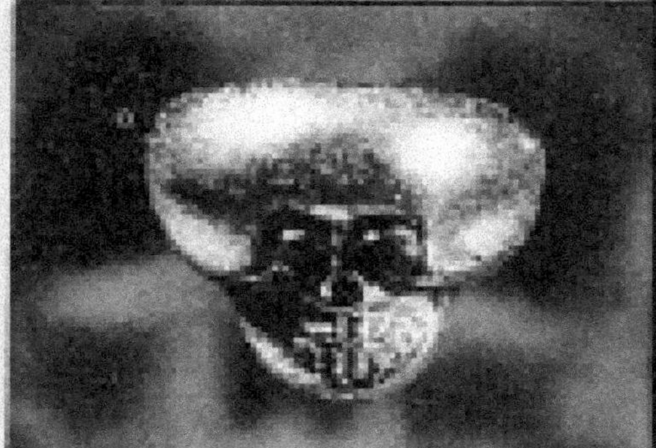

SECRET SKULL RING

Mystic skull symbol of the ancient Aztecs, later copied by the fierce pirates who sailed the seven seas. The romance and adventure is all embodied into the unique and latest style of this massive, quality ring. Sculptured cheek bones, teeth, and sparkling simulated ruby eyes are blended into a finger encircling curve on this exciting new ring. Gleaming silvery finish, too. Please state ring size when ordering. Only $1 postpaid.

MR. BONES, THE POCKET SKELETON

Your own spooky mascot! Take Mr. Bones wherever you go. He's 7 inches tall, well detailed, made of vinylized rubber! Even feels creepy! Flexible and springy; the slightest movement sets him shimmering and shaking! Hang Mr. Bones from car mirror, or pin him to your lapel! Sit him down on desk, or table! For your photography, Mr. Bones makes a sensational prop for table-top photography. Only 75¢, postpaid

UNLUCKY 13 RATTLESNAKE

13 unlucky inches of wriggling rattler! Coiling fools everybody, even inches away! "Fleshy" droopy formula makes snake feel cool and slimy to the touch! Sure cure for newly friends! Just a rattler where they're bound to see it! If you want shrieks and howls at your next get-together, this UNLUCKY 13 RATTLESNAKE is for you! Camera fiends who like to shoot miniatures can turn rattler into huge "python" in table-top scene! Only 75¢, postpaid

DEVIL SPIDER

Ugh! What a little horror this guy is! Made of vinyl rubber, for that "creepy" feel! 2 inches in diameter, he really gets the screams when you lower him on a thread or send him skittering across the floor! Well detailed in black, with rough texturing! It wiggling legs start vibrating at the slightest touch! Slip him in your pocket, hang him from a car mirror, dangle him in a doorway! If you have any friends left afterwards, they'll never forget the time they combed the DEVIL SPIDER out of their hair! Only 50¢ postpaid

CASTLE DRACULA, TOPANGA, CALIFORNIA

NOVELTIES, JOKES, GAMES

Rush me the following: _______________________

____

____

____

for which I enclose $ _______________________

NAME (PLEASE PRINT) _______________________

ADDRESS _______________________

CITY _______________ ZONE _____ STATE _____

If I'm dissatisfied with my purchase, I'll return it within one week for a full refund

MEMOIRS, from page 54

in your neck!" He was actually shocked to hear me say, "Jeepers, Spence, I'm only a human being, not a real Superman, and those are real people I'm carrying!"

Whenever we get together today, twelve years later, we still laugh about this incident.

I spent one entire day dangling 15 feet above the ground, in front of what is known as a process screen showing a film of moving clouds. A giant wind machine was facing me off-camera, making it seem as if I were actually flying. The special effects men strung me up with wires encased in a metal breastplate. It was pure torture being suspended. Just lie with your chest on a chair and keep your legs stiffly on a line with your torso, and you can get an idea of the back-breaking effect.

But it was even more discomforting when the cotton-lining of my metal suit caught fire. I was flying beside an airplane with a burning bomb attached to its wing, and the strong gusts from the giant wind machine blew the sparks down my neck. I tried beating at my chest, forgetting that I was wearing armor. In desperation, I yelled at the effects men to bring me down fast, and they poured buckets of water between my chest and the suit, nearly drowning me but finally putting out the fire.

The frustrating and costly thing about this 14 hour day's shooting was that very few of the agonizing flying scenes were used in the final release print. Almost all of the film had to be junked and the sequences redone because the wires were visible. Incidentally, a few heads "rolled" because of this.

After the release of the serial, I went on tour as Superman with a troup of Hollywood stars, leading men and comedians, staging baseball games across the country for charity. I must admit I was rather reluctant to appear in public as Superman. There was always a possibility that someone out in the audience would decide to find out for himself if bullets really did bounce off my chest!

The highlight of the ball games was Superman's appearance, which we handled very dramatically. The games lasted only three innings because of the close scores—like 108 to 99. At the bottom of the third, Superman's team would be losing, but they'd have the bases loaded; only a home run would save the day. The batter had a 3-2 count on him. The next pitch would tell the story.

Over the p.a. system, Garry Moore, our announcer, would say, "It looks bad for the Actors. They need a homer to win and—uh-oh. They're sending in a pinch-hitter. Who can hit it? Who can save the game for them?"

By this time everyone had his eyes on our dugout, and Garry would continue: "Looks like there's only one man for the job, and—yes, yes, they're sending him in—it's SUPERMAN!"

I would run from the dugout, with cape flying, swinging a couple dozen balsa wood bats, while the crowds went half-mad with excitement. During the confusion, the Comedians' pitcher would substitute a plaster-of-paris baseball for the real one. I'd swing at his first pitch, after pointing towards the fence like Babe Ruth, and when I connected the ball would disintegrate. All of the players would stare up at the sky, tracing the ball's imaginary flight into outer space, and we scored the winning runs.

As I walked up to the plate on opening day at Soldier's Field in Chicago, at least a dozen photographers and newsreel men were squatting around to get a "scoop" of Superman at bat. When the pitch came, it was low, and I had to break my swing to keep from cracking a few heads and cameras. The crowd roared and held their sides. Superman, like the Mighty Casey, had struck out! . . .

and you could hear the repercussions clear back to Hollywood. However, our umpire, Hopalong Cassidy no less, awarded me another pitch on a "technicality", being fair and square as he was.

After the tour, I went to Republic for a *Radar Patrol* serial, then back to Columbia to star as the comic book character *Blackhawk*. Shortly before making *Blackhawk*, I signed to play opposite Ilona Massey on Broadway in *Angel in Paris*, and as it turned out, this was one of the reasons for my not being available to portray another super hero—Flash Gordon in a TV series filmed in Germany.

A day or two before I left for New York, I was called about playing Superman again, now on TV. I had to refuse the part because of my Broadway commitments.

People have asked me if I ever met George Reeves. I know of him, of course, since he was Superman on television, but we had never met until 1958, shortly before his untimely death.

I was with my New York agent in his office at General Artists Corporation, when one of the other agents stuck his head in the door and said, "Guess who I have in my office? Superman, that's who!"

Whereupon my agent calmly pointed at me, and said, "Yeah? Well, here's the original Superman!"

George and I met halfway between the two offices, then had lunch together, discussing the many hazards of being a Superman. On comparing notes, we had quite a few laughs. This was the only time we ever met.

Even though I have played super heroic roles, and Superman in particular, I'm afraid that none of those amazing powers have rubbed off on me. I'm sure that if someone sent me into the Empty Doom, I'd never make it back.

I've yet to test out my flying abilities. For the present I think I'll stick to TWA's Fan Jets. ●

IT, from page 7

The villain of the film, the Venusian Invader, was one of the most unusual monsters ever seen on the screen. Six weeks in the designing and construction, the horror had movable arms, claws, eyes, mouth, and antennae. Standing over six feet tall and measuring 33 feet in circumference, there was room enough inside its foam rubber hide for two full grown people, an electric light, and even a script.

On one, the Invader "bled" chocolate syrup from its blowtorched and bazooka-inflicted wounds — much to the discomfort of all concerned, including the director, who was liberally smeared with the stuff by the time the filming was over.

It's interesting to note that the dead Venusian, lying with closed eyes on the cold, hard ground of Bronson Canyon, never really got a chance to rest in peace. It came back to pseudo-life in a later AIP film titled *How to Make a Monster*, glaring down from the wall of a makeup man's living room. There, it was nearly consumed by fire as the house burned down. The Venusian's remains, now somewhat toasted around the edges, are currently in the care of its creator, Paul Blaisdell. This maker of monsters informs me that the Invader's last wish was to be placed aboard that U.S. Mariner rocket which is actually on its way to Venus now.

It seems that after such a tempestuous career in movieland, the Venusian monster yearns for the comparative peace and quiet of an alien world. ●

DAWN, from page 44

Warner Bros in 1956, it was written, produced, and directed by Irwin Allen, with technical direction of the dinosaur sequence handled by Dr Charles L. Camp, professor of Paleontology at the University of California. Sculptors Pasqual Manuelli and Hal Wilson constructed the two-to-three foot dinosaurs following the blueprints and sketches of Willis (*King Kong*) O'Brien. Seventy-three days of animation followed, under the supervision of stop-frame expert Ray Harry-

hausen. After this, the dawn age beasts in the first 20 minutes of the film looked as though they had just stepped out of a history book.

Faithful to the last detail, the Brontosaurus ("Thunder Lizard"), Stegosaurus ("Roofed Lizard"), Triceratops ("Three Horns on the Face"), and Tyrannosaurus Rex ("King of the Tyrant Lizards") crunched and munched their way across an artfully conceived Mesozoic landscape that would have done justice to a museum.

Unfortunately, the remainder of the film did little justice to the audience. Minus the dawn age beasts, the movie was nothing more than a careful compendium of beautifully photographed travelogue-like shots, padded out from ants to zebras. Looking at the colorful posters of *The Animal World* outside the theatre, depicting all those many saurians, it was hard to believe that all you saw of the beasts in the film was twenty minute's worth.

But perhaps that would account for the huge size of our dawn age dandies —they had to be that big to carry the picture on their brawny backs. ●

HAUNT ADS

Attention publishers! RICHARD NOBLE is the author of two fine manuscripts which he would like to sell. *The Frankenstein Nightmare* is possible movie material while his other book, *The Human Monsters*, deals with the 20 most bloodthirsty criminals of all time! Write to Rich for more information at 68 Green St., Augusta, Maine . . . JACK HANER of 2943 Grand Ave., Dayton 1, Ohio, is another of the many devoted Chris Lee fans of whom we are hearing so much lately. Jack is very interested in obtaining photos of Lee, and a few of the immortal Bela Lugosi also . . . . A couple of comic book fans, CHUCK MOSS, 9404 Bellevue Blvd., Omaha 41, Nebr., and LONNIE MITCHELL, of 4340 Berwick, Toledo, Ohio, are after such comic masterpieces as *Green Lantern*, *Detective Comics*, *Brave and Bold* and *Showcase*. Lon is also starting a DC Comics Club, so write to him for more information if you're interested . . . Chuck and Lonnie might find some of those comics from *CASEY BRENNAN*, who has a pile of old comics for sale. Not only that, but he's interested in buying a few himself, and can be contacted at his address, 4238 Bricker Rd., Avoca, Mich. . . . The beginning of Flash Gordon's Trip to Mars showed a Martian operating a weird drill-like device. DAVID STIDWORTHY desperately wants a still depicting this unusual scene. Anyone able to help him? Write to David at 41 Grand St. Warwick, N.J.

Another still collector, ROGER BELL, 3806 Forest Lane, Waukegan, Ill., is looking for pictures of the Wolfman. Keep an eye on this column, Roger, we may

MARTIAN MADMAN

Many thanks to MAJOR MARS for this fine foto of himself as he was seen by millions of matinee-going kiddies years ago when he toured the country with his special theatre appearances.

be printing a photo of him very soon! . . . Film Collector DANNY ALDREDGE already has the films advertised in FanMo (from Castle Dracula) and wants to hear from anyone else who collects films, or has any to trade or sell. Danny's address is 821 East 5th St., Mt. Vernon, Ind. . . . Already We've become a collector's item! KARL WAGNER, 1800 Cedar Lane, Knoxville 18, Ky., is trying to get a copy of FanMo 1, without much luck. Can any of you other FanMo fans help him out? If that fails, Karl, we suggest you send $1. to Fantastic Monsters, Topanga, Calif., for that special first issue that is already becoming so difficult to obtain. . . . Calling all 3-D buffs! 3-D fanatic BORIS MOTZ, 201 Walnut St., Leavenworth, Kansas, is interested in hearing from you, and in getting his hands on any and all 3-D material, including magazines, comics, gum cards, clippings, stills, etc. . . . Horror book collector EUGENE VAN CAR is interested in obtaining more books for his collection. Eugene lives at 670 E. Howard, Winona, Minn. . . . DARRYL LOVKOTA wants material on monsters. Anything will do, clippings, photos, what-have-you. Contact him at 1460 N. Broadway, Wahoo, Neb. He'll buy or trade . . . Movie stills from 1931 to 1962 can be obtained from ALLAN HICKS, 1781 Bruckner Blvd., Box 72, N.Y., who will send prices and list on request.

COFFIN CORNER

I had always been under the impression that *The Fiend Who Walked the West* was an original film, but my brother insists differently. Which one of us is right?— JUDY LEE, COSTA MESA, CALIFORNIA.

You win the argument, Brother Lee, Judy loses. *The Fiend Who Walked the West* is a remake of *Kiss of Death*, the film which made a star of *Richard Widmark*. (He played Tommy Udo, the sadistic young killer who pushed an old lady down the stairs in a wheelchair.)

How many times did Lon Chaney star as the Frankenstein monster? LESTER PATRICK, BEVERLY HILLS, CALIFORNIA.

Twice; both in *Ghost of Frankenstein* and in a *Tales of Tomorrow* TV show, which retold the original story.

I've been a movie fan for many years, but I have yet to discover just what the first film was that ever featured a robot. Perhaps you can enlighten both myself and other robot lovers. RAYMOND ROY, DAYTONA BEACH, FLORIDA.

Glad to, Roy. The first appearance of a robot was in the 1917 serial, *The Master Key*, starring Mr. Escape Artist himself, Harry Houdini.

Have there ever been two movie stars who played the same role in both a monster movie and a detective film? This has been a family debate for several months now. LES FUNT, WACO, TEXAS

Both Basil Rathbone and Peter Cushing played Dr. Frankenstein (Son of and Curse of, respectively) and Sherlock Holmes (Hound of the Baskervilles). It may also be interesting to note that both men are products of England.

MONSTER CLUBS

If you're interested in any of the fields covered by Fan-Mo then you should be interested in a club called *Shock!* $4.00 gets you a one month membership in this really different Science Fiction, Fantasy and Horror club. Write to the president, BOB VILLARD, 2012 Merlo Dr., Montebello, Calif.

Descendants of the Grave-yard is the eerie title of a new club headed by TED PATTERSON and DENNY GRAYSON of Mansfield, Ohio. The "new" club is in reality over 4 years old, and still going strong. For more information, contact Ted at 388 Overlook Rd.

CASEY BRENNAN can send you information regarding a club for you monster fans who collect magazines. It's called the Periodical Collectors Club, and the members collect everything from newspapers to comic books to magazines. Casey's address is 4238 Bricker Rd., Avoca, Mich.

Fantastic Monster Club Members

JOSEPH QUAM
Superior, Wis
BUDDY SAUNDERS
Trlington, Tex
STEVE KIEFER
Palm Springs, Calif
LAWRENCE GIBSON
Detroit, Mich
GREG FRASER
Los Angeles, Calif
JOHN LANGE
Los Angeles, Calif
ROGER BARBER
San Bernadino, Calif
MARTIN EVANS
Lufkin, Tex
MIKE RUDIE
Concord, Calif
GARY CORBIN
Des Moines, Iowa

RICKY LOYA
South Gate, Calif
STEVE ALDUENA
Los Angeles, Calif
FRED ROTHENHAUSLER
Compton, Calif
HENRY STANNY
Los Angeles, Calif
PATTY McKINNEY
Whittier, Calif
HENRY TOEPIEL
Baltimore, Md
ROBERT CLEMMONS
Savanna, Calif
RICKY KILZER
Nampa, Idaho
GREGG BERCOUITZ
Los Angeles, Calif
SALLY SWENSON
Berkley, Calif
PAUL RUELLE
Farmington, Mich
DANNY CUTLER
El Paso, Tex
BRUCE POTTER
Santa Ana, Calif
DAVE GIOE
Chalmette, La
BUTCH SCHRADER
Coral Gables, Fla
DAVE RICHARDSON
Lansing, Mich
JEFFREY JONES
San Diego, Calif
ROBERT VANDERJAGT
Los Angeles, Calif
JAMES DALLMEYER
Pico Rivera, Calif
JIM SHAFER
Lakewood, Calif
DAVID CRITCHFIELD
Saratoga, Calif
PATRICK PUNNELLI
Somerville, Mass
RICKY DANA
Baltimore, Md
JEFF BURNS
Dallas, Tex
RON WILSON
E. Lansing, Mich
ROBERT PAZZANO
Waltham, Mass
FRED SQUIRES
Los Angeles, Calif
TOM HUTCHINS
Des Moines, Iowa
SAMMY LUNETTA
Corona, Calif

MIKE FEGAN
Junction City, Kans
DON SMITH
Southport, Ind
BILL FARNELL
Van Nuys, Calif
JERRY UTLEY
Dallas, Tex
JACK DUDEK
Wilmington, Del
TOM HOROWITZ
Los Angeles, Calif
RICKY JAMES
Sanger, Calif
DAL RAIFORD
Kountze, Tex
MIKE VRABEL
Taylor, Mich
MARTY SILVERT
Baltimore, Md
R.L. COOK
Hopkinsville, Ky
CRAIG CHISLEBROOK
Norfolk, Va
REID FARRELL
Houston, Tex
DICK BAUMANN
Northridge, Calif
ROBERT HEWITT
Hudson, NY
JOE SPRADLIN
McKinney, Tex
DAN SABANOVICH
San Jose, Calif
SALLY RIPLEY
Stockton, Calif
MIKE NIEWIAZKI
Highland Park, Mich
VICTOR WISCOVITCH
Los Angeles, Calif
DAN ELLETT
Des Moines, Iowa
BRUCE STEFFAN
Sandston, Va
DANIEL SCAPPEROTTI
Hicksville, NY
ANN DUNNING
Wilson, Ark
JOHN DULANEY
Oklahoma, Okla
MALCOM GOODMAN
Highland Springs, Va
STEVE BRINKER
Park Ridge, Ill
DOUGLAS FINK
Fairmont, Minn
BRENT NATHAN
San Francisco, Calif
THURMAN JACKSON
Chiloquin, Ore
BILLY MEADE
Timonium, Md
JOHN KELLEY
Baltimore, Md
BOB BUTLER
Pacific Palisades, Calif
LARRY UTTERBACK
Thornton, Colo
MARY LIBBE
Walbridge, Ohio
BILLY BAUMGARDNER
Hot Springs, Ark
LEONARD DICKSON
Jackson Heights, NY
MARTIN CROCKETT
Fairfield, Conn
STEPHEN MARRIOTT
Ogden, Utah
SHARON SEAGRAVES
Cerota, Calif

PHIL GIRARD
Delano, Calif
BILL TRICE
Monroe, La
RAY HANKS
Aurora, Ill
JAMES GOLDSTEIN
Erie, Pa
RANDY KNOWLES
San Lorenzo, Calif
TOM ANDERSON
Prarie Village, Kans
ROBERT ZANDER
Wapato, Wash
TED JAKUBEK
Bayonne, NJ
JERRY YOUNKINS
Grosse Point, Mich
GEORGE CARPENTER
Coronado, Calif
STEVEN GUSTAFSON
Cambridge, Ill
KATHY MILLS
Gulfport, Miss
JEFF POLESSI
McGill, Nevada
JAY DUNCAN
El Paso, Tex
KURT STEELE
Encino, Calif
SAM APPLEBY
Concord, Calif
KYLE ZAIDEN
Dayton, Ohio
ED KLANSEK
Akron, Ohio
FLORIAN PIETRYKOWSKI
Toledo, Ohio
DALE SCHULTZ
Plymouth, Mich
BENNY CALLISON
Los Angeles, Calif

MORE NEXT ISSUE!

MARVEL MAN FAN

Horror and fantasy film fan DONALD GLUT, of Chicago, Ill, is pictured here in a scene from his latest home movie epic, Captain Marvel, inspired by the article on the serial here which appeared in FanMo 2.

Junior Fanmos

In answer to the dire threats and polite requests from many of you out there in Monsterland, we have decided to include a column listing a few of the amateur Horror, Science Fiction and Fantasy magazines you energetic folks put out. First on the list this time 'round is *The Fantasy Journal*, published by BOB GREENBERG and JIM HOLLANDER. The thick mimeographed magazine costs a mere 15c per copy, and at this writing issue 6 has been received. The magazine includes some interesting artwork and a load of informative articles plus a bit of fiction to break up the pace a little . . . Another interesting "amzine" recently received comes from across the seas in merry England *Cthulhu*, edited by Britisher MIKE PARRY. This magazine too is filled with page after page of mimeographed movie information, a lot of it written by ALAN DODD, who was responsible for England's very first amateur horror magazine, *Camber*. We regret, however, that there is no address available for this magazine which seems to be sent out free to interested parties. We attempt then, to make a plea to Mike, wherever you are, to send us an address we may publish where horror fans may write . . . *Transylvanian Newsletter* is a small newspaper-like publication that is available from HARVEY OVSHINSKY at a subscription rate of 6 issues for 30c. The *Newsletter* is intended to report the latest news in the horror world and lists of horror clubs and publications. (say, that sounds like an amateur *Tombstone Times*!)

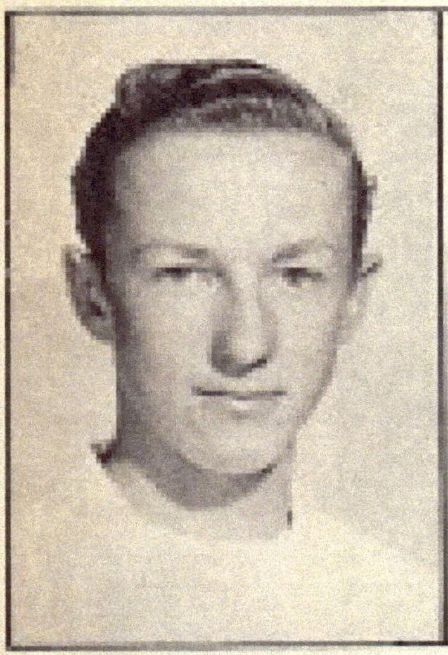

SCREEN ACE

W. ACE MASK is the editor-publisher of his own fantasy film famzine, titled *Screen Whirl*. The second issue features reviews of *Phantom of the Opera*, *Birdman of Alcatraz*, articles on werewolves, Karloff, new films. Scheduled for #3 is *House on Haunted Hill*, *New Adventures of Tarzan*, and the usual amount of interesting stories on film-making. Copies are 15c each, and may be ordered by writing Ace at 22102 Roberston Blvd., Chatsworth, Calif.

IN MEMORIAM—COUNT DOWNE

We hereby proclaim this month as National Count Downe Month, in memory of a fine old boy who finally met his match. It seems the good count was out "hunting" when he was besieged by a band of horrified villagers who just didn't understand the situation. They thought that because he had carried away three of the town's most lovely vixens and was later seen with a little blood on his teeth, he must be up to no good. The villainous villagers put a blunt end to the poor count— the blunt end of a wooden stake to be exact. With the printing of this lyric we acknowledge the loan-use of *Tombstone Times* by the World's #1 monster man, LARRY BYRD. Here he is seen in make-up for the Frankenstein Monster show for which he has been widely acclaimed.

SECRET MESSAGE FOR FANTASTIC MONSTER CLUB MEMBERS ONLY

```
I Z W G D W T T R S C E L G G D L U C K
W K Z W F L S C A S R G U Y B L G W C K
L B S B N I W G U U C O Z L C L V G U G
G N L S B G M P U C C L B G W T D Z L C
S X L B L G G X W C G G L R Y W C D L G
D S R L M W N W C L W T G Z L X
```

(Use decoding key on back of your membership card)

From
monsters to
spacemen,
everyone is
jumping over
to FANTASTIC
MONSTERS!
So don't YOU
be left out!

Be sure to get
the next
fabulous issue
of The World's
Greatest Chill
& Thrill
Magazine!

MONSTER OF THE MONTH

Friday, October 26th, 1962, less than a week before all Hallow's Eve, Boris Karloff, Lon Chaney Jr. and Peter Lorre were grandly reunited by CBS-TV for a history-making episode of the network's highly rated series *Route 66*, which stars Martin Milner and George Maharis as the roving Buz and Todd.

Titled *Lizard's Leg and Owlet's Wing*, the hour-long teleplay told the story of the three actors who meet in Chicago to thrash out differences concerning a new series of horror films they plan to produce. To avoid being recognized by their many avid fans, Karloff, Lorre and Chaney pose as members of The Society for the Preservation of Gerenuks (a species of rare African deer). When the discussion gets underway Karloff maintains that the public will no longer accept melodramatic monster films. Lorre and Chaney disagree and cook up a plan to prove their point—a plan that permits Chaney to recreate his three classic horror roles: Wolf Man, Hunchback, and the Mummy.

With the aid of coffins, candles, and their entire bag of horror props, Chaney and Lorre terrify a group of young secretaries attending a convention, proving that yesterday's terror tactics still pack a wallop. Impressed but not convinced, Karloff dons the infamous Frankenstein make-up. When the secretaries see the monstrous figure lurching down the hotel's corridors, pandemonium breaks loose. That convinces Karloff. At the fade out, Lorre and Chaney, grinning, know they've won the argument.

Hats off to CBS Television and scripter Stirling Silliphant for this magnificent addition to the Horror Hall of Fame. ●

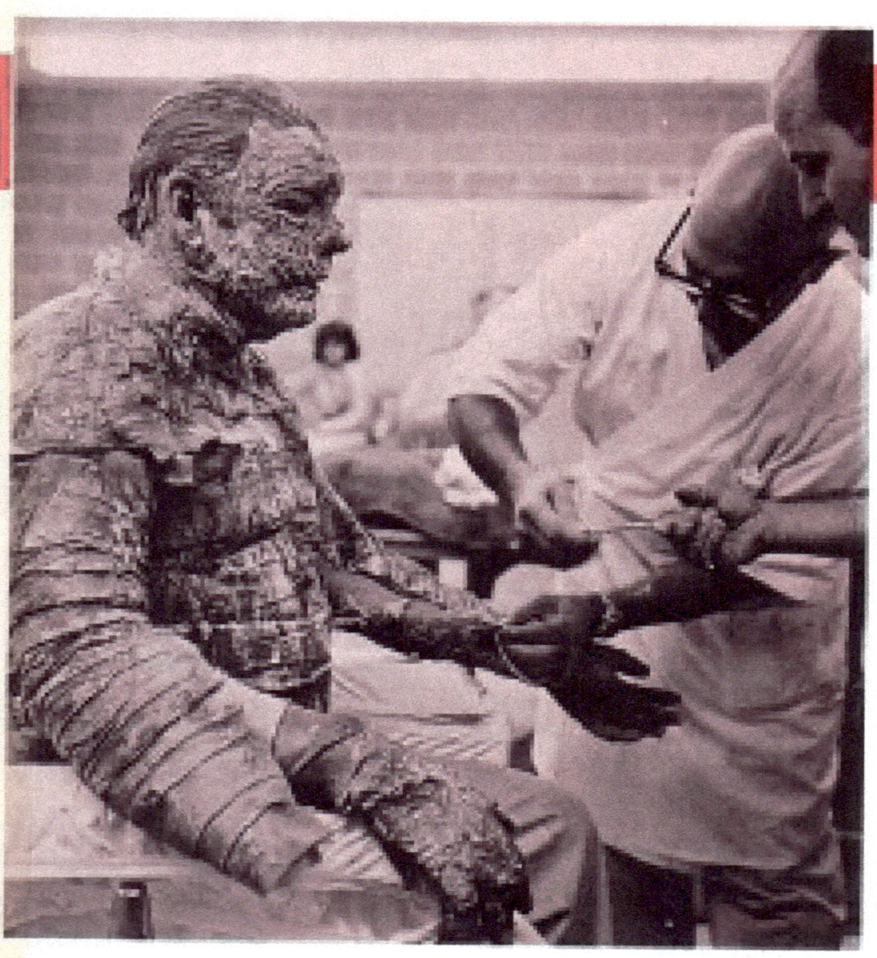

CBS-TV presents Karloff as Frankenstein, Chaney as the Wolf Man, and Lorre as his own sinister self

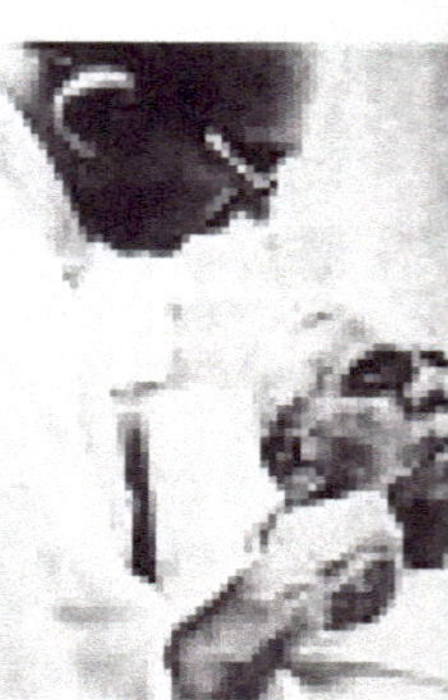

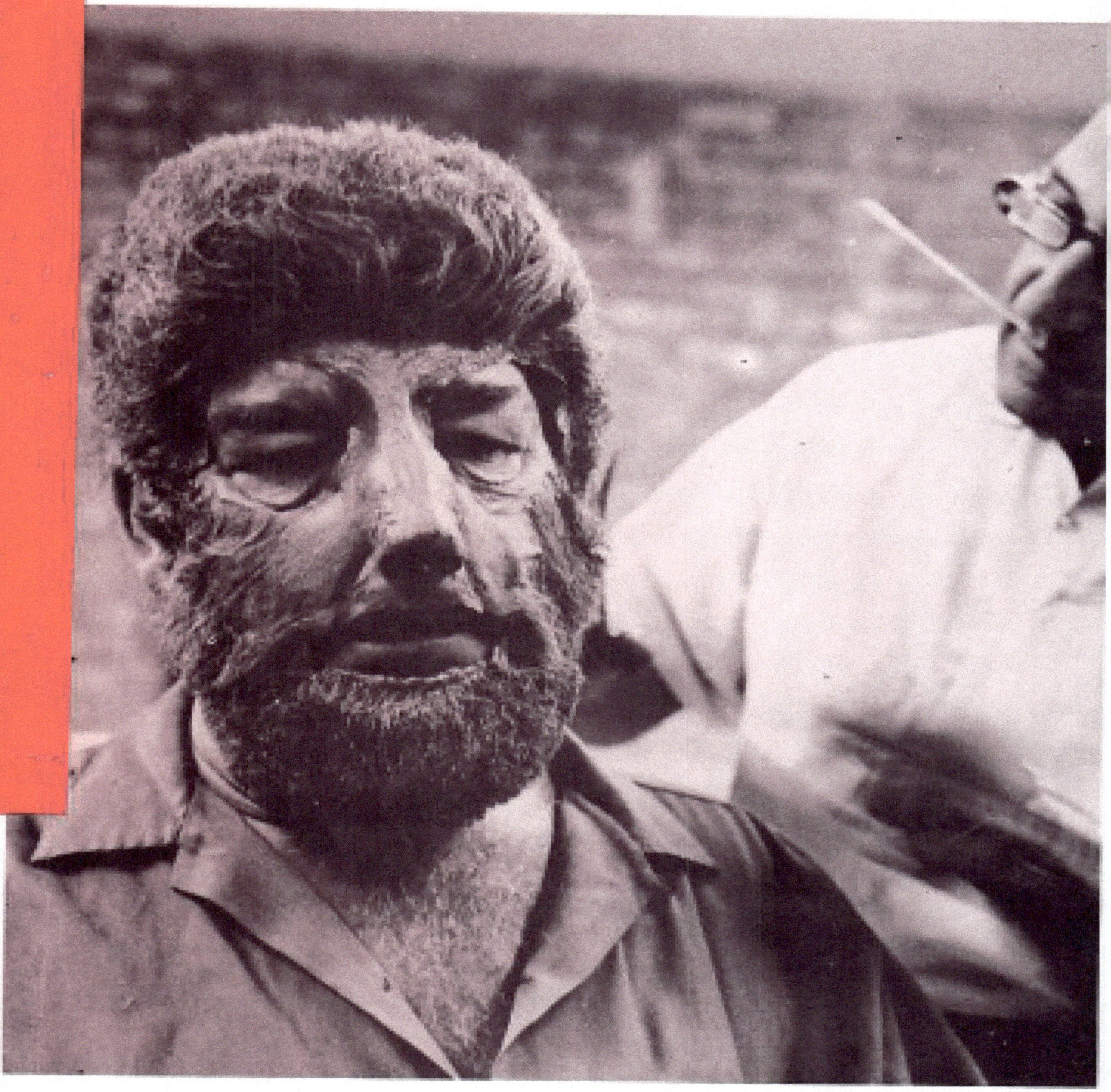

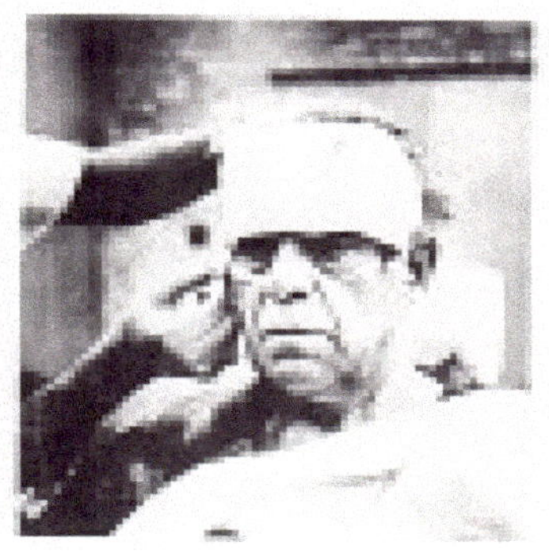
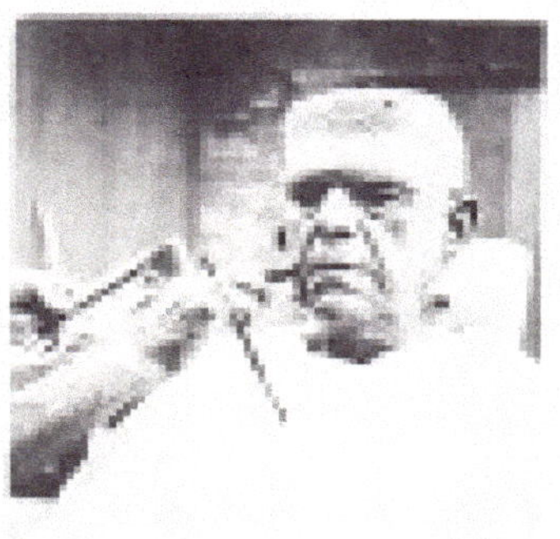

FANTASTIC
MONSTER OF THE MONTH

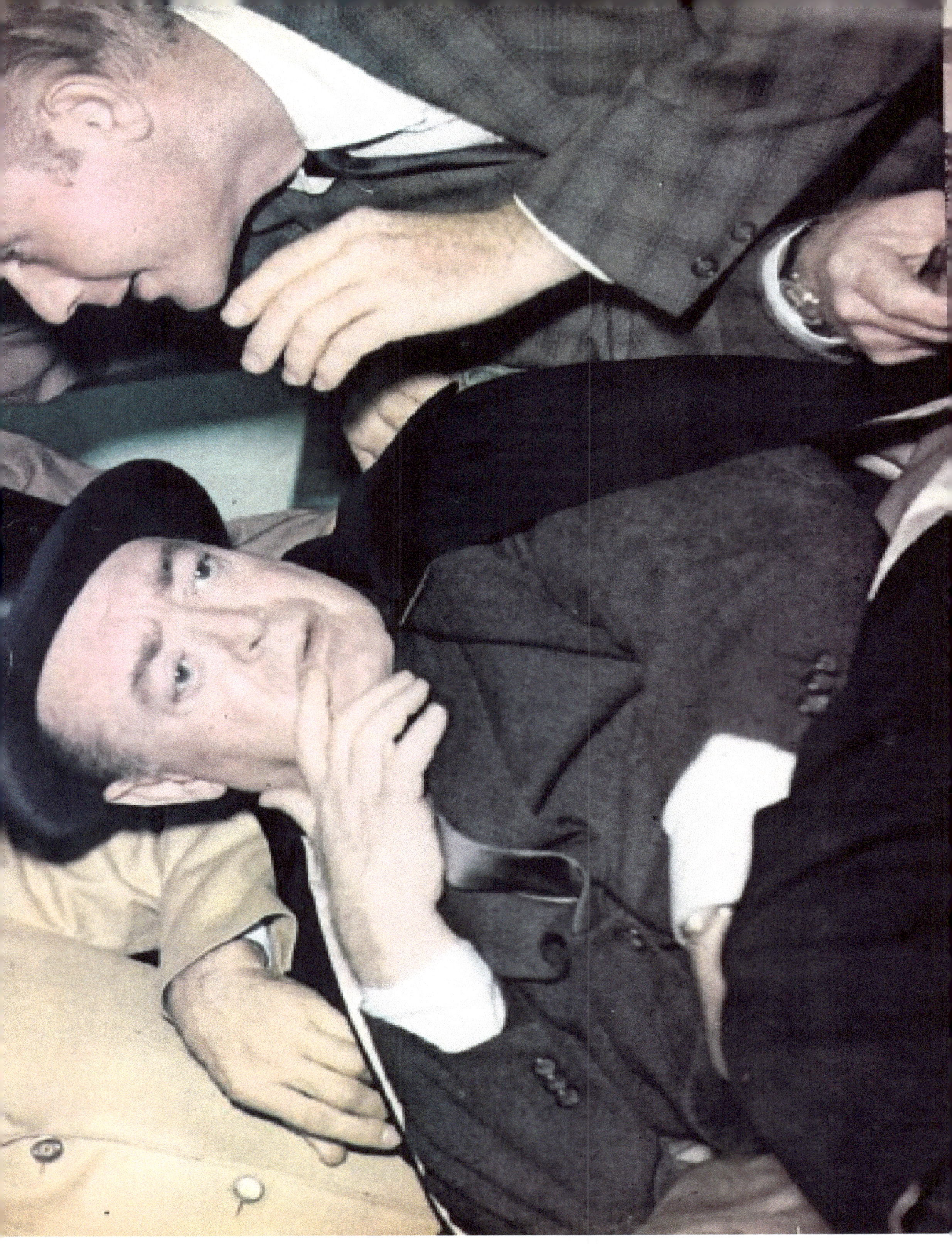

fantastic MONSTERS OF THE FILMS

WORLD'S GREATEST MONSTER MAGAZINE

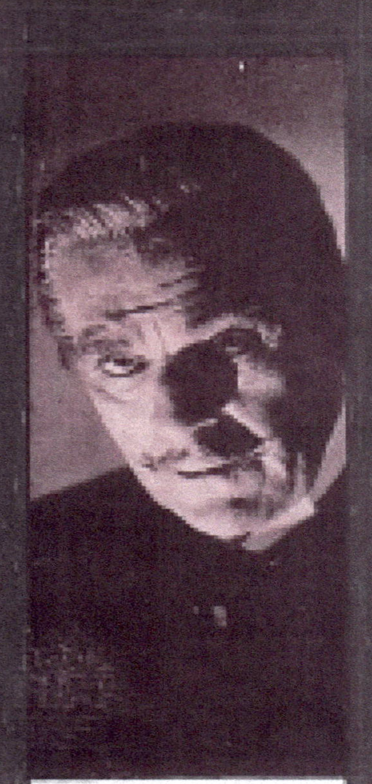

It seems definite that Hammer Films of England is going to add *Bride of Frankenstein* to their list of Universal remakes. Recalling our disappointment in their remake, *Curse of Frankenstein*, we doubt we'll be down at the local theatre when the new *Bride* opens. The original Bride—by far the best of the Frankenstein lot — should perhaps remain only in Memory and on TV rather than on the screen again.

One recent entry, *King Kong vs Godzilla*, is one we admit having passed up seeing. After scrutinizing the publicity stills, we decided there is only one Kong — the original — and this new Toho Production only stained the ape's good name. Besides, how can you have a giant ape film without Robert Armstrong?

Also, on the subject of remakes, in this issue is our beloved Mad Mummy; and you'll find a gallery of ghouls and gals herein, too. In addition, movie producer Alex Gordon gives a revealing account of his friend, the one and only Bela; and paperback novelist Judson Grey has come up with a fine little fiction shocker starring the mysterious monster-chaser, *Steelmark*.

Pleasant screams.

THE EDITORS

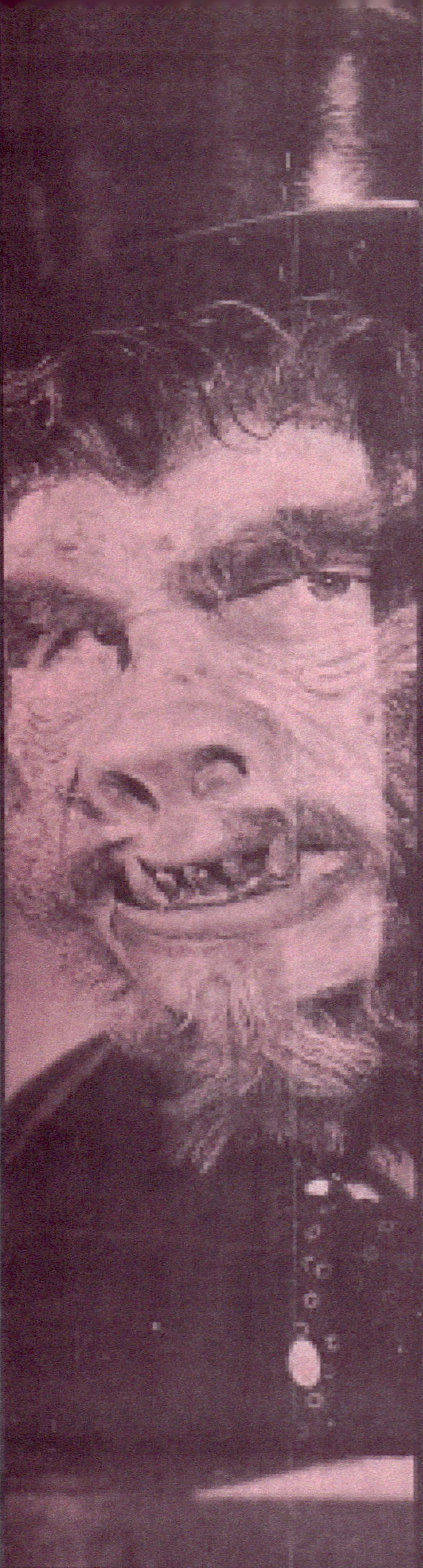

My name is Hyde. I'm a Monster. That's why I'm in this Magazine!

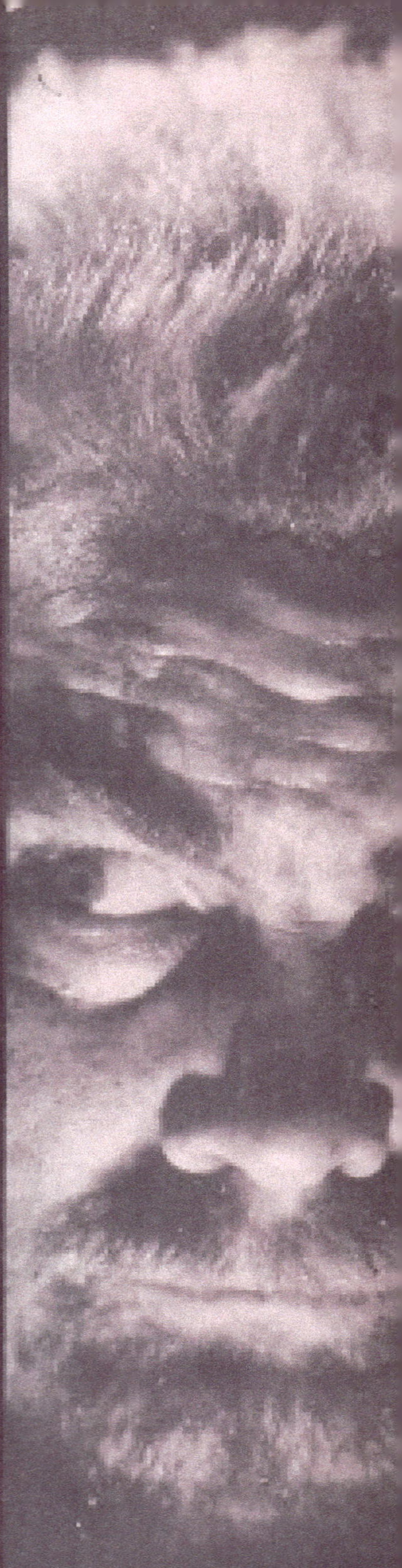

Are you looking for chills and thrills? Then FANTASTIC MONSTERS is your Ticket to Terror

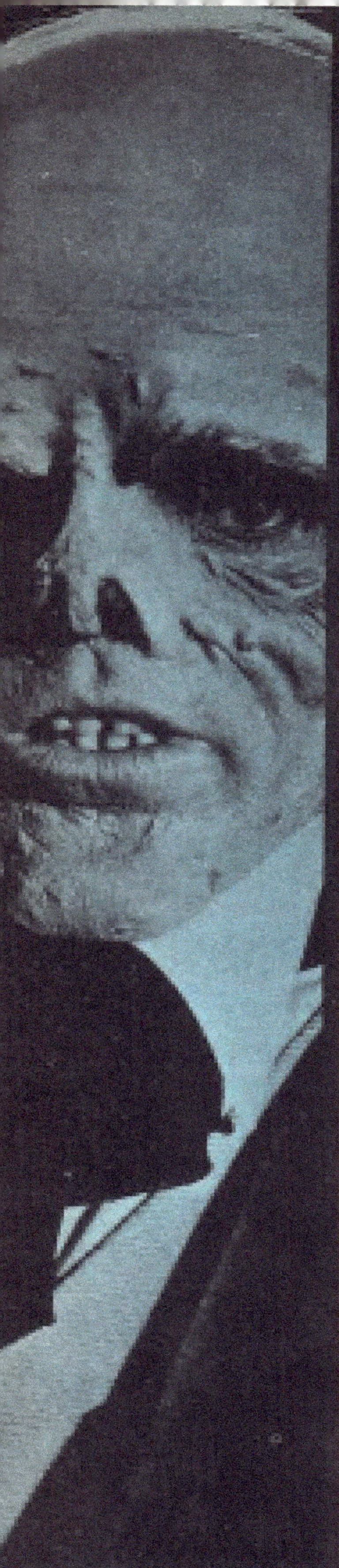

fantastic
MONSTERS
OF THE FILMS
VOL. 1 · NUMBER 5

COVER: IT
American-International's
VOODOO WOMAN

RON HAYDOCK
editor

PAUL BLAISDELL
managing editor

JIM HARMON
associate editor

BOB BURNS
research editor

LARRY BYRD
contributing editor

MAD MUMMY
crumbling editor

CREDITS & AC-
KNOWLEDGEMENTS:
Harold Aeschliman; Al-
lied Artists; Ted Bar-
nett; Columbia Pic;
Golden Eagle Films;
Bill Heffernan; Dan
Levitt; Paul Mitchell;
Kris Neville; Jack
Nicholas; Prize Comics
Group; Republic Pic;
Allan Rothmund; Uni-
versal Pic

VOLUME 1, NUMBER 5. FAN-
TASTIC MONSTERS OF THE
FILMS. PRICE 50c PER COPY.
Published bi-monthly by
Black Shield Publications
Inc. Mailing address: Post
Office Box 141, Topanga,
California. National Advertising Representatives: Harbor Company, 862 North
Fairfax, Los Angeles 46,
California. Contents Copyright 1963, by Black Shield
Publications Inc. Nothing
may be reprinted in whole
or in part without written
permission. Printed in U.S.A.
Unsolicited manuscripts must
be accompanied by stamped
self addressed envelopes;
the publisher accepts no responsibility for return. Any
similarity between people
and places mentioned in the
fiction and semi-fiction in
this magazine and any real
people and places is purely
coincidental.

TABLE OF CONTENTS

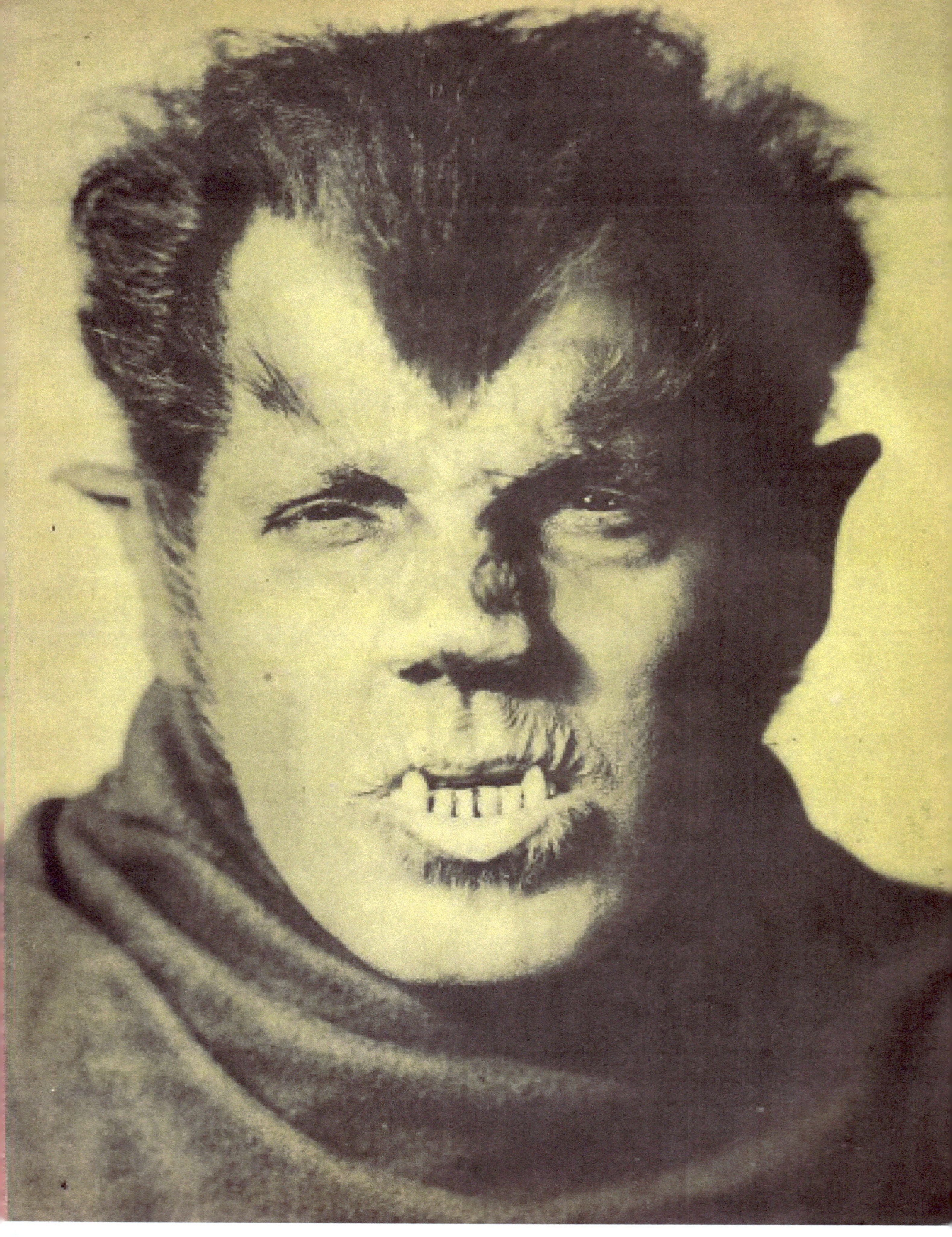

It takes more than a full moon to get a hairy horror hollering

How To Make A Werewolf Howl

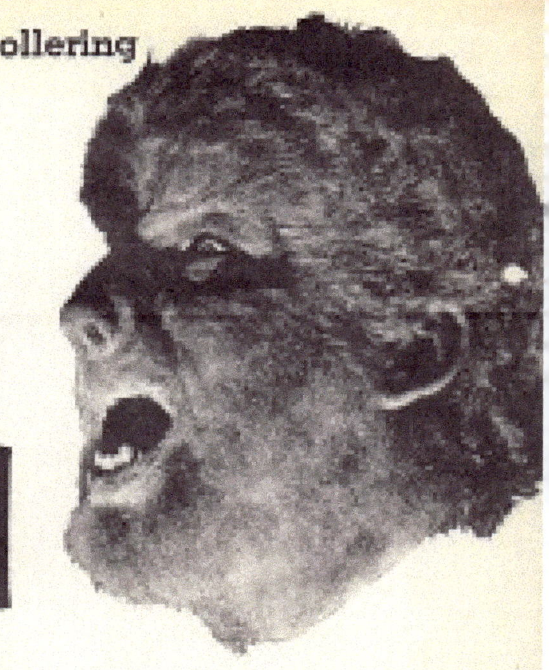

*Any film-maker worth his salt will tell you it's no simple matter to create something new and different for the screen. This axiom particularly holds true for horror pictures, where the problem is generally one of makeup, or devising a fresh, unfamiliar fright wig which (it is hoped) will in turn make the audiences' hair stand on end.

Nearly two years were spent in creating the infamous *Frankenstein*, eight months in blueprinting the bandages to be worn by *The Mummy*, one year in making a man invisible. But when it came time to introduce the very first werewolf to the screen, the main task lay not so much in the field of makeup as in the creation of a realistic (albeit blood-curdling) combination wolf-man howl.

Universal's *Werewolf of London* stalked in 1935, but three years previous another movie character presented much the same "sound" problem—Tarzan of the Apes. After many fruitless attempts at recording a half-man, half-gorilla cry, MGM's sound technicians finally came up with the idea of recording J o h n n y Weissmuller vocalizing an Australian yodel, and playing it back at three times the normal speed. ●

by Ron Haydock

Below, Comic Lou Costello and creeper Lon Chaney Jr in ABBOTT AND COSTELLO MEET FRANKENSTEIN for Universal

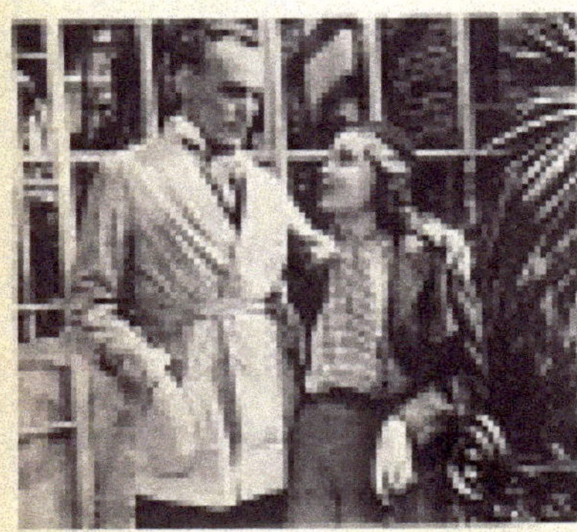

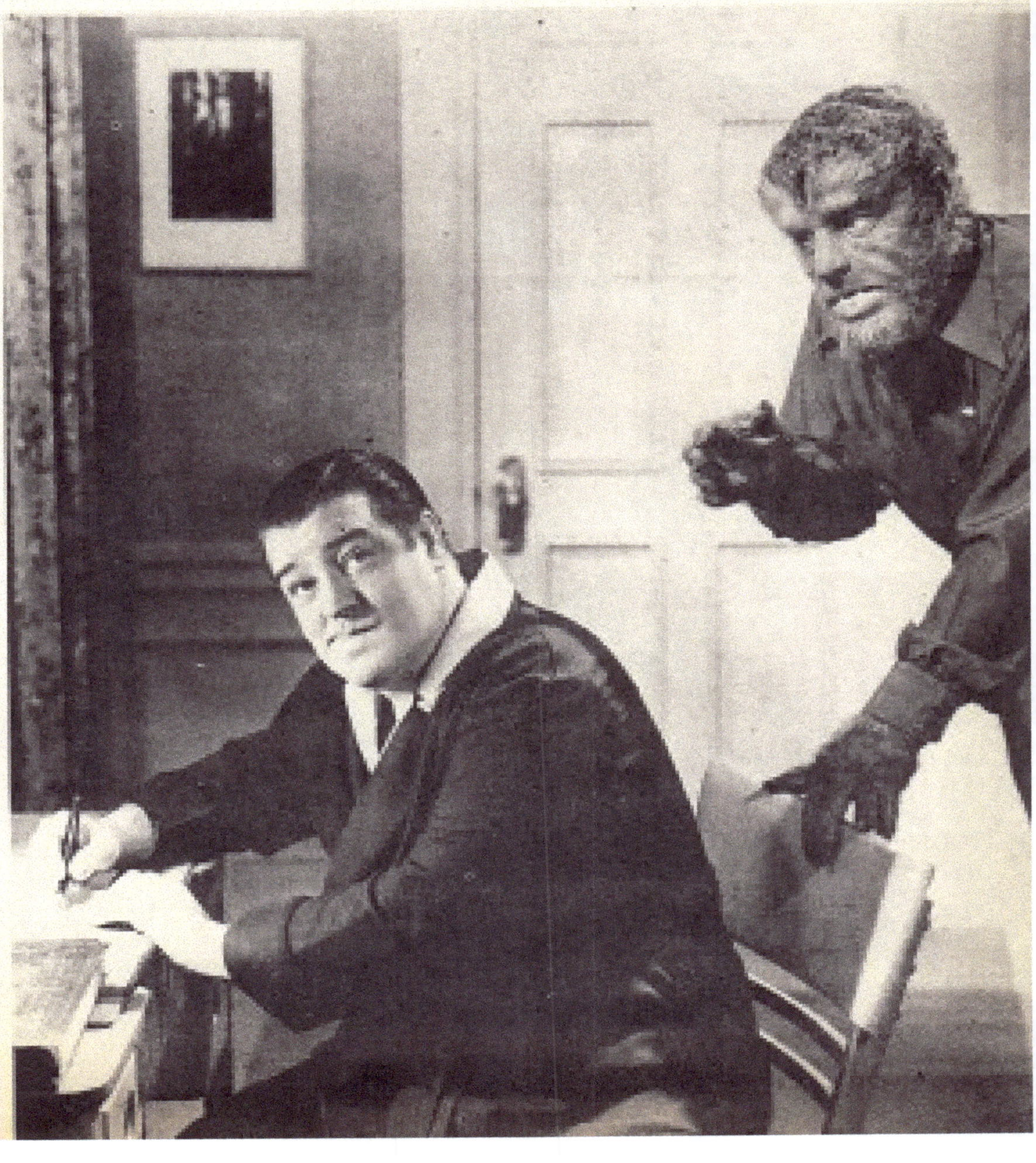

The note sought for London's werewolf, played by Henry Hull, was one of ferocity, mixed with protest and near human grief. What key should be selected for this howl? How long should each howl endure? What animals should be tested for the best sound? These were moot points threshed out in hours of discussion between director Stuart Walker and Gil Kurland, Universal's sound supervisor.

Hyena shrieks, wildcat yowls, and bear growls were found unsatisfactory. Visits to the zoo by night and day failed to elicit a single adequate yelp from the big grey lobos or coyotes or even the jackals.

While on location in Alaska for another Universal film, Kurland was able to record the bay of a wild timber wolf, full of menace and curdling with melancholy, and upon his return to Hollywood, he played the recording for Walker.

Although Walker was satisfied with the genuine wolf howl, he decided the human element in the voice was still lacking. Using a sound mixer, Kurland blended the timber wolf's baying with Indian yells, crowd roars, every tragic cry in his sound library, but to no effect. Valerie Hobson, Lester Matthews, Warner "Charlie Chan" Oland, and the other members of the cast tried their luck at supplying the right whoop, but their sounds were too flat.

Then Walker hit on the notion of seeing what Hull himself could do. As the record was played, Hull shouted with it, and reports filtered back from the mixer's booth that this attempt was more encouraging. However, only certain notes would blend effectively with the baying. At Walker's direction, Kurland edited out all of Hull's high notes, re-recorded the remains, and a realistically terrifying howl was finally throated by the London werewolf.

Six years later the second werewolf film was produced, The Wolf Man, also from Universal, but the painstaking Walker-Kurland-Hull yelp was nowhere to be heard. Although the current Tarzan, Jock Mahoney, is still voicing the original Weissmuller cry, it seems that all werewolves after Hull's prefer to yip and yap on their own.

Why not? They have a howl of a time. ●

Mauraded to launch upon an unsuspecting villager is Lon Chaney Jr in FRANKENSTEIN MEETS THE WOLF MAN (Universal, 1943)

Hammer Films' technicolor werewolf puts his curse and claws on Yvonne Romain (CURSE OF THE WEREWOLF, 1961)

1. Completed clay head with clay ear and teeth. These will be molded separately.

2. The "cured" front half of the rubber head is removed from its mold.

3. "Monster" foot is constructed like the head, but designed to fit over a pair of "sneakers".

4. Fabric body, completely covered with overlapping rubber "scales".

The DEVIL'S WORKSHOP

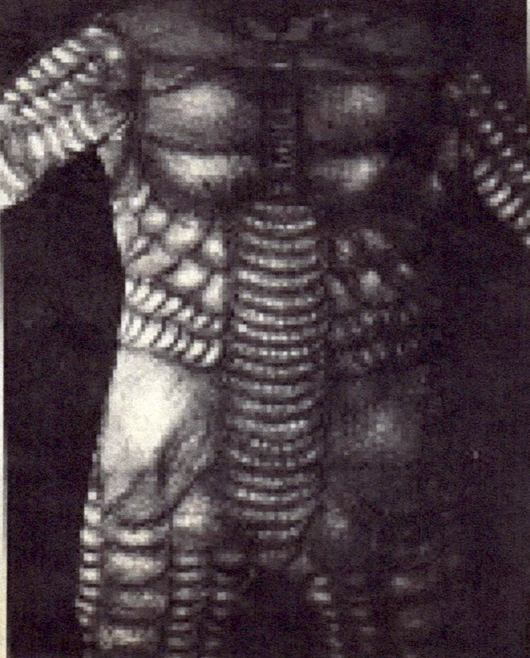

After many letters asking "What advantage does the professional prop or monster builder have over the amateur?", we've decided to come up with a two word answer—a deadline.

Proof? Well, if all the uncompleted amateur theatrical props and masks could be completed tomorrow, there would be regiments of countless thousands of monsters ready to march on Hollywood!

A pretty broad statement to make, but the sad fact is that most amateur projects run out of enthusiasm long before they run out of time or money. This is where the completion date, known as a "deadline", helps the professional. He knows that the project has to be completed by a certain date. If it isn't, he's not doing his share of the teamwork, and consequently his "team mates", who are working on the many other facets of the movie, are going to be slowed down, too.

After the original sketches of It— The Terror from Beyond Space were approved by producer Bob Kent, director Eddie Cahn, and script writer Jerry Bixby, it was time for the "prop builders" to go to work, and this is how they did it—and on time.

First, a clay head was constructed over a plaster replica of a normal human being's head and shoulders. This would insure a reasonably good fit, when it came time to wear the completed rubber head. The script called for a scaly desert creature that lived on Mars, and the sketches were carefully followed. (In issue No. 4 of FANTASTIC MONSTERS, Bill Malone described a method of insuring that a mask will fit your face. His didn't need a plaster replica, and was effective, simple and cheap.)

When the clay head for It was completed, a row of aluminum plates, the size of playing cards, were pushed into the clay. They ran up the side of the neck, over the top of the head and down the other side, dividing the head into two parts, front and back. Casting plaster was mixed with water to the consistency of heavy whipping cream and brushed into the first half of the head. Since the plaster mold was to be a large, strong one, a layer of wet burlap strips was applied over this first layer of plaster before

turn to page 3

The blow-by-blow
account of how the
monstrous It—
The Terror From
Beyond Space
was created for
Movies

by Paul Blaisdell

Ray Corrigan, as "It",
stalks after the crew of
an Earth-bound space-
ship!

STEELMASK Meets The Zombie Master

by Judson Grey

Once shadowy phantoms stalked fiends in human and inhuman form in the pages of pulp magazines, on chilly radio airwaves, in movie chapterplays. Return with FANTASTIC MONSTERS to those thrills of yesteryear with a new monster chaser, STEELMASK

From the shadows of Granger Avenue came a faint metallic glint, a glimmer of reflected light that would have told a knowing passerby that in that gloom lurked the trench-coated figure who wore beneath his wide-brimmed hat the symbol of his name, a name known throughout the teeming, multi-racial underworld of Los Angeles—the name of Steelmask.

The agent of the night was following a man who was just coming into the circle of light thrown by the corner streetlamp. In his strange career, Steelmask had shadowed many who sought to evade the clutches of law and order, but this man he followed this night was different from all the others. The man Steelmask followed in the lurking darkness was a corpse, a walking dead man!

In the illumination of the streetlamp the fact that he was dead was inescapable. Death was in his eyes, written on his face with patterns of decay. Yet he walked on with the animation, and the lifelessness of a robot.

From his watching place, Steelmask nodded to himself. He had seen this

turn to page 84

REVENGE OF THE SON OF THE MAD MUMMY STRIKES BACK

Our Crumbling Editor Returns for Another in his series of Articles — Attacking all Series Sequels as Crummy Editions

Friends, out there in Monsterland, I come before you this time with a deadly serious subject. As if worms and rats were not enough, this thing has been gnawing away at me lately. I am a Mummy with civic pride, and if there's anything I hate it is to see a Monster cheapened. When a monster has done his duty once, I say he shouldn't have to be made to do it all over again. The second time is never as good as the first.

Go back to Frankenstein in 1932. There, with Karloff as the Monster, was the classic in its entirety, based on the novel by Mary Shelly, a recognized literary milestone for centuries. Universal made it, but not content with this giant of horror, they had to keep adding chapters and with each new Frankenstein film, the quality dropped. Not only the quality dropped, so did the monster.

First, the Frankenstein Monster dropped through the floor of a burning mill into the waters below. But back he came in The Bride of Frankenstein to get another hot flash when he and his mate are blown up by a runaway electric generator. Now, in The Son Frankie sparks anew with menace to finally get tarred without feathers in bubbling tar pits. From bubbling tar he goes to a bubbling brook unleashed from a dam apparently washing the Monster up in The Ghost. But the water is frozen and preserves Frankie as well as Birdseye could do for the time he Meets the Wolf Man. Once again, that treacherously unreliable dam gives away and only the ministrations of the Mad

Left: The Frankenstein Monster, captured and jailed by local constables in Universal's BRIDE OF FRANKENSTEIN. Right: Boris Karloff as the original FRANKENSTEIN monster in 1932

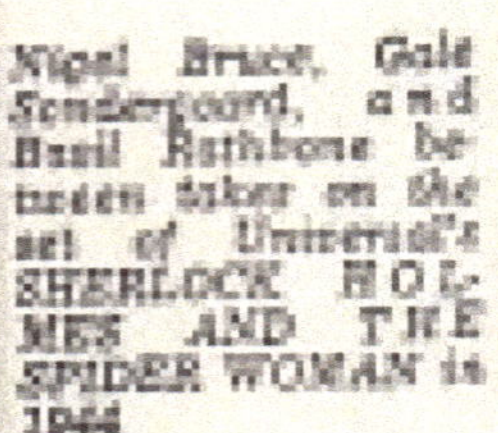

Hammer's CURSE OF FRANKEN-
STEIN boasted Christopher Lee as
the first technicolor Frankenstein
Monster

Nigel Bruce, Gale
Sondergaard, and
Basil Rathbone be-
tween takes on the
set of Universal's
SHERLOCK HOL-
MES AND THE
SPIDER WOMAN in
1944

Doctor could revive him for a visit to
The House of Frankenstein. Inspite
of being sunk in quicksand, the
Monster pulls out for guesting at the
House of Dracula where another Mad
Doctor's lab collapses on him. But
Frankie wakes up in a horror museum
when Abbott & Costello Meet Frankenstein—only to fall through a burning deck into the waters below, almost exactly where he started out in
1932.

I ask you—is it reasonable to expect
anybody to go through all that? Especially a member of the movie
audience?

Of course, I happen to be a Mummy
and I was entombed for five thousand
years before coming back to life, but
bear in mind I don't spend five
thousand years in a tomb every day
of the week!

Just look at what happened to the
Monster during those seven Universal
pictures. He started off played by
the Master himself, Boris Karloff.
Then the series went through such
horror stars as Lugosi and Lon
Chaney Jr. to wind up portrayed by
Glenn Strange, whose primary film
career is one of being a villain in
Westerns! Some people insist Strange
was the best monster of all, but I
think he should have stuck to water

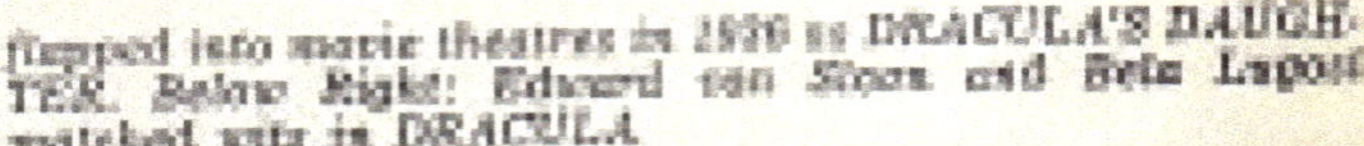

Below: SON OF DRACULA, a relatively important Universal film, starred Lon Chaney Jr, shown here choking the life out of co-star J. Edward Bromber. Center: Gloria Holden flipped into movie theatres in 1936 as DRACULA'S DAUGH-TER. Below Right: Edward van Sloan and Bela Lugosi matched wits in DRACULA.

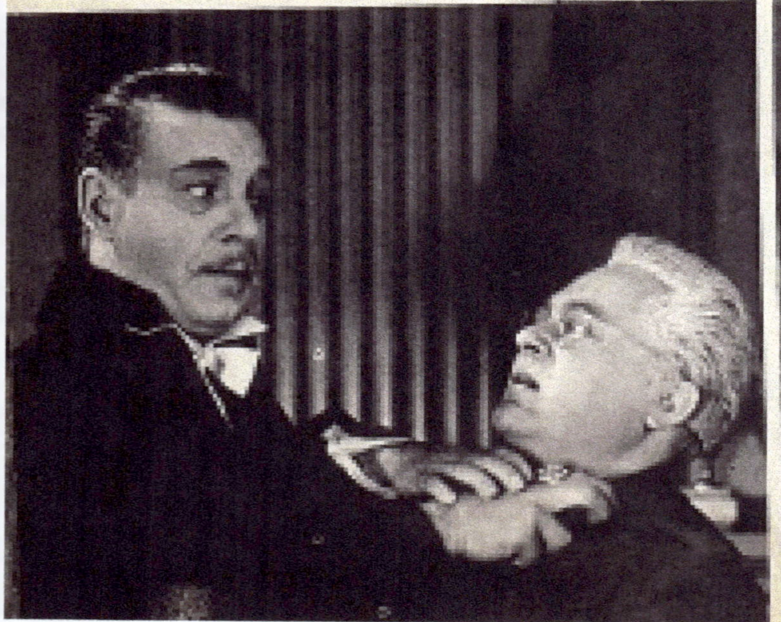

ing the horses for the pause.

That's what they did to Frankenstein, and they didn't do much better by Dracula. The version of 1931 starring Bela Lugosi was a good film, as good as possible with those primitive sound facilities influencing even the visual aspects of the movie, and Lugosi was pretty weird as the vampire king. Yet, just because they thought they could make some more money, Universal offered a slew of new Draculas, including the above-mentioned House twosome.

The first Dracula sequel was *Dracula's Daughter*. In this one, the Viscount of Vampires didn't make an appearance, only his love-sick daughter to final-reel it with an arrow through her heart—and not Cupid's. In the next one, Dracula himself was back, or at least his Son. But the Con was Lon Chaney Jr—then in a rather pudgy period, looking like the best fed vampire this side of Transylvania.

Then, of course, there are those Hammer Frankenstein and Dracula pictures from England in recent years.

These aren't really sequels—they come under the heading of re-makes. After careful consideration, I have decided that I am less against remakes than sequels. Films like *Curse*

turn to page 62

Right: Julie Adams came face-to-fish with THE CREATURE FROM THE BLACK LAGOON in 1954

The strangest Frankenstein Monster of them all!

Tormented by the angry elements of nature, he drew life itself from the lightning that flayed him. Hating the world, he developed an almost child-like love for a little girl. Obeying an impulse, he crushed to death his only friend—and wept. Mute, he spoke. And submitting to an operation to make him a creature of good, he became even more fearsome than ever.

This was the Monster of *The Ghost of Frankenstein*. In the world behind the camera, his story was equally strange.

On a Friday the 13th, in March, twenty-one years ago, Universal Pictures released the fourth Frankenstein film, with a star as astonishing to the fantastic film fan as the screenplay itself, and with an audacity seldom matched in motion picture history. For in the role of the Monster—the role Boris Karloff had made famous in *Frankenstein* and *The Bride of Frankenstein* and *The Son of Frankenstein*—Universal had cast Lon Chaney, Jr., fresh from his triumph as the Wolf Man. The critical applause for Chaney's performance as "Lennie" in John Steinbeck's great motion picture, *Of Mice and Men*, still rang in the theaters of the nation.

FANTASTIC MONSTERS presents the King of the Monsters

The GHOST of FRANKENSTEIN

by Paul Severn

Eleven years before, in *Frankenstein*, Universal had made another gamble, selecting an unknown Boris Karloff. But he had rejected this new role, and never again would he play the Monster. Now, the motion picture world wondered if the film studio had created its own Frankenstein Monster. Could anyone other than Karloff play the part convincingly? The answer came on that evening in 1942.

Audience tension mounted as the

(above, left) Ygor the mad shepherd unearths the infamous Monster of Frankenstein. (left) Leyland Hodgson, Sir Cedric Hardwicke, Evelyn Ankers, and Ralph Bellamy discuss the strange happenings in the town of Vasaria.

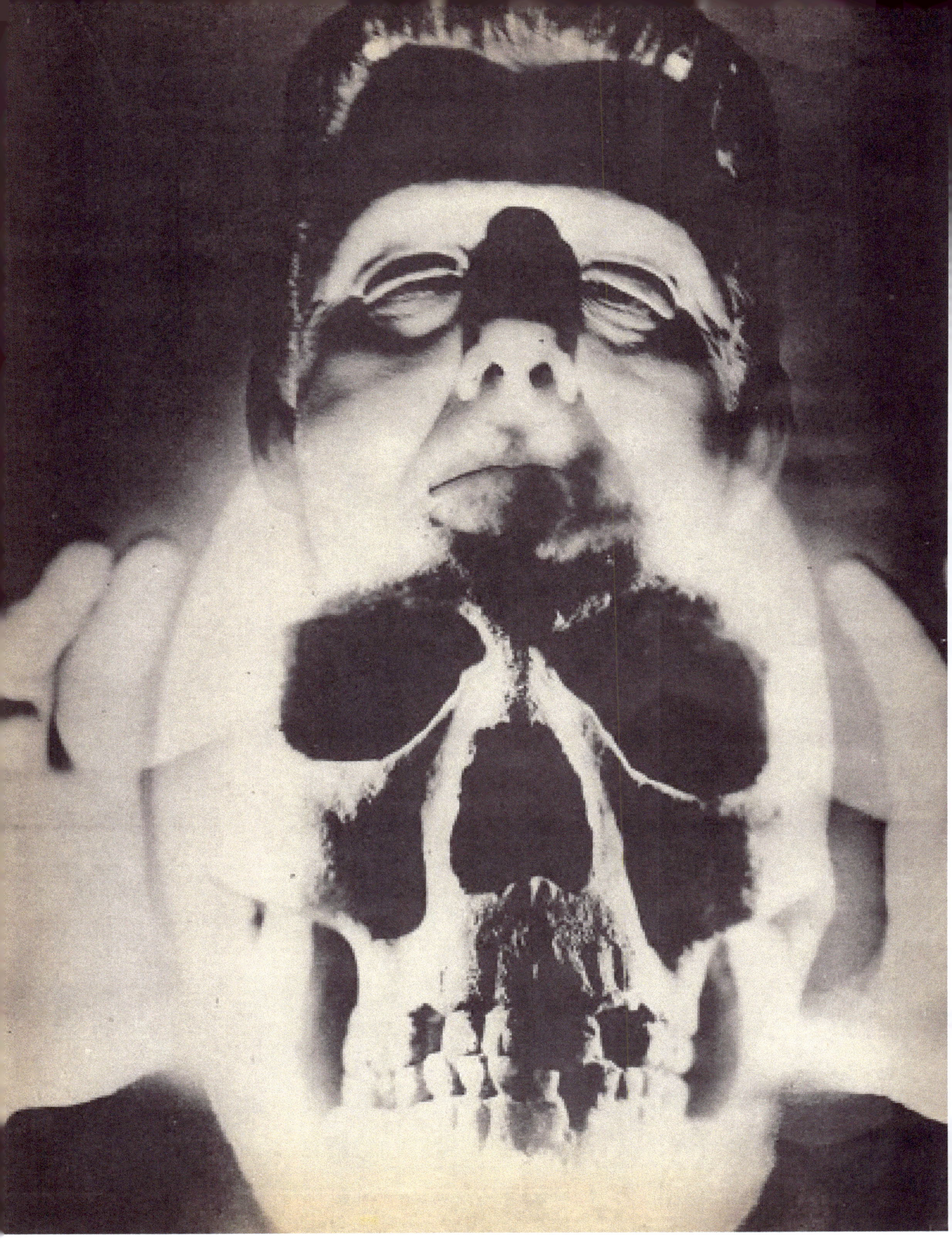

credits, one by one, flashed upon the screen. Original Story by Eric Taylor. Screen Play by W. Scott Darling. Produced by GEORGE WAGGNER. Directed by Eric C. Kenton. And then the events that concluded *The Son of Frankenstein* were played again. The Frankenstein villagers — their torches blazing in the night—were at Frankenstein castle, the Monster trapped within. Dynamite was laid against the castle walls, fuses were lit. The castle was blown into rubble, and Frankenstein's Monster buried in the midst of it. So had ended *The Son of Frankenstein.*

But now, with the villagers gone, a scarred, crook-necked, figure slogged through the silent ruins, a battered shepherd's horn slung across his back. It was Ygor, the crippled madman who had survived his own hanging. He probed the gutted remains, digging deeper than the superstitious villagers had ever dared. And there, as his eyes glittered with feverish excitement, he found the Monster imprisoned in a tomb of sulphur.

Slowly, the immense body stirred. The sulphur that obscured his features fell away, bit by bit. He stood. And for the first time, the audiences of the world saw Lon Chaney, Jr. as the Frankenstein Monster.

This was not Karloff's creature. The makeup was the same, but that was all. Chaney's Monster was massively huge, a great, dumb, tormented brute more animal than man—yet looking more man-like than Karloff ever had—heavy-faced, heavy-lidded, a column of living, hating, undirected power. There were no signs of the fleshless, almost esthetic, features of Karloff's broken-souled creation. Chaney's Monster was the 'Lennie' he had played in John Steinbeck's drama —big, strong, witless Lennie—turned irrevocably bad, demonically insane. And yet, the portrayal was right. Every good actor brings something different to a role—and the Monster was no exception.

Universal's gamble at the box office had paid off.

The rest of the players were as astonishing as Chaney. Bela Lugosi, a star in *Dracula,* accepted a more featured role to recreate the part of Ygor, the mad shepherd. Sir Cedric Hardwicke, knighted only eight years before for his contributions to the English theater, became the tragic figure of Ludwig Frankenstein, his father's second son. Beautiful Evelyn Ankers played Elsa, his daughter. Ralph Bellamy, to star as Franklin D. Roosevelt on the stage and screen in the award-winning *Sunrise at Campobello,* became Elsa's fiance and the public prosecutor who stalked the Monster. Lionel Atwill of England, with more than a score of medical roles behind him, was Dr. Bohmer, Frankenstein's jealous assistant. Barton Yarborough, the immortal "Doc Long" of radio's classic shocker *I Love a Mystery,* portrayed Kettering, a good man of science who was destroyed by the

(left) Sir Cedric Hardwicke as Dr. Ludwig Frankenstein shoots life-giving electricity into his father's creature

(above) The Monster is attracted to a child, Cloestine. (below) The colossal creation of Frankenstein is enraged at being captured by the local constables

Monster. And four-year-old Janet Ann Gallow — possibly the youngest featured player in horror movie history —was Cloestine, the tiny child the Monster came to love. It was a near brilliant cast, and they gave their roles all of the variety and scope that was demanded of them.

Unmaimed, the Monster had survived the dynamite blasts, the collapsing masonry and timbers, and the entombment, but his battered body was gravely weakened and his electrical life fluid ebbed. Ygor, his friend, led him haltingly out of the ruins of the castle and away from the Frankenstein countryside. Suddenly, in a majestic and awesome scene, the lowering skies stormed and great fingers of lightning flailed out blindly, lashing the stricken creature—and as they did, life and strength coursed through him once again. He would need more if he were to long survive, but now Ygor could guide him to Victor Frankenstein's other son.

In Vasaria, where Dr. Ludwig Frankenstein had been living incognito, the Monster escaped from Ygor and roamed the village streets. There, he found tiny Cloestine, and the child, unafraid of him—like no one else he had ever known—attracted the Monster. He carried her away, only to be discovered by the villagers and pursued over the roofs and street archways. Finally, the mob overcame the weakened creature and imprisoned him.

Meanwhile, Ygor threatened Dr. Frankenstein with exposure if the Monster's artificial life were not renewed. Although he realized his sanitarium and all his life's work would be forfeit if his real identity were known. Frankenstein refused. But when Erik Ernst, the public prosecutor and his daughter's fiance, asked for his medical opinion of the Monster, chained now in the village courtroom, he was forced to examine him, and there, the Monster, deprived of Cloestine and seeing the son of his creator, went mad, smashing the massive chair he was chained to in fragments and battering the police senseless — escaping only after Ludwig Frankenstein had faced him down, as one might a wild animal.

With Ygor, the Monster went to the sanitarium. Enraged, he strangled Frankenstein's assistant, Dr. Kettering; and Elsa, after a terrifying experience with the Monster, begged her father to destroy it—but Frankenstein, shocked by Kettering's death, decided upon a more daring course. He would transplant Kettering's brain into the skull of the creature his father had created, making him at last the instrument of good that Victor Frankenstein had intended.

But the Monster, in one of the most powerful and moving scenes in the film, had accidently crushed his only friend, Ygor, to death. While he grieved, Dr. Bohner, an assistant of Frankenstein's and blindly jealous of his success, replaced Dr. Kettering's brain with that of the criminally in-

turn to page 42

The Monster is evidently "burned to death" in the closing minutes of the film.

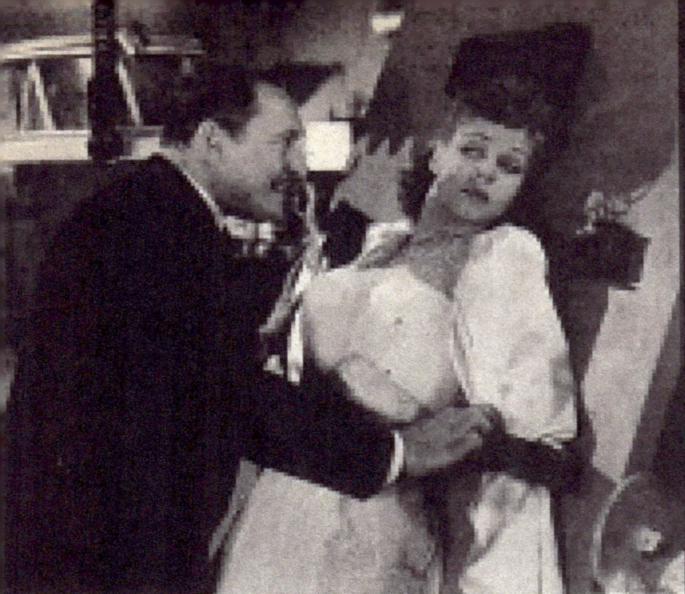

Yes, Mrs. Fitzsimmons, my invention will wash and dry that dress right on you!

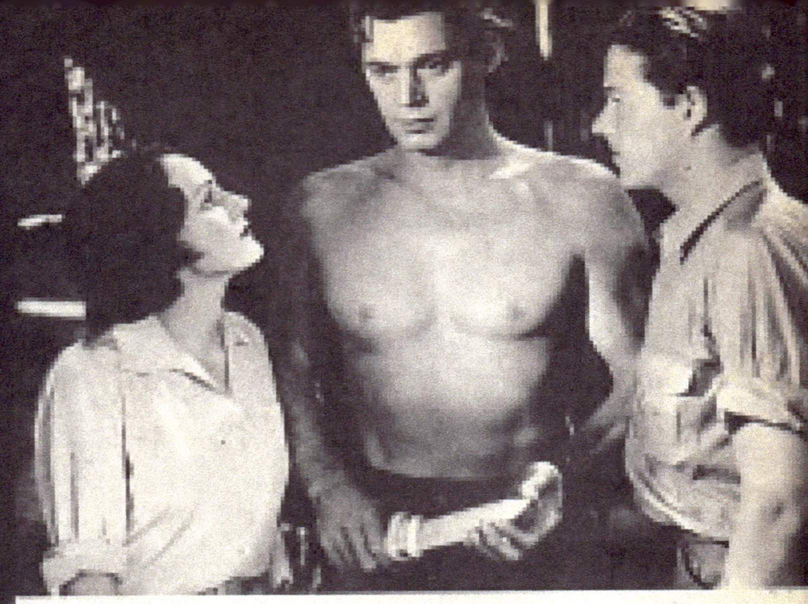

Won't you please give the young fellow back his knife?

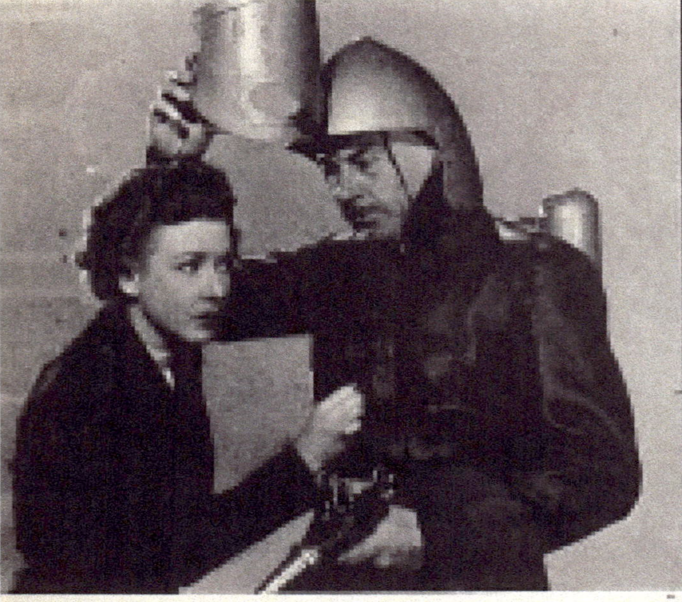

At the tone the time will be 6:59 and ten seconds . . .

Dead Time Tales

Based on the Nightmares of The Wizard of Ooze

Face it, Herbie—your teeth just aren't sharp enough for the Dracula bit!

Professor—enter one more Twist contest and you're through here!

Hey you guys—The Shadow's back on radio!

You act like a smile would break your face!

Dear, Elvis has not gone into the army forever!

Mister, like it or not, I'm taking her in the next time she bangs you up this bad!

All these bells are giving me a lousy headache!

I did not steal your hair-do, Gretchen!

They Came from Outer Space— Multi-tentacled Plant Monsters, lashing out with their Deadly Stingers to strike Mankind blind

(left to right) Janina Faye, Alison Leggatt, Howard Keel, Janette Scott, and Mervyn Johns—temporarily safe from the man-eating Triffids

THE DAY OF THE

An army of Triffids is momentarily baffled by an electrified fence

Science-fiction author John Wyndham, who has been acclaimed by SF buffs as "the modern H.G. Wells", has just had another of his best-seller novels adapted into a motion picture —Day of the Triffids.

Wyndham's Village of the Damned, based on his book The Midwich Cuckoos, proved to be one of the few fantasy film highlights of 1960, and we can expect no less a treat from his latest, the Triffids film, an SF spectacle in technicolor and Cinemascope, released by Allied Artists.

The story tells of the disasterous effects of a meteorite shower, its brilliance leaving most of the world's population blinded; and the threat made against civilization by the giant Triffids, mobile plant monsters with lethal stinging powers that multiply at an alarming rate.

Howard Keel (in a non-singing role) and French beauty Nicole Maurey are among the fortunate few who miraculously escape blindness in London. Keel, as an American seaman, and Miss Maurey, a chatelaine, join to care for large numbers of the visionless, until finally they are forced to flee for their lives from the invading Triffids.

TRIFFIDS

Unknown to them, a man-wife team of scientists (Kieron Moore and Janette Scott) are laboring up in their lighthouse home-laboratory in the hopes of discovering a way to destroy the man-killing plants. And while they labor, the Triffid monsters are already beginning to sprout up amidst the rocks on which the lighthouse stands . . .

As the film reels on, Koel and curvaceous Nicole meet up with the two scientists and become involved in countless numbers of skirmishes with the deadly monsters from space, until at long last the Secret of Successful Triffid Destruction is discovered.

Triffids is the first picture to be made by Philip Yordan's Security Pictures, Limited, a new production company with an ambitious future program of filming other world-wide best-selling novels. Yordan, who scripted Triffids, is well-qualified for such projects. Not only is he the Academy Award winning author of outstanding scenarios like El Cid and King of Kings, but he's also responsible for turning in the screenplay on George Pal's production of H.G. Wells' The Time Machine.

FANTASTIC MONSTERS' editor Ron Haydock cornered the Triffids' striking French star, Miss Nicole Maurey, at a recent Hollywood press gathering and asked her if she found co-starring with monsters any different than co-starring with Bing Crosby, Charlton Heston, Rex Harrison, and Alec Guiness as she has in previous films.

"Yes," she replied with a wink. "Monsters have more arms." ●

French beauty Nicole Maurey models up with one of the monstrous Triffids

THE MONSTER OF
FRANKENSTEIN
10¢
APRIL-MAY 1954 No. 30
MORE NEW THRILLS AND CHILLS WITH THE WORLD'S MOST FAMOUS HORROR CHARACTER!
A DEMENTED SCULPTOR DISSATISFIED WITH HIS MINIATURE BRONZE STATUE OF THE FRANKENSTEIN MONSTER DECIDES TO MAKE A LIFE-SIZE STATUE BY ENCASING THE MONSTER IN MOLTEN BRONZE.

Born on the Screen, later Broadcast on Radio, the Most Celebrated of All Monsters made his bow in Collector's Item Comic Magazines in 1946 — an Exclusive FANTASTIC MONSTERS Feature by Richard Kyle

The Illustrated Monster

by Richard Kyle

An humorous dinosaur shrinks in size while the Monster wonders what is going on in "How I Had (and Lost) a Pet Dinosaur" in FRANKENSTEIN No. 5.

Villainous symphony conductor Jerome is surprised by a visit from the Monster in the story "Three-Fold Horror and Revenge" (FRANKENSTEIN No. 31). Below: Dick Briefer's comical Monster meets up with the famous horror actor Boris Karload in FRANKENSTEIN No. 11.

FRANKENSTEIN MEETS CLEOPATRA.

How does that grab you?

Well, a few years ago—back in 1946 —you could have seen it, and in color, too. It co-starred Moish the Mummy. You've heard of him. About the same time, you could have dropped in one evening at Awful Annie's while a happy-go-lucky Monster belted a little bat brew with the old witch. Or maybe you'd have journeyed with the Frankenstein Monster to the Wild West where he shot it out with the local heavy and made the countryside safe for decent folks. Or been in the crowd the day the city unveiled a statue to him because of his outstanding personality and kindly humanitarianism.

You could have seen this all, really.

Not in a movie, of course, or a book—but in the pages of one of the nuttiest, most waaaaay out comic magazines ever published, Frankenstein.

And would you like to thrill as an evil, hating, incredibly powerful Frankenstein Monster struggles against a horde of the undead, or robs the grave of its victims, or fights to the death a great white werewolf, or takes as a mate a female monster as evil and hating and cruel as the Monster himself?

You could have seen that, too, just a couple of years later—and in the pages of the same magazine, drawn by the same artist, and published by the same Price Comics Group.

The Frankenstein Monster's comic book adventures started in 1946 when the Monster with the "outstanding personality and kindly humanitarian-ism" was invented. The scientist who did the job was sort of slap-dash about his work (he got the Monster's nose on above his eyes) and pretty careless with explosives (he managed to blow himself up) but all-in-all he must have been okay because Frankenstein (the scientist named his Monster after the book, and made the same mistake a lot of other people have) had a heart of gold that was as big as all outdoors. He was kind of simple-minded, too, but you can't win 'em all.

After his inventor was blown to smithereens, Frankenstein went to live in an old house down by the cemetery. He was a friendly guy and pretty soon he got to know all the ghouls and vampires and werewolves and witches in the neighborhood. He had a pet spider, and in fact, there wasn't much of anything he didn't like. One day a couple of kids came by while he was building something in his workshop, and they asked him if it was a bird house. "Nope," he said, "a rat house! Lot's of bird houses around. Not enough rat houses."

Like everybody else, he had to have money to keep the bacon and eggs coming in (Franky cooked his over a Bunsen burner), and so he had quite a few jobs. Once he was president of the Institute for the Rehabilitation of Maladjusted Ghosts. And a little while later he ran a drug store, with Awful Annie, the witch, filling in for the pharmacist. While he was a laboratory assistant he fought a giant chicken liver that threatened to conquer the world. And in the last days of radio, he played the most fear-

turn to page 56

Before he joined FANTASTIC MONSTERS, Paul Blaisdell gloried in one of the most horrible reputations in Hollywood

My Friend, The Fiend

Exclusive Story by Jim Harmon

As I headed for Paul Blaisdell's home that chilly Fall night, I realized that I was in for one of the tightest spots of my entire career.

A magazine writer leads a dangerous life. In my time I've been trapped in quicksand, picked up bodily by raging hurricanes, braved perilous mountain trails to the mountain-top castle of a millionaire horror producer from the days of radio; but never had I let myself in for anything like this meeting with the man who called himself Blaisdell.

In a flash of lightning I saw the house nestled in the woods of Topanga, California. Yes, the house was there—on the other side of a canyon through which boiled a torrential river. Bridging this chasm was a flimsy suspension foot-bridge, fashioned of rope and wooden slats. I knew there was no turning back now. Stepping out on the bridge, I felt the ropes sway with me, the slats snap and crack under my step. And then, as I reached the middle of the span, as it swayed to and fro over the raging water below, as the bridge crackled with tension, something flew at me from the lodge-like house, something flying, on the wings of night!

Many things flashed through my mind at that moment. One of the things I remembered was my first contact with Paul Blaisdell many years before.

At that time, young Blaisdell, who came from a good family, was making something of a name for himself as an artist—A magazine illustrator, he had done impressive cover paint-

...ings of space creatures and rocket-
craft for such magazines as Fantasy
and Science Fiction and one we were
both connected with, Spaceway. While
at Spaceway, Blaisdell was appointed
art director and I, editor, of a forthcoming magazine called only "X",
which was killed off by Korean War
restrictions.

Although we did "X" together,
Blaisdell and I worked by mail and
we never met. I did receive several
letters from what seemed to be an
intelligent young man who loved art,
books, and his bride, Jackie (perhaps
not in that order).

Imagine my surprise when Paul
Blaisdell mentioned going to work
for horror movies, making monsters!
Again and again, as I sat before my
fire, sipping tea, I marvelled at these
strange letters my friend Paul was
beginning to send.

"Dear Jim," one read, "I am now
the She-Creature. I come from beneath the sea to wreak horror and
destruction on unsuspecting humans."

Could this be my old friend, the
artist, the quiet man who loved books
and paintings?

More and more, Paul Blaisdell's let-
ters spoke of doing films for Roger
Corman, Jim Nicholson and Samuel
Z. Arkoff at American-International.

Blaisdell went from working in
She Creature with Chester Morris
(the movies' Boston Blackie) to mar-
shalling genuine dwarfs in monster
makeup also created by Blaisdell
for the 1957 release, Invasion Of The
Saucer Men.

In one letter, Paul Blaisdell told
how at a studio party celebrating the
completion of the film, everyone forgot the little men until Paul remembered them and helped them out
of their stifling head masks.

Another problem for the rapidly
rising master of makeup came when
one-time Western star, Crash Corrigan

landed the title role in *IT . . . The Terror From Beyond Space*. Unlike such cowboy greats as Tom Mix, or Col. Tim McCoy, Corrigan hadn't kept his slim ranginess into mature years, and costumer Blaisdell had difficulty building Corrigan's chest to even it with the waistline—but versatile Paul once again did the impossible.

The list of films that Paul Blaisdell was working on was growing larger, while his science fiction Illustrating was being pressed out by movie commitments.

As time went on, I heard of Paul working on *The Undead*, in which he portrays a decaying body with great skill; on *Day The World Ended* where he does the 3-Eyed Atomic Mutant, making up with histrionic skill for a minimum of makeup; returning in his She-Creature costume for *Ghost of Dragstrip Hollow*.

Still the movie credits rolled on and Blaisdell's star was blazing brightly. (For the record, Blaisdell is pronounced like a burning meadow—Blaze-dell.) For *Attack of the Puppet People*, Paul developed the technique of using a double set of props to create the illusion of giant objects and small size actors. Next to an ultra-small doorknob a performer would appear huge, but when somebody was next to a colossal oversize doorknob he would appear a tiny man from another world. This technique was used in later films such as *The Incredible Shrinking Man* and the TV series, *World of Giants*.

Paul and wife Jackie at home. Left: Blaisdell and Marla English, during a filming break on the set of VOODOO WOMAN. Below: Paul's collection of antique airplanes, all built by himself, is second to none

I lost touch with Blaisdell but I heard more reports of his work on *The Amazing Colossal Man*, *Cat Girl*, *Voodoo Woman*, *The Beast with a Million Eyes*, and at last report I heard he was involved in his own production, *The CWF Monster*, a condensed version of which he sells to private collectors.

Finally, after some years, during which time I moved from the Mid-West to California, the name of Paul Blaisdell came again to my attention when Ron Haydock was assembling his staff for FANTASTIC MONSTERS Magazine. Both Paul and I were involved, and I ventured out to his canyon home—ventured out to trod the swaying suspension bridge and face the flying night creature!

From the doorway, Paul called out to me, "Don't worry, Jim—it's just a vampire bat." He went on to explain to me that it was a prop from *Not of This Earth* he used to scare off autograph hounds.

Finally meeting Paul Blaisdell in person, I discovered he was much like I had pictured him before I learned he made monster movies. Besides being an actor who had starred in more monster roles than Karloff, and a makeup technician on a par with Bud Westmore, Paul also contributed to the cinema plotlines of his vehicles, and is the author of many magazine articles and short stories, making him well-qualified for FANTASTIC MONSTERS' Editorial Director.

But I still made him cross that suspension bridge ahead of me as I went back to the road. I wasn't going to leave Blaisdell on the other side of that rope bridge with his collection of guns—and knives.

HORROR SCOPE

We had dinner with one of our favorite people, Vincent Price, the night before he jetted out to Spain to take the lead in *The Night Creatures*, a frightening vampire tale scripted by Richard Matheson from his own novel, *I Am Legend* (Gold Medal, 50c). Over choice sirloins, Vincent pointed out that American-International was going to serve horror fans another Terror Trio dish, *Comedy of Terror*, with Peter Lorre, Boris Karloff, and himself. Vincent expected shooting to start in early July.

AIP has also contracted Lorre to another thriller, this one to co-star Frankie Avalon (!), with script again from the mighty pen of Matheson. Titled *It's Alive*, the film is based on a Matheson short story, *Being*. AIP has just released Roger Corman's *The Terror* with Dear Boris, and is currently in pre-production planning of a sci-fi spectacular, *War of the Planets*, to be filmed in color and wide screen. One other tantalizing tidbit of terror from AIP to keep an eye open for is Ray Milland as *The Man with the X-Ray Eyes*.

The Big News around FANTASTIC MONSTERS, however, is that staffer Jim Harmon's shocking paperback, *The Man Who Made Maniacs* (Epic Books, 50c), is under consideration for filming by one of Hollywood's major studios. Watch this column for further news about Harmon's horror.

Kent Taylor, Allison Hayes, Richard Arlen, and Tristram Coffin are four of the screen favorites in *Tomorrow You Die* from Herts-Lion. Producer Tom Corradine has completed *Depths of the Unknown*, and George Nader has been signed by Al Zugsmith for a *Great Space Adventure*.

We ran into that mad mad cartoonist Charles Addams on the set of a Hitchcock teleplay, and were reminded of the fact that serial veteran William Schallert was cast in "The Rising of the Moon" segment of The Lloyd Bridges Show on CBS-TV, with script by Cyril "Forbidden Planet" Hume. (Addams said he was scouting the Hitchcock set for new characters to draw upon.)

While Tarzan producer Sy Weintraub is busy getting Jock Mahoney a new loincloth for Jock's second ape-man epic, ex-tree swinger Gordon Scott is filming *The Shortest Day* in Rome. Tarzan himself, Johnny Weissmuller, has temporarily shifted his tree house to Chicago, where he's representing various commercial concerns.

It looks like Jerry Bloom's *Face of Evil* is going to be another rock & rolling monster picture. We thought we'd seen the last of these films years ago. On the other hand, *The Madwoman of Chaillot* promises to be a flicker worth seeing, as does Pat Frank's filmed novel, *Forbidden Area*. QUESTION OF THE MONTH— Whatever happened to Kane Richmond? ●

Currently exposed at local theatres is Vincent Price's *CONFESSIONS OF AN OPIUM EATER* from Allied Artists. Center: A huge Triton emerges from the sea and holds back crashing rocks so the Argo can pass in this scene from the new Ray Harryhausen-Charles Schneer epic *JASON'S SEARCH FOR THE GOLDEN FLEECE* (Columbia). Below: Janette Scott is starred in William Castle's latest thriller for Columbia—*THE OLD DARK HOUSE*

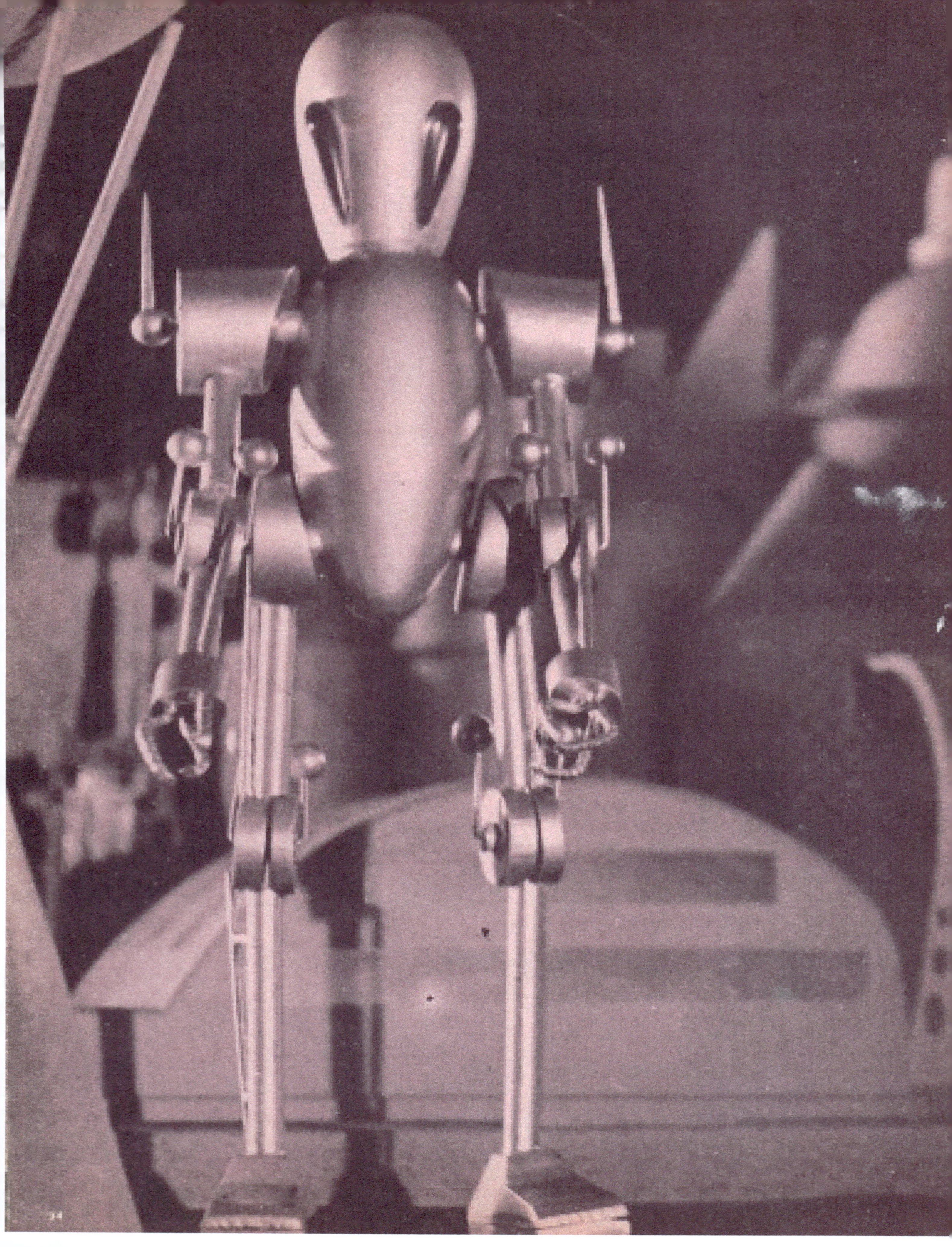

THE COMING OF THE ROBOTS

by Jim Harmon

Machine-Made Men and Vice-Verse—the Story of the Creation of Metal Monsters in Books, Science and Movies by FANTASTIC MONSTERS' Own Science Fiction Authority—Jim Harmon

The only female robot ever to grace the screen, from the 1926 silent classic *METROPOLIS*

The image of the man-made man, the slave creature of some unfleshy substance, has strode across the imagination of a restless world for centuries. Probably the most celebrated of all robots is from one of the world's great books, which was made even more famous in a motion picture classic. That robot is, of course, the Monster of Frankenstein.

For those people who insist on thinking of a robot as only a collection of animated sections of stove pipe, the idea of the Frankenstein Monster as a robot may seem odd. However, a robot doesn't have to be made of metal. Any artificially made man-like creature—whether of iron, plastic, or synthetic flesh—is a robot, generally speaking. In science-fiction novels today, though, non-metal, human-appearing robots like the Monster portrayed by Karloff are specifically referred to as "androids".

That particular type of robot, the android, was actually the first creature to be called a "robot". This was in a Czech stage play of 1924, *R.U.R.* ("Rossum's Universal Robots") by Karel Capek. Artificial men are mass-produced, sold as workers and soldiers, and eventually revolt to wipe out their creators, the standard performance of mechanical men in fiction.

Of course, these flesh robots are

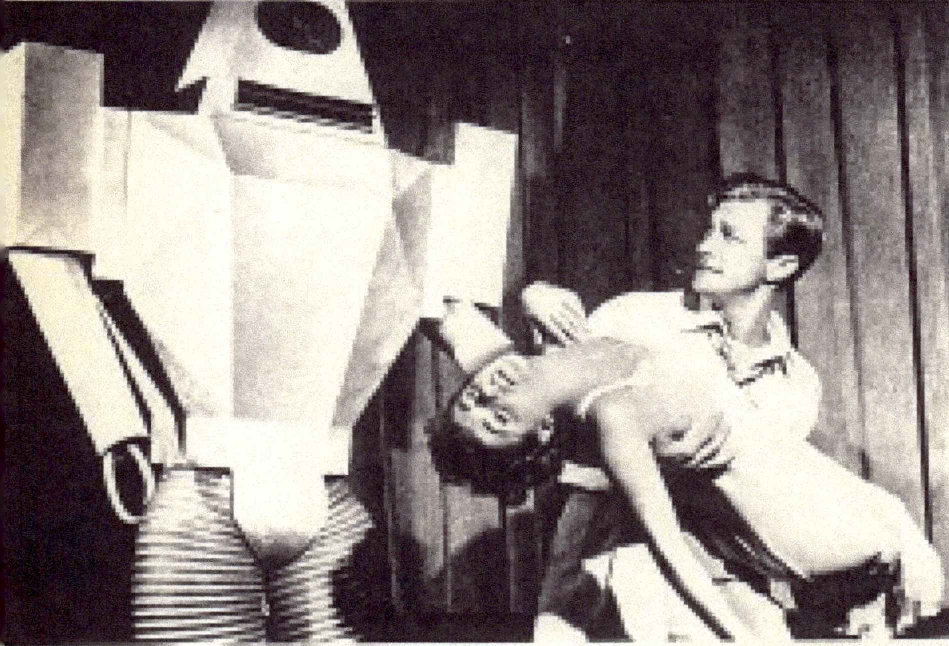

At Left: Mad scientist Bela Lugosi orders his sickly robot friend to commit more foul deeds in THE PHANTOM CREEPS (1939). Top: Ada Ince and her metallic boyfriend in THE VANISHING SHADOW (Universal, 1934). Middle: Richard Denning and Kathleen Crowley are menaced by a recalling iron man (TARGET EARTH, Allied Artists, 1954). Right: Robby the Robot and Anne Francis between takes on MGM's super-science fiction film THE FORBIDDEN PLANET

not the first synthetic men in history, only the first to earn the word "robot" (from the Czech *roboto* meaning "servitude").

Mary Shelley's book about Dr. Victor von Frankenstein and his Monster creation was an early robot story in 1816, but even this was not the first. In Ancient Greece, there was the tale of Talos, a "brazen man" built by ingenious Daidalos for the Crete King, Minos. During the Sixteenth and Seventeenth Centuries, many a European alchemist constructed a "braten head" of metal which was supposed to speak great truths. (None are reliably reported to have actually worked). According to Jewish folklore of the same period, Rabbi Low breathed the breath of life into a creature he constructed of clay, The Golem—a subject of several early silent movies.

Down through the years other mechanical men have included the "Steam Man" built by Dime Novel boy inventor, Frank Reade; Dorothy's Tin Woodman companion in L. Frank Baum's *Wizard of Oz*; and a comic strip of World War One about Fritz von Blitz, an iron-headed German mechanical man. (Even today, there is a comic book robot hero, *Iron Man*.)

Early silents featured several "meat" robots (as Dorothy might say in *Oz*) like the Golem, and Frankenstein (the Shelley story was an early Edison venture of the late 1890's). Yet the first iron-and-rivet-mechanical man robot didn't appear on movie screens until 1916 in a serial starring the great magician Houdini variously titled *The Master Key* and *The Master Mystery*.

Since then, robots have been an SF mainstay of movies in general, and were darlings of serials particularly.

A Mascot series of serials combining elements of science fiction and the Western, variously starring Tom Mix, Ken Maynard, Gene Autry, and Crash Corrigan, produced several faintly comical-looking robots. Autry in *The Phantom Empire* and Corrigan's *Undersea Kingdom*. While Mascot was busy, the fun went on at Universal with Bela Lugosi in the title role of *The Phantom Creeps*, menacing the world with a robot whose metal features were fused into a classic case of acid indigestion.

Meanwhile, Universal also brought on the *Flash Gordon* serials and *Buck Rogers* with episodes of metal man menace. (In contrast, the Buck Rogers radio series of the '40s gave Buck a "good guy" robot sidekick, "One".)

Hollywood offered miscellaneous serial metal men in *The Vanishing Shadow*, *The Monster and the Ape*, and others; then the very same *Undersea Kingdom* robots reappeared in later Republic serials like *Zombies of the Stratosphere* and its feature-length version, *Satan's Satellites*. The *Phantom Empire* metal menace walked again in the theatre serial version of the television epic, *Captain Video*. Soon after this film—which might have better been called "Captain Movie" — chapterplays closed their final robot episode.

Of course, robots got into feature-length movies early, and have stayed in focus. Fritz Lang's classic silent

turn to page 56

WORKSHOP, from page 8

died. Extra layers of plaster and burlap were built up, until the mold was over an inch thick. When the casting plaster burlap mixture was thoroughly dry, a similar mold was made over the back half of the head. This, when dry, completed the mold for the entire head. The two halves were pried apart with a screwdriver, and all clay "scraps" were carefully removed from the mold.

At this point, a recount of the materials used involved the following: Modelling clay from the five and ten cent store. A sheet of "do it yourself" aluminum from the local hardware store, and some casting plaster from the local lumber company. Empty potato sacks from the grocery store provided the burlap strips. The phone book, as usual, gave us the nearest company that sold liquid latex rubber, and a few quarts were purchased for the next phase of the operation.

The liquid latex was applied inside the head mold until sufficient layers were built up to the desired thickness. Each layer of latex was allowed to dry at room temperature, according to the instructions on the jar. A few drops of brown poster paint were mixed with each application of rubber to give the final product a desert-beige "lizard" color. When dry, the two halves of the head were peeled from their respective molds and seamed together with additional applications of latex. Ears for the head and teeth for the mouth were cast in rubber, following the same clay-to-plaster mold technique as the head. Artificial eyes were also made at this point, but discarded later in favor of letting the actor (Ray Corrigan) use his real eyes, for greater realism and better vision.

Additional shading and coloring with make-up and grease paint would "polish off" the head, but there still remained the hands, feet, and body to be constructed. There were two ways this could be accomplished. The first way would be to construct a giant mold of the body in two parts, similar to the one for the head. This idea was discarded on the grounds that it would be a clumsy, time consuming operation that, while effective, could only be indulged in by the largest of studios.

A study of some old-fashioned suits of armor seemed to indicate a faster and more time-proven way. Half a dozen one piece molds of lizard-like "scales" were made up, in varying sizes, over original clay modellings. A multitude of rubber castings was made from these plaster molds. These, in turn, were glued over a proper-size suit of heavy winter underwear, with a good brand of "contact bond" cement. The whole effect was remarkably like Medieval armor, in that the overlapping allowed for bending and flexing on the part of the actor, while still retaining enough rigidity so that the suit tended to support its own weight. "Claws" were constructed in the same way, over heavy work gloves, and the three toed "feet" were built over a pair of "sneakers". Entry into the suit was effected by a "zipper" that ran the entire length of the spine, and was concealed by the "lizard man's" backbone.

The completed suit was given final minor adjustments, to insure adequate fit and ventilation; then, in Jerry Bixby's action filled script, Ray Corrigan in full monster dress, went on to survive heavy caliber gunfire, grenades, Bazooka shells and a radio-active furnace!

From the time of the agreed-upon sketches to the completion of the operable suit, six weeks elapsed. The deadline? The "prop builders" beat it by 24 hours. It, The Terror From Beyond Space became It, the terror that got there on time!

EDITOR'S NOTE: Paul Blaisdell very modestly neglected to mention that the "prop builders" he refers to in this article are his wife Jackie and himself. ●

VAMPIRE CHECKLIST

After reading VAMPIRE BATS IN MY BELFRY (FanMo No. 1) and Al Eck's title additions (GHOUL CALL, FanMo No. 2), I also would like to add a number of vampire titles to the list. Some of them are not very well known.

DRACULA (1931), Mexican film with Carlos Villarias; DRACULA'S DAUGHTER (1936) with Gloria Holden; NIGHT OF THE GHOULS (1959) with Keene Duncan; VAMPYR or STRANGE ADVENTURES OF DAVID GREY (1932), French; VAMPIRE BAT (1933) with Lionel Atwill; VAMPIRES OF WARSAW (1914), silent; THE VAMPIRE'S TRAIL (1914), silent; LE VAMPIRE, French documentary with stock scenes from NOSFERATU; OLD MOTHER RILEY MEETS THE VAMPIRE or VAMPIRES OVER LONDON (1952), British, with Bela Lugosi; LONDON AFTER MIDNIGHT (1927), Lon Chaney silent; EL VAMPIRO (1956) and WORLD OF THE VAMPIRES (1962), both Mexican; VAMPIRES VS HERCULES (1962), Italian; VAMPIRE AND THE BALLERINA (1962), Italian; THE VAMPIRE'S GHOST (1945) with John Abbott; and finally BLOOD OF THE VAMPIRE (1958) from Universal.

Ronald Borst
Waymont, Pa.

And to Ronald's staggering list we'll add MACISTE AGAINST THE VAMPIRES (1962), Italian, starring Gordon "Tarzan" Scott; and BLOOD AND ROSES (1961), also an Italian film—Ed.

WISE GUY

I've been reading and buying monster magazines ever since they first came out five years ago, and naturally I bought yours when it first appeared.

After comparing FANTASTIC MONSTERS to all the others, I've reached a conclusion. My favorite magazine is still MAD MAGAZINE.

Doug Bohadlo
Western Springs, Ill

SUBTLE REACTION

Wow! Wow! Wow! I dig your mag a lot! Never stop printing it! It's great! Terrific! Best yet! Keep it coming! Wow! Wow! Wow!

Charles "WOW" Casey
Brunswick, Ga

MOVIES VS MAGS

Frankly, I'm very glad that there are magazines like FANTASTIC MONSTERS being published. Probably unlike most of your readers, I have stopped going to see the new horror films. With monster magazines on the stands, I can put down my 50c, buy the mag, read about the new films, and enjoy myself. The point I'm trying to make is that seeing almost all of the new films is a waste of money and time.

There was a period a few years back when the movies were all about teenage and giant monsters. These left me disgusted. I thought that after HOUSE OF USHER bigger and better films would be made, but not so. All of AIP's movies are the same as USHER. Every one has Vincent Price in it, and they're not very good in my estimation. The trouble is that AIP is the only one making horror films these days. Any other films that might come out are either as bad as AIP's or worse.

So I hope the monster mags are around for a long time yet. At least I can see the photos from the new films, and so save myself money and disappointment by not going to theater to see the films themselves.

William Lynch
St Louis, Mo

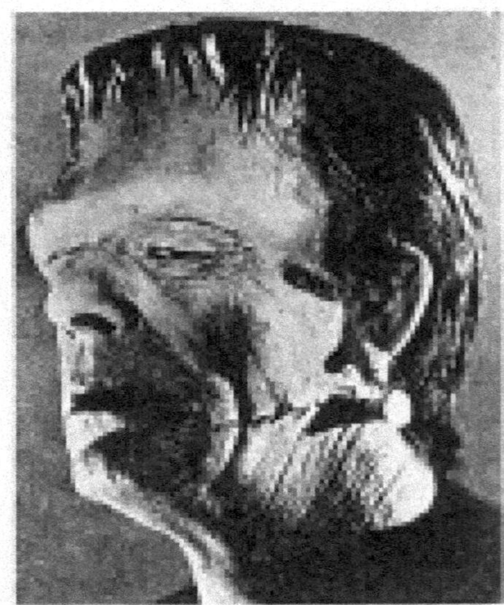

HOUSE SETTLING

I'd like to settle a confusing point about HOUSE OF FRANKENSTEIN and HOUSE OF DRACULA. The Frankenstein film, despite misleading television listings, was made in 1944 but released in January of 1945. The Dracula film was made in 1945 and released in December of that year. Amen.

Joseph Marchello
Forest Hills, NY

FANS WIN OUT

Your magazine can do only good for the monster world and its fans. By your efforts, you are forcing rival publications to do better, to outdo themselves. Consequently, the monster field of publications and information will be vastly improved, and we'll owe it to you.

Thomas Roark
Lancaster, Pa

KONG QUESTIONED

The third issue of FANTASTIC MONSTERS features a Movie Preview entitled KING KONG VS GODZILLA. After reading the article and looking at the photos (which appear "rigged") I am in doubt as to whether there is such a movie—and from Toho Productions at that!

Not only that, but on page 31 "Kong" is the real Kong (the original) and this photo is obviously "spliced" in with the shot of Godzilla, who looks as though even he doesn't belong in that Japanese setting!

So back to my question—is there or is there not a film called KING KONG VS GODZILLA? If there is, I know it's going to be a riot!

Frankie Larkin
Hollywood, Calif.

By the time you read this, Frankie, KING KONG VS GODZILLA will be in general release here in the U.S. All of the photos used in Douglas Ripley's article on the film are absolutely authentic and came to us directly from Toho. Actually, we're surprised at all the letters we've received from readers like yourself who thought we were pulling a hoax. Perhaps this strong reaction to our article indicates what fans think of seeing Kong and Godzilla together in a film; namely, that the idea is so absurd who can possibly believe such a motion picture exists?—Ed.

MONSTROUS FICTION

I just finished reading THE CAVE CREATURE by Jameson Harvey in No. 3. When I read Robert Bloch's BLACK LOTUS (FanMo No. 1) I thought you had a novel idea over your competitor trash magazines, but I've changed my mind after reading THE CAVE CREATURE.

I wonder how authors like Harvey have enough nerve or even sense to ask a magazine, even one like yours, to run a story like that? I enjoy reading a good short sci-fi story every now and then, but I don't know what to call THE CAVE CREATURE.

Charles Bell
Whiteland, Ind.

What do you think of this issue's fiction selection, STEELMASK MEETS THE ZOMBIE MASTER? Its author, Judson Grey, like Jameson Harvey, has written innumerable paperbacks—Ed.

MORE QUICKIES

I'd like to see an article on the silent horror films of Europe, like ORLAMUNDE and ONESIME HORLOGER.

Ronald Matthies
Banning, Calif

I live monsters, I talk monsters, I breathe monsters. I absolutely thrive on creatures or things that walk, crawl, sneak, slink, stomp, growl, snarl, bite, melt, ooze, squeeze, or snort!

Mark Gish
Frederick, Okla

A PUN IS NO FUN

Though I appreciate the generally serious tone of FANTASTIC MONSTERS, I heartily disagree with ol' Lloyd Fradkin (GHOUL CALL, FanMo No. 2) about the Mad Mummy and DEAD TIME TALES. In my opinion, they prove that even humor can be high class and entertaining without the need of descending to puns.

Susan Willard
Joppa, Md

Two out of every three readers would like to see the Mad Mummy keep his job here at FanMo. However, a crisis has arisen which we have brought to your attention in the Editor's Note at the conclusion of this issue's Mad Mummy article. The fate of the Crumbling Kharis is now in your hands.—Ed.

MONSTER BINDERS

My club members and I are eagerly waiting for binders for our copies of FanMo.

John Wash (Pres.)
Monsters Fan Club
Minneapolis, Minn.

How many of you other readers are interested in obtaining binders for FANTASTIC MONSTERS issues? If we get enough response, we'll start our assembly line going.—Ed.

SHARP REQUEST

I've seen THE TIME MACHINE and found it one of the best movies since Disney released his adaption of 20,000 LEAGUES UNDER THE SEA. Both are my favorites. But I have not been a monster magazine bug for long and I have no magazines with articles on these two greats. Will you please feature pictures of the time machine itself and the Nautilus?

Larry Sharp
Bellflower, Calif

You'll find a shot of the time machine in FanMo No. 4, Larry, in Mike Minor's article THROUGH SPACE AND TIME WITH GEORGE PAL. We couldn't help but spot your pet parakeet perching on your head in the above photo, and we're wondering if you're telling us that FANTASTIC MONSTERS is for the birds.—Ed.

BAT MAN RETURNS

I hope you can find a spot in FanMo for a picture of me as Count Dracula.

Victor Wiseevitch
Los Angeles, Calif

Listen, Vic—it's like we told you in last issue's GHOUL CALL—we don't have any room for your picture. Stop asking us about it.—Ed.

QUICKIES

Your magazine could be improved if you ran a feature on INVASION OF THE SAUCER MEN and included a pinup of one of the Saucer Men.

Wesley Bailey
Fort Wayne, Ind

As far as I'm concerned, the Mad Mummy is great. It shows a monster's point-of-view and his feelings.

Michael Jaworski
Sunnyvale, Calif

Considering all the films Abbott & Costello made in connection with monsters, I think it would be fitting to no an article on them.

G.R. Guy
East Hartford, Conn

The color tinting of photos presents a relief from the normal black and white photos.

Chet Wyszynski
Des Plaines, Ill.

I think FANTASTIC MONSTERS is the nicest thing that ever happened to monster lovers.

Butch Williams
Donna, Texas

I wish you'd drop DEVIL'S WORKSHOP and put something else in its place because I just don't care to know how to build my own monsters.

Ed Kocur
Brookfield, Ill

Let's have more on Karloff!

Paul Mitchell
Louisville, Ky

Would you please send me a shrunken head of a monster like the She Creature?

David Castro
Savanna, Ill

ADDRESS ALL CARDS, LETTERS, CUNEIFORMS, AND CAREFULLY WRAPPED BRICKBATS TO:
GHOUL CALL
FANTASTIC MONSTERS
TOPANGA, CALIFORNIA

At Left: FANTASTIC MONSTERS' choice for the New Queen of the Screamers is the vivacious British beauty, Miss Hazel Court; pictured here with the All-Time King of the Creepers, Boris Karloff, on the set of THE RAVEN for American-International

SCREEN SCREAM QUEENS

Whether Monsters and Mad Men prowl during the night or day, you can always be sure they've got claws and fangs ready to snatch up another Helpless Movie Heroine — FANTASTIC MONSTERS presents a healthy handful of Cinemaland's Shrieking Sirens

Oscar Homolka and John Barrymore, captured by the beauty of THE INVISIBLE WOMAN (Universal, 1941)

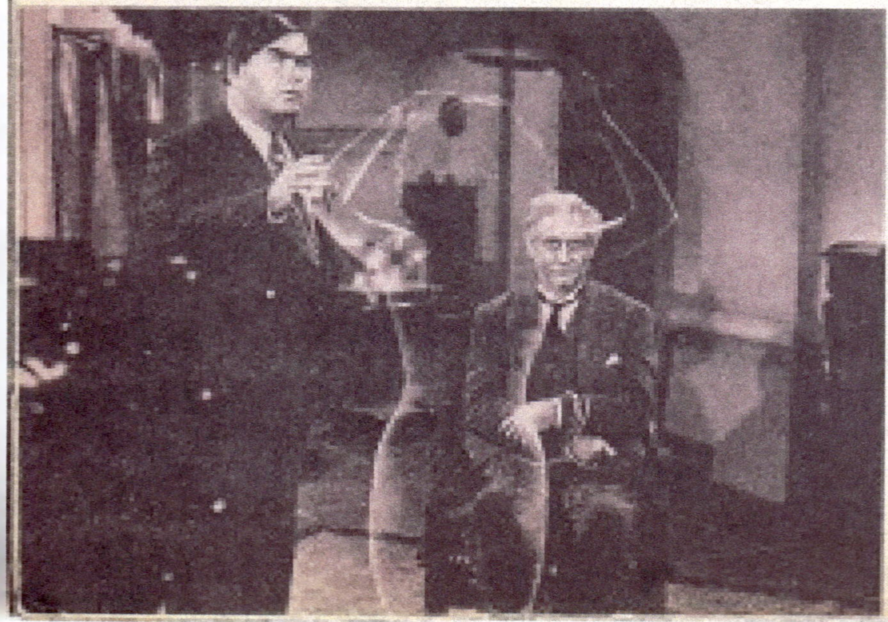

Mexico's own Evelyn Ankers—Evangelina Elizondo—is carried off by one of the werewolf servants from THE CASTLE OF THE MONSTERS

Below Left: Lon Chaney Jr as THE MAN-MADE MONSTER *confronts an harassed Anne Nagel and a helpless Lionel Atwill (Universal, 1941)*

Above: A friendly picnic is not exactly what Africa's giant lady-killer has in mind for Carol Thurston (Columbia's KILLER APE, *1953)*

*Below: Victor Maddern, as a deformed hunchback, is about to prove to Barbara Shelley that he's quite a cut-up (*BLOOD OF THE VAMPIRE, *1958)*

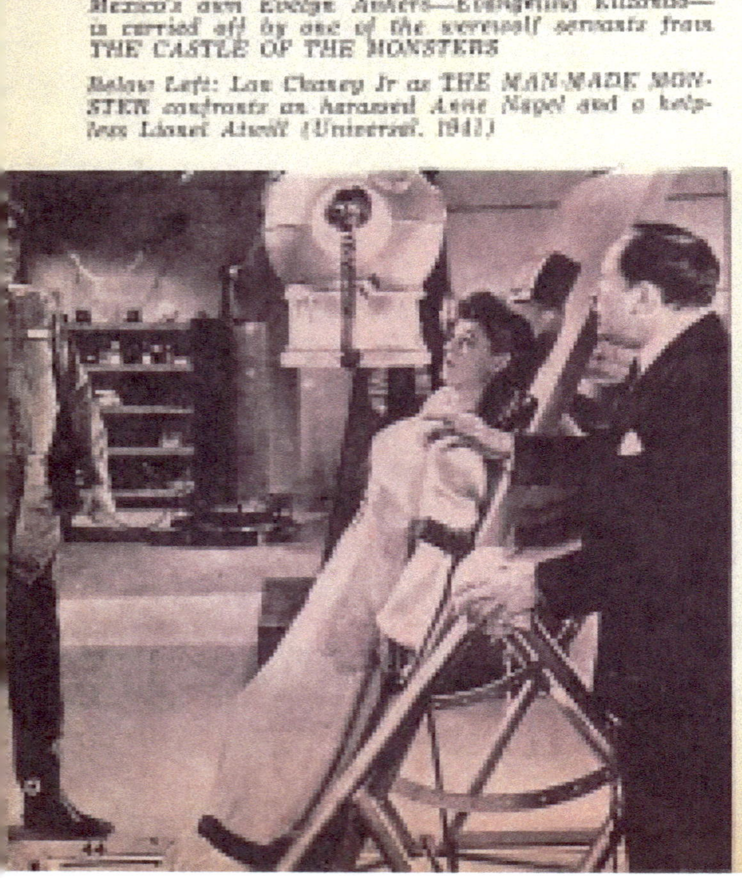

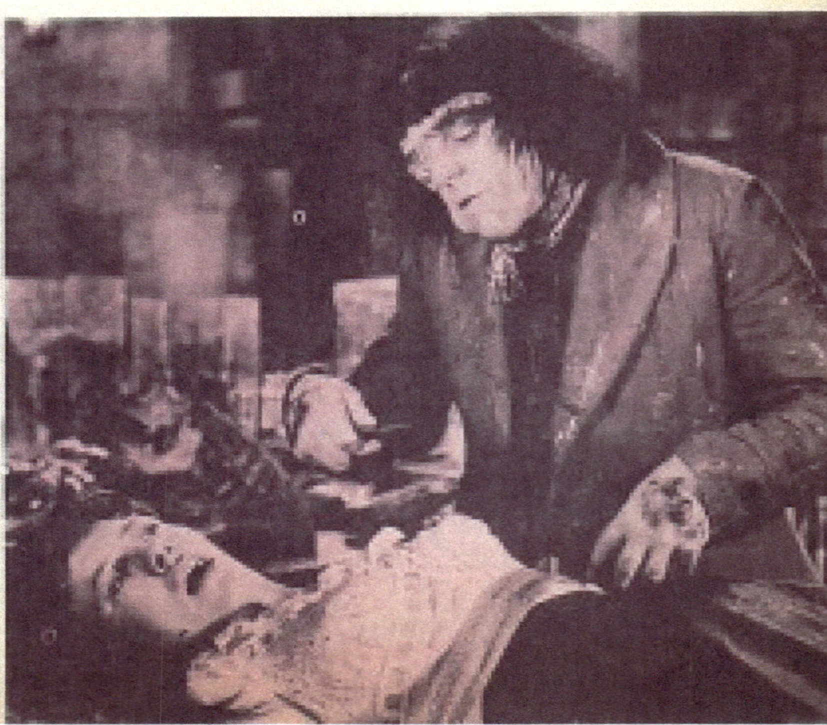

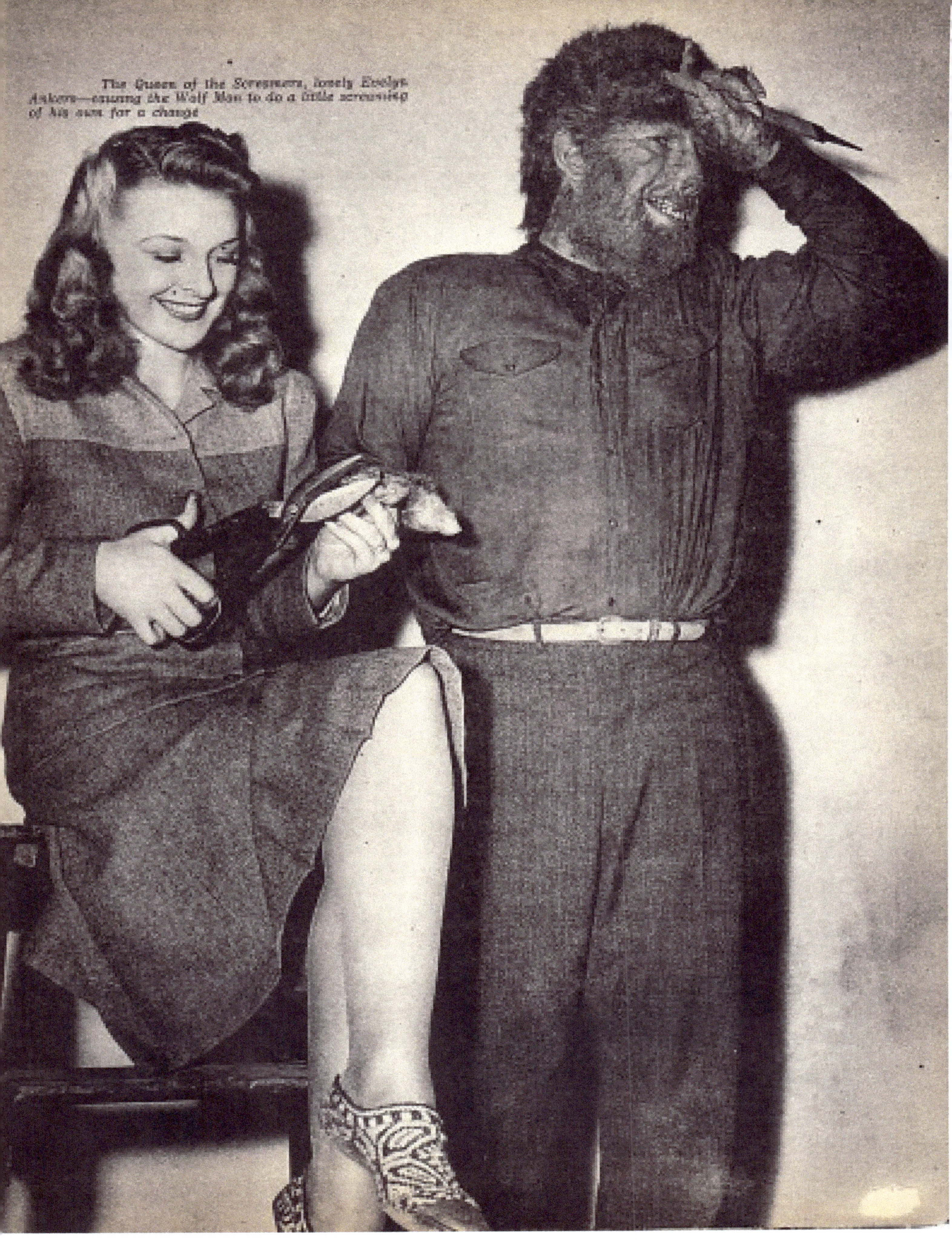

The Queen of the Screamers, lovely Evelyn Ankers—causing the Wolf Man to do a little screaming of his own for a change

My Favorite Vampire

by ALEX GORDON

From left to right are Alex Gordon, Bela, Lillian Lugosi, Richard Gordon, and Western film historian William Everson at New York City's Tokay restaurant in 1952

When I was a boy in England, I was a very frustrated youth. Under the British movie censorship classification, horror pictures cannot be seen by anyone under the age of sixteen. Therefore, it was not until many years later that I was able to see the Bela Lugosi films.

The first time I ever saw Bela on the screen was in *Postal Inspector*, a 1936 picture in which he played a gangster. I was also able to see *The Invisible Ray*, which he did with Boris Karloff, and which somehow escaped the adult horror classification. And ever since those early days, I had hoped that some day I would have the opportunity to meet Bela in person. This did not happen until 1950, after I had come to the United States and was living in New York.

At the time, Bela was doing *Arsenic and Old Lace* on the stage at the Sea Cliff Summer Theatre, and my brother Richard and I went down to try and meet him. We waited near the theatre for hours, and finally Bela—with his wife Lillian—drove up. We went up and introduced ourselves. They were both extremely pleasant and suggested we join them for dinner. They took us to an excellent Hungarian restaurant where Bela was the center of attraction, the owner and other patrons being thrilled to see him.

After dinner, we went back to the theatre and saw the show; and afterwards spent more time with the Lugosis and made a date to see them later.

One of the things Bela wanted most to do was tour England with a new production of *Dracula*. He had made movies in England—*The Mystery of the Marie Celeste*, *Dark Eyes of London*—but had never appeared on the stage there. Happily, my brother, who represents British movie producers (such as the makers of the "Carry On" pictures) was able to arrange not only such a tour, but also for Bela to make another movie in England.

Soon after that, in 1953, I became an independent producer in Hollywood after years of work in publicity and writing, and of course wanted to make a picture with Bela. We spent much time together, finally evolving a script entitled *The Atomic Monster*. For various reasons, however, this picture did not get off the ground. Meanwhile, American distributors were reluctant to buy *Old Mother Riley Meets the Vampire*—a film we had done with Bela in England—because of the British humor which they considered unsuitable for American audiences. Therefore, we put a new title on the picture, *Vampire over London*, but still no one wanted it. I cut out all of Bela's scenes and tried to make a new movie to be called *King Robot*, using all the scenes Bela was in and shooting new ones to match for the rest of the story.

However, Bela had been very ill for awhile and was very thin and haggard looking, and he did not match the original footage anymore. So we had to scrap that idea.

While I was trying to set up a new picture, to star Bela and Boris Karloff, an independent producer rewrote my "Atomic Monster" script and made a very low budget picture vaguely based on it called *Bride of the Monster*. Poor Bela looked so very old and ill in it that a double had to be used for many of his scenes.

One of his great hopes was to remake *Dracula* in color and widescreen, and he thought the resurgence of horror movies in Hollywood after

Film producer Alex Gordon and Western favorite Raymond Hatton on the set of Alex's 1956 release DAY THE WORLD ENDED

Richard Gordon and Bela clown it up during break in filming of VAMPIRE OVER LONDON (1950)

Bela and his second wife, Beatrice Woodruff Weeks of San Francisco (1934)

Photo taken on the day of Bela's marriage to Lillian, formerly his secretary. Below: Bela Jr's first haircut (1940)

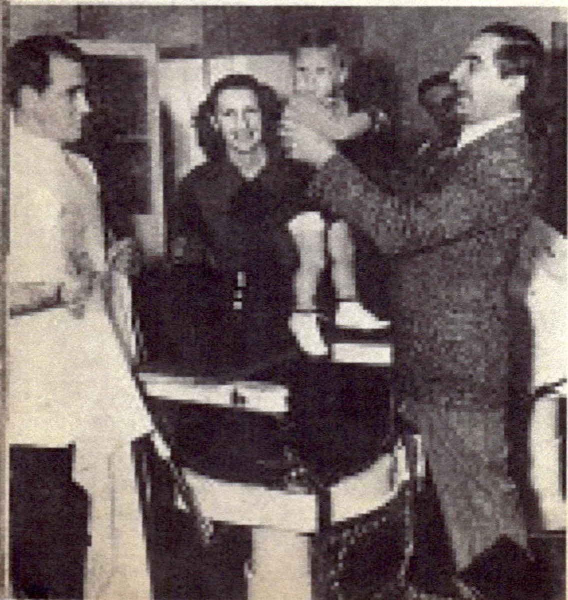

The Lugosi family in 1933—Lillian, Be

House of Wax in 1953 would mark a comeback for him. But the studios seemed to prefer other actors, like Christopher Lee when they made Horror of Dracula in color in England.

The premiere of House of Wax, incidentally, was quite an event. Warner Brothers thought up a publicity stunt to have horror stars attend the premiere at the Paramount Theatre in downtown Los Angeles. They called Bela and asked him if he would go. Bela did not want to, but I persuaded him, as I thought it would be good publicity for our projected new picture with him and Karloff. Warners' sent a limousine to pick us up at Bela's apartment, and Bela was dressed in his Dracula cape. What he did not know was that the publicity boys wanted him to lead a gorilla (a man in a skin) on a chain into the lobby of the theatre—and I was afraid to tell him. The limousine made a stop at a large hotel, and Bela immediately asked what the stop was for. I timidly told him it was to pick up a gorilla. At first it seemed he hadn't heard right, then he roared, "Gorilla?!" It took all my powers of persuasion to keep him from taking a taxi home.

When we drove up at the Paramount, there was a mass of photographers, newsmen, TV cameras, and hundreds of people milling around. Bela was, of course, the center of attention when he exited from the car with the gorilla on the chain. The gorilla chased after some girls while Bela shouted to me what we wanted him to do. We manipulated him over to a Red Cross stand where two nurses were selling milk for the Red Cross. The idea was to have a shot of Bela drinking milk instead of blood, but in all the bedlam he thought they wanted him to do a Dracula bit, and he suddenly grabbed the nurses by the necks. They were so surprised and shocked that they threw the milk all over him!

Finally I got him inside the lobby, where a female radio—TV interviewer grabbed hold of him. I should explain here that Bela was a little hard of hearing in one ear, and he had asked for a list of questions ahead of time so that he could memorize the answers when they brought him up to the microphone. With all the noise and confusion, he felt he might not be able to hear the questions properly. Needless to say, the interviewer had mislaid her copy of the questions, and started asking Bela the questions out of context with his prepared answers. I think I can leave the results to your imagination.

By the time I had him seated in the auditorium, we were both completely exhausted, though the photographers had enjoyed an absolute field day. Bela did not want to stay for the film, so we left by a back door after it had started. I did not hear the end of THAT adventure for a long time.

Another incident I remember well was when Bela was to do the Red Skelton Show, on which Peter Lorre and Lon Chaney Jr were to appear in a sketch with him. Bela was worried about the show because he knew that Red did not stick to the script but adlibbed most of the show. And

Bela was a stage actor who had to learn his lines and was not used to adlibbing.

Red treated him well, but he did use adlibs which almost threw Bela. But the comedian managed to fill in so well that the audience never knew. However, it was an unhappy experience for Bela. He always preferred to work from a prepared script.

When the original Dracula was reissued once more, as it was at regular intervals, we went to see it, and Bela enjoyed it again. Actually, he almost lived the part at times. When he was on tour, he could not stand the hard mattresses in most of the hotels as he had trouble with his back. So he would place his beautiful silk-lined coffin from the theatre in the middle of his hotel room and sleep in it. This is absolutely true and no publicity story. It was not done for effect, just plain comfort.

Bela was a delightful companion, gracious, and kind and with a good sense of humor. He was also a man of many moods, and sometimes he would sink into deep despair. Bela loved good cigars, and he also became interested in religion, hypnosis, and philosophy. He was very particular about many little things. He once asked me to sort out his desk and papers, and I found receipted bills and other statements going back twenty years, which he thought he should keep for tax and book-keeping purposes. He also kept a large collection of stills from his movies in scrapbooks.

When he lived in his small Hollywood apartment, he would call me to walk up to the corner with him at 11 pm to pick up the next morning's LA Times. It had to be the 11 pm edition, and he was quite upset if he did not get it. He liked to keep up with all the latest news and was extremely well-informed about world events.

But his daily dream was to make a good comeback, and he, like so many other former great stars, found it impossible to realize that Hollywood did not want him anymore. It is so ironic that stars like Bela Lugosi are so fondly remembered by audiences the world over, and yet were unable to get a job right here in Hollywood. It is something I have always found hard to understand. Since I became a movie producer, I have always tried to use as many old-timers in my pictures as possible, despite enormous resistance from distributors, financiers, and exhibitors who consider them "has-beens".

In a way, I think Bela regretted having turned down the role of the Frankenstein Monster in the original movie that made Boris Karloff famous. Not many remember that Bela was actually a Shakespearean actor and a romantic star before he did *Dracula* and became typed in horror pictures. He played Hamlet and even Uncas in *The Last of the Mohicans*, among many other roles. I always thought the old Universal film, *The Raven*, was one of Bela's best roles, as well as *The Invisible Ray*, and of course his role of Ygor in the later Frankenstein pictures was unforgettable.

It is strange for me now to see and hear Bela on TV in his old movies. It is as though he is still around and as though that friendly, uniquely unforgettable voice is still calling. His friends and fans will never forget him. ●

...and Bela    *Bela, relaxing at home (1933)*

Producer Herman Cohen bravely uncages a Maniacal Zoo-keeper, a Black Magic Animal Cult, and a Horde of the Wildest Jungle Beasts this side of Africa

BLACK ZOO

Black Zoo is the movie chiller that gave Hollywood a thrill when one of its big cats escaped. Then it surprised the wild animal-wise town with something new in beasts—the spectacle of four-legged blood brothers being down together like so many delegates to a United Nations of fang and claw.

Filmed in color and Panavision, Black Zoo is the most ambitious project undertaken to date by Herman Cohen, the young producer whose *I Was A Teenage Werewolf* in 1957 started the new cycle of terror movies.

Black Zoo stars Michael Gough (of *Horror of Dracula, Konga* fame) in the role of a zoo-keeper who doesn't want to sell his property for a tract development. Pressured by threats from speculators, his brain snaps and he decides to do away with all of his "enemies" by sending his pet lions, tigers, panthers, and cougars after them.

Gough gains sympathizers to his cause when he attends a meeting of The True Believers, a cult of animal worshippers, presided over at a flaming brazier by the bearded high priest Radu (played by Oren Curtis).

These are the incredible beginnings of Black Zoo, which also boasts the acting talents of Elisha Cook, Virginia Gray, Jeanne Cooper, Jerome Cowan, and singing idol Rod Lauren; and is an Allied Artists release.

Though there's plenty of action, suspense, and thrills in the film, more than one Hollywood observer has commented that Herman Cohen should have also filmed the thrills that went on during the shooting of Black Zoo. The plot may not have been much, but the plight of the actors, actresses, director, stagehands, publicity men, press corps, and the wild animal trainers themselves, was enough to make news on radio and television, newspapers and magazines.

For one scene, Ralph Heller, the head trainer, had to bring an African lion, a Bengal tigress, a black panther, and a cougar into a parlor and get them to lie down quietly on couches and chairs. For another, he had to gather two African lions and a lioness, the panther and a cheetah in peace around an open grave. ●

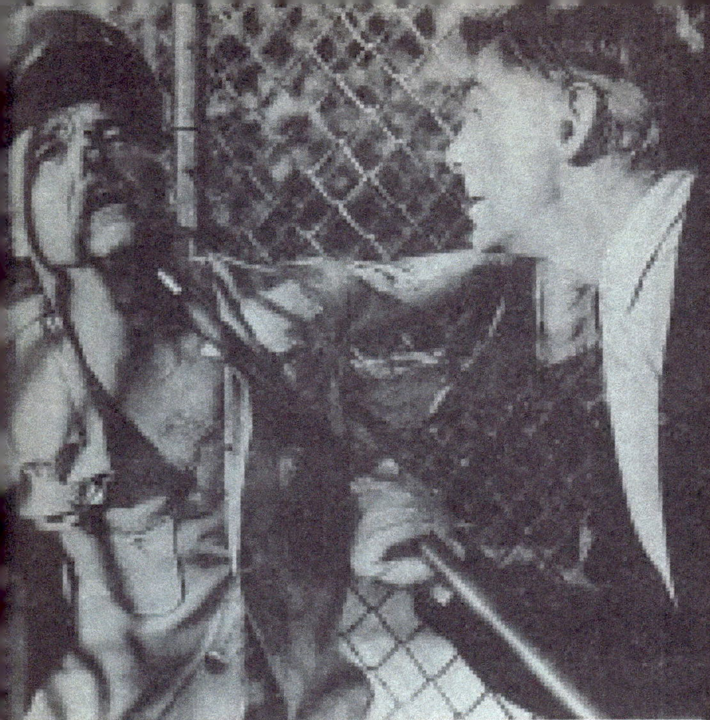

Gough deals out punishment to Elisha Cook for shooting one of his pet tigers

Herman Cohen has a script conference with Chico, the cougar. Below: Gough meets black magic fanatic Reds

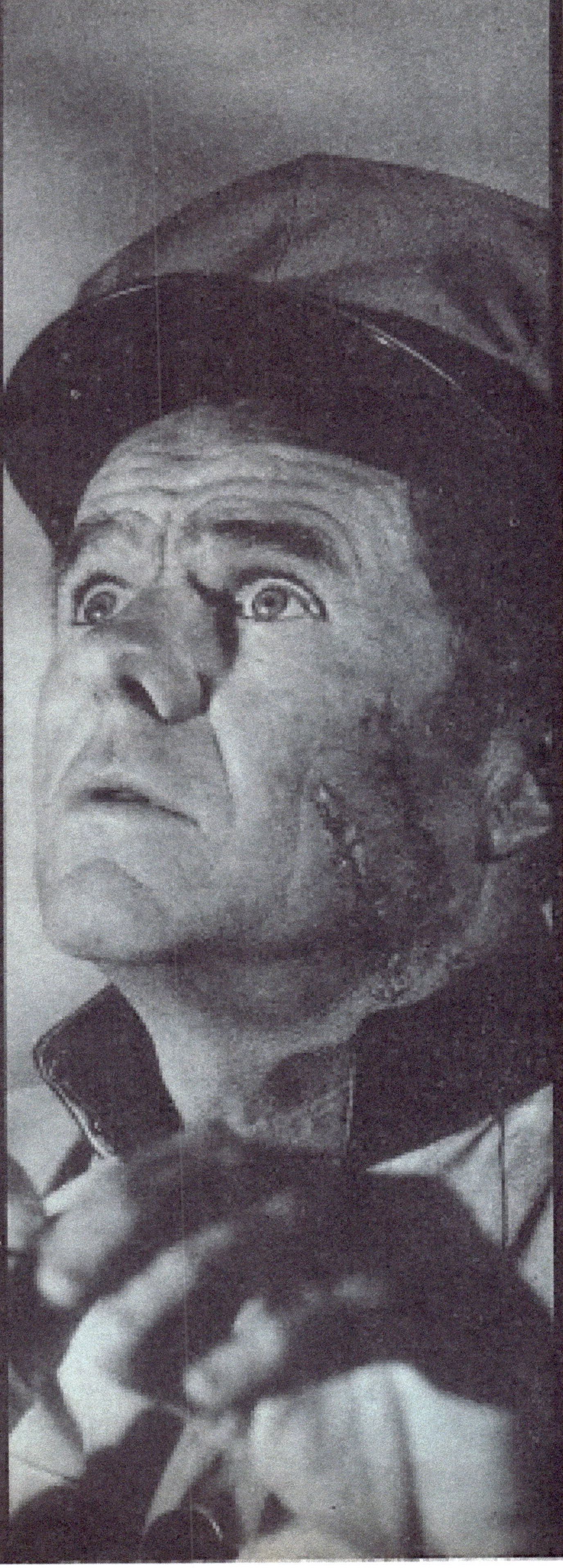

Elisha Cook barely escapes alive after he's thrown into a lion's cage

Rada, high priest of the True Believers, the sinister animal-worshipping cult

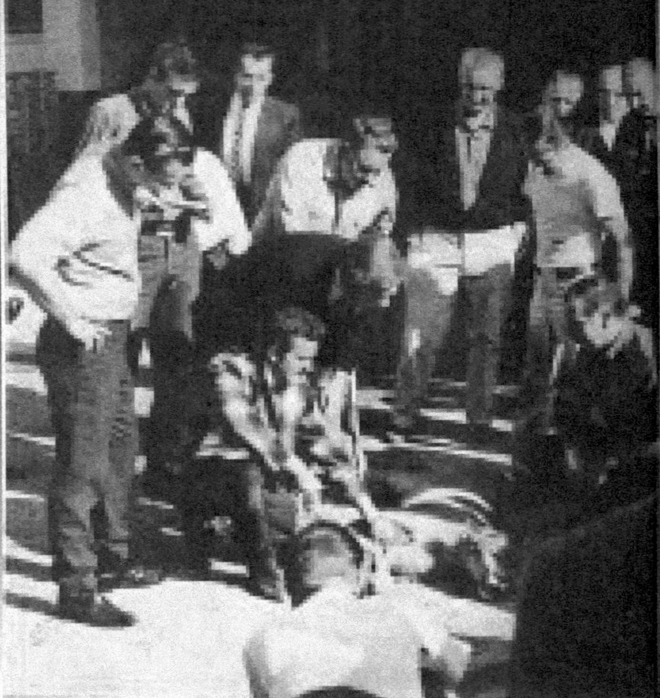

After 10 minutes of freedom on Producers Studio lot, Chico, a 300-pound cougar, was finally captured by trainer Ralph Helfer, squatting at left. Star Michael Gough leans over beside Helfer, and producer Cohen squats at right. Below: Producer Herman Cohen and Michael Gough with a friendly 600-pound tiger named Patricia. Earlier, Patsy mauled her trainer.

These animals are natural enemies.

With the help of a dozen assistants, Helfer accomplished both feats—the first time to his knowledge, he told a FANTASTIC MONSTERS interviewer, that such combinations of wild animals had ever been worked successfully except in the arena and except with the aid of whips, chairs, and banging pistols to keep them snarling, in line. Helfer uses no guns, whips, chairs or nets. "That's the old fear method," he said. "I teach that by first learning the natures of the animals you can win their trust and make them want to please you."

He accomplished the fore-mentioned feats, but he didn't do it without mishaps.

Ron Adams, an assistant trainer, was bitten on the forearm by a lion. But it seemed that the great cat, able to crush the arm or tear it from its socket, exercised conscious restraint: the teeth neither punctured a vein nor ripped a single tendon.

In two other incidents, the second lion and the tigress bolted from the sound stage. But the lion, at large on the studio lot, ran straight for the refuge of an open cage, and the tigress, after making it to an adjoining (and fortunately empty) stage, was re-captured by the trainers after a few anxious minutes.

turn to page 55

Cohen and Heller pose with the jungle beasts on the set. Never before had blood enemies like these as sorted big cats been worked in "integration"

STEELMASK, from page 11

work before, in Haiti, in the Central American jungles. Even orthodox science had come to admit the existence of such men as these, created through the use of forbidden drugs. Yes, Steelmask knew he followed one of the living dead, a zombie.

Even as the master of midnight watched, the zombie entered an apparently abandoned building that had been once part of a minor movie studio, long since closed.

Steelmask glided to the side of the building and with the remarkable athletic agility he had developed in simple necessity for staying alive, the silent avenger climbed the Spanish-influence decorations that ran up the wall.

At the top, he gingerly tested a tiny balcony meant only for ornament, and

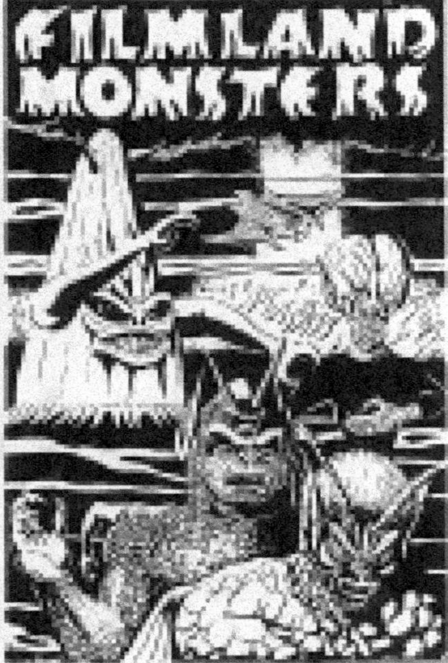

FILMLAND MONSTERS

Your Hollywood horrors can come <u>home</u> to roost!

decided that while it gave a little under his weight, it would hold him for a time. Peering through a window crusted with the dirt of many years, Steelmask followed a strange scene below. Through the use of his keen senses and his ability to read lips, Night's Agent was a silent, unseen partner in the conversation that went on thirty feet below him in the midst of a deserted auditorium.

"Give it over to me!" snapped a stooped, glowering figure at the approaching man with the face of death.

Silently, the zombie brought an oilskin packet from his jacket, handed it to the hunchback, then fell.

The man with the crevout glanced from the fallen zombie to the hunchback. "What's wrong with him?"

"Dead," explained the hunchback, tearing open the pack. "Really dead. He served his function. He delivered the drug." The little man rubbed a pinch of yellow-white powder between his fingers, and smiled.

"That's enough of the stuff to turn everybody in Los Angeles into zombies!" Crevout demanded.

The little man nodded briskly. "Yes, yes. Interjected into the city's water supply, everybody who drinks it will become a mindless automaton—a zombie if you will. The word need have no superstitious connotations. Zombies are merely ones who have had the higher reasoning faculties burned from their brains by this rare Central American herb just now fetched me from my off-shore launch by our late friend."

Crevout ran a palm over his bristles. "Knocking out everybody in L.A. with the stuff sounds like a good idea—if it works."

"It will," the little man said confidently. "You will have your loot—and I will have my revenge!"

"Sure, Doc, sure," Crevout said soothingly, "you deserve it."

"I was going to be the greatest actor and make-up technician in motion picture history. I—Doctor Proteus—but my career was cut short by that falling Kleig light that left me actually deformed. I couldn't play a hunchback in every picture, they said. But—" Proteus chuckled—"I am about to be the star of the greatest horror story ever told—turning an entire city into millions of mindless zombies. Nothing can stop me! Nobody!"

Nobody except Steelmask, thought the shadowy avenger high above. He had come to a difficult decision. For the first time in his career, Steelmask was going to kill a man in cold blood. Too much was at stake—millions of lives. Proteus had to die, the secret of his drug dying with him.

Securing his nylon climbing rope to the rail of the tiny balcony, Steelmask kicked open the small window and went through like a surging billow of black smoke.

Expertly, Steelmask slid down the rope as it played out, dropping down towards the figures of Proteus and Crevout who stood over the dead victim of zombyism.

As they saw the figure coming down at them, both the gangster and the deranged scientist set up calls for help, and instantly Steelmask saw that he had made what might well be a fatal mistake. These two were not

alone!

Doors opened on either side of the huge room. Through one door poured a horde of professional criminals, all heavily armed to guard this meeting place with revolvers, automatics, shotguns and submachine guns. And through the other door came a troop of dead men, the mindless slave victims of Proteus' evil discovery.

Steelmask found himself in the middle of a veritable army of brutal and unkillable monsters, all bent on his destruction.

This was no time for the mercy blasts of his gas gun, Steelmask knew. As he struck the floor, still determined to destroy this evil, even at the cost of his own life, twin Colt automatics were in his fists, spurting orange flame in the semi-darkness.

In answer to the thunder of Steelmask's big guns came the piping whine of the ineffectual .32's and .38's the gangsters carried, while one of the mob blazed away with a stream of sub-machine gun slugs.

Even as Steelmask's singing bullets took their toll among the killers, he triumphed in the knowledge that he would not have to destroy his own code of honor, that now if Proteus was to die, he would die in honest battle, as Steelmask fought in self-defense for his own life against overwhelming odds.

Besides summoning his horde of marching zombies, Proteus took a more personal hand as he drew a scalpel-thin knife and launched himself at the metal-masked manhunter.

Turning swiftly, Steelmask took Proteus' blade, caught it as the stiletto slid down the barrel of his gun. Twisting his gun sharply, Steelmask jerked the blade from the maniac's grasp and sent it flying from the barrel of the automatic.

A smashing elbow from Steelmask sent the scientist reeling backwards.

Now, the marching platoon of zombies was drawing near, their hands clutching for Steelmask. The avenger's guns spoke, but without effect against the walking dead.

But as one crook gathered up the submachine gun fallen from limp hands of another, Steelmask knew his only chance was to get these two hordes caught in their own cross attacks.

Diving forward, Steelmask was aware of the ruthless thug following him with the barrel of the machine gun, heedless of the mindless mass behind the manhunter.

Steelmask dropped to the floor, a burst of machine gun fire slicing over his head, ripping through the marching zombies, literally cutting them down.

One well-placed shot from Steelmask's automatic put the machine gunner out of commission, but he quickly saw a new menace. Crevout, the mob leader, had opened a compartment in the floor, opened a black bag and removed a small bottle.

"Okay, Ironhead," he called tauntingly at Steelmask, "see how you like drinking nitro!"

As the bottle came towards him, Steelmask threw himself forward as if to meet it in an apparently suicidal lunge.

turn to page 57

Radio's
invisible man—
The Shadow—
is once again
chilling
the airwaves

TERROR IN THE AIR

In the third issue of FANTASTIC MONSTERS we ran a short feature titled *The Afternoon Radio Died.* Despite its ominous heading, we concluded: "You can't kill the magic of radio. Magic never dies. It only sleeps." And true to our words, the magic of the imagination that lies in radio went to sleep with the closing of *Suspense* and *Johnny Dollar* on network radio, but, almost immediately, syndicated radio stations (including WGN Chicago, 5:30 Sundays) revived radio wizardry with the return of the master of invisibility, *The Shadow.*

These Shadow shows are recordings

Radio Historian Harmon casts a scrutinizing eye on present entertainment while surrounded by the Past

of the original broadcasts of the '40s, preserved from the lamentable junking that befell the records of so many programs when the files of reference copies grew too big for station storage space. But some time ago, the quick purchase of these ejected transcriptions by promoter Charles Michaelson saved the Mysterious Aide to the Forces of Law and Order from oblivion. Today, if you want to hear these eerie classics, requests to your local stations may prove to them that there is an eager audience.

For immediate listening to another all-time great mystery-horror show, *Lights Out* is now on a Capitol LP by author Arch Obeler, under the title DROP DEAD! Included is the most famous of all Obeler productions, the tale of the Chicken Heart that grows to swallow the entire world. Other famous series of crime and shock—I Love a Mystery, Mr Keen, Big Town—are represented with signature music and jacket photos on Columbia Records' MORE RADIO'S GREAT OLD THEMES, performed by Frank DeVol's Orchestra. The performers in DROP DEAD! incidentally include Mercedes McCambridge (Jack, Doc & Reggie's heroine in the above-mentioned ILAM) as Gell as Hal "Great Gildersleeve" Perry and Forrest Lewis, who was both Doc Green and Wash in Tom Mix and his Straight Shooters.

Curley Bradley, once known as 'Tom Mix of Radio"—the cowboy detective who sometimes rode Tony on the trail of Flying Saucers, death rays, and Shadow-like invisible man—today is the manager of a radio station in Nevada. Curley's rival for Radio's Greatest Western Hero, Brace Beemer, once the legendary masked Lone Ranger, rests on his Oxford, Michigan ranch, only occasionally giving displays of marksmanship, trick-riding, and whip-cracking astride his stallion, Silver's Pride, for open-mouthed youngsters. Brace is hoping to come to television in a part to match his present Wagonmaster-like image.

In Hollywood, Don Douglas works for a private police agency, a job worthy of his *John Steele, Adventurer* role. Russell Thorson (almost every major radio station's hero one season or another—Lone Ranger, Tom Mix, Jack, Packard in ILAM, Paul Barbour in *One Man's Family*) does movie-TV character roles; while the original "Jack Packard", Michael Raffetto, rests a now easily irritated throat except for an occasional TV role, such as a ship captain in *Hawaiian Eye.* And in New York, many memorable radio actors like Lon Clark (*Nick Carter*) have joined Bret Morrison (*The Shadow himself*) in dubbing English voices onto foreign movies.

All these great but generally unseen stars wait in a kind of ghostly happy hunting ground, alive but nearly forgotten by a TV bored public, waiting, just waiting to recreate the most imaginative, best-loved popular entertainment form in history—radio.

—JIM HARMON

MONSTER, from page 29

The hideous Monster is fascinated by the first baby he has ever seen. (FRANKENSTEIN No. 32)

some monster of them all, the Boon, but the public got tired of him because they thought he was a phony.

After work, he met a lot of interesting people. Micha Goss, for one. Micha didn't have a head, and his marriage was going down the drain until Franky introduced him to Harry Shortenbred, who had a head but no body to go with it. And then there was Zara, who was a good vampire, sorta, a baby-sitter out of Awful Annie's Baby-Sitting Agency. And Chester Dominous, half man and half horse, a centaur down his his back. Franky even met Boris Karloaf, the famous movie Master of Horror, and accidentally scared the daylights out of the poor fellow.

In the winter of 1943, Franky decided to take Moish the Mummy home to Egypt. Moish had his own room in Frankenstein's house, with sand all over the floor and a stuffed camel standing in the shade of a potted palm and a miniature pyramid sitting back in one corner, but he was homesick.

All the ghouls and vampires came down to see Moish off. Harris, the ghoul, patted him on his shoulder wrappings and said, "So long, Moish! Be careful you don't get sunstroke!", and Marvin, the vampire, said "Bon voyage, Moish." and Mildred, the vampire, said, "Watch out Cleopatra don't come back to life and try to make you!"

"All set, Moish?" said Franky when the boat docked. "We're in Egypt, land of the pyramids, the sphinx, and the Nile. Feel better?"

"I should hope to kiss a camel!" said Moish.

But they had an unnerving experience with a movie company making a Cleopatra picture — and who can blame them? — so Moish decided America was the place for him. Egypt was a nice place to visit, but he didn't want to be dead there.

Then, probably the only comic book in history with a split personality, Frankenstein came down with schizophrenia. Artist Dick Briefer—after a slight pause for retooling—turned his pen from the wild little cartoons of Franky and his wierdo friends to a serious and horrifying portrayal of the modern-day adventures of the Monster from Mary Shelley's terrifying, century-old novel, Frankenstein.

Gone, now, was every vestige of humor. Scarred, broken-toothed, scowling — inutterably hideous — the Monster's colossal, hate-filled body shambled across the world, killing, maiming, destroying. Born of death, he had no love for life; agonized by the unending artificial existence his creator had forced upon him, he was driven to a ferocity and cruelty beyond that of any beast.

And yet, somewhere within him, there was a love of beauty. And a need for a companion, someone like himself.

Once, a scientist gave him that companion, a monster-woman, and although she was as cruel as he—and even more mad, perhaps—he grew to love her. But in the end, the scientist, insane himself, destroyed her. The Monster befriended a blinded circus giantess, and a mob slew her. He captured a beautiful woman, and in anger, when he saw she only feared him, he almost killed her. The world would not let him have love and he could not take it; he could only revenge himself upon the universe that bound him. And he was hunted by men with a viciousness no less than his own.

He prowled the earth, riddled by bullets, seared by flame, maimed by iron-jawed animal traps, attacked by the creatures of the next world as well as this, enslaved by grave robbers and greedy showmen—and yet he always gave back more than he got. He was hate and revenge and power eternal.

Or almost eternal, for in 1954 he died. A censorship board was formed then, the Comics Code Authority, to control the content of comic magazines. It outlawed all horror stories, even ones based upon an acknowledged classic of world literature. As long as that code exists, there will be no son of Frankenstein . . . .

EDITOR'S NOTE: As we go to press with this article, Dell Publishing Co., has issued the first in a proposed series of Frankenstein comic magazines. However, the Dell Frankenstein is in no way a continuation or revival of the original character as published by the Prize Comics Group. Dell, which does not subscribe to the Comics Code Authority — it has its own Dell Code—is currently also publishing Dracula, Mummy, and Creature from the Black Lagoon magazines. ●

ROBOTS, from page 37

Metropolis featured a metal maid of haunting beauty. The whole world was haunted by a robot from space, Gort, and his plea to mankind's conscience for peace in one of the very best SF films, The Day the Earth Stood Still. Another space opera of top entertainment value, Forbidden Planet, presented friendly Robbie the Robot, who later saw action in Invisible Boy, and on a TV segment of The Thin Man. A current theatre release returns to the classic creation vs. creator theme in Revolt of the Humanoids, the synthetic flesh android robots of Jack Williamson's SF novel.

Science fiction has parented many robot stories from the time of Capek's R.U.R. Prominent among contemporary robotics authors are Isaac Asimov (the formulator of SF's standard "laws of robotics"), Lester del Rey, Clifford Simak, and Robert Heinlein.

Years back, Heinlein wrote of a huge man with muscles so weak that he needed artificial robot arms to work for him. The story, the man, and his robot arms were all called Waldo. This science fiction description inspired the actual creation of artificial arms which are today used to handle radioactive materials too dangerous to be touched by human hands. The actual robot arms are still called "waldoes".

Even more familiar than robot arms are robot brains, sometimes called "thinking machines", "mechanical brains", or more properly cybernetic calculators. These machines can "remember" much information on punched-out tapes, in chains of diodes and transistor patterns, and can quickly sort out this information and put it together for an answer. But these robot brains are only our slaves, only able to answer the questions we ask. And asking the right questions is a highly skilled science.

In our modern world, robots usually come in "pieces"—arms, brains, etc. A few full-fledged robots have been built — from marvelously eerie 18th Century lifesize dolls to the 1939 New York World's Fair electronic man— but a robot is only an imitation of a man, and not a very good one. Man is far better for any generalized purpose—we only need parts of robots for certain specific jobs.

Yet, not only in movies, but in real life, robots are being constantly improved. New developments in biochemistry promise "thinking machines" made not of metal but of biochemical matter—synthetic flesh.

Science may one day be able to make a very good imitation of a man —even something superior to a man. Then, humanity's problem will be the same as Dr. Frankenstein's—to be able to live with our own creation.

●

ZOO, from page 52

Then the cougar brought squads of Los Angeles police swarming down on Producers Studio, where the picture was filming, when he escaped through an electrician's crawl hole in the stage floor. With the police blocking off surrounding streets, neighbors peeking timidly through their curtains, and studio employes warned to stay indoors, Hoffer descended into the darkness under the stage and collared the varmint.

Two other men were injured by animals.

It took seven stitches to sew trainer Frank Lamping's right nostril back in place when he was clawed by the 600-pound tigress while wrestling with her for a scene. But that, he explained, had been "an accident."

Then there was the scene in which Michael Gough was holding in his arms a five-month-old tiger named John F. Kennedy. The President's namesake sank fangs through coat and shirt and nipped the actor on the forearm.

Meanwhile Cohen's animal actors

were running up what was probably the biggest food bill in the trade. It took a daily ration of 210 pounds of meat, 15 loaves of bread, and one crate of assorted vegetables to feed the hungry bunch — lions, tigers, cheetahs, leopards, jaguars, panther, and Himalayan bear. With horse meat at .30 a pound, bread (wholesale) at .10 a loaf, and the greens at $1 a crate, the board bill came to $1,358.

Black Zoo may have established a new show-business headache record, too. Forrest Duncwood, registered nurse, administered more than 400 aspirin tablets to cast and crew—more, he said, than he had given members of any other film troupe in 30 years' experience. He attributed the epidemic to "tension on the set" —understandable when you consider that the movie men were working within easy reach of the uncaged beasts.

If you think all this has discouraged Herman Cohen on making more wild animal epics, you're wrong. Planned next is *The Haunted Jungle*, to be followed by additional jungle beast blockbusters.

For the meantime, though, *Black Zoo* is one film that guarantees everyone a roaring good time. ●

STEELMASK, *from page 54*

The bottle struck the floor, and the tremendous explosion that followed registered as another California earthquake.

When the fumes cleared, Steelmask climbed to his feet, his clothing not even harmed. For in going to meet the point of the explosion, Steelmask had followed a fact of any physics textbook, a fact used by movie stuntmen and circus performers to stay alive—namely that the lines of force in an explosion go outward. At the center where Steelmask was, there was little explosive force.

But another figure rose from the debris and fallen bodies. Proteus stood unsteadily, training a gun on Steelmask.

"Before I die," the mad man said, "and before you do. I intend to see behind your celebrated steel mask. Enemy of Old."

Without hesitation, Steelmask removed the metal shield from his features.

Doctor Proteus took one look at what lay behind the Steelmask itself, and his heart stopped. It stayed stopped. He fell dead. The shock was enough to finish the work of the explosion.

Steelmask refastened the metal symbol of justice.

Yes, he thought, to look upon the face of Steelmask was enough to strike the fear of death into the unjust. For while Proteus had let his deformity drive him into bitter destructiveness, the man ,who had become Steelmask had reacted to his disfiguration in a war against international gangsters by burying his identity and devoting himself to the cause of humanity. And unlike the renown of others, Steelmask wore his mask not to conceal his face but to conceal the fact that he had no face. ●

DOG IN THE SKY

by Redd Boggs

The great husky sniffed LeBlanc's tracks in the snow to where they ended, then lifted his blunt muzzle and raised a long quivering howl to the moon at the edge of the sky.

Sgt. Foster shivered under his fur parka. The evidence was plainly etched on the frozen expanse of the tundra. LeBlanc had burst from his hut and plunged with long leaping steps across the snow. Thirty yards away his tracks ended in mid-leap and then did not return. LeBlanc had disappeared from the face of the earth. Sgt. Foster and the trapper Kravik, who had stumbled into the Mountie station with news of the mystery, had searched hundreds of yards in all directions without picking up a fresh trail. Kravik kicked off his snowshoes and built a fire on the stay grate, and in spite of the cold Sgt. Foster welcomed the warmth and the light of the small blaze.

"The Wendigo, Sergeant, the Wendigo!" Kravik muttered, hunkering down before the fire. "LeBlanc has been snatched away by the great black monster that prowls these barrens and feeds on defenceless men."

Sgt. Foster hadn't spent twenty years on this frozen frontier without learning a certain respect for native superstitions, but he shook his head. "No, Kravik, LeBlanc wasn't snatched away by any horrible monster. Can't you read the story in the tracks out there? He dashed out of this hut and ran across the snow as if he'd seen the Union of Paradise opening before him. He wasn't taken away—he was lured. He saw the vamp of his own free will."

Kravik thought for a long while, then laughed grimly. "LeBlanc had an old dream he'd dreamed often these polar nights. He dreamed he'd formed a doorway opening out of these Arctic wastes right into a strange tropic land, with a blue sun blazing down and towering green trees gently waving in the warm wind. Did you notice, Sergeant? His tracks were cut deep in the snow and frozen iron-hard, as if the snow was wet when he walked there. And we haven't had a thaw in three months! Maybe LeBlanc's dream finally came true! There's only one thing wrong with such a theory, Sergeant."

The Mountie smiled. "It's your theory, Kravik."

"Maybe LeBlanc did see a door opening before him, leading into a warmer brighter world, and maybe he ran to enter before the door swung closed. But he wouldn't have left his dog behind. Listen to the brute." Outside in the night the husky raised another plaintive howl to the cold moon.

The fire fell into red embers and died. The two men, tired from long miles on the trail, rolled into their blankets and slept. Hours later, in the pit of night, Sgt. Foster wakened to the urgent yelp of Kravik's husky and to Kravik's hand on his shoulder.

"Sergeant, look! Look!"

Sgt. Foster sprang up and ran to the door, shoved aside the wolfhide curtain. A billow of tropic heat washed over him as he stepped outside. The deep snow in front of the hut was turning to slush and puddles. Westward a vast blue radiance, like the light of a fantastic dawn never before seen on this planet, was fading from the star-slot heavens. But the Mountie didn't have time to watch the streams of blue light disappear as if a door were closing. He was too busy listening.

Somewhere, far overhead in the weirdly luminous air, faint but persistent like the yelvent of Canadian geese whooming away on their annual migration southward, he heard the deep-throated bark of a husky. There was a joyous note in that bark, as if the dog were greeting someone.

"LeBlanc came back for his dog," said Kravik. Together the two men stared into the sky, trying to see the path the dog was traveling to be reunited with his master. ●

THE ADVENTURES OF SPY S

Alan Armstrong, secretly Spy Smasher, searches for spies to smash

The Mighty Hero from the pages of WHIZ COMICS smashes his way through a great Republic serial

Spy Smasher smashed spies!

That's a pretty obvious statement to make, but it captures part of the thrill of a movie hero whose serial adventures quickened pulses and tightened viewers' grips on the arm-rests of their theatre seats during World War II. He was a dashing hero whose theme of rooting out and demolishing enemy agents is as timely and as exciting today as it was in 1942.

Spy Smasher was one of the last great serials made during the war, when patriotic fervor ran high and the figure of a mysterious, heroic, lone battler against Nazi spies and saboteurs could stir the imaginations of the most jaded Saturday afternoon movie-goers.

The twelve chapter story opened in occupied France, where brutal Nazi occupation forces had virtually enslaved an entire gallant nation to make the French help them in their vicious march to world domination. A mysterious American agent has been smuggled into the occupied nation to try to gather some clue to the identity of the Mask, known head of the German spy network in America. The American agent, of course, is Spy Smasher, whose secret identity as Alan Armstrong is protected by the aviator's helmet and goggles which he wears at all times. The helmet, goggles, aviator's suit and flowing cape which made up Spy Smasher's costume were already familiar to millions of comic book readers who flocked to their local bijous to see their hero brought to life by the granite-jawed and steely-eyed Kane Richmond.

Captured by German soldiers, Spy Smasher is sentenced to die before a firing squad, but before he can be executed, a daring French patriot leads a split-second raid and spirits him out of the country. Home in America, Spy Smasher enlists the aid of his twin brother Jack, also played by Kane Richmond in a rare and skillful use of the split-screen techni-

by Dick Lupoff

MASHER

Above: Spy Smasher gets the drop on The Mask and his thugs. At Left: Villainous Ken Terrell prepares to ray down Spy Smasher's airplane

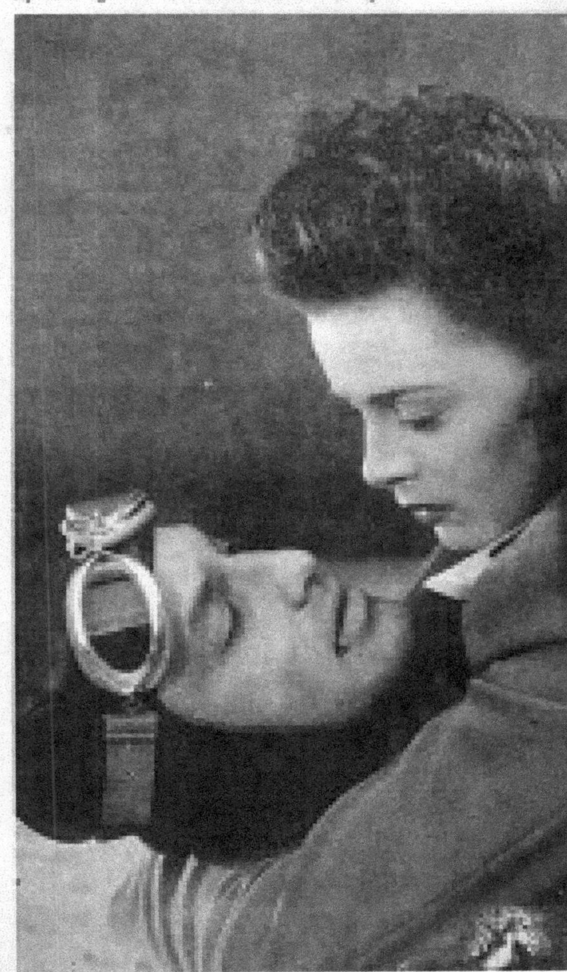

This ad appeared in Fawcett magazines. Captain Marvel, who starred in films two years earlier, greets Spy Smasher upon his Hollywood arrival. Below: Spy Smasher fans received this membership card when they saw the first chapter of the Republic serial

que in a serial. Alan and Jack together uncover an incredible plot by the Mask to murder Admiral Corby (Sam Flint), chief of the U.S. Foreign Service. Corby's daughter Eve (Marguerite Chapman) is—in the movie—Jack's fiancee. In the original comic book stories she had been *Alan's* fiancee; but such is the way of the Hollywood adapter.

Striving to protect Admiral Corby, the brothers uncover a counterfeit plot through which the Mask had hoped to wreck America's economy and national war effort, and Spy Smasher is led into a chase into a railroad tunnel, where he races the villains in a handcar only to face a flood of burning oil which they have released. Spy Smasher attempts to outrace the plunging, flaming torrent, but it is about to catch him when—wham!—there is a blinding, ear-shattering explosion and the chapter is over.

Is that enough to fill an opening chapter of a serial? It certainly is—in fact it's enough to fill many a feature-length movie, but Spy Smasher careened and cavorted through twelve incredible installments before he finally defeated the Mask's foul machinations, and every chapter ended with a chilling climax that left the most inveterate cliffhanger fan half-convinced that Spy Smasher couldn't possibly escape alive.

But he always did.

Chapter 2 opened in classic fashion, with a recap of the events leading up to that shattering explosion. For one moment, the camera cut to the advancing flames in the former episode, but this time it stayed on Spy Smasher, who produced a hand-grenade from his pocket. By setting off the grenade in the tunnel, he brought down a section of walls and ceiling, cutting off the advancing oil, and making good his escape.

This wasn't quite a "cheat"—an unfair explanation of how a hero escaped from an impossible trap by actually changing what had gone before. It was a time-honored technique of showing the hidden instant of action that the camera had not revealed in the previous episode.

In chapter after chapter Alan Armstrong and his brother Jack, Admiral Corby and his daughter Eve, chased (and were chased by) the Mask and minions through an incredible series of cliffhangers and escapes, many so great that only the greatest can be recounted here. Such as:

Chapter 5—Spy Smasher is trapped at the bottom of an elevator shaft as the heavy car descends faster and faster, seeming in the climatic moment to crush the life from Spy Smasher! (A classic cliffhanger.)

Chapter 6—Spy Smasher is battling the Mask in a timber sawmill. The hero is knocked unconscious by a terrific blow that sends him sprawling onto a conveyor belt that leads straight to a screaming buzz-saw! (Another classic.)

Chapter 9—Spy Smasher and his brother Jack have thwarted the Mask's attempt to hijack a transcontinental express train, but the Mask and his henchmen escape in an automobile. Spy Smasher and one of the henchmen are battling it out on the roof of the car as it plunges into a mountainous chasm! (Still another classic.)

But the best cliffhanger of them all is the one at the end of chapter 11.

The Mask's number two man has captured Eve Corby, but before she can be spirited away the brave girl leaves behind a clue as to her destination. Spy Smasher's brother Jack, a real All-American boy, discovers the clue and notifies Alan. Together they give chase, but are unable to rescue Eve.

Despondent, the Armstrong brothers return home, where they receive a telephone call from the Mask's assistant, offering to release Eve if Spy Smasher will give himself up to the Mask. The dashing hero walks willingly into a certain death trap, knowing that Eve has been released. His body is riddled with bullets, then falls ten stories to a deserted street. He is good and dead, no cutting away at the crucial moment this time. And just to be good and sure, the Mask pulls away Spy Smasher's goggles and helmet, revealing the heroic features of Kane Richmond. There can be no doubt about it this time, Spy Smasher is dead.

In the twelfth and concluding chapter, Spy Smasher discovers that the Mask and his henchmen have decided to flee from America in a submarine. They are just pulling away from shore but have not yet submerged. Spy Smasher pursues them in a speedboat, rams the sub and is thrown clear.

turn to page 62

Kane Richmond and Marguerite Chapman in "Hero's Death", chapter 11 of the great *SPY SMASHER* epic

SMASHER, from page 61

He swims to shore in time to see the submarine explode, ending once and for all the menace of the Mask.

Oh, and as for that cliffhanger in chapter 11. Well, it really was the face of Kane Richmond we saw when Spy Smasher's helmet was removed, but it wasn't Alan Armstrong who was wearing the costume. It was his brother Jack, also played, you will remember, by the same Kane Richmond.

And this ended Spy Smasher, one of the great serials of a great era.

Spy Smasher was a good product, all right, but Republic Studios and Fawcett Publications weren't about to let the serial rise or fall on its own merits. Together they mounted a promotion campaign, essentially similar to those used on many serials (and on many feature pictures to this day), but bigger and brassier than almost any other.

The character Spy Smasher was appearing in both WHIZ COMICS and in his own SPY SMASHER COMICS, plus several of the lesser lights of Fawcett's once mighty comic book line. In many Fawcett comics, special ads proclaimed the virtues of the Spy Smasher serial, and one issue of SPY SMASHER COMICS carried a cover photo of Richmond in his uniform.

Fawcett controlled a string of movie magazines and the serial was featured in all of these. Fawcett magazines also carried coupons for their readers to return, asking theatre managers who were not featuring the serial to do so. Dozens of prepared news stories were printed up, ready for reprinting by local newspapers. Headlines on a few read: "SPY SMASHER" EXCITING NEW SERIAL ABOUT NAZI SPY RING ... KANE RICHMOND PLAYS DOUBLE PART IN NEW REPUBLIC SERIAL. There were even ready-to-use cuts of scenes from the film, complete with captions. Delivery trucks delivering Fawcett publications carried signs promoting *Spy Smasher*, as did newsstands themselves.

And when you got to the theatre, the promotion was just starting. There were, of course, the conventional banners, posters, lobby cards, and stills, but there was more to come. Copies of SPY SMASHER COMICS were specially distributed to theatre managers, as was a special little 100-page book titled SPY SMASHER AND THE RED DEATH, written by Otto Binder. Spy Smasher Club buttons were distributed by the tens of thousands, and a "Spy Smasher Victory Battalion" membership card, signed by Spy Smasher himself (in a curiously feminine-looking handwriting) was available at showings of the first chapter. The final icing on the promotional cake of Spy Smasher was an autographed picture, suitable for framing, of the mighty hero. Exploitation indeed!

And where is Spy Smasher today? Well, the buttons, four-color Fan Photos, membership cards, and dime books by Otto Binder are rare items, seldom seen and worth many dollars each to rabid collectors. The Spy Smasher comic feature has been de-funct for well over a decade.

The movie itself? Well, put it this way. The author of this article is an active member of four different film societies, all of which specialize in rare old pictures, most of them far older than *Spy Smasher*. Yet none of the four has ever succeeded in turning up a print. Searches of commercial film catalogs and TV film libraries fail to turn it up. Try to ask Republic Studios and it turns out that Republic no longer exists.

Spy Smasher once rose to the heights of glory. There now exists of him hardly a trace, except in Memory. ●

REVENGE, from page 15

of *Frankenstein* and *Horror of Dracula* do have something on their side—Christopher Lee and Peter Cushing, if no other things. But even in this Hammer series, the sequels like *Revenge of Frankenstein* and *Brides of Dracula* turned out ghosts of their former selves. Personally, skinny monsters and bland vampires make my bandages crawl.

Hammer did do another successful remake, *Hound of the Baskervilles* with Peter Cushing as Sherlock Holmes. Hammer's entry was a full-fledged horror film, unlike 20th Century-Fox's earlier polite mystery from the Conan Doyle classic. When Universal took over Holmes from Fox they did cast Basil Rathbone in *Sherlock Holmes Meets the Spider Woman* (and her accomplice, the original Mad Scientist, Professor Moriarity). *The Spider Woman Strikes Back* later, again with Gale Sondergaard but without Sherlock Holmes. The web of mystery the Spider Woman spun was pretty flimsy without the Great Detective in its center.

The mystery and menace played out in the U-I Creature pictures as the series went on, too. The Creature from the Black Lagoon stood out—in 3-D—and with Julia Adams, Richard Denning and Richard Carlson. But the gill-man popped up from the depths of the Amazon River (where he has supposedly been bombed to death) for *The Revenge of the Creature*. Personally, I was glad to see him go down for the third time in *The Creature Walks Among Us*.

With the Creature, I have covered almost all the Universal horror series epics. I have saved the best for last. Can you guess what it is? No, it isn't *The Wolf Man*.

The Mummy, of course!

I thought the original *Mummy* with Boris Karloff was just fine, as I commented in a previous FANTASTIC MONSTERS. But then for the next one, *The Mummy's Hand*, they have to get Tom Tyler, a cowboy, to portray the Mummy. I ask you: would he have to be entirely wrapped in bandages for saddle sores? Of course, they got a good horror man for *The Mummy's Ghost* and the rest with Lon Chaney Jr. But then, Universal had the effrontery to have the Mummy wind up the same way as Frankenstein, Dracula, the Wolf Man, the Invisible Man, even Jekyll and Hyde—straight men for Abbott and Costello. Stooges for a pair of comics!

That's probably what turned me against all "Son of", "Return of", "Revenge of", "Strikes Back" pictures. I'm still smarting about it beneath these moldering wrappings!

EDITOR'S NOTE: I regret to inform you readers of a foul and fantastic deed! Your editor, suspecting something was wrong with the above column—it read somehow unlike the Mad Mummy—dashed into the Mummy's office here at Black Shield Publications and immediately spotted an IMPOSTER beneath phony mummy wrappings. Tearing these rags aside, I uncovered Jay Judson, a renegade literary critic. Judson snarled out the startling news that he and a band of other literary critics had taken justice into their own hands and had KIDNAPPED the Mad Mummy in order to protect the youth of America from his influence. So saying, Judson made his escape. Therefore, FANTASTIC MONSTERS hereby offers a

REWARD

for information on the whereabouts of the Mad Mummy and for information leading to the capture of his kidnappers! America, Be Alert! ●

GHOST, from page 20

came Ygor.

The operation successfully completed, Frankenstein closed the final switch, sending artificial electrical life into the Monster. And Ygor, shrieking his hate through the Monster's lips, went berserk, hurling Bohmer back into the laboratory apparatus, electrocuting him and starting a fire that swept the sanitarium, destroying it. In the midst of the flames, beside his father's creature, Ludwig Frankenstein perished.

So ended the strangest of all Frankenstein films, with the crippled shepherd and the mindless Monster welded into one terrible being.

Yet, strangely, outstanding as it is *The Ghost of Frankenstein* cannot take its place beside the earlier classic films of Karloff. Despite the astonishing and inventive story—and the vast power of such scenes as the lightning storm, Ygor's death and the final terrifying passages as the Monster burns, his flesh blistering in the heat, while the sanitarium falls—and despite the performances of the players, the motion picture falls short of greatness. If a little more effort had been made to give it the size and scope of the earlier Frankenstein productions; if, like the earlier films, the camera work had been truly distinguished, if the makeup department, a major here once, had adapted the Monster's makeup to conform with Chaney's utterly different face, if that had happened, perhaps *The Ghost of Frankenstein* could have been truly memorable. Nonetheless, it stands out as a milestone in horror film production.

But strangest of all, as though mind had weirdly triumphed over matter the Monster's terrible new brain-shaped flesh as well as emotion. For in the sequel, *Frankenstein Meets the Wolf Man*, Bela Lugosi—Ygor—portrayed, for the only time, Victor Frankenstein's awesome, indestructible creation. ●

HAUNT ADS

Unusual and interesting horror and jungle film publicity material can be obtained from FRANK LARKIN, 2026 N. Ivar, Hollywood 28, Calif. Write to Frank for more information and prices. . . . FanMo reader response to his radio articles has inspired our own JIM HARMON to issue RADIOHERO, a non-commercial, mimeographed "fanzine". The Shadow, Jimmy Allen and RON HAYDOCK's Captain Midnight highlight the first issue "Limited Edition", which can be had for 50c from RADIOHERO c/o Black Shield, Topanga, Calif. Also wanted at the same address. Trades or sales of recordings of many radio shows like I Love A Mystery, Tom Mix, or information about possible runs of radio character dramas on local stations anywhere. Such news starts from RADIO HERO. . . . DOUGLAS HIGLEY has three classic terrorpics for sale, available in 8mm for all you home movie fans. Cabinet Of Dr. Caligari —$39, Phantom Of The Opera—$45, and Terror Of Dracula—$9.95. The films, or information regarding their purchase may be had from DOUG at 59181 Ke Nui Rd, Haleiwa, Oahu, Hawaii. . . . CALVIN RUSH would like to get his hands on any Justice Society Of America comics, plus Justice League Of America comic #1 and Flash comic #32. CAL will pay 15c for each if you'll send them to 218 North Hancock, Ottumwa, Iowa. . . . Anyone selling posters and stills from the old serials will find a ready customer in RUSSELL BALL, who lives at 1242 West 24th St, Los Angeles 7, Calif. . . . ROBERT SKOLMOWSKI would like to hear from other fans who write fantasy, science fiction, or horror stories as a hobby, or are amateurs trying to break into the pro-

BLOWING HIS OWN HORNS

Our recently appointed editor at Tombstone Times, LARRY BYRD, displays his hairy growths with a great deal of pride. Since his appointment, Mr. Byrd has noticed a definite growth in the horns due, he says, "to spending countless hours trying to decipher a portion of the poison-pen letters that have flooded our offices for TOMBSTONE TIMES.

COFFIN CORNER

Keep up the Flash Gordon stories and stuff! Could your "Coffin Corner" section tell me just when the original Flash Gordon stories were started? — SALVATORE ROMANO, BROOKLYN, N.Y.

You're a little vague about which 'original' Flash Gordon stories you mean. The newspaper comic strip was originated in January, 1934; while the film version began just a year later, in 1936.

Explain the "R.I.P." seen on tombstones in comic books and motion pictures. — CRAIG ELFNER, RED LION, PA.

Are you kidding, Craig? We thought everyone knew that R.I.P. stood for "Rest In Peace", or "Pieces," depending on the way in which the individual had died!

Would you please explain Tanna Leaves to me? I have heard of them, and seen them mentioned in monster magazines, but I don't know what they are. Please give me the story behind them— NORM PHILLION, FENTON, MICH.

As most every monster fan knows, Tanna Leaves (in dried form) were used by Egyptian Priests to brew a sort of tea or soup which was fed to THE MUMMY to keep him alive over thousands of years. They were supposed to have looked a great deal like Eucalyptus leaves.

fessional field. He has an idea that may be of interest to you. Write him at 3060 Nebraska Ave., Toledo 7, Ohio. . . . Searching for a particular horror still? CARL CAUDILL of 620 Bayview Ave., Millbrae, Calif., has a number of stills available, and will trade or sell . . . . Send a self-addressed, stamped envelope to GARY SCHWENDER, 9-12 Fair Haven Pl, Fair Lawn, N.J., for a free catalog of 2nd-hand mystery, horror, and science-fiction books he has for sale. . . . Wanted: the first four issues of WRESTLING REVIEW magazine, any fanzines, and all monster magazines. Send your lists to DAVID JONES, 324 Avenue "A", Battle Creek, Mich. David is also the editor of the new amateur horror magazine, Dante's INFERNO, which can be had from DAVID at the same address. This new amateur magazine features articles, stories, and a lithographed cover illustration by none other than LARRY BYRD, the editor of TT. . . . More horror stills, pressbooks, etc., can be had from RICH WANNEN, 341 Sheffield Ave., Webster Groves 19, Mo. Write to Rich for a list of available material. . . . A flare has been sent up by BILL BIRTCIL, 1620 Deerwood Dr., W. Sacramento, Calif., who desperately wants information regarding Monster and comic book fan magazines. We suggest that all you fan editors contact BILL, and tell him about your own publication. . . . Another Bela Lugosi fan is seeking material on the late, great horror star. SEAN HUGHES, who resides at 7616 Willow Glen Rd., Hollywood 46, Calif., requests any authentic photographs, autographs, stills, posters, pressbooks, scripts, etc., from any of the films in which Lugosi appeared, especially Dracula. . . . GEORGE BERCOVITZ, 350 N. Detroit St., Los Angeles 36, Calif., wants information and material regarding Lon Chaney Sr. . . . and to finish off the column for this trip, BARBARA MIDGETT is desperately looking for a 14 year-old pen-pal. (BARBARA, we suggest you contact SUSAN MUNSEY, 1736 Carlyon Ave., E. Cleveland 12, Ohio)

FANTASTIC MONSTERS CLUB MEMBERS

GARY MEYERS
Redmond, Oregon
JERRY McNAMARA
Phoenix, Arizona
EDDIE CORTEZ
Brooklyn, N.Y.
STEVEN HYLAND
New Hope, Minn.
RON HALL
Madison, Wisc.
LEROY DRESSLER
Bradford, Pa.
MICHAEL BRADSTONE
Dayton, Ohio
FRANK SILVA
E. Providence, R. I.
ALLEN ORCUTT
Whittier, Calif.
RICHARD WOLLETT
Pittsburgh, Pa.
RANDAL KIRSH
Los Angeles, Calif.
STEPHANIE CIOFFI
New York, N. Y.
BILLY TAYLOR
Oakland, Calif.
CHRIS HICKS
Lakewood, Calif.
DENNIS GATES
Cleveland, Ohio
DOUGLAS JUSKA
Oakhurst, N. J.
LARRY OSBORN
Lansing, Mich.
MARILYN FROST
Fairborn, Ohio
GARY BEYMER
Richland, Wash.
FRED GRAYBAR
Palos Park, Ill.
SANDRA STEWART
Long Beach, Calif.
TOM SCHULTZ
Dayton, Ohio
ROGER STROBEL
San Francisco, Calif.
CREIGHTON WREN
Charlotte, N. C.
ROSALIE CARATELLO
Chester, Pa.

LARRY ROGERS
Marengo, Ohio
RON RYAN
Astoria, N. Y.
BILLY RUZICKA
Cicero, Ill.
DAVID STAVEN
Fresno, Calif.
MIKE EVANS
Arlington, Texas
DUNCAN HARP
New York, N. Y.
DENNIS McCOY
Ripon, Calif.
DAVID BOWMAN
Buckley, Wash.
MIKE GARRETT
Birmingham, Ala.
FRANK PODOJIL
Parma, Ohio
KEITH HURD
W. Farmington, Ohio
CHESTER SOBOSLAY
Pittsburgh, Pa.
CLEVELAND SANFORD
Erie, Pa.
BOB AMBROSE
Anniston, Ala.
BOBBY URIG
Dayton, Ohio
GREG URBAN
Mequon, Wisc.
JAMES SHAPIRO
Los Angeles, Calif.
RALPH RICHARDSON
Estacada, Oregon
JOHNNY GOODMAN
Bloomington, Ind.
ED KEMPINSKI
Chicago, Ill.
JAMES PANYARD
Detroit, Mich.
JAMES JONES
Cincinnati, Ohio
MICHAEL KLINKERT
San Diego, Calif.
MIKE GRAY
Toledo, Ohio
TOMMY WRIGHT
San Antonio, Texas

MORE NEXT ISSUE!

NEW COMIX STRIP

This issue brings with it, what we hope will become a regular feature—a refreshing new comic strip by that talented cartoonist, CHUCK SCARBOROUGH. MOSE, as the strip's denizen here is called, is slightly reminiscent of MELVIN MOLE of old MAD comics fame, yet has his own inimitable sense of humor. We hope to have lots of comment on this new strip, and if the reactions are as favorable as we expect them to be, the possibility of still another strip is very probable.

HORRORZINES

Here is a handful of recent monster film fan publications:

DANTE'S INFERNO—Dave Jones, 324 Avenue 'A', Battle Creek, Mich—30c an issue; $1 now available.

STRANGE AND TERRIFYING FICTION—Duncan Harp, 114 West 70th St, New York 23 NY—25c per copy.

THE PHANTOM—Dave Butler, 1441 Willowmont, San Jose 24 Calif—10c an issue.

TRANSYLVANIAN NEWSLETTER—Harvey Ovshinsky, 10047 Forrer, Detroit 35 Mich—25c per copy (bi-monthly).

FANTASY FLICKERS—Chet Wyszynski, 1738 Morse Ave, Des Plaines, Ill.

MENACE—John Berry, 35 Dusenberry Rd, Bronxville 8 NY.

We'd also like to mention the latest project of DONALD SHAY, editor of the now-extinct KALEIDOSCOPE. Don is currently assembling two special film booklets—one each on the first two FLASH GORDON serials. The booklets will not only include chapter-by-chapter descriptions of the stories but also a Collector's sprinkling of scene stills.

If you'd like more information about the Flash books, contact Don at 11 Wintergreen Ave, MD #15, Newburgh, N.Y.

SUPER-FAN

Once again the pages of TOMBSTONE TIMES are adorned by the efforts of DONALD GLUT, a "glutton for publicity", who has sent us more photographs and information regarding his film work and disguises—inventing more than any other monster fan to date! This time Don gives us his concept of SUPERMAN.

A Batty Count

Pictured here is the infamous COUNT VICTOR WISCONTEC, who recently contracted an important survey across the country. Count Wiscontec tells us: "After two years, my group had 31% fewer cavities with Crest."

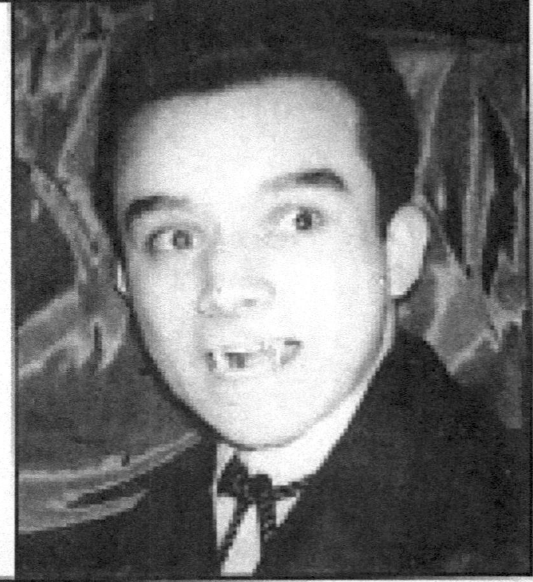

HERO #2. Published by Larry Herndon, 3320 Walnut St., Carrollton, Texas, features articles on Conan the Conqueror, the Blue Beetle by Howard Keltner, serious reviews of the comics edited by Stan Lee of Atlas, plus art by B. Green, Al Kuhfeld and Bud Saunders. Check with Larry for price.

ALTER EGO #4, edited by Jerry G. Bails at 17645 Gaylord, Detroit 40, Mich. This issue, completely offset, boasts the Comic Book Alley Awards for 1961, plus articles by Roy Thomas, Ed Lahmann, and Fanite's own Ron Haydock, with art by Ronn Foss, Harry Thomas, and the Jack Kirby. 50c gets you this fine, almost professionally reproduced magazine.

COMIC ART #4, the recent issue, is now out of print; however, a limited number of copies of #3 (sold on an advance basis) can still be had from the publishers — Don and Maggie Thompson, 29 College Place, Oberlin, Ohio.

Other comic fan magazines are listed below, and further information regarding these can be had by mailing a self-addressed, stamped envelope to the addresses given.
ROCKET'S BLAST—G.B. Love, 9812 S.W. 212 St., Miami 57, Fla.
MASQUERADER — Mike Vosburg, 2348 Avalon, Pontiac, Mich.
THE COMIC FAN—Buddy Saunders, 1405 Joyce, Arlington 2, Texas
COMIC HEROES REVISITED—Bernie Bubnis Jr., 48 Walnut Ave., Farmington, N.Y.
SPOTLITE—Parley Holman, 3938 S. 3300 East, Salt Lake City, Utah
KOMIX ILLUSTRATED — Billy J. White, 487 Sardis, Columbia, Mo.
HEADLINE — Steve Snider, 7014 Roberts Ct., University City 30, Mo.
FAN TO FAN — Robert Butts, 719 Pierce St., South Bend, Ind.
COMIC HEROES UNLIMITED — S.B. Love, 9812 S.W. 212 St., Miami 57, Fla.
THE COMIX—John Wright, P.O. Box 1277, Port Elizabeth, So. Africa
SUPER HERO—Mike Tuohey, 16857 Sunderland, Detroit 19, Mich.
THE COMIC WORLD—Robert Jennings, 3819 Chambers Dr., Nashville 11, Tenn.

Meteor Monster

Ambitious young monster fans from Rosemont, Pennsylvania, display their creation for a home horror film, the design of which was modeled after Paul Blaisdell's It Conquered The World monster. The team of young movie makers is headed by WALTER SHANK, a long time monster fan and avid reader of Fanite. Others in the picture are CHUCK HODGKINSON and Shank's sister, PEGGY.

ZIP!
YOU'VE JUST
BEEN ZAPPED!

Universal's Classic **WOLF MAN**

MONSTER OF THE MONTH

We thought nothing would be more appropriate for this special "Beauty & Beast" issue of FANTASTIC MONSTERS than a Full-Color Monster Pinup of Evelyn Ankers and Lon Chaney Jr. in a classic pose from an equally classic motion picture—*The Wolf Man*.

The Wolf Man was produced in 1941 especially to celebrate Universal's tenth anniversary in the horror film field. A decade previous, the studio took what everybody thought was too great a financial risk in producing and releasing a talking screen version of Bram Stoker's *Dracula*. The daring risk proved so lucrative, however, that *Frankenstein* soon followed; and afterwards, no season had passed without one or more spectral thrillers on the Universal schedule.

The Invisible Man, The Black Cat, Bride of Frankenstein, The Raven, The Invisible Ray, The Old Dark House—these are a few of the fine horror films Universal released between 1931 and 1941. And their ten year celebration picture—*The Wolf Man*—was indeed a tremendous addition to the annals of classic horror films.

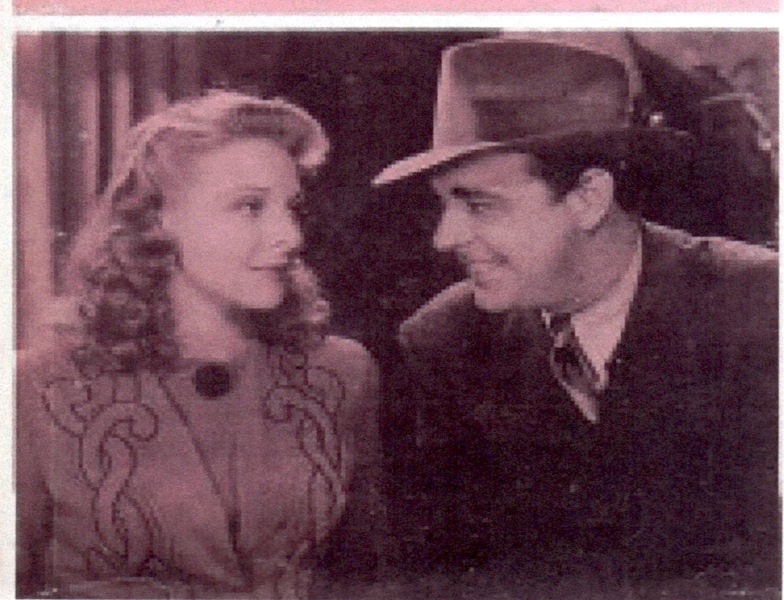

FANTASTIC
MONSTER
OF THE
MONTH

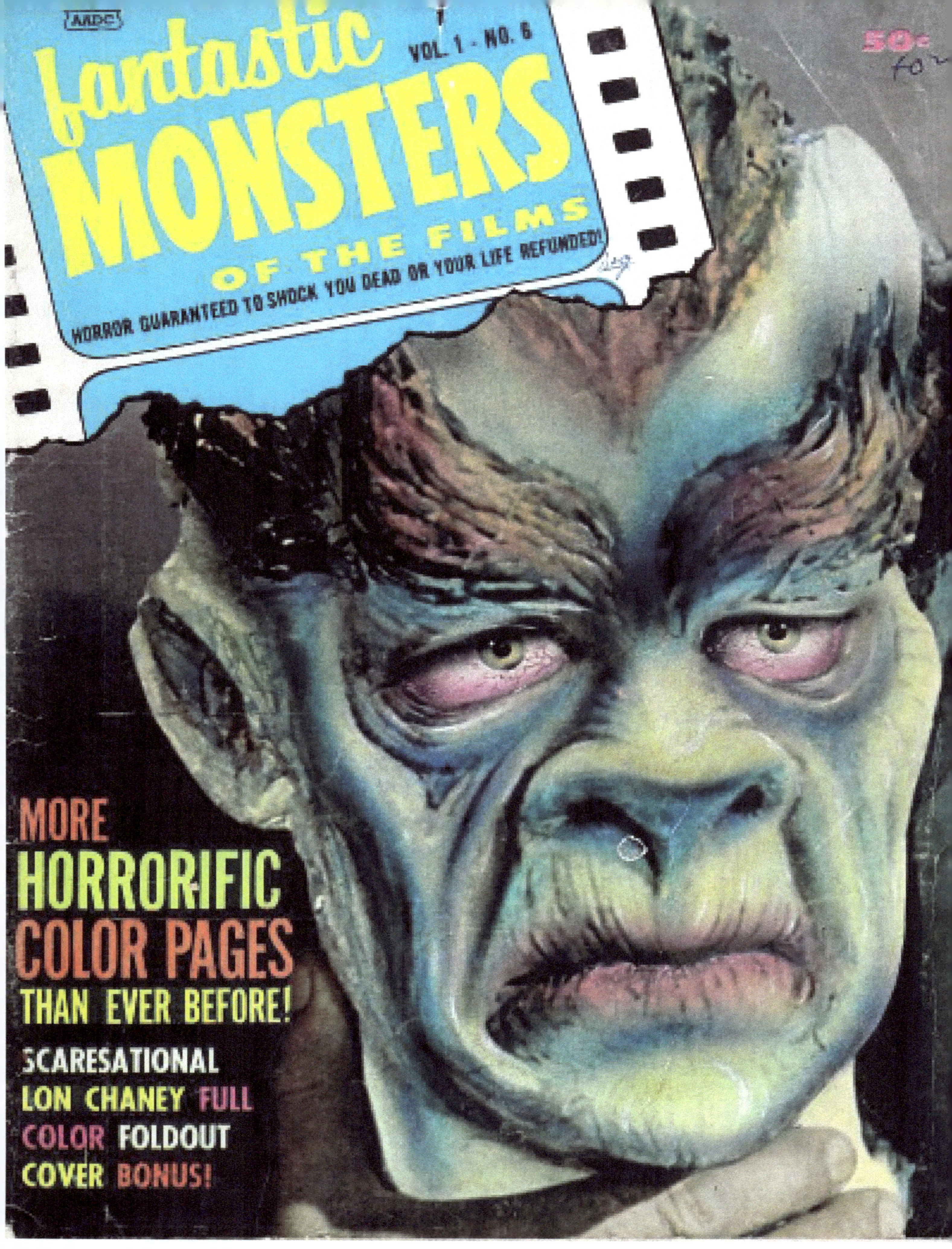

MDC
fantastic
MONSTERS
OF THE FILMS
VOL. 1 - NO. 6
50c
HORROR GUARANTEED TO SHOCK YOU DEAD OR YOUR LIFE REFUNDED!
MORE
HORRORIFIC
COLOR PAGES
THAN EVER BEFORE!
SCARESATIONAL
LON CHANEY FULL
COLOR FOLDOUT
COVER BONUS!

BRIDE OF FRANKENSTEIN

MONSTERSCOPE

Introducing another
great new Fantastic Monsters Collector's
Photo Feature

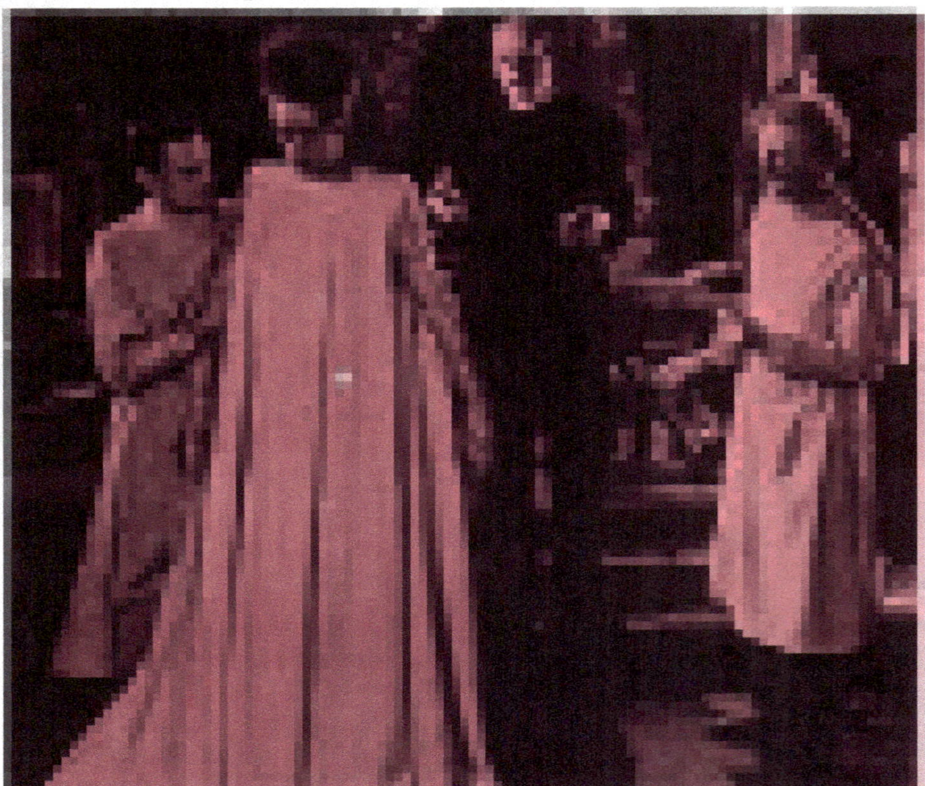

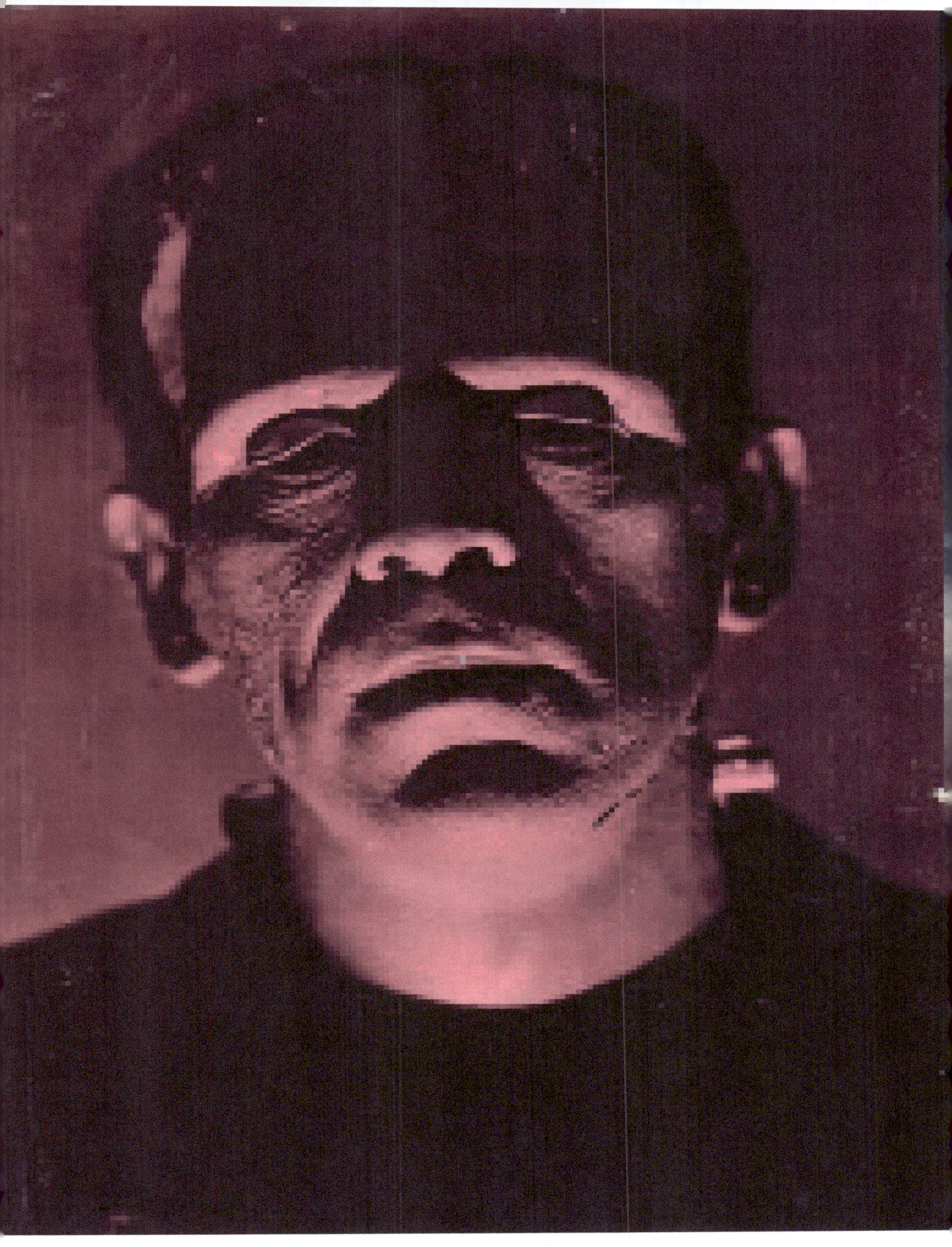

MONSTER OF THE MONTH

Universal-International's
DINOSAURUS

Hollywood's craziest audition was held for the sound testings to provide "voices" for a Tyrannosaurus and a Brontosaurus who *were* among the prehistoric stars of Dinosaurus, released by Universal-International in 1960.

An estimated 250 sounds were tested by producer Jack Harris and his technicians to select those used as prehistoric dialogue for the film. Among the weird sounds checked were snake kisses, combined with bear growls, squealing brakes mixed with the screech of an owl, and the moans of a wild pig.

They also experimented with a variety of animal noises combined with sandpaper scraping, jet planes, and human sneezing. They sought maximum effect rather than authenticity—of course!

But, as producer Harris put it, "Who can tell if the sounds are correct or not?"

fantastic
MONSTERS
OF THE FILMS
VOL. 1 • NUMBER 6

RON HAYDOCK
editor

PAUL BLAISDELL
managing editor

JIM HARMON
associate editor

BOB BURNS
research editor

LARRY BYRD
contributing editor

MAD MUMMY
crumbling editor

CREDITS & ACKNOWLEDGE-MENTS: Art: Ron Haydock, Gumby S. Brown, Kathy Byrnz, Lon Chaney Jr. Columbia Pix, Roger Corman, Dynamo, TV, Maxwell Gaines, Marty Holmers, Joan Haydock, Jack Hafner, Alan Barbour, Bill Kramer, Del Levitt, Bill Morris, George Pandora, Ray Smith, David Soorak, Dick Sheppard, Universal Pix, Frank Wee, Public Relations.

VOLUME 1, NUMBER 6, FANTASTIC MONSTERS OF THE FILMS, PRICE 35c PER COPY. Published bi-monthly by Black Shield Publications Inc. Mailing address: Post Office Box 181, Torrance, California. National Advertising Representatives: Master Company, 883 North Fairfax, Los Angeles 46, California. Contents Copyright 1963 by Black Shield Publications Inc. Nothing may be reprinted in whole or in part without written permission. Printed in U.S.A. Unsolicited manuscripts must be accompanied by stamped self-addressed envelopes. The publisher accepts no responsibility for their return. Any similarity between people and photos involved in the fiction and non-fiction in this magazine and any real people and places is purely coincidental.

TABLE OF CONTENTS

NEXT ISSUE—THE WINNERS OF FANTASTIC MONSTERS-GOLDEN EAGLE FILMS' NAME THE NAMELESS MONSTER CONTEST! ARE YOU ONE OF THE LUCKY 51 WINNERS? FIND OUT IN FANTASTIC MONSTERS No. 7!

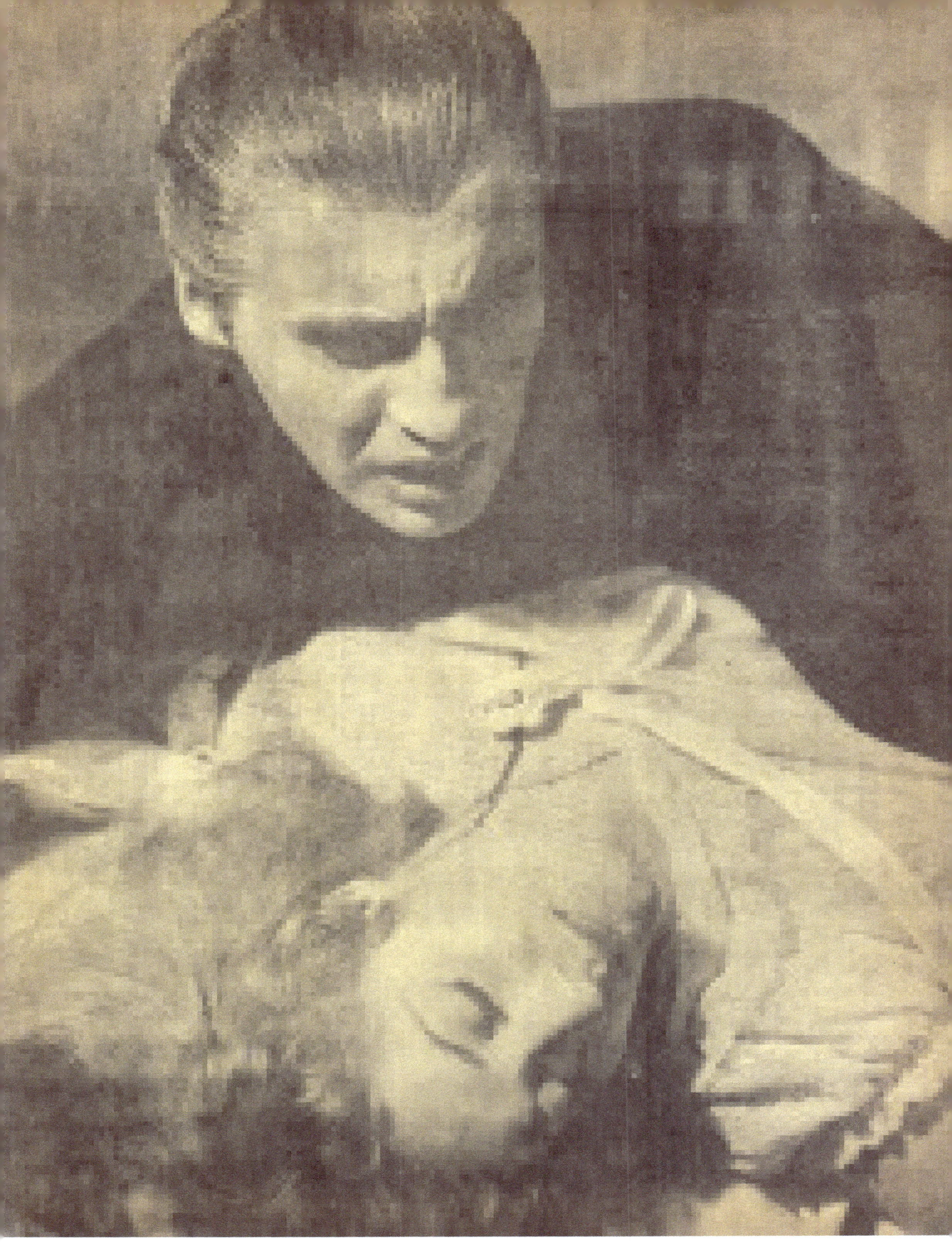

HORROR OF DRACULA

by Vincent Lewis

5 Years ago Hammer Films of England unearthed a Count Dracula more Horrendous than any other Screen Vampire in the History of Horror Films —Reviewed by Vincent Lewis

I remember switching on my radio in early summer, 1958, and hearing a maniacal announcer in an echo chamber screaming at the top of his voice. What he was screaming was this:

"It's all new! . . . the great all-time shock story by Bram Stoker! . . . HORROR OF DRACULA! . . . the story of the terrifying lover who died—yet lived! . . . and of the women who, one by one, became the grisly dead-alive brides of Dracula! . . . HORROR OF DRACULA! . . . starring Peter Cushing, Michael Gough — with Christopher Lee as the blood-lusting Dracula! . . . HORROR OF DRACULA! . . . the unforgettable story of Count Dracula—who has been rising every night for 500 years from his coffin-bed—silently to seek the warm blood he needs to keep himself alive—and to turn each of his victims into a human vampire! . . . HORROR OF DRACULA! . . . but don't dare see it alone—the chill of the tomb won't leave your blood for hours! . . . HORROR OF DRACULA! . . . in Technicolor!"

Shades of Bela Lugosi! I thought. An "all new" Dracula film! And in blood-curdling technicolor, too!

However, even after being frightened half to death by this "Shriek, Shudder and Shock" radio announcement, I admit I didn't rush right down to my favorite neighborhood theatre to see the film. It was during this period that I had practically given up all hope of ever again seeing a worthwhile horror movie. What with abominations like *Frankenstein's Daughter*, *The Giant Leeches*, and *I Was a Teenage Bloodbeast with Ivy League Electrodes* continually and persistently vomiting out of Hollywood, I decided it was safer (and cheaper) to stay at home watching the great old Universal horror films on TV's *Shock Theatre*.

Some weeks afterwards, though, after reading favorable reviews in trade papers, I took my life and money in hand and cautiously approached the box-office of the movie house running *Horror of Dracula*. I can happily report I stayed to see the film twice; and days later returned for another viewing—this time with a squad of friends. (I had convinced them there was at least one bright beacon shining in the fog-shrouded moors of horror movieland.)

The Hammer Dracula is one of the extremely few fantastic films released during the last decade that not only miraculously managed to live up to a horror film's typical "Chills and Thrills, Blood and Thunder" exploitation, but also turned out to be a remarkably entertaining—that is, terrifying — motion picture. Too, the film is a rare example of an excellent color horror flicker.

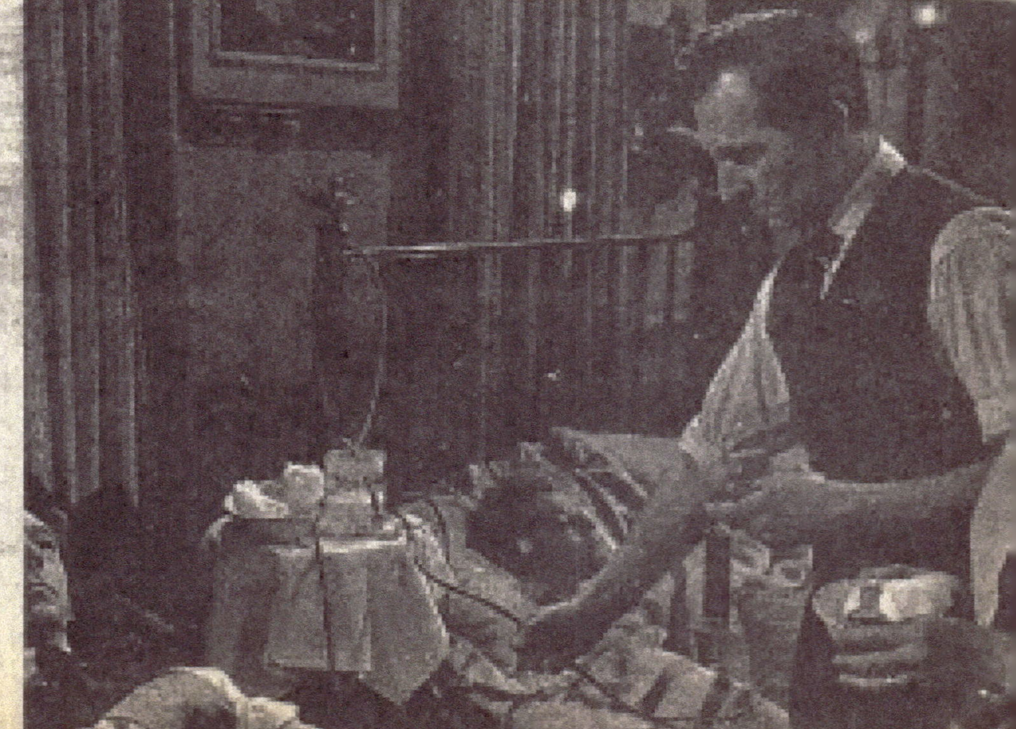

Peter Cushing supervises Michael Gough's blood transfusion to his wife, Melissa Stribling, after she has been bitten by Dracula

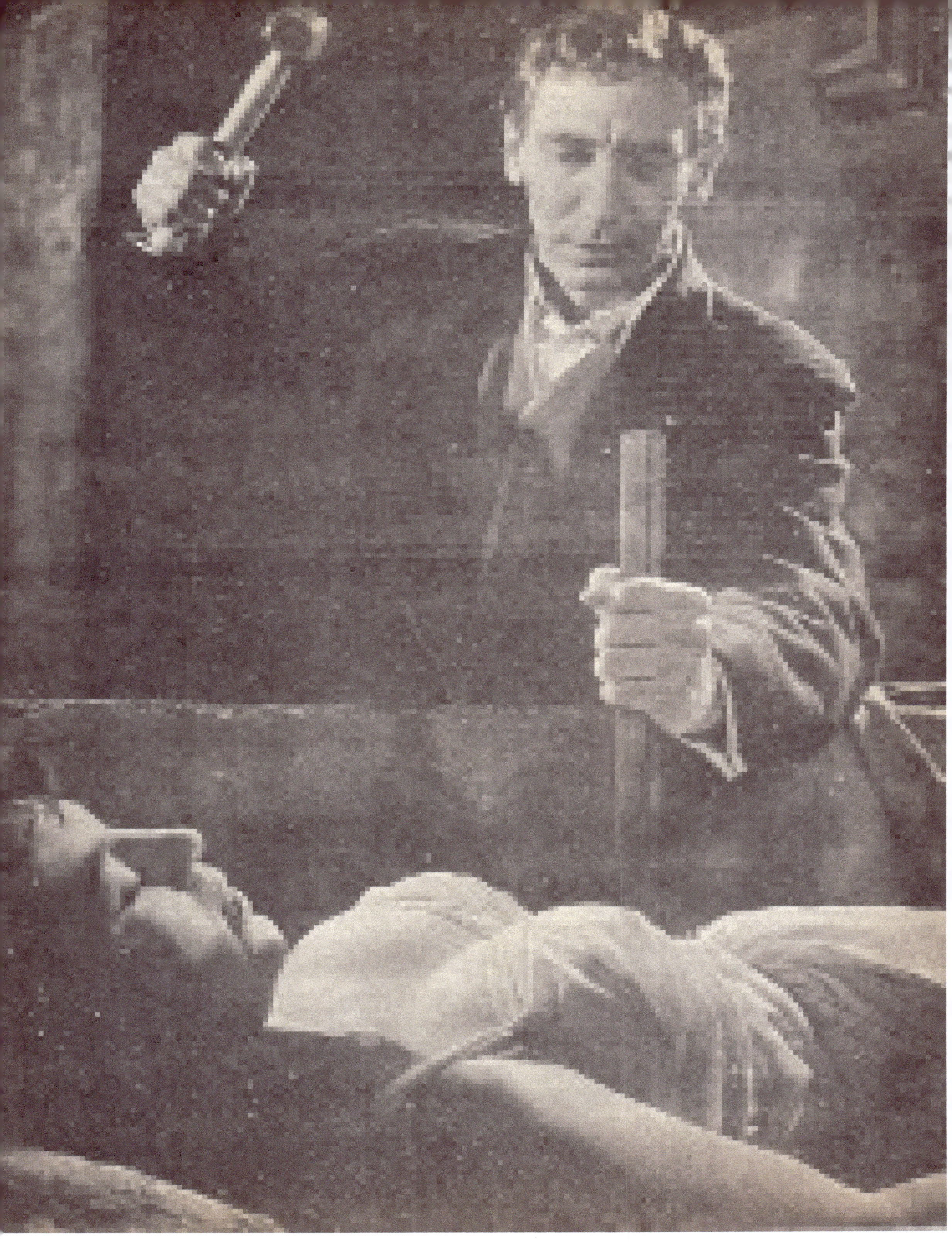

Hammer's vampire is, of course, a remake of the 1931 *Dracula* with Lugosi (which is a remake of the silent *Nosferatu*), but this reviewer joins the many others who contend the Hammer version is far superior to the Lugosi starrer. Actually, about the only thing the 1931 film holds over the 1958 release is the fact that it's the original talking Dracula.

I've screened the Lugosi film at least a half dozen times and still can't believe how dull and boring it is. This may have been the picture that brought Lugosi fame, but as a film it does not hold up over the years; unlike, for example, Karloff's *Bride of Frankenstein*, which is still as exciting as it was when originally released in 1935. On the other claw, this reviewer feels secure in predicting that 30 years from now, audiences will still be frightened out of their seats by Hammer's Dracula.

Jimmy Sangster's script and Terence Fisher's directing move the *Horror* story along at a furious pace, and, of course, the photography and art direction is much improved over the Universal "classic". Peter Cushing, the Movies' Modern Basil Rathbone, is a perfect Van Helsing, pursuing the infamous Dracula from one British graveyard to another; and the women in the cast include three of England's most glamorous actresses, Mellam Stribling, Carol Marsh, and Valerie Gaunt, who portrays the vampire woman.

Then there is Christopher Lee as Count Dracula . . .

I don't necessarily believe in vampires, but if such creatures do exist, they must certainly look and act as evil as Lee's Dracula. What a fiend! Some critics have already labelled his performance of the horrendous vampire man as classical as Karloff's *Frankenstein*, and I have to agree. In comparison to Lee's deathly sinister portrayal, Lugosi's Dracula is today not only completely out-dated but in many instances utterly ludicrous.

There is one scene in *Horror* that stands far out among all the rest; and the effect it had upon the audience must surely be likened to the classic reaction of audiences the world over when they first glimpsed Karloff in *Frankenstein*. This scene is, simply enough, a cut to Dracula's lurching face, his eyes blood-red, hating; mouth opened wide; lips pulled back over pointed yellow teeth stained crimson—easily one of the most effective and shocking cuts ever seen in the horror films. (The shot Mr Lewis refers to was reproduced in full color on the cover of FANTASTIC MONSTERS No. 1—ED.)

Two years later, in 1960, Hammer Films again delved into the Dracula legend, miscasting a blond vampire as the star of *Brides of Dracula* (Cushing, though, was once again Van Helsing). This sequel could in no way match the impact and shock of their first Dracula picture.

Hammer has gone on to bigger shock films since *Horror*, but unfortunately none have been any better. Of all the many fantastic films released within the last decade, only a handful are redeemable; and of these, *Horror of Dracula* is perhaps not only the best of the lot but also one of the all-time great terror productions.

And as for me, I'd sooner meet up with Bela Lugosi in a dark alley anytime—rather than take my chances with Christopher Lee as Dracula.

*

John Van Eyssen as Johnathan Harker puts a pointed end to vampire woman Valerie Gaunt

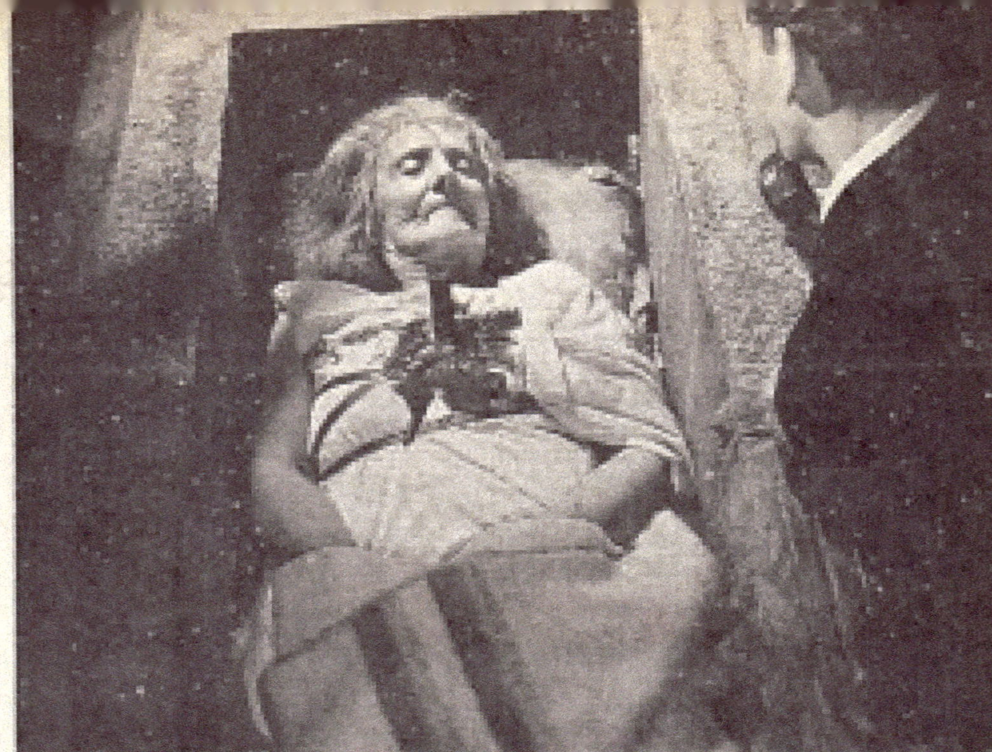

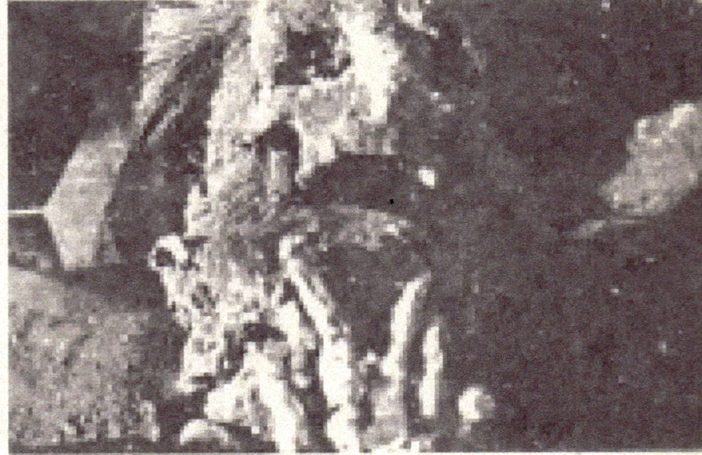

Above: Johnathan Harker drives a stake through the heart of one of Dracula's many deadline brides. Right: Affected by sunlight, the vampire man dies a hideous death. Below: Count Dracula meets his match

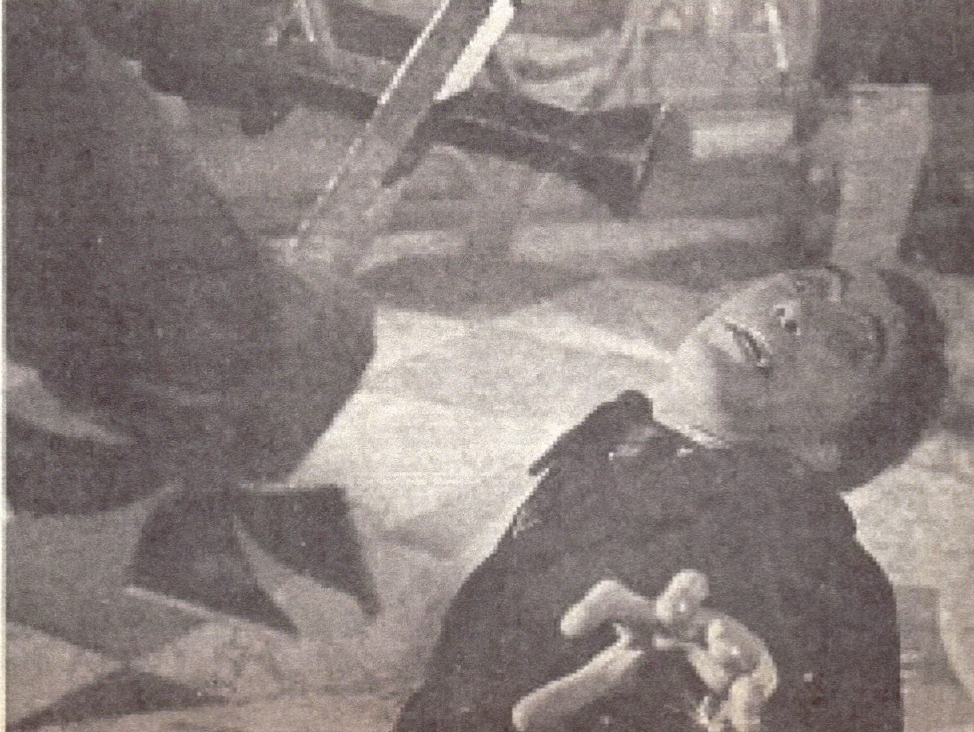

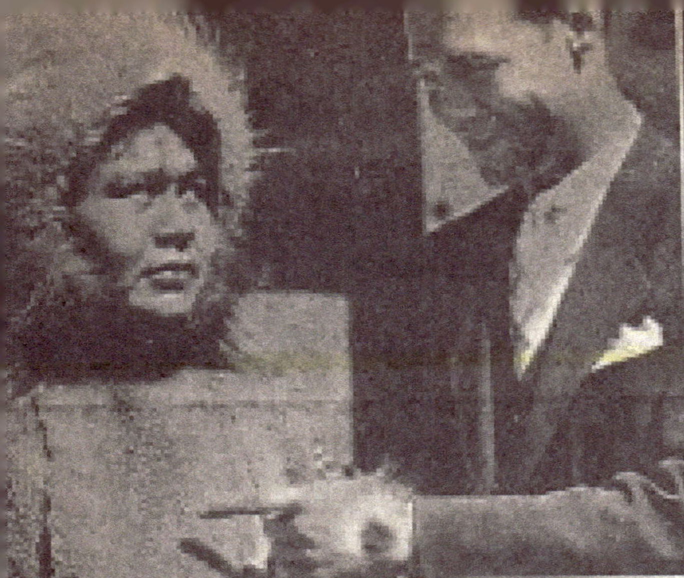

My name is Bibby. What's yours?

You slim guys don't know what it's like to wear one of those dad-ratted girdles!

Greetings . . . from . . . Uncle . . . Sam . . .

Dead Time Tales

Courtesy of the Brothers Grimm

You must have faith, George. Soupy Sales WILL be back on TV again.

Just one drop of Formula I with Formula 2 and—POOF—there goes perspiration!

[illegible caption]

[illegible caption]

[illegible caption]

[illegible caption]

[illegible caption]

[illegible caption]

THE INCREDIBLY STRANGE CREA

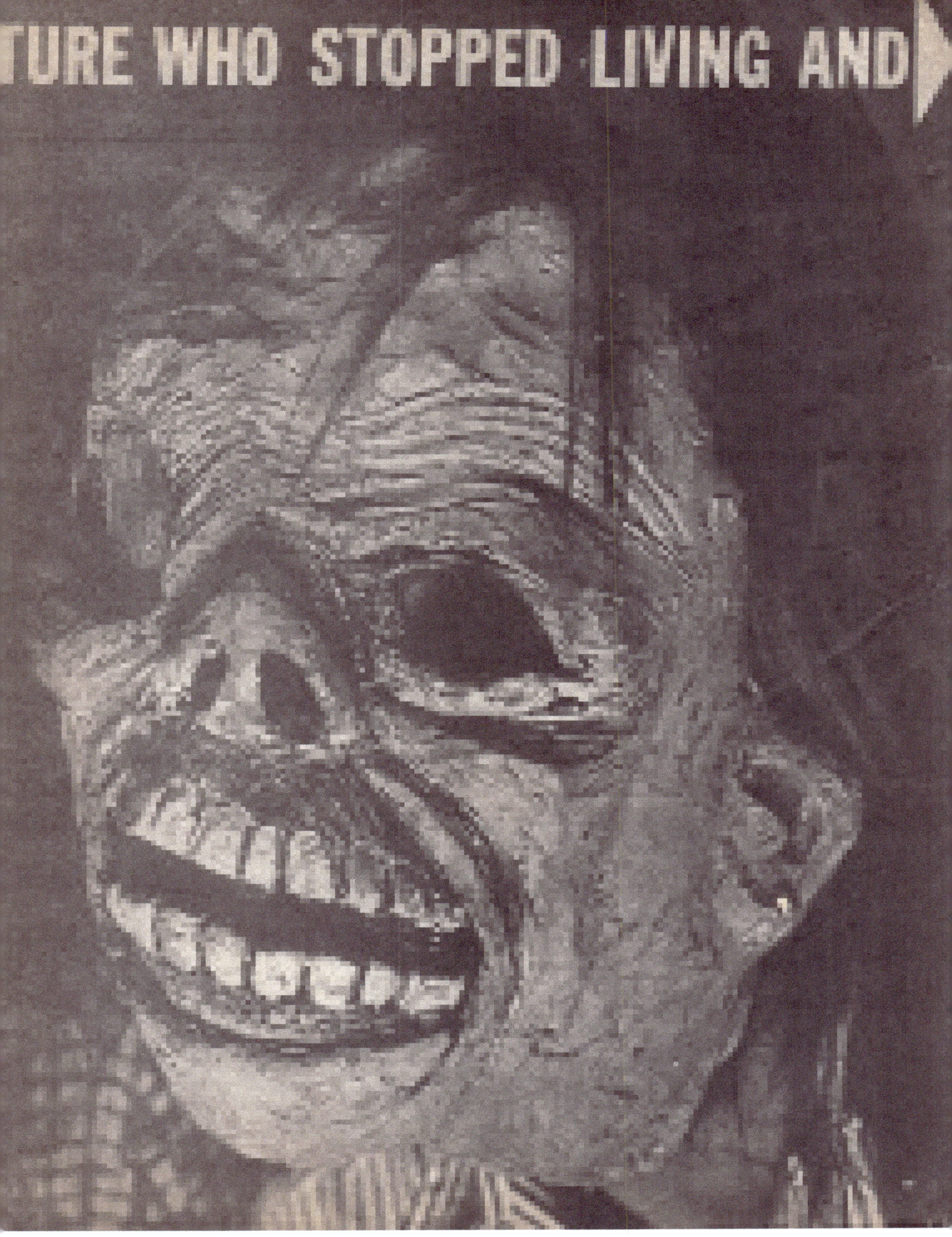

TURE WHO STOPPED LIVING AND

BECAME A CRAZY MIXED UP ZOMBIE by TITUS MOEDE

Jerry the zombie cuts into Marge's dance act

After breaking from their cage, the monsters start attacking everybody they see—even themselves

Look out Horror Fans—the crypt has been opened again and out of it has emerged one of the most terrifying pieces of psychological warfare ever launched against the human race.

The Incredibly Strange Creature Who Stopped Living And Became A Crazy Mixed Up zombie is due to invade the local theatres soon. This is a George J. Morgan-Ray Dennis Steckler production under the a b l e (twisted) direction of Steckler himself. Steckler, warped from early childhood, has been planning this mass assault on humanity for the last few years. Gathering two ex-trunk murderers, Gene Pollock and Robert Silliphant (brother of the creator of TV's *Route 66*), he had them adapt a screenplay from an original story by E.M. Kayke; then commissioned monster craftsman Tom Scherman to design and construct a set of special monster makeups for the film. This accomplished, Steckler set about evolving his insidious plan. Dragging the backpaths of cemeterys, he finally located a leading man—Cash Flagg, a lady killer in his own right. Cash shortly showed up for shooting with his first victim, Carolyn Brandt. And soon, other faces were seen haunting the set.

The Incredibly Strange Creature revolves around the demented antics of a fortune teller named Estrella (Brett O'Hara). Estrella, who has more complexes than Marquis De Sade, and a face that could only lead to a foundling home, derives her kicks from pouring acid in the faces of her reluctant boyfriends.

Marge (Carolyn Brandt), a dancer at a local club, stumbles into Estrella's tent at a sideshow for a quick peek into the future. She gets a long look at Estrella's experiments, though. Panicked, Marge flees; leaving her purse behind. Not one to miss an opportunity for playing a practical joke, Estrella devises a plan to kill Marge. With the aid of her sister Carmelita (Erina Enyo) as bait, she lures a passing stranger—Jerry (Cash Flagg)—off the midway. She uses Jerry's weak mind, and hypnotism, and winds him up like a clock and sends him after Marge. Arriving at the nightclub, Jerry cuts into Marge's act —and also into her. He wakes the next morning with a headache and a convenient loss of memory, and later that afternoon visits his girlfriend Angie (Sharon Walsh) who he tries to strangle for an encore. But he fails miserably, and leaves. Driving in his car, he is made disturbingly aware of last night's events through a news broadcast. He returns to Carmelita's place to initiate his own form of the game Twenty Questions.

While he is enroute another problem develops. Stella (Toni Camel), who works in the girlie show with Carmelita, pays an ill-advised visit to Estrella. The seer, thinking Stella is getting wise, takes out her copy of "Medieval Tortures" by the late Machiavelli, into the already-boiling cauldron jumps our blissful young hero—and being painted like a retriever prepares to stage the last act of the Sabre Dance on Stella.

Finishing his knifing practice, Jerry returns to Estrella, who throws acid in his face and puts him in with the rest of her experiments. These "experiments" can be totally qualified as "monsters". They escape from their cage and conjure up a few sadistic pranks of their own—such as strangling Estrella, Carmelita, and a demented hunchback (Dan Russe). Having completed this, they devise a new game which they call "The Zombie Stomp".

But after a few more killings, the police arrive on the scene and dispatch the monsters as well as a few paying customers. Jerry, who now has become one of the acid clan, decides his presence is no longer needed, and slips out a back window into the night. Window-jumping becomes a popular sport as soon after half the remaining cast exits in pursuit of him.

There is a chase sequence that comes to a finish in an hilariously happy way: our hero gets nailed, his best friend gets his girl, and everyone in the theatre gets up to get popcorn . . . .

This is a picture not to miss. It's apt to kill you—as it did half the cast!

*

Jill Carson and friends

Robert Silliphant, Don Marquis, and Don Smiley wear monster makeup

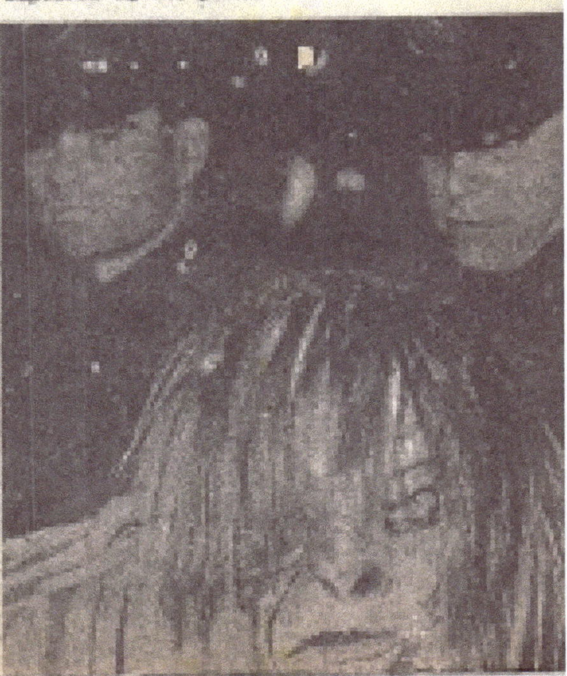

Captured by the police

This could be American-International's Most Important Horror Film Yet—Special Editorial by Ron Haydock

HAUNTED PALACE

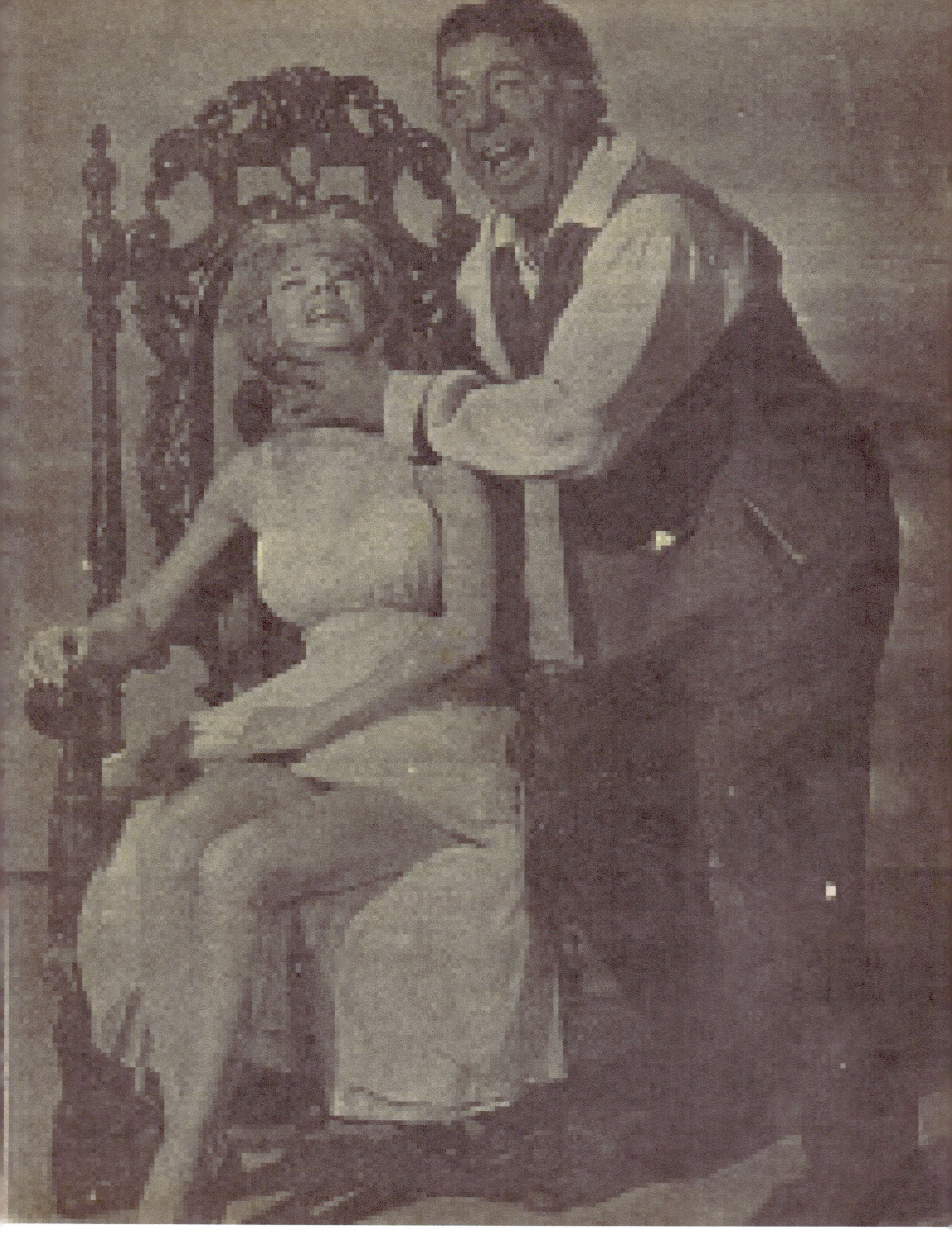

Today, some six or seven years later, the studio that once released such abominations as *Teenage Frankenstein* is producing films based on the classic works of Edgar Allan Poe, H.G. Wells, and Jules Verne. *The Premature Burial*, *Pit and the Pendulum*, *Master of the World*, *Poe's Tales of Terror* have already been screened; *Wells' When the Sleeper Wakes* is forthcoming.

In short, the studio has grown-up—considerably.

While there have been innumerable pros and cons voiced by serious students of horror films regarding the actual qualitative merits of recent AIP productions like *The Raven* and *House of Usher*, there is one indisputable fact that must be recognized and — more important — realized by everyone: American-International Pictures is the only major motion picture studio producing thrillers on any regular basis. Universal, Columbia, Allied Artists, and other film companies only occasionally release horror films today; and when they do, it's more than likely that the respective film is simply the product of an independent producer or, even more likely, the American release of a British or German or Japanese title.

In summation then, AIP is the studio we must look to for quality American horror and fantasy pictures today—and in the foreseeable future.

Their latest is *The Haunted Palace*, a color film based on the Poe poem of the same name and also H.P. Lovecraft's classic story "The Strange Case of Charles Dexter Ward." Vincent Price, Lon Chaney Jr, Debra Paget, and Frank Maxwell are the stars.

Briefly, *The Haunted Palace* is the story of a haunted village as well as a haunted palace with the terrifying spell emanating from the palace and cast over a whole village and its inhabitants. It is also the story of a man—or a warlock—a practitioner of the black magic of necromancy —whose curse haunts an entire community for a century after he is burnt alive by an enraged mob for his occult work.

One hundred years later, the descendant of the warlock returns to the scene of the curse where his body is possessed by the evil ancestor. Mixed with the black magic of necromancy are strange mutant creatures and warlocks, plus typical shock elements such as return from the dead, revenge, diabolical torture, and human beings haunted by strange desires and even stranger fears.

And *The Haunted Palace* could very well be the most significant terror film AIP has yet produced.

I spent many hours (if not days) on the set—watching the shooting; talking with Vince, Lon, Debra, stillman Bill Creamer, director Roger Corman, publicity man Roy Smith, others; absorbing the atmosphere (and consequently choking on the thick clouds of synthetic fog belched out by the fog machine); gulping down the free coffee; and, in general, simply "sniffing around", as Bob Bloch would say. (and, since no one else will ever report it, I was on hand when Roger Corman phoned FANTASTIC MONSTERS to ask Paul

A human sacrifice to the monster than lurks in the pit. Below, left, Price is haunted by his evil ancestor depicted on the painting. Below, right, one of the many grisly mutant monsters from the black pit of horrors within the haunted palace

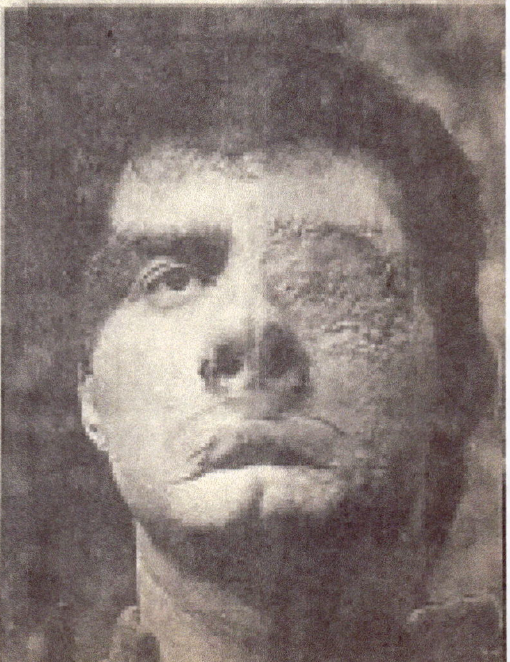

Price, Leo Gordon, and Chaney plan their next evil deed

Rehearsing the grand entrance scene

Blaisdell's knowledgeable assistance in ironing out some technical difficulties concerning the gruesome monster makeups seen in the film.)

However . . .

Everyone I talked to on the set had some comment to make about the film. "It's going to be a good one," said Vincent Price. "Our biggest," said Roy Smith with a confident nod. "In order of their importance, I would say Palace, The Raven, and The Terror in 1963," said Roger Corman.

And this writer will say that Palace is AIP's best film to date.

This is not to suggest that the film is by any means a perfect horror production. There are flaws in direction, lighting, other areas. But, on the other hand, these same flaws are existent to some degree in nearly every motion picture ever made, though Citizen Kane may be an exception. This writer also strongly doubts that the Palace will go down in film history as another Bride of Frankenstein, Invisible Man, or Wolf Man, or that the picture is the "best" AIP is capable of producing. All the above statement means to imply is that here for once is a brand-new horror film with a good script (by Charles Beaumont), treated for the most part in deadly seriousness; with competent acting and direction, and with talent-casting and production that more than faintly harkens back to those old (and great) Universal pictures of the 1930s and early '40s. And—unlike so very many thrillers of these times, both from AIP and others—The Haunted Palace should prove to be a frighteningly enjoyable film to see.

One of its merits is that a "handsome young Pretty Boy" has not been awkwardly cast in any of the lead roles. The stars and character actors are professionals who have been around for years, who know their business, who can act when called upon to do so, and who have that magical gift called screen presence. In all fairness to Hollywood's young talent, though, there are two comparatively unknown actresses cast in secondary roles who handle their parts with believability — which is something that most of today's young "stars" cannot seem to satisfactorily accomplish for any theatregoer who possesses critical faculties even one iota above those of an amoeba's.

And if you're a fan of the older and much-loved films like the Frankenstein series—and who isn't?—you're going to get a genuine kick out of seeing the AIP descendants of the torch-wielding Universal villagers rushing to storm the haunted palace and destroy the evils that dwell within.

The film is a step forward in the right direction—to when major studios and independent producers will be earnestly trying to make better and better films. The Haunted Palace isn't a GREAT BIG STEP, but at least AIP president James Nicholson and vice-president Sam Z. Arkoff have kicked off the tasteless blue suede shoes worn by that teenage werewolf, and have slipped their feet into a pair of wedding boots.

The Haunted Palace seems to be their most encouraging catch yet.

*

Reading from "The Necronomicon" at the opening of the program.

John Burke, Television Terror and Master of Make-up hosts WSUN-TV's Late-night Horror Show as . . .

THE OUTSIDER

by Larry M. Byrd

The room is silent; the only light visible is that which radiates from a television set. On the glowing screen can be seen a deserted graveyard—with tree branches swaying in the breeze to the sound of lonely rain drops giving way to a moaning wind; and in the background the haunting strains of "The Sick Rose" provide an eerie dancing melody for the swaying branches and moss. A lone figure makes his way through the graveyard carrying a lantern, saying, *"I ride with the nightwind and sleep within the catacombs of Pephren-Ka. I know the dark side of the moon . . . I am THE OUTSIDER!"*

This eerie beginning marks the opening of another Friday night for thousands of TV viewers, both young and old, in the Tampa-St. Petersburg, Florida, viewing area. This program, *Nightmare Theatre*, is a great deal different than *Shock Theatre* or similar shows seen by nearly every horror movie enthusiast from coast to coast. *Nightmare Theatre* is handled with expert care by expert technicians, who treat the classic horror film screenings as the incredible tales of the nether world they are rather than as laughable and ridiculous fairy tales.

Heading the crew of WSUN-TV monster makers is John Burke, the talented host of the show. Burke has been a horror buff and make-up enthusiast for as long as he can remember, doing incredible make-up for numerous stage and TV productions in years past. This interest shows in his work, which ranks alongside the accomplishments of the greatest of make-up magicians. He's also the father of four intelligent and attractive children, who consider Daddy a remarkable story teller—whether he's weaving a tale of chills for his viewing audience, or simply reading them a bedtime story.

You might expect John to give you a cold slimy paw for a handshake, or sneak up on you with a hearty "Boo!" when your back is turned, but you couldn't be farther from the truth. You'll be relieved and pleasantly surprised to find that he's as tame and mild a man as ever walked the face of the earth. In his spare time John can be found with a little-known green thumb in his tremendous rock garden, of which he is justifiably proud. All in all, an unusually surprising man to be scaring the wits out of a sizable group of late nite television viewers.

The show, which runs old horror films, makes for exciting viewing. When the time comes for a break, you're not suddenly jolted by a blasting pain reliever commercial or a tasteless bid for an underarm deodorant that "isn't a sticky roll-on". No, instead you're led painlessly and effortlessly into the commercial message by a cleverly planned "bridge". During the showing of *Hunchback Of Notre Dame*, for example, break time came while Quasimodo was scaling the walls of the huge cathedral. The crew switched to John in hunchback make-up and also climbing cathedral walls, built specially for this break by the WSUN-TV technicians. John, then cleverly led into the commercial and back into the film itself. When the commercial was through, you hardly

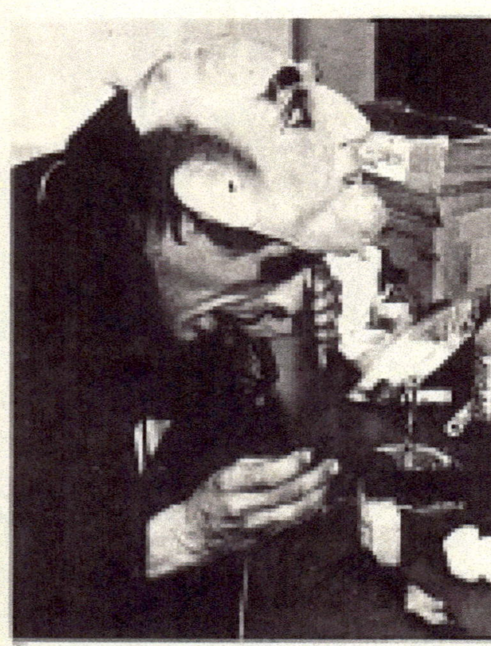

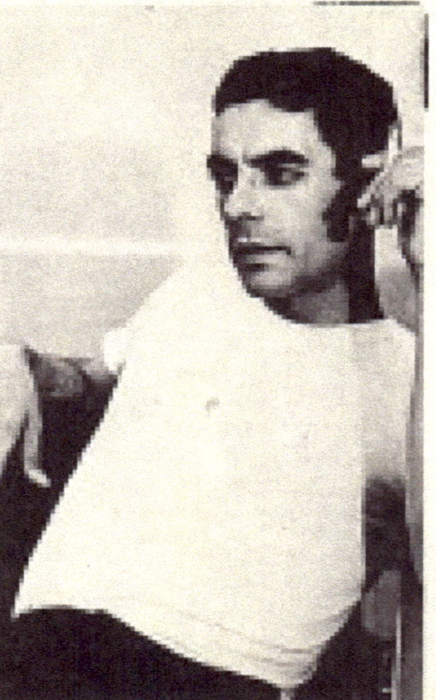

Because all shows are 'live' and very quick character changes are necessary, John Burke always keeps his first makeup change under The Outsider mask. Here John is applying the finishing touches for a psycho part for Boris Karloff's BEDLAM. At left, John Burke, the Terror of Tampa, during a brief break after a rundown on the night's show.

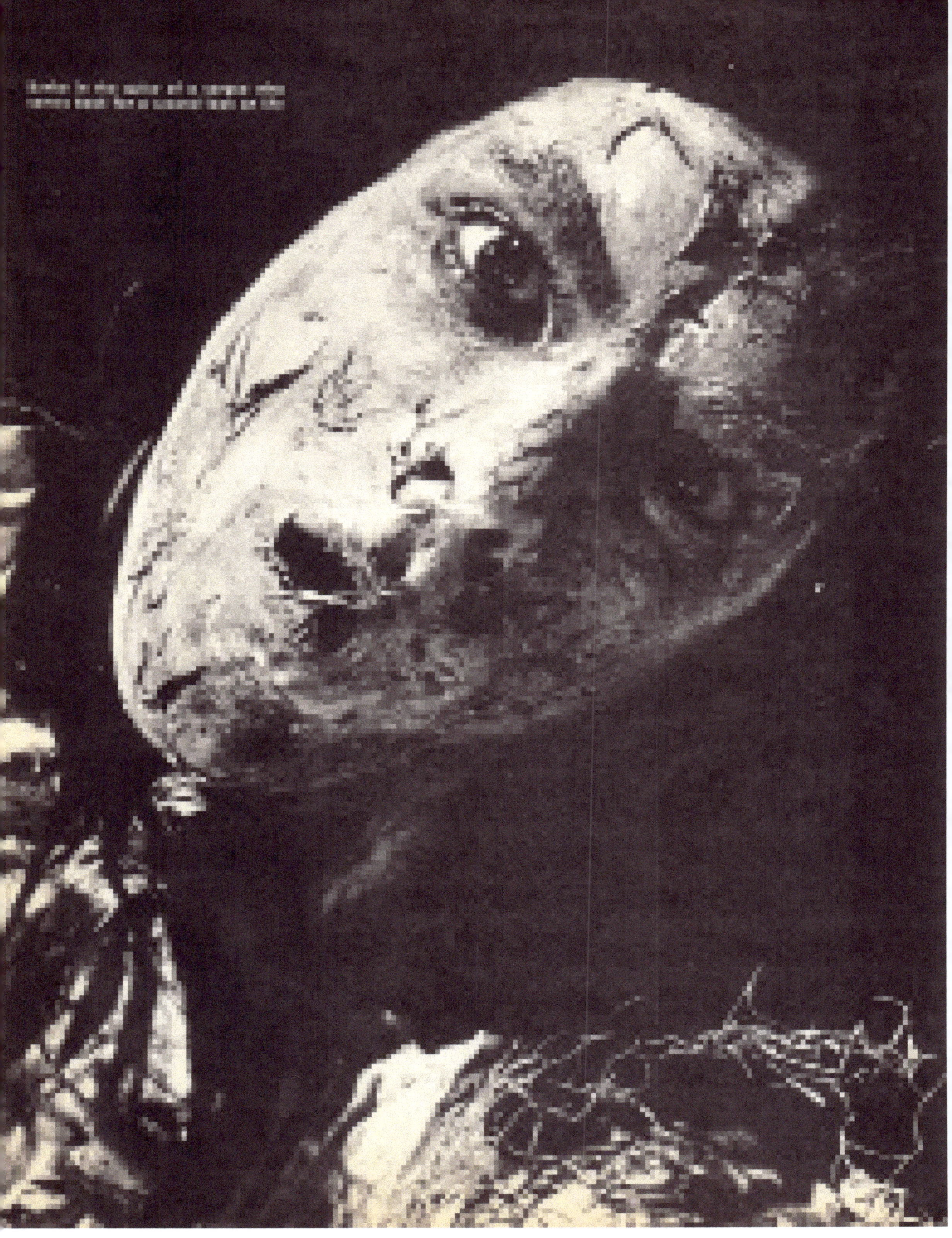

realized that you had not been watching the film all along. Other shows have attempted this, but none have come quite so close to perfection as John Burke's *Nightmare Theatre*.

John explains that he originated the show and its host over a year ago, taking his name and a great deal of the text from a short story titled "The Outsider" by the late master of horror-fiction, Howard Phillips Lovecraft. As an example: when the Outsider makes his entrance he approaches a crypt, kneels, and pushes back the stone lid. As it falls, a thunderclap is heard. He then pushes aside a bony arm and removes a huge dusty volume titled *The Necronomicon*. Speaking directly to the book Burke says, "Deep within the dusty crypt the eldritch hands of the mad Abdul Alhazred clutch the dread *Necronomicon*, so ancient it was old ere Babylon was new. In your curious pages monstrous secrets lie." He then turns the pages and depending on the film slated for that evening's viewing, continues. If, for instance, the film was *The Legend Of Sleepy Hollow*, The Outsider would go on with his narrative with, "Ah there . . . Sleepy Hollow, a strange little valley nestled among the hills . . ." and the scene would fade into the film itself. In this way, John is able to set the mood and give a little background before the film itself begins.

When the movie comes to a close, the graveyard comes back into view. The Outsider ends the story himself, always leaving some measure of doubt in the minds of the viewers as to the actual outcome. Again using the Sleepy Hollow picture as an example, The Outsider would close with: "And they lived happily ever after. Our story ends as all good fairy tales must, but is it a fairy tale after all? And did they live happily ever after? . . . I wonder. Once the shadows of the dark world have been called forth, they continue to walk the nightside, seeking . . . ever seeking. And beware to him that first disturbed their restless slumber . . ."

A wolf howls in the foggy distance as the Outsider turns, puts the book and the stone lid in place, picks up his lantern and turns to face the viewer . . . "You there, beyond the wall of sleep . . . take heed!" He turns and slowly limps off into the distance with the wind and night noises howling behind him, leaving his viewers to sleep in peace . . . or at least try!

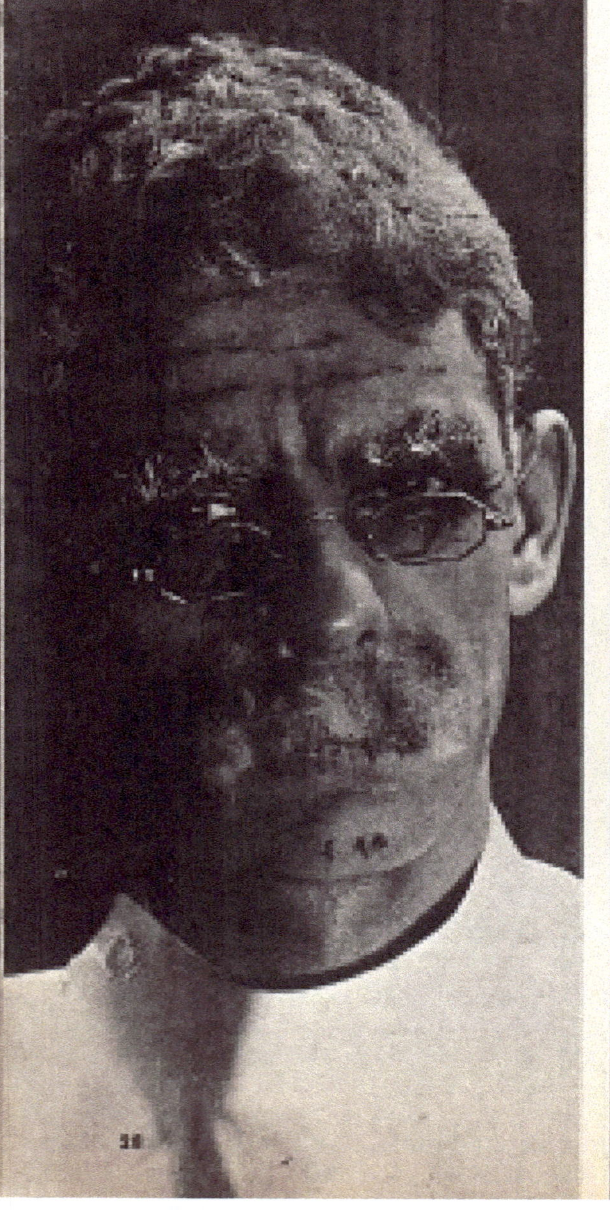

There's always clowning at rehearsals. Here The Outsider scares the hair straight up on cameraman Frank Moglia. Below, The old faithful, "a mad doctor", is one of the many roles Burke portrays on his highly acclaimed TV show. At right, This Chinese Mandarin is actually Burke

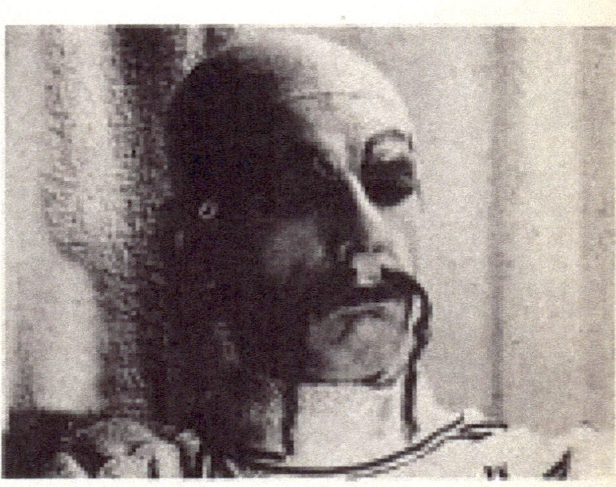

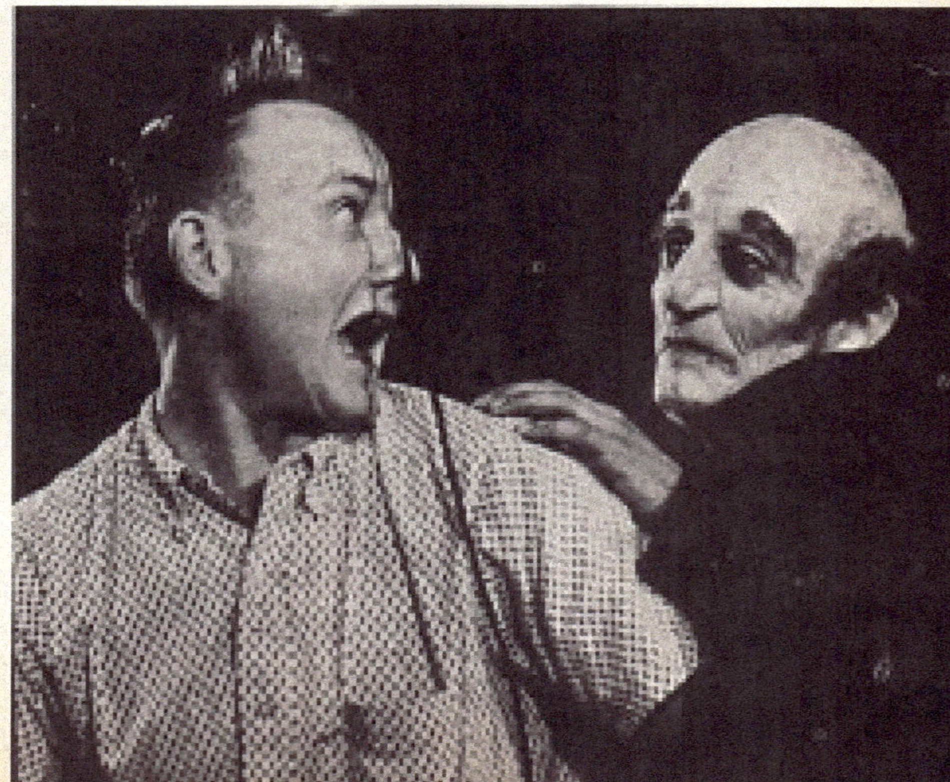

HORROR RECORDS

Here's a list of horror records your readers can buy at their local record shop.

OUT OF THIS WORLD by Dave Barry, HOUSE OF HORRORS by Merv Griffin, THE HORROR SHOW by Sharkey Todd, CHA CHA WITH ZOMBIES by The Upperclassmen, THE FANG by Nervous Norvus, TRANSYLVANIA by the Mysterians, BEAUTY AND THE BEAST by Danny Davis, THE PROWLER by The Idols, FLYING SAUCER GOES WEST by Buchman & Goodman, MAD MARTIAN PINSTRIPPER by Jerry Madison, and THE COOL GHOUL by Sharkey Todd.

Jerry Ayers
Louisville, Ky.

Also available is GWENDOLYN AND THE WEREWOLF by Hutch Davies, and BE-BOP-A-JEAN by Ron Haydock & The Boppers on the Cha-Cha label—Ed.

SHADOW MAN

"Who knows what evil lurks in the hearts of men? THE SHADOW knows! Heh-heh-heh-heh!"

With these words, The Shadow returned to the airwaves of the CBS radio station in St. Louis, Missouri, KMOX, at 6:35 Sunday evening, Jan. 13, 1963.

"The Shadow, Lamont Cranston, a man of wealth, student of science and a master of other peoples' minds, devoted his life to righting wrong, protecting the innocent and punishing the guilty. Using advance methods that may ultimately become available to all law enforcement agencies, Cranston is known as THE SHADOW! Never seen, only heard. As haunting to superstitious minds as a ghost. As inevitable as a guilty conscience."

As an introduction it's not bad, but I still prefer the old one. It went something like this. ". . . Lamont Cranston, who long ago in the Orient learned an amazing secret. The power to cloud mens' minds so that they could not see him."

Maybe the writers felt that they needed a more realistic approach to hold an audience who had never heard of the Shadow. Yet I feel that there is too much emphasis on realism. So much so that it is even invading escapist media. We listen to programs to escape from reality. We don't need to be convinced that such a person might really exist.

As I sat there and listened to the program progress, I was a little disappointed. Had I too been affected by an age of cynicism and sarcasm? Maybe as a small boy I wasn't as skeptical and as eager to reject as I am now. I could not help but lose my childhood, but did I also lose my sense of wonder?

Then I heard his laugh! That laugh that used to send shivers down my spine. I could feel the hairs on the back of my head start to bristle. It was the same identical laugh that the Shadow had used so long ago. I leaned back and smiled, content in the knowledge that I still had the gift of imagination.

Add to I Love a Mystery covered in FANTASTIC MONSTERS, The Shadow, as another giant of the Golden Age of Radio.

Jack Cascio
Naperville, Ill.

No sooner requested than done, Jack. There's a Shadow article in this issue. We hope that you and the million other Shadow fans enjoy it.—Ed.

SPECIAL REQUEST DEPT

Will you print my picture in FANTASTIC MONSTERS?

Fred Chodkowski
Torance, Calif.

Well . . . okay—Ed.

SATISFIED READER

You have been getting letters telling how perfect your mag is. They are saying how intelligent your articles are, how many unused pictures you have (Ha!!! That's a laugh!) And one such writer stated that you were the first monster mag to have colored covers. Again I am forced into laughing for you weren't the first! And why are all your articles written by your staff? Do Ray Harryhausen, Boris Karloff, Bert Gordon, etc, think you're contaminated? Let's face it—you aren't the best monster mag in the world!

Bill Moreing
Atherton, Calif.

You're being unfair, Bill. While it's true that most of the material to appear in FANTASTIC MONSTERS is staff-written, it's also true that we have brought our readers articles by stars like Vincent Price and Kirk Alyn; film producers like Alex Gordon; movie historians like Richard Lupoff, Don Sheppard, Richard Kyle, Paul Severn, Douglas Hinley, Don Gilbert, Larry Byrd, others; fiction from recognized authors like Jim Harmon and Robert Bloch. And we have many more "guest writers" scheduled for future issues, including some of the biggest names in the motion picture industry. If you'll take the trouble to check "Ghoul Call" in past numbers, you'll find that the letter writer who stated FANTASTIC MONSTERS was the first fantasy film publication to use "colored covers" was referring to the indisputable fact that FanMo was the first indeed to use actual color PHOTOS of monsters for covers and not PAINTINGS. But you're right, Bill—we aren't "the best monster mag in the world" nor do we claim to be. All we (humbly) state is that "FANTASTIC MONSTERS is the GREATEST Monster Magazine in the World!"—Ed.

HOW-TO FAN

I really enjoyed Don Sheppard's HOW TO MAKE A FRANKENSTEIN MONSTER in FANTASTIC MONSTERS #3. I hope you are planning to run articles on How-to-make other horror movie monsters like the Wolf Man, Creature from the Black Lagoon, and others.

John Copeland
Ogden, Utah

Wait'll you read HOW TO MAKE A MUMMY in a future FanMo! WOW!—Ed.

MISPLACED APE-ZINE

I have followed all of your interesting issues right from the start, but I have one BIG complaint. In #3 you did not list ALL of the important Edgar Rice Burroughs fanzines. We have published 45 issues of Norb's Notes which is more issues THAN ALL OF THE FOUR YOU NAMED ON PAGE 64 have published in a COMBINED EFFORT. Also, our total mailing list is as large as any of theirs. We also publish Cinema, Comics & Collecting, which is also devoted in part to Edgar Rice Burroughs and Tarzan. However, we also include Flash Gordon, Buck Rogers, et al. If anyone is interested have them write for details or they may send a buck donation for the CC&C Yearbook (40 pages). Thank you.

Charles Reinsel
120 Eighth Ave
Clarion, Pa

Y'r welcome—Ed.

PRICELESS ARTICLE

In FANTASTIC MONSTERS #4 Mr Vincent Price wrote an article defending horror films. A similar article by Mr Price appeared in Look Magazine (Apr 23, 1963). I wish to salute Mr Price for his fine opinions. I sincerely believe horror films are much more satisfying, enjoyable, and much better for a person's character than the degrading, sick, worn-out movies released these days. And it is my opinion that the "splendid personages" who review movies for newspapers and magazines are out of their cotton-pickin' minds! They give good horror films tremendously unfair write-ups, and they give good write-ups for the SICK movies!

Jerry Younkin
Grosse Pointe, Mich

PARENT PROBLEMS

I like your magazine very much even though I am a girl and I am only ten years old. My mother and my father both yell at me because I read your magazine. They say it is junk. But I like to learn how monsters are made. I've always been interested in any kind of monsters. My girl friend likes them too, and we both get yelled at. But we just keep on reading and watching the monster movies on TV. Everytime I go to watch one on TV my mother keeps yelling at me and says I'm stupid for watching them. So then I move closer to the TV so I can hear it, and then my father yells. He says I will ruin my eyes. But I like them very much. And I will keep reading your wonderful magazine no matter what the zirk in school say or anything.

Elaine Ann Hendershot
Dover, N.J.

Perhaps you can convince your mother and father about monster films by showing them Vincent Price's article IN DEFENSE OF HORROR FILMS in our fourth issue, Elaine. If you do, please let us know what happens—Ed.

NOT TO BE CONTINUED

I think Manuel Moese's suggestion (GHOUL CALL, FANMO #3 on running a chapter of a serial per issue is all wet and here's why: FANMO is published six times a year and most serials run from ten to 15 chapters. By Manuel's method, reviewing a twelve chapter serial would take 2½ YEARS! This would be, of course, much too long, so keep everything the way it is. And how about having the Mad Mummy review the Captain America serial? I'd like to see the 2,000 year old humor of MM thrown on this great serial here.

Dave Bibby
Verona, N.J.

As soon as we can locate the Crumbling Kharis, we'll see what we can do about getting him acquainted with Captain America. But until he shows up—until he can escape from his captors (see special MM page in this issue)—we'll all have to wait for the historic American meeting—Ed.

MONSTERS ON PARADE

There are quite a few macabre and fantasy films coming up, so here goes: Boris Karloff next is LADY OF THE SHADOWS which will probably be released following his long over-due DOCTOR OF SEVEN DIALS co-starring Chris Lee as a graverobber. THE BAD FLOWER is a vampire tale from Korea. THE DEVIL'S CASTLE is a Turkish release resembling BLUEBEARD. Two spots once occupied by Chaney Sr are being taken over by the undead in VAMPIRE OF THE OPERA and THE VAMPIRE OF NOTRE DAME. Devil worshippers and cannibals terrorize England in THE HELL FIRE CLUB. THE CREATURE FROM THE BLACK LAGOON is satirized in THE CREATURE FROM HIGHGATE POND. Tor Johnson plays an atomic monster in BEAST OF YUCCA FLATS. In ATOM AGE VAMPIRE a doctor resorts to grisly means to repair the face of a horribly mutilated girl. And the silent DR MABUSE series faces a comeback in DEVILISH DR MABUSE, INVISIBLE DR MABUSE, THOUSAND EYES OF DR MABUSE and IN THE STEEL NET OF DR MABUSE.

David Szurek
Detroit, Mich

Karloff's LADY OF THE SHADOWS film has been retitled. It is now called THE TERROR. Ye Editor was consulted on the title change by producer Roger Corman—Ed.

QUICKIES

I bought FANMO #1 and #2 but soon tore them in half, and burned them.

Eddie Christofferson
Olympia, Wash

Sheppard's HOW TO MAKE A FRANKENSTEIN MONSTER in #3 talked me out of wanting to have the "joy" of being a movieland monster.

Terry Baark
Lancaster, Pa

Why do you ruin the mag by putting in all the crummy, stinky, junky space stories?

Robert Barnes
Miami, Fla

MASTER MAGICIANS OF MOVIELAND in #3 was very interesting. I never tire of seeing candid photos of horror producers and stars.

John Mullet
Bontoul, Ill

I want to marry the Mad Mummy. Other girls may have husbands who are plumbers, welders, and what-not, but I'd have the only husband who is a Mummy!

Judy Bohadlo
Brookfield, Ill

Boy Karloff is lost—Haunted by a beckoning She-Ghost...in a new Technicolor Thriller from Roger Corman's Filmgroup

THE TERROR

THE COMPLETE BELA LUGOSI

Today, more than Six Years after his death, the man who is called Champion of the Undead has a larger following of Fans than at any time during his 37 Year Long Motion Picture Career. FAMOUS MONSTERS presents the First Published Listing of Bela Lugosi's Screen Appearances—Compiled by BILL OBBAGY

Karloff and Lugosi in Edgar Allan
Poe's THE RAVEN

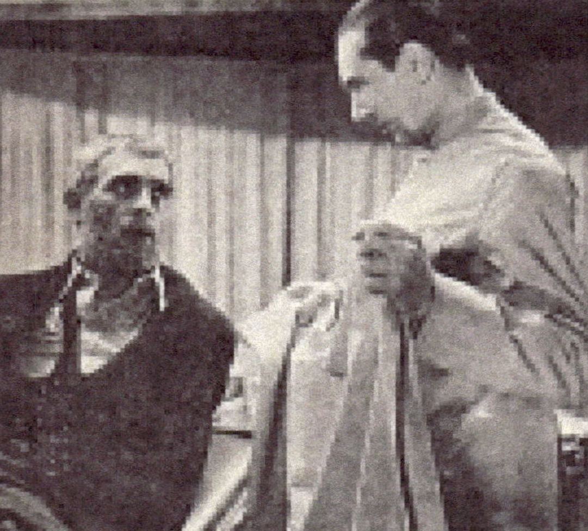

On the set of SON OF FRANKEN-
STEIN

Lugosi in his one-time appearance as
the Frankenstein Monster, seen here
with Lon Chaney Jr

NOW YOU CAN HEAR THESE TERROR-TALES!

Horror beyond imagination!

A study in terrifying evil!

You've heard of records in a humorous vein? — Well, this album can only be called HORROR IN A JUGULAR VEIN. A frightening narration from the stories of the old master of horror himself — Edgar Allan Poe. "THE PIT AND THE PENDULUM" is tough enough on your nerves, but wait until you hear "THE TELLTALE HEART!" #M-36 — ONLY $1.98

ALL 12" LP RECORDS
ALL 33 RPM

A COMPLETE COLLECTION OF THE MACABRE

A CLASSIC OF HORROR spoaken from the heart (with the right kind of background music, of corpse). The idea of hearing this narrative in your own home is enough to scare you out of your wits! Put the lights out and have your blood curdled by the tale of THE BLACK CAT, written by Edgar Allan Poe. It's HORRIFIC! #M-37 — ONLY $2.98

ALL 12" LP RECORDS
ALL 33 RPM

CLASSIC TALES OF TERROR to make you shiver in your boots. Be prepared for streaming suspense and maniacal action when you listen to these spine-tingling, chilling narrations penned by the master of the macabre, Edgar Allan Poe. "MASQUE OF THE RED DEATH" and "THE PREMATURE BURIAL" are among his best and most terrifying tales. #M-38 — ONLY $2.98 ★

PERFECT FOR EERIE MIDNIGHT GHOUL PARTIES

HOUSE OF FRIGHT—

A grim, ghostly, spine-chilling, nerve-wracking tale of horror that will leave you with lingering fright, written by the all time master of thriller-chillers—Edgar Allan Poe. You will remember "THE HOUSE OF USHER" (his most famous tale) with shuddering fear every time you're alone in a dark house or on a deserted street! #M39—ONLY $2.98

★ Narrated by Richard Taylor

RUSH YOUR ORDER NOW   CLIP THIS COUPON   USE AS ORDER BLANK   MAIL TODAY!

Please Rush Me The Following Long-Playing Albums: NO C.O.D.'s

- ☐ NIGHTMARE —— $1.98 Plus 25¢ Postage and Handling
- ☐ HORROR —— $2.98 Plus 25¢ Postage and Handling
- ☐ TERROR —— $2.98 Plus 25¢ Postage and Handling
- ☐ FRIGHT —— $4.98 Plus 25¢ Postage and Handling

I Enclose $ .... ☐ CASH ☐ CHECK ☐ MONEY ORDER

RANDOM RECORDS, C/o Black Shield
P.O. BOX 141 • TOPANGA, CALIFORNIA

NAME .... AGE ....

ADDRESS ....

CITY .... ZONE .... STATE ....

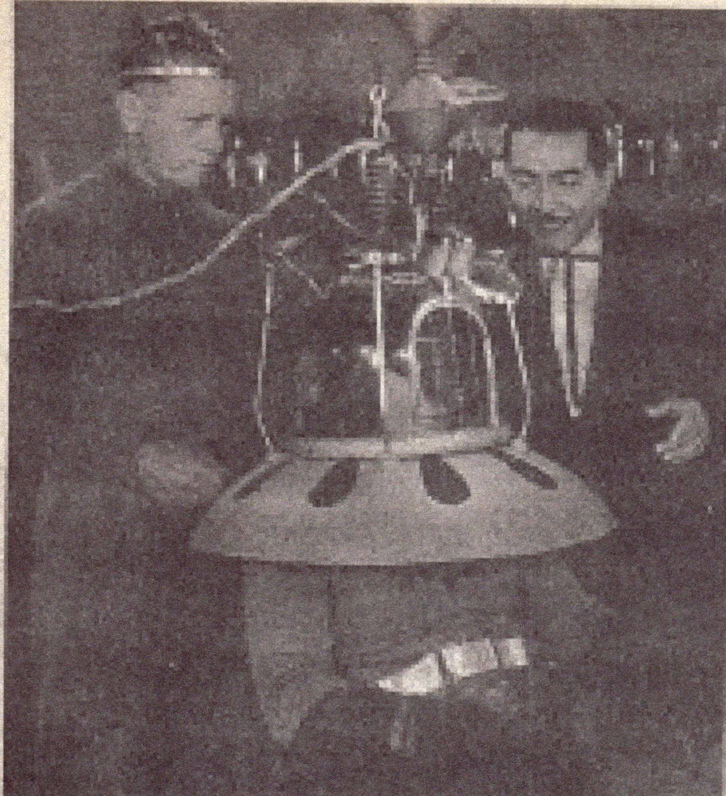

News of the Latest Horror Films and Facts about a Great New Screen Publication

American-International continues to be the only major motion picture studio producing horror films on a grand scale. *Dementia 13*, *The Haunted Palace*, *Fear*, *X—The Man with the X-Ray Eyes*, and *Nightmare* are already scheduled for release; and future filming plans include *It's Alive* with Peter Lorre and Elsa Lanchester, *Black Sabbath* starring Karloff; *Masque of the Red Death* and *When the Sleeper Wakes* with Vincent Price; *War of the Planets*, *The Dunwich Horror*, and *Something in the Walls*.

AIP recently signed Robert Dillon to their growing staff. His first assignment will be producing and directing the Lorre starrer *It's Alive*. In the past, Dillon scripted Columbia's *The Candy Web* and *The Old Dark House*.

Author Ray Bradbury's celebrated novel *Fahrenheit 451* (Ballantine, 50c) will be filmed in Germany this year. Other foreign productions due to reel off at local American theatres in the coming months include Orson Welles as *King of Atlantis*, Mexico's *Castle of the Monsters*; *The Wolf Woman* and *Werewolf in a Girl's Dormitory* from Germany; and *The Ghost of Elisha Dawn*, a Yugoslavian color release. Japan's new *Gorath* has been described by critic David Soures as "the Japanese version of George Pal's *When Worlds Collide*."

Two old horror-fantasy radio programs slated for a TV revival next season are *I Love a Mystery* and *Witches Tales*, the latter hosted by Vincent Price—who hunts more "never seen" TV horror anthology shows than anybody else we know. Kirk Alyn and Spencer Bennet, star and director of the *Superman* serials, are currently planning a brand-new adventure series for television. And we suggest you check your local radio log for the broadcast time of the *General Electric Stereo Drama* program. Recently heard on this excellent series was Joseph Cotten in *The Fall of the House of Usher*, and Agnes Moorehead in *Turn of the Screw* (which was the basis for the recent film chiller *The Innocents*).

Alex "She Creature" Gordon intends to film a Fu-Manchu novel shortly; and another Gordon—this one named Bert—will soon be filming the classic *Food of the Gods* by H.G. Wells. The ever-popular ape-man Tarzan has completed his latest for producer Sy Weintraub—*Tarzan Faces Three Challenges*.

The first issue of a new motion picture publication—*Screen Facts*, "The Magazine of Hollywood's Past"—recently crossed our desk, and we would like to highly recommend this fine, authorative (and illustrated) periodical to anyone interested in any phase of movies. SF #1 features articles by Alan Barbour, William Everson, Earl Michael, Clifford McCarty, and Edward Connor on "The Silent Serials", "Saga of Frankenstein" (with a photo of the Edison monster), "The Republic Serials", Miklos Rozsa, and the life story of film Bad Guy Roy Barcroft. Copies may be obtained from the publisher, Alan Barbour, for 75c each. Address Screen Facts, Dept RH, PO Box 154, Kew Gardens 15, NY.

HORROR SCOPE

MASTER OF THE STRATOSPHERE

by RON HAYDOCK

TV's Cosmic Crimebuster rocketed his way to Hollywood in 1951 to star in a 15 Chapter Serial Spectacle

Al Hodge (standing) and Don Hasting were Dumont TV's Captain Video and Ranger

During the dawning electronic-atomic age of the late 1940s and early 50s probably the greatest, most popular single fictional television hero was a dynamic scientist-soldier who, with his teenage assistant, rocketed up one side of the Milky Way and down the other to combat the forces of interstellar evil.

This fearless scientific champion of cosmic justice operated on Earth from a secret mountain retreat (the location of which was known only to a select few); and to the agressors of the universe he offered no quarter, nor asked none. He used his fantastically thorough knowledge of super-science to wage war on evil, and it was a running and thrill-blazed campaign which his fans were allowed to tune in on for half an hour each weekday evening on the Dumont Television Network.

His name was Captain Video; and by his fearless exploits on Earth and in outer space, he won the undying favor and admiration of millions of young Americans.

The Master of the Stratosphere, clad in his goggled football helmet and space togs, armed with not only two experienced fists but also a ray gun (just in case), was created especially for TV by the Dumont people. And on TV, there were two Captain Videos. Richard Coogan was the original Video, during the length of his stay mainly confined to Earth battling a criminal mastermind named Dr Pauli. Aiding Coogan was Don Hastings as Video's young sidekick, the Video Ranger.

Video, the Ranger, and Dr Tobor prepare to blast off for Planet Atoma

Serial stars Judd Holdren and Larry Stewart capture Vulturan agent William Fawcett on planet Theros (Fawcett's spacesuit courtesy of George Pal). At right, The Video Ranger is about to have his thoughts screened by the "Electronic Mind Reader" machine

When newspapers, magazines, and Hollywood seriously turned their thoughts to man's racing to the moon and beyond, around 1950, Captain Video also gave the intriguing possibilities his attention. Coogan, a former Broadway actor who was by then tiring of the Video role he had been playing for two years, resigned his claim to the Master of the Stratosphere title, and radio announcer Al Hodge immediately stepped in to fill Captain Video's famed lace boots. Hodge as Video soon constructed a rocketship capable of piloting around the universe, and with blasting continuing as the Ranger he blasted into some of the wildest (and well-written) adventures ever seen on 'live' TV.

Manufacturers were quick to capitalize on Video's tremendous success, producing official Captain Video merchandise of all types: dishes, bedspreads, trading cards, sweaters, play suits, shirts, trousers, wallets, comic books, stationery, pajamas, dolls, and even an "authentic" Radio Scillograph tor which permitted "honorary" Video Rangers to communicate with each other over sizable distances. It was the greatest merchandising campaign since Superman.

But there was another facet of exploitation looming up on Captain Video's scanner—Hollywood. For the first time in television history a program specifically created for the medium was being enthusiastically

turn to page 50

SHADO

W STRIKES BACK

By Jim Harmon

The Shadow Knows the Evil of Men — and does something about it in Fiction, Length, Screen Shockers in Serer-Science Serials, and the Classic Radio Show of Yesterday — and TODAY!

Those shows that everyone knows to be radio's all-time classics—*I Love a Mystery, This Man, Lights Out, One Man's Family*—THE SHADOW alone remains to chill the nervous with his ghostly laughter.

Unlike the latday used role radio network plays (*Johnny Dollar* and *Suspense*) The Shadow has a just claim on the honor of having the stage of the Theatre of the Mind to himself. While not intellectual fare, *The Shadow* represents many angles of radio's popular entertainment. When not using his hypnotic power to cloud men's minds so that they can not see him, Lamont Cranston is a private eye, not unlike Nick Carter and Sam Spade. His long-suffering girl friend shares the fate of soap opera heroines in the Helen Trent tradition, and the light exchanges between them are Gildersleeve-like domestic humor. Then when Cranston exits, The Shadow is revealed as a fantasy character with near supernatural power, the original costume crimefighter, forerunner of The double-identified Lone Ranger and Superman.

Because you can't see The Shadow, he is the perfect character for radio. He has been in movies, comic books, pulp magazines, hardcover novels, but he is best where he originated—on radio.

Even before Street & Smith's long-running *Shadow Magazine*, the Master of Darkness was on the air. In the early 'thirties, a radio anthology of mystery plays from Street & Smith magazine stories was hosted not by an Alfred Hitchcock or Boris Karloff as on TV, but by a mysterious figure who knew he knew what evil lurked in the hearts of men—The Shadow.

In those days, young Orson Welles took the role, and the role grew with him until the program became entirely about the one-time host, The Shadow. The show's owner, the Publishing company, named its magazine about the Cloaked One, and Orson Welles stepped aside to begin figuring how to scare the pants off the country with his convincingly real "Invasion from Mars" broadcast, making way for a series of radio actors, finally Bret Morrison, the best-remembered of all chuckling Shadows. Morrison today does movie-film voice dubbing, being a mild-mannered recorder for a great metropolitan newsreel.

Whether with Welles or Bret Morrison, generations have thrilled to the Shadow's radio adventures, and continue to do so. Scoffers say the stories are standardized — they always deal with some kind of leering supernatural or super-scientific menace; and investigator Cranston usually only becomes the Shadow twice during each half-hour story! once to question that reluctant witness, and the second time to nail the villain and usually to rescue his friend and companion Margo Lane (who alone knows to whom the voice of the invisible Shadow belongs).

The Shadow radio shows may be predictable—but part of what you can predict about them is chills and thrills.

THE SHADOW RETURNS to the warehouse to instruct his cab driver friend Shrevie what to do with an unconscious villain

Kane Richmond as Lamont Cranston is questioned by Police Commissioner Weston who wants to know what became of THE MISSING LADY (Monogram, 1946)

Margo Lane (Barbara Reed), Lamont Cranston (Kane Richmond) and friend Shrevie (Frank Scully) keep an eye open for danger in THE SHADOW RETURNS (Monogram, 1946)

One random factor has caused the Shadow's image to change slightly from one media to another. In the old comic books and newspaper strips, like on the radio, The Shadow could become as invisible as H. G. Wells' Invisible Man (and then, in the comics, he was printed entirely in blue, no black outlines over) but in the magazine novels, he only wrapped himself in a black cloak and slouch hat and skulked through the shadows deftly enough to be practically invisible—if you didn't look too close. There's an example of this in the Feb. 1946 *Shadow Magazine* novel, *Crime Out of Mind* by Maxwell Grant (pen name for one-time magician Walter Gibson) . . . . It was living blackness, cloaked in the sable-hued garb that symbolized The Shadow! The Shadow let go with a hard, side-arm throw, sending the loaded .45 ahead of him as he completed his whirl to produce another automatic from beneath his cloak. By then, the Shadow's fling had scored. (When it came to throwing things, the crook whose knife was dislodged by the Shadow's hurled gun tried using his Monte captive.) As the girl came flying headlong, The Shadow gave a sardonic laugh and with it seemed to dwindle, only to come upward from his stooping twist to pluck the girl almost as she struck the floor.

On the radio, the Shadow plucked another girl — Margo Lane — from danger many times. He saved her from the mad sculptor who built his statues from clay mixed with the blood of his models. There was a last-minute rescue from the man who had the touch of death, and whose chain of murders was running Cranston's friend, Police Commissioner Weston, ragged before the Shadow chased the killer away from Margo, into some high tension lines. turn to page 50

The mysterious Shadow (on the left) tangles with a notorious criminal in a Bowery flophouse during his search for THE MISSING LADY

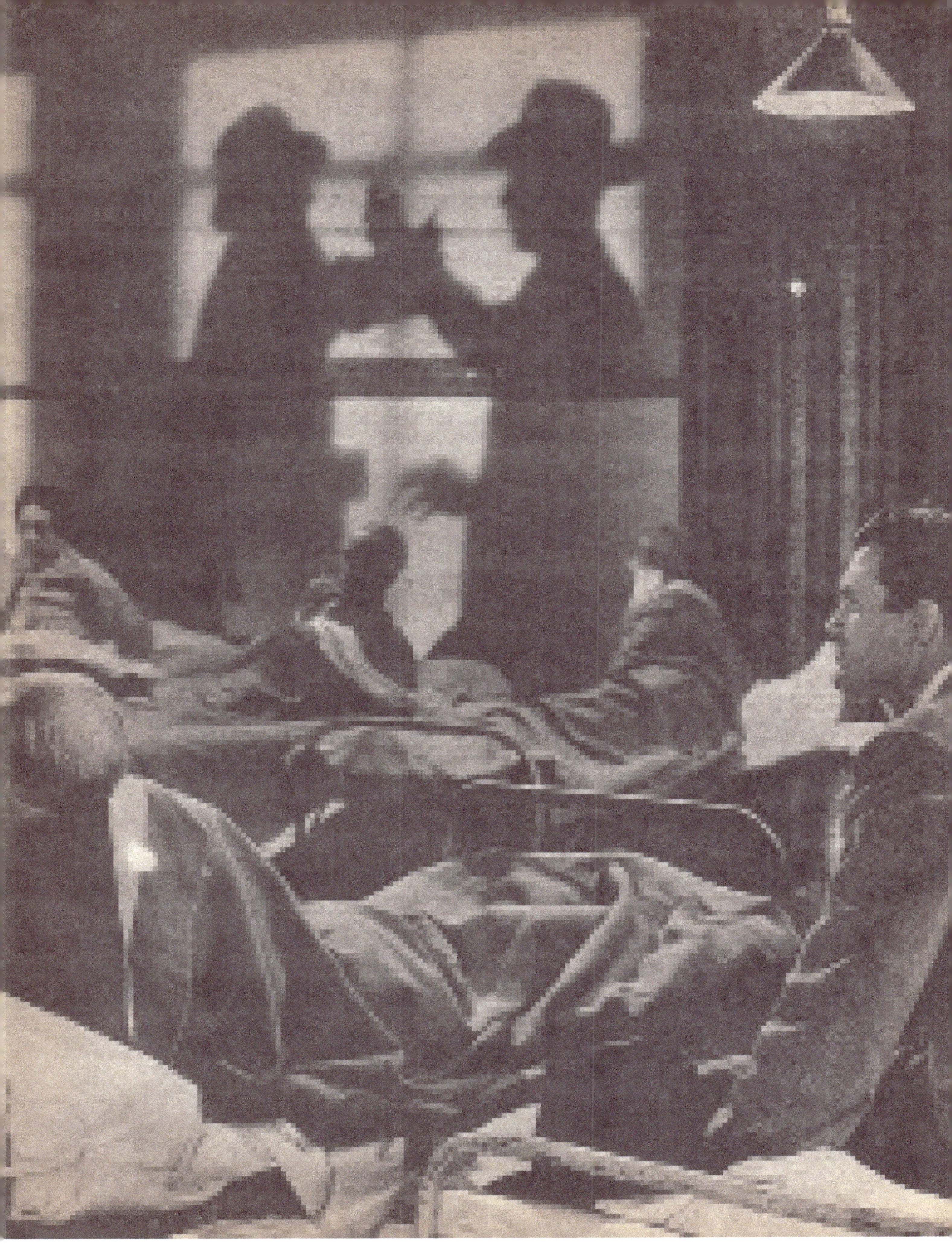

SHADOW, from page 48

But in the abandoned subway tunnel where the "ghost train" runs beneath the grounds of the Carnival of Death, it is Margo who throws Cranston a plank to help him get out of a pit of quicksand. The two of them can stand facing The Werewolf of Hamilton Mansion, or having a river fall on them in a mile-deep tunnel during Smuthig Murder, or being caught in an airplane dogfight when Death Rider High; but the thing that really dumbfounds both Lamont and Margo is when Cranston seems to lose his power of hypnotic invisibility in The Shadow's Revenge.

Of course, ways of getting around the Shadow's ultimate camouflage were always being tried by villains—particularly in the scripts by science-fiction writers like Max Ehrlich and Alfred Bester. One simpler way was just using a thick rug to show up the footprints of the invisible Shadow; but another enterprising crook used a television camera that couldn't be hypnotized, and way back in the late 'thirties, visitors from another planet tried something like radar to spot mind-clouding Cranston.

Tight spots all, but Cranston and Margo always manage to squeeze by.

One of the most painful difficulties the accident-prone Margo found herself in was reproduced in Norman Weiser's Writer's Radio Theatre 1940-41 (Harper). The Jerry Devine script concerns a killer in a New England town who is disguising himself as a ghost, and who has captured Margo—or "Margot" as its occasionally spelled.

EDWARD: In the days of the Puritans they had a very satisfactory method for dealing with meddlers . . . they branded them upon the forehead . . . Soon, young lady, soon you shall feel the searing agony of that brand biting into your flesh . . . (Laughing) Prepare yourself, Miss Lane . . . I have the iron ready now . . .

MARGOT: Keep it away from me . . . (Screaming) Keep it away!

SHADOW: Drop that iron, Mr. Darow!

EDWARD: Who was that . . .

SHADOW: (Laughs) I am the Shadow!

Yes, Lamont Cranston is and always will be The Shadow—the voice of the spirit of imagination that is radio drama.

●

VIDEO, from page 44

adapted by the movies.

Captain Video was scheduled to blast his way through fifteen chapters of continued cinema, produced and directed by Sam Katzman and Spencer G. Bennet, the veteran film-makers responsible for serializing Superman, Vigilante, Batman, and other colorful super-heroes. And to top it off, they were going to film Video in color—at least, in part.

The serial, released in 1951 by Columbia Pictures, had tinted scenes by Cinecolor whenever Captain Video and the Ranger (played by Judd Holdren and Larry Stewart) landed on a distant planet. It was a sequence of dazzling green for planet Theros, pink for Atoma.

Captain Video may have been wildly scientific on TV, but in the bigger budget serial he used every type of super-scientific gadget and device conceivable, including many which were not. There was, for example, the Ozonator, which emits a static spark that clears the air of poisonous fumes; Isotopic Radiation Curtain, which causes a truck or other vehicle to vanish; Optican Scillometer, a seeing device that can penetrate any object; Radionic Directional Beam, a small gadget which sends out an electronic impulse which can be traced, and a Radionic Guide to pick up the impulse; Door Hinge Recorder, a tiny recording instrument set in an ordinary door hinge (!); Mu-Ray Camera, which can photograph people after they have left a room or area, an after-image gadget. In all, Captain Video was surrounded by a total of exactly 52 cosmic whats-its.

Columbia propman Wes Morton, whose mind-shattering chore it was to construct all of these gadgets, told this writer he vividly remembers running to Katzman and Bennet hoping they could solve a most perplexing problem for him.

"I've built a Polarized Blast Furnace," he said to the two serial veterans, "and an Atomic Eye, a Gravitational Decelerator, and a Concussion Comet. But," he cried, "will you please tell me how in Sam Hill do you make a Psychosomatic Plunger?!"

(Morton learned exactly what the device was—a Video invention which turn to page 54

MONSTER CLUBS

COFFIN CORNER

ALEX RAYMOND, Lonaville, Texas asks us, "In what film did the monstrous Gocko appear?"

Al, the creature you're speaking of was seen in the 1936 Flash Gordon epic, starring Buster Crabbe.

"I seem to recall seeing a picture in which Superman had a battle with the Mummy. Could you freshen my memory?" asks SAM SHERMAN, Brooklyn, N.Y.

The only picture we have been able to find like that was a 1943 Paramount Superman cartoon titled The Mummy Strikes.

"A friend recently told me that he'd heard of a film years ago called Bride Of Frankenstein. I told him he was nuts, but maybe you know of such a film." STANLEY HARDY, Hollywood, Calif.

The film you're speaking of was actually released, but under the changed title of Abbott and Costello meet Frankenstein.

JUDSON GREY of Chicago, Ill. thought he was tripping us up when he dared us to tell him, "What famous western star once played The Mummy?"

Sorry, Jud, but you fooled us! Tom Tyler played the bandaged Egyptian in The Mummy's Hand.

For FANTASTIC MONSTER fans—The FANTASTIC MONSTERS FAN CLUB presided over by Charles Grazer, 510 Rindale St., Brooklyn 7, N.Y. sounds interesting. Write to Charles for information.

Ronald Borst of 1118 Kirby, Chicago 39, Ill. is also

OUR APOLOGIES...

We sincerely apologize to ardent monster-maker Val Warren for having mistakenly labeled his photo which appeared in FmMs #4 as being one of Count Dorko's Schockeaps. It meant that a drawing of Warren's and on the picture for Val and we mistakenly thought the star was Gerard himself. Sorry, VAL, and to help make up for our goof, here's another shot of Val the Vampire.

publishes it's own fan magazine titled THE HORROR EXPRESS and is currently seeking new members from all over the country. Leslie's address is 4013 36th St., Lake ...

Pictured is Bob McCague, director of the MOVIE COLLECTOR'S CLUB, in his office as he begins work on another issue of the club's publication, the Reel Scene.

If you collect any movie-related material (movie stills, posters, pressbooks, etc.) you'll be interested in this club. They publish a quarterly journal in which members advertise their movie-related wares and items for sale or trade, as well as articles on the members and their interests.

For information and a 20 page sample copy of the journal, send 25c to:
MOVIE COLLECTORS CLUB
Painter Department
Post Office Box B190
Cleveland 1, Ohio

You French-type werewolves should be interested in Leslie Ida's club, THE LOUP-GAROUS. The club

HAUNT ADS

We've been receiving letters by the pile from individuals wanting both to sell stills (and other movie related material) and to buy them. Feeling that this probably represented a large percentage of our readers, we decided to list here separately a few of these people for your information and use.

WANTED: POSTERS AND STILLS—FLORIAN PIETRYKOWSKI JR.—933 Waverly Ave.—Toledo 7, Ohio—Lugosi as Dracula, Day The Earth Stood Still and Tarzan — TOMMY WEST — 2232 Euclid — Wichita, Kansas—She Creature, It Destroyed The World — ROBERT KOZICKI—5443 S. Rutherford—Chicago 38, Ill.—all — LEE WOODWARD—113 Park St.—Jamestown, N.Y. — all—GUY GUDEN—1013 S. Malden—Fullerton, Calif. — all, also scripts, fan mags—BORIS MOTZ — 318½ Delaware—Leavenworth, Kansas—all Frankenstein and other "classic" films— CHARLES W. BAILEY—3010 Bernhart—Fort Wayne, Ind.—Battle Beyond The Sun—TARLTON INGALLS—3 Club Rd.—Baltimore 10, Md. — all — BOB TOSKL—6632 Russell Ave., S.—Minneapolis 23, Minn.—all—MARY ROLAND—18-a, Stockleigh Rd.—St. Leonard's on Sea,—Sussex, England—Christopher Lee—KENNETH DIXON—674 Buttonwood Dr.—Springfield, Pa.—Tarzan, Batman, Buck Rogers and Flash Gordon—SUSAN MUNSEY—1736 Canyon Ave.—E. Cleveland 12, Ohio—Zacherle — JAMES CHENOWITH — Y.M.C.A.—Colorado Springs, Colo. — The Thing — PETER CASICA—811 Beaconsfield—Grosse Pointe 30, Mich.—Gill Man, Robby the Robot and Gort — CHARLES GREGOR — 510 Hinsdale St. — Brooklyn 7, N.Y.—How To Make a Monster, Teenage Frankenstein.

FOR SALE — MALCOM WILLITS—P.O. Box 85343—Santa Western Station, L.A. 27 — stills, etc; free 3-page list—ITALO PATUELLO—9 S. Putnam — Buffalo 13, N.Y.—Phantom Of The Opera posters, masks; sale by bid—ALLEN WHITE—Route 2—Estill Spgs, Tenn — posters, 11 x 14's—DUNCAN HARP—114 W. 70th St.— New York 23, N.Y.—7th Voyage of Sinbad stills.

Both GARY MARTIN, 608 Browning Dr., Arlington, Texas, and EDWIN HURHAY, 2540 Chapel Hill Rd., Durham, N.C., are looking for old comic books. Fellas, you might try one of the following individuals: "I have Monster magazines, comic books and a 500 page book on Poe for sale," says MIKE GARRETT, 6801 3rd Ave. Birmingham 12, Ala. . . . JEB HOCKMAN has back issues of FANMO and lots of old Mad comics for sale and also wants to trade them for movie posters and other monster material. His address is P.O. Box 362, Front Royal, Va. . . . If you're looking for any DC comics from 1958 to 1962 you might get them from DANNY PHELAN, 1226 Frame St. Charleston, W. Va. . . . DUNCAN HARP is selling his entire collection of monster and space comics for 5c each, so send an inquiry to DUNCAN at 114 W. 70th St., New York 23, N.Y. . . . Three high school monster fans wish to correspond with anybody, anywhere, by use of recorded tape. For details, write to GARY SCHWINDER, 9-12 Fair Haven Pl., Fair Lawn, N.J. . . . All issues of World Famous Monsters are desperately being sought by David Jones, who insists he'll pay fair prices. Write to him at 354 Avenue "A", Battle Creek, Mich. . . . For "13 ghosts" out there in monsterland, there are 13 fine masks, all different, for sale for $1.50 each by G.R. GUY GORDON says he'll throw in a 3-fingered hand and a "bloody stump" for a prompt reply, and his address is 23 Canterbury St., E. Hartford 8, Conn. . . . DOUGLAS BUGLEV, 59181 Ke Nui Rd., Haleiwa, Oahu, Hawaii, will pay $1 for the Amazing Stories edition of 20 Million Miles to Earth if it's in good condition . . . A number of pocketbooks from motion pictures are available from CHRIS BROOKS, Lower River Rd., Harrisville, Pa. who wants to trade them for pressbooks, posters, stills and other related movie material . . . $2 is offered by JEFF FERGUSON, 17 Dapplegray Ln., Rolling Hills, Calif. for a copy of the paperback edition of The Creature From the Black Lagoon. JEFF also offers $5 for the hardbound edition from the same film . . . BILLY BURFORD, 2128 N.E. 23, Portland, Oregon, wants to know who will sell him a model of the rocketship which was used in the film, First Spaceship On Venus. He is also looking for movie stills.

DON GLUT, by now a tradition with TOMBSTONE TIMES, here depicts the blood-drinking Count from another of his many fantastic amateur films. This one is Dragstrip Dracula, a sort of teenage terror whose favorite drink is a "bloody Mary"!

DRAGSTRIP DRACULA

A Pox On You

So the legend goes . . . SHEVA is the evil sorcerer, dead for many hundreds of years, who rises from his coffin to bring his fantastic curses to the modern world. With his evil magic he can summon terrifying creatures such as the Human Race has never seen. With the strength of Frankenstein, the savagery and animalistic instincts of the Wolfman, plus the hypnotic power of Dracula, he is a true master of horror. It is said that one look at his face can bring death within an hour, too bad if you looked.

Jerry Ayers as "Sheva"

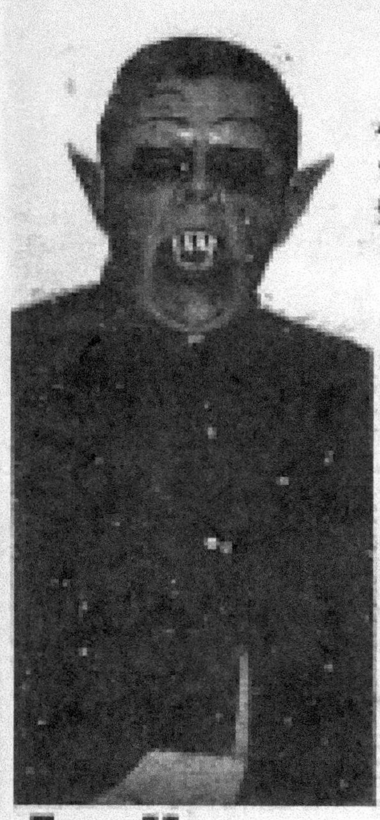

HORRORZINES

More monster film fan magazines are listed here this issue, along with one that isn't . . .

FANTI — "a complete change in the concept of a science fiction magazine," reports it's co-editor, the inventive KEITH NORD-STROM, residing at 301 Mott Ave., Santa Cruz, Calif. The first issue is now in production.

TRANSYLVANIAN CAR-RIER—a monster newspaper. Editors are calling for pub-lishable material. Write to BILL PORTMUELLER, 918 N. Martel, Los Angeles 36, Calif.

HEROES — not a monster magazine, but all sorts of in-formation and news regard-ing your favorite comic heroes. 15c per copy from JEFFREY GELB, 125 Glen Ellyn Way, Rochester 18, N.Y.

VAMPIRE'S CRYPT—The improved efforts of ACE MASK, well known for his previous attempt, SCREEN WHIRL. Interesting material and beautiful printed covers. Send 25c to ACE at 48156 N. 3 Points Rd., Lancaster, Calif.

Foo, Man, Chew?

Make-up enthusiast and FANTASTIC MONSTERS fan G.R. GUY demonstrates for us his latest achievement— The Chinese Vampire. We think that with such impres-sive dental protrusions, he might have no trouble at all getting a job. After all, he could always chop-suey!

Lazy Lycanthrope

Our Tombstone Times Edi-tor, LARRY BYRD, here shows us his terrible afflic-tion. No, he's not a werewolf, his disease is far more hor-rible—he's a monster fan! His werewolf antics are done the easy way—with make-up. This particular shot is from his monster stage show, which has received much favorable comment.

FANTASTIC MONSTER CLUB
BLACK SHIELD PRODUCTIONS INC.
P.O. BOX 141 • TOPANGA, CALIFORNIA

Enclosed is $3.00 ☐ cash, ☐ check, ☐ money order, for one full year's subscription to Fantastic Monsters of the Films magazine (6 big issues) plus an official mem-bership in the Fantastic Monster Club. In addition to the magazine I will receive my official membership card, free monster photo and exclusive member's bulletin.

Name: ____

Address: ____

City: _________________________ Zone: ____ State: ______

VIDEO, from page 50

causes momentary insanity when turned on its victims—but "knowing this didn't solve the problem of building the darn thing, though the information helped—I think!")

The culprit responsible for giving Morton his special effects headaches was writer George Plympton, who started writing serials back in the great silent era. Plympton adapted Video from TV to the movie screen, then handed the actual scripting task to his staff of chapterplay scenarists: Royal K. Cole, Sherman Lowe, and Joseph Poland.

Aside from concocting all of the forementioned gadgets, Plympton had Captain Video and the Ranger up against an out-of-this-world menace in the person of Vultura, dictator of the distant planet Atoma. Vultura was a scientific fiend who planned on crowning himself the King of the Universe. But, of course, he hadn't reckoned that the courageous Captain Video would take a hand in the matter.

The serial opens as Video traces an unusual cosmic disturbance to the lab of Dr Tober (George Eldridge), who, it turns out, is keeping secret his nefarious affiliation with Vultura (Gene Roth). When Video discovers that Tober has suddenly disappeared (Vultura has ordered the man to

rocket to planet Atoma), he sets up his Scanner in time to catch a fleeting glimpse of Tober's Atoma-bound spaceship. Video and the Ranger follow in their own rocket — unaware that Vultura has been keeping a close watch on their own activities through his Scanner!

Vultura grins fiendishly, sets the dials on his Concussion Comet panelboard, and causes a comet to move directly into Video's special course. The directed comet smashes into the Video ship, and the screen explodes with the impact of the serial's initial cliffhanger.

Throughout the length and breadth of the galactic chapterplay, Video and the Ranger fight for their lives (as well as the fate of the entire universe) as they slowly but surely, over 14 more weeks of action, rocket in on Vultura and blast his conquest plan into hunks of space junk. They fight for their lives when robots manipulated by Vultura attack the Ranger and carry him unconscious into a blazing chemical plant. It's up to valiant Video to dash into the fiery inferno and quench the Ranger-enveloping flames with his Vapo-projector.

Video is overcome by a Paralysis Gas Bomb, and he awakes to the frightening knowledge that he is being frozen into a huge cake of ice. He manages, though, to contact the Ranger with his Radionic Directional

Beam, and the Ranger comes to the rescue with an ice-melting thingamajig called the Thermoid Transmitter.

One of the most unusual, if not the wackiest chapter ending ever, occurred in episode 9 when Video finds himself suddenly engulfed in flames. He tests the mysterious flames (in chapter 6) with his unique little Thermograph and discovers to our amusement that the flames are cold!

Vultura finally gets his in "Video Vs Vultura", the concluding installment. Video and the Ranger have cleverly disguised themselves as Vulturan officers and have snuck into Vultura's lab on Atoma. With a cry of alarm, the Mad Monarch jumps to his disintegrator ray cannon and turns it on them. The cosmic crimebusters dodge the blast in time—and suddenly one of Vultura's henchmen becomes a Good Guy and turns the deadly ray on his leader!

In the wink of an eye, and the flash of a sizzling ray spray, the Mad Monarch vanishes to wherever it is that all Mad Monarchs vanish to when their 15 chapter life span is up.

Judd Holdren, who later went to Republic Pictures to star as Commando Cody, Sky Marshall of the Universe, was a convincing and formidable Captain Video. Decked out in his (some think) UCLA football helmet and army outfit, he slipped through the serial with two-fisted gusto, typical of the original TV hero. However, most all who have viewed the Video serial have agreed that one of the film's sorespots was the casting of Larry Stewart, a real life airplane pilot, as the Video Ranger. The little known fact is that Larry Stewart—not his real name—who awkwardly and unconvincingly portrayed the Ranger was actually the casting director's son!

The scientist-soldier Dumont created continued thrilling his fans on TV for a few more years after the Columbia serial release. Then, quite suddenly, he disappeared from the TV screen. Press notices told of rising production costs for the 'live' adventure show, and the all-too apparent trend towards filmed TV programs only served to hasten the Captain's departure.

But Captain Video—whether on TV in the persons of Richard Coogan and Al Hodge, or in the serial with Judd Holdren—left behind him a universe of cherished memories for those who braved with him the monumental dangers of outer space villains and cosmic weapons. His unfortunate demise on TV signalled the end of an era of television programming which viewers cannot hope ever to witness again. There were, of course, other rocketkids and ray gun happy heroes on TV—special effectswise, Tom Corbett . . . Space Cadet was the best—but Captain Video, for the amazing chap he proved many times over to be, was something special. A super scientific hero among heroes, a Master of the Stratosphere who asked no quarter and gave none; the Conqueror of Space who operated right here on Earth from that terribly secret mountain retreat, waging his unrelenting war against the aggressors of the universe—that was Captain Video . . .

*

Horrors of the Hollywood Museum

by Ron Haydock

Front entrance to the Los Angeles County-Hollywood Museum, to be built across from the world-famous Hollywood Bowl (Wm. L. Pereira & Associates, Architects)

Marty Halperin sat back in the easy chair of his swank Beverly Hills apartment, one arm idly resting on a stack of recorded tape reels. "Yes, Ron," he said, "the Hollywood Museum wants to preserve all the horror and fantasy classics of movies, television, and don't let us forget—radio."

With Mr. Halperin around as well as FANTASTIC MONSTERS' own audiphile (nut on old radio) Jim Harmon in the opposite armchair, it was difficult for me to forget such monster and menace radio shows as *Lights Out* and *I Love a Mystery*. Even though Marty Halperin is a leading member of the Radio Acquisitions Committee, I managed to learn that all the old classics of film fantasy will be preserved in the vaults of the Hollywood Museum—from Edison's *Frankenstein* in the Gay (and Ghastly) 'Nineties, through the terror triumphs of Lon Chaney, Sr. in *The Hunchback* and others; to the latest American International offering with Karloff, Lorre, and Vincent Price.

It is even my hope and suggestion that the original make-up for such classic creatures as Karloff's Frankenstein Monster and Chaney Jr's Wolf Man will be on display at the Museum.

However, with Halperin and Harmon on hand the discussion quickly turned back to radio. Jim revealed that he had uncovered a complete 13 chapter radio serial of *Frankenstein* done back in the dim red dawn of history—say, about 1930.

I juggled my coffee cup impatient to inquire whether the museum had acquired all chapters to the silent movie serial starring Boris Karloff while Marty Halperin and our associate editor compared which chapters they had of Carlton E. Morse's *I Love a Mystery*—which, they tell me, was radio's greatest program.

However, I learned that the Museum would like to have still further chapters of ILAM as well as many other radio greats. It was an unfortunate fact that the stations themselves or the program's producers did not retain recordings of the many fine programs broadcast during radio's Golden Age.

The Museum urgently requests all public-spirited citizens who have any type of recording of old radio shows—tape, home disc, wire, 16 inch transcriptions or whatever—to make copies of these programs available so they may be preserved for history.

Among the shows needed is *Inner Sanctum*, with its chuckling host Raymond opening the squeaking door to the horrors within. *The Mysterious Traveler*, *Hermit's Cave*, *Whistler*, *Shadow*, *Witch's Tales*, *Peter Quill*, *Lights out*, and *Stay Tuned for Terror* also offered adventures into the unknown.

Dimension X and *X Minus 1* offered science fiction terror, and there were other space flights with *Buck Rogers* and radio versions of *Space Cadet* and *Space Patrol*. *Superman* also took to the air en route to outer space, and radio episodes of the Man of Steel are urgently needed for museum archives.

While not horror shows, FanMo also passes on as a public service the museum's want list for such shows as *Captain Midnight*, *Tom Mix*, *Green Hornet*, *Gangbusters*, *Lone Ranger*, *Orphan Annie*, *Sea Hound*, *Ma Perkins*, *Mr. District Attorney*, *Mary Marlin*, and *Terris*, as well as comedy-radio shows like *Jack Benny*, *Fred Allen*, *Fibber McGee*. In fact, ALL radio programs.

After running through some of the Museum's wants as well as showing Jim and me some of his own usable personal collection, Marty Halperin finally revealed why he had invited the FanMo staff over. In recognition for his efforts in preserving radio drama, Jim Harmon was made a member of the Radio Acquisitions Sub-Committee.

Personally, I will be devoting my efforts to uncovering old film classics, but associate Jim will be working with Marty Halperin and other Committee members such as Ken Carpenter and Marvin Miller and Chairman Hatfield Weedin on Radio Acquisitions. Information or recordings for the Museum may be sent to Jim Harmon, Black Shield Publications, Inc., Topanga, Calif.

MAD
MUMMY
STILL
MISSING!

American-International's
I WAS A TEENAGE WEREWOLF

VAMPIRES
WEREWOLVES
MONSTERS
GHOULS
ROBOTS
FIENDS
MUMMIES
mutations
Wierd Creatures
MADMEN

the supernatural

(t) American - International's THE
HAUNTED PALACE; (m) INCRED-
IBLY STRANGE CREATURE; (b) Kar-
loff in CBS-TV's "Lizard's Leg &
Owlet's Wing" episode of ROUTE 66

fantastic
MONSTERS
OF THE FILMS
GASP!
'Curse OF
The
FACELESS
Man
KARLOFF
EVIL!
FRANKENSTEIN'S
MONSTER!
BELA

KING KONG IN

No. 2 in Fantastic Monsters Great New Collectors Item Series

!

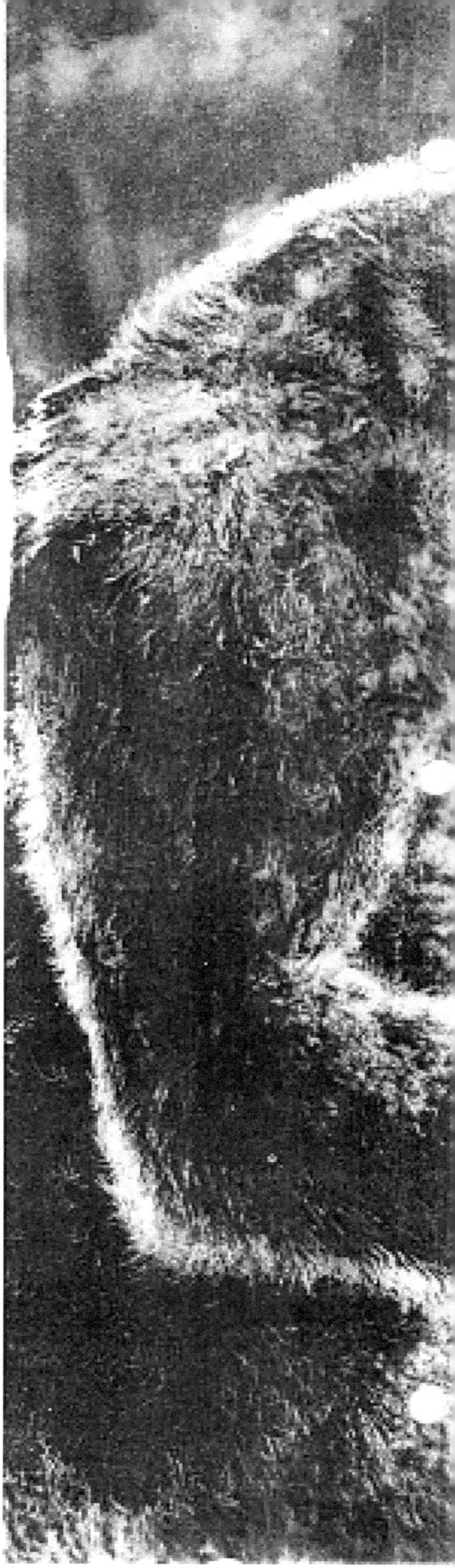

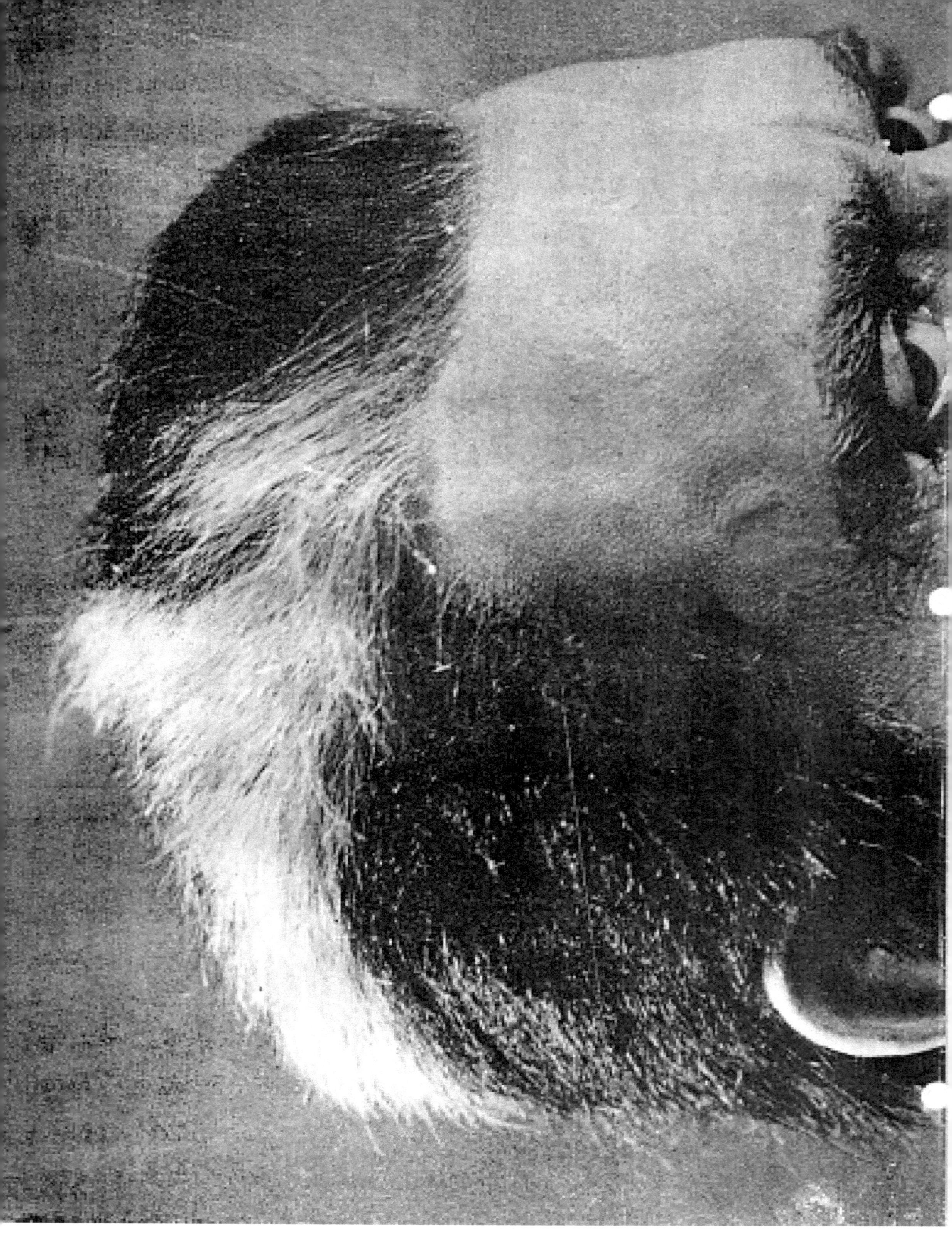

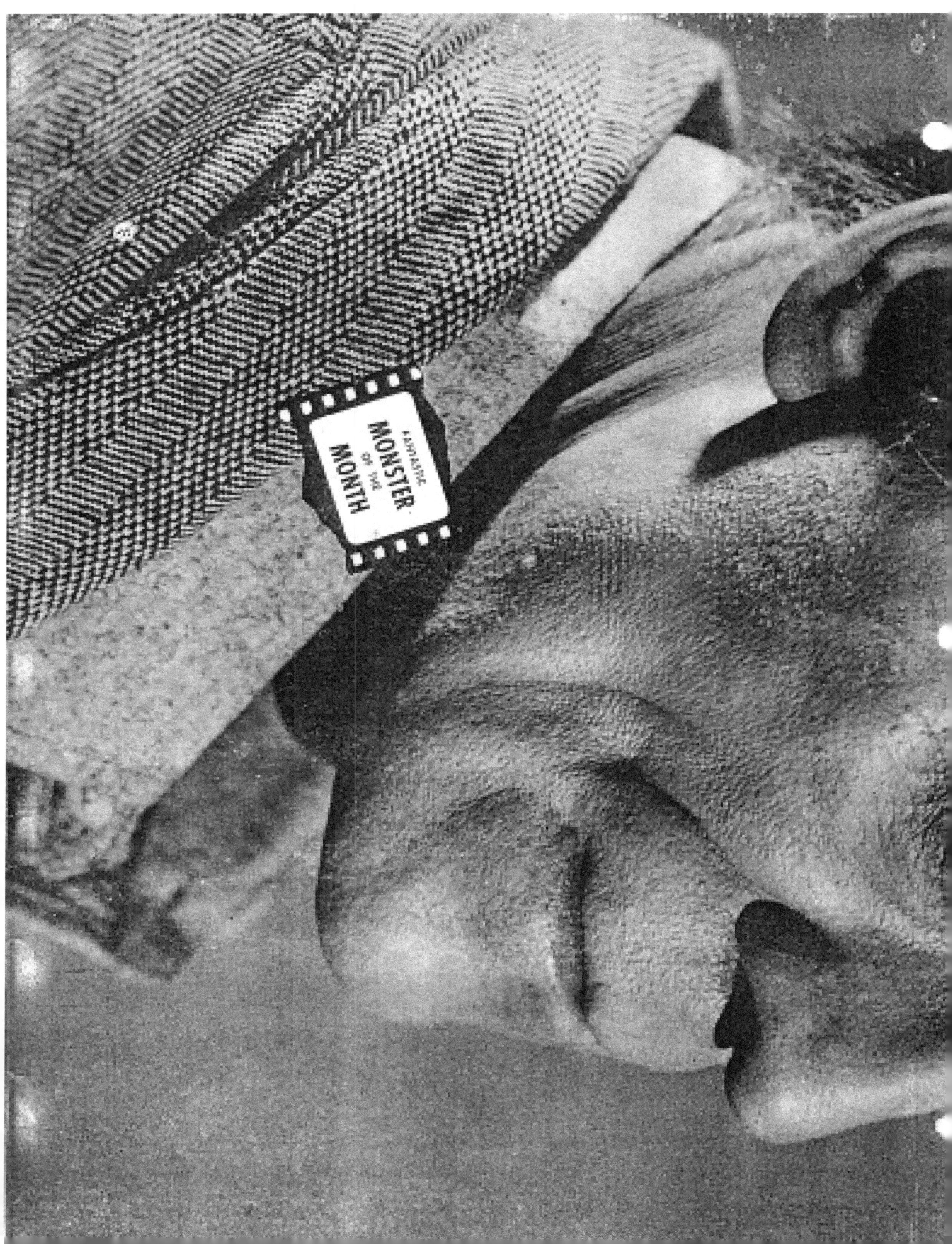
A FAMOUS MONSTERS
MONSTER
OF THE
MONTH

SON OF FRANKENSTEIN
—by LARRY BYRD

MONSTER OF THE MONTH

MONSTERS
OF THE FILMS
VOL. 2 • NUMBER 1

Karloff the Uncanny in Warner Bros THE WALKING DEAD

Because we've received literally thousands upon thousands of "We-want-more-Boris" letters from enthusiastic Karloff followers the world over, the next issue of FANTASTIC MONSTERS will be a special Karloff edition.

Along with various articles and short features on the King of Horror Films, there will be an unprecedented Collectors Section of giant Karloff pinups, prepared especially for this much-requested issue.

BE SURE TO RESERVE YOUR COPY OF FANTASTIC MONSTERS No. 8 AT YOUR FAVORITE NEWSSTAND—NOW! YOU WON'T WANT TO MISS OUT ON GETTING YOUR COPY OF THIS HISTORY-MAKING KARLOFF EDITION!

Black • Shield
MAGAZINE •

PAUL BLAISDELL
publisher

RON HAYDOCK
editor

JIRO TOMIYAMA
art & production

JIM HARMON
associate editor

BOB BURNS
research editor

LARRY BYRD
contributing editor

JACKIE BLAISDELL
circulation manager

MAD MUMMY
kidnapped editor

CREDITS & ACKNOWLEDGEMENTS: Paramount Pic: Ted Barnet; Allied Artists: Roy Smith; Milt Moritz; AIP, Cayuga Prod; CBS-TV; Richard Kyle; Dan Levitt; Universal Pic; Jack Nicholas; Columbia Pic

VOLUME 2, NUMBER 1, FANTASTIC MONSTERS OF THE FILMS. PRICE 35¢ PER COPY. Published bi-monthly by Black Shield Publications Inc. Mailing address: Post Office Box 141, Topanga, California. National Advertising Representatives: Harbor Company, 862 North Fairfax, Los Angeles 46, California. Contents Copyright 1963, by Black Shield Publications Inc. Nothing may be reprinted in whole or in part without written permission. Printed in U.S.A. Unsolicited manuscripts must be accompanied by stamped, self-addressed envelopes. The publisher accepts no responsibility for return. Any similarity between people and places mentioned in the fiction and semi-fiction in this magazine and any real people and places is purely coincidental.

TABLE OF CONTENTS

COVER—KARLOFF AND BELA LUGOSI IN SON OF FRANKENSTEIN—by LARRY BYRD

Bob and Paulette Goddard in Paramount's THE GHOST BREAKERS

10

HOW TO HANDLE A GHOST

by BOB HOPE

Bob Hope may not be a Monster, but he's one of the most Fantastic Talents of our time, well deserving of making the Big Time in FANTASTIC MONSTERS with Rare Scenes from his Celebrated Spook Show, THE GHOST BREAKERS—with Captions by the Wizard of Wit Himself

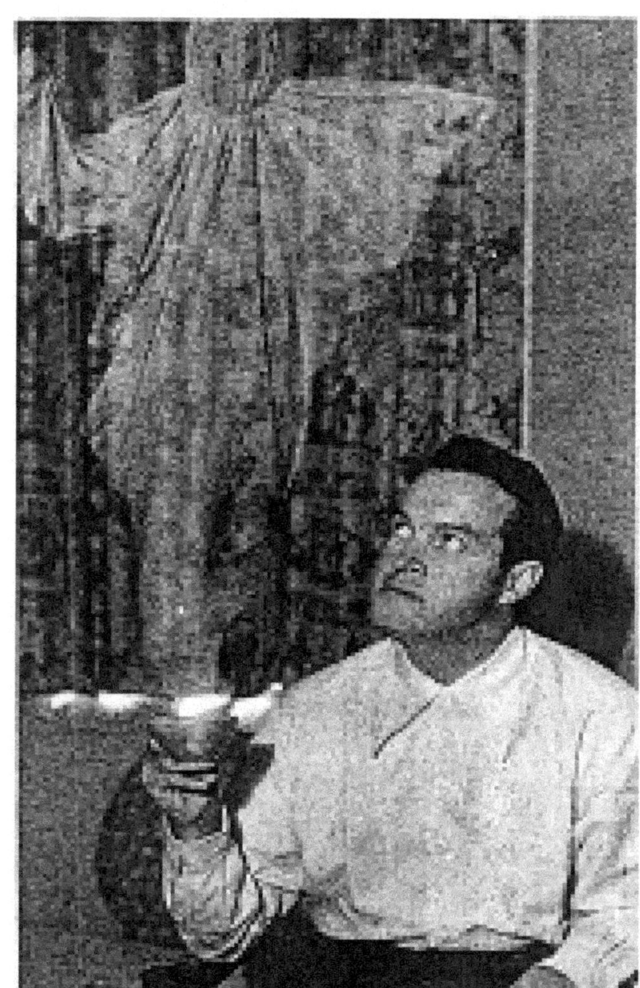

"A little ghost in your coffee won't make it any the worse."

"Don't, for heaven's sake, get your haunt sore by refusing to allow him (or her) to put sugar in your oatmeal."

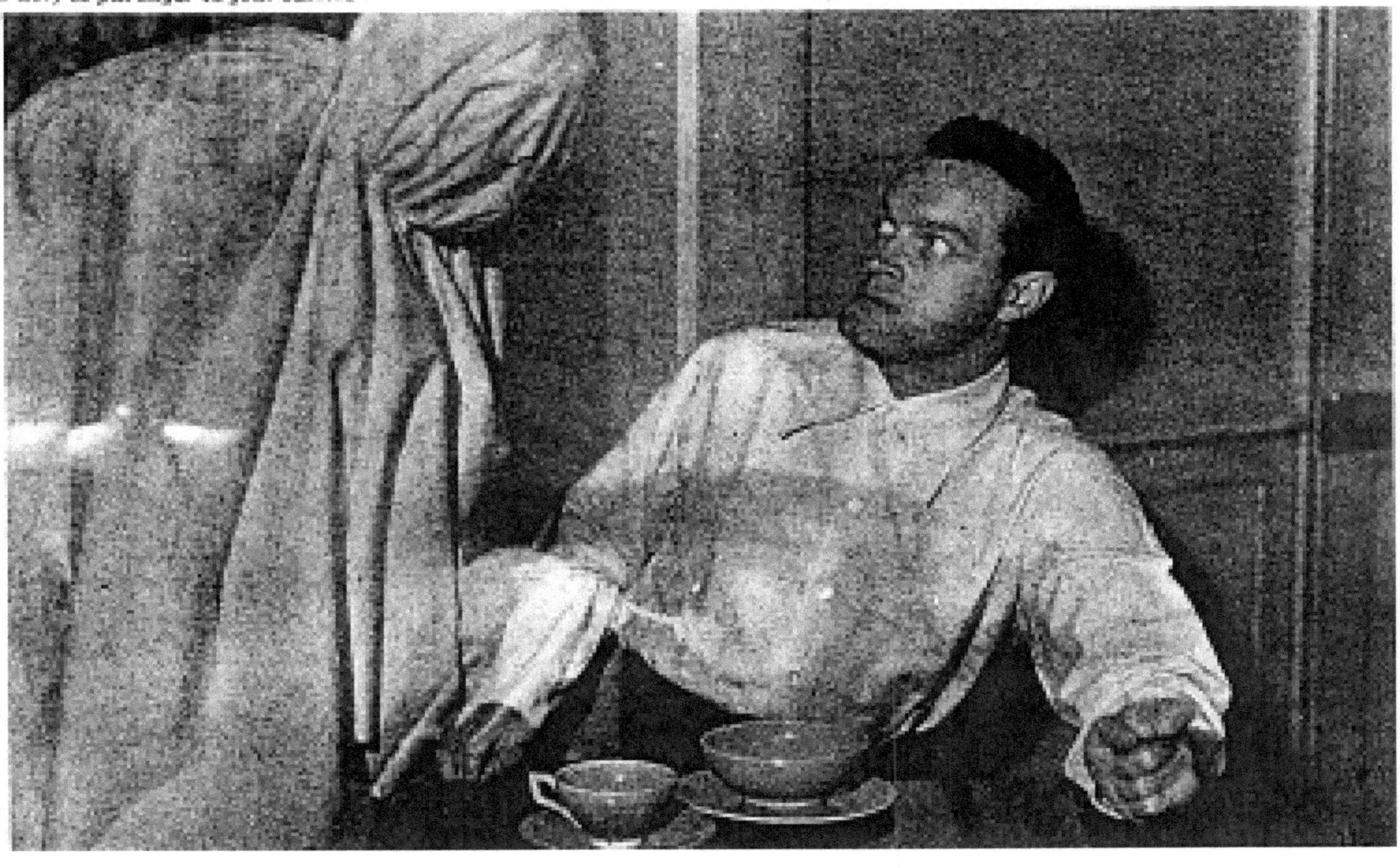

Price and Philip Ahn, as the proprietor of an antique shop, exchange notes on mysterious legends surrounding a Chinese Dragon statue

Vincent Price
in
CONFESSIONS OF AN OPIUM EATER

A new Price Terrorizer from Allied Artists—the Tension-packed Tale of a Lone Adventurer battling slave-running Hatchet Men at the Turn of the Century

(above) Charles Horvath creates the role of a Tong Hatchet Man posing as a mangled auction attendant; (right) Captured by slave runners, very Chinese girls are shipped to San Francisco in cages; (below) mangled skeleton found on a beach near San Francisco is mute evidence of the fatal treatment given same Chinese women while being smuggled into San Francisco to be auctioned as brides

THE METALOGEN MONSTER

A Mechanical Man clashes with an Ape named Thor in a Columbia Pictures Super-Serial Science-Fantasy Spectacular

by RON HAYDOCK

I remember looking through a telescope and seeing a robot monster and a huge ape wrestling with each other atop a nearby factory building.

I remember marveling at the sight of a super-scientific "monster-making" machine that shot sparks, hummed, whined, lit up, and was, of course, utterly fantastic.

I also recall entering a contest to name as many film monsters that I could because the first ten prizes were free tickets to my local theatre.

And lastly, I (grimly) remember having to finally pay my way into that same local theatre . . . .

These are a few of the memories that come to mind whenever anyone mentions *The Monster and the Ape*, a Columbia Pictures movie serial released in 1945. According to *Boxoffice*, a theatre trade magazine, Columbia has recently re-released this episode tale of the man-made machine man and his hairy little nemesis, Thor the ape, but I strongly doubt that any theatres running the re-release are exploiting the film this way they did in 1945.

turn the page

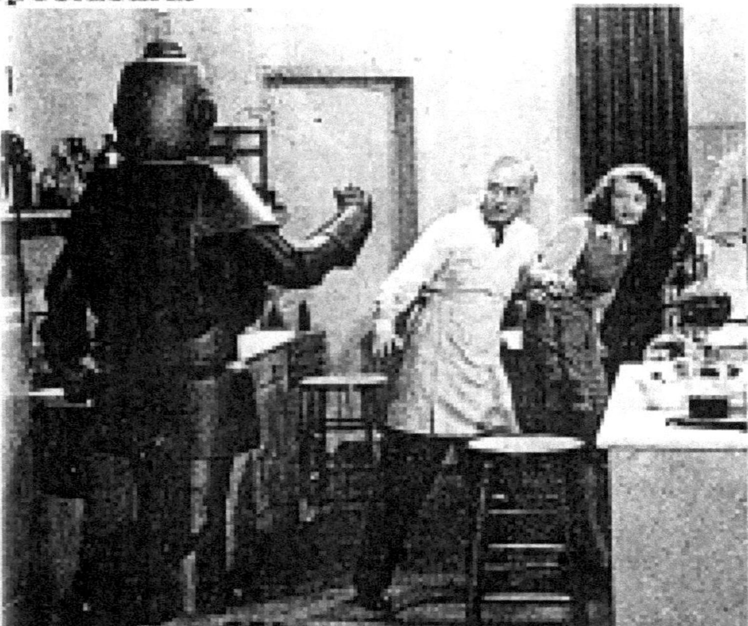

Morgan and Ruthless menaced by the Metalogen Monster

Macready and friend on a filming break

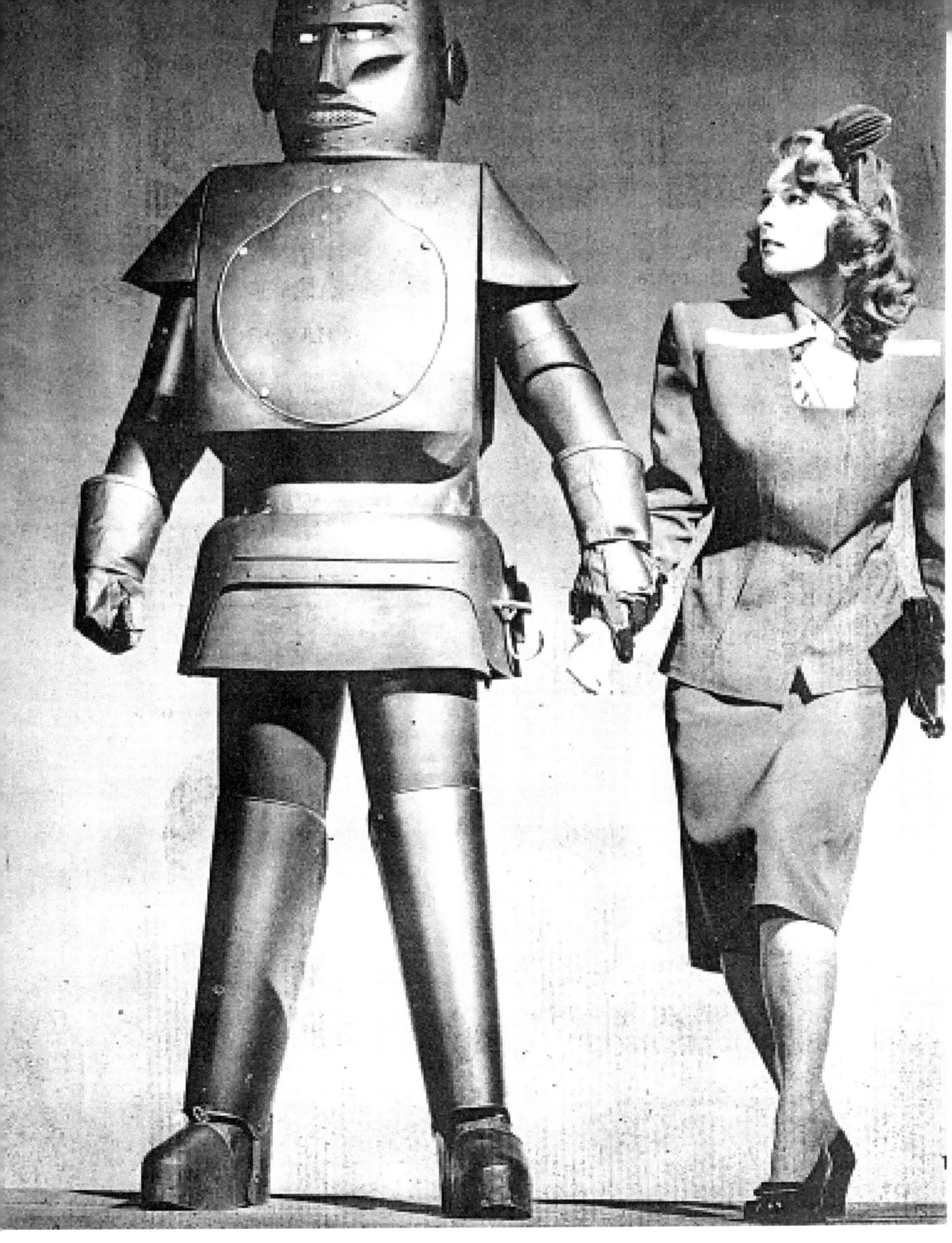

Lowery, Mathews, and Morgan do not know it, but that's George Macready in makeup posing as a friendly scientist to gain their confidence.

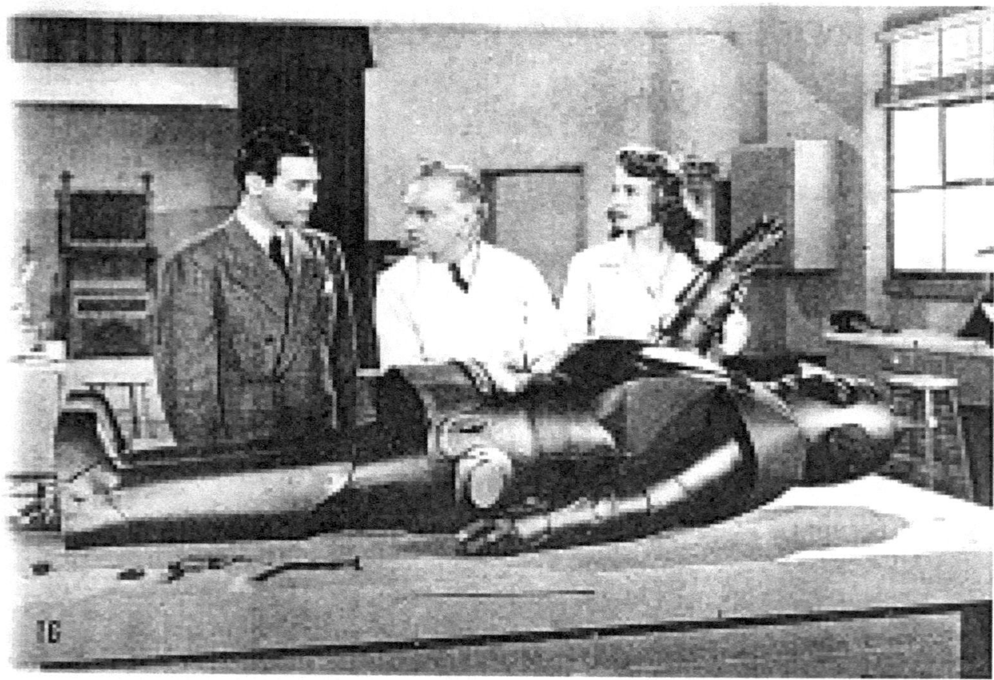

The robot and ape wrestling atop the factory building . . . the "monster-making" machine . . . the movie monster contest—just three of the many exploitation gimmicks that heralded the showing of the serial at theatres back in 1945. Of course, not every theatre in every town set up a telescope in the lobby, aimed at two stunt men across the street on the roof of a building, or constructed the weird "monster-making" machine, or even held the film creature contest. One theatre in St. Louis simply obtained a quantity of small punched-out pieces of metal from a nearby metal-stamping mill and hired "street bally men" to distribute them. The metal pieces were slipped into small brown envelopes upon which was printed: THIS IS METALOGEN, THE METAL THAT POWERS THE MECHANICAL MAN IN "THE MONSTER AND THE APE." A line followed which told you where you can see the film: COMING SOON (or NOW PLAYING) AT THE BIJOU THEATRE.

Some theatres — probably — didn't bother to exploit the serial at all.

However, whether accompanied by colorful ballyhoo or not, the chapterplay was a success during its times and is still being enjoyed by those who are seeing the current re-release.

The stars of the film are Robert Lowery, who later played comic strip hero Batman; Carole Mathews, former "Miss Chicago"; Ralph Morgan, well-known actor; and George Macready, who plays the major villain. Macready, incidentally, once operated an art gallery in Hollywood with another favorite Menace Man—Vincent Price.

The serial's various excitements include an electronic energizer—instant death for those who stray into the path of its rays; speeding autos plunging from cliffs, avalanches, explosions, and other typical cliffhanger elements. And there is, of course, the ape Thor who lends his own brand of excitement to the film.

The monster of the title—a robot named the Metalogen Man, after the unearthly material used in its manufacture—is devised by a group of scientists to help solve the manpower needs of a large company. After the mechanical monster is successfully demonstrated, three of the scientists are murdered by Thor, while a mysterious radio voice claims ownership of the robot. The robot itself disappears and is found to be stolen.

The shape of thrills to come is indicated by the names of subsequent episodes—"A Fiend in Disguise," "The Secret Tunnel," "Forty Thousand Volts," "The Mad Professor," "Gorilla at Large," and others.

Macready the Villainous is one of the scientists who helps to create the mechanical monster and who then manipulates it to his own evil ends. And pitted against him are Lowery, Morgan, and Miss Mathews—who soon find themselves battling against a twisted triumph of modern science and the ape which seems to have come unchanged out of the dark past of the world.

A newspaper article of 1945 tells about the (humorous) meeting of Thor the ape and his co-star, the Metalogen Monster:

turn to page 48

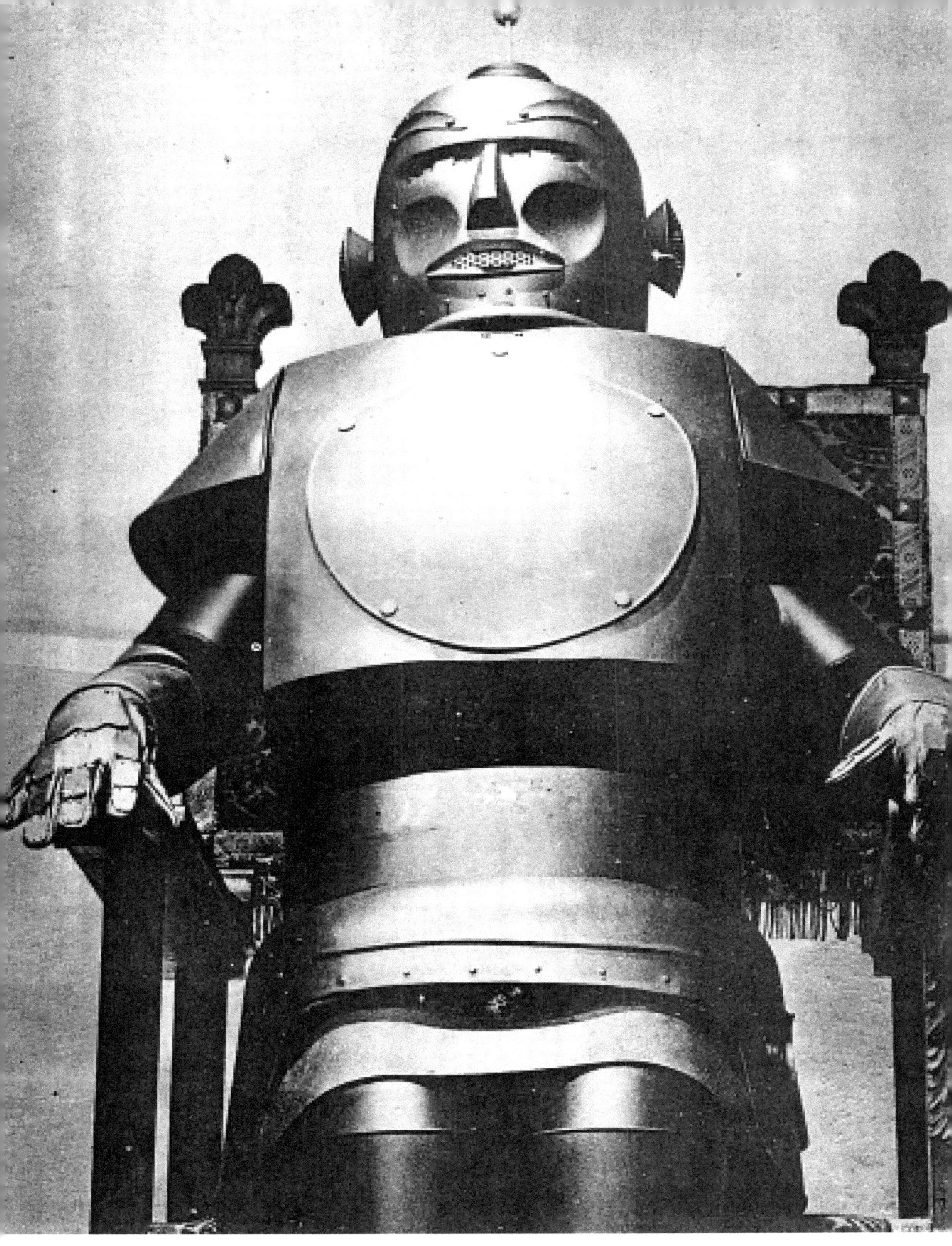

American-International's *X — The Man with the X-Ray Eyes*, a James H. Nicholson-Samuel Z. Arkoff production filmed in color and wide screen, stars Ray Milland in the role of a brilliant doctor who seeks to improve upon the limited and imperfect mechanical devices which assist a doctor in his work.

Calling upon the new worlds of knowledge opened by the discovery of the fantastic and as yet only partially explored "miracle" powers of the products of atomic energy, the film tells of a strange new experiment designed to increase the seeing ability of man's eyes.

Scientists know that man's eyes are a remarkable optical instrument, and we know that discoveries every day make possible stronger and more powerful microscopes and telescopes. With the amazing new electron microscope and other new devices, man is today probing deeper and deeper into the infinitesimally tiny mystery world of matter.

Why not then, as Ray Milland as "Dr. Xavier" reasons, cannot man give to his own natural optical instrument the power he has given to the new microscopes he has developed?

Such is the basis of the story of *X* — a new film from AIP that you're not going to want to miss.

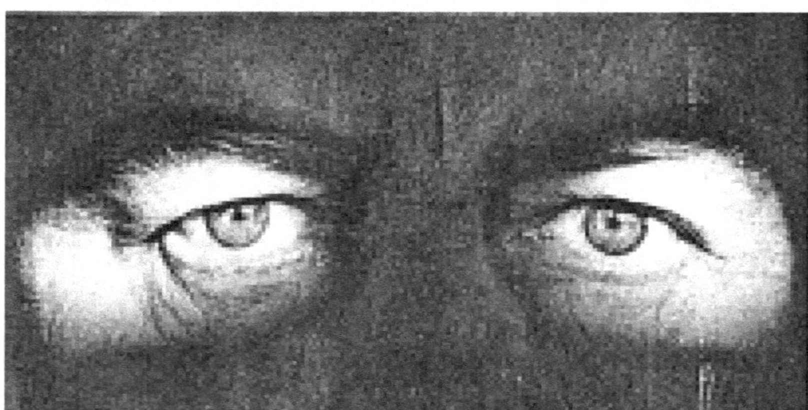

ARTY
THE
BLACK S

A Horror Horde of Monster Mutants Walks the Earth

At the time of its release in 1956, United Artists' film *Black Sleep* looked like it was going to be the best horror film since Universal's *House of Frankenstein*, released some dozen years previous.

When you took a long look at the various newspaper ads announcing the opening of the film in your town, you sat right back with a giddy grin and mumble, "This is one horror pic I'd better not miss! Look at that cast!"

Yes—that cast . . .

Basil Rathbone—Akim Tamiroff—Lon Chaney—John Carradine—Bela Lugosi—Tor Johnson!

One would think that any film with such an impressive array of horror stars can't be all bad. *Black Sleep*, however, proved to fans that you just can't have the top names in horrordom in a film and—presto—you automatically have a great, memorable motion picture.

Black Sleep, for the most part, was a boring and trite tale of a mad doctor involved in the usual illegal practices of all mad doctors. And to add salt to the wound, Bela Lugosi and Lon Chaney—more so than any of the other stars—were handed roles they could do practically nothing with. Bela was a deaf mute servant named Casimir, walking through his scenes making a few motions with his hands, and that's about all. Chaney was just a simple madman.

turn the page

21

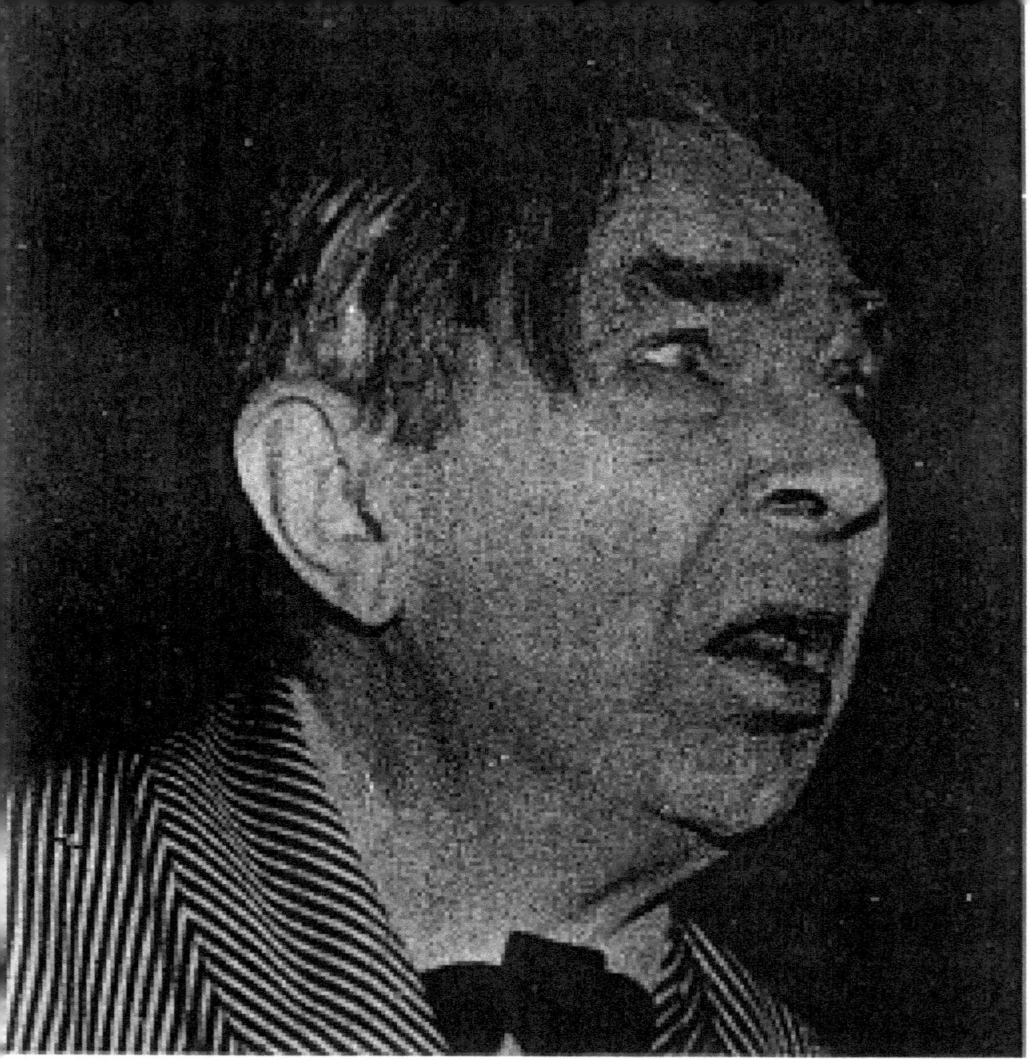

...ter seeing the film you wondered ... the producers—Aubrey Schenck ... Howard Koch—bothered to cast ... out names in the films when they ... ld have gotten unknowns for much ... salary. But, of course, the answer ... this is obvious. The point is that ... imir could very well have been ... rtrayed by an unknown rather than ... la and the role would still have ... me off as unexciting as it did.

Black Sleep is a good example of ... used talent.

Briefly, the story takes place in ... ngland during the 1870s. Sir Joel ... adman (Basil Rathbone), a surgeon, ... discover a cure for a strange ... disease suffered by his wife ... (Ouanna Gardner). He uses an an-cient drug that puts people into a sleep resembling death called "The Black Sleep."

Odo (Akim Tamiroff) supplies Cad-man with victims for his experiments, one of whom is Gordon Ramsay (Herbert Rudley), who has been framed for murder.

The victims all become mutants as a result of the experiments, and, naturally, they hate Cadman. They wait for the day they can escape from their cells in the foul dungeons of Castle Cadman, and destroy the doctor.

In the meantime, though, Ramsay falls in love with Laurie (Patricia Blake), one of Cadman's unwilling assistants.

Through an accident, the mutants escape and kill Cadman and his wife and set after Laurie and Ramsay. The fortunate arrival of the police save the two. Odo confesses to the murder which Ramsay had been framed with, and the two lovers return to London to start life anew.

turn the page

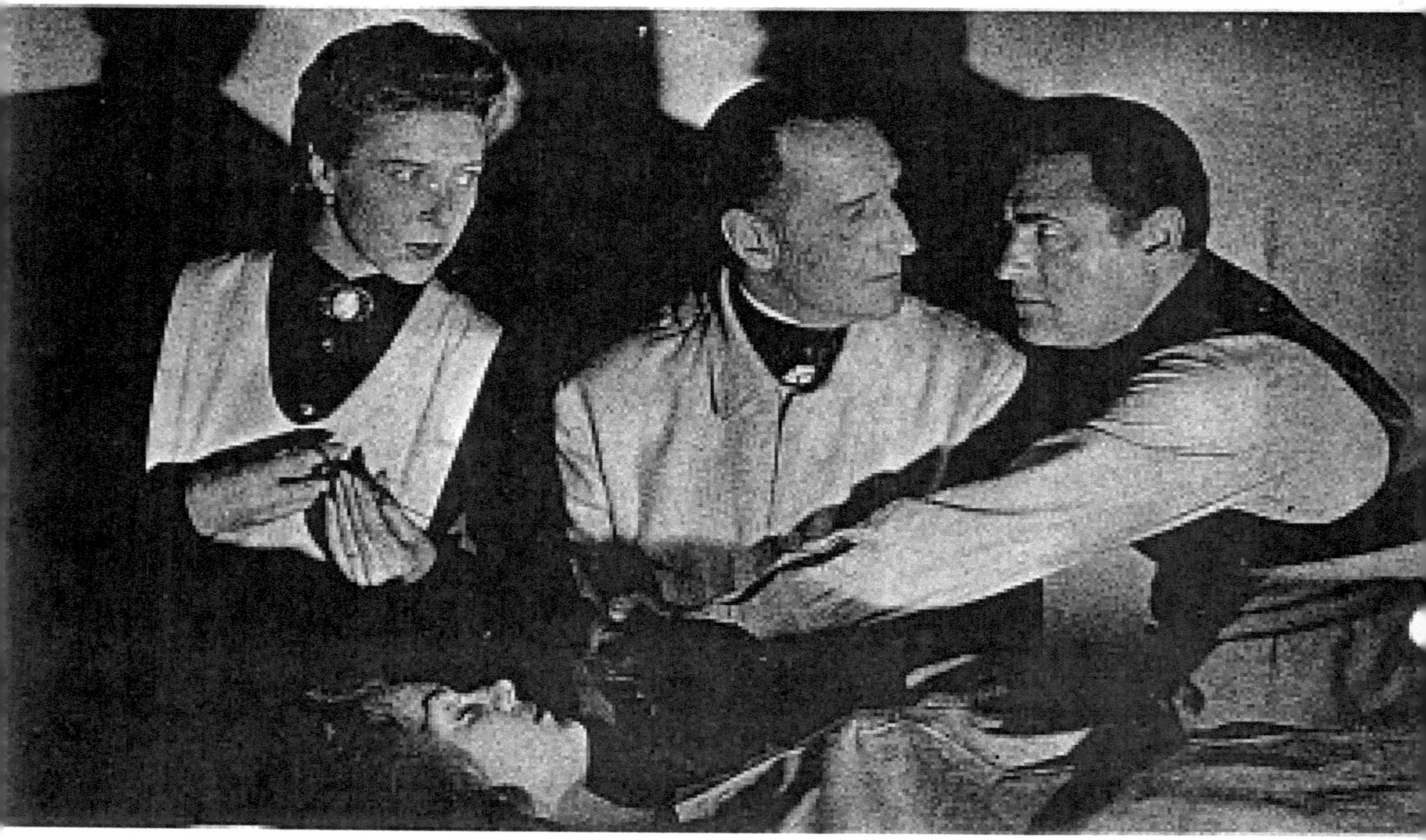

Bela Lugosi as servant Casimir

'The Mad Doctor and His Monster Mu-
ants' Pictured here are (left to
right) John Carradine, Lon Chaney,
Tor Johnson, George Sanders, Basil
Rathbone, and Sally Yarnell.

Herbert Rudley tries to prevent an operation on Patricia Blake (on table)
as Phyllis Stanley stands by with mad
surgeon Basil Rathbone

While the acting and story was unimpressive, the makeup seen in the film was the opposite. The various mutant monsters caged in the dungeon of the castle were the products of two artists, Volpe and George Bau.

Volpe designed the "characters" with color etchings while makeup artist Bau took charge of the task of making the material and applying it on the actors.

Another satisfactory accomplishment of theirs was the creation of a "Brain" which was used in an operation scene. It had to be designed, molded, and baked into soft rubber. Many models were molded but didn't turn out right, and the experts had to keep at it until they came up with a perfect specimen. It had to be colored and made to actually pulsate like living tissue.

In addition, actor George Sawaya's head was cast; and, through various processes, the life-like result was made so that Basil Rathbone could "operate" on it and actually "cut" through various layers of skin, bone, and membranes.

There were a lot of weird props dug up for the film, too. A four hundred year old rare book in Hindustani was one. Others included: an operating table of the 1870s; a Leyden jar (which was one of the first electrical devices in that era); human skulls; old time tatto blocks and equipment; manacles; an authentic 1870 London delivery wagon.

In short, *Black Sleep* had everything necessary for the making of a good old eerie thriller. Instead—had it not been for the Name Value of the Cast—*Black Sleep* would be talked about today in the same breath as *I Was A Teenage Frankenstein*, *Missile to the Moon*, and *Frankenstein's Daughter*.

Too, this was Bela Lugosi's second-to-last film, and it was a shame not to hear that magnificent voice of his.

The *Black Sleep*—a choice example of Hollywood at its inept best.◼

Tiny Terror on TV

Agnes Moorehead starred in one of the most unforgettable television episodes when she appeared on Rod Serling's CBS-TV *Twilight Zone* in the story "The Invaders," scripted by Richard Matheson.

Miss Moorehead spoke not one single word throughout the entire 26½ minute tale!

The character she portrayed was a woman whose lonely existence is one night shattered when she is attacked by two strange robot-like creatures from another planet. As the sole occupant of the crude farmhouse, her only problem previous to this frightening encounter had been acquiring enough food to eat. But suddenly, unexpectedly, she is forced to repel the attack of a spaceship which crashes through her roof and settles to rest up in her attic.

The *switch-ending*—that of the spaceship and its occupants coming from Earth and not to Earth—coupled with Miss Moorehead's accomplished dramatics caused this particular *Twilight Zone* episode to be one of the most talked-about in the show's history.◼

A Handful of Celebrated Hollywood Horrors take a quick trip South of the Border to appear in EL CASTILLO DE LOS MONSTRUOS

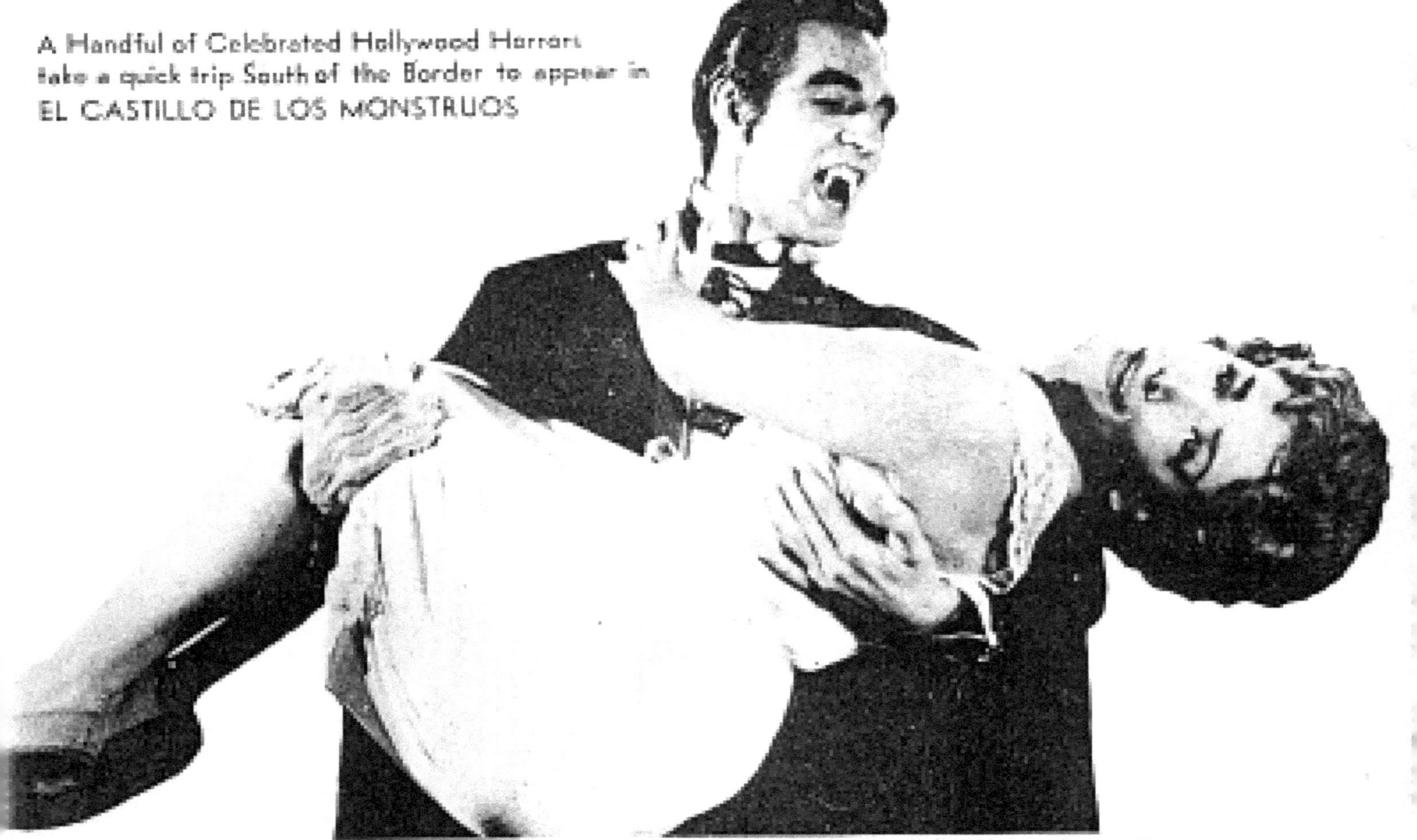

CASTLE OF THE MONSTERS

The Frankenstein Monster!—The Wolf Man!—Dracula!—The Mummy!—Creature from the Black Lagoon! All of these famous movieland monsters have joined forces to haunt a newlywed couple visiting a Mexican castle of horrors.

This is the story basis for the Mexican film *El Castillo De Los Monstruos—Castle of the Monsters.*

Of course, all of our favorite fiends of filmland look rather shoddy in this *Producciones Sotomayor, S.A.* release, but that's the way tortilla crumbles.

One of Mexico's favorite comedians, Clavillazo, is the human star of the film. It seems that he and his new bride, Evangelina Elizondo, are touring the countryside on their honeymoon, when suddenly—unexpectedly—their car runs out of gas. A savage thunderstorm is in the brewing, too.

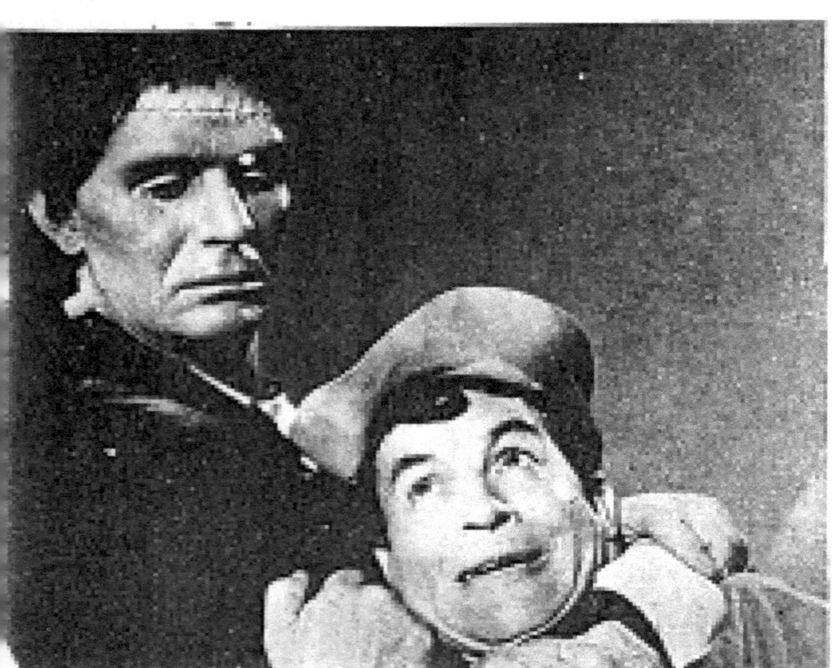

Castle of Monsters doorman, the Frankenstein Monster, greets guest Clavillazo

turn the page

Cassie and vampire Dracula play a game of life and death

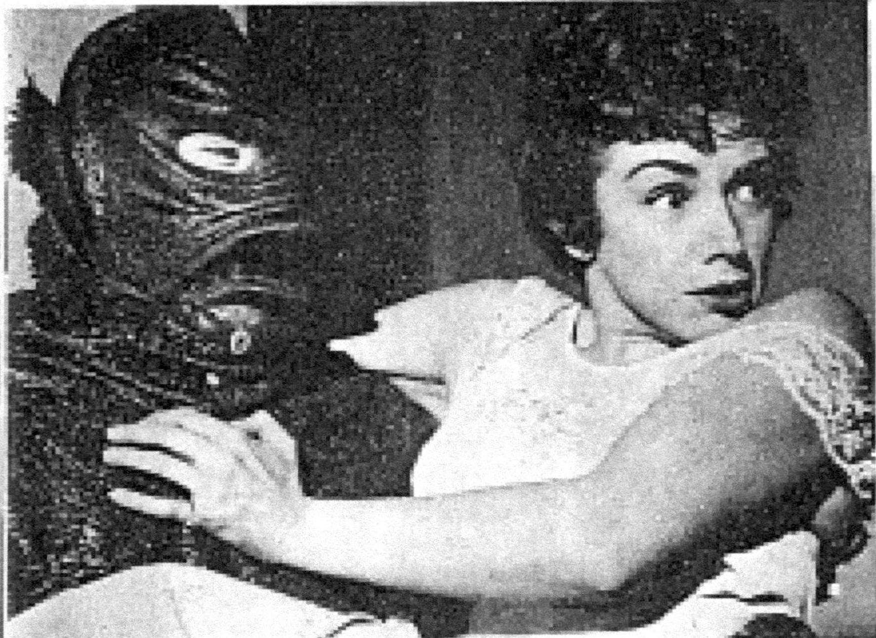

Frankenstein Monster and Wolf Man are about to give Clavillazo a hand

Clavillazo and Evangelina spot a castle off in the distance and decide to go there, hoping to get some gas from the owner.

It's pouring cats and Mexican jumping beans by the time the two of them reach the dry safety of the castle. No one is around—and they begin to search the musty old place.

They became separated in due time, and that's when things start happening.

Evangelina is attacked by the infamous Black Lagoon creature, but manages to break away—only to be menaced by the vampire man, Dracula.

Clavillazo suddenly feels claws about his neck and looks up to see some hideous creature grinning into his face. Dealing the beast a fast one-two, the comic darts off into another part of the castle, frantically searching for his bride.

She, meanwhile, is being chased by the Mummy; and seconds before she bumps smack into her bewildered lover, he is confronted by the Frankenstein Monster and Dracula—who are out after the girl.

This is the pace for the rest of the film. In the end, naturally, Clav and Evangelina scurry out of the castle of monsters, racing down the road as fast as their shaky legs will carry them.

But if you want to know what all of our favorite creeps are doing at the castle in the first place, you'll have to see the film. ■

Creature from the Black Lagoon and heroine Evangelina

Vincent Price as THE

by VINCENT LEWIS

Son of Frankenstein is without a doubt the last great Frankenstein film from Universal Pictures. For that matter, it is the last great Frankenstein film from any studio.

Scanning the list of titles in the celebrated series, we see the original *Frankenstein*, *Bride*, *Son*, *Ghost*, *Meets Wolf Man*, *House* and the *House of Dracula* sequel, *Abbott & Costello*; then two Hammer Films offerings in technicolor—*Curse* and *Revenge*, followed by various 35mm abominations such as *I Was A Teenage Frankenstein* and *Frankenstein's Daughter*, to name just two of the many atrocities that screamed at local theatres during the past few years.

There are some so-called "students" of horror films who will argue endlessly that *Meets Wolf Man*, for example, is certainly one of the better Frankenstein films. As far as this reviewer is concerned, there are two separate stables of Frankenstein films: first one comprising the first three films; the second sheltering all the titles that followed, whether produced by Universal or not.

On these terms, I will agree that *Meets Wolf Man* is indeed one of the better films of the series—in the *second* stable, of course. At that, undoubtedly the best in the second string is the *Abbott & Costello* picture, even though it is a comedy.

One of the points that qualifies *Son of Frankenstein* for placement in position number three in the first stable is the fact that here is Karloff for the last time portraying the now-famous Monster. Lon Chaney, Bela Lugosi, Glenn Strange, Christopher Lee, and others portrayed the Monster in later films, but none of them could possibly equal the dramatic genius of Karloff in the role.

turn the page

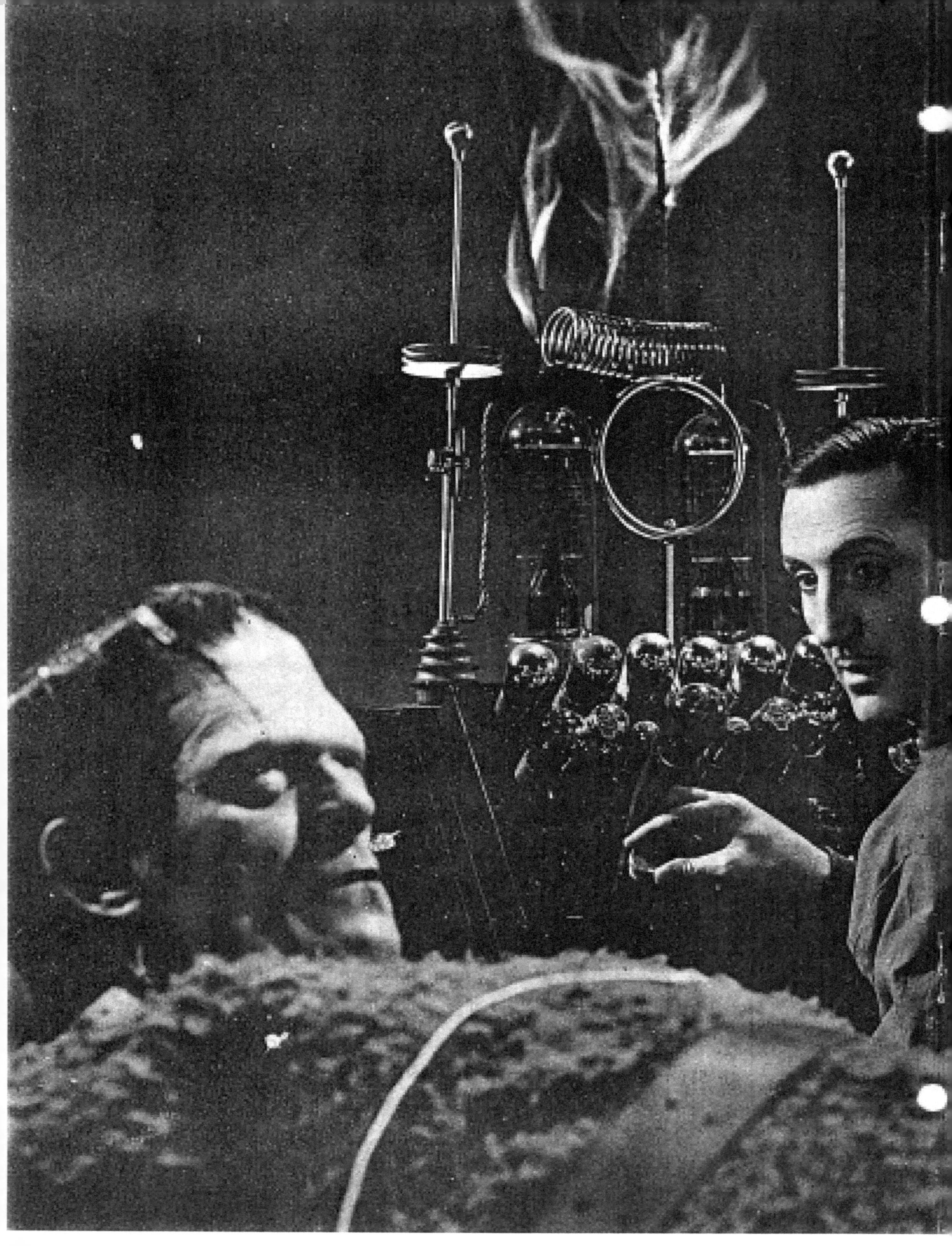

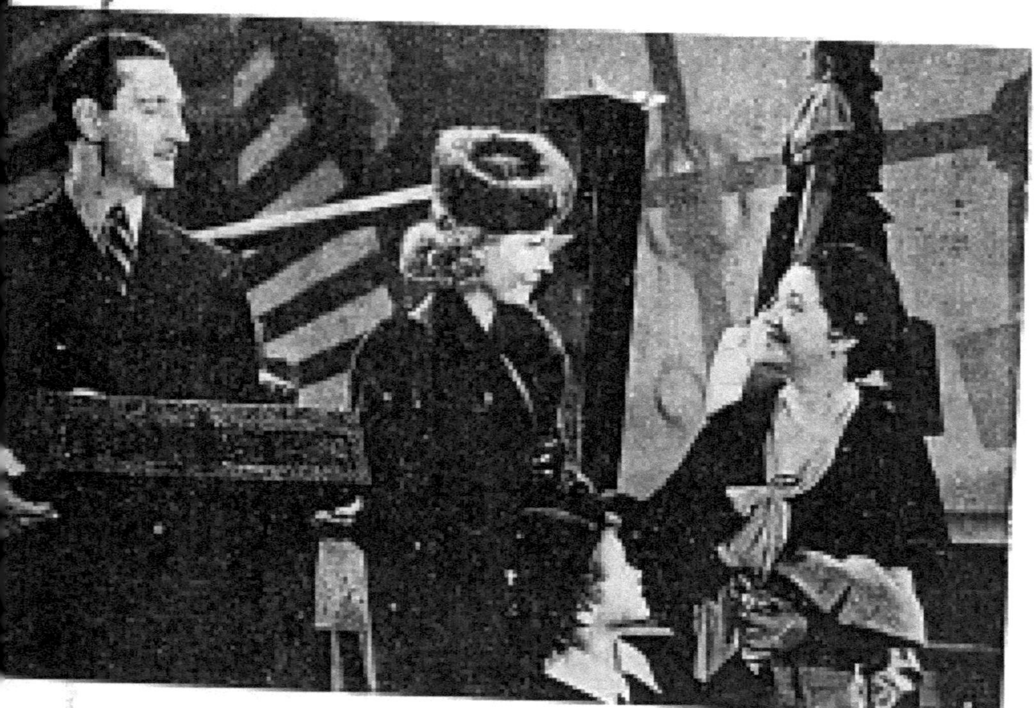

Too, and probably most important, this film represents the last time audiences were given the Frankenstein Monster as a pitiful creature and not as some huge lumbering ox who stiff-legs around the set, grunting and groaning like an ape, making his much-awaited appearance not until the last reel.

When Karloff vacated the role after this film, it seemed as if the studio couldn't care less about producing their next Frankenstein film with any degree of intelligence or artistic merit. *Ghost of* was the first of the second stable films, and I know that all who saw it during its original release were vastly disappointed.

Son was an original screenplay by Willis Cooper, produced and directed for Universal by Rowland Lee. Lionel Atwill, Josephine Hutchinson, and Edgar Norton were in featured roles. The massive sets were designed by Jack Otterson, and the eerie lighting and camera effects were handled by George Robinson.

In the story, Basil Rathbone assumes the mantle of Baron Wolf von Frankenstein, possessor of the dread heritage of the family, who returns to his ancestral castle twenty-five years after his father's death, as stipulated by the elder Frankenstein's will.

There, he stumbles upon his father's grim creation, the hair-raising Monster of Destruction and Pity, played by Karloff.

Soon afterwards, Wolf encounters Ygor (Lugosi), the crazed, broken-necked shepherd, who insists Wolf take up his father's experiments with life and death and restore the electrical power to the giant creation. This the young Frankenstein does, and later lives to regret.

Ygor, who had been sentenced to hang for grave-robbing and who escaped from his fate by a miracle and with a broken neck, thinks of revenge now. He plans to use the revived Monster in his scheme. Afraid that Wolf will destroy the Monster should he learn of Ygor's plans, the mad shepherd tries to kill the scientist but is accidentally killed himself. Blindly striking out to avenge Ygor, the Monster kidnaps Wolf's little boy to kill him. But Wolf arrives in time to save the child, and sends a post hurtling at the creature, knocking him off balance and flipping him into a bubbling pit of molten lava.

Lionel Atwill gave an excellent performance as a police inspector whose arm has been torn off by the Monster sometime previous.

And Bela Lugosi probably gave his most memorable performance since *Dracula* as the shepherd Ygor. As a matter of fact, this writer believes that the role of Ygor is by far Lugosi's best.

turn the page

ABOVE: The Monster backs away towards the sulphur pits; RIGHT: Actor is floored by the fact that the Monster likes to read books; BELOW: Ygor brings the Monster to the lab

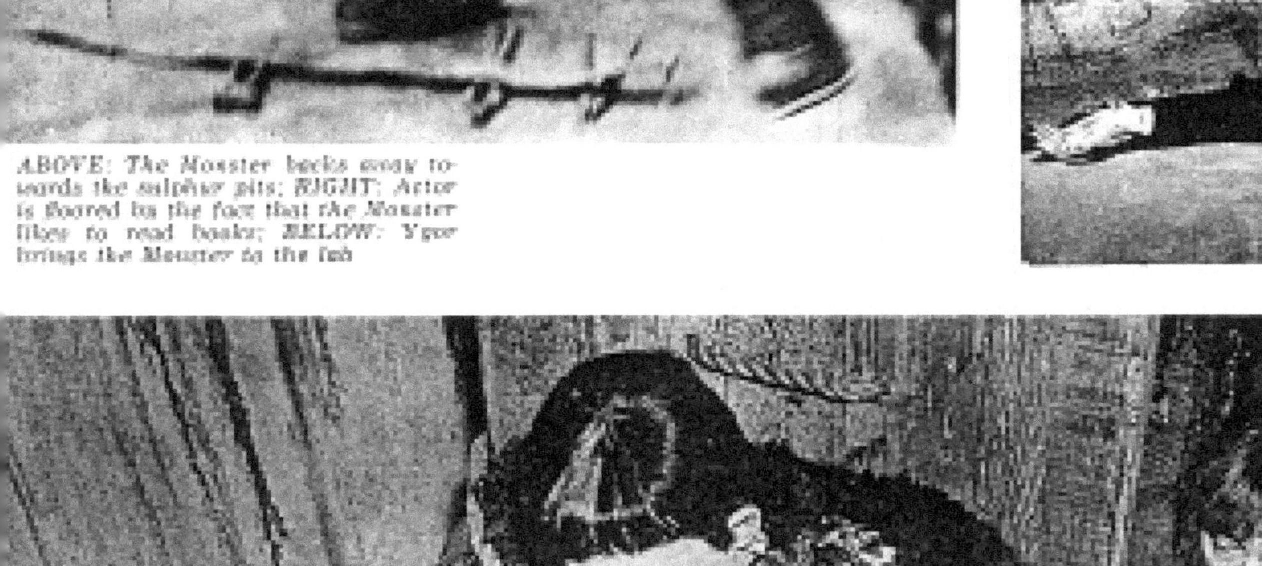

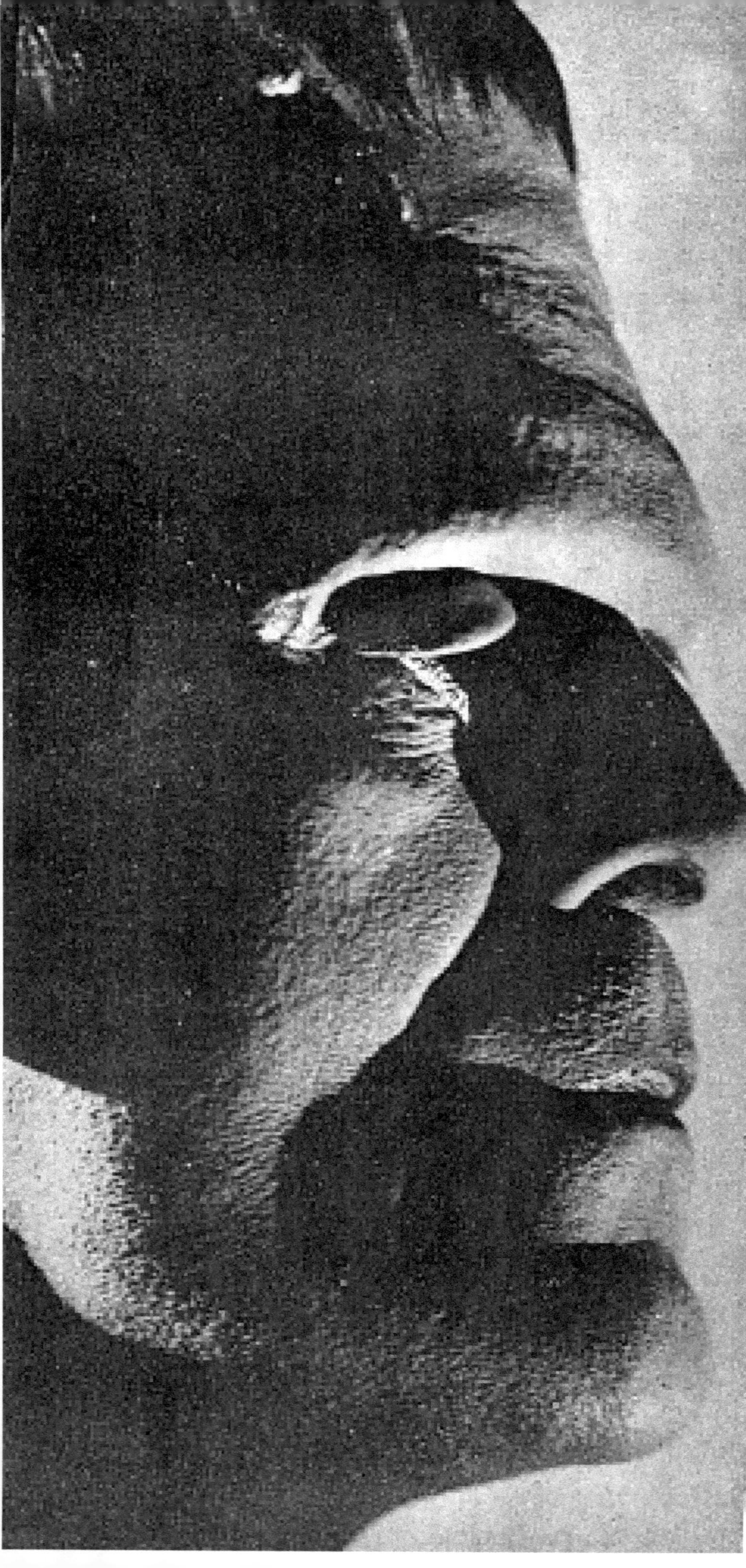

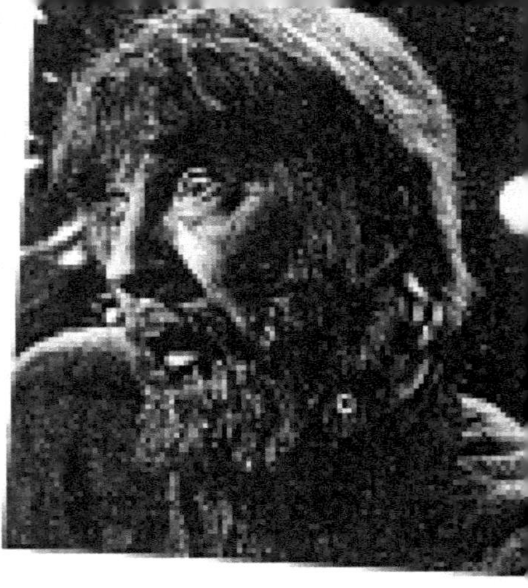

Rathbone, I'm afraid, is guilty of over-acting in this film—particularly in the sequence where he is tossing darts while being questioned by Atwill as to what he knows, if anything, about a monstrous being who is running rampant around the countryside scaring and sometimes killing local villagers.

Karloff's portrayal of the Monster is truly not as magnificent as in the second picture, Bride. An interesting footnote to Karloff in Son is the fact that technicians constructed a permanent double for him made of half-inch iron piping. It moved on rubber tired wheels. The body was merely an upright pole, but at the top of the pole—some seven feet above the floor—was fixed a plaster mask. This mask was an exact likeness of Karloff as the Monster. It was covered with the same gray-green greasepaint, and a scar was made on the right cheek. There were the same sort of big metal clamps in the fake skull as were used to fasten the sections of the Monster's head on Karloff. The main reason for the construction of this thing is that it was used as a "stand-in" for Karloff before the cameras began grinding away on a scene. To make up a regular human stand-in for Karloff would have taken eight hours every day, just as it did for the star.■

GHOULITA FAN CLUB

I would like to announce that membership in the GHOULITA FAN CLUB is now open. Membership fee is 50c, for which you receive a photo of Ghoulita, club badge, membership card, and club pencil. Address all mail to:

MARK SHEPARD, Pres
GHOULITA FAN CLUB
16167 ADLON ROAD
ENCINO, CALIFORNIA

Pictured above is Mark Shepard and Hollywood's favorite TV female fiend, the Mae West of the Graveyard — GHOULITA. The gorgeous (?) ghoul gal is the hostess of KCOP-TV's Saturday night horror show program "Jeepers Creepers," which has proven to be a fantastic hit with California viewers.—Ed.

SPECIAL REQUEST DEPT.

Is it possible for you to print a picture of me as the Frankenstein Monster?

JIM KELLY
PHILADELPHIA, PA

No.—Ed.

ANGRY READER

I must express my resentment concerning a letter sent in by Bill Page of Oklahoma which appeared in GHOUL CALL in FANTASTIC MONSTERS #4.

I am sure there must be others who read the letter who will agree with me that Vincent Price is one of the few fine actors of our time. Mr Price is not only an outstanding actor who, I think, portrays Edgar Allan Poe's characters expertly, but he is also one of the most intelligent and recognize human beings of our era, and he should be respected for all these rare qualities. Those who display similar opinions to that of Bill Page, such as "Getting sick and tired of seeing Price in AIP films," undoubtedly do not appreciate the type of high-quality acting which Mr Price represents in the whole area of the motion picture industry.

I say, Vincent Price portrays Poe's subjects as well as or better than anyone else ever brought into the production of these films, and, may I add, with power and a quality which is so very hard to find in many other actors. If you agree with Bill Page and eliminate Mr Price from the production of these films, you will also be eliminating a most important factor involved in the enjoyment and excitement of these film thrillers.

BONNIE IVONE
BROOKLYN, NY

MAD MUMMY MUMBLINGS

If you wanted a long title for the Mad Mummy's column in FANMO #5 why didn't you use one like THE RETURN OF THE REVENGE OF THE CURSE ON THE HOUSE OF THE GHOST OF THE SON OF THE MAD MUMMY VS THE HORROR OF THE BRIDE OF THE SECOND SON OF WOLF MAN'S DAUGHTER—1970?

WERNER LEUPOLD
SARATOGA, CALIF

I'm glad the Mad Mummy was kidnapped. I only wish I was one of the renegade literary critics who helped cart him off. I hope you never find him.

ED KOCAR
BROOKFIELD, ILL

Why don't you put out a special issue of your magazine that contains nothing but all of the Mad Mummy articles together?

PAUL MITCHELL
LOUISVILLE, KY

FRANKENSTEIN FINE

I think Paul Severn's article on GHOST OF FRANKENSTEIN in #5 was great, and I would like to know if you could add more stories and pictures of Karloff as Frankenstein in future issues?

LARRY RAY
SACTO, CALIF

You'll find a lot of info and pix of Karloff in our next edition, Larry. Over twenty-five pages will be devoted to the King of Horror Films—Ed.

CRITIC OF THE MONTH.

I find the latest issue of FANMO (#5) not up to par with previous issues. The cover wasn't colorful enough. Haydock's HOW TO MAKE A WEREWOLF HOWL was ok, but at the bottom of the first page I saw a dot, denoting that the article was over when it really wasn't. DEVIL'S WORKSHOP was, as usual, very interesting. STEELMASK MEETS THE ZOMBIE MASTER was good. I liked the surprise ending. REVENGE OF THE SON OF THE MAD MUMMY STRIKES BACK gave your magazine a very definite anti-sequel, anti-remake policy. The Mad Mummy shouldn't have used BRIDE OF FRANKENSTEIN as an example, however, because most people consider it to be better than the original. Also, what he says about HORROR OF DRACULA is rather vague. Everyone I know who has seen that movie considers it to be better than the original DRACULA.

GHOST OF FRANKENSTEIN review was very disappointing. In the review itself, Mr Severn started off on the wrong foot (or is it paw?) by giving the film opening wrong. What happened was that the villagers were about to dynamite castle Frankenstein when Ygor appeared. He tumbled huge concrete blocks down on them, in a futile attempt to stop them. But, as the charges went off, the castle shook and huge blocks caved in. Ygor, amidst all this destruction, made his perilous way through the falling rubble and masonry to the bottom of the sulphur pit; where, sticking out of a pile of bricks, he saw a hand. Working feverishly, he soon had the entire Frankenstein Monster uncovered. Another thing—the Monster did not crush Ygor to death. But my biggest gripe was that writer Severn never even mentioned the fact that since Ygor's blood-type had been different from that of the Monster's, Ygor had gone BLIND, which was the reason for his having gone berserk. Mr Severn also neglected to mention what he meant when he stated that the camera work was not distinguished, and that the makeup department had or adapted Chaney's face to conform with Karloff's.

DAY OF THE TRIFFIDS article was good, but who drew those eyes on the triffid on page 27? FRANKENSTEIN . . . THE ILLUSTRATED MONSTER, I enjoyed. MY FRIEND THE FIEND was also interesting; and COMING OF THE ROBOTS was fine. What movie was that robot on page 34 from? Writer Jim Harmon erred when he said the robot in METROPOLIS was the only female automaton on the screen. There was a female robot in CREATION OF THE HUMANOIDS.

SCREEN SCREAM QUEENS was good. Alex Gordon's MY FAVORITE VAMPIRE was my favorite article in the issue. I liked the stills of Lugosi, too. How about showing a photo of Bela being made up as the Frankenstein Monster by Jack Pierce? BLACK ZOO article fine. ADVENTURES OF SPY SMASHER by Richard Lupoff was my second favorite article. MONSTER OF THE MONTH pinup was ok, except you forgot Evelyn Ankers' hair is red, not blonde, and that the Wolf Man's coat is a dirty reddish-brown. (If you doubt me, check a WOLF MAN movie poster.)

On the whole, however, I think FANTASTIC MONSTERS is an excellent magazine. Finally—BRING BACK THE MAD MUMMY!

JEFF KNOREY
(no address)

The robot photo in COMING OF THE ROBOTS is from an experimental color film produced by Golden Eagle Films for American-International Pictures—Ed.

from Fellow Monsters

SUPERMAN FAN

The article on the Superman serials by Kirk Alyn in #4 was terrific. Congratulations to Kirk on a fine article. I really appreciate stories like this with little-known, behind-the-scenes facts. The pictures which accompanied the article were also terrific. Kirk has been my favorite actor ever since 1948 when the first Superman serial was released. I hope to see more articles like MEMOIRS OF A SUPERMAN in future issues.
JOHN SKILLIN
UPPER MONTCLAIR, NJ

MORE MONSTERS

We, the members of The League of Vampires and Werewolves, believe that your magazine is one of the best to come along in many years. The idea of having color monster photos was a brainstorm. Some of your stories are very ghoulish and enjoyable to read, but we have been reading some letters sent in by various readers who are asking for more stories on space films and movie serials. We feel that if you print such stories, you will lose some of your readers. We hope that in the future you will refrain from running articles on outer space movies and serials. After all, FANTASTIC MONSTERS is a MONSTER MAGAZINE!
ROBERT MARTIN, Sec
12318 PRESTON WAY
LOS ANGELES 66, CALIF

PRICE COLLECTOR

Until about two years ago I had never heard of an actor named Vincent Price. But since seeing him in FALL OF THE HOUSE OF USHER, I have never missed one of his films. The current one showing in London is TALES OF TERROR, and my friends and I rate it the best he has made yet.

The reason why your magazine appeals to me is because you include thousands of pictures of him from his films BUT—you have not yet written anything about Vincent himself; if he is married or not, when he first started in films, and so on. I am sure that many of his fans like myself would very much like to know all about him. So how about doing an article on him in a future issue? In fact, I implore you to. I have my own personal scrap book on him, and so far have his photos and information on his films, but I don't have a life story. I look forward to reading his biography soon in FANTASTIC MONSTERS.
VICKY EVANS
LONDON, ENGLAND

A Vincent Price article is in the making, Vicky. In the meantime, we suggest that you and all other Price fans read Vincent's excellent book, "I Like What I Know," which was published a few years ago. Incidentally, how many of you readers knew that Vincent once starred in Poe's PIT AND THE PENDULUM—on RADIO? This was years before he made the AIP film version of the classic tale.
—Ed.

ALEX & BELA

Movie producer Alex Gordon's article on Bela Lugosi (MY FAVORITE VAMPIRE, FANTASTIC MONSTERS #5) brought to mind a question which has been bothering me for years. Why aren't we allowed to see Bela's VAMPIRE OVER LONDON film? According to Mr Gordon, he has had a tough time trying to sell it to American distributors. In view of the current cycle of horror films, most of which are very bad, VAMPIRE OVER LONDON can't be THAT bad that no one will show it.

I only wish Bela were alive today to enjoy all the free publicity he has been getting in FANTASTIC MONSTERS and its competitors, as well as in hundreds of amateur horrorzines across the country. Considering that Bela is still one of the three top horror favorites (the other two being Karloff and Chaney Jr) even though he is no longer with us, Mr Gordon should realize that he has not written an article on his one-time friend for fans of FANMO alone—but for all of Bela's fans all over the world! So who not let the millions of fans of the greatest Dracula of all time see VAMPIRE OVER LONDON, one of his last films?

There is even a fan club devoted entirely to Bela's memory. I am a member, and all Lugosi fans should contact the president of the club and join. He is Bill Obbagy, C o The American Bela Lugosi Fan Club, 11818 Forest Ave, Cleveland 20, Ohio.
FRANKIE LARKIN
HOLLYWOOD, CALIF

SATISFIED READER

I've just finished reading GHOUL CALL in previous issues and there are a few things bothering me. In several issues The Mad Mummy was derided and criticized. I think this moldy member of your staff is GREAT! I always enjoy reading his articles. Your fiction stories also have been criticized unjustly. Don't drop them. They're tops! As for you guys who are constantly criticizing FANMO, here's what I have to say to you: I'd like to see you try and do better! I think FANMO is the GREATEST!
JEFF JONES
SAN DIEGO, CALIF

QUICKIES

After reading Judson Grey's STEEL MASK MEETS THE ZOMBIE MASTER in #5 I thought it was really great! Please—more Steelmask stories!
ROGER LESSER
DENVER, COLO

I abhor your magazine! FANTASTIC MONSTERS is the biggest waste of time, space, and money yet!
GALEN PEOPLES
(no address)

GREATEST HORROR EVER HEARD !

ONLY IN "RADIOHERO" CAN YOU SEE THE PICTURES AND STORIES OF THE PHANTOM HEROES AND VILLAINOUS MONSTERS BROADCAST DURING THE GOLDEN AGE OF RADIO—AND THEN LOST FOREVER EXCEPT IN THE FILES OF JIM HARMON, THE WORLD'S GREATEST EXPERT ON RADIO CLASSICS!

HERE THEY ARE! HORRORS AND MONSTERS TOO MIGHTY FOR ANY MOVIE SCREEN! *The Temple of Vampires, the Werewolf Who was Beloved, The Secret Mountain-top of the Superman Challenged by the Greatest Threesome since the Three Musketeers—JACK, DOC AND REGGIE IN "I LOVE A MYSTERY"! The Hound of Hell, the Slavering Beast whose Fiery Teeth Brought a Cursed Agony worse than Death until he met the Greatest Foe of Evil of all Time — SHERLOCK HOLMES! The Monster of the Mansion, the Phantom Train of the Abandoned Subway with its Car-load of Corpses, the Man with the Touch of Death All Battled by the Master of Men's Minds—the Invisible Man whose Power Could Control the Entire World —THE SHADOW!*

AND THERE'S MORE!

Now RADIOHERO brings you pictures and stories of Golden Age Radio's Heroes as they appear in

MOVIE SERIALS!
COMIC BOOKS!
PULP FICTION MAGAZINES!
BIG LITTLE BOOKS!
PREMIUMS!

Yes, now it's

"RADIOHERO" — The Magazine of the Golden Age of Heroes, Villains, Thrills, and Smiles. Edited by Jim Harmon, Famous Science Fiction Star, with Redd Boggs, Western Authority, and Teen-Age Horror Expert, Don Glut, Special Consultant; Ron Haydock, Editor of the World's Greatest Monster Magazine, FANTASTIC MONSTERS! Only these geniuses could bring you the GREATEST THRILL MAGAZINE OF ALL TIME...

"RADIOHERO"—

Sold by Mail Only! 60¢ per trial copy. Now before the price may go up—Six Tremendous Issues of this Handsome Limited Edition—Only $3.00!

JIM HARMON, RADIOHERO

—Topanga, Calif.

"When Thor first met us with his co-title performer during the production of *The Monster and the Ape*, he momentarily went on a sit-down strike.

"Thor was mildly curious about the Metalogen Man, while the huge robot was standing still. However, when it started walking, Thor backed into a corner with ludicrous alacrity.

"Little by little, the great ape was coaxed out of his voluntary retreat by his trainer. The robot raised its hand in friendly greeting and, once again, Thor decided that discretion was the better part of valor. It was not until the robot's eyes lit up that Thor surrendered—to curiosity. He stopped his backtracking and slowly came up to the robot. Tentatively, he put his huge paw up to the eyes. All at once, the lights went out. Thor took his paw away quickly, but this time stood his ground. Cautiously, he sniffed at the robot.

"That's enough,' said director Howard Bretherton, they're acquainted now.'

"Thor was taken back to his corner. Later, during a scene which did not include the ape or the robot, a terrific clanking noise was heard offstage. There was Thor, conducting a personal investigation of the robot. Apparently he was trying to find out what happened to those lights, for he was poking his huge fingers at the robot's glass eyes!"

The two stunt men in robot and ape costumes fighting atop a building, the contest, the "Disease of Metalogen" may be gone forever, but the serial is still around today. We suggest you request your favorite theatre to run it. It's a grand way to spend fifteen Saturday afternoons.●

MONSTER MOVIE ADS!

Half the fun of a new Horror, Science-fiction, Terror, or Monster Movie is seeing the films' advertising in newspapers, magazines, and on TV! And as is too often the case, the advertising is so much better than the picture itself! We know there are many of you Out There who make collections of fantasy film ads, and we'll be giving you pages in each issue you can clip out and put in your scrapbooks. In times to come you'll see the original advertisements for such classic films as BRIDE OF FRANKENSTEIN, THE WOLF MAN, HOUSE OF DRACULA, and many more! And for those of you who don't collect the movie ads, we hope you'll get a kick out of seeing them again in this magazine—or maybe even seeing them for the first time!

ELECTRONIC WAR ERUPTS FROM OUTER SPACE...
M-G-M PRESENTS
"THE MYSTERIANS"
in BIG SCREEN COLOR!
WHO CAN SAY IT WILL NOT HAPPEN?
A TOHO PRODUCTION

CAN YOU TAKE "THE REVENGE OF FRANKENSTEIN"?
WARNING! Be sure you can take this tremendous adventure into terror!
PLEASE don't scream too loudly— you may scare those waiting to get into the theatre!!!
IN SUPERNATURAL TECHNICOLOR
THE WHOLE WORLD TREMBLES BEFORE THE NEW FRANKENSTEIN!
starring
PETER CUSHING · EUNICE GAYSON · FRANCIS MATTHEWS · MICHAEL GWYNN
Written by   Produced by   Directed by
JIMMY SANGSTER · ANTHONY HINDS · TERENCE FISHER · A HAMMER FILM PRODUCTION
A COLUMBIA PICTURE

Night Creatures in Eastman COLOR
THEIR OATH WAS... TERROR!
THEIR CRY... BLOOD!
PETER CUSHING
NO WOMAN ALIVE IS SAFE from the MOST FRIGHTENING FIEND IN THE HISTORY OF HORROR!

BLOOD OF THE VAMPIRE
ALL NEW in Eastman COLOR
DONALD WOLFIT · BARBARA SHELLEY
VINCENT BALL and VICTOR MADDERN   Produced by ROBERT S. BAKER and MONTY BERMAN
Directed by HENRY CASS · Story and Screenplay by JIMMY (FRANKENSTEIN) SANGSTER
An EROS FILMS LTD. Production · A UNIVERSAL-INTERNATIONAL Release

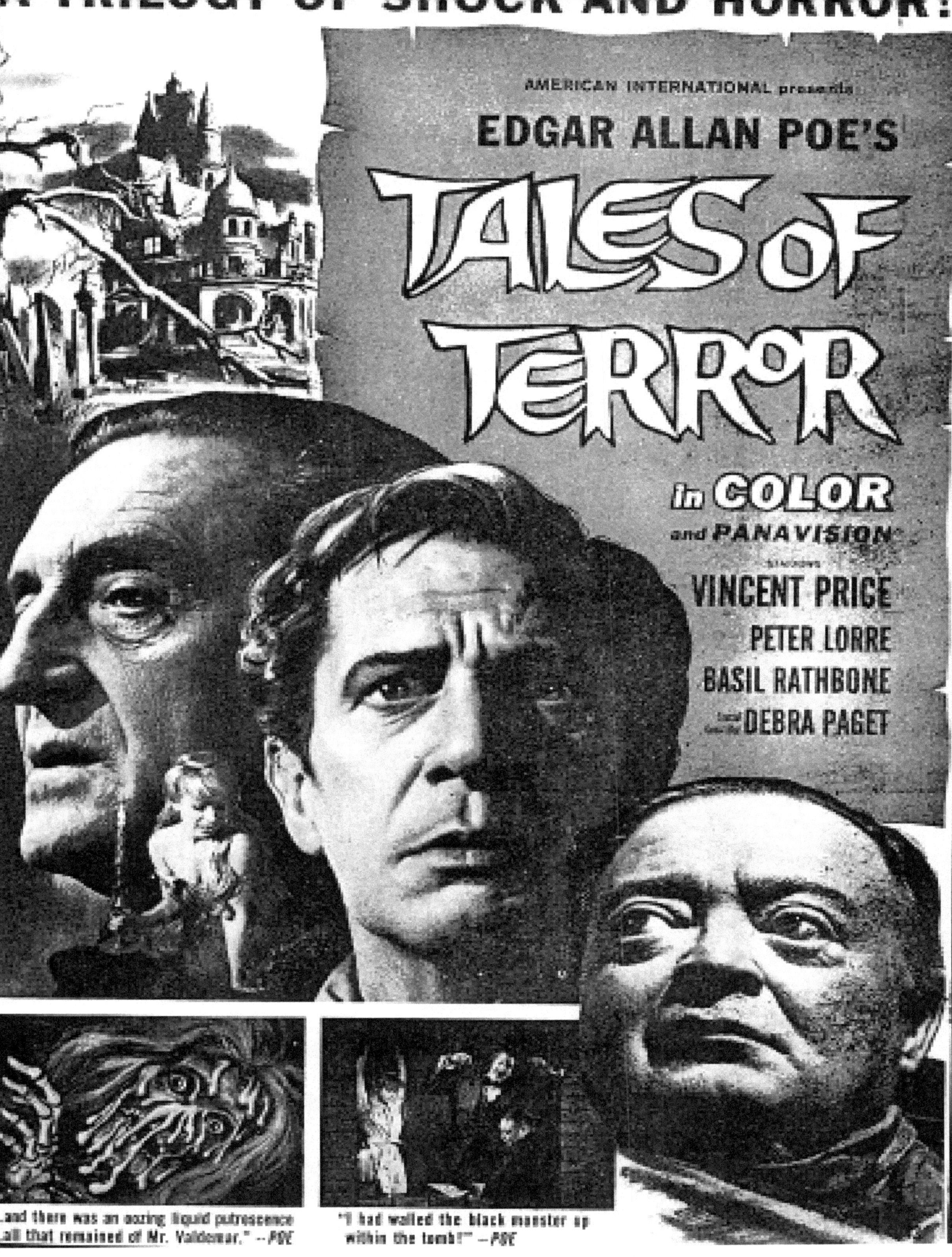
A TRILOGY OF SHOCK AND HORROR!
AMERICAN INTERNATIONAL presents
EDGAR ALLAN POE'S
TALES OF TERROR
in COLOR
and PANAVISION
STARRING
VINCENT PRICE
PETER LORRE
BASIL RATHBONE
and Introducing DEBRA PAGET
...and there was an oozing liquid putrescence all that remained of Mr. Valdemar." —POE
"I had walled the black monster up within the tomb!" —POE

TARANT

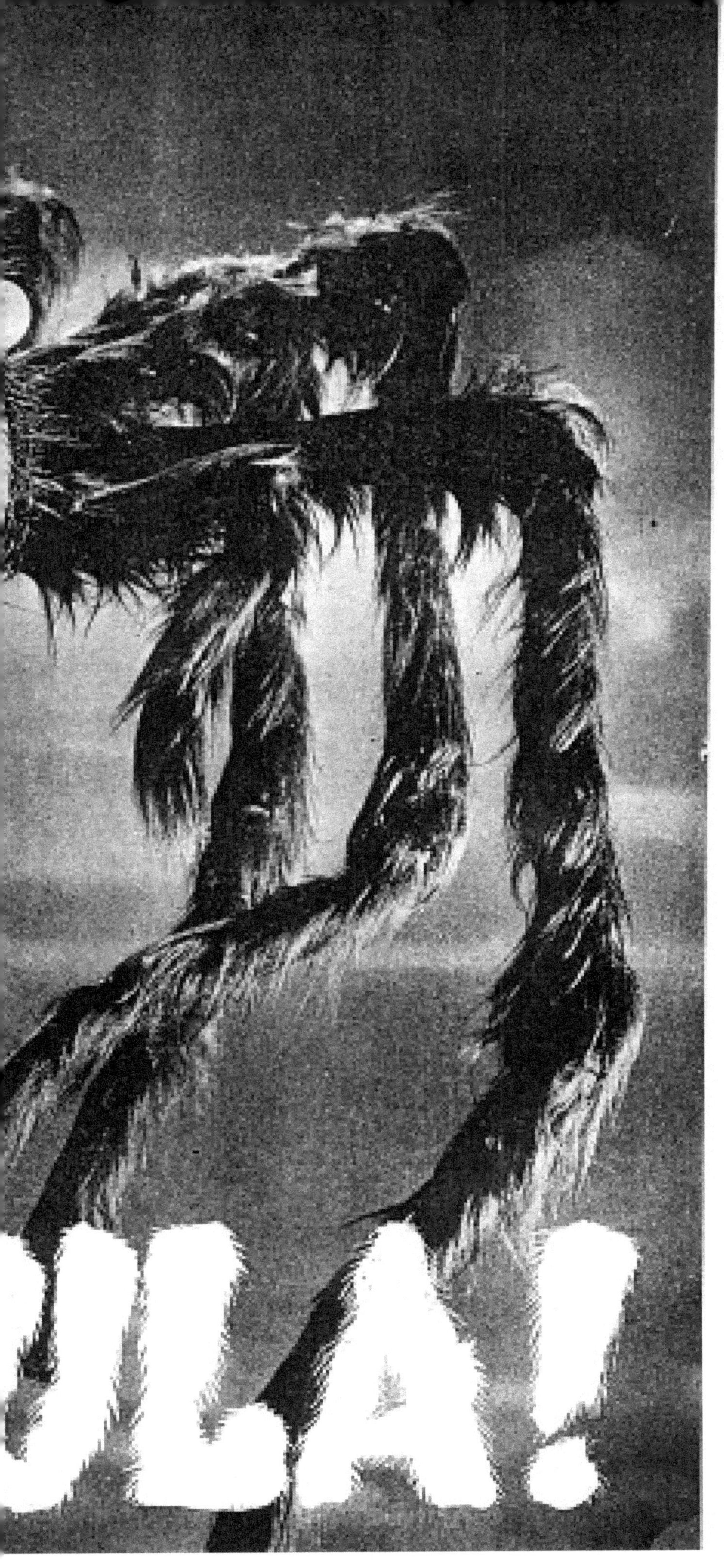

Fantastic Monsters interviews Monster-Chaser John Agar on the subject of co-starring with a 60 foot high Spider

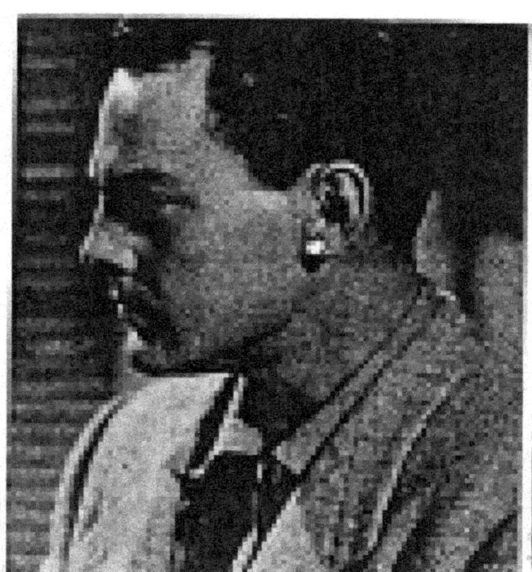

"Every actor should emote opposite a tarantula at least once during his screen career!"

This is the considered opinion of John Agar, who starred opposite Mara Corday and Leo G. Carroll—and a giant tarantula—in Universal-International's 1955 science-fiction adventure release, *Tarantula*.

"Co-starring with a spider 60 feet high and 50 feet wide," John Agar went on, "is an experience no man can easily forget. It adds to an actor's stature."

One could not be quite certain whether John was kidding. He said this was the first time in his professional life that he had come smack up against such a mammoth scene stealer, and he did not know what to do about it.

He admitted that trying to keep a monster from stealing important scenes kept him on his toes; and this he heartily recommended for the edification of every player who is sincere about his work.

"If Donald O'Connor could take it from Francis in those talking mule pictures," Agar said, "I decided I was ready to level with that hairy old spider."

Tarantula was produced by William Alland, the man responsible for shrinking the incredible man on the screen two years later and whisking audiences away to the planet Metaluna in *This Island Earth* shortly before the filming of the spider film.

The grotesque makeups seen in *Tarantula* were created by the well-known Bud Westmore.

Fortunately for John, he didn't have to undergo any physical changes in the picture—unlike some of his co-stars.

"No," he said, "all I had to do was battle a spider bigger than a two-story house!"

turn the page

... gets a sympathetic assignment as a scientist who is called in to investigate strange goings-on at a desert laboratory where experiments are being carried on to develop an artificial nutrient.

When two scientists die under mysterious circumstances with greatly swollen features near Desert Rock Arizona, immediate suspicion is cast on their remaining colleague, Prof. Gerald Deemer (played by Leo G. Carroll, "Topper" on TV).

Dr. Matt Hastings (Agar) thus investigates the situation.

After the subsequent mysterious killings of human beings as well as herds of cattle, Hastings arrives at the conclusion that the killer is a giant spider—a tarantula that has escaped from Prof. Deemer's lab. Hastings believes that because of the nutrient injections, the once normal-sized spider has now grown to huge proportions.

Deemer discovers that he has been injected with the deadly nutrient while unconscious after a fight with one of the mad scientists who died in agony experimenting with themselves.

Approaching his own death rather casually, Deemer explains to a new female colleague—scientist Stephanie Clayton (Mara Corday)—that he has been searching for an atomically stabilized nutritional formula which will feed the world's masses when they grow too large for the food supply in a few generations.

Deemer realizes, however, that the nutrient he has developed is highly unstable—and when injected into a human, it will cause tremendous glandular changes.

Meanwhile—the tarantula, now as big as a barn, attacks the little town of Desert Rock. Jumping to the defense are Hastings and a squad of highway patrolmen.

But it is they and not the monster who are almost destroyed!

There seems little left to do but call in the Air Force—who sends a pair of jets streaking across the sky and over the doomed town just in time to drop napalm bombs on the creature and destroy the beast before it can cause further damage.

The bombs burn the spider to death, and the reign of terror is over—leaving Hastings and Stephanie to walk arm in arm into the sunset. . . .

Actually, *Tarantula* was not John Agar's first encounter co-starring with "scene-stealing monsters."

Shortly before appearing opposite the spider, John shared the billing with the now-famous Gill Man, in the 3-D thriller, *Revenge of the Creature*.

Another picture in which John came face-to-face with the unearthly was *Brain from Planet Arous*. However, in this film, it was a turnabout—John metamorphisized into a monster!

With a grin, the handsome actor suddenly recalled that the U-I spider movie was really not the first time he came to grips with a tarantula.

turn the page

● *This deformed creature, victim of lab experiment, staggers to his bloated death*

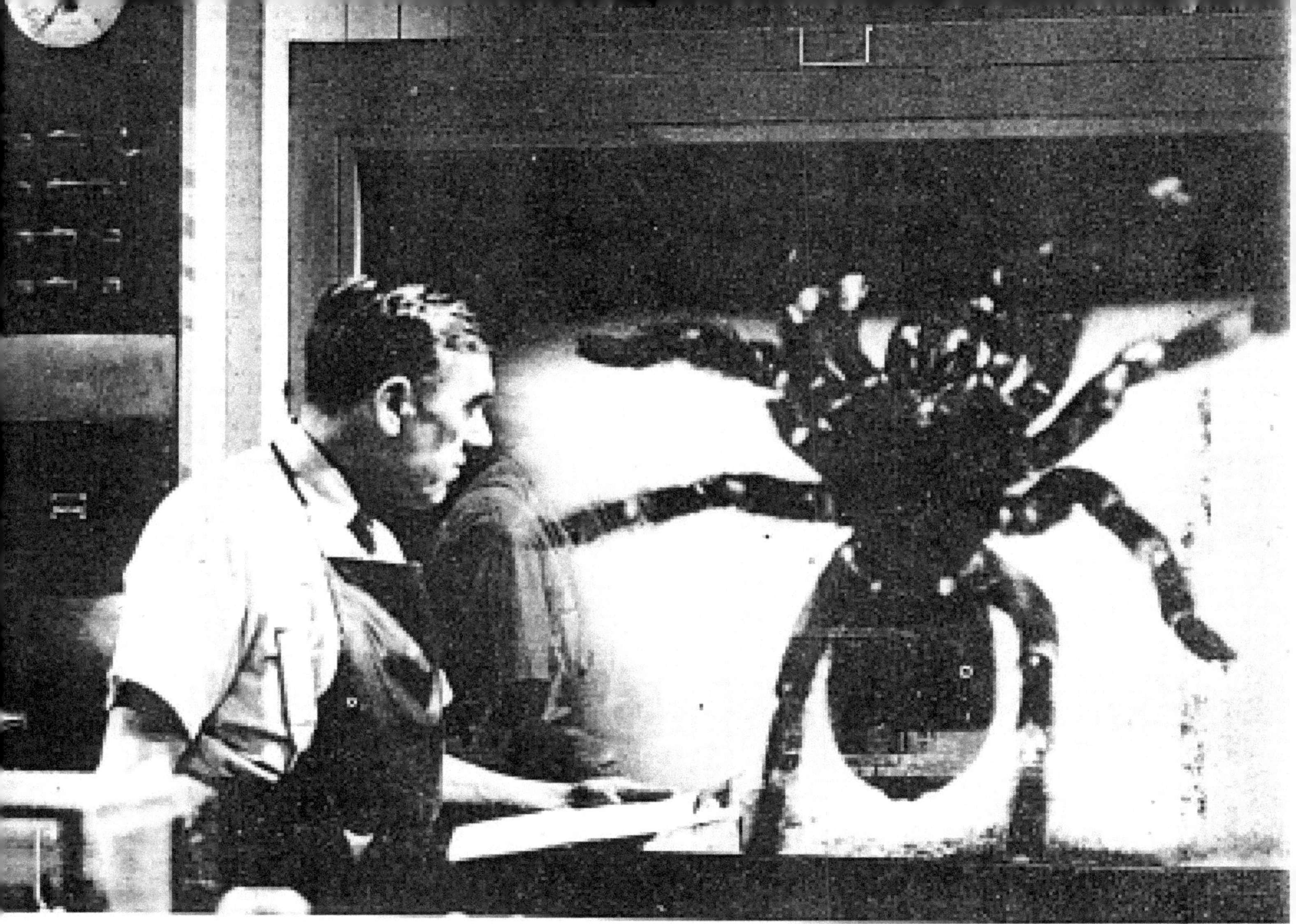

Leo G. Carroll gazes in wonder at the size of his pet tarantula

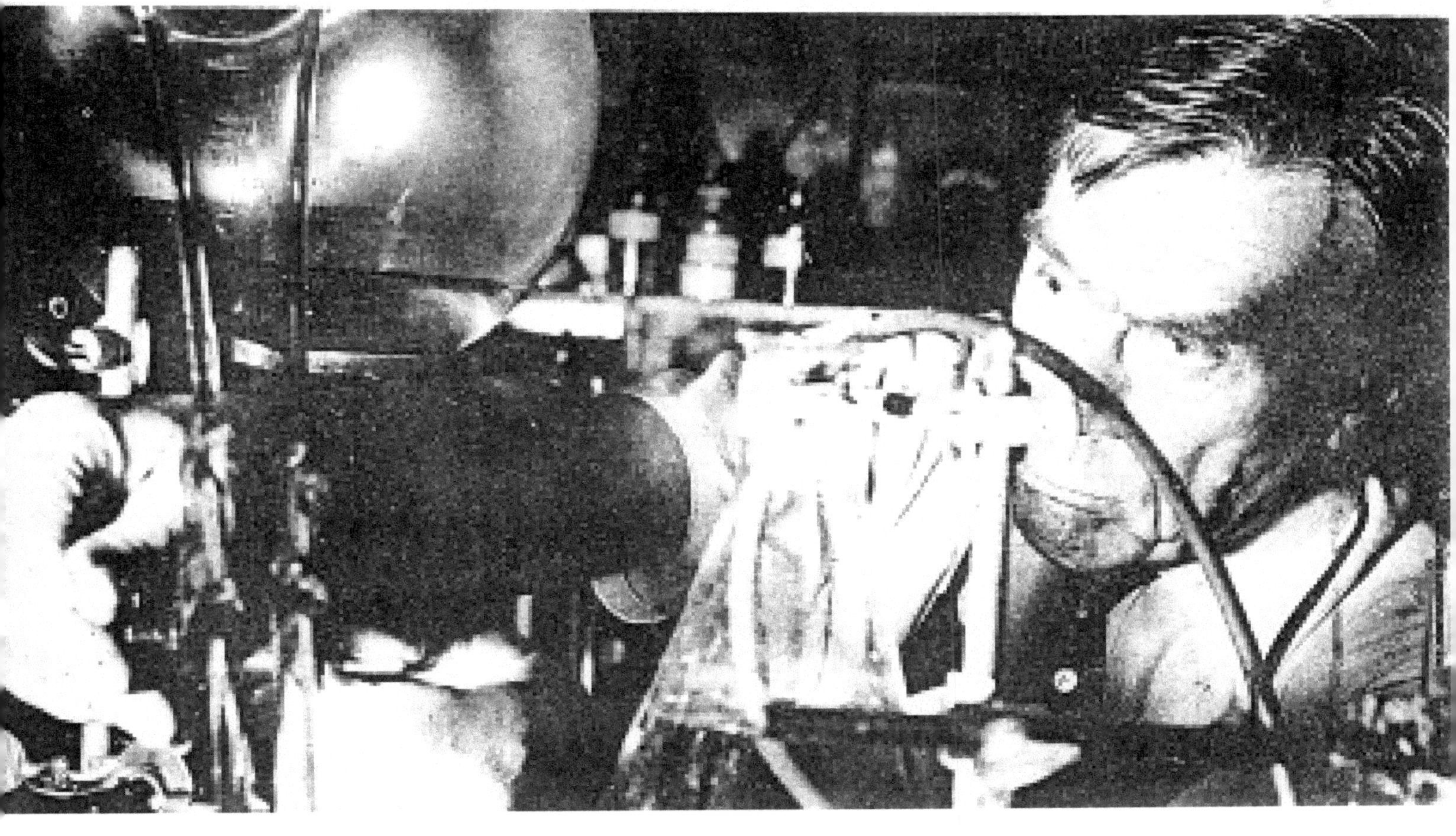

"When I was a child," he not
fondly remembered. "I was bitten b
a tarantula and spent an entire wee
in the hospital letting the docto
drain the poison from me and recupe
ating."

He added that he was glad t
was no such thing as a 60 foot spide
romping around in his childhood.

In conclusion, John said, "I believ
that every actor should be given th
opportunity of co-starring with a mon
ster at least once—if only to tell h
grandchildren about the experience
As a matter of fact, it's getting so tha
your prestige isn't worth a nickel un
less you have a monster to your cred
its!"

ABOVE, John Agar, Ed Rand, and Nestor Paiva—on the scene of the latest cattle killing; BELOW, state police and deputies flee in terror after laying dynamite charges in a vain effort to stop the giant spider.

Leo G. Carroll is attacked by Ed Parker who also portrays one of the many ill-fated experimenters working with the deadly menace.

A quick course about a curse—the
doom of a man from a 2000 year
old race who tries to save face,
with nothing for a base
"Curse Of The FACELESS Man"
50

by DON SHEPPARD

Some remarkable new faces zoned into view in 1958. Satirist Stan Freberg aired the panel panic *Face the Funnies* for CBS-Radio, while Audrey Hepburn danced the lighter fantastic with her own MGM-style *Funnyface*. Spencer Tracy had already done an about-face as Dr Jekyll and Claude Rains had managed to lose his while sealing *La Tosca* as the Opera's pet Phantom.

But actor Bob Bryant was faced with the problem that he had none. No face, that is.

Bryant was cast by producer Robert Kent for the role of Quintillus, a 2000 year old Gladiator who had been entombed in molten stone on the last day of Pompeii, when the city sank beneath the eruption of Mount Vesuvius.

Being buried in stone for 2000 years doesn't do your looks much service. So when Quintillus is uncovered by a group of archeologists, generaled by Dr Paul Mallon (Richard Anderson), the Pompeian has a face that might have been around the world in 80 days in a cement mixer, followed by a ten round travelog with King Kong. It is a face that isn't much—in fact nothing.

The Curse of the Faceless Man was scripted by an honest-to-Zeus science-fiction writer, Jerome Bixby, 35 year old author of some 180 sci-fi stories. Selected by producer Kent, Bixby represents an unusual choice in Hollywood to write an SF film. Such pictures are generally assigned to Western or love story screenplay creators who know or care nothing about fantasy and horror, unlike the talented Bixby who always does the best with the elements given him.

The problem of faceless Quintillus' lack of physiognomy, the story develops, doesn't mean he hasn't eyes for the beauty of Dr Mallon's fiancee, Tina. (That's curvaceous Elaine Edwards.) The gladiator is more than glad to see in her the reincarnation of his long-stoned girlfriend from Pompeii, despite Tina's screaming denials.

Scooping her up and away into the heated countryside of Southern Italy, the Faceless Man believes he is saving Tina from the dangerously percolating Mount Vesuvius he left thousands of years behind him.

Mallon & Co. are quick to horse; but meanwhile, the Faceless Man plunges into the Adriatic sea, the helpless girl in his arms.

As the man of stone splashes into the sea spray, the cooling water washes against his petrified body, and then pieces of stone begin to crack away, his giant form disintegrating in the ocean after the dry centuries.

The pursuing Mallon tries a Johnny Weissmuller, breast-stroking out to his drowning girlfriend, towing her back to the safety of the shore.

Deciding to fly back to the States to get married, Mallon and Tina leave dead Pompeii to its dust, now that the gladiator with no face has come to be equally bodiless.

BACK ISSUES!

How many have you missed?

Here's your ghoulden opportunity to get the big Collectors Item back issues that you missed! Stocks of some issues are frighteningly low, so send in your order today! Only $1.00 each — while they last!

#2—Monster COLOR pinup of Metaluna Mutant from This Island Earth; Yanan the Unbelievable; First Spaceship on Venus; Mad Mummy Writhes Again; Devil's Workshop; 3-D shots that pop off the pages; Devil's Messenger; Robby the Robot; Ados of Captain Marvel; World of Giants TV show; Castle of Karloff; Frankenstein; Dracula; Wolf Man in Hollywood; Rod Serling's life story; Michael Rennie as Dr Jekyll-Mr Hyde; Tombstone Times; Rubber Face

#3—Monster COLOR pinup of Black Lagoon Creature; How to Make a Frankenstein Monster; Tower of London; Master Magicians of Monsterland; Devil Commands; Mad Mummy Meets Flash Gordon; I Love A Mystery; Blackhawk; King Kong in Baddies; Shocker Sleeper; Belfry of Bela; 3 Stooges Meet the Martians; Dead Time Tales; Cave Creature; Tombstone Times; Dr Cyclops and the Big Eye; Horrorscope; Ghoul Cult; Shock Shop; Filmland Fiends; Karloff as Frankenstein

#4—Monster COLOR pinup of Karloff as Frankenstein, Chaney as Wolf Man, and Peter Lorre; Jr Conquered the World; Devil's Workshop; Monster of Planet X; I Was A Teenage Mad Mummy; Horrorscope; Karloff and Price in Malice in Wonderland; Invidious Dr Ng; George Pal life story; King Kong and prehistoric monsters; Kirk Alyn's Memoirs of a Superman; Bowery Boys Meet the Monsters; Depending Horror Films by Vincent Price; Chamber of Chaney

#5—Monster COLOR pinup of Chaney and Ankers in Wolf Man; How to Make a Werewolf Howl; Steelnecks Meets Zombie Master; Son of the Mad Mummy; Ghost of Frankenstein; Adventures of Spy Smasher; Alias Gordon's I Remember Bela Lugosi; Screen Scream Queens; Frankenstein the Illustrated Monster in comic books; Coming of the Robots; Black Zoo; Day of the Triffids; Horrorscope; Terror in the Air; Dog in the Sky; Tombstone Times by Larry Burd; Dead Time Tales

#6—Monster COLOR pinup of Lon Chaney in The Haunted Palace; Karloff as The Terror; Bride of Frankenstein in MonsterScope; Captain Video by Ron Haydock; Complete Checklist of Bela Lugosi films; Horror of Dracula; TV's The Outsider; Shadow Strikes Back; Incredibly Strange Creature Who Stopped Living and Became a Crazy Mixed Up Zombie; pix of Jim Harmon; Horrors of the Hollywood Museum; Dinosaurus pinup; Tombstone Times; Mad Mummy Kidnapped

ONLY $1.00 PER COPY — WHILE THEY LAST!

*

FANTASTIC MONSTERS BACK ISSUES, TOPANGA, CALIFORNIA

I enclose $______ for the issues I have circled below.

☐ Issue #2 ($1)   ☐ Issue #5 ($1)
☐ Issue #3 ($1)   ☐ Issue #6 ($1)
☐ Issue #4 ($1)

NAME_______________________

ADDRESS____________________

CITY________________ ZONE____ STATE________

VOLUME 2 ☆ ☆ ☆ ☆ ☆ FIVE SCAR FINAL — ALL THE NEWS UNFIT TO PRINT ☆ ☆ ☆ ☆ ☆ NUMBER 1

CREEPY CLUBS

A letter was recently received at our offices from a hitherto unknown organization, THE BELA LUGOSI FAN CLUB. Until this letter came we knew only of Bill Obbagy's memorial organization for Bela. However, we recommend this club for all the many Lugosi fans the world over. The club is centered at 200 K St., S. Boston 27, Mass., and is headed by JAMES BOWEN. Dues are $1 yearly, for which members receive the club badge, bulletin and photos of Bela and other monsters.

JOPLIN SOCIETY OF MONSTERS—A club for Missouri monster folk, is headed by STEVE MURRAY, who lives at 2711 Connor, Joplin, Mo. Write to Steve for information.

GHOULITA FAN CLUB — for all the Los Angeles area horror fans of the witch-like woman who hosts the Jeepers Creepers TV show, has recently gotten under way under the supervision of MARK SHEPARD of 16047 Adlon Rd., Encino, Calif. MARK tells us that for the 50c membership fee you will receive a membership card, "Ghoulita pencils," photo, and a club badge.

MONSTERS INTERNATIONAL—is a club designed for monsters all over the world! Members have already been accepted from all over the world, and new members are continually invited. The club also publishes their own horror magazine, Alien, mentioned in our amateur magazine column. Write to ROBERT BELL, 336 E. 198th St., Bronx 58, N.Y.

INTERNATIONAL GEORGE PAL FAN CLUB— for serious-minded fans of such films as The Time Machine, Atlantis, and Brothers Grimm. Dues are $1.50 and members receive 6 issues of the club magazine, member-

• IN A CLANKY MOOD •

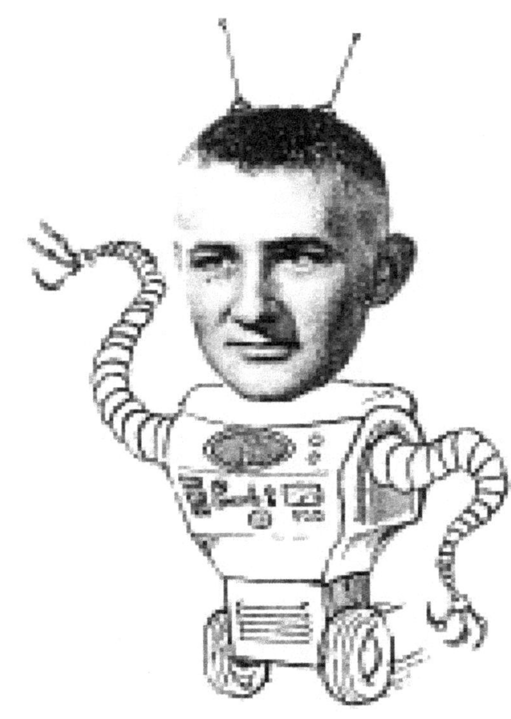

Tombstone Times' nuts-and-bolts editor LARRY BYRD, after a long session with the postcards, crayon-scrawled letters, and neatly wrapped bombs which come into our office, turns them into a fairly legible fan news-paper section. Larry offers to take all criticism on his "tin-chin."

ship card, certificate, and a number of other surprises. The address is 415 N. 19th St., Apt. 150, Phoenix 6, Ariz.

Another FANTASTIC MONSTERS FAN CLUB has popped up! This one, to which free membership is offered, is headed by CRAIG SUWALSKI, 5333 W. George, Chicago, Ill.

Any of the club presidents who would like a mention in this column need only send information and a set of the club paraphernalia to TOMBSTONE TIMES, TOPANGA, CALIFORNIA.

COFFIN CORNER

A question often asked, but very difficult to answer properly, comes to us from ANDY ROLPH, Eastown, Kentucky —"What in the world was the very first horror film, and who starred in it?"

I'm sure you'll agree that it would be next to impossible to determine just when someone first experimented with motion picture film along macabre lines. The very first film of any great importance, however, seems to be the classic "Cabinet of Dr. Caligari," made in 1919 and starred Conrad Veidt, Werner Krause and Lil Dagover —LB

Who really thought up the idea of a "phantom" below the Paris Opera House? There wasn't really such a fellow was there? — Sarah Kire, Perris, Calif.

The character often credited to the great Lon Chaney —Erik the Paris Phantom— was obviously quite alive in the mind of one Gaston Leroux. Gaston, now deceased, wrote the novel "Phantom of The Opera" from which the successive films have been taken—LB

What year was "The Day The Earth Stood Still" released? — DONALD GREY, Brookfield, Ill.

1951—LB

What were the "Tales of Frankenstein," with Anton Differing?—BILL DRUMELLER, Richmond, Va.

In an attempt to clear this up once and for all, the title was that of a proposed television series in England, the pilot for which was by Hammer Films. This pilot film has been making the rounds here in the states recently on various half-hour anthology shows, and reports have it that the picture is surprisingly good, making one wonder just why the British powers-that-be decided against the series—LB

53

HAUNT ADS

L. BUBAN, who has a collection of horror and western posters, advertisements and pressbooks, is seeking the help of fellow FANMO readers in building up his collection. If you have any horror or western advertisement material, we suggest that you contact him at his address, 301 W. 12th Ave., Homestead, Penna. Make-up enthusiast, G. ROSS GUY of 25 Canterbury St. E. Hartford 8, Conn., is interested in corresponding with serious make-up fans. ROSS is also in the process of beginning a memorial magazine for Bela Lugosi and would appreciate the help of you loyal Lugosi lovers in preparing the first issue. . . . To complete his hideous "coffin," in which he wishes to place a vampire, CLARK WILKINSON is searching for a head to use on the body of his bat man. CLARK, who lives at 585 4th Ave., Baraboo, Wisconsin, cautions readers that he merely wants a movie prop or some other sort of fake head, rather than the real thing! . . . WILLIAM WATKINS of 914 N. Calhoun St., Baltimore 17, Md., has a large amount of advertising material for sale from serials. He tells us this material includes 1-sheets, 3-sheets, 11x14s and a few stills to boot. . . . BILL, we suggest you get in touch with FRANK MASARI, 119 Seaside Ave., Stamford, Conn. who is madly searching the world for all information and material from the classic Flash Gordon's Trip to Mars. . . . Another young fan who is interested in starting his own amateur magazine is JOE VONDERWISH. Joe is seeking photos, articles and stories from amateur fans like himself to help get the little publication going and asks that you write to him at 4120 Edith Ave., Cincinnati 27, Ohio. . . . Horror and science fiction paperbacks can now be obtained at the low price of 4 for $1 from DENNIS BRIGHTWELL, 1223 Creston Ave., Des Moines 15, Iowa. DENNIS suggests that he can't guarantee your preferences at such prices, though he will certainly try to please one and all. Money will be cheerfully refunded if you are not satisfied. . . . An English fan of Vincent Price, Miss Vikky Evans, 41 Prince Of Wales Rd., Kentish Town, London N.W. England, wants all the American Price fans to help her fill her scrapbooks on Vincent with articles, clippings and photos from American magazines and newspapers. . . . GREGORY FELDMAN, a discriminating comic collector, is in search of a number of older comics which he is willing to trade for or buy, and requests that anyone interested write to him at 9540 S. Bennett, Chicago 17, Ill. . . . Another comic fan, who tells us he has hundreds of comics in the horror vein, wishes to expand his collection to the thousands! Send a list of prices, condition, etc., to ROGER HOWELL, Box 457, Weaverville, N.C. . . . In the glossy still department JOEY AUSTIN of 1518 S.E. Blvd., Salem, Ohio, is diligently looking for giant size photos such as the one offered in our "Name the Nameless Monster" contest. . . . DAVID WILLIAMS wants good action stills from The Birds to show his friends and help him in his own amateur aviatical melodrama based on Hitchcock's masterpiece. He can be contacted at 42 Walnut St., Lewiston, Maine. . . . Horror man BORIS MOTZ, of 313½ Delaware, Leavenworth, Kansas, is still searching for old 3-D comics, magazines, gum cards, movie clips, etc., and asks that you write to him if you have anything pertaining to 3-D or horror films for sale. . . . If you've got any stills from War of The Worlds, you've got a buyer in JIMMY BOLLINGER, 801 S. Church St., Brady, Texas, who is also interested in buying and trading other monster pics. . . .

RICK ADAMS of 670 E. 18th St., Eugene, Oregon, offers 50c apiece for 8x10 stills in good condition depicting the harpies, skeleton warriors, or the hydro from Ray Harryhausen's latest masterpiece, Jason and the Argonauts. RICK also has a number of wallet size monster pictures for sale at $1 for 25 different ones. . . . A beginning still collector, CHARLES HARRIS of 1926 McClellan Way, Stockton, Calif., is looking for almost any good horror stills, to help get his collection on a sounder footing. CHARLES is also looking for back issues of FANMO. . . . Both LARRY LIVEL, 510 Ave. "F" Fort Dodge, Iowa, and RICHARD PRESCOTT of 11 Wadsworth, E. Tawas, Mich., are willing to pay $1 in cold cash for the first rare edition of our magazine.●

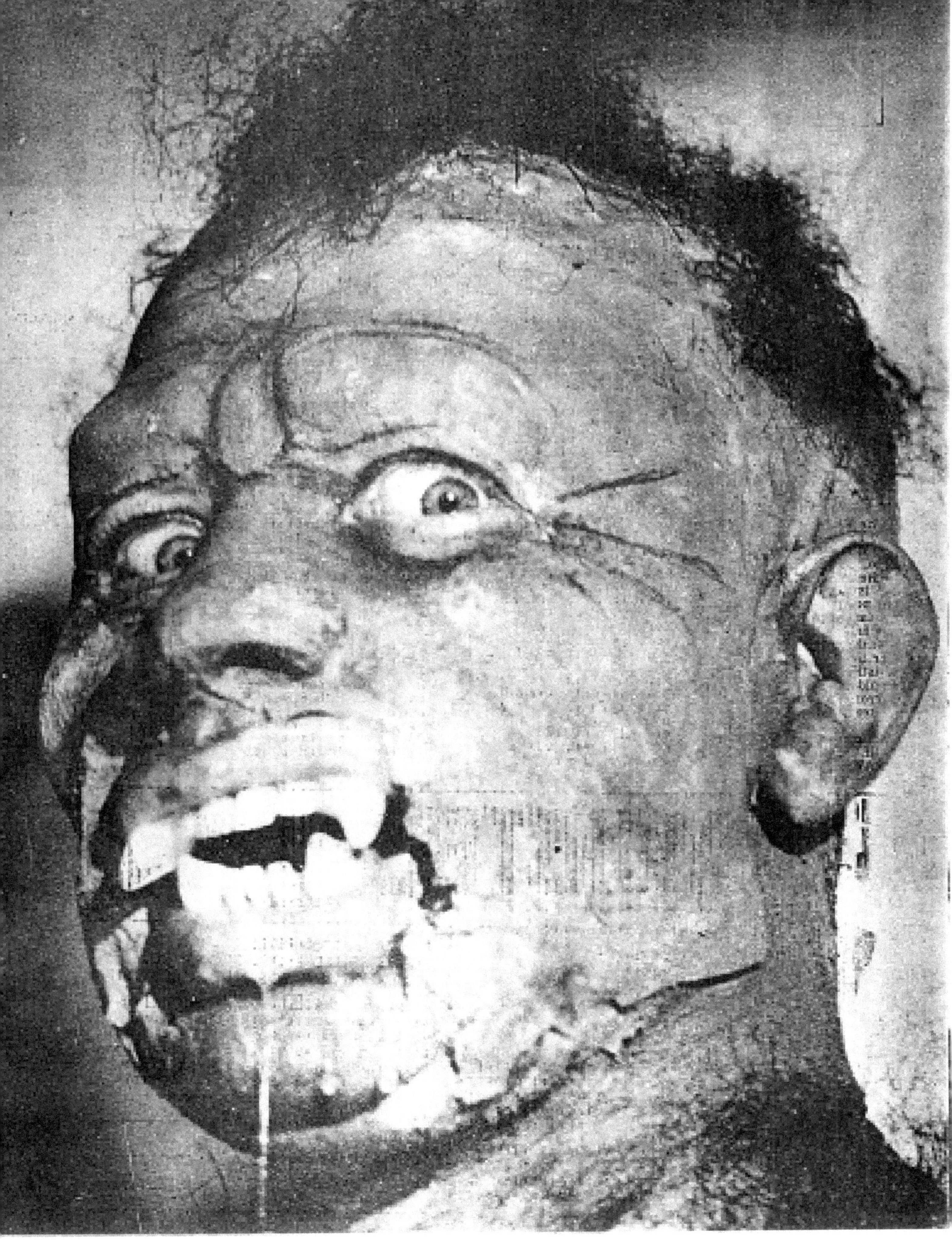

NOW YOU CAN HEAR THESE TERROR-TALES!

Horror beyond imagination! A study in terrifying evil!

You've heard of records in a humorous vein? — Well, this album can only be called HORROR IN A JUGULAR VEIN. A frightening narration from the stories of the old master of horror himself — Edgar Allan Poe. "THE PIT AND THE PENDULUM" is tough enough on your nerves, but wait until you hear "THE TELLTALE HEART!" #M-36 — ONLY $1.98

ALL 12" LP RECORDS ALL 33 RPM

A COMPLETE COLLECTION OF THE MACABRE

A CLASSIC OF HORROR spoken from the heart (with the right kind of background music, of corpse). The idea of hearing this narrative in your own home is enough to scare you out of your wits! Put the lights out and have your blood curdled by the tale of THE BLACK CAT, written by Edgar Allan Poe. It's HORRIFIC! #M-37 — ONLY $2.98

ALL 12" LP RECORDS ALL 33 RPM

CLASSIC TALES OF TERROR to make you shiver in your boots. Be prepared for screaming suspense and maniacal action when you listen to these spine-tingling, chilling narrations penned by the master of the macabre, Edgar Allan Poe. "MASQUE OF THE RED DEATH" and "THE PREMATURE BURIAL" are among his best and most terrifying tales. #M-38 — ONLY $2.98 *

PERFECT FOR EERIE MIDNIGHT GHOUL PARTIES

HOUSE OF FRIGHT—

A grim, ghostly, spine-chilling, nerve-wracking tale of horror that will leave you with lingering fright, written by the all time master of thriller-chillers—Edgar Allan Poe. You will remember "THE HOUSE OF USHER" (his most famous tale) with shuddering fear every time you're alone in a dark house or on a deserted street! #M39—ONLY $2.98*

Narrated by Richard Taylor

RUSH YOUR ORDER NOW • CLIP THIS COUPON • USE AS ORDER BLANK • MAIL TODAY

Please Rush Me The Following Long-Playing Albums: NO C.O.D.'s

☐ NIGHTMARE —— $1.98 Plus 25¢ Postage and Handling
☐ HORROR —— $2.98 Plus 25¢ Postage and Handling
☐ TERROR —— $2.98 Plus 25¢ Postage and Handling
☐ FRIGHT —— $4.98 Plus 25¢ Postage and Handling

I Enclose $ ______ ☐ CASH ☐ CHECK ☐ MONEY ORDER

RANDOM RECORDS, C/o Black Shield
P.O. BOX 141 • TOPANGA, CALIFORNIA

NAME ________________________ AGE ______

ADDRESS ________________________

CITY ____________ ZONE ____ STATE ______

Sheila as Nyoka in Edgar Rice Burroughs' JUNGLE GIRL

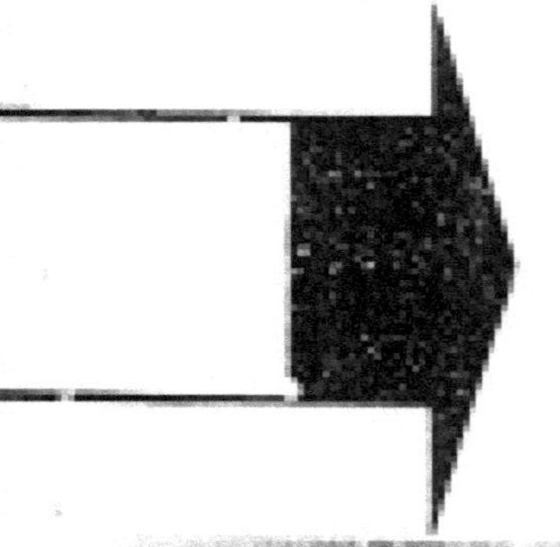

DON'T YOU DARE BUY THE NEXT ISSUE OF FANTASTIC MONSTERS!

●

. . . Don't dare buy it, that is, unless you want to shudder & shake, quiver, crumble & quake with cursed nightmares for the rest of your life—and afterwards!

BECAUSE—the next insidiously diabolical, cadaverously chillifying issue will be—THE GREATEST, MOST HORRIPULATING SINGLE ISSUE OF ANY MONSTER MAGAZINE EVER PUBLISHED IN THE HISTORY OF MANKIND!!!

BECAUSE—in FANTASTIC MONSTERS #6 you're going to thrill and gasp to—

—over 25 shock-traumatic pages of petrifying pictures and peril-packed pinups of the most bestial boogy man ever seen on the scream screen—the one, the unholy only—KARLOFF THE UNCANNY, Master of Monstrous Movie Macabre, Grand Guignol of Gore!

YOU ASKED FOR IT!—and Editor Ron Haydock is going to give it to you —with both bloody barrels!

KARLOFF—revealing the dark and devilish secrets locked from mortal eyes in THE BLACK ROOM!

KARLOFF—in a spine-crushing photo gallery—depicting the Demon Boy Wonder as you have never seen him before!

KARLOFF—invading gloomy graveyards, armed with pick and shovel, chilling the dead—as THE BODY SNATCHER!

KARLOFF—in exclusive FANTASTIC MONSTERS KARLOFF CUT OUTS—fearsome full-length standups to make you the eerie envy of your fiendish friends! Scusticological!!!

PLUS—more creepy Karloff than you can shake a voodoo stick at!

PLUS—hellish exposé of the satanic DEVIL DOG OF DEVONSHIRE!

PLUS—terror tale of the mutant monstrosity that stalked human prey on THE DAY THE WORLD ENDED!

PLUS—life story of HAZEL COURT, Britain's buxom beast-battling beauty!

PLUS—BRIDE OF MONSTER MOVIE ADS, TOMBSTONE TIMES, scaresational color pinups of MONSTER THAT CHALLENGED THE WORLD, FRANKENSTEIN, BLACK LAGOON CREATURE—and MORE, MORE, MORE!!!

All this is lurking for YOU—in the next bone-snapping issue of—FANTASTIC MONSTERS, World's Greatest Monster Magazine!●

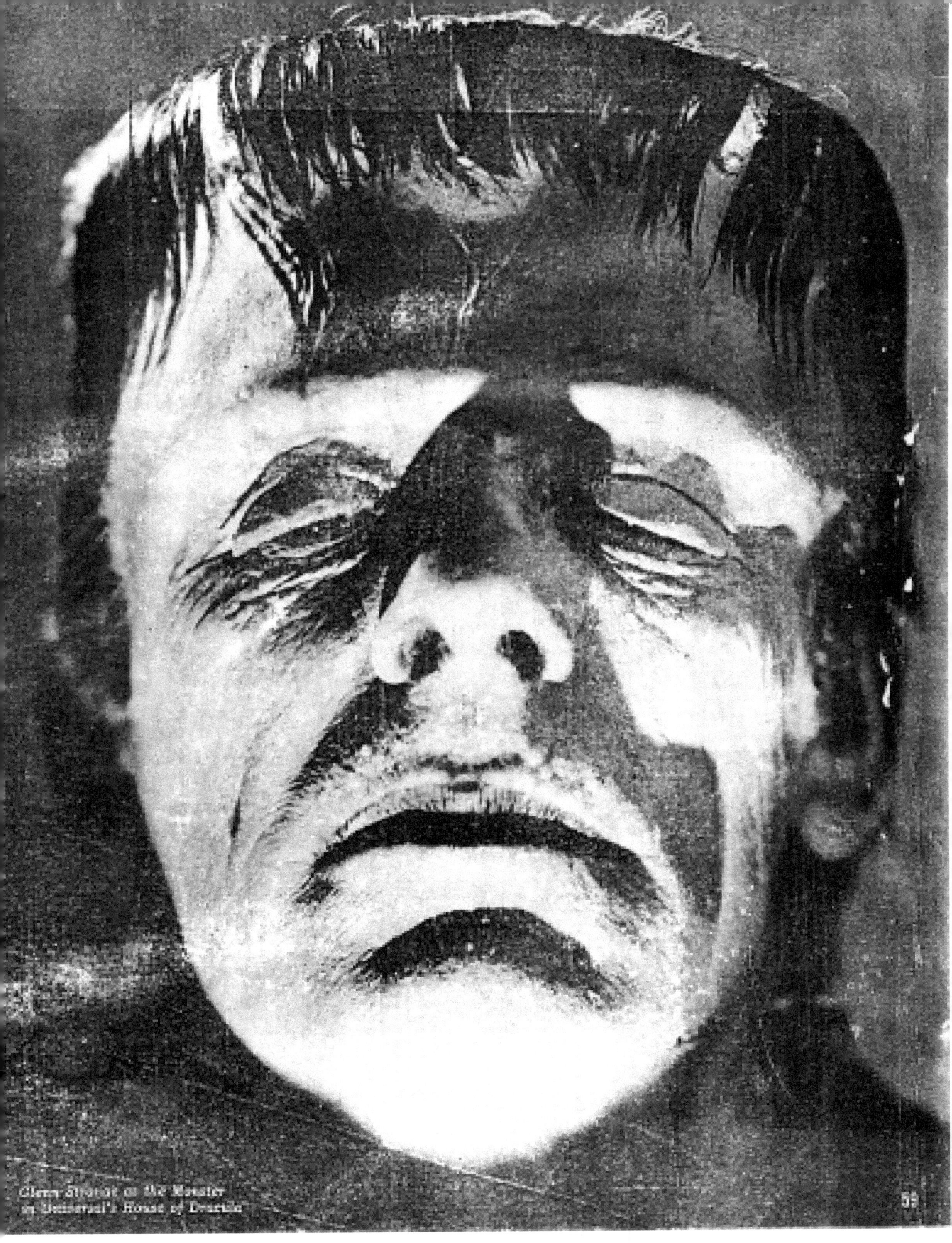

Glenn Strange as the Monster
in Universal's House of Dracula

!Blood!
BEASTS!
BEAUTIES
!!!!!

DEATH!

CHILLS!

*Shock!

fantastic

Like what you see keep up
with all we do visit us at
moonmochibooks.com
&
Perfectcommandoproductions.com

Thank you
for your
purchase

Look for these other titles from this and our other imprints.

変態

Blue Sky

A Zombie Christmas Carol
ABCs of Bombers
ABCs of Fighter Planes
ABCs of Military Helicopters
ABCs of Tanks and other Fighting Vehicles
ABCs of Naval Weaponry
American Manga-ka
Cheney's Got A Gun
Curse Renorn Vol.1
Eternal Damnation Vol.1
Eternal Damnation Vol.2
Five Little Elves Wrapping Christmas Gifts
Five Little Pumpkins Sitting on a Fence
Five Little Turkeys Sitting on a Porch
Five Silly Turkeys Staning in a Row
Holiday 4-Pack
Geshia
Hitokiri Vol.1
Hitokiri Vol.2
Iron Ace Vol.1
King Kong
My First Cavity Search
Spooky Letters
Zombie Dinosaurs Awakening Vol.1
Nemalorn
The Creation of the Priestess
Fairy Tale Twist
Fairy Tale Twist 2
Perfect Commando Productions Presents Heroes of long ago:
When Worlds Collide

Iron Fossil Express
Castle Academy Magic Tarot Card Fight Vol.1
Quickies Vol.1
Farmlords Vol.1
Punished By Haloween Vol.1
Women in Black Vol.1
Merry Clause Vol.1
Éirinn go Brách Vol.1
Éirinn go Brách Vol.2
Éirinn go Brách Iathghlas Criostail Vol.1
Pride & Prejudice(Yaoi)
Disciples Vol.1

Perfect Commando Productions Presents
Heroes of Long:
The Ghost Rider Collection 1
The Ghost Rider Collection 2